Louise Brindley was born in Darlington, County Durham, and at the age of four moved with her family to Scarborough, North Yorkshire. The moment she saw the sea and the sand, she knew she could be happy with the town and countryside destined to become her new home. All Louise Brindley's writings reflect her knowledge of, and deep affection for, the North East, with special attention to the Yorkshire coast.

Louise Brindley

TANQUILLAN

CORGI BOOKS

TANQUILLAN

A CORGI BOOK   0 552 12564 4

First publication in Great Britain

PRINTING HISTORY

Corgi edition published 1986

Copyright © Louise Brindley 1986

This book is set in 10/11 pt Ehrhardt

Corgi Books are published by Transworld Publishers Ltd.,
61–63 Uxbridge Road, Ealing, London W5 5SA,
in Australia by Transworld Publishers (Aust.) Pty. Ltd.,
25 Harley Crescent, Condell Park, NSW 2200, and in New
Zealand by Transworld Publishers (N.Z.) Ltd., Cnr. Moselle
and Waipareira Avenues, Henderson, Auckland.

Printed and bound in Great Britain by
Cox & Wyman Ltd, Reading

To Olga and Peggy, and that September Sunday
morning long ago.

PART ONE

CHAPTER ONE

Snow, soft and sparkling by early morning gaslight, flurried up beneath Filly Grayler's determinedly wielded sweeping-brush, and spun in feathery arcs as she cleared a path from the side door to the kerb. Then, hitching up her skirts, back she trooped to pick up her box of cleaning materials, stopping momentarily to glance with quiet satisfaction at the door with its patterns of stained-glass lozenges, tinted rich amethyst, ruby and aquamarine, of which she was inordinately proud. Other doors in the neighbouring houses had glass upper panels, but none was as colourful as hers, and in summertime, or whenever the sun shone, the carpet in the narrow passage leading to the stairs and the house above the shop, seemed awash with precious gems.

Frank, her eldest son, would come out presently to take down the shutters and swish away the snow from the pavement fronting the shop with its 'Albert Grayler and Sons, Family Grocers' fascia. By that time, Filly would have polished, to pristine brightness, the brass door-knocker, letter-box and bell-pull, knowing that Albert's customers expected to see everything spotless. Besides, one could always tell how other people lived by the freshness of their curtains, precisely executed yellow-stone edging to their steps, and the colour of their washing strung out to dry.

Her name was Felicity, but her husband with his penchant for nicknames called her Filly. During their courtship she had reminded him of a neat chestnut foal, spare and glossy, with her softly folded brown hair, slim waist and well-turned ankles. Now her waistline had thickened with the five children she had borne, but she was still a handsome woman, spry and worksharp.

Frank emerged, whistling, from the shop, and started taking down the shutters, heaving them in his brawny arms as effortlessly as if they were dominoes or playing cards. The milkman's float, with its clanking churns and plodding horse, appeared at the entrance to the square. A tall woman in black made her way precariously to the shop, clinging to the garden railings for support, planting her feet carefully in the snow. Filly smiled. Her day had begun. This was a moment to treasure, when blinds were rolled up and gaslight glowed at bedroom windows on a winter Monday morning.

Now the shutters were down, Filly could see her husband moving heavily behind the wide mahogany counter, pad and pencil in hand, checking stock on the towering shelves, counting the tins of fruit and salmon beneath the patterned jars of crystallised ginger in plaited straw baskets, and the huge black and gold tea-canisters on the highest shelf of all.

To chase away the gloom of an early January morning, Albert had lit the gas-jets which threw warm pools of light on the brass scales and its symmetrical pyramid of weights. The shop seemed to Filly an Aladdin's cave of shine and shadows as the flickering lights caught the gleam of brass and gold, and glinted on the edges of the biscuit-tins and the bacon-slicer.

Giving the door-knocker a final rub, she entered the shop to dust the counter, lifting her head to catch the fragrance of spices and roasted coffee beans which pervaded the air like incense in a church, immutably blended with the strange, pungent smell of soap and firelighters; the long rolls of bacon hanging, muslin-covered, from hooks in the ceiling; the queer, dusty scent of tea from a newly-opened chest in the warehouse behind the shop.

The dairy round the corner exuded a totally different smell, a cool milkiness which reminded Filly of the days when her children were babies. She loved that dairy with its spotless marble slabs, white and gold patterned milk-bowls, and the china swans in the window filled with speckled brown eggs.

The butchers and the greengrocers possessed their own ingrained and unmistakable odours too, as did the ironmongers and the chemists, and if she were led blindfold into any one of those neighbouring shops, she would know as soon as she crossed the threshold which one she was in: would have instantly recognized the warm, sickly smell of meat, offal, and newly-made sausages in Mr Franks's establishment, without having to look at the stiff carcases slung from meat-hooks, the pools of blood in the sawdust, or the trays of savoury ducks, pork pies, and pease-pudding in the window.

Equally, she would have known at once the chemists by the faint scent of violet soap, cachous and lavender-water intermingled with the indeterminate, clinical smell of lint and bandages, tincture of quinine and camphorated oil: the red sealing-wax Mr Bland blobbed onto the wrapped-up prescriptions: the strange effluvia of tinware, dishcloths and paraffin in Mr Eustace's ironmongery store, and the strong, often unpleasant odour of sprouts, turnips, earthy potatoes and over-ripe bananas in Mr Wells's greengrocery shop.

Filly Grayler loved all the strange, exotic fragrances which permeated her life. They were part and parcel of being a housewife, a mother and a woman. She liked nothing better than to set off to the shops with a basket on her arm to chat to the other tradespeople, to pay her milk bill, decide what to give her family for Sunday dinner, and root among the vegetables to procure the firmest carrots, the soundest onions, the least scarred potatoes.

She had married young – too young in her mother's opinion, when, at seventeen, she announced that she was engaged to Albert Grayler. But even then she had known that what she most wanted from life was a home of her own, and children. A country girl born and bred, she had become inured to cooking, housework, and helping, since she left the village school, to take care of her three brothers. But that did not satisfy Filly, who had never cared for any of the village lads who made sheep's eyes at her on Sunday school outings.

She had daydreamed, at times, about the kind of man she wanted to marry; would stop what she was doing to stare out of the window at the humped hayricks in the farmyard behind the cottage, and the thick muddy tracks leading down to the village, the clucking hens, and the slow procession of cows to the milking-shed, thinking what a waste of time it was cooking and cleaning for her brothers when she might have a man of her own to care for. She imagined that man as tall and good-looking, with the manners of a gentleman – a doctor perhaps, or a curate. But what hope had she of finding such a man, stuck away in a village? And what if her fine, young shapely body had sagged to middle age before she met a man she wanted to marry?

In burgeoning springtime, when the fields were starred with buttercups, and primroses lay thick beneath the hedgerows, she would experience an intense longing to procreate, would watch the skittering lambs and new-born calves with a passionate awareness of their innocence; their dependence on food from their mothers; and yet she herself was innocent of the meaning of sexuality between a man and a woman; she simply loved young, tender, growing things. Filly's maternal instincts were as deeply planted as the great elms near the churchyard gate.

She had first seen Albert Grayler behind the counter of the village shop when her mother sent her down to buy a bag of flour and a twist of yeast, and wondered who he was and what he was doing there, regarding him suspiciously as folk were inclined to regard strangers in a close community. Then Mrs Good, the grocer's wife, came from the back room, to tell a group of village women that her husband had been taken bad in the night. 'Oh,' they said, making questionmarks with their eyebrows and glancing at the woman's bulge under her flowered pinny. 'Oh, and how are you going to manage the shop and all when your time comes, with Samuel taken bad?' And 'How bad is he? He seemed well enough yesterday morning humping boxes from the wagon to the lean-to.'

Well, that was the way of things with men who lifted too heavy loads. Samuel had complained, at tea, that his back was giving him hell. At four o'clock in the morning she was rubbing him with wintergreen. And she couldn't manage the shop, the house, the kids, and Samuel all by herself, not in her condition, which was why she was glad of Albert, Sam's friend, who had come to stay for a few days until his own shop was ready to move into. And how relieved she had felt when he had offered to help out in the shop, being a grocer himself with a First Class Certificate.

'Oh.' They had all turned to look at Albert then, nodding their heads and making clucking noises of approval of this Sir Galahad of the bacon-slicer, now that he had been explained to their satisfaction: a comely enough young chap, despite his oddly-coloured hair – ginger to put it mildly – and his wiry moustache. Not exactly handsome, but possessed of a good heart despite his physical shortcomings – *and* a friend of Samuel's, which spoke volumes in his favour. And, 'Where is your shop, mister?' one of the women enquired, so that she could pass on the information to her neighbours who might not have heard about Samuel's being taken bad in the night.

'In Scarborough, ma'am,' Albert replied civilly, giving her the benefit of his engaging smile and twinkling blue eyes which creased at the corners as if he had done a great deal of smiling in his time.

'Oh well, did you ever? I wish you good luck, young man.'

'Thank you very much, ma'am.'

Felicity, standing at the far end of the counter, one leg crossed behind the other, twisting the money her mother had given her in the corner of her handkerchief, flushed crimson when Albert asked her what he could get for her, thinking that she had never seen a pair of arms like his before, with fine golden hairs glinting in the sunlight shining through the shop window, to where his shirt-sleeves stopped just above the hefty muscles of his upper arms.

Her brothers, Jim, Ted, and Arthur, had strong arms of course, as farm-labourers were bound to have, but not golden arms, nor soft hands with nicely-shaped nails.

It was soon round the village that Samuel Good was on his deathbed. They had almost got the wreath ordered and the plot chosen when Sam appeared behind the counter once more, limping slightly and stinking of wintergreen. The drama was over. But what had happened to that nice young chap with the ginger hair and moustache? Why, he'd gone about his own business. Married? No, Albert wasn't married. Never had much chance when his mother was alive, being a possessive

13

kind of woman. Ay, Albert and Sam had known each other for a long time. Came from Stockton way, did Albert, where Sam lived as a boy. They'd kept in touch ever since. 'Albert should do well in a nice little corner shop of his own,' Mrs Good said.

Young Felicity Stephenson had kept her ears open and her mouth closed. Her mother wanted to know what ailed her, why she kept on mooning about the house instead of getting on with her work. The dream man she wished to marry had emerged from the mist at last, with several real physical attributes, penny-gold hair, moustache, and golden arms. She had thought that she would never see Albert again once he started up his corner grocery store in Scarborough. Then one evening in church her mother had poked her sharply in the ribs and asked, in a fierce whisper, who the chap with the ginger nut was, sitting near the pipe-organ, because he had never taken his eyes off her since she came in. 'Don't look across at him!'

But Filly had peeped between her fingers when she should have been praying, and suddenly a delicious feeling of relief, as warm and heady as communion wine, had flooded through her when Albert smiled at her across his hymn book. She had known then, as certainly as she knew spring would follow winter, that this was the man she was going to marry, and despite her mother's opposition to her engagement because of the difference in their ages, she *had* married him, a year later, in that very church.

Never had she found reason to regret that marriage. She had found, in Albert, a warmth, charm and dedication to his family which had never ceased to surprise and delight her. As the woman in black who had planted her feet so carefully in the snow, pinged open the shop door, Filly gave the counter a final swipe with her duster, while Albert, in his clean cotton coat with the bone bachelor-buttons, turned, smiling, to greet his first customer of the day.

Busying herself in dusting the tiny office where Albert added up his accounts, Filly recalled the day when they came to view this property. Just after the birth of their second son, Harry, that was, when the house above the corner shop had seemed too cramped to contain a growing family, and Albert had said that it was time they moved on to something bigger and better, a shop on Scarborough's South Cliff, where the "nobs" lived.

The empty shop and the house above it had seemed enormous to Filly at the time. She had never felt so small in all her life as they explored together the long creaking passages, and stood in the bay-windowed living-room with its dusty corners, treacle-coloured paint and torn wallpaper.

'How long has it been empty?' She had peered cautiously into dark cupboards, afraid of mice, then stared up at the flaking ceiling with its central rosette and ornate mouldings. She stifled a sneeze as a shower of dust descended from the paper blind Albert had opened to see the view from the window.

'Almost three years.'

'But it's terrible! *Awful!*'

'Even so, it has possibilities, and there isn't another grocer's shop nearer than Ramshill Road,' Albert said patiently.

Filly had yanked away a strip of wallpaper, revealing the dusty layers beneath, wrinkled her nose, and dusted her hands with her pocket handkerchief.

'Have you thought how much we'll need to spend on it to make it right?' She had stared in disgust at the pile of soot in the fireplace. 'Can we really afford it?'

Albert tugged his moustache. 'The rent's a bit steep,' he admitted, 'twelve-and-a-tanner a week, but it's got everything I need. That big room behind the shop would make a fine warehouse and I could stable the horse in the yard.'

'Horse? We haven't got a horse!'

'Not yet, but we will have. I'll need a horse for the deliveries.'

'Then you'll need a man to drive the horse, I suppose! And have you thought how much stair-carpet we'll need? And how shall we be able to afford furniture for all these rooms?' She had counted up on her fingers, 'Six bedrooms, dining-room, sitting-room, kitchen, and three flights of stairs.'

'You think we shouldn't take it then?'

She hated to disappoint him, but she had to be practical. She had wandered then to the bay window overlooking a long rectangle of fresh green grass and budding trees, surrounded with solidly-built Victorian houses; houses bespeaking respectability yet frilled with unexpected iron balconies catching the sunlight of an April Sunday morning.

A flicker of pure happiness had invaded her heart as she looked out at the square. The sound of birdsong, the exuberant shrilling of a blackbird in a lilac tree, the close proximity of other shops hidden from view behind all those russet bricks and balconies had lifted her spirit to a feeling of hope that she might make something of this creaking skeleton of a house after all.

Listening intently, she heard the murmur of the sea in the distance, scarcely a stone's throw away, and shivered with delight as she imagined herself wheeling her children along the Esplanade with its elegant buildings and wide sea views; taking them to Sunday school in the church across the way.

Albert had slipped his arm about her waist as he stood quietly beside her, looking down at the long garden interspersed with meandering paths and hemmed about with iron railings, knowing his Filly so well: sensing her new-born excitement, 'Well, what do you think?'

'You know very well what I think! We'll take it!'

As Albert bent to kiss her, she had started making plans. From that moment, her energies were channelled into turning the house into a home; in giving birth to three more children, Joe, Maggie and Charlotte.

Now, on this bitterly cold January morning in the year of our Lord 1914, Felicity Grayler went upstairs to make herself a cup of tea.

Life had been good to her. Frank, her eldest son, and Harry, worked for their father, and there was plenty to keep them busy in the shop and warehouse; manhandling the kegs of butter, the heavy boxes of dried fruit – sticky dates, currants and sultanas for the apprentices to sort, wash, dry and pack. Frank was in charge of the warehouse, Harry in charge of orders and deliveries, and of the delivery horse, Nobby, which he groomed with a kind of fanatical devotion, whistling about the cobbled yard, sleeves rolled back, polishing the harness and brasses. That done, he would exchange corduroy breeches for neat navy blue jacket and trousers, white shirt, collar and tie, and set off on his calls for orders from the hotels and boarding houses, and those gentry families who would never dream of setting foot across the threshold of a grocer's shop.

Joe, her third child, had found himself a steady clerking job at the harbourmaster's office, one reason why Filly seldom patronised Mr Roe's fishmongery round the corner in South Street. Not that she would have been in any doubt about that particular aroma in a state of blindfold. And although she had felt slightly nervous about explaining to the aptly named Mr Roe that her son now brought home all the fish she required fresh from the sheds as one of the perks of his job, Mr Roe had been very decent about it, and still tipped his straw boater to her whenever she passed his shop.

Maggie and Charlotte both worked at Mrs Hollister's fashion workroom in St Nicholas Street. Not that Filly was entirely happy about that, having been there on two or three occasions to take her girls meat-paste sandwiches and slabs of moist currant cake when they had a rush order and could not get home for their dinner. A dingier place she had never seen. She had felt like taking a bucket of hot soda water and a scrubbing-brush to it, and a wash-leather to clean the grime off the windows. Nor did she like Mrs Hollister, who reminded her of a pouter-pigeon strutting about the place and issuing orders.

Maggie would be leaving soon to get married. It was Charlotte Filly worried about, her beautiful, mysterious Charlotte with her crown of shining copper hair and skin the colour of cream fresh from the dairy, tinged a delicate wild-rose pink on her planed cheekbones.

The beauty of her youngest child caught Filly unaware at times. She would find herself marvelling at the fleeting expressions of joy, wonder and thoughtfulness in those hazel-green eyes which reminded her, absurdly, of spring catkins framed with thickets of black lashes.

Maggie, with her brown hair, plump cheeks and grey-blue eyes, took after herself, and so did Joe. The other two boys favoured Albert. Frank in particular had inherited his father's crinkly ginger hair, and his fine flourishing moustache turned up at the ends, which gave him the appearance of Frans Hals's

Laughing Cavalier. But Charlotte's hair was the deep, glowing red of burnished copper. Even at birth, her hair had quiffed up in a fuzzy red coxcomb above her beautifully modelled little face; had burned like a tiny copper flame about the shawl Filly had knitted to receive her, so that when Albert saw his youngest daughter for the first time, lying in her mother's arms in the big front bedroom, he had burst out laughing.

'Good lord, a copper-knob,' he exclaimed proudly. 'That's what we'll call her – Copper!'

'That we will not,' Filly said indignantly, irritably aware of the binder the midwife had strapped round her under the clean flannelette nightgown. 'We'll call her Charlotte Mary after my mother.'

But Albert had always called Charlotte 'Copper', and Filly knew that she was her husband's favourite child; knew also that she had never understood Charlotte the way she understood Maggie who possessed no hidden depths, who was not the least bit clever nor even very pretty.

Charlotte possessed both brains and beauty, which was why, Filly reckoned, Mrs Hollister's workroom was not good enough for her. Not that Charlotte complained about it as the plump, extrovert Maggie often did.

In the warmth of her kitchen, Filly thought about her two daughters and the differences between them. Maggie butted her way through life like a sturdy coble thrusting to harbour against a choppy sea, while Charlotte resembled a gracefully-built yacht whose captain knew all about currents, and used his skill to tack serenely with the wind.

Maggie seldom looked at a book. Charlotte, on the other hand, paid weekly visits to the penny library in town, bringing home with her books on every subject under the sun. By the time she left school, she had read most of the classics, and poetry enough to make one's head spin.

'You'll strain your eyes with all that close print,' Filly would say impatiently, whilst the over-plump Maggie would tease her sister unmercifully about always having her head stuck in a book.

'When are you going to get yourself a young man, our

Charlotte?' Maggie would say, glancing with satisfaction at the engagement ring Bob Masters had given her; waving her podgy left hand so that the small band of rubies and diamond chippings caught the light. 'That would cure you of wanting to read about love all the time. Or are you waiting for a knight in shining armour to sweep you off your feet and carry you away on horseback?'

But Charlotte seldom took umbrage. Even when Maggie prised the books from her hands and made game of them, she betrayed no sense of pique at her sister's teasing intrusion into her quiet world of prose and poetry.

Often enough it was Filly who lost her temper. 'For heaven's sake, Maggie, that's enough! Stop it, do you hear me!'

'Oh well, if you can't take a joke.' Maggie's colour would mount suddenly. 'But Charlotte will end up an old maid if she isn't careful!'

'I've told you, Maggie, that's enough!' Perhaps it was the smugness and the faint inflexion of jealousy in Maggie's voice that worried Filly so much.

But why should Maggie feel jealous of Charlotte? Maggie, after all, had what she wanted from life. She and Bob Masters had started courting as soon as Maggie left school at fourteen – if all that standing about and giggling on street corners could be termed courting, and strolling along the sea-front in summertime with other girls of her own age, making sheep's eyes at the boys. Soon they had begun to pair off. Maggie had paired off with Bob. It was as simple as that.

Not that Filly had anything against Bob, who seemed a steady enough lad despite his inability to string two words together whenever he arrived on the doorstep to escort his intended to one of those new fangled picture shows. At least Bob was a good worker, with a trade at his fingertips. There would always be a reasonable living for joiners and undertakers, and Cowlings was one of the best firms of undertakers in town. Besides which, Bob hadn't squandered his money, but had gone, as regular as clockwork, every pay-day, to put a pound of his wages into the Penny Bank until he had saved enough for a deposit on a two-up two-down house in Garibaldi Street. And how could Filly possibly condemn Maggie for knowing her own mind? The girl was simply following in her own footsteps in wanting a home of her own and a husband to care for.

It had been an understood thing that Bob and Maggie would eventually get engaged, but it had to be done according to custom, with Bob asking Albert's permission before buying the ring, and saying how he intended to support his elder daughter. That over and done with, came the tears and congratulations and the engagement party, with everyone dressed in their best clothes the following Sunday, and Bob's parents as guests of honour.

Filly had set the table herself with her best lace cloth, starched doilies, and Albert's mother's cut-glass bowl with the silver rim for the fruit salad. If only Bob had not such distressing acne, she thought, baking a rich fruit cake, and sausage rolls: if only his cap-dangling servility did not irritate her so much. But he was Maggie's choice, and she must make the best of her future son-in-law.

But even as Filly set the sausage rolls to cool, she knew that Charlotte would never follow the same pattern. Impossible to think of Charlotte ever coming home, blushing, to say that she wished to marry some spotty youth she had met on a street corner.

This extraordinary knowledge and certainly worried Filly. It was as if Charlotte did not quite belong in their world, as if her looks, grace, and intelligence held her apart from the rest of the family – all except Joe, and Albert, who were members of her charmed circle.

Joe and Charlotte had been indivisible since childhood, and Filly knew that her younger daughter loved Albert more than she loved her. It was always to Albert or Joey that Charlotte turned in time of trouble, never herself.

Filly paused to wonder if she too was jealous of Charlotte. But no, that was ridiculous. She loved her youngest, most beautiful child with all her heart.

CHAPTER TWO

Albert Grayler preferred to shave in the scullery. There, in front of the mirror suspended from the window-catch, he could see to sweep his razor in precise arabesques over his florid cheeks, and swill away the foam, with walrus grunts of enjoyment, before putting on his collar and tie.

The bathroom he had installed as an emblem of his success held no delights for him. Too cold and clinical to suit his taste for warmth and companionship, he still liked to bath in front of the fire on Friday nights when the lads were out playing billiards and the girls had gone to the pictures. Then he could splash and splutter to his heart's content, and get Filly to flannel his back for him.

Equally, he enjoyed early mornings in the warmth of the kitchen, eating his breakfast at the square wooden table, knowing the day would bring the steady tread of housewifely footsteps to his shop.

Almost bald now, with a simple, childlike faith in God, Albert asked nothing more of his Maker than to keep his world intact, his family beside him. Even now, as he ate with relish his best smoked bacon, eggs and blackpudding, he knew that Frank and Harry were busy downstairs opening the shop. Frank would be stacking the shutters in the warehouse, Harry feeding and watering the horse, while the apprentices, under Frank's directions, would have made a start bagging sugar and smashing the unwieldy slabs of caked salt and soda – the self-same jobs he had done when he was apprenticed to a master grocer.

He sighed, replete and happy, swallowed his last mouthful of tea, and pushed back his chair. 'Best be getting down now,' he said. 'Station morning.'

Filly watched, from the kitchen window, the scene in the yard below: Harry harnessing the horse to the van; Frank and the apprentices carrying out the empty kegs and boxes, loading them ready for the station goods train to return to the factories at a substantial discount.

When all was ready, Frank rolled down and buckled in place the back flap over the tail-board, while Harry mounted the driver's seat, slapped the reins over the horse's broad back, and the van moved forward slowly over the snow-covered cobbles. Filly watched, out of sight, the horse seeking purchase for its hooves along the slippery lane; heard Frank's laughter as he called out to his father, and hooked back the double gates. Except for the snow, this was no different from any other station morning. Why then did she feel suddenly afraid, as if the pattern of her life was about to change?

Turning away from the window, shivering as if a goose had walked over her grave, Filly remembered Christmas Day when her brothers, their wives and children, arrived in their Sunday best clothes, bringing with them a great bundle of holly, brightly-wrapped presents, and a brace of pheasant.

'Oh, you shouldn't have!' She had held the dead birds at arm's length, hating the thought of having to pluck them, as they all trooped upstairs laughing and calling out 'Merry Christmas everyone!'

Her mind flicked back to the scene in the sitting-room: the blazing coal fire in the grate, the baubled and candled Christmas tree in the bay window; the ecstatic faces of the children as they unwrapped their presents, until the carpet was littered with string and paper and torn greetings cards. How much in her element she had been then, with everyone crowded together, laughing and talking and drinking ginger wine, in an all-pervading atmosphere of warmth and geniality, with the scent of roast goose and sage-and-onion stuffing floating through from the kitchen.

Then the women had tied on their aprons to help with the dishing-up, while Charlotte and Maggie saw to the table, setting it with the best silver, and colourful paper crackers.

When everything was ready, Filly had taken off her apron and bustled into the sitting-room, flushed and excited because this was Christmas Day; because all the people she loved were gathered together under one roof. The men were standing near the fire. Albert was saying that no-one would dare to meddle with Britain as long as the Fleet remained at full strength and the men of the National Reserve stood ready to defend their country if the need arose.

At that moment, it had seemed to her as if a great bird with dark wings hovered over the house, dispelling the brightness of her day. She had rounded on Albert fiercely. 'Is that all you can find to talk about, today of all days!'

'No need to get upset, love,' Albert said mildly.

'Upset! The birthday of the Prince of Peace, and all you can find to talk about is war!'

'You've got it all wrong, Filly. I was just saying . . .'

'I know what you were saying. I heard you!'

She had tried to put it out of her mind, but the seed had been sown. If war came, her sons would be taken away from her.

Now, as she walked slowly to the foot of the stairs to call the girls, she laid her head briefly on the furled newel which reminded her of a glossy snail's shell. Then, straightening up, she shouted, 'Come on, you two! It has turned seven o'clock!'

Her face softened suddenly at the sight of shining brass stair-rods holding the strip of red, patterned carpet; the flickering gaslight on the landing beneath its white, etched globe.

Things that shone and gleamed had always fascinated Filly Grayler, filling her with a sense of warmth and security: the kind of homeliness she found in the crackling of a coal fire on a wild winter day; toasting muffins at tea-time; night-lights floating in water; candles, in the church across the way, blobbing haloes of light against the shadows.

It was the ordinary things of life which most pleased her: cooking and mending, washing her men's clothes; making starch, watching the rough white lumps turn pale blue and opaque as she poured on the boiling water; clean sheets on the washing-line, cracking smartly in the wind.

Smoothing the curled newel with the palm of her hand, Filly

experienced a sense of pride, of almost sensual pleasure, that she with her strong body and capable hands should have created this home and filled it with a family to be proud of. That family seemed to her a warm tide lapping about her, turning to her for comfort and sustenance.

It had not been easy making this house into a home. She remembered the utter exhaustion of whitewashing the high ceilings, papering walls, chivvying the dust and dirt from dark corners, sitting in sale rooms bidding for furniture and carpets; sewing curtains, caring at the same time for her husband and children, giving birth again, again and again, nursing her babies, bathing their tiny bodies, loving them, always loving them, even when her temper frayed and she had wept out her tiredness and frustration in Albert's arms.

No one knew what this house had cost her in terms of sheer physical exhaustion, but she did not regret one minute of her labour if only she could feel certain that her home would remain safe and impregnable. This was why she could not bear talk of war; the stupidity of men who made war; those thin-lipped politicians in Whitehall who herded clean-limbed boys into tents to make soldiers of them.

Charlotte Grayler stretched her toes luxuriously beneath the bedclothes to derive the last sensation of warmth before stepping on to the cold linoleum.

'One, two, three,' she counted desperately, before taking the dreaded plunge. Then half-frozen, she pattered to the window, lifted the edge of the blind with its swinging ivory acorn, and saw by the flickering light of a street lamp, the square below, with every tree and spotted laurel starched to immobility in the frosty air.

'What time is it?' Maggie opened one eye, groaned and turned over in the double bed she shared with her sister.

'Time you were up.' Charlotte groped for the matches to light the gas. In its familiar glow, the bedroom sprang to life: the brass bedstead, the honeysuckle wallpaper, wardrobe, and marble-topped wash-stand.

Maggie's clothes were slung pell-mell on a chair, her stays

festooned over the chair-back, just as she had taken them off. Maggie couldn't care tuppence if her garments were creased when she put them on again. All she cared about, when she undressed, was getting into bed as quickly as possible. 'How you can be bothered to fold everything up, Charlotte, I just don't know,' she would mutter. 'Your feet will be like blocks of ice by the time you've finished messing about, and I'll have them to warm up. You're too finicky, that's your trouble.'

'I'm not finicky, I just don't like wearing creased clothes,' Charlotte would say, folding her things away in the chest of drawers.

Now, as she unfolded them and put them on, her glance lingered on the book she had brought home from the penny library. Shivering with cold, she could not resist turning the pages, to drown almost with pleasure in reading Shelley's incomparable lines:

'The One remains, the many change and pass;
Heaven's light forever shines, Earth's shadows fly;
Life, like a dome of many-coloured glass,
Stains the white radiance of Eternity.'

'Now what are you doing?' Maggie struggled up in bed, yawning and stretching her arms.

'Nothing.' Charlotte closed the book and scurried off to the bathroom. There she recited the words of 'Adonais' aloud as she washed her face, neck and slender young arms with violet-scented soap, brushed her teeth with gritty tooth-powder, and skewered her bright auburn hair with a handful of hairpins, noticing herself in her brothers' shaving mirror as she did so, seeing, as if for the first time, the way her shoulders sloped to the neckline of her modesty-vest; deriving no pleasure from her appearance, seeing no beauty in the burning flame of her hair, pale skin, greenish-brown eyes, slanting eyebrows, and the thinness of her body encased in flannelette underwear.

Nature, she felt, had treated her unfairly in lumbering her with such uncompromisingly red hair. And yet what did looks matter as long as there was poetry in the world. On Saturday afternoon she would ask the librarian for a book on the life of

Percy Bysshe Shelley. Reading it, she would forget about her red hair and skinny body. What mattered most to Charlotte was the amazing precision of words strung together like pearls, honed to their essentials, confined within an exact framework of strophe, metre, iambics, yet emerging as fluid as water to convey the lucid perfection of the poet's imagery.

Maggie turned up her nose at the black pudding, declaring she would be sick all over her sewing-machine if she ate it. 'Can you imagine Mrs Hollister's face if I was?'

'Really, Maggie,' Filly said disapprovingly. 'She'd give you the sack as likely as not.'

'I wouldn't care tuppence if she did. I'm sick to death of that silly job anyway. I wouldn't mind if she ever gave me and the other girls anything decent to do. But no, it's always Charlotte who gets the plum jobs.'

Maggie's tone, Filly noticed, was tinged with real envy. 'That's not Charlotte's fault,' she said tartly, springing to the defence of her youngest child, who seemed too preoccupied to even notice what they were talking about.

'I know it isn't.' Maggie lavishly buttered a slice of bread. 'To tell you the truth, I wouldn't have one of those "plum" jobs on my shoulders for all the world. After all,' she added, with a touch of sagacity that surprised her mother, 'if anything went wrong with one of Lady Tanquillan's dresses, it would be Charlotte, not me, who'd get the blame.'

Filly's brow puckered. 'You and Charlotte haven't fallen out, have you?' she asked, worried about that hard note of envy in Maggie's voice.

'Lord no,' Maggie reached for the marmalade, 'whatever gave you that idea? I'd have a job to fall out with Charlotte about anything, seeing she never listens to a word I say.'

Filly glanced at Charlotte over the rim of her teacup and wondered what was going on in her mind at the moment; difficult to tell by that faraway expression on her face. And yet Charlotte could be stung to anger, as Filly knew to her cost. Her thoughts turned back to the argument, bordering on a quarrel, she'd had with Charlotte when she mentioned that the

Reverend John Spalding might make her a good husband.

Filly's sharp eyes had been quick to notice the lightening of the reverend gentleman's face whenever Charlotte walked into his church, the way his eyes kept straying in her direction from the pulpit, his eagerness to shake hands with her after the service. The man was a widower, quite handsome in a scholarly, aesthetic way. It was only natural, Filly thought, for a man in his position to be on the lookout for a new wife.

When she had voiced that opinion to Charlotte, the girl rounded on her fiercely. 'Marry Mr Spalding!' she said in a shocked voice. 'If ever you say anything so silly again, I shall stop going to church. I mean it!'

'But why? I only meant . . .'

'Because I couldn't bear it. I couldn't bear – *him*!'

'But you enjoy going to church.'

'I go to church to worship God,' Charlotte's cheeks had flushed crimson, 'not to think about getting myself a husband. And when I marry – *if* I marry – it will be for love and for no other reason, and I shouldn't care two pins if the man I married were an atheist, if I truly loved him.'

It was then Filly knew she came nowhere near understanding Charlotte, and even Albert had not been on her side when she tried to explain her feelings to him. He had simply smiled and advised her to leave the lass alone. 'After all, she's got a good head on her shoulders,' he'd said lazily.

'That's what worries me. Don't you realize, Albert, that Charlotte has outgrown us? At seventeen, she is far older, mentally, than we are. I mean to say, girls of seventeen shouldn't know about atheists, should they?'

'Probably not.' Albert sighed contentedly as he slipped down beside his wife in the feather bed.

'No, Albert! Don't!' Filly thrust aside his warm, exploring hand. 'I'm serious! If you'd seen the look on her face. Marry for love, indeed! And not caring tuppence if she married an atheist! Do you know what an atheist is?'

'Not really. Do you?' Albert yawned.

'Yes, because I looked it up in the dictionary. An atheist is someone who doesn't believe in God.'

'I don't know what you're making such a fuss about,' Albert said. 'Charlotte believes in God, doesn't she?'

'Yes. At least I *think* she does. Oh, I just don't know what she believes – or what she's thinking about half the time. I know what Maggie's thinking, right enough, because she comes straight out with it. But not Charlotte.'

'You're making a mountain out of a molehill,' Albert said comfortingly. 'Come on now, go to sleep.'

'It's all those damned books she reads,' Filly said bitterly.

Walking with Maggie across the snow-filmed square, Charlotte quietly absorbed the beauty of the trees hung with mysterious snow-blossoms. Turning the corner onto the Esplanade, she noticed that the sea was streaked saffron with the first light of morning, beneath fleecy cloud-banks massed on the horizon.

She walked uprightly, drinking in the beauty of the scene, the bay cut with shimmering shafts of light, the huddled, snow-covered roofs of the fishermen's cottages clustered near the harbour, the buildings fringing the curving Esplanade, the Crown Hotel with its central apex and Corinthian pillars, lace-like balconies and tall French windows.

Maggie, floundering along beside her, noticed nothing except the wetness of her skirts and the state of her feet. 'God, I hate snow,' she wailed, clutching Charlotte's arm for support. 'Just imagine having to sit in that rotten workroom with wet feet. And I bet the snow has turned to nothing but slush in town!'

She was right: in the main street and the streets radiating from it, the snow was churned to a mud-like morass by the hooves of delivery horses – great Suffolk Punches rumbling beer barrels from the breweries to the hotel vaults. The slush had been further trampled by the feet of all those people hurrying to get to work on time: heavily-booted workmen, hunched into greatcoats, on their way to the station coal-yards, mews and warehouses; shop assistants, waitresses, barmaids, cashiers, clerks and errand boys, their faces pinched with the cold.

'I'll bet anything you like,' Maggie chuntered as they turned into St Nicholas Street, 'that old Aggie Hollister hasn't even lit the stove to keep us warm. I'll be glad when I leave that rotten job! Bob wants to bring forward the date of our wedding, and I've a good mind to do it. After all, why not? The house is as good as ready, so we might just as well get married at Easter instead of August Bank Holiday. Are you listening to me?'

'Yes, of course I am.' Charlotte turned her eyes from their contemplation of the white roof-tops bordering St Nicholas Street. 'Why shouldn't you get married at Easter if that's what you want.' She tucked her slim, gloved hand affectionately into the crook of Maggie's elbow. 'I'll still have plenty of time to make the dresses.'

Maggie said unexpectedly, 'I would like to get married as soon as possible. I just have the feeling that something awful is going to happen . . .'

'A – war, you mean?'

'I suppose it sounds daft, but the boys are always on about it. If it happened, Bob would have to go. So would Frank, Harry and Joe. That's right, isn't it?'

Charlotte shivered suddenly, fighting off a strange sense of despair, remembering a nightmare she'd had recently, a terrible dream of marching men in a wilderness of barbed wire and skeletal trees where no birds sang.

They walked together up the dim staircase to the workroom, Maggie stamping her feet and blowing on her hands. They joined the other girls taking off their coats and pinning up their skirts near a cold grey stove filled with the ashes of a long-dead fire.

'God,' Maggie exploded, 'I knew that old bitch wouldn't have lit a fire for us. It's not good enough, and I've a mind to tell her so!'

It was a long, low room with a dozen sewing-machines set up under a series of arched windows. Gaslight threw wavering shadows across the ceiling, showing up the cobwebs strung from the beams. Near the entrance was a glass-partitioned room marked Private – it was Mrs Hollister's cutting-out room, filled with paper patterns, tailors' dummies, and shelves piled high with bolts of material.

29

A door on the landing led to her living quarters, while the ground-floor salon – Agnes's pride and joy – was choc-a-bloc with gilded chairs, tables, and sofas upholstered in plum-coloured velvet: the fitting-rooms discreetly hidden behind a plethora of potted palms. The salon windows, fronting St Nicholas Street, were draped with lace curtains pendent from brass rods, and kept sparklingly clean in contrast to the ones in the room above.

The forthright Maggie declared that the salon reminded her of a high-class funeral parlour with the corpses, in their frilly petticoats and boned corsets, standing up instead of lying down. A pity Mrs Hollister's fancy customers couldn't take a look upstairs! They'd skedaddle, shrieking, into St Nicholas Street if they did.

Winding thread onto the spool, Charlotte felt the silky softness of the material beneath her fingers; such expensive material, a deep gentian blue in colour.

Agnes Hollister was shrewd enough to have realized that Charlotte was far and away her best seamstress, that she could rely on Charlotte not to wrinkle or botch the dresses for her most valued client – Lady Tanquillan.

Not that Mrs Hollister deluded herself into thinking that her ladyship's most fashionable clothes were entrusted to herself to make. Hardly likely that a rich, titled woman would trot off to dine in Mayfair wearing any other than a Bond Street creation. Agnes Hollister also knew, and deeply resented the fact, that Lady Tanquillan regarded her as an ill-bred fool, as dispensable as a bandage on a cut finger when the finger has healed. Moreover, she knew that the first badly-made or ill-fitting garment would deprive her not only of Lady Tanquillan's custom, but that of her sheep-like followers of fashion, those equally patronizing Scarborough friends of hers who appeared to float through life in a series of fashionable frocks, feathered hats and antelope suede gloves.

These considerations rendered Mrs Hollister impossibly short-tempered on occasions. She felt, at times, like a plump salmon fighting its way upstream against a tide of debt and threatened disaster. It was all George Hollister's fault, that feckless husband of hers who had left her for a cheap bitch of a barmaid just after she had signed the lease on the salon. To mitigate the pangs of loneliness, Agnes kept a secret 'friend' securely locked in a cupboard in her sitting-room, a friend to which she turned increasingly for solace as time went by.

The only person she trusted absolutely was Charlotte Grayler, whom she could rely on to handle whatever material she was given with a sureness of touch which delighted her employer. Not that Agnes ever said so – the girl might become swelled-headed if she did. But it was Charlotte who made up Lady Tanquillan's dresses. It was Charlotte she relied on to turn back the satin cuffs just so. It was Charlotte who understood the patterns almost as well as she herself did.

Almost, but not quite, Mrs Hollister thought, pursing her thick lips, and it never paid to let a member of the staff believe herself to be indispensable. One must always keep one jump ahead in the fashion game. To this end, Agnes spent her lonely evenings in her eyrie above the shop poring through fashion periodicals, her plump hand trembling slightly on the whisky bottle beside her, plotting and planning ways and means of expanding her business without the undeniable advantage of capital, worrying about the overheads which threatened to engulf her, dreading the grim spectre of bankruptcy with its attendant shame and publicity, regretting her lost youth, regretting, even more, her lost husband.

The next morning, recovered from her hangover, she would be up and doing, her dark hair dressed pompadour style, her lorgnette dangling between her breasts, to make the best of whatever life was left to her, snappish, overtly proud and domineering to cover up her loneliness and fears.

That snowy morning in January, Charlotte frowned over the dress she was sewing. Something was wrong with it. When Mrs Hollister swept into the workroom, Charlotte asked her for a word in private. The other girls glanced up expectantly. Maggie, wide-eyed with curiosity, wondered if Charlotte was going to complain about the stove.

'Yes, Charlotte, what is it?' Agnes closed the door of the cutting-out room firmly behind her.

'I'm sorry, but the dress for Lady Tanquillan. I'm afraid there's been a mistake in the cutting out. Or perhaps the pattern was wrong.'

'A – mistake? But that's impossible!' Beads of perspiration gathered on Agnes's forehead. 'I would have noticed at once if that was so.'

'But it *is* wrong, Mrs Hollister. The back panel's too narrow.'

Agnes moistened her lips with her tongue. 'Let me see it. And please don't mention this to anyone else.'

'What's going on?' Maggie hissed, as Charlotte came into the workroom. 'Have you told her we're frozen to the marrow?'

Charlotte gathered up the dress and went back to the cutting-out room. She felt a wave of pity for Mrs Hollister. As Agnes crumpled suddenly, Charlotte saw, for the first time, the frightened human being behind the stern façade. The dress was a disaster.

'Oh, God! What on earth shall I do? Lady Tanquillan is coming for a fitting this afternoon!'

'Have we enough material left to re-cut the back panel?'

Agnes sat down heavily on a chair. 'Not enough to re-cut the whole of it.' She began to cry. Charlotte laid her hand gently on the woman's heaving shoulders. 'Perhaps if we cut another panel, we could join the two with lace to match the bodice and cuffs,' she suggested.

'No, that wouldn't do.' Mrs Hollister dried her eyes. 'Lady Tanquillan would realize at once that the dress had been badly cut.'

'But if the pattern was wrong?'

'I should have noticed. It's all my fault. Now I shall lose her custom.'

'I'm so sorry, Mrs Hollister. But couldn't you simply explain things to her?'

'You don't know Lady Tanquillan,' Agnes Hollister said bitterly.

The crisis was averted at the last moment. At noon, Lady

Tanquillan's driver, ill-at-ease in the plum-coloured fashion showroom, handed in a note cancelling the dress and the fitting. Her ladyship had been called away to attend a funeral.

Charlotte could not sleep. It was close on midnight when she got up and stole down to the kitchen, knowing that Joe would be there studying for an accountancy exam which, if he passed it, would mean promotion and better wages.

Joe was sitting at the table, his books spread around him. The fire had sunk to embers but the room was still warm, redolent with the scent of cooking, starch, and clean linen strung on the ceiling rack to air.

He glanced up at her and smiled. How tired he looked, but how determined. Dear Joe, Charlotte thought, not so tall as Frank and Harry, with soft brown hair and deep blue eyes, the one she had always thought of as her 'little' brother because he had never seemed quite as robust as the others.

'Have I disturbed you?' She spoke gently.

Joe grinned. 'No, I was just about to pack up.' He gathered his papers together. 'I think I'm wasting my time going in for these exams. I'm not cut out as a book-keeper, but I'd like to take on a more responsible job: earn a bit more money.'

'Because of Annie, you mean?'

Joe's face softened. 'Yes, because of Annie. If I get promoted, I'll ask her to marry me.'

'I don't think Annie would mind one way or the other.' Charlotte sat down on the chair opposite, thinking about the girl Joe was in love with, a shy little creature with no outstandingly beautiful features; as thin and understated as a birch sapling in a springtime wood – until she smiled at Joe, when her face became suddenly radiantly alive and lovely.

'I'm glad you and Annie get along so well together,' Joe said simply. 'But why are you up so late? Is anything wrong?'

Charlotte frowned. 'You know the Tanquillans, don't you?'

'Yes. What about them?'

'What kind of people are they?'

'I don't know. It's difficult to say. The only one I know well is Rowan Tanquillan. Why do you ask?'

Charlotte explained briefly about the dress. 'Mrs Hollister was in tears over it. It seemed all wrong to me that one person should wield such power over another. Everyone is liable to make mistakes. Perhaps Mrs Hollister had cut out the pattern wrongly, I don't know, but I never saw anyone so upset before.

'Then Lady Tanquillan sent a note cancelling the dress with no apology or mention of payment for the time and material wasted. So even if the dress had been perfectly all right, Mrs Hollister would still have been the loser.'

'I see what you mean.' Joe sighed. 'They are too rich for their own good, I guess. But that doesn't apply to Rowan.'

Charlotte inclined her head. 'Who is – Rowan?'

'Sir Gervaise's son,' Joe explained. 'The old man is a real bastard. None of the workmen like him, but Rowan's different. It's odd, really, but I can never think of Rowan as a Tanquillan. Everyone likes and respects him, but then, he respects the workmen.' Joe yawned and stretched his arms. 'God, I'm tired!' He smiled. 'You mustn't worry too much. It will all be the same a hundred years hence.'

He crossed to the fire and put up the guard. 'Better get back to bed now. You'll be tired out in the morning.' He put out the light.

'Yes, I suppose you are right. But I can't help worrying, not just about the Tanquillans. They are not important.' She stood beside him, looking down into the embers of the dying fire. 'Joe, be honest with me. Do you think there's going to be a war?'

'Yes, I do.'

'But *why?*'

Joe ran his fingers through his hair; his bright young face seemed suddenly much older. 'How the hell should I know? It has to do with territorial rights; with general dissatisfaction; with boredom too, in my opinion.'

'*Boredom?*' Charlotte frowned disbelievingly.

'Among the upper classes, I mean. Men who are tired of fox-hunting as a sport. Men who can't wait to get into a fight to prove themselves better than the other fellow. That's what I believe. Wars are created by the politicians; the generals, the men in Whitehall. It's all a crazy game to them!'

Charlotte asked, in a low, frightened voice, 'When will it come?'

'I don't know,' Joe said wearily. 'When something happens to trigger it off, I guess. The Germans are arming to the teeth, and so are the Russians. All I know is that it *will* come: that nothing we can say or do will prevent it.'

'Oh, *Joe!*'

He held out his hands to her. 'I'm sorry, I shouldn't have said that. I didn't mean to frighten you.'

'No, don't feel sorry.' Charlotte clasped her brother's hands tightly in hers. 'We have always been truthful with each other. Just one thing. Whatever happens, don't go and get yourself killed! Promise? I couldn't live without you, Joey!'

CHAPTER THREE

Snow had turned to powdery sleet as the Tanquillans walked beneath tugging black umbrellas to the graveside. The parson and the bearers felt the full force of the wind as they filed solemnly in front of the mourners. The pages of the prayer book fluttered in the parson's cold fingers, his white surplice billowed about his knees, revealing the soaked hem of his cassock and the fact that his shoes needed heeling. The bearers inclined their heads away from the coffin digging into their shoulders as they carried Oliver Tanquillan to his last resting-place, a melancholy spot beneath wind-racked elms in a London cemetery.

Mouldering leaves combined with the slush to make the path more difficult. Rachel Tanquillan, walking stiffly beneath the plunging umbrella held by her husband, thought that Oliver had been a nuisance in life and was proving equally so in death, and yet her pale set face beneath a clinging black veil revealed nothing of her feelings. She simply wished the charade over and done with as quickly as possible, and hoped the child would not become hysterical when her father's coffin was lowered into the ground.

Glancing over her shoulder, she saw that the girl was walking quietly enough beside Rowan, her thin, gloved hand in his, her tear-stained face beneath her black tam-o'-shanter set in a stubborn, mutinous mask.

Her ladyship experienced a sudden surge of anger that the wretched child was now their responsibility since there was no-one else to care for her except, possibly, Gervaise's Aunt Kitty. And why should not that crazy old spinster be asked to take the girl off their hands, at least during the summer holidays? It was unthinkable that she and Gervaise should be saddled with a rebellious thirteen-year-old brat when they went abroad in July.

Hatred of her late brother-in-law, who had lived impecuniously and died such a shameful death, welled up inside her, and yet her pinched face with its aquiline nose and piercing grey eyes gave nothing away. She merely walked along the path in front of her, holding up her skirt with an elegantly-gloved hand.

Sir Gervaise, walking stolidly beside his wife, knew exactly what was going through that coolly analytical brain of hers, and he shared her dislike of this funeral, with its disturbing undertones, as much as he had despised his brother Oliver, whose way of life had scarcely complemented his own.

Deepset eyes watering with the cold, Gervaise glanced with distaste at the coffin with its tilting family wreaths, experiencing the same bitterness towards Oliver dead as he had done when he was alive. His only satisfaction lay in the knowledge that never again would he be called on to pay his brother's debts. And yet Oliver, as poor as he was, had bequeathed him one legacy he had rather done without – his child, Alice, whom he detested as much as the father, an unattractive girl whose presence in his household would prove a constant thorn in his flesh.

As the wind came whistling between the macabre reminders of man's mortality, bending and shaking the elms near the graveyard wall, Gervaise thought that a suitable boarding-school must be found for Alice as soon as possible, although considerable string-pulling would be needed to persuade any headmistress to accept a girl whose uncontrollable temper had already shattered the calm of his house in Eaton Square.

The whole thing was monstrous: Oliver's death and having his child thrust upon him to care for and educate. He remembered the shockingness of the scene he had witnessed the day he was called to his brother's rooms in Highgate. The seedy pawnbroker's shop down a narrow side street had been the venue for a group of gossiping sightseers as his carriage drew up outside it.

The crones standing on the pavement, pulling shawls about their shoulders in the biting snow-flurries, had reminded him of knitting-women round a guillotine. Bad news travelled fast. They craned their necks as the pawnbroker hurried down the steps, babbling of how he had found his lodger in a pool of blood. 'He must have fallen and struck his head on the fender,' the man said. 'The kid ran down to tell us her father had been taken ill. Of course we saw in a jiffy that he was as dead as mutton. My missus dragged the kid out of the room then. Scream! I've never heard anything like it! She clawed at my poor wife: made her hand bleed!'

Gervaise listened in silence as he mounted the stairs. Inside his brother's room, he was obliged to take out his handkerchief. The stench was appalling. Oliver's body lay near the fireplace. A syrupy pool of blood, coagulated like clotted cream, stained the cinder-strewn hearth.

'Have you sent for the police?'

'Gawd no, sir.' The pawnbroker wiped his forehead with a spotted handkerchief. 'I thought I'd better send for you, sir, knowing you were his brother.'

'Then I suggest you send for them at once.'

Gervaise glanced round the room where his brother had lived out his miserable existence. What he saw shocked his deepest sensibilities. An animal, he thought, would not have fouled its lair in such a manner.

The slatted blinds, held with yellowing calico strips, were half closed. Filtering daylight revealed the unmade bed, the litter of whisky bottles on the bedside table. A stained tumbler half full of the stuff stood amid the litter of books and papers on a chenille-covered table in the centre of the room, beside his brother's typewriter.

The place smelt sourly of whisky, and something else besides. With a sense of utter revulsion, Gervaise saw that the dead man's trousers were soaked with urine. He must have clutched, as he fell, the strip of chenille bordering the mantelpiece, ripping away the dusty, bobbled green fabric which remained grasped in his dead fingers. He had brought down with it an avalanche of rubbish: letters, a brass spillholder, and several cheap ornaments which lay smashed among the blood, cinders and fire-tongs in the hearth.

'My God,' Gervaise muttered. But his invocation had nothing to do with pity or regret that his only brother lay dead. It was a cry of disgust, disgust, which struck him as a physical blow, that a Tanquillan had chosen to live and die in such squalor. Even the sight of the blood-let which had robbed his brother of life had not moved him to pity.

'Ay, it's a bad business,' the pawnbroker said heavily. 'And what's to be done about the girl? She can't stay here, sir, that's certain. And there's a matter of rent owing, and those broken ornaments. Who's going to pay for them, I should like to know?'

Gervaise drew out his wallet, threw, contemptuously, a couple of notes on the table.

'Oh, thank you, sir. Very generous of you, I'm sure. But what about the girl?'

'She will come with me.' Time, Gervaise thought, might eventually blot out the memory of that room, but he was now saddled with the detestable spawn of his brother's loins, his half-witted child, Alice, whose keening could be clearly heard from another room.

Alice Tanquillan held onto Rowan's hand as to a lifeline, the only comforting touch she had known since her father died. Shocked and bewildered, the girl had found herself suddenly wrenched from her own environment and taken to her uncle's house in Eaton Square.

Stumbling along the path to the graveside, she remembered the carriage ride through the streets of London as a nightmare as she had screamed and screamed to be taken back to her father. Ignoring her pleas, her uncle hustled her indoors, bruising her arm, telling her to be quiet, to control herself. Servants turned away shocked faces as she struggled to free herself of her uncle's grip and shouted at him that he was a pig, and she hated him.

Writhing and wriggling like a worm, Alice had managed to free herself momentarily, and blundered into an elegant side table, upsetting a blue and white flower-container. Suddenly, there at her feet lay the shattered fragments, a scattering of soil, and a heap of broken hyacinths.

Breathing heavily, Sir Gervaise had rung for a servant. 'Take her upstairs to the nursery for the time being, Mrs Pritchard, and turn the key on her,' he snapped.

In a room on the top floor, with bars to the windows, Alice had cried herself sick with terror. Shivering and moaning, she climbed onto a window seat, and banged at the glass with her clenched fists. Daylight was fading. The sky above Eaton Square was heavy with grey, scurrying clouds. She had sunk down then in her prison-house, wailing like a banshee, a high, keening note of grief which brought her uncle hurrying upstairs in a temper.

'How dare you make such a hideous noise?' he said sternly.

'I – I want my father!'

'Your father is dead! The sooner you get that into your head, the better!'

She had watched, in horrid fascination, the pale lips beneath his prickly moustache mouthing words which made no sense to her. Springing up, she cried out, 'It's a lie! He isn't dead, he isn't! He *isn't*!' She knew her uncle was lying: trying to keep her away from the man who was all the world to her, Oliver Tanquillan with his quietly amused brown eyes, clean-shaven top lip, whisky breath and warm, loving nature. 'Won't you take me back to him? *Please*, Uncle Gervaise!'

'I have just told you,' Gervaise spoke with the clipped accents of a schoolmaster attempting to hammer the multiplication table into the head of an idiot child, 'that your father is dead! You will remain here until I have made other arrangements for you. But understand this, I will not tolerate having my home turned into a bear-garden.'

'But you are not going to keep me locked up? I couldn't bear that!' She had torn at his sleeve, half wild with terror.

'Let go of my arm this instant!' But she had clung to him, whimpering, as he laid his hand on the doorknob.

He was sweating profusely by that time, his mottled cheeks flushed red with anger. She had stepped away from him then, trembling and proud, her thin shoulders drawn back. 'I shall hate you as long as I live,' she said in a low voice, 'just as my father hated you. But no, he didn't exactly hate you, he just felt sorry for you. I know because he told me so. He called you a self-seeking bastard who would sell his soul for a government contract.'

'How *dare* you!' The very air between them had seemed charged with Tanquillan's sense of outrage as he strode from the room, locking the door behind him.

Two servants came up later, carrying clean bed-linen, sticks and coal to light a fire, and a tray with milk and sandwiches.

Standing near the old rocking-horse, Alice watched them make up the bed. 'I want to go to the lavatory,' she said in a clear voice. 'I shall wet my knickers otherwise.'

The younger of the two maids, Irish by her accent, glanced anxiously in her direction. 'You're not to be let out, miss. Master's orders. I'll fetch you a chamber-pot.'

'Please, won't you let me out?' Alice crept forward. 'You see, I must go back to my father. He'll be so anxious about me.'

The two exchanged glances. 'I'm ever so sorry, miss,' the Irish girl said compassionately, 'but it would be more than our jobs are worth. I'll just nip and get you a chamber, then you must try to eat your supper, and go to bed like a good girl.'

'I don't want any supper. I just want to go to my father,' Alice said patiently.

'Oh lor',' said the Irish girl, 'I'm not sure I like this business at all, at all. But Madam's coming from Scarborough soon. She'll know what to do.'

When Madam arrived, Alice was made to bath and brush her tangled hair before being marched down to the drawing-room. Mrs Pritchard, the housekeeper, a tall woman in black with pince-nez glasses cutting furrows into the sides of her nose, and an expression of extreme distaste on her equine face, had walked beside her like a wardress, gripping her arm.

Inside the room, a thin woman in grey was seated near the fire, a woman whose cold, disapproving eyes matched the colour of her dress.

Tears welled up in Alice's eyes. Her legs shook so much that she could scarcely stand up by herself as the housekeeper turned and closed the heavy double doors behind her. Then suddenly a tall, dark-haired young man with compassionate eyes stepped forward from the window to take her trembling hands in his.

'I am your cousin Rowan,' he said. 'Poor Alice. I am so sorry about your father.'

Now, walking to the graveside, it was Rowan's hand that steadied her. When the coffin was lowered into the ground and the parson intoned the final prayer of committal, it was for Rowan's sake that Alice Tanquillan did not give way to hysteria.

It was Rowan who gently reminded her that now was the time to throw on her father's coffin the bunch of snowdrops clutched tightly in her hand.

Poor little scrap, he thought, as the flowers descended in a shower, and spread out in their green and white-belled innocence on the coffin lid.

Then he took her hand and led her away from the gaping hole in the ground, along the paths bordered with weeping angels and all the scrolls and cherubs attendant on the forgotten dead, and sat beside her in the carriage that rolled away the living to the house in Eaton Square.

CHAPTER FOUR

Rowan stood near the drawing-room window, looking out at the lights of Eaton Square. How strange, he thought, all these rooms, like cells, containing their own secret prisoners. Poor Alice alone in his old nursery on the top floor, his mother resting in her bedroom, his father in the library, himself in this pretentious drawing-room – and Oliver Tanquillan locked forever in that tucked-away corner of Highgate Cemetery. The man they had buried as a stranger because he had not conformed to the accepted notions of how a Tanquillan should live and die.

As a boy, Rowan had listened to the story of his uncle's downfall. How, in announcing his intention to become a writer, in defying Grandfather Tanquillan, he had brought about the stroke from which the old man had never recovered.

Sir Gervaise spoke bitterly about his father's decline in health; branded Oliver a rogue and a murderer. But Oliver had paid the price of his folly. When Grandfather Tanquillan's will was read, his younger son was left penniless. Rowan had never understood why. What was so unforgivable in a young man's desire to make his own way in life?

When he had dared to voice that question, he was taken into his father's study and lectured so long and earnestly about Duty and Responsibility that he had never raised the subject again. He was ten years old at the time.

After that dressing-down, his Uncle Oliver had assumed the role of knight errant in Rowan's mind: Don Quixote tilting at forbidden windmills. Later, he had discovered a photograph of Oliver in a forgotten family album tucked away in a nursery cupboard. The photograph, that of a slim youth of sixteen or so, with a thatch of dark curly hair, shy smile, his hands tucked nonchalantly in the pockets of a cricket blazer, might have been a photograph of himself at the same age.

His father's words echoed back to him. 'I want it clearly understood, Rowan, that you are never to mention your uncle's name again. So far as this family is concerned, he is dead.'

His 'dead' uncle, however, had a way of springing up like a jack-in-the-box occasionally. Rowan always knew by the grim set of his father's lips whenever Oliver's letters were handed to him at the breakfast table; knew that it was not brotherly love which prompted Gervaise to send whatever sum of money was requested, but a deeply entrenched fear that Oliver might land himself in bankruptcy court and bring the family name to the attention of the newspapers.

When Oliver married, he sent a scrawled invitation to his wedding. Rowan secretly applauded the tongue-in-cheek impudence of the man. What a sublime gesture. Now he thought of the child born of that marriage. What would become of Alice now that her parents were dead? She seemed to him a starved scrap of a girl, warped by circumstance, marginally unstable. Did she know that her mother had died in a mental institution? Poor Alice seemed to him, because of her inbuilt genes of madness and instability, desperately in need of love and friendship.

He swished the curtains together impatiently, shutting out the view of the square, and turned to the piano, picking out a tune on the keys. Providing even a little stability for Alice was the least he could offer, by way of recompense, his shy knight errant Oliver Tanquillan; not that his championship would meet with his parents' approval, nor could he imagine his fiancée, Romilly Beresford, taking to that oddly unattractive cousin of his.

The Grayler lads, their girlfriends, Maggie, Bob Masters, and Charlotte, began the steep ascent of Scarborough's Oliver's Mount, dragging their toboggans behind them, panting and laughing in the piercingly cold air which stung to crimson the girls' cheeks, and made their eyes water.

Tall Frank Grayler, with his striding walk and Laughing Cavalier moustache, was the leader, a role he naturally assumed as the first-born. Clinging desperately to his hand, Madge Robinson, a girl with a determined chin and full red pouting lips, urged him not to walk so fast. 'You *are* a beast, Frankie! You know my legs are only half the length of yours,' she cried, her strong white teeth gleaming brightly in the winter sunlight.

Turning to laugh at her, Frank experienced a strong desire to kiss those pouting lips of hers, to feel those splendid teeth digging into his bottom lip. Twenty-two now, it was high time he thought of settling down, but giving up his freedom required a great deal of thought since he had long ago discovered his irresistibility to the female sex, and it would seem foolish to deprive womankind in general by marrying just one of them. Even so, every time Frank Grayler felt Madge's teeth digging into his bottom lip, he felt all male, and if he did not soon make up his mind to marry her, Madge's teeth might bite, with equal fervour, some other fellow's bottom lip.

Madge, whose pout belied her cool, appraising brown eyes, had wanted Frank from the minute she saw him lifting down the shutters of his father's shop one morning on her way to work. Expert in the art of flirtation, she had marched past him, head in air, her skirts frothing about her slender ankles encased in neat black boots, happy in the knowledge that she had chosen to wear her new grey costume and best hat. When she heard his low whistle of approval, she had glanced back at him saucily over her shoulder, then raised her chin in pretended disdain.

Soon she had taken to walking past the shop every morning at the same time, knowing that she had made a favourable impression on him. Before long, they had started walking out together in the evenings, nipping into shelters in the Spa gardens for a kiss and a cuddle.

Men, in Madge's experience, preferred stupid girls to strong-minded ones, and so she had giggled a great deal at his jokes: urged him to let her feel his muscles, stroked his moustache with butterfly fingertips, driving him half crazy with her nonsense. But it was best, she considered coolly, not to let his love-making get out of hand during those nocturnal excursions to the Spa shelters. 'Oh don't,' she would cry when his kisses became too demanding. 'If you think I'm that kind of girl, well I'm not, that's all!' All pretended virtue, she would slide away from him, pat her hair and rearrange her hat, knowing that she had aroused his passion to fever-pitch by her teasing. It was all part of her plan.

Harry's girl, Connie, fair-haired and full-bosomed, puffed along the path declaring that she would never make it to the top of the hill. 'Oh do stop a minute, Harry,' she wailed. At nineteen, Connie felt her life to be overshadowed by the size of her bust, and she had taken to walking with her shoulders bent forward to hide it. Now the straps of the 'miracle' brassiere she had sent away for were fairly killing her, gouging into her soft fat shoulders and chafing her tender flesh, so that all she could think about, as she clung to Harry's hand, was her bust and the pain it was causing her. 'Aw, come on,' Harry said impatiently, embarrassed by her puffing and panting, catching Frank's look of amusement, knowing his brother's low opinion of fat girls.

Joe and Annie walked quietly together, hand in hand, followed by Bob and Maggie. Charlotte dawdled along the path behind them, listening with half an ear to her companions, feasting her eyes on the wintry sky above the trees. Far below, near the road leading out of town, a curving lake, the colour of pewter, reflected the pinkness of the sky. Through a gap in the trees she watched a group of girls, carrying tea-trays as toboggans, stream across the road from a school on the lower slopes: heard their laughter on the crystal-clear air.

Struggling up the path, Maggie said crossly, 'I'm going as fast as I can! I'm not a mountain-goat, Bob Masters!' All hot and bothered, she turned to Charlotte. 'What are you hanging back for?' she demanded, angry because her sister looked so calm, cool and collected.

'I was just watching the girls from Queen Margaret's School.'

'Where?'

'Down there.'

'Oh, those silly, rich little sods! I have no patience with them! Mincing round town as if they owned the place, just because they go to boarding-school and their fathers have pots of money,' Maggie snapped, tossing her head.

'They're not mincing now at any rate,' Bob retorted, nettled by Maggie's carping.

'Oh, I suppose you wish you were down there with them, instead of up here with me,' Maggie flashed back at him.

'Don't talk so daft, Maggie! Come on, give me your hand, it's slippery just here.'

'Oh, daft now, am I?'

'Bob didn't mean anything,' Charlotte said, as Maggie was hauled up the path, slipping and sliding, showing her petticoats and plump calves above her tightly-laced boots.

When she was safely landed, Bob turned to help Charlotte, grasping her hand firmly in his, experiencing, at her touch, a strange tingling sensation down his spine, a strong physical desire to keep her hand in his. The intensity of his feeling showed momentarily in his eyes before he turned away, embarrassed, to catch hold of the toboggan, hoping against hope that Maggie hadn't noticed, but he knew she had. She was struggling up the path alone now, her back rigid with disapproval. 'Here, wait for me,' he called out to her.

'I can manage by myself!'

'You'll fall if you're not careful!'

'A fat lot you'd care if I did!' Anger brought tears to Maggie's eyes.

'I don't know what's come over you just lately,' Bob said, bewildered by the turn of events.

Maggie herself scarcely knew. She simply felt out of step with life. Perhaps it had to do with her wedding: the prospect of finding herself alone with Bob on their wedding night. Until the date had been brought forward, she had not given much thought to what would happen to her after the church ceremony: what she would have to do on her honeymoon.

Like most girls of her generation, Maggie was ignorant of the facts of life. The subject remained taboo. Fearfully, she had leafed through the pages of her mother's prayer book to read the wedding service.

'With my body I thee worship.' Oh God, she thought, what

does that mean? For the first time in her life, the extroverted Maggie found herself locked away mentally with secret doubts and fears, wishing she had never promised to get married at all. Now here was Bob attempting to slip his arm round her waist, trying to coax her into a better frame of mind. 'Get off!' she said icily, coldly jealous because she had seen the way he looked at Charlotte, wanting to get back at her sister in some way.

Her chance came when Herbert Franks, the butcher's son, whom Charlotte disliked, shouted to them to wait for him. Maggie smiled grimly at Charlotte's discomfiture. 'Well, why don't you wait for him? He's got his eye on you!'

'I have no intention of waiting for him.' Charlotte remembered the day her mother had sent her round to the butcher's for an extra pound of sausages. Herbert was standing behind the counter wearing a blood-smeared apron, sharpening a knife, grinning at her, showing his pyorrhoea-pitted gums. Suddenly he had picked up a rabbit, slung it on a chopping-board, and sliced off its paws. 'Here,' he laughed, 'take one for luck!'

'*No!*' She had backed away from the counter, horrified by his cruelty.

'Don't tell me you're squeamish about rabbits,' he'd snorted. 'Why, they're nothing but vermin. Watch!' He had picked up a pathetic heap of fur and skinned it, exposing to Charlotte's shocked eyes the animal's naked pink flesh and quivering guts. 'Here, where are you off to?' he had called after her as she stumbled out of the shop, a handkerchief clasped to her trembling lips. 'You've forgotten the sausages.'

At home, sickness had overwhelmed her. She had spent a good half-hour incarcerated in the lavatory. When she emerged, pale and shaken, Filly was on the landing, wringing her hands. 'Whatever's wrong?' she asked.

'I can't explain. But please, Mother, don't ask me to eat meat ever again.'

'Eh? Why not?' Filly had slipped her arm round her waist, failing to understand what ailed her daughter. Sickness, in her book, meant one of two things, pregnancy, or eating something disagreeable, bad meat or fish, or too many sweets.

'Because I can't bear the thought of animals being killed,' Charlotte said, remembering the pig slung between two hooks with blood dripping from its snout in Mr Franks's shop: the heap of chitterlings on a tray in the window, the pig's dead eyes framed with pointed pink lashes – and the rabbit on Herbert Franks's chopping-board.

'You are far too sensitive, that's your trouble,' Filly said inadequately. 'Come on, love, don't cry. Everyone eats meat. It must be all right because it says so in the Bible.'

'I don't care what it says in the Bible.' Charlotte pushed back her tear-wet hair. 'I'll never eat meat again as long as I live.'

'What will you eat then?' Filly was a great believer in good meat dinners with plenty of gravy.

'I – I don't know. Cheese and vegetables, I suppose. Anything, just as long as it doesn't cause suffering to a living creature.'

When the matter was aired at suppertime, Harry, who loved his horse with a fanatical devotion, sided with Charlotte. 'Sis is right,' he said flatly, 'I've been inside the slaughterhouse, and it made me sick.'

'Hold on, son.' Albert laid down his knife and fork. 'No need to go into detail, is there?'

Maggie said airily, helping herself to another sausage, 'Our Charlotte's always getting a bee in her bonnet over something or other.'

'And that's enough from you, young lady,' Albert said. 'If Charlotte chooses not to eat meat, that's entirely up to her.'

From that day, Charlotte had stuck to her guns. Now the thought of joining forces with Herbert Franks for the afternoon made her feel physically ill.

'Oh, go on, Charlotte,' Maggie said slyly. 'Give the lad a chance. I'll ask him to come with us if you are too shy. I'll invite him to have tea with us as well, if you like.'

'Don't you dare, Maggie. I mean it,' Charlotte said in a low voice.

'Leave her be, Maggie,' Bob advised.

'Well I like that! Whose side are you on anyway, Bob Masters?' Joe and Annie heard the argument. Joe said quietly,

'For God's sake, Maggie, mind your own business and leave Charlotte to mind hers. You know she can't stand the sight of Herbert Franks.'

Annie tucked her hand into Charlotte's elbow. 'You are welcome to come with Joe and me,' she said timidly.

'Thanks, Annie, but I'm going home.'

'Then we'll go with you, won't we Joe?'

'No, I don't want to spoil your afternoon,' Charlotte said.

'It's spoilt already, thanks to you,' Maggie snapped.

'Maggie! Is that what you really think?'

'Yes. Oh, I don't know!' Shamefaced at the stricken expression in Charlotte's eyes, Maggie mumbled, 'Why must you act so stuck-up and awkward? At least Herbert Franks would be someone for you to pair off with.'

Joe was angry then. 'How many more times do you need telling, Maggie. Charlotte doesn't want to pair off with Herbert Franks.'

'It's all right, Joe. Please don't say any more.' Charlotte turned back down the path as Herbert hove into view. 'Where are you off to then, Miss Prim and Proper?' he called after her.

'Oh, let her go,' Maggie sang out in a high-pitched voice, 'she's too good for the likes of us!'

Oh, Adonais, Adonais. Charlotte leaned against a tree, sobbing. Presently, when she was calmer, she lifted her eyes to the sky. The wood was still now and silent, beautiful in its winter simplicity.

> 'Life, like a dome of many-coloured glass,
> Stains the white radiance of Eternity.'

It was true. Charlotte noticed, with a quickening of her pulse, the colours of the wood; deep violet shadows beneath umber branches, the great expanse of pink sky with its masses of billowing clouds like soft, warm feather pillows, the whiteness of the snow, the pearl-grey wings of wood-pigeons.

Nearing the road, she heard the sound of laughter and turned to watch the girls of Queen Margaret's School rocketing down the slopes on their tea-trays. Down the field they sped, rolling and tumbling with the abandonment of puppies into the soft snow near the hedge-bottom.

How wonderful it must be to have a decent education, she thought. Teachers capable of answering questions, of stretching the mind, implanting new ideas. To have a room of one's own. If only her mother would let her move up into one of the attics. The thought excited Charlotte. How wonderful that would be. A room with a little writing-desk and a shelf for her books.

Deep in thought, determined to broach the subject of the attic room to her mother as soon as she got home, Charlotte walked quickly down the road past the school.

Equally thoughtful, head bent, feeling like a traitor, Rowan Tanquillan hurried up the school drive to the gates. Poor Alice, he thought, how would she fare alone in a strange atmosphere of green paint and slippery linoleum, desks and chalk-dust?

The girl he bumped into appeared from nowhere. 'I – I beg your pardon,' she said breathlessly, cheeks flushed beneath the green tam-o'-shanter pulled down over her bright red hair.

'Not at all. My fault entirely. I wasn't looking where I was going,' Rowan said.

'Neither was I.' They smiled at each other uncertainly.

'I haven't – hurt you?'

'No, of course not.' Charlotte hurried on down the road.

A quotation sprang to Rowan's mind. Something from a poem he had learned as a boy:

> 'Sir Lancelot mused a little space,
> He said, she has a lovely face . . .'

He wondered briefly who the girl was and where she was going, before his thoughts turned again to Alice Tanquillan.

CHAPTER FIVE

Romilly Beresford could not imagine life without Rowan. Their families had been neighbours before she and Rowan were born. They had played together under the watchful eyes of their respective nannies, he a solemn, handsome little boy, she a plain, colourless little girl tormented by the occasional presence of other, prettier girls who came to nursery tea, torn with jealousy if Rowan so much as smiled at them, when she would burst into tears and declare that she did not want any jelly. Rowan was *her* property. She wanted him all to herself. Her tears and tantrums were to gain his attention, to make him look at her, not at those silly little ninnies with their rosebud mouths and stupid ringlets.

She had made up her mind that one day she would marry Rowan, when she grew up to be beautiful. It had never entered her mind that she would always be plain, that nothing could ever alter her slightly bulbous forehead or the sharp, bony bridge to her nose. Romilly's only claim to beauty lay in her softly waving brown hair which her nanny made her wear scraped back from her brow and tied with a bow of ribbon, because it was less troublesome that way.

In vain she had begged to have her hair cut in a fringe. 'A *fringe*? The very idea, miss! Nasty, floppy things. You'll go cross-eyed. *Ask* your mother then. She'll say the same! Madam's very proud of your hair the way it is.'

One night Romilly slid out of bed to stare at her reflection by candlelight. No one knew or understood how much she loathed that bulging forehead of hers. In a frenzy, she picked up a pair of nail-scissors and clipped away at the front of her hair until the dressing-table was littered with tresses. When she had finished, she saw, with horror, the jagged ends of her butchery, and wept bitterly because she had made herself look even uglier.

Her mother was coldly furious next morning. 'What on earth possessed you to do such a stupid thing?' Emily Beresford stared at her daughter as if she had contracted some loathsome disease. 'You've ruined your hair, your looks.'

'Looks! I haven't any looks!' Romilly's eyes were red-rimmed with weeping. 'Nothing I could do to myself would make any difference!' She had flung herself away from her mother, crying bitterly, and raced upstairs to her room. She was fourteen at the time, long past nursery-days and nannies, a leggy schoolgirl, unpopular with other girls of her age, morbidly obsessed with her appearance.

Emily Beresford, smelling deliciously of French perfume, rustled into the room after her. Her daughter was stretched across the bed, shoulders heaving, head buried in the pillows. 'I'm sorry I spoke so sharply,' Emily said. 'I was shocked, to put it mildly. If you had asked my permission . . .'

'You'd have said no.'

'Oh, my dear.' Emily sat down on the edge of the bed. 'I've always been so proud of your hair.' She touched Romilly's shoulder. 'Come now, sit up. We must discuss what's to be done about it. More importantly, why you cut your hair in the first place.'

'I – I'm so tired of being – ugly.' The words came in a long, shuddering sigh.

'*Ugly!* What utter nonsense!' Emily spoke lightly. 'Why, my dear girl, you're not at all ugly. You have a lovely clear skin, slender hands and feet, a good figure, pretty hair. More than that, you have a great deal of intelligence. It is up to you to use that intelligence to make the most of yourself.'

'I don't understand.'

'If you'll just sit up and stop crying, I'll try to explain. That's better.' Emily gave Romilly her handkerchief. 'I've never told this to anyone before, but there was a time when I believed myself to be – not ugly – but unattractive. Then, at finishing school, I learned some very important lessons. How to move

53

gracefully, to hold my head correctly, to smile charmingly – especially at your father.' She said teasingly, 'As you will learn to smile at Rowan. I imagine he is at the bottom of all this.'

A hot tide of colour suffused Romilly's face. 'Rowan?' she murmured.

'There's no need to blush, my dear. I think I understand. You are very fond of him, aren't you?'

Relief flooded through Romilly because her mother was smiling. She said childishly, 'But Rowan isn't fond of me.'

'He will be, if you are clever enough.' Emily carefully considered her daughter's hair. She said, 'Perhaps cutting that fringe wasn't such a bad idea after all. I think I had better make an appointment for you, with Monsieur Jacques, to have it properly cut. But you must promise me that you will never cut the rest of your hair.' She gathered up the soft mass and drew it back from Romilly's tear-stained face, revealing the slim column of her throat. 'Ah yes,' she nodded, 'when you are older and put up your hair, it will look quite charming.'

'Oh Mummy, do you really think so?'

'Yes, I do.'

From then on, Romilly became a quiet observer of her mother's friends when they came to tea, and she began to realize that charm could be spread like honey on bread. She noticed their clothes, how they dressed their hair, held their shoulders, fluttered their hands, walked into a room. In the privacy of her bedroom she would emulate them, gesturing, smiling, even curtseying in front of the cheval-glass.

Often, she pretended the mirror to be Rowan Tanquillan. She would walk towards it breathlessly, her head held a little to one side, discovering, through trial and error, that if she pulled her fringe down closer to her eyebrows her eyes seemed larger, the bridge of her nose less conspicuous. Then she would kiss the mirror, clouding the glass with the soft emanation of breath from her parted lips.

Romilly's headmistress wrote to her parents in complimentary terms, commending their daughter's academic improvement. Her praise was sincere. Even so, as she penned her report, she could not help wondering what had brought about Romilly's newly-acquired interest in her lessons, what had caused the metamorphosis of a round-shouldered school-girl to a model of deportment.

But that growing-up period was fraught with misery for Romilly, who felt that she was not growing up fast enough. Rowan was slightly older than herself. What if he should meet another girl; become engaged to marry her?

Their paths had diverged suddenly. She saw little of him these days. When they did meet, she felt utterly tongue-tied and stupid. None of the tricks she practised in the secrecy of her bedroom seemed to work when she met him face to face.

It was so unfair. At nineteen, going on twenty, almost six feet tall, with broad shoulders, clean-shaven chin and top lip, Rowan seemed a man, herself nothing but a wretched school-girl. All she did was peg away at her school lessons, while Rowan was abroad in France, Italy and Germany, learning about wine, cheeses, silk and lace manufacture; everything relevant to foreign imports to Britain. He would pay flying visits to England from time to time, strong and suntanned, glowing with health and vitality, and she would watch him talking to her parents in that easy, relaxed way of his; longing to touch him, to have him smile at her, kiss her, to feel the warmth of his hand in hers, to look at her with the sudden realization that she was no longer a child but a woman, to notice the slimness of her waist, the delicacy of her complexion, the abundant hair, worn up now and thickly coiled at the nape of her neck. But he appeared not to notice her at all, and the realization made her feel even duller, more stupid.

When, during a courtesy call on her parents, he said that he was going to Scarborough to look after his father's interests there, Romilly felt she would choke with misery.

'How long shall you remain there?' Emily Beresford glanced at her daughter as she asked the question, knowing exactly what was going through her mind at the time.

'Indefinitely,' Rowan said. 'It's a question of making my home there from now on. I've always liked Scarborough, and my being there permanently will come as a relief to my father.'

Romilly's father, Edmund Beresford, greying, charming,

cultured, the director of a publishing firm, leaned forward interestedly. 'You'll live in the Chalice Walk house, I suppose?'

Rowan smiled. 'My parents expect me to do so, of course.'

'But you have your own ideas?'

'Yes, sir. I've made enquiries about a fisherman's cottage near the harbour. Just a small place. As a matter of fact, I've already signed the deeds for it.'

'A – fisherman's cottage?' Emily raised her eyebrows. 'But who would look after you?' The notion of a Tanquillan living in a fisherman's cottage slightly bewildered her.

Rowan laughed. 'No-one, Mrs Beresford. I'll look after myself. I like the idea of being independent.'

'A healthy attitude, my boy,' Beresford chuckled. 'Every young man should learn how to fend for himself.'

Noticing the anguished expression on her daughter's face, Emily adroitly changed the subject. 'Romilly is going to France next month,' she said brightly, 'to a finishing school near Paris.'

'Oh how splendid for you, Romilly,' Rowan said, smiling at her. Not really seeing me at all, she thought desperately. 'Are you looking forward to it?'

'Yes,' she said stiffly, twisting her hands in her lap, wanting to cry out, 'No! I shall hate it!'

When Rowan had taken his leave, Emily hurried upstairs to Romilly's bedroom.

'I told you so! He doesn't even *like* me!' Romilly burst into a storm of tears. 'He doesn't even *see* me!'

'Not at the moment, perhaps. But he will. Just wait a little while longer.'

'*Wait!* I shan't see him again for two years!' Romilly cried. 'All those things you told me! None of them is true. I've tried so hard, but it's no use!'

'Nonsense,' Emily said calmly. 'You are still shy and a little gauche, that's all. That is why you must make the most of your time abroad. Finishing school will teach you to broaden your outlook, how to project your personality, if you are prepared to set aside the mistaken notion that only beautiful women get what they want from life.'

'But what if he meets someone in Scarborough? What if he marries someone else?'

'That is hardly likely, in my opinion. Rowan has a job to do. Knowing him, he'll give his work all his time and attention before he starts thinking about marriage.' Emily paused. 'Perhaps I shouldn't tell you this, but Rowan is scarcely likely to marry against his parents' wishes, and the Tanquillans have clear-cut ideas about the girl they would like their son to marry.'

Romilly's eyes widened suddenly. 'You mean – me?'

'Now will you go to Paris like a good girl?'

'Yes. Yes, I will!' Light-headed with happiness, Romilly caught hold of her mother's hands. 'Thank you, Mummy. Thank you for telling me.'

Emily thought, with a deep sense of relief, that Romilly was almost pretty when she was happy.

CHAPTER SIX

Sir Gervaise had pulled strings to get Alice a place at Queen Margaret's School. For one thing term had already begun, and it was usual practice for the headmistress to interview prospective pupils and their parents before acceptance. But Gervaise Tanquillan had a way of overriding normal procedures. His ruthless determination had brought him what he most valued in life, his knighthood, his wife, his wealth and his position in society. In the case of his brother's child, he required a speedy solution to his immediate problems concerning her. Queen Margaret's, a not too expensive boarding-school far removed from London, offered such a solution. He wrote to the headmistress personally.

The lady replied that she would be pleased to take his niece as a boarder, for a limited period at any rate, until she assessed the child's potential as a student. Queen Margaret's held a high reputation which she felt it her duty to maintain. In view of the tragic circumstances, however, she would relax the rules on this occasion and accept Alice mid-term, waiving the usual entrance examination. It was a letter which stated between the lines that everything rested with the pupil, no matter who her sponsor might be.

Gervaise called Rowan to his study and showed him the letter. 'I leave it to you,' he said, 'to tell the girl what has been arranged.'

'*School!*' Alice cried. 'In *Scarborough?*' Her poor, tormented mind could not grasp what he said. London was the only place she knew. She felt lacerated, betrayed. Leaving London meant leaving her father. 'I won't go,' she said passionately, 'I won't go! I'll kill myself first!'

She ran to the barred nursery window to beat her hands impotently against the glass. Rowan saw, with infinite pity, the heaving of her thin shoulders beneath the ugly mourning dress she wore, and strode across to her. Taking her flaying hands in his, he pulled her gently but firmly to the fire, made her sit down, and mopped her streaming eyes with his handkerchief.

She faced him hostilely, as if he had delivered her into the hands of uncaring enemies. 'You won't be alone, you know. I'll be there,' he said. 'Try to think of it as a new beginning. A kind of freedom. You trust me, don't you?'

'*No!*'

'I'll call for you every Saturday afternoon and take you out to tea. As many chocolate eclairs as you can eat. Then we shall walk along the beach together. I'll show you my cottage and the office where I work. You'll like the sea, Alice, and the harbour. We'll hire a rowing-boat and go fishing.'

'Really, Rowan? Just the two of us?'

'Of course.'

Her lips trembled. 'I've never been to school before, except a silly little school with two old women in charge. My father taught me after that.' She reached up and flung her arms round his neck. 'Oh Rowan,' she whispered, 'I miss him so. But I love you.'

A knock came at the door. The servant said quietly, 'Mrs Beresford and Miss Romilly are downstairs in the drawing-room.'

'Thank you. Tell them I'll be down in a few minutes.' Rowan frowned, wishing the interruption had not happened just then. He ruffled Alice's hair. 'Feeling better now, Scrap?'

'Who is Romilly?' A cold note of jealousy crept into Alice's voice.

'Romilly is my fiancée,' he said lightly.

'Fiancée?' Alice stared at him wildly. 'Does that mean you are going to marry her?'

'Yes, eventually.'

'But you said there'd be just the two of us. You lied to me, and I hate you!'

59

'No, Alice, I did not lie to you. Nothing has changed. We are going to Scarborough together the day after tomorrow.'

'But when you get married, she will go to Scarborough, too! You'll love her more than you love me!'

He said quietly, 'I'll come back later, Scrap.'

She backed away from him like a wild creature. 'I don't want you to come back – ever!' she muttered hoarsely. 'And I won't go to Scarborough with you!'

When he had gone, she sank to her knees. Tears flooded between her fingers. When she could cry no more, she got up, opened the door, stole on to the landing, and hung over the banister, staring down at the great well of the staircase and the tessellated hall far below. One spring and she would lie there on those cold marble slabs like a broken pawn on a giant chessboard.

The Beresfords had just returned from an extended family visit to Scotland where they had stayed, with Edmund's mother, for Christmas and the new year, despite Romilly's pleading to be allowed to stay in London to spend Christmas with Rowan.

'You know that is out of the question.' Emily had remained obdurate. 'Arrangements have been made. Rowan will spend Christmas with his family and travel to Scotland in the new year.'

But Rowan had not gone to Scotland as planned. The sudden death of his uncle had prevented his doing so. Truth to tell, he had felt relieved to be spared the ordeal of appearing among a bevy of Beresford uncles and aunts as Romilly's fiancé. As he walked slowly downstairs, it occurred to him that he had seen Romilly only twice since their engagement. How incredible that after such a short separation he could not bring her face clearly to mind. Drawing in a deep breath, he entered the room.

'Rowan, *darling*!' Romilly jumped up with the eagerness of a child; held up her face to be kissed, and hung on to his arm, treating him with a playful possessiveness which irked him, glancing coyly beneath the brim of her hat, spreading out the fingers of her left hand on his coat sleeve, smiling as the light caught the sparkling sapphire and diamond engagement ring she wore.

'Come, sit with me.' She patted the sofa cushions to indicate the exact spot, and began talking, in a high-pitched voice, about Scotland; how disappointed she was when she received the telegram cancelling his visit.

Emily Beresford reminded her, with a veiled warning glance, that they should remember the reason for the cancellation.

Romilly flushed. 'Oh yes, of course. I'm sorry. But I did write to Rowan about it at the time.'

Emily said sympathetically, 'We were all very sorry, Rachel. What an appalling thing to have happened. It was very sudden, I gather.'

Rachel's eyelids flickered momentarily. This was a subject she had wished to avoid. She had no desire to talk about Oliver Tanquillan or the presence of his child under her roof. 'Yes, it was very sudden,' she said calmly.

'I never knew you had an uncle,' Romilly said artlessly, gazing up at Rowan. 'How odd that you had never mentioned him before.

'My husband and his brother were never very close,' Rachel said coolly. 'I suppose one could describe Oliver as the black sheep of the family.' She wondered if Emily knew the truth, if a breath of scandal had ever reached her ears. Probably not. In the event, what did it matter now? Oliver was dead and buried. She turned the subject adroitly. 'How well you are looking, Romilly,' she said.

'Thank you, Lady Tanquillan. I *feel* well . . .'

Rowan glanced covertly at Romilly's face as she chattered on about Scotland, noticing the high-bridged nose and pale blue eyes, the upswept coil of hair on which rested a fashionable, feathered hat, the slight swell of her breasts beneath the green basqued blouse, the fox furs draped round her shoulders.

In his present analytical mood, she seemed to Rowan less of a flesh and blood woman than a work of art. Somewhere beneath that fashionable, perfumed façade must lurk the Romilly of long ago, who had cheated at hide and seek and burst into tears whenever she wished to draw attention to herself. God, what had he been thinking about to fall into the trap so easily?

The tide of conversation washed over him as he remembered the day, last October, when he came to London to attend Romilly's coming-of-age party, summoned by a letter from his mother who made it plain that she expected him to be there.

His first impulse had been to ignore the letter, to cut the strings manipulated by parental puppeteers, but he had no valid reason not to go. He caught the train reluctantly, glimpsing as it pulled out of Scarborough station the tall houses bordering Westwood, the smooth uplifted breast of Oliver's Mount washed with a tide of autumn leaves. Leaning his head against the seat, he thought, with distaste, of London, which seemed to him a desert, totally restrictive and curiously lacking the vitality he had learned to value in the north of England: a kind of puppet theatre where human beings jerked on carefully manipulated strings, playing out their little dramas and comedies against an artificial background of extreme wealth or soul-destroying poverty.

As the train clattered on, he knew he would miss, even for a few days, the warm comfort of his cottage near the harbour where he lived as he chose to live – eating whenever he felt hungry, sinking his teeth into crusty bread spread thick with butter; bringing home fish fresh from the sheds, cooking it over the kitchen fire, watching, with a strange sense of euphoria, firelight dancing on the walls and rafters. Or, when the notion took him, striding down the cobbled street to a Sandside pub to drink ale with the locals, sinking into his narrow bed afterwards, replete and curiously happy.

In a moment of folly he had exchanged that freedom for chains. Conditioned to do what his puppeteers expected of him, he had dressed for Romilly's party, hearing, as he wrestled with his tie and brushed his hair, the sound of music and laughter drifting up from the house next door. Light spilled on to the steps when the door opened, as a liveried footman took his mother's wrap. He recalled that moment of sheer surprise when an elegant, poised, smiling young woman wearing a close-fitting ivory dress swept forward to greet them, her gloved hands extended in welcome.

'Why, Rowan! Is it really you? You've grown even taller since we last met!'

'Romilly?' He had not been able to take in the metamorphosis of gauche chrysalis to self-assured social butterfly. 'I scarcely recognized you.'

'I shall take that as a compliment. How long is it, by the way, since our last meeting?' She knew exactly how long it had been. She had counted the days, hours, years. 'Well, aren't you going to ask me to dance?'

He smiled down at her, holding her hands lightly in his. 'You might regret it. I'm not a very good dancer.'

She laughed, glancing up at him under her softly curling fringe. 'Do you remember the last time we danced together?'

'No, I'm afraid I don't.'

'Have you forgotten Miss Elsom's Dancing Academy? One two three, turn. You wore a sailor-suit and dancing pumps. I wore a white dress with a blue sash. You hid in a corner when Miss Elsom called your name, when it was your turn to dance with me.'

'Did I? I don't remember. What a beastly kid I must have been.' He led her to the shining expanse of maplewood laid down in the conservatory, where the band was playing beneath brilliantly coloured Chinese lanterns.

When the waltz ended and the band struck up a tango, he had laughingly refused to attempt it. Then Romilly tucked her hand in his arm and led him through the open French windows. Her dress glimmered softly by moonlight as she leaned on the wrought-iron balustrade overlooking the garden where they had played together as children. He remembered the faint, sad tang of autumn in the falling leaves, the trace of smoke from an earlier bonfire. 'You mustn't catch cold,' he said.

'Cold! I'm far too excited to feel cold.' She laid a hand on his sleeve. 'Oh Rowan, I've missed you so much. But I don't suppose that you have missed me at all – or even thought about me. No, don't bother to deny it. Why should you? You have your own life to lead now. But you must tell me all about it, about your work, about Scarborough.'

That was the start of it, he thought. Romilly's apparent

interest in his work, linked to the changes he observed in her, the way she had managed to arouse his sense of protectiveness when she shivered slightly and said, 'I do feel a little bit cold after all. Shall we go in and have supper?'

'I should have made you wear a wrap.' He put his arm round her waist to lead her indoors; carried her plate and napkin to a quiet corner of the conservatory. The band had packed up their instruments for the intermission and gone through to the servants' quarters for beer and sandwiches. He went back to the buffet for champagne, pushing his way through the crowd of formally dressed men and elegant women choosing food, not that there was anything formal in their behaviour. Most of them were young and totally uninhibited, Romilly's friends, he supposed, the kind of people he had grown away from in Scarborough.

The older generation were seated at tables. He recognized most of them. His parents and the Beresfords were together at a table in a corner of the room; the younger element had carried their plates to the great hall staircase to perch on the steps.

'Do you still play the piano?' Romilly asked, when he returned with the champagne.

'Not very often nowadays.'

'I wish you'd play for me now. *Please*, Rowan.'

'I – I couldn't possibly. Not here. Not now.'

'Why not? You play so beautifully. Just for me. After all, it is my birthday.'

And so he had crossed to the piano on the rostrum and played Chopin's Waltz in C Sharp Minor, while Romilly clasped her hands ecstatically beneath the swaying Chinese lanterns.

Yes, that was the start of it. Urged by his mother to stay on in London just a little while longer because she saw him so seldom these days, it had seemed natural enough to escort the new, work-of-art, Romilly to art galleries, concerts and the theatre. 'But I must get back to work soon, Mother,' he said, puzzled by Rachel's insistence that he should remain, neglecting to add that he had had quite enough of London for the time being.

'Your father agrees with me that you need a break,' she said.

'Yes, but I've been here almost a week now.'

'Just a few more days, darling, to please me.'

And so the pearly October days drew in to the first rain and fog of November. On a grey, rain-soaked afternoon, at tea with his mother and Romilly in the drawing-room, he announced casually that he had decided to return to Scarborough the next day. He might have dropped a bombshell. There was a moment's stunned silence before Romilly made a hurried excuse to leave.

'Really Rowan, that was extremely tactless of you!' Rachel was coldly furious with him.

'I don't understand. Is Romilly ill?' In her hasty departure she had left her gloves on her chair, her tea untasted.

'Are you blind? Can't you see the child is head over heels in love with you?'

'Romilly – in love with me?' He laughed, genuinely amused at the idea.

'I see nothing whatever to laugh about. I'm surprised at you, Rowan, for being so insensitive.'

'I beg your pardon, Mother. But I've known Romilly all my life. I think of her as a sister. Nothing more than that.'

'Oh, you men are such idiots at times! You've paid court to the child since the night of the party. Can you blame her if she thought . . . Can you blame your father or myself for hoping that you would ask Romilly to marry you? You've had your taste of freedom. Now it is high time you settled down.'

He said angrily, 'And what if I don't feel inclined to settle down with a girl I'm not in love with?'

'Don't be so ridiculous. Of course you must settle down. Romilly will make you a charming wife.' Knowing his innate kindness, Rachel tried another tack. 'I think it would be cruel of you not to propose to the poor child after raising her hopes.'

'I've told you, Mother. I think of Romilly as a sister, that's all.'

'Then I strongly advise you to start thinking of her differently from now on.'

'That is a monstrous suggestion.' He had turned away abruptly. 'I think we should end this conversation.'

Rachel knew that she had handled him wrongly. 'Rowan,

darling, don't be angry with me,' she begged. 'I only want what is best for you.' She felt more than a little angry with herself, knowing that she had let the situation get out of hand. Losing one's temper with Rowan had never paid dividends. Her son could be reasoned with, never pushed. She had noticed a new firmness about him recently. His boyhood compliance had toughened to a man's independence. 'I really believed that you had grown to care for Romilly. At least promise me that you will say goodbye to her before you leave.'

'Of course I shall. How could I do otherwise?'

He had made the gloves an excuse to call on Romilly the next morning. Unhappiness was stamped in every line of her. All her new-found confidence was gone. She appeared as someone who has suffered a sudden bereavement. For an instant he glimpsed the old Romilly, the plain child who had cried when she could not get her own way. Curiously, it was this remembered vulnerability that touched him to a genuine concern that he had made her unhappy. He could see that she had been crying. There was an almost shocking apathy about her as she turned her back on him.

'When are you going away?' She asked dully.

'This afternoon.' He hesitated. 'Romilly, I'm so sorry. I meant to make you happy.'

'You did make me happy. I shall think of the time we've spent together as the happiest I've ever known.'

He touched her arm gently, not fully understanding her grief, with no way of knowing that, having expended every ounce of her charm on him, Romilly now believed herself to be a failure. She had lost him. She had lost Rowan after all the waiting and hoping. Never would she come so close to him again. Slow racking sobs shook her thin body.

'Don't, Romilly,' he said softly. 'Please don't cry. I've been happy too.'

Her reaction stunned him. She swung round, caught his hand and pressed it passionately to her lips. 'There. Now you know how I feel about you,' she gasped. 'Goodbye, Rowan.' She ran to the door.

'Wait.' He strode after her, wanting to explain his own feelings, to set things straight between them. Seizing her by the shoulders, he said, 'You mustn't be so upset. We'll meet again soon. I'll be home for Christmas.'

'No. I shan't be here then. It could be years before we meet again. Not that you'll care, because you have never really cared about me at all, have you?'

Bewildered, out of his depth, he shook her slightly to make her see sense. 'Don't say that. Of course I care about you.'

She relaxed suddenly against him, eyes closed, as if she was about to faint. He put his arms round her to save her from falling. She opened her eyes and held up her face to his, lips slightly parted, eyes shining.

'Feeling better?' He kissed her as one might kiss a child; was totally unprepared for the sudden shaking of her body, the way her lips fastened eagerly on his, her expression of radiant happiness when she stepped away from him.

'Oh Rowan, *darling*! I knew it all along. Why didn't you tell me?'

'Tell you . . . ?'

'How much you care for me. I should be very cross with you, but I'll forgive you.' She ran her fingers through his hair. 'Everything is really all right then, after all? We *are* engaged, aren't we? We are going to be married?'

As the conversation turned inevitably to their wedding, and Romilly tilted her head like that of an enquiring robin, Rowan remembered that moment's hesitation which had cost him his freedom. He had started to say that she had misunderstood his kiss, but how could he have borne to extinguish the light of happiness in her eyes? Cruelty was not in his nature. 'If that's what you really want,' he said slowly.

'Oh, I do! It's what I've always dreamed of. I've loved you all my life!'

The trap was sprung.

Now, 'I think we should have a June wedding,' Romilly was saying, 'and a honeymoon in Paris. I adore Paris, don't you Rowan? Isn't it all exciting? So much to think of, so many plans to make.' She sighed ecstatically. 'We haven't even discussed yet where we shall live in Scarborough, and we must settle on something soon. Are you listening to me, darling?'

Rachel smiled indulgently. 'It occurred to me that you might live at the house in Chalice Walk until you have had time to look at other properties. That would solve your immediate problem.'

Romilly clasped her hands delightedly. 'Oh, how kind and generous of you, dear Tante Rachel. I can't wait to see it. You must describe it to me in detail, Rowan.'

'Better still,' Rachel suggested, 'if you went to look at it. Perhaps you and I, Emily, and Romilly, might go to Scarborough next week: join Rowan there.'

'But I thought you said he was going the day after tomorrow, Tante Rachel. Wouldn't it be nice if we could all travel together?'

'Really, my dear,' Emily threw her daughter another warning glance, 'you must learn to curb your impatience. Lady Tanquillan has invited us to go next week, not this.'

Romilly pouted slightly. 'I'm sorry. I just thought it would be nicer for Rowan not to travel alone.'

Rowan glanced at his mother. How hard she had tried to keep off the subject of Alice. He said, with a certain degree of satisfaction, 'But I'm not travelling alone, I'm going with Alice.'

'Alice? Who on earth is she?' Romilly's colour mounted.

The young idiot, Rachel thought, why drag Alice into the conversation? Had he done so deliberately to embarrass her? Too late now. She said lightly, 'Alice is our niece, Rowan's cousin. The child is going to a boarding-school in Scarborough.'

'Oh, I see,' Romilly said. Then, as Rowan got to his feet, 'Where are you going?'

'Speaking of Alice reminded me that she was rather upset when I left her,' Rowan replied. 'Naturally so, since she has never been away to school before. I think I should go to her now, if you'll excuse me.'

'That is hardly necessary,' Rachel said coldly.

'I happen to think otherwise. She is, after all, just a child, a lonely, unhappy child.'

'But we haven't settled our wedding date,' Romilly said in a high-pitched voice.

'No, I'm sorry. Perhaps we can discuss that later.' Rowan did not give a damn at that moment for wedding plans. He had the strangest feeling that Alice was in some kind of danger, that he must go to her at once.

As he strode purposefully upstairs to the top landing, he saw that Alice was poised on the banister, her back to the wall, staring down at the chequered hall below. 'Don't come any closer,' she warned him. 'I shall jump if you do.'

'You'll do no such thing,' he said calmly. 'Get down at once!'

She stared at him wildly. 'Why should I? I'd be better off dead. Nobody would care!'

'I would care.' His heart lurched as her foot slipped. He lunged forward, caught her in his arms and pulled her to safety. 'You stupid little fool,' he groaned, smoothing her hair from her ravaged face. 'Haven't you the sense you were born with?' He lifted her up and carried her back to the nursery, laid her on the bed and sat beside her, scarcely able to speak for the pounding of his heart.

She stared up at him. 'Don't you love me the least little bit?' she whispered.

'It depends what you mean by love.'

'I once read a book,' she said, 'all about love. It made me ache, somehow, down here.' She held his hand to her thin belly. 'I can't quite explain it. I just wanted someone to take away the pain inside me. I want you to take the pain away.'

Eyes dark with anguish, he said, 'I'm afraid I can't do that, Alice.'

'But you will take Romilly's pain away, won't you?'

'Probably not, Scrap. You won't understand this, but try to remember it. I have never loved anyone – any woman – in my life. Perhaps I'm incapable of loving anyone enough to assuage their pain in living.'

'Not even Romilly?' she begged.

'Go to sleep now.'

'Please kiss me.'

He touched her forehead with his lips and sat beside her for a little while, stroking her hair, experiencing, deep within his own body, a longing for love which had so far eluded him. Not the love of a child or a child-woman, but that of a real woman. A woman with a mind to match her beauty. Someone who cared nothing about wealth or position, a woman who would be content to share his life as he wished to live it, simply and fully, without complications.

CHAPTER SEVEN

Steam eddied and flattened beneath the vaulted glass roof of King's Cross station. Alice clung to Rowan's hand, too frightened to speak. He stopped at the bookstall to buy a newspaper. Uncertain February sunshine filtered between the high-flung arches as they walked together to the train. The porter put their luggage on the rack in a first-class compartment. Alice perched on the edge of the window seat. Her face, Rowan noticed, was chalk-white, her shoulders hunched with tension. Feeling in his pocket, he handed her a few pennies for chocolate.

'Where?' she asked uncertainly.

'See that red machine on the platform?'

'Yes.'

'Put your money in, a penny at a time, and pull out the drawer.'

'By myself?'

'Of course.'

'What if the train goes without me?' The thought of being left alone among a crowd of milling strangers made her tremble.

'It won't. Go on, Scrap.' He watched her, a lost, lonely little figure, feeding her pennies into the machine. He had wanted to break her tension, to make her act independently to help her conquer her dread of this strange new experience. She had never been on a train before.

She returned smiling, and showed him the chocolate. Six penny bars in silver paper and red wrappers. He could have wept. 'Don't eat them all before lunch,' he said.

'Lunch? You mean here on the train?'

'Yes, of course.'

'Oh, *Rowan*!' The colour came back to her cheeks, her eyes began to sparkle.

London slid away from them, a vast, amorphous octopus under a pale winter sky. Tonight they would stay at the house in Chalice Walk. Tomorrow he must take Alice to school. Then would come the tears he dreaded. 'Sufficient unto the day is the evil thereof.' He would make today as happy as possible for her.

He unfolded his newspaper. Nothing but rumours of war, disturbing news of growing unease between nations. Wealthy German families were being taxed to the hilt to underwrite Germany's armament programme. France and Germany were at each other's throats, Russia's desire for an interest in the Slav Balkans was increasing, alliances were being formed – Germany with Austria and Italy, France with Russia. The German Emperor hinted that only the superiority of the British Navy had prevented his joining in the recent Boer War on the opposing side. Now, apparently obsessed by his envy of British naval power, the Kaiser had begun to build up his own fleet.

The situation was fraught with danger. What would it take, Rowan wondered, to trigger the coming Armegeddon. He had no doubt that it would come, that its coming would sweep the world like raging tongues of fire. And yet there remained, in Britain, amongst politicians who should know better, a kind of lazy arrogance which irked him; the kind of arrogance prevalent in slow cricket matches at Lords.

Alice sat bolt upright in the dining-car, as prim and proper as a child at a party, saying 'Yes please,' and 'No thank you,' to the waiter. A firm 'No' to the Brown Windsor soup, 'Yes' to the roast lamb and mint sauce. A shuddering 'No' to the carrots, a shining 'Oh yes, please' to apple tart and custard.

She looked almost pretty, Rowan thought, when she laughed. 'Listen,' he said. 'Can you hear what the wheels are saying?'

'No. What?'

'I think I can, I think I can, I think I can.'

'Oh yes. That's right!'

'And when they are going uphill. "Noooo, I'm sure I can't,

I'm sure I can't, I'm sure I can't.'"

She clapped her hands delightedly.

When they had finished luncheon, she fell fast asleep in the compartment, her chocolate bars beside her.

Looking at her, Rowan uttered a silent prayer to the God he scarcely believed in. Help me to keep her safe. He was thinking of Oliver Tanquillan at the time.

Daylight was fading when they reached Scarborough. Alice was solemn now, tired and fretful after the long journey. Lomas, the coachman, was on the platform to help with the luggage – a stocky, middle-aged Yorkshireman, amiable and weather-beaten, who doubled as gardner-cum-odd-job-man in his spare time.

'Up you go, miss,' he said cheerfully, helping Alice into the carriage and tucking a rug round her knees. 'Not far to go now.' But Alice remained silently mistrustful of the stranger with his queer way of speaking, refusing to smile, inching closer to Rowan as the carriage moved out of the station yard.

'Well, here we are, Scrap.'

Alice stared at the house. 'I'm not going in,' she said flatly, overwhelmed by the strangeness of everything.

'Oh, that's rather a pity isn't it?' Rowan said easily, dismounting; holding out his hand to her. 'I daresay Mrs Lomas has tea ready for us.'

'Mrs Lomas?' Alice frowned. 'Who's she?'

'Mrs Lomas is the housekeeper. Come in and meet her.' Smiling, he coaxed Alice over the threshold of the house in Chalice Walk. She reminded him of a small, mistreated animal uncertain of human motives. He made an unusual to-do about helping Lomas carry in the luggage, giving Alice time to look round her. Perhaps, he thought, she had expected cold black and white marble and frowning portraits, reminders of her stay at the house in Eaton Square. But this house was far less imposing, with its warmly carpeted hall and unpretentious staircase. He threw his hat and gloves on the central octagonal table, his coat over a chair. 'That's my music room,' he said, 'the room straight ahead. The drawing-room's on the right, the library on the left. Here, let me take your things. I'll show you round the house after tea. Ah, here's Mrs Lomas.'

'Good afternoon, sir.' The housekeeper appeared, smiling, smoothing the back of her hair with a practised hand to encompass stray locks which might have escaped her tortoiseshell combs: a plump, rosy-cheeked woman wearing a plain black skirt and a crisp white blouse fastened with a garnet brooch. 'Tea's just on ready, Mr Rowan. I've lit the fire in the music room.' She smiled warmly at Alice. 'Perhaps the young lady would like to see her room. Come along, my dear, I expect you're cold and tired after that long journey, and wanting your tea.'

Thankfully, Alice made no demur. Whistling his relief, Rowan went into the music room. He was standing near the French windows leading to the terrace when the girl came downstairs, hands and face washed, her long brown hair tied back with a clean blue ribbon. Thank God for Mrs Lomas, he thought.

Alice was happy again. 'My room has pink curtains and a bedspread to match,' she said. 'Oh!' she clasped her hands ecstatically, 'a terrace! May I stand on it for just a little while?'

'Yes, if you like. But it's cold out.' He opened the windows for her. She ran to the balustrade. 'It's like standing on the edge of the world,' she cried. 'I feel I could take off and fly like an eagle. Oh, look at the sky. Isn't it beautiful? All those little, delicious pink clouds!' She leaned forward. 'Is that the garden? Isn't it queer, all those paths and trees? To think I'm standing above the treetops. I've never been higher up than trees before! Do the paths lead down to the sea? I've never seen the sea before either. I can't imagine what it looks like.' She turned to him, her face alight with joy. 'I want to see it now. Please, Rowan!'

Smiling at her childishness, he said, 'After tea. Come on, Scrap. You can pour out.'

'Very well.' She sat in a wing chair near the fire, tongue-tied again as the housekeeper brought in the tea things: a silver tea-kettle and hot-water jug, followed by the housemaid with a tray of sandwiches, scones and chocolate cake.

'Can you manage to pour out, miss?'

'Oh yes.' Alice's thin hand trembled on the milk jug. 'I'm used to it. I always poured out for my father.' She nibbled a sandwich. When the servants had gone, 'It must be very pleasant to be rich,' she said. 'Father and I were very poor, you know, but I didn't mind. I loved him just as he was. I wouldn't give tuppence to be rich except that . . .' her eyes filled with tears, 'except that I wish my father hadn't been quite so poor. He felt it, you know, being cast off as a leper. That's why I hate all the Tanquillans – except you – because they made him suffer so much.'

'Money doesn't ensure happiness, Scrap,' Rowan said slowly. 'I've been happier in my cottage near the harbour than anywhere else on earth. It's people, not riches, that matter. Being with someone you love.'

Shadows were trapped in the bare, overhanging branches of the trees as they set off together down the garden paths to the valley. Clumps of snowdrops gleamed whitely against dark shrubberies. The garden was a steep maze of criss-crossing paths overhung with trees, crowded with fleshy-leaved rhododendrons.

Alice clung desperately to Rowan's hand. She gave a shrill little scream as a ghostly white figure loomed out of the darkness. 'Oh! What is it?' she cried.

'Don't worry. It's only a statue. Minerva, I think.'

'I don't like it!'

'Neither do I.' He swore softly. 'We should have left this until morning.'

'No,' she said stubbornly. 'I want to go now.'

'Very well, if you insist. But don't blame me if we break our necks. God, how I hate this damned garden.'

'That's the second time you've said "damned",' she re-primanded him. 'I've never heard you swear before.'

'I beg your pardon, Scrap.' He fumbled with the gate. 'I shall probably swear again in a minute.'

'My father used to swear at times, you know. He used "bloody" quite a lot. I liked to hear him swear because he

75

worked better when he was angry. "I'll show the bloody lot of them," he would say. When he wasn't angry, he would call himself a failure.'

'I can understand that,' Rowan said softly.

Walking sedately beside him, Alice said, 'You pretended to like the house for my sake. But you don't really like it very much, do you? Why not?'

Startled by her perspicacity, he replied, 'It's hard to explain.' How could he possibly tell a mere child about puppets and puppeteers? It wasn't the house he hated so much as the memories connected with it – the prison-house of his childhood. 'You must not do this, Master Rowan. You must not do that, Master Rowan. Little boys should be seen and not heard.' With the sea calling to him, and the warm sand under a hot, summer sun, sand on which the poor children ran barefoot and happy.

Alice said, 'You haven't explained anything yet.'

'Let's not talk about that. You wanted to look at the sea. Well, we're almost there. Hold your breath, Alice, then tell me what you think of it.'

The valley had widened to a curving road beneath the spandrels of a high-flung bridge. Beyond it, the sea lapped the shore, a grey, diffuse, constantly moving mass, overlaid with fitful moonlight.

Rowan had not been prepared for Alice Tanquillan's reaction to her first meeting with the sea. She stood stock-still for a moment as if drawing in, with her very breath, the sight and sound of it, holding out her arms as if to embrace it, her head thrown back in ecstasy, her face transfigured. 'This is my place forever now,' she whispered. 'My place on earth and in heaven. Amen.'

Her attitudes, Rowan knew to his cost, were all exaggerated. She hated and loved with equal intensity. He could not help thinking, as she stood there like an acolyte at some vast, grey altar, that this was a child born for tragedy.

Alice spoke little over dinner, and ate practically nothing, and yet she seemed curiously contented, strangely fulfilled. When he suggested that it was time she went to bed, she made no protest.

'Goodnight then, Scrap.'

'May we go out again tomorrow morning early? I should like to look at the sea again.'

'Yes, of course.'

'I shan't mind school so much now,' she said. 'Whenever I am unhappy I shall think of the sea. It will comfort me to know it's there, that nobody can take it away from me.' She threw her arms round Rowan's neck. 'No-one can ever take you away from me either. I shall always love you.'

Gently disengaging her arms, he said, 'You are very tired. Go to bed now, Scrap.'

'You must stop calling me that,' she said calmly, 'I'm not a child. You must call me Alice from now on. Goodnight, Rowan darling.'

The poor kid, he thought, when she had gone. But at least she had experienced an overwhelming love for two people, her father and himself.

He touched the keys of the piano, absent-mindedly at first; began picking out a melody he had started to compose years ago. An unfinished melody – unfinished as so much in his life seemed unfinished – or never even attempted. The music reflected his pent-up emotion in a minor key. Then the mood changed. The second movement of his symphony soared in catatonic scales to a tremendous climax. Suddenly he stopped playing, closed the piano, and crossed restlessly to the window. The sky was bathed with the quiet radiance of a quarter moon riding high among a constellation of stars. Romilly's face swam before him, that eager, watchful face of hers beneath its fringe of softly waving hair. He imagined telling Romilly that he did not love her as a man should love the woman he married; asking her to release him from their engagement. He knew he could not do it. Cruelty to him remained the ultimate sin. On their wedding night he would make love to her physically because he must. What he could never give her was his heart, mind and spirit, without which physical love possessed little, if any, meaning at all.

Queen Margaret's School crowned a ribbon-like road at the base of Oliver's Mount. Alice thought at first that the white lodge, guarding the entrance, *was* the school, had felt, at its homely appearance, a sense of relief, despite the itching of her legs beneath the crackling navy blue skirt of her brand-new school uniform. When she realized that the many-gabled and chimney-stacked house in the distance was Queen Margaret's, she gave way to panic.

'Rowan!' she cried. 'Don't make me go in! Please don't!'

'You'll be all right, Alice, I promise.' He clasped her hand tightly in his. 'It can't be as bad as all that. Look! The girls are going tobogganing on tea-trays.'

That was all very well for him to say, but even Rowan could not understand her loneliness as the door opened and the smell of chalk-dust hit her nostrils. The only formal schooling she had ever received was at a kindergarten with elderly ladies in charge. The mother she could scarcely remember had taken her there, leaving her in the narrow hallway with a brief goodbye kiss and a warning to be a 'good girl'.

Then the thin woman with the dark frenetic eyes and high-pitched girlish voice had mysteriously gone away. Alice did not know where to because her father wouldn't talk about it. She had asked him one day if her mother had gone to Jesus, because another child's mother had gone to Him and she wondered if they might meet each other in heaven. She had not understood her father's grief, his muttered words, 'I only wish to God she had.'

When, after her mother's strange disappearance, Oliver told her that she would not be going back to the kindergarten, that he was going to teach her himself, she was wild with joy. They had moved then from Islington to Highgate, to the rooms over the pawnshop, where she would perch on her bed in the tiny, squeezed room near the kitchen, and stare out of the window at other windows across an alley, listening to the strange sounds that drifted up to her through the grimy lace curtains: the shuffling footsteps of dustbin scavengers, the screaming of children playing ball or marking out hop-scotch squares, the clink of a tossed pebble, the quarrelling of men and women behind the torn blinds of the houses opposite.

She had not minded, as long as she could be with her father. She had never cared for other children, and she had hated the silly, elderly women at the kindergarten. She loved being taught by Oliver, sitting beside him at the square table in the living-room. Her father had a way of making lessons come alive for her. Geography was not just a dull business of maps and atlases and tracing the outline of countries. He had told her about the starving Indians who begged their bread in the gutters, making her feel their poverty, the heat and dust, the sores on their bodies, their crippled limbs displayed for baksheesh; the caste system, the terrible gulf between the maharajahs in their palaces with their jewel-bedecked elephants and the dusty beggars displaying their sores for money.

Oliver had lighted for her the flames of Jeanne d'Arc's funeral pyre in the marketplace at Rouen; had made her visualize the paper-white skin and high ruffs of the proud Elizabeth of England; reduced her to tears over the execution of Mary, Queen of Scots.

Sometimes he had told her that she must not disturb him today because he had an article to write, a crust to earn. Then she would go quietly to her room overlooking the alley and listen to the staccato pounding of his typewriter keys. If his writing had gone well, they would walk together along the high street to buy their supper, savoury ducks or saveloys, crusty bread from the baker, or little pots of meat-paste and a few over-ripe bananas, because the ones turning black were cheaper than the fine yellow ones.

But if his writing had gone badly, he would send her out alone to do the shopping, leaning his head in his hands, saying, 'I'm a failure, Alice. Your father is a failure. Take notice, child. Take a good look at me so that you will know what a failure looks like.' Then she would fling herself into his arms, crying, 'No! No, you're not a failure!' And she would know, when she kissed him, that he had been drinking that amber-coloured stuff he kept hidden in his bedside cupboard.

Her father's death had left a gaping hole in her life, as if someone had cruelly torn away a gossamer spider's web, leaving no remnant of its quiet industry. When Oliver died, Alice had felt as vulnerable as a spider robbed of its home, scuttling frantically to find a quiet corner in which to hide, hating the relentless hands of those who had torn down her old web of security leaving nothing to replace it.

Now she stared about her in terror and dug her fingernails into Rowan's hand as the maidservant ushered them across the hall to the Headmistress's study.

This Rowan had feared most, the handing over of poor Alice to a new regime which might engulf her. The choice was not his. He had crossed swords with his father on the child's behalf, had begged him to consider engaging a governess, to spare her the ordeal of a boarding-school, to no avail. Now all he could do was kneel beside her to dry her tears. 'Don't forget, Alice,' he said, feeling like a murderer, 'I am close by if you need me.'

She seemed so vulnerable in her ill-fitting school uniform with her hair bound up in pigtails. He was close to tears himself as the study opened and he heard the squeak of the girl's new shoes on the polished linoleum.

The door closed behind him. He could hear, on the still air, the sound of laughter as the girls he had noticed earlier hurtled down the slope on their tea-trays. Deep in thought, he collided with someone as he turned to latch the gates – a girl with bright red hair beneath a green Tam-o'-Shanter and a remarkably lovely face.

'Sir Lancelot mused a little space . . .'

CHAPTER EIGHT

Emily Beresford shivered slightly as she stepped from the train, and pulled her furs more closely about her shoulders as she faced the bitter north-east wind blowing in from the sea. There was no sign of Rowan on the platform or in the station yard. God, what an end to a journey, she thought, as the wind scurried stinging hailstones against her cheeks, and Romilly's lower lip began to tremble.

Of course the child must feel bitterly disappointed, having spent the past hour powdering her nose at frequent intervals, settling her hat, twitching her hair into place, and chattering like a parakeet, saying brightly that she hoped Rowan would not catch his death of cold waiting on a draughty station platform for the train to arrive.

'I'm sure there's a simple explanation, darling,' Emily said, as the Tanquillan coachman stepped forward to take charge of their luggage. But Emily could tell, by the grim expression on Rachel's face and the ramrod set of her shoulders, that she was far from pleased by her son's non-appearance. She spoke sharply to the driver as he opened the carriage door. 'Where is my son at the moment?'

'I couldn't say for certain, your ladyship. At the harbour as likely as not. He sent a message to the house about meeting the train.'

'Indeed! Well please do hurry with the luggage. We are half-frozen.'

So you are, Lomas thought as he struggled with the cases and cast covert glances at Romilly. If that was Mr Rowan's intended – well! He had seen livelier-looking girls in the Sally Army band. The mother, on the other hand, was what Lomas thought of as 'a fine figure of a woman'. At least she had smiled at him and said 'Thank you' when he helped her into the carriage.

'I really cannot imagine what has happened to prevent Rowan meeting us,' Rachel said.

'Please don't worry. I'm sure there's a simple explanation.' Emily smiled charmingly, wondering at the same time if she had, from the best possible motives, condemned her daughter to a loveless marriage. Or perhaps condemned was too strong a term. All the same, she had been guilty of collusion with the Tanquillans in engineering the engagement, in wanting her child's happiness. If only the young idiot had been at the station to meet her. She wondered if Romilly realized that Rowan was not in love with her.

Emily's delight, when Romilly had burst into her room with news of her engagement, had turned to silent dismay when she knew that Rowan had not done the asking. Impatient to hear the details, anxious to know exactly what had been said in the drawing-room that day, she had pumped her daughter unmercifully when Romilly frowned and said that she could not remember very clearly what had happened.

'Nonsense, darling! You must remember. Or perhaps you don't want to tell me.'

'No, Mummy, it isn't that.'

'What then?'

Romilly bit her lip. 'I don't know. It just – happened. Rowan put his hands on my shoulders. Then he – kissed me.'

'Yes, and then what?'

'I looked up at him and said . . . that is, I asked him why he hadn't told me before how much he cared for me. Oh, it all happened so fast. I felt as if fireworks were exploding in my head. Well, after he'd kissed me, I told him how much I loved him. . . .' Romilly laughed excitedly. 'Then I said something about being engaged now. And Rowan – oh, he was so kind and understanding – well, he said he wanted me to be happy.'

And Rowan was too much of a gentleman to tell you he didn't love you, Emily thought dully. She could picture the whole scene then. Romilly had literally thrown herself at Rowan with all the petulance of a child determined to have her own way. And yet she had believed that Rowan was beginning to show signs of interest in Romilly. If only her daughter had waited a little while longer; given Rowan enough time to make up his own mind. Perhaps another year or two. But patience had never been Romilly's strong point.

Rowan was undoubtedly a gentleman, but he was nobody's fool. One serious quarrel between them, and Romilly's happiness might dissolve like mist on a May morning. Not that Romilly looked very happy at the moment, with her sullen expression and pushed-out underlip.

I really must speak to her, Emily thought desperately as the carriage moved forward. The silence was becoming unbearable. To break it, she said brightly, 'I had no idea that Scarborough was so grand a place. The buildings are really magnificent.'

She spoke the truth. She had not been prepared for the town's solid Victorian grandeur: the grey bulk of the Pavilion Hotel near the station, her glimpse of the main street on the left, or the splendid toll-bridge ahead, spanning the deep cleft of the valley road which cut, like a shining artery, the town from east to west; the tall Victorian houses rising, church-spire punctuated, beyond the bridge.

She caught Rachel's eye as she spoke. Each knew what the other was thinking, that Romilly must be made to snap out of her mood of sullen indifference if her eventual meeting with Rowan was not to end in disaster.

If Rowan really loved me, Romilly thought, he would have moved heaven and earth to meet me. One would think he did not love me at all. He might at least have sent a note of explanation. After all, we are engaged to be married.

God in heaven, Emily thought, why is Romilly so unlike myself? Why is she so dull and stupid? Why must I always speak to her as a child? But I suppose I must keep on doing so, because that is what she expects of me.

Leaning forward, Emily asked, 'What do you think of your future home? Isn't it exciting to think that you and Rowan will soon be settled here together?'

'Yes,' Romilly stared thoughtfully at the passing houses. 'Yes, it is.'

Emily breathed a sigh of relief. The atmosphere lightened as Rachel leaned forward to point out where the house lay, on the far side of a garden hedged about with spiked railings and bordered with tall, balconied houses.

A lamplighter was making his rounds, leaving in his wake glowing primrose circles on wet pavements. As the carriage ground to a halt, Romilly thought disappointedly that the Tanquillan house was much smaller than she had imagined; sandwiched between two more imposing houses built of the same honey-coloured sandstone. Her initial disappointment, however, gave way to pleasure when she crossed the threshold into a hall with a curving banister leading to a gallery, and saw, with delight, the great bowl of out-of-season azaleas on the polished octagonal table, the gleam of lamp and firelight from the drawing-room: inhaled the fragrance of bees-wax polish, and something else beside – the tang of sea from a distance; the curious smell of bladderwrack borne inland from the shore.

Tea was served in the drawing-room. Firelight flickered on the silver tray and tea-kettle; glinted warmly on the delicate porcelain cups and saucers. Lamplight shone on corner cupboards filled with Meissen china; gilded side tables, famille rose jardinières, and plumply-cushioned armchairs. It was an L-shaped room, the dining-room forming the foot of the L, a long, picture-hung room behind double doors.

Emily and Rachel were seated near an ornate marble fireplace. Romilly was standing near a window overlooking a lily-pond, scarcely discernible in the dusk, gazing out at a laburnum tree which tapped the glass with ghostly fingers.

She walked, shivering slightly, to the fire as a servant came to close the curtains against the encroaching night. Still no sign of Rowan.

Romilly's mood of optimism on entering the house had dulled now to a nervous despair that something untoward had happened to him. An accident perhaps. She sat holding her teacup in trembling fingers, nibbled at an egg and cress sandwich as if it would choke her to swallow it, her eyes fixed on the door: willing him to walk through it.

Suddenly the outer door slammed. She rose quickly to her feet, listening. And there he was, his face stung with the cold. 'I'm so sorry to be late.' He threw his coat on a chair and hurried forward to greet everyone, filling the room with his presence. Romilly's world steadied on its axis as she looked at him. How tall he was, how vibrant, how full of life. She clung to his sleeve. 'Where have you been? I thought something dreadful had happened to you.'

'I'm sorry, Romilly,' he said. 'I was detained at the harbour. There's been some trouble.'

Rachel leaned forward in her chair, a frown between her eyebrows. 'What do you mean? What kind of trouble?'

'Talk of a strike.'

'Then your father must be informed at once.'

Rowan held his hands to the fire. 'Don't worry, I have already sent him a telegram recommending a settlement.'

'You've done *what*! But he will never agree to that without a fight. Knowing your father, he will come up at once to look into the matter.'

'But why?' Rowan said impatiently. 'Why fight at all? The poor devils are asking little enough. Sixpence a week extra, to which they are more than entitled in my opinion.'

'And you have told them that? Really, Rowan, I fail to understand you. Have you any idea what such a settlement will mean to the company in pounds, shillings and pence?'

'Have you any idea, Mother, what non-settlement will mean to the men?'

'That is beside the point.' Rachel drummed her fingers impatiently on the chair-arm. 'In any case, this is not the time or the place to discuss it.'

'I'm sorry, but I think it is very much to the point,' Rowan said stubbornly. His thoughts were all of the men he had just left, honest, decent men who trusted him to do what was best for them.

Emily stirred uneasily, watching her daughter's face, praying that she would have the sense not to interfere. But Romilly, bitterly disappointed and piqued at not being the centre of attention, cried petulantly, 'But if they have been able to manage so far, why are they asking for more money now?'

'Romilly, my dear, I don't think you should question Rowan on that score.' Emily spoke with scarcely-veiled impatience.

'I'll be happy to explain, if I can,' Rowan said. 'For one thing, these are hard-working men with wives and families to support, and God knows things are tough enough for them as it is. Now they are faced with increased taxation. A country arming for war does not do so without considerable cost to the tax-payer. The men need more money.'

'And so we are virtually to pay their taxes for them. That's what it amounts to,' Rachel said coldly. 'It is always the same with that type of person, given a banner to wave, a hook on which to hang their constant demands. War! There isn't going to be a war. It's all alarmist propaganda!'

'I hope to God you are right, Mother,' Rowan said wearily.

Romilly pressed her hands to her ears. 'I can't bear it,' she cried. 'All this talk of a strike, and war! You haven't even asked about our journey yet!'

'I'm sorry. I'm afraid I got rather carried away.' Rowan's contrition was genuine. Emily had always liked him. Now he seemed a different person from the shy, somewhat diffident youngster she remembered, who used to play, as a child, in the garden of the Eaton Square house. He was very much a man now, and she found his new forthrightness and vitality, linked to his old charm and sensitivity, infinitely attractive and refreshing.

She thought, as she looked at him standing there so tall and strong and erect, that Rowan had never succumbed to the weaknesses and follies of most young men of his class, who cared more for sport, hunting, shooting and fishing, than their fellow human beings. Whilst she secretly applauded his attitude to life, she could not help wondering if Romilly would be happy with the man he had become.

She said as much to Romilly when they were dressing for dinner in adjoining rooms with the connecting door open, with Romilly seated at her dressing-table, fussing with her hair.

Emily walked through into Romilly's room. Laying her hands gently on her daughter's shoulders, she said, 'You know, my dear, you should try to be more sympathetic towards Rowan. He is a man now, with a man's duties and re-sponsibilities to shoulder. That is the way of the world.' She smiled. 'Who was it said that men must work and women must weep . . . ?'

Romilly laid down her hairbrush. 'What do you mean?' she asked, staring hostilely at her mother's face reflected in the mirror. 'What a curious thing to say! I have no intention of weeping over stupid strikes and sixpence a week increases!'

Emily sighed, and tried again. 'I am simply trying to point out that you *should* care. What concerns Rowan must concern you also – if you are to be happy together.' She paused. She *had* to say it. 'Romilly, are you quite sure that you will be happy with Rowan?'

Romilly's cheeks flushed scarlet beneath her softly curled fringe. She said waspishly, 'How could you ask such a question? Of course I'll be happy with Rowan. I love him more than anyone else in the world! I just felt angry and disappointed, that's all, because he did not come to the station to meet me. Then, when he walked into the drawing-room and started talking about that stupid strike, I couldn't help saying what I did! How would *you* have felt if you were me?' She stood up jerkily to smooth her dress and rearrange the lace evening shawl about her shoulders.

'I know, darling, I know. I might have felt angry and disappointed too, in your place. All I'm trying to say is, you must try to put aside your own feelings once in a while: try to take an interest in Rowan's work; try to understand how important it is to him.'

'You needn't worry, Mummy,' Romilly said calmly, peering at herself in the wardrobe mirror, 'I shall take an interest in Rowan's work if it kills me. It is just so frightfully dull and boring.'

After dinner, when she and Rowan were alone together in the music room, Romilly said, 'You haven't kissed me properly yet.

Please kiss me now, darling.' She held up her face, eyes closed, lips parted.

If we are to have any chance of happiness, he thought, I must be fair to her. He hated himself, as he bent to kiss her, for his inability to give her, spontaneously, the affection she craved.

Reassured by his kiss, she rested her hands on his shoulders. 'now you must tell me all about the strike,' she said solemnly, like a child repeating a lesson.

She perched on his lap, hands linked round his neck, and said in that same childish way, 'When we are married, we must share all our troubles.' Her fingers strayed to the back of his head, exploring the nape of his neck. 'I couldn't help noticing how preoccupied you were at dinner. Please explain things to me. I've never really understood what your work entails.'

'Very well, I'll do my best.' He wished she had chosen to sit elsewhere. 'You know, of course, that the Tanquillan Company has agents the world over, in every major continental city; the Far East – China, India. My father takes care of the London office, whilst I am in charge of the Northern. My main concern lies with the shipment of goods to and from Newcastle, Aberdeen, and Rotterdam.'

'How fascinating.' Romilly twisted his hair with her fingers. 'How – romantic . . .'

'It isn't all that romantic,' Rowan said wryly. 'My ships bring in scrap-iron, salt, cement, potatoes, cured fish, and manure.'

'Oh, is that all?' Romilly sighed, bored to distraction, wishing that he would kiss her again.

'I'll take you down to the harbour tomorrow, if you like,' he said. 'Perhaps you would like to see a ship unloaded; look round the warehouses.'

'Mmmm, yes, that would be nice,' she murmured, standing up to smooth her dress and glance at herself in a mirror before crossing the room to the piano. Opening the lid, she ran her fingers lightly over the keys. 'Please play for me now,' she said.

Rowan said quietly, 'Very well, if you wish. What would you like to hear?'

'Chopin's Waltz in C Sharp Minor,' she said dreamily, 'to remind me of – that night . . .'

'Night? Which – night?'

'The night of my party,' Romilly said impatiently. 'Surely you haven't forgotten?'

Rowan had forgotten. He had preferred to forget sitting at that piano on the rostrum like a performing monkey, surrounded by simpering girls and their escorts who had crowded into the conservatory when they heard the music: had begged him, when he had finished with Chopin, for the latest dance tunes.

Romilly slid next to him on the piano-stool, and slipped her arms round his waist. 'We'll have such wonderful musical evenings, when we are married,' she breathed ecstatically, buoyant now because she had succeeded in turning the conversation away from scrap-iron, salt, cement, potatoes, cured fish, and manure.

Eyes half closed, she glanced round the room with its glowing fire, shining lamps, warmly carpeted floor, and deep red velvet curtains.

Listening to the music, watching Rowan's hands on the keys, she thought, he's mine now, and nothing on God's earth can take him away from me.

Soon, she would stand with Rowan before God's altar in St Peter's church in Eaton Square; would hear him say: 'With this ring, I thee wed; with my body I thee worship.' It was all to come: the church, the flowers, the solemn organ music – her wedding day. Her wedding night.

I shall have his child as quickly as possible, she thought, tracing the curve of his cheek with her fingertips. I shall have Rowan's son. We will call him Beresford. Beresford Tanquillan.

A memory of finishing school flashed into her mind at that moment: something she wanted to forget, but could not.

One summer evening, when crystal-clear light bathed the fields and orchards fronting the chateau, she had watched, from her bedroom window, a girl and boy darting among the trees, a peasant couple from the village who neither knew nor cared that they were trespassing on private property.

The girl's long fair hair spilled carelessly about her

shoulders. She wore a short muslin dress; her legs were bare. The lad was dressed, peasant-style, in breeches and a cotton shirt, the sleeves rolled back to reveal his sinewy arms.

They had played together for a long time between the fruit-laden apple boughs, and Romilly had stood quite still, hiding behind the curtains, her heart thumping in her chest, knowing that theirs was a kind of mating dance. She had laved her lips nervously with her tongue, knowing that she should turn away – but she could not, gripped, as she was, by a strange, unwholesome excitement: the trembling of her own limbs, a feeling of mounting desire within her own body.

At last, the boy caught the girl by the wrists and forced her down into the long, sweet grass.

She had cried out then, and run blindly from the room to the refectory: trying desperately to behave as if nothing had happened to her. But something *had* happened.

She, Romilly Beresford, had touched on sexual knowledge and desire in a way that had stunned and slightly shocked her, not because of what she had witnessed, but because she had so enjoyed it. Because she had wanted, with all her heart, to be that girl with the long fair hair, lying in the arms of her lover.

CHAPTER NINE

A shroud of mist enfolded the sea, a white, vaporous wall sweeping along the coastline, shutting out the view of the high cliffs, blanketing the bay, probing inland with ghostly fingers.

Standing forlornly at the end of the jetty, Alice heard the grating roar of the tide beyond that great white wall, the splintering sound of the waves washing up on the rocks beneath.

When the fog lifts, she thought, they will find me sprawled face down on those rocks. Then perhaps they would feel sorry for her – her aunt and uncle and Rowan. She wanted to break Aunt Rachel's air of calm indifference, to hurt and shock Uncle Gervaise who had so hurt her father. Perhaps even Rowan would love her more when she was dead.

She had walked out of the school quite recklessly, dressed in her Sunday black skirt, white blouse and basqued jacket, her hat tilted accurately above her eyebrows, smoothing on her gloves as if she were going to church, carrying her psalter to allay suspicion if the porter stepped out of his lodge to challenge her. But nobody had noticed her departure. There had come a sickening moment of fear as she passed the lodge gates. When the school was out of sight, she had started to run, feeling the breath catch in her throat as she hurried down the long road to the sea.

Dying, she supposed, would be rather like going to church, as cold and awesome as waxen lilies arranged at an altar, a newly-dug grave or weeping cherubs in the Highgate cemetery.

Her thin legs trembled as she ran, tears streamed down her face. She had promised Rowan that she would try to like school, but she hated it; hated everything about it – the cold linoleum and green-painted walls, the laughing groups of girls who clattered about the place on their way to lessons, leaving her stranded like a crab in a rock-pool; having to share a dormitory with those mysterious self-assured beings who ignored her, knowing that she was not, and never could be their equal.

She loathed the long tables in the refectory, the food she could not swallow, the classrooms with their tall narrow windows and smell of chalk-dust, the blackboards on which the double Dutch lessons were scrawled, the books that did not interest her, the depressing view of mud-filmed paths and patchwork allotments from the dormitory windows, the endless cold which numbed her brain and fingers. Above all she hated the school uniform which robbed her of her own identity.

Raising her white, tear-stained face to the blanket of mist rolling in from the sea, she nerved herself to step into that comforting shroud of oblivion. She could taste salt spray on her lips, her eyes were dazzled by a myriad dancing flecks like bright dust motes floating and dissolving in the fog. Moistening her tongue, she began to pray aloud: 'Our Father, Who art in Heaven . . .'

Charlotte had gone out early for a walk along the beach. The jetty was deserted except for the figure of a girl standing with her eyes closed. Something about the girl's attitude made Charlotte stand still, pulse racing, afraid that if she made a sudden movement the child would take fright and go over the edge. She said in a low, clear voice, 'Don't you think you had better step back a little? These stones are very slippery. You don't want to fall . . . ?'

Alice opened her eyes; glanced fearfully over her shoulder. 'Keep away from me,' she cried. 'I'm going to jump!'

Oh God, Charlotte thought wildly, what shall I do? Instinct warned her to keep talking as naturally as possible. 'My name is Charlotte Grayler, what's yours?'

'Alice Tanquillan.' She hadn't meant to say it.

'Tanquillan?'

'I suppose you've heard of my uncle,' Alice said bitterly. 'He hates me because of my father. Aunt Rachel hates me too. Everyone hates me!'

'I don't hate you.'

'That's because you don't know me. You'd hate me too if you did.'

'What makes you so sure?' Charlotte spoke calmly, but her legs were shaking, her palms felt clammy. She knew instinctively that she must not take a step forward. If she did, the girl might jump. There was something about her, a certain tension and wariness, that made Charlotte feel sure she meant what she said. 'Nobody is ever alone in the world. There's always someone. Won't you let me help you? You are welcome to come home with me.'

'No! You can't trick me! You think I'm mad. You are trying to humour me, that's all! Keep away from me!'

Taking her courage in both hands, Charlotte turned away and began to walk slowly back along the jetty. Wet stones gleamed dully at her feet. She could hear the pulsating beat of the tide on the rocks below, the whisper of her skirts about her ankles, the tap-tap of her shoes on the cobbles. Every sound seemed exaggerated in the still air. What if the child jumped now? Would she ever be able to forgive herself? Her withdrawal gave Alice Tanquillan a second alternative. What if she chose to ignore that alternative?

She sobbed inwardly with relief when she heard stumbling footsteps behind her, and turned, arms outstretched to gather the weeping child in a loving embrace. 'Don't cry,' she said softly. 'You are safe now. Quite safe. I'll look after you.'

'You shouldn't have brought that girl here,' Filly said in a hoarse voice. 'Whatever made you do such a thing?'

'What else could I have done?'

'You could have taken her back to her own people where she belongs,' Filly said irritably, beside herself with worry.

'But don't you see, Mother? That's the last thing I could have done!'

Filly twisted her hands nervously in her apron. 'All this fussation just on dinnertime. Just fancy, a young girl like that wanting to do away with herself. She must be out of her mind!'

'Please, Mum, lower your voice. She might be awake now.'

Charlotte tiptoed to the sitting-room, but Alice was still fast asleep on the sofa.

'I wish to God your father would come in.' Filly was out of her depth in this situation. The dinner was past being ready, the joint ready for carving, the cabbage soggy, the potatoes nearly boiled dry, and there were Albert and the boys downing pints of beer at the Ramshill pub without a care in the world.

'Joe will know what to do,' Charlotte said, having more faith in Joey than his brothers or her father. Albert would come home slightly befuddled, so would Frank and Harry – but not Joe.

'Then Joe had better take the girl back to where she belongs this afternoon,' Filly said firmly. 'Yes, that's the best plan.' Felicity Grayler possessed a superstitious dread of abnormality in any shape or form. Senility in old folk she understood and made allowances for – after all, she had nursed her own mother through her last illness, spooning her food as if she were a child. She had not liked doing it, or watching her mother's withered hands pluck, pluck, plucking at the sheets, but she had done it just the same. What she could not tolerate was abnormality in the young. She had always dreaded the possibility that one of her children might be born with queer eyes and drooling lips.

'Ah, there they are now!' Filly hovered on the landing as Albert's head appeared on the stairs. 'About time too!'

'What is it, Ma?' Harry recognized at once the danger signals in Filly's flushed face and sharp tongue.

'You might well ask. Charlotte's brought the Tanquillan girl home with her.'

'Eh, whassamatter?' Albert stared at his wife bemusedly.

'What are you talking about, Ma?' Frank steered his father into the kitchen. 'What Tanquillan girl? I didn't know there was a Tanquillan girl.'

'Well there is, and she's asleep on the front room sofa!'

They had all crowded into the kitchen now. Filly threw up her hands at a sudden smell of burning from one of the pans on the fire. 'Tell them, Charlotte! There now, the potatoes are burnt black!'

Charlotte said, 'I found her on the jetty . . .'

Frank laughed.

'It's nothing to laugh about,' Filly cried, rushing the burnt pan to the sink. 'She was going to throw herself into the sea!'

'*What?*' Frank raised his eyebrows.

Beside herself, what with the Tanquillan girl and the burnt potatoes, Filly said, 'And if three great strapping fellers like you can't keep their father sober, you should be ashamed of yourselves. I'll put a stop to these Sunday dinnertimes, you see if I don't.'

'It does Dad good to meet his pals,' Harry chipped in. 'I can't see any harm in it myself.'

'I'm as sober as a judge,' Albert said. 'I only had two pints and a game of dominoes.'

Filly rounded on him fiercely. 'If you'd come home at the proper time, none of this would have happened!'

'Eh?'

Charlotte signalled to Joe with her eyes. They went into the dining-room together. 'I'd better explain things to you. Mum's so worked up. I think she's upset because – well . . .'

Joe smiled. 'I know.'

'I had to bring the girl here. She's got it into her head that everyone hates her. You know the Tanquillans. Mum thinks that you had better take Alice home. But I'm not sure about that. She trusts me, you see. What do you think, Joe?'

'Did she really mean to kill herself, or was it just play-acting?' Joe asked, frowning.

'I think she did mean to. She talked so wildly and looked so strange.'

'The poor kid.' Joe thought for a minute. 'I think you had better be the one to take her back, if she must go back – and I suppose she must. I'll go with you, if you like.'

'Thanks, Joe. I think I can manage on my own. It might be better that way.' Charlotte gave a rueful smile. 'I couldn't think properly in the kitchen with everyone talking at once.'

'Charlotte, there's something I want to tell you.'

'What, Joey?'

He said shyly, 'I've asked Annie to marry me. I asked her last

95

night. I know I'm not earning much, but I couldn't risk losing her.'

'Oh Joe!' Charlotte threw her arms round him, 'I'm so glad. You and Annie belong together, I've always known that.'

'I couldn't keep it to myself any longer. I wanted you to be the first to know. But don't tell the others, will you?'

'No! I won't go back! You can't make me!' Alice tugged away from Charlotte's restraining hand. 'I trusted you. Now I hate you!'

'I haven't any choice. Believe me, Alice, I don't want to take you back, but what else can I do?'

'You could have let me drown! I'd rather be dead than face them. You don't know what they're like.'

They were standing on a path leading through the Spa gardens to the bridge. Alice had walked here with Rowan on her first night in Scarborough. The mist had lifted, scurried away by a freshening wind, but the sky was still grey and overcast. Alice had walked stiffly, mutinously, at first, dragging her feet, refusing to speak. Now that she had managed to free herself of Charlotte's hand, she faced her wildly, in a blind panic. Words came bubbling from her lips, incoherent words which made little sense to Charlotte at first.

'They killed him, you know, as surely as if they had stuck a knife into him. They put him in a hole in the ground. I thought, if I died too, we'd be together again. Uncle took me away; locked me up. I broke a vase. The flowers were there at my feet, the stems were broken. Then Rowan came. I adore Rowan, but he doesn't love me as much as I love him. The cemetery. It was so – *cold*. The statues were watching me all the time. I threw snowdrops on the coffin lid. They'll all be dead and rotten now, won't they? All dead and buried and crawling with worms. Oh, *Charlotte*! I want him so. I want my father!'

Suddenly Alice was sobbing in Charlotte's arms.

'Hush, darling.'

Then Alice began to laugh hysterically. 'If you could have seen my uncle's face when I told him how much I hated him. I thought he would burst, he was so angry. They made me go to school, you know, because I was a thorn in their flesh. My father was a thorn in their flesh too, that's why they hated him so much, because he was poor. But he was far cleverer than any of them, except Rowan. You mustn't blame Rowan. I love Rowan.'

In that instant, Charlotte knew how slim was the borderline between sanity and madness, between laughter and tears. But the girl's laughter had died now. She was weeping again, trembling from head to toe, struggling with the dark images that invaded her mind. The wind came rustling through the branches of the trees bordering the path, a seagull keened overhead. Charlotte drew the girl to a bench, held her tightly, making the small, comforting sounds that one would make to a baby afraid of the dark. When Alice seemed calmer, Charlotte whispered, 'Don't be afraid any more. Look, here's sixpenny-worth of courage for you.'

She had found the coin in her pocket. Holding it up, she slipped it into Alice's hand. To her infinite relief the notion appealed to the child. Bribery in the shape of a sixpence, she thought. But the value of the coin was immaterial, as she had meant it to be. Alice understood that too. What mattered was the talisman quality of the coin, the idea that courage could be given as a gift.

CHAPTER TEN

Charlotte was to remember the events that followed with the clear precision of a pen and ink drawing, or a Chinese painting done with great simplicity in vibrant colours: honey-coloured stone, the glinting of a garnet brooch worn by the housekeeper; gleaming wood; pink azaleas in a blue bowl, fragile petals as pink as a winter sunrise.

'Oh, *there* you are, miss! What a hue and cry there's been over you,' the housekeeper said. 'You had better go to the music room at once. The family's there discussing what's to be done about you.'

She could not have said anything worse so far as Alice was concerned. The child dug her nails into Charlotte's hand, her eyes round with terror. 'I can't go into that room on my own. Promise you won't leave me alone with them!'

'Perhaps you'd better go with her,' Mrs Lomas advised. 'If you'll tell me your name, I'll announce you.'

'My name is Charlotte Grayler.'

'Follow me, please.'

'You won't tell them where you found me, will you Charlotte? Uncle Gervaise might lock me up again . . .'

'Don't worry. You can trust me.'

The scene resembled a tableau with the people in the room frozen to immobility at their entrance. It seemed to Charlotte that every detail of that room and its occupants would be forever imprinted in her memory – the wide French windows leading to a terrace, the colour and the texture of the curtains, the ornaments and pictures, and one picture in particular, that of a woman with a brown-haired boy beside her. There was no mistaking the original of that portrait: she was sitting in a high-backed chair near the fire, a thin fashionably dressed woman with coldly appraising eyes. The heavy diamond rings on her fingers flashed prisms of colour. Lady Tanquillan. Charlotte knew at once why Alice hated her. The way she used her lorgnette to observe the girl from head to foot was tantamount to an insult.

A man in an immaculately tailored grey suit was standing near the fireplace, a portly figure with veined cheeks, thinning grey hair, and soft plump hands, wearing gold-framed glasses; lips set in a thin line beneath his bristling moustache. Sir Gervaise Tanquillan. His eyes behind the glasses were pale blue, as cold as icicles.

A slender young woman with coiled hair and a fringe was standing near the piano. The stiffness of her pose, the pale face and high-bridged nose, reminded Charlotte of a painting by Van Eyck she had seen in a book borrowed from the penny library. Another woman, with dark hair, was standing near the window. She turned slightly and smiled as Charlotte and Alice entered the room.

A young man with dark curly hair was seated at the piano. Charlotte strove to remember where she had seen him before. In that moment when their eyes met, she could have sworn he recognized her too. Or was it simply that he reminded her of another painting in that borrowed book – a painting by Ford Madox Brown. Only that matchless painter could have captured so much controlled awareness and grace, the warm flush of colour beneath the skin texture, the compassionate expression in those dark eyes.

The silence was broken when Sir Gervaise said in a cold clipped voice, 'I suppose we should thank you, Miss Grayler, for returning my niece to us. I was about to notify the police of her disappearance.'

As Charlotte laid her arm across the girl's shoulders, she could feel the heaving of the blades beneath her jacket, the softness of her hair brushing her fingers. 'I require no thanks,' Charlotte began, but Sir Gervaise interrupted impatiently. 'Have you any idea the trouble you have caused?' he said, speaking to Alice. 'The embarrassment to your headmistress and myself, the serious nature of this incident. I want to know why you absented yourself from school in such a fashion, and where you have been all day. Well, I'm waiting!'

Alice began to whimper, unable to speak for the lump in her throat. She clung to Charlotte, who said quietly, 'I – I think Alice is too upset to explain anything at the moment.'

'In that case, Miss Grayler, you had better speak for her. Where did you find my niece? Under what circumstances?'

As young and inexperienced as she was, and overawed by the grandeur of the surroundings and the powerful, intimidating personality of Sir Gervaise, Charlotte had no intention of speaking in a room full of strangers on such a personal matter. 'I'm sorry,' she said, 'may I be allowed to talk to you in private?'

'Really,' Lady Tanquillan raised her eyebrows, 'that is hardly necessary. You may answer my husband's questions here and now.'

She would be grateful to Rowan Tanquillan all her life for the way he intervened at that moment. 'Come here, Alice,' he said gently, beckoning her to the piano. 'Listen. Do you know this tune?' Smiling at her, he began to play 'Sur le pont d'Avignon'. And, 'Oh yes,' she cried, running across the room to him, 'my father taught it to me.'

Charlotte noticed that the girl with the coiled hair moved jealously away from the piano as Alice approached. Then Rowan said quietly, 'Wouldn't it be better, Mother, if you went with Miss Grayler to the library? I'm sure she has her reasons for wanting to discuss things in private.'

Sir Gervaise and his wife exchanged glances. Lady Tanquillan rose to her feet. 'Very well,' she said. 'You had better come with me, Miss Grayler.'

Charlotte smiled her gratitude to Rowan as her ladyship led the way to a book-lined study, a cold, dark, inhospitable room with a mottled marble fireplace which reminded her of brawn in a butcher's shop window.

The walls above the shelves were hung with hunting scenes. The air was musty as if the room was not used very often. The books appeared to be largely unread: ponderous tomes bound in thick leather, put there for show. Everything about the room was stiffly formal: the leather armchairs placed with almost mathematical precision on the rug-strewn floor, the mahogany desk near the window set out with a leather-bound blotter, silver-framed photographs, and ink-stands. Charlotte noticed, through the heavily curtained window, that the mist was rolling in again from the sea.

Lady Tanquillan seated herself near the desk. Charlotte recognized the dress she wore as one she had made up for her, a cream lace tunic over a moiré underdress. Her hair, a dusty wheat colour, was sculpted to her narrow head and knotted into a chignon at the nape of her neck. Charlotte remained standing.

'You do realize the seriousness of this matter?' Lady Tanquillan had asked coldly. 'My niece has caused a great deal of trouble in running away from school, for what reason I cannot imagine.'

'I think she was very unhappy there,' Charlotte said.

Rachel Tanquillan raised her eyebrows. 'But this is incredible. Don't you think it an impertinence that you should voice an opinion?'

'I'm sorry, your ladyship. I didn't mean to be impertinent. But I think that if Alice is sent back to school, she will run away again.'

Rachel's lips tightened, 'Where did you find her?'

'Near the harbour. I noticed that she seemed lost, so I took her home with me, She slept for a while, then we gave her some dinner, She was tired and very hungry.'

'Ah. I see now why you wished to speak in private.' Lady Tanquillan opened the gilt bag she had laid on the desk. 'I should have realized that you would expect payment, a reward for your trouble. Will this do?'

Charlotte's cheeks burned with shame as she looked at the carelessly tossed five-pound note on the desk. She said in a low voice, 'You are wrong, your ladyship. I require no reward. I brought Alice home because she would never have come by herself.' Tears stung behind her lids. 'That is all I have to say, except that I should like to say goodbye to her before I leave.'

Anger flared in Rachel's eyes. 'I see no necessity for that, Miss Grayler.' The girl's quietly self-contained pride and bearing had outmatched her own. 'I hardly think that my niece would notice the departure of a – stranger.'

'Even so, with your permission . . .'

Alice was still near the piano. 'Miss Grayler is leaving now,' Rachel said in a coolly impassive voice. The girl stared at Charlotte, her pleasure in the music forgotten. 'No,' she cried, 'you mustn't go! *Please* don't go!'

'You will say goodbye to Miss Grayler at once, Alice!' Rachel's voice was no longer cool or impassive. Alice cowered against the piano. Then, 'No,' she shouted, 'I will not stay here without Charlotte! I'd sooner be dead!' She sprang towards the French windows leading to the terrace.

'Alice! Come back!' Rowan was on his feet in an instant, but the girl was out of the window, running along the terrace, racing down the steps near the lily-pond, screaming as she ran.

Charlotte stood for a moment, transfixed. Then, not stopping to think, not caring a jot for the Tanquillans, she darted after her, calling out, 'Alice! Come back!'

The terrace was wreathed in mist. Daylight was fading. Picking up her skirts, Charlotte stumbled down the steps to the garden, then stood still for a second, perplexed, not knowing which path to take. There were so many of them, steep muddy paths criss-crossed like a tangled skein of wool.

Footsteps came after her. Turning, she saw Rowan hurrying down the steps behind her. Then she remembered where she had seen him before – near the gates of Queen Margaret's School. He was the man she had bumped into that day on Oliver's Mount.

'I'll call Lomas,' he said tautly. 'You had better stay here, Miss Grayler. The paths are too treacherous.' He smiled suddenly. 'Don't worry, we'll find her.'

Charlotte said urgently, 'I do hope so. I'm so afraid she might try to . . .'

'What?' Rowan gripped her arm. 'Might try to do what? You can tell me. You *must* tell me!'

'But I promised I wouldn't.'

'*Please*, Miss Grayler.'

'I think she might try to kill herself. That's what she meant to do when I found her this morning on the jetty.'

'My God! I'll fetch Lomas at once. She can't have got that far. But what about you? You're shivering.'

'Never mind about me! Just find Alice.' When he had gone, she sat down on a stone seat near the lily-pond, half expecting Sir Gervaise to join in the search. The lights of the music room shone onto the terrace from the open French windows. Suddenly Lomas appeared, pulling on his jacket, pounding along the path, swearing softly under his breath as he slipped on a patch of mud. 'This bloody garden!' he muttered, plunging down a path beneath the overhanging trees.

Rowan called to him, 'Get down to the valley gate as fast as you can!'

The mist was thicker than ever now, rolling in like a dense grey wall. Someone closed the music room window. The lights in the drawing-room came on, slanting down over the lily-pond, illuminating the fleshy lily-pads, shining into the cold, still water. Charlotte rose to pace restlessly, hearing in the distance the dull drum-beat of the sea.

A few hours ago she had not known that Alice Tanquillan existed. Now the girl seemed an integral part of her life. What was happening down there in the garden? She could bear the waiting no longer, and began to walk down one of the paths, her feet slipping and sliding, her skirts catching on the bushes bordering the path. Suddenly her Tam-o'-Shanter was snatched from her head by an overhanging branch. Her heart was pounding in her chest. Somewhere in that strange wilderness of a garden was a little lost girl, terrified out of her wits. 'Oh, Alice,' she murmured, and found that she was crying.

Realizing the futility of attempting to join in the search, she turned back to the seat by the pool, thinking that if Sir Gervaise had possessed one ounce of compassion, he would have been outdoors now with a lantern to help look for his brother's child. What kind of a man was he to stand aside when his own flesh and blood was in danger?

Suddenly a hoarse cry came out of the darkness. 'It's all right, sir. I've got her!'

Lomas appeared, dragging Alice by the hand. The girl shook herself free and ran into Charlotte's arms, sobbing as if her heart would break, as fragile, Charlotte thought, holding her and smoothing back her hair from her tear-stained cheeks, as a bird or a tiny, helpless animal.

Rowan hurried up the path after Lomas, dusting his hands on his trousers, brushing dead leaves from his hair. 'Thank God she's safe,' he said breathlessly. 'Where did you find her?'

'Hiding behind Minerva.' Lomas grinned. 'Gave me a hell of a fright, she did.'

'Thanks, Lomas. You'd better go back and finish your tea now.' Rowan returned the man's smile. Turning, he caught his breath at the glory of Charlotte's hair burning like a flame in the light from the overhead window.

She reminded him of one of the Florentine Madonnas in his Aunt Kitty's drawing-room at Grey Wethers.

'You won't go away and leave me, will you Charlotte?' the child said in a muffled voice.

'I must, darling. But remember your sixpennyworth of courage. You haven't lost it, have you?'

The girl felt in her pocket. 'No, here it is. But I don't want you to leave me.'

Charlotte looked up helplessly at Rowan. 'I don't know what to do now,' she said.

Kneeling beside Alice, he said quietly, 'Don't worry, Scrap. You will see Charlotte again soon, I promise.' His eyes met hers as he spoke. 'I'll take her indoors now. The poor kid's half asleep.'

He lifted up the child in his arms, feeling the weight of her head lolling against his shoulder. Her eyes were closed now, her limbs as relaxed and sprawling as those of a rag doll. 'Please come too, Charlotte,' he said. 'I'll ask Lomas to drive you home.'

'No, I'll walk,' Charlotte said awkwardly. 'Please, I'd much rather.'

'But you can't possibly walk home alone. I won't hear of it. You can't simply disappear – after all you have done for us.'

The thought of losing her so suddenly seemed unbearable to

Rowan, but Alice was already fast asleep in his arms.

Charlotte said, 'If I may just go out by the front door. I'll walk over the Spa bridge. It isn't far from there.'

She walked with him along the terrace, through the music room, across the hall; felt in her coat pocket for her Tam-o'-Shanter, and opened the door. 'Goodnight,' she said, 'I hope all goes well with Alice.'

'Charlotte. Where shall we find you if – if we need you?'

'I think you know my brother Joe,' she replied quietly. 'He works at the harbour.'

It seemed like a dream to her afterwards, the misty garden, the lights of that strange, unhappy house shining down into the lily-pond, the sound of the sea in the distance, a simple French nursery jingle played on a piano, the feeling that something magical and mysterious had happened to her as Rowan Tanquillan knelt beside her: his words, 'You will see Charlotte again soon, I promise.' She had felt, at that moment, as if he was speaking, not to Alice, but herself.

Later that night, in the silence of her cold attic room, she looked at her naked reflection in the wardrobe mirror. It was the first time in her life she had ever done so; had ever wondered about her body. But then, never in her life before had she felt such a strange desire, such a longing to love and be loved. She saw, by the flickering light of a candle, the firm uplift of her breasts, the long clean sweep of her limbs; saw her smooth young body as a vessel, a chalice filled with the sweet warm wine of youth.

She knew then, with an instinct as old as time, that she loved Rowan Tanquillan.

CHAPTER ELEVEN

The scene with Alice could not have happened at a worse time from Rachel's point of view, with Romilly and her mother present to witness the girl's abominable behaviour. Thankfully Gervaise had been present to lend his support, since he had come up from London to arbitrate in the matter of the strike.

Emily Beresford's charm and understanding had gone some way towards soothing Rachel's ruffled calm. Romilly, on the other hand, had betrayed, because of Rowan's obvious interest in the child, a jealous antipathy towards her. To make matters worse, Gervaise had received a letter from the headmistress of Queen Margaret's declining to reinstate Alice as a pupil in view of her wanton flouting of rules and regulations in absenting herself without permission and, in so doing, precipitating a crisis totally unacceptable to the good name and reputation of her school.

The Tanquillans found themselves contemplating the same problem that had faced them in London at the time of Oliver's death – what to do about his daughter. Another school in another town, Rachel suggested. 'With the same, possibly even worse results,' Gervaise said grimly. 'The girl is ineducable, aggressive, totally lacking in social values.'

Rowan said quietly, 'That is scarcely her fault. In any case, I don't believe that Alice is ineducable. She is highly intelligent and eager to learn. She has been handled wrongly, that's all.'

Gervaise said pointedly, 'Perhaps she would be better handled by the authorities, by people qualified to deal with children of her kind.'

Rowan turned impatiently from his examination of the Constable painting over the mantelpiece which he had always disliked, nettled by his father's dark allusion to 'the authorities'.

'I don't know what you mean,' he said.

'I am speaking of government-sponsored institutes for the mentally retarded.' Gervaise poured himself a stiff whisky, satisfied that he had hit upon the only real solution to the problem. He had reckoned without his son's reaction. 'That is outrageous! You cannot condemn Oliver's child to such a place.' It was the first time Rowan had spoken the forbidden name. He did so now with force and vigour.

The family conclave was taking place in the drawing-room. Emily had tactfully withdrawn, taking Romilly with her.

Rachel said, 'It is rather Oliver Tanquillan who has condemned us to a life of misery over the wretched girl.'

'I cannot understand your attitude, Rowan,' Gervaise said angrily. 'What else is there to do with her under the circumstances?'

'I've already told you what I would do. Why not engage a governess? At least give the girl a chance to learn.'

Rachel drummed her fingers impatiently. 'A governess,' she said scornfully. 'And where do you suppose she would be taught?'

'Here, of course.'

'*Here?* That is out of the question!'

'I can't see why.' Rowan faced her coolly. 'The rooms on the top floor are not in use. You and Father are seldom in residence. The old nursery could be utilized as a schoolroom . . .'

Rachel interrupted heatedly. 'And where do you suppose we would find a governess willing to take charge of a tiresome, abnormal child twenty-four hours a day? That is what your suggestion amounts to. One could hardly expect the house-keeper to be responsible for her after lessons.'

'I realize that. So why not engage someone to act as a companion? That would seem to me the sensible thing to do.'

Rowan thought for a moment that his father would have a heart attack. '*What?*' he spluttered. 'Are you out of your mind? Are you seriously suggesting that I should pay two people to take care of one simple-minded girl?'

Rowan said, in a carefully controlled voice, 'That might prove a better alternative from a discretionary viewpoint.'

'What do you mean?' Gervaise stared at his son over the rim of his glass.

'I was thinking of you, Father. Authoritarians have a way of probing matters very carefully. You have always gone to such lengths not to disclose your relationship to Oliver Tanquillan. Would you really care to do so now?'

Gervaise made no reply as he turned to the sideboard to replenish his glass, but Rowan could tell that the argument made sense to him.

Rachel, on the other hand, remained hostilely unconvinced. 'And what do you suppose will happen when you bring Romilly here as your wife? I hardly think that she will care for the idea of sharing her home with a nuisance of a child and two other women.'

His mother was right about that, Rowan thought, but he refused to be beaten. 'There is no reason why Romilly should ever come into contact with them,' he said. 'The upper floor is a self-contained unit. They could use the back stairs to the kitchen. I always used to when I was a boy, remember?'

Heartily sick of the discussion, Rachel glanced across at her husband. 'It is up to you, Gervaise,' she said. 'I'm tired, and I'm going to my room.'

'Damnation!' Gervaise swallowed his whisky at a gulp as his wife rose to her feet. 'Very well. But I warn you, Rowan, if this plan of yours goes wrong, if we have any more trouble with Alice, I shall have my own way in this matter, and there's an end of it.'

Rachel turned at the door. 'You do realize that I am now saddled with the job of finding two people trustworthy enough to be left alone in this house with the servants? I totally disapprove the idea of strangers wandering at will in my home.'

'I imagine that whomever you decide to appoint as governess would come armed with suitable credentials,' Rowan said. 'As for the companion, there is someone known to you who might be persuaded to look after Alice.'

Charlotte and Maggie walked into town one Saturday afternoon to shop for Maggie's wedding-dress material. It was an afternoon of brief showers, and bitterly cold. Early lamplight gleamed on wet pavements, on glistening tram-lines and overhead wires. People hurried along beneath bucking umbrellas. Bright sparks and the scent of roasting coffee beans issued from the side window of a grocer's shop in the main street. Maggie was in a bad mood, sulky and hard to please, at odds with her sister over the incident on Oliver's Mount when Bob had taken her hand to help her up the path, and Charlotte's removal of her belongings to the attic as a result of the row over Herbert Franks. Maggie had never come up against Charlotte in quite the same way before, had never thought the day would come when her quiet, normally serene sister would react so strongly to words spoken in the heat of the moment. While Filly had wrung her hands in despair over the contretemps, Maggie had assumed a 'don't care, it's not my fault' attitude, even in the matter of her wedding-dress material.

'We'd better try here,' Charlotte said, stopping to look in the windows of the busiest draper's in town.

'Please yourself,' Maggie said offhandedly, staring at the stalactites of puffy eiderdowns draped from brass rods, and the wax dummies robed à la mode.

'I'm not here to please myself,' Charlotte reminded her sister. 'I'm here to please you.'

'Oh come on then,' Maggie said shortly. 'Let's get inside. My feet are frozen.'

They walked together into the shop with its long oak counters, shelves, glass showcases, and pressurized pipes hissing money on its way to the counting-house. Charlotte forgot Maggie's awkwardness as she sniffed the indefinable scent of new linen and looked, with pleasure, at the little chests of drawers on the counters containing cotton reels and embroidery silks and egg-eyed needles. The shop intrigued her. As a little girl, she had waited, with a kind of nervous excitement, for the metal change-containers to explode from the chutes into the wire baskets. She had adored the metal-tipped yardsticks and snapping scissors, the great rolls of brown paper and string, the deft way the assistants wrapped up the parcels and tucked in the ends.

Perhaps it was her liking for that particular shop that had decided her to become a dressmaker. The shelves behind the material counter were stacked with bolts of fabric: sateen, duvetyn, organdie, lace, prints, serges, silks, and satins.

'We'd like to see some wedding-dress material,' Charlotte told the assistant, since the unpredictable Maggie had seated herself on a bentwood chair near the counter and was busy examining her fingernails.

Soon the counter was snowed under with clouds of white stuff deftly spun from the bolts by an obliging elderly lady who said, 'May I suggest, miss, that an off-white colour would look lovely with your red hair?'

Charlotte flushed. 'It isn't for me,' she said, 'it's for my sister.'

Nettled, Maggie muttered, 'It's no use, I can't make my mind up. I'm hungry.'

Charlotte sighed. 'We'd better go and have a cup of tea then, and come back later.' Maggie got to her feet and marched off without a word. 'How could you?' Charlotte said reproachfully when they were outside. 'Wasting the woman's time like that.'

'That's what she's there for, isn't it?'

Sitting at a tiled table with a brown teapot between them, Maggie bit into an eclair so fiercely that the cream squeezed out of it onto her face, then she couldn't find her handkerchief.

'Here, use mine.' Charlotte wrinkled her brow. 'Please, Maggie, can't we be friends? I'm sorry about – everything.' She wished she could find the right words to explain how she had felt that day on Oliver's Mount, how much she had hated the thought of being paired off with Herbert Franks.

Slightly mollified by Charlotte's capitulation, Maggie wiped the cream from her face. 'I don't know what you are talking about,' she said carelessly.

'Yes you do, Maggie. I've said I'm sorry. What more can I say? And what about the material? We must get it today or I'll never get your dress finished on time.'

Maggie remembered, with a feeling of panic, the other thing that was worrying her. Charlotte was quick to notice the stricken expression in her sister's eyes. She said gently, 'Why don't you have the white satin? Come on, Maggie, we'd better get back to the shop before it closes.'

And so the white satin was measured, wrapped up, and slung carelessly into Maggie's shopping bag. 'Thank God that's done with,' Maggie said dourly as the pair of them walked home in the blustery twilight.

Charlotte couldn't bear to see Maggie like this, wounded and unhappy. 'What is really bothering you?' she asked. 'I know there's something. Can't you tell me?'

'Nothing you'd understand,' Maggie said breathlessly, and yet she needed to talk to someone. She blurted suddenly, 'It's all very well for you. You're not the one getting married.'

Talking was difficult with the wind boring into their faces. Charlotte said, 'I don't understand. You and Bob are happy together, aren't you?'

'Yes. No. Oh, I don't know! It's the wedding, if you must know. The thought of standing there in front of all those people – saying things.'

'What kind of things?' Charlotte tucked her hand in Maggie's arm.

Flustered and tearful, hot and uncomfortable from struggling uphill in the teeth of the wind, Maggie snapped, 'Indecent things – about bodies – and procreation. I don't know anything about bodies, and I'm not sure that I want to find out.' She clung onto her hat as a gust of wind threatened to lift it from her head.

'Here, give me your shopping bag, I'll carry it.' Charlotte clung onto her own hat. 'If that's what's bothering you, why don't you ask Mother?'

'I tried to,' Maggie said despairingly. 'It only made things worse. She went all pink and said it's something nice people don't talk about. God, it was awful! Tell me the truth, Charlotte. You've read a lot of books. Do you know what happens to a woman on her wedding night?'

'No, I don't.' Charlotte remembered, with a feeling of guilt, that she had wondered about that herself ever since the night she stood naked in front of her wardrobe mirror; how, afterwards, she had pulled on her nightgown and prayed God's forgiveness, not just because she had looked at her own body, with pleasure, for the first time, but because of the strange flickerings of hitherto unknown desires buried deep within her tender young flesh. She dared go no further than that, and yet . . .

Lifting her eyes to the darkening sky heavy with scudding clouds, seeing the winking lights of the town glowing like bright fireflies in the dusk, she knew that those deep, tender, unexplored desires had to do with Rowan Tanquillan. Even as she lay tossing in bed that night, she ached to feel his arms around her, to hold him close to her, to bring to fruition all her hidden longings and desires. But how could she help or advise her sister, when she was just as ignorant as Maggie about the nature of sexuality between a man and a woman? And yet Charlotte believed, if Maggie did not, that love, whatever that meant, was nothing to be afraid of, with the right person. Therein lay the difference between the two sisters. Maggie liked everything cut and dried. Charlotte was content to believe that the very nature of love lay beyond explanations.

'You've gone very quiet all of a sudden.' Maggie said. 'What's on your mind?'

'Just that if you love Bob, and he loves you, everything will be all right.'

Maggie snorted her disgust. 'That's all very well, but how do babies come? A lot of women die, don't they, when they have babies? I heard Mum and Aunt Clara talking about it at Christmas. Aunt said that she didn't give much for Mary Phillips's chances when her time came. Then they saw me standing in the doorway, and Mum poked Clara in the ribs and told her to be quiet.'

'But Mary had her baby,' Charlotte said, 'and she didn't die.'

'Yes I know. But what made Mary have a baby in the first place? That's what I don't understand. I wonder if the boys know. Perhaps I'd better ask Frank or Harry.'

Maggie giggled nervously. 'Perhaps it has to do with the way they're made.'

They turned together into St Martin's Square. The shop lights gleamed on the wet surface of the road. They could see

Albert behind the counter as they opened the side door and went upstairs.

Filly was on the landing, holding a letter in her hand. 'It's for you, Charlotte,' she said. 'It came by the four o'clock post.'

'For me?' Charlotte turned the thick envelope in her cold fingers, frowning at the decisive, flowing handwriting stabbed, with black ink and a thick nib, into the white paper. 'I wonder who it's from.'

'You won't know unless you open it,' said the ever-practical Filly, brushing back her hair with her hand, her face pink from baking and bending down to look in the oven.

Charlotte tore open the letter. 'It's from Lady Tanquillan,' she said disbelievingly.

'Lady Tanquillan? Oh my God! Well, go on, read it!'

'She wants to see us . . .'

'Us? What do you mean, "us"? Now what's gone wrong?' Filly's inborn dread of 'getting out of her depth', her inborn shibboleths concerning what she thought of as the 'gentry' came uppermost at once.

'You'd better read it for yourself.' Charlotte handed the letter to Filly who promptly sat down on a chair and fanned her hot cheeks with a tea-towel, certain that the missive contained bad news; disgrace for the Grayler family. 'It must be about that niece of hers,' she wailed. 'I knew no good would come of bringing her here. Oh dear, I can't read it, my hands are shaking so.'

'For heaven's sake, Ma, let me read it.' Maggie grabbed the letter. 'Well, whatever next? Her ladyship wants to see you and Dad and Charlotte tomorrow in connection with . . .' Maggie quickly scanned the page and threw the letter contemptuously on the table. 'It's nothing to get hot and bothered about. Seems there's a job going as companion to the Tanquillan lass. You might have known her ladyship wouldn't be bothered with the likes of us unless she wanted something from us.'

'Well, of all things!' Filly picked up the letter and read it avidly, now that the spectre of solicitors and prison had been dispelled. She read aloud: 'If you are interested, Miss Grayler, perhaps you and your parents would care to discuss the matter with me on Sunday at two o'clock.'

Charlotte put on the kettle for a cup of tea, thinking of her previous encounter with Lady Tanquillan, which she had not mentioned to her parents. Indeed, she had told her family little about the day she returned Alice to the house in Chalice Walk, to Filly's disgust, and nothing whatever about the escapade in the garden or her own part in that curiously dramatic game of hide and seek.

Mazed by the turn of events, Filly sat open-mouthed, her mind busy with the implications of the letter. The Tanquillans, of all people, wanting her daughter to work for them. That would mean Charlotte handing in her notice to Mrs Hollister, and a good thing too. That job had never been good enough for her.

But herself and Albert having to meet a real lady in her own drawing-room! She couldn't see Albert agreeing to that. And what on earth would she wear? All these thoughts flooded Filly's mind in a matter of seconds, making her feel dizzy.

Of course, she could wear her new hat with the violets on the brim and the fox-fur necklet with the beady eyes and limp paws she had paid five shillings for at the church jumble sale. That would smarten up her grey coat with the frogging, although she had not worn that coat recently because it had started to pull a little at the waist since she had grown stouter.

Still, it was smarter than her brown coat, and perhaps Charlotte could alter the buttons, or extend the frogging in some way before the interview.

She put the matter to Charlotte as she carried the teapot to the table. 'I don't know what your father will wear, though. You know how much he hates getting dressed up to visit people, and his best suit smells of mothballs.'

'I shouldn't worry about that,' Charlotte said, getting out the cups and saucers, 'because I'm not going.'

'*Not going?* Why ever not?' Filly cried. 'It's the chance of a lifetime. A chance to better yourself. You don't want to spend the rest of your life at Mrs Hollister's?'

'I don't mind Mrs Hollister's,' Charlotte said quietly, 'I'm used to it, and I enjoy sewing. What do I know about being a companion? What would the Tanquillans expect of me?'

'That's why they want to see you, isn't it?' Maggie retorted, taking off her hat and helping herself to a freshly-baked jam tart. 'Besides, I thought you were mad keen on that queer niece of theirs.'

Maggie's comment stirred Charlotte to the remembrance of the stricken look on Alice's face that evening in the garden, her anguished words: 'I don't want you to leave me alone here.' She also remembered that carelessly tossed five-pound note in the library. If only she could think clearly, but it was difficult to think at all with her mother and Maggie voicing their opinions over the teacups.

'Please don't let us talk about it any more just now,' she said. 'Maggie, show Mum your wedding-dress material.'

'Humph,' said Maggie, getting out the brown paper parcel, 'I had begun to think that no-one was interested in *my* affairs.' She felt more cheerful now, since she had voiced her secret fears about her wedding.

'Of course we're interested,' Filly said heatedly, wondering what was going on in Charlotte's mind. 'Only for heaven's sake don't unwrap it on the table among the baking things. It will get all over sticky with jam, if you do.'

Charlotte thought, perhaps I was wrong to say no straight off like that. I was thinking of myself, not Alice.

'Oh, that's lovely,' Filly said admiringly as Maggie unwrapped the satin.

'So it should be,' Maggie grumbled. 'Six yards at two and eleven. I'll be skint for a month!'

'Did you buy a pattern?'

'Yes. That cost a tanner extra! Well, what do you think?'

'It's very nice.'

'Yeah, neat but not gaudy, as the devil said when he painted his tail pea-green,' chuntered the irrepressible Maggie.

'I could alter the buttons on your grey coat tonight, Mum,' Charlotte said slowly.

Filly raised her eyebrows in surprise. 'Oh, does that mean you are going to see Lady Tanquillan after all?' She would never understand Charlotte if she lived to be a hundred.

'I think I should.' She could not bear to think of Alice Tanquillan's bitter disappointment if she failed her now.

CHAPTER TWELVE

To Filly's amazement, Albert proved amenable over the interview. 'I want to make sure,' he said, 'that Copper gets a fair crack of the whip. The Tanquillans are not noted for their generosity, so it's only right and proper that I should go with her to see justice done.'

'You make it sound like a boxing-match,' Filly said with some exasperation. 'Just don't start throwing spanners in the works and not letting anyone else get a word in edgeways, that's all.'

'As if I would,' Albert said reproachfully. He winked at Charlotte. 'As a matter of fact, Filly, you needn't bother to go with us if you don't want to. I am quite capable of handling this on my own.'

'What? Not go with you!' Filly bridled. 'Of course I'm going! I've steamed up the ears on my fox-fur especially! Besides, I've always wanted to look inside that house, so don't think you're going to do me out of that, Albert Grayler, because you're not!'

Charlotte smiled at her father. A deep bond of affection had always existed between them. She loved her mother, but she had never felt as close to her as she did to her father. Since babyhood, she had been her father's girl. It was to Albert she had turned for comfort in her childhood crises. Her mother was often too tired or too irritable to mete out comfort, too concerned with treating all her children the same, so that her impartiality got in the way of her sympathy. Filly had often meted out clips on the ears all round when she caught the boys fighting with each other. Equally, she had always been quick to defend Charlotte when Maggie's teasing went too far; an avenging angel whenever the lads had made Maggie cry.

Growing up, the older boys and Maggie had become more their mother's. Not so Charlotte. The deep affection she felt for her father had never changed throughout the years. Now all they meant to each other was expressed, not so much in words but in quiet laughter, as if their heartstrings were tied together in an invisible knot of understanding. Nobody else called Charlotte 'Copper'. Nobody, save Charlotte, ever called Albert 'Dadda', her secret name for him, spoken aloud only when they were alone together. Charlotte loved her mother. She adored her father.

'It's not much of a house from the outside.' Filly twitched the limp paws of her fox-fur necklet and settled her hat more securely on her head. 'Well, go on, ring the bell, Albert.'

'Give me a chance, Mother.' It struck him momentarily how odd it was that he should now refer to the slim, starry-eyed girl he had proposed to at a village dance, as 'Mother'. Memory played strange tricks at times. Surely this stout little woman who had borne him five children could not be that laughing girl with her hair caught back in a tortoiseshell slide. He still loved her, but what had become of all the passion he had felt for her then? As the housekeeper opened the door and showed them in, Albert Grayler experienced an inexplicable yearning for his lost youth.

'Her ladyship is waiting for you in the library.'

The library, Charlotte thought, that dark room with its shelves of unread books. She hated the thought of going into that room again.

Filly was thinking what a grand house it was inside. She felt as if she was in a museum or an art gallery with everything in such a state of polish, with all those pictures on the walls. She glanced nervously at her husband, who seemed entirely at ease in such posh surroundings. He was a fine-looking knowledgeable man, no doubt about that.

'Ah, Mr and Mrs Grayler, Miss Grayler. Please sit down.' Rachel Tanquillan did not shake hands. She seated herself in a wing chair near the fireplace and waited until they were settled. 'I'll come straight to the point. You received my letter?'

What a daft question, Filly thought, staring at the rings on her ladyship's fingers, we wouldn't have come otherwise.

'And you have met my niece, Alice?'

'Yes, ma'am,' Albert said easily.

Rachel inclined her head slightly. 'We have decided to appoint a governess and a companion for the child.' She glanced coolly at Charlotte sitting quietly between her parents. 'The position I have offered your daughter would entail seeing to the girl's welfare between lessons. The governess alone could not undertake the duties of teaching and guardianship combined, you understand.'

'Not quite, your ladyship.' Albert smiled disarmingly. 'I've heard that you and your husband are not often in residence here, understandably of course, since you live in London. Is it your intention to leave your niece in sole charge of my daughter and the governess? I should not want Charlotte to shoulder too much responsibility. She is still very young, you know.'

Rachel coloured slightly. 'There is no question of that. There are servants in the house when my husband and I are not in residence. Your daughter's role would not prove too arduous. All I require is a trustworthy person to oversee my niece's leisure pursuits.' She hesitated. 'I should be less than honest if I did not tell you that Alice has formed a strong attachment to your daughter. I am prepared to pay well for her services.' She wanted the whole thing settled as quickly as possible. Rowan had suggested this grocer's daughter as a likely companion for Alice, but she had swept that notion aside at first and applied to the labour exchange. Now time was running short, and she had been forced to the conclusion that Charlotte Grayler, as much as she disliked her, might prove a better proposition than any of the other young women she had interviewed.

'Albert cleared his throat. 'Financial considerations come second to my daughter's happiness, your ladyship.' He winked at Charlotte. 'My wife and I are mainly concerned with the exact nature of the work entailed.'

Rachel opened her handbag. 'Here is the list of duties. Perhaps you would care to look at it.'

Filly craned her neck to look over Albert's shoulder.

Charlotte neither moved nor spoke. Suddenly a light knock came at the door, and the 'Van Eyck painting' stood there, dressed for going out, wearing a pencil-slim skirt, elegantly tailored jacket, and a wide-brimmed hat trimmed with ruched green ribbon.

'Oh, I didn't realize you were busy, Tante Rachel,' Romilly said in a high-pitched voice. 'Rowan and I are going for a walk on the Spa. We'll be back in time for tea.'

'Have a good time, my dear,' Rachel smiled. 'Tell Rowan to wear his overcoat.'

Romilly laughed. 'I'll tell him, but it won't do a scrap of good. That fiancé of mine never listens to a word I say.' She stared coolly at Charlotte as she spoke. 'Well, au revoir.'

Charlotte's face drained suddenly of colour. She clenched her hands tightly in her lap. The room swam away from her momentarily.

Albert handed back the list to Lady Tanquillan. 'That seems reasonable enough,' he said. 'Now perhaps we had better discuss the financial arrangements.'

Charlotte heard his voice as someone in a dream. Rowan is engaged to marry that girl, she thought despairingly. And to think that I believed for one moment . . . She felt sick with shame.

Albert was saying, 'It is entirely up to my daughter, of course. My wife and I will not attempt to influence her one way or the other. May we have a little time to think about it?'

'Certainly you may.' Lady Tanquillan rose from her chair and rang the bell for the housekeeper to show them out. 'But you will let me know as quickly as possible? My husband and I are returning to London in a day or so.'

'I'll put a letter in the post tomorrow.' Albert straightened up. 'Thank you, your ladyship, for explaining everything so clearly.'

Things might have turned out very differently had not Alice Tanquillan bounded downstairs just as they were about to leave.

'Have you talked to my aunt?' she begged, clinging to

Charlotte's waist. 'Have you said yes?' Her hair was in disarray, her eyes bright with hope. 'Oh, *please* say yes. I need you so much.'

Charlotte smoothed back the girl's hair from her hot, sticky forehead. 'Don't worry, Alice,' she said, 'everything will turn out all right, you'll see.' She could have wept, as she knelt beside her, to think that at least one person in the world wanted her.

In that moment, Charlotte's decision was made. She could not bear to extinguish that look of hope in the child's eyes. But Filly, who had been in favour of Charlotte taking the job an hour ago, had changed her mind in view of Lady Tanquillan's total disregard of herself as Charlotte's mother.

'I've never felt so small in all my life,' she chuntered, marching, head up, across the Spa bridge, twitching at her fox-fur necklet, her face suffused with righteous anger. 'I'm telling you now, our Charlotte, you'd be soft in the head to work for a stuck-up madam like her. Who does she think she is – God Almighty?'

'I don't care tuppence for Lady Tanquillan,' Charlotte said, 'it's Alice I'm worried about.'

'Ha,' Filly snapped, clinging to her hat and her fur at the same time. 'That's all well and good, but why should you worry your head about *her*? What do you think, Albert?'

'I think we should talk about it when we get home.' He tucked his hand into his wife's elbow. 'We agreed, didn't we, that the final decision rests with Charlotte?' He cast an understanding glance at his daughter.

Charlotte stopped for a moment to look at the sea moving restlessly in great breakers across the bay, as if irritated by the wind whipping its surface.

Bright shafts of light cut the low-hanging clouds, spotlighting the peaked crests of the waves. Spume streamed back from the breakers, a fine spindrift as delicate as mist or rainbows. So much for dreams, Charlotte thought, watching the slow march of the waves to the shore. So much for the longings and desires which had disturbed her sleep. She was nothing but a silly, romantic little fool in believing that their meeting in the garden had meant something special to Rowan, as it had to herself.

Filly turned with a flurry of skirts, her cheeks pink with indignation. 'You are not going to take that job Charlotte, and that's flat! You speak to her, Albert. Try to make her see sense.'

Seated in his favourite chair by the fire, his feet encased in leather slippers, his favourite pipe in hand, Albert said quietly, 'Now, Filly, no need to get so excited. We haven't talked the matter over yet. We agreed, didn't we, that the final decision rests with Copper?'

The argument dragged on, interspersed by Filly's quick excursions to the kitchen to start getting the tea ready, while Charlotte set the dining-room table.

Soon the boys would come in, bringing with them their respective girlfriends. Then, Charlotte thought, the argument would become even more involved as her brothers added their opinions. That was the way of things in the Grayler family.

She went through the kitchen to butter the bread, while Filly sliced the cold ham and grumbled about the high-handedness of rich folk who thought they could ride roughshod over the poor.

'That's not quite fair, Mother. Lady Tanquillan didn't exactly ride roughshod over us.'

'Ha,' grumbled the affronted Filly, 'she didn't exactly lean over backwards to be pleasant neither. Fancy not shaking hands – as if we weren't good enough. And did you see the way she looked at my hat?'

The passage door slammed suddenly. The boys were home, trooping upstairs with their girls, bringing with them a breath of cold air, filling the house with vitality and laughter as they took off their outdoor things and hung them on the antlered hall-stand on the landing. The girls, on the other hand, were naturally restrained, with Filly keeping a sharp eye and ear open for any breach of propriety.

The boys poked their heads round the kitchen door. Frank wandered in, gave Filly a resounding kiss on the cheek, and tweaked her apron strings undone.

'Now you get from under my feet, Frank Grayler, or you

won't get any tea! That goes for the rest of you. Go and sit in the front room until you're called,' Filly said indignantly.

Madge Robinson enquired pertly, 'Is there anything I can do to help you, Mrs Grayler?'

'No there isn't!' Filly had no great opinion of Frank's girl, nor did she care for Harry's. The only one she liked was Joe's girl, Annie. Quiet little Annie who did not stop to primp in the hall mirror as Madge did. Annie was the only one Filly would allow in her kitchen, which had caused a few words between herself and Frank on two or three occasions. 'Why won't you let Madge help with the washing-up if she wants to, Ma?' he'd asked. 'Because I want to hang on to my best china,' she told him.

When the cold ham and pickles, the bread and butter, the dishes of peaches and strawberry jelly, the scones, jam and the chocolate cake had been set out, Maggie and Bob arrived. They had been to the house in Garibaldi Street to measure up for curtains. But Maggie seemed out of sorts with Bob. Filly wondered why.

Inevitably, over tea, the subject of Charlotte, the Tanquillans and the job she had been offered cropped up, broached by Filly who believed in getting everything – except war and childbirth – dragged out into the open. Frank and Harry hooted with laughter at the idea of Charlotte becoming a companion. Not Joe. Joe merely glanced across the table at his sister's flushed cheeks and downcast eyes, while Annie, sitting next to Charlotte, touched her hand sympathetically under the tablecloth.

Maggie said that she couldn't understand what all the fuss was about, seeing that old Aggie Hollister's was never good enough for Charlotte anyway.

'I expect they'll make you wear a cap and apron,' Frank said cheerfully, spreading a great deal of mustard on his plate. He winked at Madge as he spoke. They'd had a fine afternoon together on the beach, throwing stones into the sea with the others. But just once he had managed to pull her behind a rock for a passionate kiss and, well, it had happened again, that feeling of sublime masculinity as she dug into his lips with her teeth. Now he had made up his mind. Tonight he would ask her to marry him.

'A cap and apron indeed,' Filly said crossly. 'Charlotte's to be a companion, not a housemaid.'

'What does Charlotte think?' Joe asked quietly. 'It's up to her to decide what she wants to do.'

'But what about the kid?' Frank butted in. 'She's a few pence short of a pound, isn't she?'

Madge giggled. She knew she had Frank where she wanted him at last. Filly gave her an icy glance across the chocolate cake.

Joe said, 'She seemed a nice little kid to me.'

'She tried to do away with herself,' Frank reminded him. 'What's nice about that?'

Annie spoke up bravely. 'Who are we to condemn? There, but for the grace of God . . .' She squeezed Charlotte's fingers. Her plain little face flushed crimson, her eyes sparkled.

Albert laid down his knife and fork. 'I think we've said enough on the subject. Joe's right. Copper must make up her own mind. Now why don't we talk about something else for a change?' He smiled at Annie. Filly felt suddenly jealous.

'I'll clear the plates,' Annie said quietly to break the tension. Then Harry began to talk about the new snooker table at the National Reserve club room.

Albert doesn't love me the way he used to, Filly thought dully as she served the jelly.

Charlotte was reading by the fire. Annie and Joe were playing dominoes, with Albert, in the sitting-room, Frank and the others had gone out again. Filly wondered, as she moved about the kitchen getting her menfolk's clean cotton coats ready for Monday morning, what was in Frank's mind concerning that Madge Robinson. Frank had always been a bit of a handful, she thought fondly, the handsome, devil-may-care one, the ring-leader, a terror for the lasses. But she didn't want him to marry anyone just yet, especially not Madge with her saucy eyes and buck teeth, nipped-in waist and voluptuous bosom. There were so many things she wanted to tell Frank, if she knew how, about life and marriage. She had tried once or twice: 'Life isn't a bed of roses, you know, and neither is marriage. It's damned hard work.' She had meant much more than that but could not find the words. How could a mother tell her son, in clichés, that passion is a short-lived flower?

When she had finished what she was doing, she turned out the light and stood by the kitchen window staring at a wavering gas-lamp in the lane, one bright, effulgent blob of warmth in the enfolding darkness. Standing there, she thought about her life and her family: Harry, not quite as tall and handsome as Frank, who had always seemed to stand in Frank's shadow, lacking his older brother's ebullience and charm; quieter, more self-contained, kinder perhaps, with a great tenderness and respect for animals. She thought of Joe who was all kindness, who had tried so hard to follow in his brothers' dare-devil footsteps as a child, but never could. She remembered the day she had seen Joey walking along the high wall behind the house, egged on by his brothers, how she had run, screaming, into the yard. She would never forget Joe's pale, terrified face, as he balanced there on the uneven bricks, moving forward inch by inch. She had set about Frank and Harry in no uncertain manner. 'Get him down before he falls and kills himself,' she shouted. But Joe would not be got down. She had watched, heart in mouth, as he continued to inch his way forward. Joe had won his brothers' respect that day.

They never dared him again afterwards.

She thought of Maggie and Bob, remembered that Maggie had come to her shyly, diffidently, to ask questions that she could not answer. What happened to a woman on her wedding night was not something to be talked about between mother and daughter. It had shamed Filly to think that Maggie might wonder what happened between herself and Albert, occasionally, even now. Filly was still a comparatively young woman, and Albert was not an old man despite the difference in their ages. Her desire to procreate had nothing to do with sexuality or sexual desire. She had wanted children, not sexual fulfilment. How could she have wanted that since she had not known what it meant at the time? Now that she had had her children, the act of love seemed superfluous to her. She had become too totally involved in the family she had created to care whether Albert made love to her or not. And yet she was still capable of jealousy. She still wanted to come first with him. Staring into the darkness at the wavering gaslight, she knew that she felt jealous of Charlotte at times because Albert thought so much of the girl.

She had felt so nervous and jumpy of late, what with Maggie's wedding to arrange, and the thousand and one things she would have to see to before then, the invitations, the church, the flowers, the reception. Life had never seemed so difficult before, with talk of war on everyone's lips, and now this business with the Tanquillans. Why did she worry more about Charlotte than all her other children put together? She wanted the girl to get on in the world, so why should she stand in her way? Filly faced the truth. She could not bear the thought of change. She hated the thought of growing old, of losing Albert's love.

It seemed to Filly Grayler that her safe, secure little world was crumbling away beneath her feet. Soon she must part with her sons when they got married, or if war came. But she dared not think of that too deeply lest it undermined her strength and willpower to carry on with her work. If only she could go back in time to when her children were young, when they still needed her. If only she could return to the days when she carried Charlotte in her womb, when she had felt supremely confident of her role in life. Now the wind of change was blowing in the air about her head. She felt its coldness in her bones, its chill at her heart.

Turning away from the window, she felt for her pocket-handkerchief to dry the tears that lay on her cheeks. Then she crossed the room and stood quietly on the landing for a little while before braving the sitting-room with its shabby furniture and warm, glancing firelight.

Sitting down in the chair opposite Charlotte's, she heard the soft click of the dominoes on the chenille-covered table, saw the marble clock on the mantelpiece, Albert's pipe-rack next to the shining brass ornaments, the pictures on the walls, 'The Fisher

Lassie' and 'A Stag at Bay'; noticed the way the firelight shone on Charlotte's hair. She picked up her work-basket and began darning socks, wondering what her mother would have said if she could see her. Not that Filly had ever seen much sense or reason in the supposed wickedness of working on the Sabbath day. Meals had to be cooked on a Sunday as well as every other day of the week. Women gave birth on a Sunday, people died on a Sunday.

Charlotte glanced up from the book she was reading. 'Can you see, Mother?' she asked. 'Would you like to change places with me? The light's better here.'

If only I could change places with you, my Charlotte, Filly thought. If only I had my life to live all over again, what wouldn't I do with it? But what could she have done differently? What would she have changed? Change lay in others as well as herself.

Knowing that she had been too harsh at times, too dogmatic, she said, 'About this job. You must take it if you want to.'

CHAPTER THIRTEEN

Charlotte worked her week's notice at Mrs Hollister's with a tight feeling of misery in her heart. The dusty workroom had never looked more dingy or felt so cold, and yet she regretted leaving Mrs Hollister whose dark reproachful eyes followed her with the sad intensity of one who has received an unexpected blow from a friend. Charlotte had the feeling that she would never be so carefree again, that she was closing a chapter of her life which had meant a great deal to her, and she remembered only the good things about it.

On the last afternoon, when she put aside her sewing and covered her machine for the last time, Charlotte turned back for one final look at the room with all its memories. The girls were putting on their outdoor things for going home; queuing up at the cutting-out room window to receive their wages. They had clubbed together to buy Charlotte a scented handkerchief sachet with violet ribbons. When her turn came to be paid, Agnes Hollister said: 'Well, goodbye, Charlotte. I still think that you are making a big mistake.'

'I'm very sorry, Mrs Hollister.'

'We might have gone into partnership one of these days, you know. You are simply wasting your talent.' Agnes spoke with her eyes fixed on some rapidly dissolving dream of the future. When everyone had gone, she locked up, climbed the stairs to her rooms over the shop, and stood for a moment looking out at the darkening sky over the rooftops of St Nicholas Street, her hand trembling on the curtains. I shall never find another girl like Charlotte, she thought. Then, shivering, she turned to her amber-coloured friend in the sideboard cupboard. The only one who had not, so far, deserted her.

Jenny Carfax approached her new job with some scepticism and no little trepidation. Life in a seaside town in the north of England would prove as different from her student days at Somerville College, Oxford, as one could possibly imagine. At least, she thought, as the driver helped her down with her trunk and cases, it would prove a challenge.

This was the day before Lady Tanquillan and the Beresfords returned to London. Sir Gervaise had already gone back to Eaton Square, since the strike had been settled, to his own satisfaction, by the acceptance of a threepence a week increase which the men had perforce agreed to, not without protest. There had been ugly scenes at the harbour when his carriage was jostled, and he had walked to his office through a forest of waving fists and verbal abuse.

Rooms on the top floor of the house in Chalice Walk had been cleaned and made ready for Alice and the governess. A small room across a narrow landing had been allotted to Charlotte. She was there, arranging her things in the chest of drawers, when she heard the bumping of something heavy on the stairs, and a light, girlish voice saying something to the man – Lomas presumably – doing the bumping. Alice had been whisked away by Mrs Lomas to look at some new kittens in the garden shed, to keep her from underfoot while the governess was getting herself settled. Having finished her unpacking, Charlotte went into the schoolroom. Suddenly a girl with a mass of dark hair drawn back from a heart-shaped face, wearing a baggy oatmeal-coloured skirt, high-collared blouse, a long, loose oatmeal cardigan, and a broad-brimmed black hat with a drooping ostrich feather, appeared in the doorway. 'Hello,' she said brightly, 'I'm Jenny Carfax.'

'My name is Charlotte Grayler. I'm the – companion.'

'God, what a relief!' Jenny laughed. 'The very word "companion" struck fear to my heart. I had visualized you as sixty at least with a face like a prune.' She unpinned her hat, tossed it carelessly on a chair, and tripped to the window to look at the view. 'Mind if I open it to let in a bit of fresh air?' She flung wide the sash and leaned out to peer at the garden below. 'How curious,' she said, turning back into the room, 'it looks more like an obstacle course than a garden. But the whole set-up seems a little odd to me. This child I am going to teach – has she two heads and webbed feet? I asked to meet her at my interview, but the idea sank like a lead weight. To be honest, I very nearly told her ladyship to jump into her lily-pond, but certain aspects of the job appealed to me, especially knowing that I'd be left alone to teach the child in my own way.' She pulled a wry face. 'I say, there isn't a lunatic wife locked away somewhere?'

'I don't think so,' Charlotte said shyly, 'and no Mr Rochester either, more's the pity.'

Jenny clasped her hands together ecstatically. 'Oh joy, oh bliss! A Brontëophile! And I thought that I was about to waste my sweetness on the desert air of a seaside resort! I can feel it in my bones that we are going to be good friends, Charlotte.'

Romilly had put off her visit to the harbour until the last possible minute, and Rowan had not pressed her to look at the cottage until the strike was settled and the tense atmosphere had cooled somewhat.

Romilly thought it strangely eccentric of Rowan choosing to live in a fisherman's hovel, and she had not enjoyed poking round the warehouses on the quayside since they contained nothing of interest, nor did she relish the idea of looking round a two-up two-down house sandwiched in a row of identical cottages in a narrow side street.

The large, beamed, sparsely furnished room in which she found herself, with its tiny windows and inglenook fireplace, failed to arouse her enthusiasm.

She stared with distaste at the ship's wheel mounted above the fireplace, uncaring of its history, and the figurehead of a woman, battered by countless tides to a sun, salt and wind-bleached monotone.

Rowan realized at once his mistake in taking her there, knowing she would never understand what the cottage meant to him; that this, the oldest part of Scarborough, was the sturdy root from which the town had sprung when the Vikings landed long ago, in the mists of time; that there remained, in their descendants, something of that Nordic heritage of strong shoulders, blue eyes, and a passionate love of the sea in the young fishermen busy about their boats. Men who whistled and sang about their work, the scent of the sea trapped in their heavy woollen ganzies. Nor would she understand, if he told her, the significance of his proud-breasted figurehead, his salt-bleached Helen of Troy who had known the freedom of the sea.

He watched Romilly closely as she moved about the room: noticed the disapproving expression on her face as she glanced out of the window where a group of women, with shawls over their heads, stood gossiping together on the pavement.

She said suddenly, 'You will sell this place when we are married?'

'I hadn't thought of it.' He was standing near the uncarpeted oak staircase leading to the rooms above, his hand resting on the banister. 'Why do you ask?'

She frowned, pulling her furs closer about her shoulders. 'But why on earth would you want to keep it?'

'You never know, it might come in useful one day.'

She sighed impatiently. 'Why is it you always fob me off with half answers? It was kind of your mother to let us have Chalice Walk for the time being, but we cannot possibly live there indefinitely. I should like a house on the Esplanade. And, of course, we must have a place in London.'

She walked slowly towards him and laid her hand on his. 'Why is it you always back away from important issues? You do realize, don't you, that I am going home tomorrow to start making arrangements for our wedding, and yet you have made no suggestions of your own. And I am not very happy about Chalice Walk being turned into a kindergarten.'

'Arrangements had to be made for Alice.'

'Alice!' She turned away in a huff. 'It seems to me that your precious Alice takes precedence over everyone else, including me!' She wanted his reassurance that she was talking nonsense, to have him take her in his arms and tell her that she was the most important person in his life.

All he said was, 'We'd better be going now. It's getting late.'

Rowan came face to face with Charlotte that evening on the back stairs. She did not see him at first on the shadowy half-landing, and flattened herself against the banister to let him pass. 'I'm sorry,' she faltered, 'I was on my way to the kitchen for Alice's milk and biscuits.'

'Charlotte! I might have guessed it. We have a penchant for bumping into each other, it seems. I was just on my way to say goodnight to her. Please don't run away. Tell me, how are things going?'

'Very well on the whole. Alice and Miss Carfax seem to have taken to each other. Miss Carfax is a very good teacher, and Alice seems much happier now.'

Rowan breathed a sigh of relief. 'Thank God for small mercies.' He paused. 'Charlotte, I can't thank you enough for coming here, for taking care of the child. You have given up a great deal, I know – your old job for one thing, and your family to some extent. It can't have been easy for you taking on a new way of life: sleeping under a strange roof . . .'

He noticed, by the faint light of the landing window, that her hand was trembling on the banister. 'I must have frightened you,' he said gently, 'looming out of the shadows the way I did. I suppose I should have come up by the front stairs, but I always came this way when I was a boy, and old habits die hard.'

'I really must go now,' she said, beginning to edge past him. The warmth of his presence was like a heady drug, robbing her of lucid thought, coherent speech.

Realizing her intense nervousness, he said slowly, 'You're not afraid of me, are you?'

'No, of course not.' But that was untrue. She was all too afraid of the emotions this man aroused in her.

'Tell me, do you like your room?' He experienced, as he asked the question, a strong desire to take her in his arms, to touch her hair, to kiss away the tears that seemed so close to the surface.

He thought of Romilly as he had seen her a few minutes ago,

giving the maid explicit instructions about packing her clothes correctly. He had stopped at her door to say that Lomas would bring the carriage round at eight o'clock in the morning in time for the early train, but for once she had scarcely noticed his presence in her anxiety to make sure that the maid did not crease her dresses.

'My room?' Charlotte said softly. 'Yes, I do like it very much. There's a shelf for my books.' She spoke as if that were the greatest treasure on earth.

Rowan thought again of Romilly, busy with her jewel-case, intent on arranging her rings, bracelets and necklaces in the padded velvet compartments while the maid struggled to pack all the shoes, gloves, hats and accessories Romilly had brought with her from London.

The pale ghost of the girl he was engaged to marry seemed to hover between himself and the girl he loved.

The realization that he had loved Charlotte since that night in the garden came to Rowan as a blinding revelation. He felt suddenly warm, at peace, drained and contented as he drew her into his arms and kissed her gently on the lips.

Next morning, he watched the train move out of the station with a mounting sense of relief. At the last moment, Romilly had leaned out of the carriage window to fling her arms round his neck and cover his lips with moist kisses.

'Oh, darling,' she cried, 'I shall miss you so. You will write to me, won't you?'

All he could see now was the fluttering of her lace-edged handkerchief. Turning away, his light-headed feeling of release, of freedom, suddenly forsook him. He was not free at all.

He remembered the moment he had kissed Charlotte; the pale oval of her face seen in the shadows, her low cry of anguish as she pulled away from him and ran quickly down the stairs to the kitchen.

If this is love, Charlotte thought, I cannot think how I shall learn to live with the pain of it. If only Rowan had not kissed her. If only, meeting him again, she had discovered one flaw in him. It was all too easy, she imagined, to imbue certain people with characteristics of kindness and gentleness which they did not actually possess, but this was not true of Rowan.

She had known, at the touch of his lips on hers, that he was all she had imagined him to be, and more, an opinion strengthened by his compassionate concern for Alice, his interest in the girl's welfare – and her own.

If only he had held her roughly; kissed her savagely. She would have been repelled by his closeness: would have struggled to free herself. But his lips were tender, his arms gentle. She had experienced, at the moment he kissed her, an overwhelming sense of peace and happiness, quickly followed by the onrush of guilt as she remembered that Rowan Tanquillan was not hers to love, that they were worlds apart from each other in circumstance and upbringing: that one kiss could never break down the barriers between them. If anything, they seemed even more insurmountable now.

Jenny was quick to realize that Oliver Tanquillan's unorthodox teaching methods had borne fruit so far as Alice was concerned. She found his child to be intelligent, quick and eager to learn. The girl's grown-up vocabulary and odd turns of phrase vastly amused her.

Unorthodox herself, Jenny was happy to teach more by discussion than from books, as Oliver had done, catering to Alice's curiosity about the world and everything in it.

Somerville had disabused Jenny of valuing lessons learned by rote. There, essay-writing was something to be tackled at the last possible minute, by midnight oil or candlelight, after long lazy afternoons on the Cherwell followed by firelight discussions, toasted muffins, coffee and cakes, with an argumentative circle of friends sprawled on cushions to debate some knotty political problem or other. And so it delighted her to walk along the seashore with Alice and Charlotte, laughing and talking; feeding ideas into the girl's receptive mind. And it was not just Alice who benefited from her lessons, Jenny felt, as she became increasingly aware of Charlotte Grayler's bright intelligence.

One night, Jenny confided in Charlotte that she wanted to be a writer. They were sitting near the fire at the time, in Jenny's room. Charlotte had put down her book to listen, and left it open on her chair when she went down to the kitchen to make their suppertime cocoa.

When she returned, Jenny glanced up at her, frowning slightly. 'I hadn't realized you were interested in poetry,' she said, 'especially that of John Donne. "To make one little room an everywhere." What a surprising person you are. I've often wondered what goes on in that quiet little head of yours.'

Charlotte flushed crimson as she closed the book, and said, remembering Maggie's teasing as she did so, 'I've always loved poetry, though I'm not sure I understand John Donne very well.'

'I don't believe that for one moment,' Jenny replied. 'You're just being modest. Are you afraid to admit that you are an intellectual? Is that it? Has someone made you afraid of what you feel and think? You know, Charlotte, I met women at Oxford who were not half as clever as I suspect you are.'

'Clever? I'm not the least bit clever! I only wish I were!'

'You have an untutored mind, of course, but what possibilities I see in you! I mean it,' Jenny said. 'There's no end to what you could make of yourself if you tried. What a waste of talent, hiding yourself away here.'

'What about you, Jenny? Aren't you wasting your own talent?'

'It's different for me. But don't tell me that you intend to squander your life by marrying the first man to ask you, and saddling yourself with four or five children.' She leaned back in her chair to sip her cocoa, and looked at Charlotte over the top of the pince-nez glasses she affected to give herself 'stature', to live up to her reputation as a 'blue-stocking'. Those glasses, she felt certain, had been the deciding factor in convincing Lady Tanquillan that she would make a satisfactory governess.

'I don't think I shall ever marry,' Charlotte said slowly, wishing Jenny would change the subject.

'Nonsense,' Jenny snorted. 'You are not only clever, you are beautiful. Surely you must know that you are! With your looks and brains there's no telling what you could do.' Jenny warmed to her theme. 'The day is coming, my girl, when women will take their rightful place in the world. Doesn't it seem criminal to you that we women are not even allowed to vote, that men still look upon us as chattels?' She stared into the fire as if she could see, in the flames, a vision of a brave new world. 'I wouldn't have missed Oxford for the world. The true value of education lies in being taught to think for one's self.' An idea occurred to her. 'I'm starting Alice on French, soon. Why not join in? I could teach you at the same time.'

'Would you, Jenny? Would you really?'

'Why not?' Jenny chuckled. 'Two for the price of one!'

'Lady Tanquillan would not approve.'

'Who's to tell her?' Jenny had gazed owlishly at Charlotte over her spectacles.

Maggie stood as stiffly as a wax dummy in her tacked-together wedding-dress, giving herself agonized glances in the wardrobe mirror. 'Why ever did I choose white satin?' she wailed. 'I look like a tub of lard!'

Filly appeared, screwing up her eyes against another crisis in the Grayler family.

'What do you think, Mother?' Maggie demanded, making wings of her arms so that the satin strained tightly across her bust and the underseams began to gape.

'It fits you a treat,' Filly said, 'or it would if you'd stop waving your arms about. You're not going into church flapping like a chicken, are you?'

'It feels like a strait-jacket!' Maggie complained.

Charlotte knelt back on her heels. 'It could do with a bit of trimming,' she said. 'I've got some lace in my work-basket.'

'Well I'd better get on.' Filly hitched up the pile of crocheted valances in her arms. 'I've got this lot to wash and starch.' Off she bustled. Maggie's wedding meant spring-cleaning the house from top to bottom, washing and starching everything in sight, from bolsters to antimacassars, serviettes to doilies. The house was beginning to reek of disinfectant and Monkey Brand soap. The idea that people might go poking about her house looking for dust under the beds and finding it, appalled Filly.

Romilly Beresford glanced at the menu for her wedding reception. Fortnum and Mason were doing the catering. Her pencil hovered over the list: smoked salmon, turkey and venison patties . . . She must remember to tell Fortnums that her grandmother was sending fresh salmon and trout from Scotland. There would be a marquee on the lawn, the house would be filled with white roses and red carnations. The three-tier wedding cake would stand on a special table in the dining-room. She was lying on her bed, chin cradled in cupped hands, alternately scribbling and dreaming. First Paris, then Dijon. She knew a marvellous restaurant there where the chef's Coquille St Jacques was out of this world. From Dijon, she and Rowan would drift on to the romantic Auvergne, from there to Nice, to laze in the sun. Romilly could see it all, the sun-drenched days and cool evenings with Rowan beside her. She imagined standing with him on some shaded balcony overlooking the Mediterranean, his arms about her, her head resting against his shoulder; imagined some cool bedroom, herself in a white negligée, waiting for him to come to her.

Her wedding-dress was a dream of thick oyster satin falling to a fan-shaped train sewn with seed pearls. She would wear her grandmother's veil, carry pale creamy orchids and tea-roses, wear, in her ears, her father's gift to her, two perfectly matched diamonds in a pearl setting.

CHAPTER FOURTEEN

Maggie's wedding day dawned fair and clear, with the bride-to-be buried in a mound of bedclothes, wishing herself dead. I can't go through with it, she thought despairingly. But when Filly brought up a breakfast tray with a plate of bacon and eggs, a pile of toast, and a pot of strong tea, she struggled up in bed and polished off the lot with a kind of nervous relish.

'Well, you've got a fine day for it, thank God,' Filly commented, opening the curtains, 'and everything's ready.' She had been up since the crack of dawn making sausage rolls and ham sandwiches. 'There'll be a right old crush in the dining-room, but I can't help that. Lord, I hope your Aunt Clara doesn't forget to bring those extra plates she promised me.'

Bob stood before the swing-mirror in his bedroom trying to get his parting right, his mind reeling with the beer he had consumed at his stag party the night before, and the advice he had received from his workmates, all of them married, with families. 'You mean to tell me,' one of the older men had said, with a broad wink at the others, 'that you've never had carnal knowledge of that lass you're gonna marry? No? Well I'll be damned! Going to the "aisle altar hymn" a buck virgin are you? You do surprise me, Bob, you really do.'

'Maggie isn't that kind of girl,' Bob said helplessly. 'We've never . . . I mean, she wouldn't like it.' He had no head for drink, the crowded pub atmosphere bewildered him.

'She'd better like it tomorrow night,' the older one chuckled, swallowing his beer without his lips touching the glass, 'or you'll be in for a heap of trouble. Let her know who's master right off. Stand no nonsense.' He wiped his moustache with the back of his hand.

'Well, I don't know,' Bob said uneasily, flushing to the roots of his hair, 'Maggie's got a funny temper.'

Now his hand shook slightly as he tried to strike a centre parting, and dipped his comb in the jug of water on the washstand to make the hair on the crown of his head lie down.

Maggie moved forward stiffly on her father's arm to Mendelssohn's Wedding March and the muffled coughs of the congregation. She felt sick and cold and empty in the great church with lighted candles on the altar, the shadowy side aisles flaring away into seemingly limitless distance, and the high, echoing roof above her. She saw, in a dream, the cream jonquils arranged in brass containers near the altar steps, and thought that if the parson swung round suddenly he would knock them for six. She wished he would, or throw a sudden fit – anything to draw people's attention away from herself.

Now here it came, the part she had dreaded: 'to satisfy men's carnal lusts and appetites, like brute beasts that have no understanding.'

She farted softly into the folds of her white satin weddingdress; saw Bob's face not a foot distant from her own, and hated the sight of it.

'First it was ordained for the procreation of children . . . Secondly it was ordained for a remedy against sin and to avoid fornication . . .'

Fornication, there's a nice word to say in church!

'With this ring I thee wed, with my body I thee worship . . .'

Heat ran in waves under Maggie's corsets. Bob was putting the ring on her finger. 'For better, for worse, for richer or poorer, in sickness and in health . . .'

'Oh Perfect Love.'

Signing the register, the bride sicked up a tiny portion of fried egg into her lace-edged handkerchief.

'It all went off very nicely, love,' Filly said tearfully. Albert, in the kitchen seeing to the liquid refreshment, called out, 'Come and give me a hand with the beer – son.' It seemed daft, somehow, calling Bob 'son' but he supposed he had better start doing so.

'Don't be so soft, Albert,' Filly snapped, 'Bob's got to stand with Maggie to "receive". You'll get all the help you need with that beer when Frank arrives. Too much help, in my opinion.' She disappeared into the dining-room to make sure the sandwiches hadn't started to curl at the edges.

At that moment, the bridesmaids came upstairs like a cluster of bright summer flowers. Ha, Filly thought, trust that Madge Robinson to make straight for the looking-glass, preening herself and showing off her engagement ring. Still, it wouldn't be a show without Punch. 'You and Bob had better stand in the bay window to receive,' Filly told Maggie, 'it'll be bedlam here on the landing.'

'You look ever so nice, Maggie,' Bob said shyly, wondering vaguely if his hair was sticking up at the back.

'I don't feel very nice,' Maggie said shortly. Her corsets were killing her. She felt stiff and strange and – different. No longer Maggie Grayler but Maggie Masters. She couldn't quite take it in as Charlotte hugged her and whispered, 'Be happy, Maggie.'

Bob was worrying about his speech, feeling in his inside pocket to make sure he hadn't forgotten to bring it with him. Frank pushed through the crowd and thrust a glass of beer in his hand. 'Get that down you,' he laughed, 'it'll make you feel better.' Bob eyed the glass doubtfully.

'Put that down,' Maggie said tartly. 'The very idea! You should be ashamed of yourself, Frank Grayler!'

Bob looked round for somewhere to put the glass, and settled for the floor. People had started thronging into the room: pumping his hand, wishing him well. He hoped to God he wouldn't step back too far and send the glass flying with his heel.

He thought bemusedly how remote Maggie seemed in her white dress and orange-blossom, a different person from the girl he had cuddled in shop doorways when they were courting. He could not believe that she was really his wife; that he was now a married man with all that entailed: doing his duty on his wedding night. He wasn't entirely sure what that was. He had never made love to a woman in his life. Suppose he couldn't do whatever he was supposed to do?

How he and Maggie got to Blackpool seemed a mystery to Bob at the time and forever afterwards. He had vague recollections of balloon-like faces at the station; showers of confetti, Maggie's mother wiping the tears from her eyes, Maggie's pale, set face beneath the brim of her new straw hat; sitting together in a compartment full of people, not speaking to each other.

The boarding-house was at the far end of the promenade. He remembered feeling intensely cold as he lugged the suitcases to the front door and rang the bell, humiliated when a shower of confetti scattered from his hat-brim onto the landlady's hall carpet. The staircase was steep and narrow. Their room overlooked the promenade. He saw, through the stiffly starched lace curtains, gas-lamps spaced out like beads on a rosary. 'Can we have something to eat?' he asked the landlady. 'Not at this time of night,' she replied with a sniff. 'High tea's at six o'clock. We do a nice high tea. Nothing after. There's plenty of cafes. No suitcases on the bed, it sags the mattress.' She closed the door and departed.

'God, I'm tired,' Maggie said irritably, 'and hungry.'

'We'd best go out then, and find a cafe,' Bob said.

They walked together along the promenade and found a fish and chip parlour where Maggie wolfed haddock, chips, peas and bread and butter as if she had never had a meal in her life before. 'Aren't you going to eat anything?' she asked him accusingly as he toyed with his food.

'I'm not all that hungry,' he said, dreading going back to the digs. If only Maggie would smile at him or say something funny. He thought briefly of the painful feeling he had experienced, at times, just below his jacket, when she teased him. If this was married life, he didn't think much of it. He couldn't understand why Maggie was suddenly so distant, like a stranger. He tucked his hand into her arm on the way back to the boarding-house. 'I can smell the sea,' he said. 'Let's walk near the railings and have a look at it.'

'I look at the sea every day of my life,' Maggie snapped, wishing she could take her corsets off. Her mother had warned her that she should wear her old ones for the journey, but Maggie wouldn't listen. Besides, her new dress and jacket wouldn't have fitted her properly if she had worn the old ones. 'I don't know why you wanted to come to Blackpool in the first place,' she chuntered. 'Why couldn't we have gone to London where there's plenty going on?'

'I've always fancied Blackpool,' Bob said, squeezing her hand.

'We can't see anything anyway, it's too dark.' Maggie's new shoes were beginning to pinch.

'We'd best be getting back to the digs then,' Bob suggested, 'we can't walk about here all night.'

They unpacked in silence. When Bob had hung his things in the wardrobe, he said, 'Well, we'd better get undressed.'

Maggie turned on him. 'I'm not getting undressed in front of you, Bob Masters.'

'Eh?' He stared at his bride like a wounded dog. 'But we're married now.'

'I said I'm not getting undressed in front of you!'

'Where do you want me to go then? Shall I stand out on the landing until you're in bed?'

'I'm not getting into bed with you either.' Maggie's face puckered.

'Don't be so soft.' Bob's temper frayed suddenly. All he wanted was to get into bed and go to sleep. 'I don't know what's come over you, Maggie Grayler. It was your idea to get married at Easter instead of waiting till August Bank Holiday.'

'That's a downright lie! It was all your idea.' She began to cry. 'Oh God,' she sobbed, 'I wish I'd never got married at all.'

'Aw, come on, pet.' He put his arm round her shoulders, 'You'll feel better after a good night's sleep. You get undressed. I won't look at you if you don't want me to.'

'How many more times have I to tell you? I'm not getting into that bed with you, and that's flat!'

He'd had enough. 'Please yourself.' He began, savagely, to peel off his trousers. 'To hell with this for a lark. I'm tired out and cod frozen. You do as you like. I'm going to sleep!' Ignoring Maggie, he pulled on his pyjamas, got into bed, thumped the pillow until a shower of feathers billowed from the thin cotton cover, pulled the eiderdown under his chin, and lay there, his stomach churning with hunger and his feet like blocks of ice. A bloody fine wedding night this had turned out to be. All very well for blokes to ladle out advice at a stag party. But what the hell was a man supposed to do if his bride wouldn't even get into the same bed with him?

He awoke at two o'clock in the morning. A clock was chiming somewhere in the darkness. Groping with his hand, he encountered the huddled figure of his wife. She was lying on the very edge of the bed, on top of the bedclothes. He could hear the chattering of her teeth. What a queer noise, he thought, like a woodpecker nipping at a tree. He groaned and sat up. 'My God,' he said, 'you'll catch pneumonia. Get up a minute.' He heard a shuffling sound, a muffled sob as he pulled back the sheet. He could just see Maggie, a sacrificial lamb in a white nightgown. 'Now, get into this bed,' he said. He slipped his arm round her and held her until she was warmer. 'I wish I knew what ailed you,' he said softly, thinking what a wonderful thing it was to feel the whole length of a woman beside him. He hadn't realized it would be like this, how soft and comfortable Maggie would be without her strapping, those damned corsets that nipped her waist in like an egg-timer, and the boned bodice she wore to keep her bust in place. He touched her hair with a kind of wonderment that she had taken out all the hairpins. It felt soft and fluffy to the touch. His heart was hammering against his ribs as he slid his hand across her belly.

Maggie turned her head away. Tears oozed from the corners of her eyes as Bob began to worship her with his body.

CHAPTER FIFTEEN

Daffodils were almost over. Trees wore mantles of spring green in a world overshadowed with grim rumour.

Jenny Carfax, an avid reader of the national newspapers, marched out every morning before breakfast to buy her copy of *The Times* from a newsagent's in the main street. Soon, Charlotte began to realize how little she knew about world events, and took to going with her, hurrying along beside the intrepid Jenny, drawing in gulps of fresh air, wanting to keep up with her both mentally and physically, enjoying those early morning excursions whatever the weather. The magic of Jenny lay in her ability to imbue life with the shining qualities of hope and purpose, to comment pithily, often unexpectedly, on what she read.

'My God, Charlotte, listen to this,' she said excitedly one morning. '"In East London yesterday, suffragettes hurled stones and stink-bombs to break up a council meeting. The intruders laid about them with handbags and umbrellas, seizing confidential documents which they ripped up and tossed into the air like confetti. A spokesman for the councillors said afterwards that the attack came as a total surprise. Several arrests were made." Isn't that splendid?'

'Yes, I suppose so,' Charlotte replied doubtfully. 'But what about the violence involved?'

'Oh, heavens, girl,' Jenny said impatiently, 'how else are we to free ourselves from male domination?' She sighed. 'I have spent a good deal of time in London, so I know what I'm talking about. Most women are content to go "up West" to window-shop, to drool over the latest fashions, things they couldn't afford in a thousand years. Women like that give me the hump, not giving a damn about anything except clothes, turning their backs on the suffragettes, the *real* women, doing their fighting for them.'

She continued angrily, 'All that matters to those empty-headed nincompoops is getting married; going off on day trips to Brighton; having babies! They haven't the vision or mentality to realize, when they turn their faces away from the suffragettes and make fun of them, that those women are fighting for the betterment of all womenkind! I'm sorry, Charlotte, but I feel very deeply that it is high time we were given the right to vote, to have our say about what is happening to this world we live in.'

She paused momentarily, her bright, heart-shaped face masked with despair. 'It makes me sick to think that important politicians like Ramsay MacDonald, Lloyd George, and Asquith, are footling about in Whitehall doing absolutely nothing about votes for women. That so many women remain impassive too.

'Oh, it's so easy to turn a blind eye, to stroll down The Mall in the sunshine, thinking that as long as the royal standard flutters over Buckingham Palace we are all safe and secure, but it isn't true.' She sighed impatiently. 'Can't they see what is happening? That men are hell-bent on landing us all in another war?'

'Don't upset yourself, Jenny,' Charlotte said anxiously.

'Upset myself! It's enough to upset any woman with two ounces of brains in her head!' She grinned suddenly. 'Sorry. I do get rather carried away, don't I? But I just think that if women had their say, there wouldn't be a war. As things stand, we must needs leave everything to the men, and that cannot be either right or fair. You know, Charlotte, I believe that we are galloping, as a nation, towards a chasm. That in years to come, we will remember this Maytime of 1914 with regret for a way of life that will never come again.'

'Oh, don't, Jenny. Please don't!' Charlotte said. 'I can't bear to think about it.'

Jenny smiled. 'I know. The truth hurts, at times, doesn't it?'

Rowan wakened suddenly from a dream of Charlotte. Moonlight edged the curtains. Getting up, he crossed to the window and looked out. The night was very still except for the sound of the tide running in on the shore.

Charlotte would be sleeping now, her glorious hair a deep, shining copper against a white pillow-slip, her eyelashes fanned out in dark crescents against her cheeks. Leaning his hands on the sill, looking up at a scattering of brilliant stars above the chimney-pots, he knew that he had no right to think of Charlotte at all, engaged as he was to marry Romilly.

Romilly!

The pain of love surprised him: the inner torment and uncertainty; the long, empty days and sleep-interrupted nights; the fever and fret of loving.

He paced the room restlessly, knowing that he could not marry Romilly now. He did not want to hurt her, but he must be honest with her, must make her understand that he could not marry her, loving Charlotte as he did.

He lay down again, the pillows bunched beneath his head, knowing that he must go to London to see Romilly as soon as possible; explain things to her gently, ask her to release him from their engagement.

Scarborough's May Day horse procession was in full swing. Along the seafront, into town and back again went the great Suffolk Punches with their polished harnesses, their hooves burnished like the sun; manes plaited with red, white and blue ribbons, with hoops of flowers surmounting their hames; pacing with quiet strength and dignity between the admiring crowds lining the route.

Urchins had scrambled up lamp-posts to gain a better view. A holiday spirit was in the air, as if the town had shuffled off winter like an old worn-out cloak. Soon would come train-loads of trippers from the smoky mill towns of the West Riding. Now there were bright flowers in the parks, ducklings on the Mere, trees in leaf in Westborough, so that the horse procession wended its way in an atmosphere of light-hearted gaiety beneath an early summer sky, against a backdrop of blue sea and budding trees. On they came, the polished jockey-carriages with their brilliantly-garbed riders, the wagonettes and chara-bancs filled with laughing girls throwing flowers, the fire-engines and tradesmen's delivery-vans to the accompaniment of jingling harness and the Town Silver Band, and the cheers and chatter of the onlookers.

Alice, with Jenny and Charlotte, stood enthralled by the spectacle, wearing a new dress that Charlotte had made for her from a soft blue light woollen material. The Tanquillans had reluctantly made provision for the child's education, none for clothes. Alice had still been wearing her ugly mourning dress until Charlotte had taken it into her head to buy some material out of her own money.

'I don't see why you should beggar yourself,' Jenny had said.

'But every little girl should have at least one pretty dress,' Charlotte replied, smiling. Next day, Jenny had thrown a brown paper parcel on the school-room table. 'Philanthropy begins at home,' she said carelessly. 'It's a petticoat to go with the dress. And I've bought her a straw boater as well, for good measure.'

Now Alice stood, trembling with excitement, hearing the stirring music of the Town Band growing louder and louder until the uniformed men marched into view, followed by the first of the dray-horses with their straining shoulders and rippling hair socks.

Tears began to stream down the child's face. She grasped Charlotte's fingers tightly, her thin shoulders shaking with emotion.

'What is it?' Charlotte asked in a low voice.

'The horses! I've never seen anything so beautiful before. One day I shall own horses like these for my soul's contentment.'

Jenny and Charlotte exchanged glances. My God, Jenny thought, from the mouth of babes and sucklings . . . Charlotte said quickly, 'My brother Harry is in the procession. You remember Harry, don't you?'

'Oh yes.' Alice was suddenly quite calm again, her tears forgotten. 'I liked him better than the one with the ginger moustache who looked at me as if I'd escaped from a zoo, but not as much as the quiet one with curly hair, the one called Joe.'

As the crowds pressed forward, Charlotte said eagerly, 'There's Harry now!' She stood on tiptoe to wave.

Harry Grayler sat upright in his seat, gently shaking the reins over Nobby's back, proudly aware of his horse's well-groomed hindquarters, neat crest, and the shining scarlet ribbons he had plaited so carefully into its tail. He had been up at the crack of dawn to polish Nobby's reins, bit, bridle, collar and breeching, rubbing away until his arms ached, motivated by a strong desire to win first prize in the tradesmen's entry. More than that even, to make the judges aware of his horse: to recognize its worth.

Suddenly he caught sight of his sister in the crowd, and raised his whip to her in salute, his handsome, weather-tanned face split by a radiant smile, his broad shoulders held proudly erect.

So that is Charlotte's brother Harry, Jenny thought, raising her eyebrows in surprise. God, what a handsome man.

After the tradesmen's entries came contingents of the 5th Yorkshire Territorials, The Green Howards, marching to the music of their military band, followed by non-uniformed men of the National Reserve, men who had fought in the Boer War, who stood ready to defend their country again should the need arise. The cheers and applause of the onlookers rose to a crescendo as they swung jauntily into view.

Then came a sense of anti-climax as the procession wound its way down Westborough to the Old Town. The laughing urchins scrambled down from their lamp-post eyries to run after it, whistling and hooting, swaggering in time to the music, pretending to be soldiers.

Suddenly, 'There's Rowan,' Alice cried, darting across the road to him, twirling excitedly to show off her new dress as he smiled down at her and placed a restraining hand on her shoulder.

Jenny had not seen Rowan before, but, because his name was Tanquillan, she had been prepared to bracket him, along with his mother, as a prime snob, a bloody-minded plutocrat. For the second time that day, Jenny's eyebrows lifted to her hat-brim in surprise. First Harry Grayler, now Rowan Tanquillan! But even that staunch supporter of Women's Liberation, Jenny Carfax, could find nothing to rail against in the way Rowan Tanquillan knelt on one knee on the pavement to calm a child's excitement, apparently not caring tuppence that one knee of his trousers was covered in dust as he did so.

And then the perceptive Jenny noticed the way he glanced across the road: the expression of relief on his face when he saw Charlotte; how quickly he rose to his feet and came towards her, smiling, guiding Alice with a lean, firm hand, making sure that no harm came to the girl. But what was wrong with Charlotte? Why the flushed cheeks and nervous reaction to his approach? Why the primly-set lips as she said, 'I don't think that you have met Miss Carfax.'

'No, I haven't,' Rowan said easily, raising his hat, 'though how we have managed to miss each other, I can't imagine. How do you do, Miss Carfax? I understand that you are a marvellous teacher.'

'I do my best,' Jenny replied with a twinkle, digging her fingers into Charlotte's arm, aware of some inexplicable tension between the pair of them, Rowan and Charlotte.

So that's it, she thought, with a flash of inspiration; they're in love with each other, and Charlotte is too proud, or too daft, to admit it.

'I wonder,' Rowan said, 'if you would care to have tea with me at my cottage? It is rather a long way off, though, near the harbour. Would you mind walking so far?'

'Lead on, Macduff,' Jenny said, catching Alice by the hand; pulling her back to prevent her making a nuisance of herself, anxious to give Rowan and Charlotte some time together; noticing with satisfaction, the way he took Charlotte's arm as they walked together along the crowded pavement.

'Why have you been avoiding me, Charlotte?' Rowan asked.

'I don't know what you mean. And please let go of my arm.' She hurried on ahead of him, chin uplifted, ill at ease, but determined not to show it.

Rowan cursed under his breath as a pursuing crowd of laughing people separated them. 'You know quite well what I mean,' he said, catching up with her again. Is it because I – I kissed you?'

'I'd rather not discuss it, if you don't mind.'

God grant me patience, he thought, side-stepping into the gutter as a crowd of laughing youngsters pushed their way along the pavement towards him.

'God dammit! We *must* discuss it,' he said, gripping her elbow. 'This was the last thing I envisaged, talking to you like this! I should have waited.'

'Waited for what?' Charlotte was still her mother's daughter, a red-head into the bargain.

Anchored to her by his hand on her sleeve, uncaring of the crowds which surged around them, Rowan said quietly, 'To tell you how much I love you!'

'No. Please. You have no right to say that!'

'Because I'm engaged to Romilly Beresford? Is that it?'

'Oh no! Not just that! Don't you see, Rowan, that I don't belong to your kind of world?'

'My kind of world,' Rowan said bitterly, 'I wonder what that is.' He felt a misfit, a cipher, with his upper-class education and all the so-called privileges that money had bestowed on him.

At that moment Alice tugged away impatiently from Jenny's restraining hand. 'Wait for me, Rowan,' she cried.

Charlotte fell back a pace or two.

'Why didn't you tell me how things were between you and Rowan?' Jenny asked.

'I don't know what you mean.'

'Oh, come off it, Charlotte.' Jenny frowned. 'The man's head-over-heels in love with you, and you with him, unless I'm much mistaken.'

'You *are* mistaken!'

'You can't fool me,' Jenny said quietly, risking Charlotte's wrath.

'Oh, leave me alone, Jenny, *please*!'

'Very well, but just tell me why.'

'Why what?'

'All this high-minded self-denial.'

'Does it really matter?' At that moment, Charlotte had no

149

idea where she really belonged, either.

Despite Charlotte's rebuttal, Rowan knew that he must go to London to ask Romilly to release him from their engagement. He had watched Charlotte, the afternoon of the May Day procession, walking about his home, touching, with reverent fingers, the possessions which meant so much to him: the old ship's lanterns and logs he had acquired at auction, the flowering geraniums on the window-sills, his books and engravings. Things which Romilly had not even noticed.

He knew, as the train sped towards London, he must tell Romilly, as gently as possible, that he did not love her; brace himself to meet her storm of tears when he asked for his freedom.

As the train clattered over the rails and the carriage windows were shrouded with smoke from the engine, Rowan thought of the strike threat at the harbour, the ugly, rebarbative, yet understandable attitude of the workmen when they were forced to accept a threepence a week increase in their wages. The men were angry and bitter because their claim had not been met. They had raised their fists against his father, had called him a penny-pinching bastard, and worse. Had it not been for his own presence that day, they might have added physical violence to their abuse. He remembered the pounding of his heart as he shouted to them to remain calm; how they had fallen back, realizing that he was on their side.

Now, as the train travelled inevitably towards London, Rowan thought that he would rather face a threatening mob of underpaid workmen than Romilly Beresford.

He had warned no-one of his arrival. He alighted from a hired carriage near the steps leading up to the house in Eaton Square, and stood for a moment gathering his courage to face what must be faced.

The butler was surprised to see him. 'The family is at dinner, sir,' he said. 'Shall I tell her ladyship?'

'Thank you, but I dined on the train. I'll go to my room: join them later for coffee.'

'There are guests, Mr Rowan. Mr and Mrs Beresford and Miss Romilly.'

'I see. Thank you, Charters.'

Rowan remembered, as he went upstairs, a bull-fight he had witnessed in Pamplona; that sickening moment when the matador stood ready to plunge his sword into the creature's heart. That moment of truth which meant certain death for one or the other. Now that his moment of truth was here, he felt every bit as sick as he had done in that arena with the scent of death in the air. The crowd had not cared which died, man or beast, as long as their blood-craving found appeasement. That afternoon, the man had died. Died because his nerve failed him at the last moment. That slight moment of indecision, and the bull had plunged its horns deep into his gut, twisting his body to a grotesque question mark of suffering.

'Rowan, darling, what on earth are you doing here?' Romilly seized his arm ecstatically, triumphant because he had come to her, because he could not bear being apart from her.

The drawing-room reminded Rowan of that bull-ring at Pamplona: the eager, watchful, upturned faces, the figure of a dead man sprawled in the sand under a hot summer sun. But his moment of truth had not come yet. This was merely the parade of the picadors.

Romilly laid claim to him with flushed cheeks and a proprietary air, flicking imaginary specks of dust from his dinner-jacket.

The windows were shrouded with red velvet curtains. It was a room he had always hated. He glanced distastefully at the painting above the mantelpiece, a dreary picture with heavy overhanging trees lining a road leading to nowhere in particular. But then, he had never liked any of Constable's paintings. He preferred those of the impressionists: the light, bright, sparkling water scenes of Monet, or Degas's enchanting ballerinas.

Sofas and chairs were grouped together like a stage-setting for Oscar Wilde's *The Importance of Being Earnest*. The occupants of the room seemed, to Rowan, a group of actors speaking old familiar lines. His father, for instance, was expounding his views on the present political situation as if he really understood what he was talking about. His entry into the room had caused a momentary diversion, that was all. Gervaise was telling Romilly's father that the Germans were a cowardly lot at heart. That, if war came, they would be given the sound thrashing they so richly deserved.

Edmund Beresford nodded wearily. The old man looked tired, Rowan thought. He had always liked and respected Romilly's parents. He felt like Judas Iscariot, standing there listening, half smiling, with Romilly glancing up at him and pawing at his sleeve.

His mother, he noticed, was frowning and shaking her head. He knew what she was thinking. War was *de trop* as a topic of drawing-room conversation. He caught her puzzled glance over the coffee cups and guessed that she was wondering why he had come to London so suddenly. She would question him later, would probe and pry until she winkled out the truth. He knew exactly how it would be. Later, when the house was quiet, she would come to his room. Then he would confess his reason for coming, and she would berate him soundly as a fool; beg him to reconsider; accuse him of infidelity.

It happened exactly as he knew it would. His mother came to his room at midnight. She had read his mind: had guessed that he wished to break his engagement. Her anger was far greater than he had anticipated. He had never known her so vitriolic, so incensed.

'Have you no sense of decency?' she demanded. 'Is it possible that you have not considered the ramifications of such a step?' Her next thrust hurt him far more than he had expected. 'First Oliver Tanquillan, now my own son! I bracket the pair of you together! Bad seed! Contemptible, cowardly, destructive, dishonourable!'

He watched her as she paced the room. She wore a padded dressing-gown over her night attire. 'Just how do you intend to break the news to Romilly? And what will the Beresfords think? Do you imagine that our friendship will survive such an insult?'

The cuts came thick and fast. 'And have you thought about your father? You know that he is hoping to gain a seat in the House of Commons in the next election.' Her tactics changed suddenly. 'You are simply overwrought,' she said, touching his arm. 'You will come to your senses by morning.'

'I'm afraid not, Mother,' Rowan said briefly. 'Believe me, you have not said anything new to me. Nothing that I have not said to myself time and time again. The truth remains, I am not in love with Romilly. Our marriage would be a disaster.'

'You are talking like a child, a spoilt, petulant child,' Rachel said heatedly. 'What about Romilly's happiness? Does she mean nothing to you?'

'I told you a long time ago that I look on Romilly as a sister. Nothing more than that. For God's sake, Mother, would you want me to marry her knowing how I feel about her?'

Suddenly Rachel guessed the truth. 'You are in love with someone else, aren't you?' Her eyes narrowed to slits. 'What a fool I've been. Well, who is she, this other woman of yours?'

'Goodnight, Mother,' he said quietly.

'You fool,' she said as she quit his room. 'You utter, stupid young fool! I can guess who she is!'

Next morning, as Rachel was dressing, a maid came to her. 'Mrs Beresford's butler is here, madam,' she said. 'He wishes to speak to you immediately.'

'Mrs Beresford's butler? What does he want at this hour?'

'I'm afraid it's bad news, your ladyship.'

'Bad news?' Rachel finished dressing and hurried downstairs to find that her husband was there before her. 'What is it?' she asked. 'What's wrong?'

Gervaise held out his hands to her. 'It's Edmund Beresford,' he said, his face the colour of putty. 'He died at two o'clock this morning.'

'Edmund? But – how?'

'A sudden heart-attack, my dear.'

'I see.' An incredible sense of relief swept through Rachel Tanquillan. There could be no question of Rowan calling off his engagement to Romilly now.

The bright bubble of Romilly's happiness had burst suddenly. Always the petted and cherished child, she possessed no reserve of womanly strength to meet the blow of her father's death.

First came the stunning realization of his physical departure from the world in the drawing-together of curtains; the solemn air of mourning which overhung the house like a shroud.

Emily had not been able to persuade her daughter to look at her dead father. She would not even venture into the room where he had died. The thought of walking up to his bier terrified her. She could not bear the thought of change in anyone she loved; could not contemplate the thought of seeing her father as a stranger. She remembered, with utter revulsion, the death-masks she had seen in foreign museums.

It was Rowan who bore the full brunt of her grief and terror as she clung to him, sobbing helplessly against his shoulder, her face blotched and swollen with the tears she could not control. Hers was an hysterical grief, an outpouring of self-pity that her father had left her. 'Why did Daddy have to die now?' she sobbed. 'Just when I was so happy?'

Rowan's regard for Emily Beresford strengthened and grew as she moved, tall and calm, through the stricken house, quietly receiving her guests – those people who had come for the funeral. Her amazing fortitude in the face of her own grief moved Rowan deeply. She said to him, just before the funeral, 'Romilly's life is in your hands now, my dear. You will look after her?'

'I'll do my best, Tante Emily.' His childhood name for her sprang easily to his lips. The events of the past days had left the mark of suffering on her face. Rowan understood that a great part of that suffering lay in Romilly's reaction to her father's death.

Emily said, 'I don't think she has realized that the wedding will have to be postponed. Poor child, it will come as a bitter blow to her.' She smiled sadly. 'You have been a tower of strength to both us. How unselfish you are, Rowan, how kind.'

'Please don't.' He could scarcely prevent himself from telling her the reason for his visit to London. They were together in the library. He could see, through the open door, the Beresfords' friends and relations beginning to gather in the hall, awaiting the carriages, in deep black, the women veiled, waiting like silent figures in a Greek tragedy.

'I must go now, my dear. Take care of Romilly today. She will need all the help you can give her.' Rowan raised Emily's gloved hand to his lips and watched her as she moved uprightly to the foot of the stairs. There was no sign of Romilly. He went in search of her and found her in the conservatory, a forlorn figure in black, her face bloated with tears. 'It is almost time for me to go,' he said gently, touched by her vulnerability.

'I can't bear it,' she said. 'I feel as if a part of me is dead too.'

He took her arm, and she walked with him to the waiting carriages.

That night, when Emily, her brother-in-law Richard, his wife, and the Tanquillans were seated at the dining-table, Richard, bearded, inclined to pontificate, made some reference to his mother's state of health. News of Edmund's death had come as a great shock to the old lady – 'As it did to all of us,' he hemmed, gazing solemnly over his pince-nez spectacles. 'She felt so distressed that she could not make the journey to London on this sad occasion. Her heart, you know.' He tapped his own chest vaguely. 'However, Mother and myself very much hope that you, Emily, and Romilly, will spend the summer with us.'

'But Uncle Richard,' Romilly cried, 'have you forgotten? I am going to be married next month!'

A hush descended at the table. Emily glanced quickly at Rowan. She said, in a quiet voice, 'Let us not discuss that now, darling.'

'But I do want to talk about it now,' Romilly said defiantly. 'We cannot possibly go to Scotland! Everything is arranged.' She half rose to her feet, upsetting her wine glass as she turned to Rowan. 'Well, why don't *you* say something?'

'Please sit down, my dear,' Emily said wearily. 'You must realize that there is no question of the wedding taking place so soon after . . .' Emily's self-control almost broke.

'But Daddy would have wanted it!' Petted and spoilt, accustomed to having her own way, numbed and shocked by events, Romilly stumbled from the room, weeping hysterically.

'I am so sorry,' Emily said. 'Please excuse me. I must go to her.'

'Damned awkward, what?' Richard muttered into his beard. 'Young people these days! Overwrought. Understandably so. But a white wedding so soon after Edmund's funeral. Out of the question! A disappointment. Bound to be. Emily will make her understand.' He glanced at Rowan. 'Sorry, my boy. Damned disappointing for you too, eh?'

Rowan made no reply. He was looking at his mother, wondering what was going through her mind. She was sitting there, half smiling, fingering the stem of her wine glass.

Appointing himself host in Emily's absence, Richard suggested that they went through to the drawing-room for coffee. Rachel made an excuse not to join them. Still smiling, she walked upstairs to Romilly's bedroom.

Rowan wondered uneasily what she was about to do.

The Beresfords' relations departed for Scotland by the early train. Rachel had said little all day. When Rowan mentioned that he must be getting back to Scarborough, she merely smiled and went on arranging a bowl of long-stemmed roses in the drawing-room. 'By the way, I have invited Romilly and Emily to tea,' she said casually. 'You will be here, won't you?'

'Yes, of course, if you wish.' He could not rid himself of the feeling that his mother was up to something.

The idea of an immediate wedding by special licence was handed to him, as a fait accompli, along with a cup of tea. Emily's face still bore signs of her recent ordeal. Romilly, on the other hand, was bubbling with excitement, her grief forgotten. 'It was Tante Rachel's idea,' she said. 'Mummy made me realize that a white wedding was out of the question, then Tante Rachel suggested this alternative. Oh Rowan, isn't it splendid!'

Scarcely pausing to draw breath, she babbled on. 'Mummy made me sleep on the idea because she wanted me to be quite sure that I should not mind giving up my lovely white wedding.' She laughed delightedly. 'Isn't "sleep on it" a stupid phrase? I couldn't sleep a wink for thinking about it. I don't think I shall mind at all, as long as we are married in church . . .'

Rowan experienced a deep sense of anger against his mother. How dare she have interfered in such a way? 'It is not as simple as all that,' he said coldly, 'there are other considerations . . . my work, for one thing.'

Romilly interrupted brightly, 'If you are worried about postponing our honeymoon, I don't mind that in the least. I'll go back to Scarborough with you after the wedding.'

An angry retort sprang to his lips, but the words remained unsaid as he caught sight of Emily's suffering face – a woman he had always cared for, whose eyes were fixed on his face in a dumb appeal for clemency and understanding.

'We must give Rowan time to get used to the idea,' she said slowly. 'Perhaps he, too, would like to sleep on it.'

'But that's nonsense, Mummy!' Romilly's eyes flashed fire.

'Even so, these things cannot be arranged in a few minutes. Come now, my dear.' Emily rose to her feet. 'We'll talk about it tomorrow.'

When they had gone, Rowan turned to his mother. 'How could you have done such a thing,' he said in a low, contemptuous voice. 'You have placed me in an impossible situation! Now it will be even harder for me to tell Romilly the truth, that there isn't going to be a wedding!'

'Don't be so absurd, Rowan. Of course, there is going to be a wedding,' Rachel replied coolly. 'How impetuous you are, and how foolish. Did you really imagine that I would stand by to watch you make an idiot of yourself over a grocer's daughter? The girl may be a common thief for all we know; hardly a fit person to act as companion to a mentally sick child like Alice.'

'What the hell are you talking about?' But he knew. 'Well, it won't wash, Mother! Emotional blackmail won't work with me!'

'Emotional blackmail?' Rachel laughed as she turned to smooth her hair in front of a mirror. 'Really, darling, how absurd of you to suggest such a thing. Do you really imagine that I would go to the trouble of accusing Charlotte Grayler of theft, or sending Alice to a special school . . .'

'Oh yes, Mother.' Rowan said hoarsely. 'You would do it if it suited your purpose! My God! Have you ever stopped to wonder why I never cried for you as a child? Perhaps I knew, even then, that you didn't love me! How you must have resented bearing a child you never really wanted. But I was necessary, wasn't I? Not as a child to be loved, but as the continuation of the name of Tanquillan! A possession to be displayed along with your brooches and fingerbobs!'

Rachel turned on her son in a fury. 'How *dare* you speak to me like that?'

'It's the truth! You have dared to threaten two people I love – because I *do* love Charlotte and Alice! Christ, Mother! What kind of a woman are you?'

Beside herself with rage, Rachel snapped back at him, 'I am a realist, which you, apparently, are not! Make no mistake, Rowan, I will defend the family name whatever the cost! I don't give a damn for Charlotte Grayler or Alice Tanquillan. They are both expendable. But drive me too far, and you will realize that I mean what I say! It is all up to you!'

Rowan drew in a shuddering breath. He cared nothing for himself. Happiness was something he had never known; a bright star he had thought to be forever out of reach, something he had come close to in his music and his love for Charlotte Grayler; something he could live without so long as Charlotte, and Alice too, remained safe.

If war came, he would fight for his country to his last breath. But this was a different kind of war, in which even brave men were defeated by strategy.

'Very well, Mother, you win!' He could not bear the thought of harm coming to Charlotte.

'That is very sensible of you, my dear.' Rachel said.

'For God's sake spare me that!' He looked her straight in the face. 'I will never forgive you for what you have done!'

Romilly wore a dove-grey dress, a hat trimmed with violet ribbons, and carried a nosegay of violets and lilies of the valley. The church was lit with a myriad tapering candles, the flower-holders filled with white roses and double white lilac. She fluttered down the aisle like a violet and grey butterfly, on the arm of Sir Gervaise Tanquillan.

The parson stepped forward. 'Dearly beloved, we are gathered together here in the sight of God, and in the face of this congregation, to join together this man and this woman in holy matrimony . . .'

The sound of distant traffic filtered into the church, a reminder of the world outside. Rowan lifted his eyes to the stained-glass window above the altar. A girl with long red hair looked back at him: prisms of sunlight reflected in her eyes, her folded hands dappled with candleshine. Charlotte, he thought, with a deep sense of despair, forgive me for what I am about to do.

'Wilt thou have this woman to thy wedded wife, to live together after God's ordinance in the holy estate of matrimony? Wilt thou love her, comfort her, honour and keep her in sickness and in health and, forsaking all other, keep thee only unto her, so long as ye both shall live?'

A long silence ensued. Romilly glanced up at him fearfully beneath the brim of her ribbon-trimmed hat.

'I will,' Rowan said heavily. Oh, Charlotte, he thought. It is you I love and always will, my Rose of Sharon, my lily of the valley.

Emily's lips trembled suddenly as she struggled to hold back her tears. It was not Romilly's happiness she cared for now, but Rowan's. Rowan whom she loved as dearly as her own flesh and blood.

How unhappy he looked, how careworn. Beware of pity, she thought, masquerading as love. How she wished she had not, in her grief, asked Rowan to look after Romilly! Had not listened to Rachel Tanquillan.

She had been so weak, so stupid; an indulgent mother intent only on her child's happiness. She should have told Romilly, a long time ago, not to cry for the moon. Instead, she had gone along with this absurd charade, the marriage of the two people she loved most in the world, who would never be happy together.

The coldness of the church pressed in on her. A matter of a

few days ago she had seen her husband's coffin borne into this church: four grey walls enclosing a vast, inhospitable space filled with memorials to the long-dead.

The family had begged her not to attend Edmund's funeral; to remain at home, in a kind of discreet purdah, with the other women, but she would have none of that.

She had stood, then, alone and bewildered, understanding, for the first time in her life, what loneliness meant. Loneliness, she now knew, was a private and personal hell from which there was no escape: a clinging grey shroud shutting out the sunlight of a summer day. Loneliness was seeing other people through a veil of indifference; the memory of a love which would never come again: a drawing-down of blinds, a fruitless searching for a well-loved smile in a world of strangers.

As Romilly held out her hand to receive her wedding ring, Emily knew, with a feeling of despair, that Rowan was lonely, too; that, no matter how hard Romilly tried, she would never begin to touch the solitary core of loneliness in Rowan's heart.

CHAPTER SIXTEEN

Mrs Lomas was inured to the arrival of telegrams at the house in Chalice Walk, usually from her ladyship to inform her how many house-guests she and Sir Gervaise were bringing with them from London. 'Now what?' she would say to her husband. But the one she had just received caused her to flop suddenly onto a kitchen chair in surprise.

'What's the matter?' Lomas asked, his mouth full of bacon and egg.

'I thought Mr Rowan's wedding was to take place next month,' she frowned, 'But it says here that the house is to be made ready immediately. Mr and Mrs Tanquillan will be arriving by the evening train. The wedding must have taken place in a devil of a hurry, that's all I can say!'

Alice, who had been out to the shed to look at the kittens, caught the tail-end of the conversation. 'Whose wedding?' she asked, loitering near the door.

'What are you doing there?' Mrs Lomas said sharply. 'I thought you were in the garden.'

'I was, but I'm here now.'

'And little pitchers have long ears! Well, my advice to you, miss, is to keep out of Mrs Tanquillan's way when she arrives.'

Alice frowned. 'Mrs Tanquillan?'

'Don't stand there repeating everything I say. Mr Rowan has married that young lady of his, and I won't want you under my feet to-day of all days! Oh, my goodness! Where has Bessie got to?' The housekeeper hurried off to find the girl who came in daily to help with the rough work.

Alice slid silently through the baize door to the back stairs, and stood against the wall, trembling, her eyes as black as coal in her paper-white face, shocked by what she had heard. A terrible numbness swept over her. It couldn't be true. She began to whimper. Rowan had betrayed her. Hatred of Romilly Beresford welled up in her like poison, distilled to its purest essence, an antidote almost to pain itself. Release lay in thinking what she could do to harm her; to get even with her for stealing Rowan. The Mills of God grind slowly. She began to laugh, then tears flooded down her cheeks. She had never felt so wretched before, not even when her father died.

Jenny appeared on the landing. 'Alice, where art thou?' she sang out. 'Time for your history lesson. Why, what on earth's the matter?' She clattered downstairs. 'Why are you crying? Has one of the kittens died?'

'I'm the one who has died,' Alice said dramatically.

Jenny laughed, then just as suddenly she stopped laughing. 'What do you mean?'

'He has betrayed me!'

'I wish you would stop talking like a penny novelette,' Jenny said impatiently. '*Who* has betrayed you?'

'Rowan! He has married Romilly Beresford!'

'*What?* But I thought . . .'

'I know what you thought, that Rowan loved *me*.' Alice's breath caught on a sob. 'That's what is so terrible. He *does* love me!'

Oh God, Jenny thought. Poor Charlotte. She took Alice by the arm and led her upstairs. Even Oxford with its petty jealousies and passionate friendships was nothing compared with this. She would rather have written a French essay on the comparative genius of Balzac and Flaubert, at midnight, by candlelight, any time, than break the news of Rowan's marriage to Charlotte.

They had talked long and late about love last night. Love, Jenny said, was composed of two diametrically opposed equations, the spiritual and the physical, and one counter-balanced the other. Sitting with her feet tucked under her, Charlotte had said, 'Yes, I see that. But what about wealth and poverty? Where do they come into it?'

'They are merely conditions of Society. I know what's in

your mind. You've got it into your head that because Rowan Tanquillan is rich, he stands behind some physical barrier or other. But that's all nonsense! Wealth makes no difference at all.'

'It does to me,' Charlotte said. 'Don't you see, there are so many things he takes for granted as part of his upbringing; travel, music, education. What could I possibly give him in return?'

'Well, if you don't know *that*, my dear Charlotte!' Jenny laughed. Then, seeing the colour mount in Charlotte's cheeks, she said quickly, 'I'm sorry. I shouldn't have said that.' Jenny could have kicked herself at that moment, realizing that Charlotte knew nothing of sex. But then, Charlotte had not been to Oxford.

'I meant that Rowan may not stand behind a barrier of wealth and privilege, but his parents do, and so does the girl he is engaged to marry.' Charlotte explained.

'A girl with whom he is obviously not in love,' Jenny had been quick to point out.

'Probably not. But I couldn't bear to become a bone of contention between Rowan and Romilly,' Charlotte said quietly, 'Love is a fragile thing. I couldn't bear it if I came between them, or Rowan and his parents . . .'

'That's a poor way of looking at things,' the more practical Jenny had snorted. 'Rowan struck me as the kind of man who would fight to the death for what he wanted, so why shouldn't you?'

'The fighters in this world are not always the victors,' Charlotte said slowly, staring into the fire.

'The meek shall inherit the earth, is that what you mean?' Jenny asked, trying to come to grips with Charlotte's point of view. 'Well, I don't agree with all that Sermon on the Mount stuff! What if Rowan marries that silly little nonentity he's engaged to? What price your high-minded altruism then? You are a fool, Lottie, in my opinion. If I were you, I'd fight tooth and claw for the man I loved.' She added slyly, 'As I feel inclined to fight for your brother Harry.'

'Harry?' Charlotte had raised her eyebrows in surprise. 'But

Harry isn't in your mental class at all.'

'Ha!' Jenny snapped, 'I have yet to meet a man in my "mental class" as you call it, who was not utterly boring and physically unattractive. But why keep on harping about class all the time? I'd trade my cap and gown any day for a good, physical love affair.'

Charlotte had laughed then. 'Harry would be scared stiff of you, Jenny. He's just an ordinary man. Besides, he's walking out with a girl called Connie.'

'My God! Walking out with! What on earth does that mean? Fortunately, I don't share your high altruism, my dear Lottie. All's fair in love and war; that's my principle. One of these days I'd like to meet Harry and tell him how pleased I was that his horse won first prize in the May Day procession!'

Charlotte had been astute enough to realize that Jenny was playing the devil's advocate. Enjoying the verbal cut and thrust, she asked, 'But even if you and Harry came together, would you be entirely happy?'

'Of course not,' Jenny replied airily, 'no one in this world is ever entirely happy. Perfect happiness is an illusion, a dream, an ideal.'

'I know it is,' Charlotte said softly. 'That is what I have been trying to tell you.'

All that, now this, Jenny thought as she took Alice to her room. Her pity flowed out to the child. Useless to tell her, you are young, you will get over this in time. You don't know what love is. Anyone capable of feeling the pain of rejection was capable of experiencing love, too, in Jenny's opinion.

Those stinking, bloody Tanquillans, she thought wildly, with their rotten class distinctions and hard-as-ice bigotry. Jenny had never known servitude before: the bonds and shackles imposed on human beings obliged to earn a living to keep body and soul together. Her father had known it, of course. A poor country parson was considered less than the dust beneath the feet of those haughty parishioners of his whom he had been called on to join in matrimony, give communion to, and ultimately bury. What did the Tanquillans care for a fine person like Charlotte Grayler, worth a thousand times more than Romilly Beresford?

Why had she fought her way through university if not to raise herself above that kind of degradation? Money gave people like the Tanquillans all the power they needed to humiliate their poorer brethren – people like Charlotte and Alice, and yes, even herself. But no, Jenny thought, they shall not destroy me. Her father had worn his life away to give her the chance of a decent education. Her mother had carried on the struggle: taking in washing, giving piano lessons, slaving away day and night to see Jenny through university; had died at the age of forty-five, a worn-out shell of a woman, clasping her Bible.

The meek shall inherit the earth, Jenny thought bitterly. But she would never give in. She would fight the bloody Tanquillans, and people like them, till her dying day. They would not get the better of her.

When Charlotte walked into the schoolroom, pin-neat in a white blouse and skirt, with her shining hair braided into a coronet, and a smile on her face, Jenny's heart sank. She had just witnessed the crucifixion of one human spirit; she could scarcely bear to witness another.

'Sit down, Charlotte,' she said quietly. 'I have something to tell you.'

Romilly felt herself to be in a seventh heaven of delight. 'I am Mrs Tanquillan now,' she kept on reminding herself, looking at the wedding-ring on her finger; mentally hugging herself at the achievement of a lifelong dream. The words, 'my husband,' sprang to her lips as easily as if she had been saying them all her life. 'My husband will be along in a few minutes,' to the porters who carried their luggage to the train. 'My husband and I will take tea in the dining-car.' My husband, my husband, my husband . . .

Mrs Lomas had worked like a slave to make the house ready to receive them. Every room contained fresh flowers. She had given directions for the master bedroom to be prepared, had set a small table in the music room with crystal goblets and candles. Lomas had been down to the market for a fresh salmon which she had poached gently with herbs and shallots. She had piled a china compote dish with fresh fruit: peaches, nectarines, grapes and melon, had made a salad of endive, lettuce, cucumber and tiny radishes, and set a bottle of Sir Gervaise's prized dry white Graves in the pantry to cool.

When everything had been seen to, she walked from room to room casting a critical eye; smoothing curtains, plumping cushions, picking up fallen petals. She opened the bedroom windows leading to a stone balcony, and stood there for a few minutes looking out at the ruler-straight line of the sea on the horizon, the pink and gold of a Maytime sunset. The scent of white lilac was almost unbearably sweet. Lomas had gathered armsful of the stuff, and masses of blood-red rhododendrons for the great jardinières in the drawing-room.

But Mrs Lomas derived no particular pleasure from the results of her labour. She could not think that Mr Rowan's wife would do so either. What had possessed him to marry a girl so lacking in warmth and charm? But there was a great deal about the Tanquillans that she had never fully understood. Sir Gervaise and Lady Tanquillan had always struck her as cold fish. She had never liked either of them. The advantage of working for them lay in that they were so seldom in residence, that she and Lomas were entrusted with the upkeep of the house, had their own quarters, and were paid a fair wage for their services.

Frances Lomas thought that the disadvantages of their employment lay in that one never knew exactly when the Tanquillans would descend, bringing with them a houseful of guests. Strange things happened from time to time – turning the top floor into a school, for instance. Not that she disliked Alice Tanquillan. She felt sorry for the girl, and she had no fault to find with the governess or Charlotte Grayler, except that their being in the house meant a lot of extra cooking.

Closing the windows, she went down to the kitchen, thinking about Rowan Tanquillan. How different he was from his parents. She had often wondered how Sir Gervaise and his lady wife had ever managed to produce a son like that, whom they treated with a cool offhandedness which she could never quite fathom. There were rumours, of course, that the Tanquillan marriage had been an arranged affair, for money. She could well believe that. Servants had a way of finding out the truth about their employers, and Frances Lomas had heard it said that Rachel Tanquillan, in her younger days, and despite her fine family name, had been unable to find a husband. One woman Frances Lomas knew had put it more bawdily than that. 'Frigid, my dear, so I've heard. Wouldn't let a man within a mile of her. It's true. Lord Fitzpatrick's son – and my cousin worked for the Fitzpatricks at the time so I know what I'm talking about – said that if ever Madam Rachel had a child it would have to be by immaculate conception, and he for one didn't fancy trying to ram an iceberg!'

Mrs Lomas wondered if it was a case of the old pattern repeating itself, if pressure had been brought to bear on young Rowan to marry for social prestige. If so, God help him. But why hadn't the young fool stood up to his parents? She could have sworn that he was strongly attracted to Charlotte Grayler. Lomas had said so after that queer business a few weeks ago when the girl, Alice, had fled down the garden as if the devil was after her. What a pity, she thought, lifting the muslin to look at the salad, that young Rowan had not married someone like Charlotte, a lovely girl who would have made him happy. She couldn't imagine her Mr Rowan being happy with a stiff and starchy lass like Miss Beresford, and what a dangerous situation might arise with all three of them under the same roof.

Romilly was delighted with the house. This was the first time she had been there alone with Rowan. It was just after seven when they arrived. The sight of the little table set so romantically in the music room enchanted her. She went upstairs to change, and came down later in a full-skirted white gown with a low-cut neckline.

Rowan was on the terrace, his hands resting on the balustrade, looking down at the garden, listening to a thrush singing its heart out in a lilac tree, thinking about Charlotte, feeling his unhappiness as an almost tangible thing, a dead weight of despair that would not lift from his heart. Nothing

167

had changed. He was married to Romilly but he did not love her. He wondered how he would be able to face physical intimacy with her. But he had made a bargain; taken vows. Romilly was his wife now. She must not be hurt, must never be made to suffer for his own weakness, his concern for Alice and Charlotte.

He knew his mother too well to believe her capable of bluffing. He knew that, had he not given in to her emotional blackmail, she would have sent Alice away to spend the rest of her days shut up in an institution for mentally crippled children. God alone knew what she might have done to Charlotte, but he could hazard a guess. Gentle people like Charlotte were all too vulnerable in a situation like this. Easy to accuse someone of theft, to say, in court, this girl stole a valuable ring from my dressing-table, or a valuable miniature from my drawing-room. He preferred to hope that Rachel would not have gone that far, but he couldn't be certain.

Romilly came up to him, rested her hand lightly on his arm. 'What are you thinking about?' she asked.

He said, quite truthfully, 'I was thinking about my mother.'

'Oh. I rather hoped that you were thinking of me.'

Knowing what she wanted to hear, he said, 'You are looking very charming.' That also was the truth. Excitement had imparted a high colour to her cheeks, her eyes were bright, her slender figure emphasized by the gown she wore. She smelt deliciously of French perfume. 'Oh, isn't this heavenly,' she murmured. 'Are you as happy as I am, darling?'

'Yes, yes of course I am.'

'Then why don't you kiss me?'

He touched her cheek with his lips, took her hand and led her back into the room. Mrs Lomas knocked and entered. 'How nice everything looks,' Rowan said. 'I hope we haven't put you to too much trouble, having everything to do at such short notice.'

'Oh no, sir.' Mrs Lomas flushed with excitement. 'It was a pleasure for you and your young lady.'

Romilly said coldly, 'May I remind you that I am no longer Mr Tanquillan's "young lady" but his wife. You will refer to me as Mrs Tanquillan in future.'

'Oh, I'm sorry. I didn't mean any offence . . .' The housekeeper's pleasure gave way to agitation. Seeing her distress, with a feeling of anger that Romilly had spoken to the woman so sharply, Rowan said, 'That's quite all right, Mrs Lomas.'

'Will there be anything else, Mr Rowan?'

'Not at the moment, thank you.' When she had gone, he said quietly, 'There was no need for that.'

'Oh no? Well, I happen to think differently. I am not accustomed to being referred to so casually by a servant. I'm surprised that you did not reprimand her – or perhaps you encourage familiarity with the paid help!'

'This is Scarborough, not London,' Rowan reminded her. 'Anyway, supper's ready. Shall we begin?'

'No,' she said petulantly. 'I'm not hungry now. I'm tired. I'm going to bed!'

He let her go, making no attempt to dissuade her. Lighting a cigarette, he went out onto the terrace and smoked for a while, noticing the way the light from the valley below filtered up between the branches of the trees.

Suddenly the figure of a woman emerged from the side entrance and moved quickly between the massed lilacs and rhododendrons. It was gone in an instant, but he recognized at once that slim, upright form.

Throwing aside his cigarette, he strode quickly along the terrace, down the steps to the lily-pond, and plunged down the path she had taken, calling 'Charlotte', in a low, urgent voice.

She heard him coming after her, and slipped into the shadows near a stone archway, her heart hammering against her ribs. She had known all along that Rowan would one day marry Romilly, but she had not expected it to happen so soon; had convinced herself that she would get used to the idea in time: had braced herself to overcome all her wild hopes and dreams, to accustom herself to the inevitability of losing him. But this! She could not bear to face him now – a bridegroom on his wedding night.

Mrs Lomas had been all agog with news of the wedding

which had taken place earlier that day: eager to impart details of the supper she had prepared for the bride and groom, the flowers in their room.

Standing in the shadows, Charlotte looked up through the trees, saw, through the branches, the open windows of the master bedroom with its stone balcony: suppressed a cry as she glimpsed momentarily a white-gowned figure pacing restlessly behind the fluttering curtains. Romilly!

'Charlotte!' She heard Rowan's footsteps coming closer. Her pale green dress betrayed her. He saw it glimmering whitely in the shadows, drained of colour in the darkness. He moved quickly towards her. She turned and ran through the arch into the walled garden beyond, realizing too late that there was no escape. The high wall was faintly visible by starlight. Her skirts brushed against clumps of spiky, silver-leafed lavender bushes bordering the path, unleashing its fragrance on the night air. Great sprays of double white lilac plumed up against the imprisoning brickwork. Pink and white azaleas showered their petals about her as she hurried past them.

She seemed to Rowan a trapped bird or butterfly. He knew she was afraid of him, that he had no right to pursue her now or ever again. He had no right to speak to her of love, could never explain to her his reasons for marrying Romilly. But he must talk to her just once more to tell her that nothing had changed. Whether or not she believed him, he must tell her that he loved her. The only way he could face the future, ease the pain in his heart, lay in speaking what he knew to be the truth.

He stood quite still near the archway, looking at her, not moving, not wanting to frighten her. The soft night wind rustled the branches of the trees. Charlotte could see clearly his clean-cut features, the lean strength of him, the slight droop of his shoulders, the air of weariness about him, the sadness and longing in his eyes. She knew then that to run away from him was impossible, not just because of the walled garden, but because, even if she could scale that wall and run to the ends of the earth away from him, she would never be able to escape him. He would always be there, in her heart and mind, a living part of her own self and being.

She moved slowly towards him. He made no attempt to touch her. They stood a little apart from each other. He said, in a low voice, 'I love you, Charlotte. I shall always love you, to my life's end.'

'Yes,' she whispered, 'as I shall always love you.'

There was nothing more to say. They stood together in silence for a moment before Rowan turned away and hurried back to the house.

Romilly was waiting for him. She wore a white negligée over a white organza nightdress. She had unbraided her hair. When he entered their room she ran towards him, weeping. 'Oh darling,' she cried, 'I'm so sorry. I've spoilt everything. Please say that you forgive me!'

'There's nothing to forgive,' he said heavily. 'I should have been more patient, more understanding.' But she could not stop weeping, she flung herself into his arms sobbing hysterically, beside herself because she had ruined her wedding night. 'I was just so tired, and I did so want to be called Mrs Tanquillan.'

'Of course you are tired.' He smoothed back her hair. 'Shall I fetch you a warm drink?' He might have been speaking to a child – to Alice.

'No, I don't want a warm drink. I want you, Rowan. Don't you understand, I love you. I am your wife now. I want you to treat me as your wife. I want you to make love to me.' She threw back her head, lips parted. Tears lay on her cheeks. 'I'm a woman, not a child. Why do you always treat me as a child?'

'Perhaps because I remember you best as the little girl who used to come to nursery tea,' he said patiently.

She swayed suddenly against him. 'Well, if I am a little girl, take me to bed.'

He picked her up in his arms and carried her over to the bed, remembering as he did so how he had carried Alice to bed the day he found her poised on the banister rail threatening to jump. What was it Alice had said? 'I once read a book all about love. It made me ache, somehow. I wanted someone to take away the pain inside me. I want you to take the pain away.'

He remembered his reply to her. 'Perhaps I am incapable of loving any woman enough to assuage her pain in living.' He hadn't known of Charlotte's existence then.

He began, slowly, to undress.

CHAPTER SEVENTEEN

Rachel tapped her teeth lightly with her pen. There was no love lost between herself and Gervaise's Aunty Kitty, but she needed a favour from the old woman and thought she knew the best tactics to make sure of receiving it.

The rift in the family lute had been caused by Oliver Tanquillan, Kitty's favourite nephew, whom she considered to have been unfairly treated, and whose cause she had always espoused. The old lady had sent a wreath to his funeral along with a letter demanding to know what Gervaise intended to do about Oliver's child, a letter to which Gervaise had replied in the curtest possible manner, saying that the girl would be sent to a boarding-school as soon as a place could be found for her. Rachel had questioned her husband's wisdom at the time, but Gervaise, incensed by what he termed his aunt's damned interference, paid no attention. Now Rachel thought it was time to approach Aunt Kitty in a more conciliatory manner. She wrote:

'Dear Aunt Kitty,

Knowing how fond you were of Oliver Tanquillan, of your deep concern for his daughter's welfare, it occurred to me that you might like to see the child who is at present in Scarborough in the charge of a governess and a companion. Unfortunately, Alice disliked the idea of a boarding-school, and so in her best interests, Gervaise and I decided upon educating her privately. A complication, however, has arisen. You knew that Rowan was engaged to marry Romilly Beresford. Sadly, Romilly's father died suddenly. Rather than postpone the wedding, they were married very quietly in London, and they are now in

Scarborough – ostensibly on their honeymoon . . .' Rachel smiled to herself as she went on to say how much she and Gervaise would appreciate it if Kitty would invite Alice and her companions to Wiltshire for a few weeks to give Rowan and his bride some privacy. She also asked that Miss Grayler's parents should receive a personally written invitation 'because', she added, 'they are somewhat old-fashioned and retrogressive.'

Rachel stamped the letter and gave it to her maid to post, certain of the old woman's response to her appeal.

Kitty Tanquillan's reply came unhesitatingly.

'Dear Rachel,
    As you well know, I am a lonely old woman sadly in need of company. It will give me great pleasure to see Oliver's child again, to make up to her, in some measure, for the unkindness meted out to her father during his lifetime. I shall write to Miss Grayler's parents as you request. Knowing you as I do, my dear Rachel, I wonder what lies behind your letter. Why have I the feeling that it is not just Alice you are so anxious to remove from the house in Chalice Walk?'

Charlotte had no inkling of the invitation until she went home on Sunday to find her mother in a tizzy because of the letter from Wiltshire, from a Miss Kitty Tanquillan, written on thick cream notepaper with the name of the house, 'Grey Wethers', printed in the top right-hand corner.

'Wiltshire,' Filly cried as if it was on the dark side of the moon. 'Whatever next? You've not had time to get properly settled in the job yet! Now they want to pack you off to the back of beyond. Well, I don't know what to say I'm sure. Mind you, this Miss Tanquillan must be a real lady because of the writing-paper.' Filly looked sharply at her daughter. 'And you look as if you could do with a holiday. I've never seen you so pale and peaky before.'

'I'm all right, Mum.' Charlotte studied the letter carefully.

'Well, what do you think?' Filly asked, measuring flour into a basin.

'It's more a case of what you and Dad think,' Charlotte said, and yet the more she looked at the letter the more certain she felt that she wanted to go to Wiltshire, away from the house in Chalice Walk now that Rowan and Romilly were there together.

'Well, you might know what your dad thinks before you ask,' Filly replied, turning to the sinkful of petticoats she had started washing. 'But I'd like to have a look at that governess before I make my mind up. I don't want you going off with anyone flighty.'

'Jenny? Jenny isn't a bit flighty,' Charlotte said. 'And what are you doing? Are those my petticoats in the sink?'

'Certainly,' Filly said, plumping them up and down in the hot soapy water. 'You're not going to Wiltshire, to stay in a posh house, looking like a ragman's horse. Your best shoes will need mending too if you go. But I'm not making up my mind on the spur of the moment. I'm not saying yes until I've clapped eyes on that governess. You had better bring her to tea.'

'I can't, without Alice, and you know how you feel about her. Jenny looks after her on my day off.'

Filly sighed. 'Then you'd better bring her too.' She poured boiling water on the starch, then set about rinsing the petticoats.

'I'd rather not if everyone else is going to be here,' Charlotte said desperately. 'You know what Frank's like.' She could not bear the thought of another family inquisition.

'Frank is going to Madge Robinson's for tea.' Filly sniffed. 'He's scarcely ever indoors these days since he got himself engaged to that lass.' Filly's contempt for 'that lass' was evident in the fierce way she wrung out Charlotte's petticoats. 'Joe's going to Annie's for tea, and Maggie and Bob won't be staying after they've had their dinner, so there'll only be your dad and me, and Harry.'

'What about Connie?'

'Oh *her*!' Filly screwed up her face contemptuously, 'he's given her the go-by. About time too, the big soft thing.'

'Very well then, I'll bring Jenny and Alice.'

'You'd better flop two eggs into that bowl of flour and mix up the puddings while I hang this lot out to dry, or the dinner will never be ready on time,' Filly said, rushing down to the yard with the newly-starched petticoats.

Maggie and Bob arrived soon afterwards. The pair of them had got into the habit of having Sunday dinner with Maggie's parents, Sunday tea with Bob's. These matters had to be carefully worked out so that no-one felt slighted or took the huff. Albert and the boys were round at the pub in Ramshill for their beer and dominoes. Maggie was puffed after climbing the stairs. She wore her going-away straw hat set defiantly on her brown frizzy hair, the picture of a blowsy young matron. Bob followed her sheepishly, cap in hand, as inarticulate as usual in the presence of his mother-in-law. Maggie sank down on a kitchen chair, stuck her feet out in front of her and announced, 'I'm expecting.'

There was a moment's stunned silence before Filly burst into tears and began hugging Maggie, while Bob examined his boots intently.

Maggie did not care about having to undo her waistband to be able to sit down properly; the almost unbearable restrictions imposed by her whalebone corsets, the straining of her blouse across her bosom. She was a married woman now with a home of her own to see to, and felt happily bloated and contented as the mistress of her own kitchen and fireside, having got Bob housetrained to carry in the coal from the shed in the yard, and the dolly-tub for the Monday wash-days; to eat, without complaint, whatever she set before him, great dollops of mashed potatoes, sausages, fried onions, dripping bread and faggots, or fish and chips from the shop round the corner when she couldn't be bothered to cook anything herself. He knew his acne was getting worse as a result of all the fried food, but as long as Maggie remained cheerful and let him do what he enjoyed doing to her on Saturday nights and once during the week, he could always use sulphur lotion on his spots.

When Albert and the lads appeared, they were regaled with the news that Maggie was, as Filly put it, 'that way'. Albert shed a few tears which he tried to hide in the roller-towel, overcome with emotion that he was going to be a grandfather. He then produced a bottle of port wine from the sideboard and insisted on wetting the baby's head before dinner.

Harry hadn't much of an appetite. He was thinking about Connie. It hadn't been easy shaking her off. She had taken the news badly, making him feel guilty, now he had deserted her. He had talked it over with Frank at first when the two of them were lying on their beds like men of the world, Frank with his pillows bunched up to make a backrest against the iron bedstead, lying on top of the bedclothes with his legs crossed at the knee like a crusader, contemplating the delights of Saturday night, discussing the merits of their respective girlfriends. That was when Harry had admitted that he was getting fed up with Connie. He'd never said a word about getting engaged, but she'd been down-town and bought a pair of sheets at Hopper and Mason's, on 'spec'.

'I don't know what you were thinking about to get yourself landed with a great bovine lump like that in the first place,' Frank observed, lighting a cheroot which his mother would kill him for if she happened to smell it. He smoothed his moustache with his free hand. 'Well, you'd better do something about it right quick before you find yourself lumbered. The next thing you'll know, she'll have bought some blankets and a bed as well – and you'll find yourself tucked up as nice as nip.'

'I don't like hurting her feelings,' Harry said disconsolately.

Frank slid down on his pillows so that his knees were higher than his head, and blew smoke rings at the ceiling. He and Harry had had meaningful conversations about girls all their adult lives. Frank felt it to be a reflection on his own reputation with the lasses that his brother had started going with Connie who, as he vulgarly expressed it, 'carried all before her'. He liked his girls trim and neat, well-developed but not over-blown, with plenty to say for themselves. 'There's no need to hurt her feelings,' he said, 'just don't turn up tonight. Go down to the club room for a game of snooker instead.' He half closed his eyes in blissful contemplation of the ceiling. Life stretched before him as golden as the road to Samarkand. He could feel the powerful throb of living, the joy of it, from the tips of his moustache to the soles of his feet.

'I couldn't do that,' Harry said, opening the window before lighting his own cheroot and wafting the smoke towards it with the back of his hand. 'I'll have to tell her to her face that it's all off.' So he had told her, and she had gone off in floods of tears, blaming the size of her bust for her misfortune. It had been a miserable experience for Harry, especially when Connie accused him of leading her on, and asked him what she should do about the sheets, and the jumper she was knitting for him. 'I shall want the money for the wool,' she sniffed, and so he had stumped up the five bob, and walked down to the club room as Frank had suggested, feeling utterly wretched. He had felt rotten ever since – until Jenny came to tea.

Jenny's outmodish attire made an immediate and favourable impression on Filly, who breathed a sigh of relief that the governess could in no way be described as flighty. When she knew that Jenny's father had been a Church of England minister, she warmed to her even more, and pressed her to a second helping of strawberrry jelly.

Jenny made an immediate impact on Harry too, although he remained partially tongue-tied in her presence. It was only when she congratulated him on his success in the May Day procession, and asked him about Nobby, that he began to thaw out. 'Nobby's a fine horse,' he said, 'none better.' He offered to show her the animal after tea. Jenny smiled across the table at him. Later, she and Harry, Charlotte and Alice, went down to the yard where Charlotte's petticoats were blowing on the washing-line.

Jenny patted Nobby's nose as Harry pointed out, with pride, the rosette pinned to the stable door, whilst Alice fed sugar-lumps into the horse's nuzzling mouth. She had come to tea under duress, saying that she didn't want to go anywhere. 'Go away and leave me alone,' she had cried when Charlotte told her that she had been invited out to tea. She was lying across her bed at the time, staring moodily out of the window, thinking about Romilly Beresford.

'You know we can't leave you alone,' Charlotte said, sitting

178

beside her, understanding her suffering.

'Don't you know I'll always be alone now?' Alice muttered.

Realizing the girl's penchant for drama, Charlotte said gently, 'You mustn't just lie there feeling sorry for yourself. And you mustn't be angry with Rowan.'

Alice replied, with a curious smile, 'Oh, I'm not angry with Rowan now. Anger is too precious a thing to be diluted.'

And so the girl had suffered herself to be washed, made tidy, and taken out. She said practically nothing during tea, answering questions offhandedly, staring suspiciously at Filly who was doing her best to be pleasant. When Filly asked her about Miss Tanquillan, Alice said in that odd, grown-up way of hers, 'Oh you mean my Great-aunt Kitty. She lives in grand style and keeps horses. My father said her wealth came from the land. I will lift up mine eyes to the hills from whence cometh my help. That's a quotation from the Bible, you know.'

'Yes I know it is,' Filly said, flummoxed.

In the stable, which smelt mustily of hay and oats, leather and horseflesh, Jenny smiled at Harry. 'I once rode to hounds when I was a girl,' she said. 'The horse didn't belong to us, of course, and I wasn't very keen, so I fell off at the second fence. In any case, my sympathy lay entirely with the fox.' She laughed. 'I often wonder if I fell off on purpose. I couldn't have borne to be there at the kill.' She had slipped her spectacles into her cardigan pocket, and gazed up at Harry with unconcealed admiration.

'I hear that you and Charlotte are off to Wiltshire next week,' he mumbled, overcome by the speedwell blueness of her eyes.

'Yes, we are.' She watched his strong young fingers caressing Nobby's muzzle.

'Perhaps you'd like to go to the pictures with me when you get back.'

'I'm not sure when that will be,' she replied. 'What's wrong with tomorrow night?'

They went to the Grand Pavilion on the sea-front to see *The Curse of War*. Harry said apologetically that he should have taken her to the Picture Palace instead to see something lighter.

Jenny said it really didn't matter to her where they went, going to the pictures was a novelty in itself. They sat in the back row and held hands, after a little manoeuvring. Harry sat there like a ramrod for a good half-hour before Jenny took the initiative in letting the bag of sweets he had bought for her fall between the seats, when his groping fingers suddenly met hers.

Afterwards, they walked together along the promenade. The bay resembled a great dark millpond, moving mysteriously, reflecting light from the gas-lamps spaced at intervals along the sea-front. 'Let us walk on the sand,' Jenny suggested, 'close to the sea. I love the sound of lapping water.'

'You'll get sand in your shoes,' Harry said, as she tugged at his hand.

'I don't care, do you?'

'No, not really.' He slipped his arm round her waist, drew her close to him, and kissed her there in the darkness, with the murmuring of the sea close at hand, seeing through half closed eyes the flickering dancing lights along the shore, feeling the cold rice-pudding texture of wet sand beneath his feet.

The journey to Wiltshire was long and tedious, but Charlotte could not help revelling in the feeling of escape from Chalice Walk with all its reminders of Mrs Tanquillan: the sound of Romilly's voice on the stairs or in the garden: her garden hat and gloves on a chair in the hall, a trace of French perfume in the air.

King's Cross station overwhelmed her, but Jenny, a seasoned traveller, knew exactly how much to tip the porter who wheeled their luggage from the train to the taxi-rank. Charlotte had drawn in a deep breath to calm her nerves when she saw, not horse-drawn vehicles but new-fangled motor-cars; had scarcely dared to open her eyes as the panting, snorting thing nosed out into the traffic.

At Paddington, Jenny marched into the melee, bought tickets, found out the time of the train to Devizes, and shepherded her flock to the refreshment room for tea and sandwiches.

Fretful and tired, Alice fell asleep as soon as the train began to move. Charlotte fell silent as she watched the scenery flick past the windows, her sense of escape blunted now with fatigue and the realization that she was a long way from home.

'Homesick?' Jenny smiled at her.

Charlotte nodded. 'Just a bit.'

Jenny fell silent too, lost in thoughts of Harry Grayler, trying to equate her feelings for him with her all-too frequent condemnation of the male sex. Perhaps it was his shyness that appealed to her, his lack of arrogance, his gentleness with animals, apart from his undeniable good looks, and the respect he had shown her as they walked together, hand in hand, through the Spa gardens.

By that time, they had become burningly aware of each other, wanting to know more about each other. They had talked for a while in a shelter, looking out to sea at ships on the horizon; watching the slow passage of moving lights against the great dark arch of the sky lit with twinkling stars, breathing in the essence of the night, the scent of wild flowers growing along the paths, hearing the soft rustle of the wind among the branches of the trees.

'I wish you weren't going away, Jenny,' he said, 'I'll miss you.'

'I'll miss you, too, Harry.'

'Strange, isn't it? We hardly know each other.'

She had caught the gleam of his smile in the darkness. His hand was warm in hers.

He had kissed her then, a lingering kiss, and slipped his arms about her, so that there had seemed nothing else in the world except the steady drum-beat of his heart against hers and the masculine scent of him, compounded of his best tweed jacket, cheroots, and hair-oil which was, Jenny supposed, the way ordinary, decent young men should smell: not of sweat and chalk-dust and Havana cigars, the smell peculiar to Oxford dons.

She had pushed him away then, before she was swept away, out of her depth in a bewildering sea of emotion, realizing what might happen between them had she not done so, the suffragette side of her came uppermost at the crucial moment.

And yet, she wished, now, that her courage had not failed her when it did: that she had possessed enough wisdom and humility to tell Harry Grayler how much she wanted him.

Dusk was falling when the train pulled into Devizes station. Kitty Tanquillan had sent her coachman to meet them. The air was cool and fresh, full of late birdsong and shadows as the horse jogged along unfamiliar roads to 'Grey Wethers', a low rambling house set in a fold of quiet hills, amid rich pastureland where woolly sheep grazed and rooks made homeward for the night.

Almost sick with nervousness and fatigue, Charlotte saw the lights of the house between the trees. The horse, scenting hay and stables, trotted smartly between iron gates, along the drive to the front door. Windows were still open to catch the scent of lavender and pinks bordering the long stone terrace at the front of the house. A gentle wind sighed down from the high, curving hills in the distance. Windows pricked firefly brightness into the dusk of a June evening.

As the horse drew to a standstill, the front door opened and a woman stood silhouetted against the light from the hall, a tiny figure with untidy white hair, like a nimbus, about her wrinkled face.

'I am Kitty Tanquillan,' she said, drawing her brightly-coloured silk shawl more closely about her thin, upright shoulders. 'Come inside quickly. The night air is bad for my rheumatism. So you are my great-niece Alice? Well, why don't you kiss me, child?' She chuckled as the girl drew away from her and clung to Charlotte's waist. 'Ah well, never mind. Friendship must be earned.' She turned her penetrating eyes on Jenny. 'You must be Miss Carfax, the governess,' she said in a dry voice. 'And you,' she peered intently at Charlotte, 'are the companion.' She frowned suddenly. 'Ah yes, I was right after all! My Florentine pieta to the life! Well, don't stand about here! Rivers,' she called in an imperious tone of voice, 'where are you? Why will you persist in creeping about like a tom-cat? Show my guests to their rooms, then bring them down to the dining-room. They must be famished.'

Her face crinkled with sudden amusement. 'Rivers likes nothing better than playing the part of the old family retainer.' She glanced fondly at the old man who appeared, smiling, from the shadows. 'But why not? He runs this house and myself too, come to that, and we all play games when it suits our purpose to do so.'

Charlotte wondered briefly if Miss Tanquillan was mad. Then, catching her eye, and the old woman's mocking smile, she knew that whatever else Kitty Tanquillan might be she was certainly not that. Hers was a proud, humorous face seamed with wisdom. Her dark penetrating eyes above her hawk-like nose kindled with fun. Despite her acute homesickness, Charlotte could not help smiling back at her.

The room she was shown to was the most beautiful she had ever seen, low-ceilinged and beamed, with latticed windows overlooking the garden. A fire had been lit, not so much for warmth as a bright, welcoming glow. Charlotte saw with delight the rose-sprigged cover on the bed, the curved doors of the high, wide and handsome wardrobe inlaid with holly, the Chinese bowl on the dressing-table filled with dried lavender and rose petals which scented the air with memories of bygone summers.

A copper can of hot water had been placed on the wash-stand, and when she had washed her hands and face, she went in search of Alice: found her bouncing gaily on a four-poster bed hung with dimity curtains. 'I'm sorry now that I wouldn't kiss Great-aunt Kitty,' she laughed. 'She rather frightened me at first, you know, but I'll make it up to her for giving me such a lovely room. See, I have my own desk with locks to the drawers for my secret things.' She was fairly bubbling over with high spirits, but Charlotte did not want her to get too excited. 'We had better go down now,' she said. 'After dinner, you must get a good night's sleep.'

'I don't think I shall be able to sleep at all for thinking about tomorrow.' The wayward girl bounded downstairs to the dining-room to throw her arms around her aunt's waist and cover her face with kisses. 'I do love you, Aunt Kitty,' she cried, 'really and truly.'

Charlotte wondered at the sudden spasm of pain that crossed the old woman's face as she held the girl in her arms.

The table was set with fine Georgian silverware. After the soup, Rivers poured wine from a flagon as a maid came in with the tureens of vegetables, gravy boats, and a dish containing roast lamb for Miss Kitty to carve, which she did with the expertise of a chef in a London restaurant. Rivers handed round the plates to her guests.

'No, thank you,' Charlotte said, when it came to her turn.

Miss Tanquillan glanced at her sharply. 'Why not? Is it not cooked to your liking?'

'It isn't that, ma'am. I'm a vegetarian.'

'Are you indeed? May I ask why?'

'Because I cannot bear the thought of animals being killed, that's all.'

'Really?' Kitty Tanquillan leaned back in her chair. 'But surely, Miss Grayler, the Old Testament is filled with blood sacrifices and feasting upon the flesh of slain animals. Are you saying that you do not believe in the Old Testament?'

'As a Christian, I suppose I must.' Charlotte felt her colour rising, but she stuck to her guns. 'But acceptance of the Old Testament does not necessarily imply a belief in all its precepts. Esau, after all, had three wives.'

'Ah yes, I had forgotten that. Thank you for reminding me.' Kitty Tanquillan smiled. 'Rivers, ask Cook to prepare an omelette for Miss Grayler.'

'I would rather not put your cook to so much trouble,' Charlotte said, miserably aware of her flaming cheeks and the trembling of her legs beneath the table. 'I shall be quite content with the vegetables.'

'Even so, I insist upon your having an omelette. It's a long time to breakfast, and I should not care to have a guest of mine waking up, with hunger pains, in the middle of the night,' the old woman said.

'Esau, after all, had three wives.' She would not forget that in a hurry. Ah yes, Kitty Tanquillan thought, I can see now why Rachel wanted this girl out of the way.

CHAPTER EIGHTEEN

Brilliant shafts of dying sunlight bathed the apple trees. It was that unearthly moment when the sun sank down towards the horizon, leaving the world to shadows and starlight. Every blade of grass, each flower, stood sharply poised on the edge of night. The daisies had closed their petals.

Walking alone in the orchard, Charlotte saw that the sky was pearl-soft above the branches, feathered with tiny translucent clouds. She could smell the warm fragrance of the earth and grass beneath her feet, saw twisting spirals of smoke rising from the cottage chimneys dotted along the valley. She felt very close to Rowan here, in the silence of the orchard, with the midges brushing her cheeks and the warm night air sighing about her. She felt his presence as an almost tangible thing; thought that, if she stepped more quickly, she would meet him face to face beneath the fragrant branches. And so she did step more quickly, hearing the soft, light whisper of her skirts in the long grass, remembering the exact way his hair turned up on the nape of his neck, the way his lips curled when he smiled, the deeply-cut dimple in his chin, the low, warm timbre of his voice when he spoke her name, the strength and leanness of his clean young body.

In after years, whenever she thought of Rowan Tanquillan, she would remember the exact scent of a summertime orchard; would realize that only perfume and music possessed the power to invoke an exact image of a beloved person.

It would worry her, in time to come, that she had forgotten the essential Rowan. She would believe that age and memory played tricks, until she breathed again the scent of white lilac, lavender, the salt air of the sea, dog-roses or apple-boughs, and the exact memory of him would flood her being again, like a warm tide, and she would know that she had not forgotten anything at all.

Life at Grey Wethers proved an antidote to unhappiness. The house itself was warm and inviting; extremely old; sprawling as intimately as a relaxed companion beside a winter fire. Kitty Tanquillan had inherited Grey Wethers from a rich uncle on her mother's side, had gone there, as a girl, to learn all she could about farming, leaving behind her, with no regrets, the London life she hated. But such a step was considered unseemly for a delicately brought-up young woman educated to the finer things in life – coming-out parties, dances and theatres. When her friends and relatives told her, in no uncertain terms, that she was mad to think of burying herself in the country: that Grey Wethers, and the land surrounding it, should be sold to the highest bidder, Kitty had told *them*, in no uncertain terms, that she had no intention of giving up her uncle's legacy.

'But Kitty, you cannot possibly become a – farmer!'

Kitty merely smiled. 'Can't I?' she said. She was just turned twenty at the time, a lovely, wayward girl with a mass of dark hair and a strong determination to live her own life as she saw fit. She had known and loved Grey Wethers since childhood, and blessed the uncle who had left to her his most prized possession, knowing that she would care for it as he himself had done.

She had built her life there with all the guts and tenacity of a man; had learnt about the land from her peers, her uncle's tenant farmers and his estate manager, Gilbert Stapleford. She had thought to bypass the soft, feminine things like falling in love; marriage, having children. She had been obliged to bypass marriage, because Gilbert Stapleford was already married, with a growing family, but she had been powerless to prevent herself from falling in love with him.

Whispers of her liaison with a married man had filtered back to London. Her parents were shocked to think that a daughter of theirs should bring the family name to disrepute. There were rumours of a still-born child which Kitty neither affirmed nor denied. It was a passionate, April affair of the heart, as lovely and fleeting as the month itself. When it was over, Gilbert had gone away, taking his wife and children to another part of the country to live. But Kitty's name was forever after linked with his. She had committed an unpardonable sin in the eyes of her family, much as Oliver Tanquillan had done. But the proud and beautiful young Kitty Tanquillan had ridden out her particular storm in the place she loved most on earth, surrounded with slow country folk inured to the follies of youth, the inevitability of birth and death. These people saw life as a rich canvas of changing seasons under a changeless sky, and knew, whatever the sin and suffering, no matter how deep the pain and regret, all eventually ended in peace beneath the turf of the quiet churchyard in the valley.

On the first morning, after breakfast, Miss Kitty drove them to the farm, holding the reins of the pony-trap easily in her thin brown hands.

Along the lane they bowled, beneath the trees, beside the wild dog-roses, campion and lady's lace in the hedgerows. The Downs rose smooth and wind-rippled in the distance. Alice's face was alight with expectation. She wanted to see the horses, cows, calves and hens Aunt Kitty had told her about over breakfast.

A grey farmhouse lay beyond a cobbled yard with stables, haylofts and milking-sheds. It was a long, low building with smoke rising from its chimneys. Hens scurried, clucking their disapproval, as the trap spanked into the yard. A man emerged from the farmhouse as Miss Kitty climbed down from her seat, and came towards them at a leisurely pace, a thickset man with greying hair and the tanned skin of a countryman outdoors in all weather. His sturdy legs were encased in corduroy riding breeches and polished brown leggings, and he was pulling on a tweed jacket. Smiling, he caught the reins and looped them over a fence.

'This is my farm manager, Will Oakleigh,' Kitty said. 'Will, these are the people I told you about. Get someone to take my great-niece to look at the cows. I want to see you about those cottages in Longbarrow Lane. Have you done anything about getting the repairs started?'

'You'd best come indoors,' he said, whistling to a man busy about the barn to take charge of Alice. A couple of yellow labrador dogs appeared from the house at his whistle, tongues panting, following his every movement with their liquid brown eyes. He had appeared stiff and ill at ease until the dogs lolloped towards him. Now he bent down to caress them, more sure of himself with the dogs at his feet and the cold pipe which he had unearthed from his jacket pocket in his hand.

Obviously he was a man unused to feminine company, Jenny thought, as he unlatched the farmhouse door and stood back to let them enter. Then she noticed the man's startled expression as he looked at Charlotte standing in a patch of sunlight which touched her hair to the colour of autumn leaves, her cheeks to a warm glow, like cream on a bowl of fresh apricots. He might well look at her like that, Jenny thought, what right-minded man would not. In another time, another place, Charlotte's face might have launched a thousand ships.

The farmhouse kitchen was stone-flagged, mat-strewn, with deeply embrasured windows, broad sills, blackened beams, and a wide hearth with a log fire. Muslin-covered hams were suspended from the beams, the great oak dresser was crowded with blue and white china dishes, the chairs were well-worn, with faded chintz covers. Dust lay thick on the floor, the corners were filled with kicked-off wellingtons; door-hooks were crowded with stiff oil-skin coats. The table was littered with trugs containing eggs, fruit and vegetables; a wicker basket near the fire spilled over with a litter of squealing kittens. The dogs wandered over to them and anxiously licked their faces. The mother cat disdainfully lapped a bowl of milk in the hearth, her tail hostilely erect.

'Perhaps you'd like some tea?' Will Oakleigh asked uncertainly, twisting his pipe between his fingers.

'Oh, get on with it, man,' Kitty said, laughing. 'We haven't come to be entertained. Just show me the plans for the repairs and we'll be on our way.' She made a sudden question mark with her eyebrows 'Oh, I see. Well, you can show us the sights afterwards, if you've a mind to.'

The name of Miss Kitty's house had puzzled Charlotte. Will Oakleigh explained the reason for it. 'See those sheep over yonder,' he said, pointing with the stem of his pipe.

'Yes,' Charlotte said, falling into step with him.

'Not moving much, are they?'

'No, now you come to mention it, they're not moving at all.'

'I'm sorry, miss. They're not sheep at all, but boulders,' Will said. 'They're called wethers. The downs are littered with them. That's why the house is called Grey Wethers.'

'Oh, I see.' Charlotte smiled up at him, thinking what a strange, awkward man he was, quite good-looking, but with a curious air of reserve about him, as if he wanted to be friendly and gregarious, but didn't know how.

Alice was running ahead of them, her long dark hair in disarray, stopping now and then to ask questions. 'What's that?' she cried, catching a glimpse of water through the trees.

'We call it Sweet Water,' Will said. 'It's a natural lake fed from an underground spring. Some say it has medicinal qualities, others that nobody who swims there will ever drown. Not that I'd trust that old wives' tale myself. The lake isn't very big, but it is very deep.'

Alice ran forward, trampling the buttercups, her thin legs and the hem of her dress golden with pollen, her arms outstretched to embrace the shining water.

'Alice! Come back!' Charlotte ran after her, seized with a sudden terror, remembering that day on the jetty. She caught hold of the girl at the water's edge; swung her round, and clung to her, her forehead bathed with sweat, and sank, trembling, to her knees, holding Alice in her arms, the sky tilting above her.

Later, 'Why did you do that?' Kitty Tanquillan asked in a low voice. 'Never mind, you can tell me when we get back to the house.' She called over her shoulder, 'I'm tired, Will. I want to get home now, to rest. You may drive the trap back this evening: stay to supper if you wish.' She glanced sharply at Charlotte as they crossed the meadow to Grey Wethers. Alice was running on ahead. Jenny lagging behind. 'The way you ran after that child just now,' Kitty said, 'one might have thought that you were trying to save her from drowning. Were you?'

'I'm sorry Miss Tanquillan. I'd rather not discuss it now if you don't mind,' Charlotte said wearily.

'Very well. I'm sorry, we will talk about it later.' Kitty nodded. 'By the way, from now on, you and Jenny will call me "Miss Kitty". Is that understood?'

Will Oakleigh seemed curiously out of place at Kitty Tanquillan's dining-table. He felt out of place too, in his best suit and starched collar. Essentially an outdoor man, his good dark suit was given an airing mainly at Harvest Festival or Christmas, when the vicar asked him to read the lessons. Silent and taciturn, he had become inured to solitude since his wife, Abby, died four years ago. Now the wife of one of the farm-hand came in to 'do' for him three times a week, to dust his unused front parlour with its stiffly-arranged vases and Abby's little piano with the brass candlesticks; to turn out his bedroom and clean the kitchen. Not that that was much use, she said, since the place never stayed clean for two minutes together with all the dog and cat hairs. Then she would cluck her tongue at the pots in the sink and ask him what he would do if he ran out of plates and pans; scolding him affectionately; telling him it was high time he found himself another wife to take care of him.

But always, at the back of Will's mind, lay the thought that he had been responsible for Abby's death. They had long wanted a child, a son, to follow in his footsteps; had given up hope of ever having one. Abby was just turned forty when she told him that she was pregnant. A plump, bustling country woman, Wiltshire born and bred, she had pooh-poohed his fears that she might have a hard time of it giving birth to a first child at her age. 'You worry too much, Will,' she scoffed. 'I know I'm not all that young, but I have never had a day's illness in my life. I'll give you a son to be proud of.'

She had given him that son – stillborn – and he had stroked her hair and wept over her when she died. He had never looked at another woman since – until today – when he looked at Charlotte Grayler. Perhaps it was simply that she reminded him of Abby when she was young, for Charlotte seemed to him to possess the same shining air of unconquerability as Abby had done. Even so, he could find nothing to say to her; his conversation, directed mainly to his hostess, was all about the cottages in Longbarrow Lane and what needed to be done to make them fit for habitation.

'Will has a fine baritone voice,' Miss Kitty said after supper. 'Remember, Will, those evenings when we met for choir practice in your parlour, and Abby played the piano for us? You should not have given up the choir, and it's no use saying you are too busy. Everyone should spare the Lord two or three hours a week.' She glanced amusedly at Will's downcast face. 'But I'll say no more about that if you will sing for us now.' She crossed to the piano.

Charlotte felt intensely sorry for the man so obviously out of his element in the drawing-room. Will Oakleigh, she felt, would be far happier singing to the wind on the Downs. She sat primly beside Jenny on the sofa, hands clenched in her lap as he cleared his throat and glanced at him sympathetically.

Kitty looked at Charlotte and smiled inwardly. Did the child imagine that she wanted to make a fool of Will? On the contrary, she had noticed his interest in the girl and wished to show him off to the best advantage. 'Sing "There's no Place Like Home",' she said.

'Very well,' Will eased his collar. The power of his voice flooded the room.

My God, Jenny thought, this man could have made his living on a concert platform. She glanced sideways at Charlotte, then at Miss Kitty, and guessed that the old woman was trying her hand at match-making. The cunning old vixen!

Jenny now had her daily newspaper delivered along with Miss Tanquillan's. 'Listen to this,' she said avidly to Charlotte one morning. 'Scottish suffragettes have destroyed a water-main near Loch Katrine. I bet that put the cat among the pigeons!'

'I don't know how they dare,' Charlotte commented, not

sharing Jenny's enthusiasm for women's suffrage. 'I wouldn't have the nerve.'

'It's a good job somebody has,' Jenny retorted. 'Remember Emily Davison who threw herself under the King's horse at last year's Derby? *There* was a woman who didn't mind dying for what she believed in! But even that wasn't enough to convince the politicians. Even the King won't listen!'

'But the King isn't a politician,' Charlotte frowned.

'No, but he must have known about the suffragette demonstration in Hyde Park, since it was all done legally. But when the women formed up to march along the Mall to Buckingham Palace to present their petition, the law was out in force to prevent them. Half of them were arrested! Bundled off in police wagons! Does that seem right or fair to you?'

'No, I suppose not,' Charlotte admitted.

The weather changed suddenly. In Scarborough, the sea was lashed to fury by north-east gales. It was the worst June weather that anyone could remember.

The azaleas in the garden of the house in Chalice Walk were all dead now, their petals drifting brown and broken on the paths leading down to the sea. The blood-red rhododendrons were gone from the drawing-room, their brief moment of glory ended.

Romilly Tanquillan hugged a shawl about her shoulders, hating the moaning of the wind about the windows as she wandered aimlessly from room to room, scarcely able to bear the cold and loneliness, the utter boredom of having nothing to do.

The few people she had met since her marriage seemed to her to be small-mindedly provincial and dull; Scarborough itself a piddling place compared with London. God, how she loathed it!

Apart from the shops in the main street and the Spa, a complex of Victorian buildings, concert-hall, bandstand, and cafes, there was little of interest to divert the fashionable young Mrs Tanquillan when her husband was busy about his work at the harbour.

She had strolled, occasionally, to the Spa, before the weather broke, thinking that she would give her soul for a glimpse of Bond Street, Piccadilly, or the Mall under a bright London sky, with candled sycamores in full leaf, and the great buildings she knew and loved aglow with summertime; Eaton Square with its march of symmetrical houses, its great shining width and eternal comings and goings; the parade of nannies with their charges in the Square's gardens; hansom cabs at midnight, the swish of ball-gowns, attentive servants and champagne breakfasts.

Instead, she had perforce watched from the spa bridge the capering crowds on the sands below: those brainless idiots from the mill-towns of the West Riding, there on a day's outing. Shameless women running into the sea to paddle, their skirts tucked up above their knees; flat-capped men lying out on the beach; old women devouring whelks and ice-cream cornets; mill-lads mounted on donkeys; screaming urchins running wild along the sea-front with its clanging trams and fish-and-chip parlours, fortune-tellers, and souvenir shops; couples strolling along arm in arm, their hands filled with gimcrack ornaments fashioned from sea-shells; men, with knotted handkerchiefs on their heads, reeling drunkenly from the pubs when they closed.

Even on the spa itself, that haven for the elite who stayed in splendid isolation at the hotels on the Esplanade, indulged in light orchestral music, promenaded in their fashionable clothes, and chatted discreetly over afternoon tea, the thin screams of the mill-town masses could be heard in the distance.

Romilly was sick and tired of the house in Chalice Walk. It was not, and never could be, her home. She wanted her own house, the excitement of choosing her own furniture and carpets; she longed to invite her London friends for weekends, to plan parties and picnics. She had said as much to Rowan over and over again, but he seemed so moody and preoccupied when he came home from that beastly, boring job of his, scarcely noticing the trouble she had taken with the menus, the hours she had spent over her toilette.

Staring out of the music room window at the storm-tossed sky, Romilly felt she would go mad if Rowan did not take her soon to London. Perhaps there, away from the town which so depressed her, she would be able to rekindle his interest in making love to her.

It had been so wonderful that first night, feeling the full weight of his body on hers: the slow, pulsing rhythm which had caused her to cry out in ecstasy as she fingered, with joy, the lean, firm flesh of him; the hair at the nape of his neck.

But ever since that night he had seemed so distant, so tired, so disinterested in love-making. Romilly pushed aside the thought that, on that first night, he had seemed a different person, making love to another woman.

CHAPTER NINETEEN

Devizes, with its bustling market square, fascinated Alice. She could not get enough of watching the splashing fountain between the market stalls piled high with fruit and vegetables, glowing succulent oranges and fine yellow bananas – so different from the brown, spotted fruit she and her father used to buy in Highgate market. She would finger, greedily, the creamy cauliflowers, golden carrots and fresh green runner beans; caress the baskets of eggs, and plunge her face into bunches of garden pinks and sweet williams, as if she could never have enough of food and fragrance. Charlotte needed to keep a wary eye open as the child wandered between the stalls, stopping to gloat over the silvery-scaled fish – herring, haddock, salmon and grayling, the chunks of meat – brisket, silverside, rump, pork chops, and saddles of lamb.

'If only my father had been able to afford decent food,' Alice said, 'he might be alive now. He never got enough to eat, you know. He would buy two savoury ducks and give them both to me. He would pretend not to be very hungry, but he was. He was always very hungry. I pretend that I am buying him some good rich meat and eggs and vegetables to nourish him as he deserved to be nourished. I know it's too late, but I buy him everything he needs in my mind, and give it to him with my love. I buy him flowers too, for his soul.'

Alice was growing taller by the minute, it seemed to Charlotte, and filling out too. She needed some new clothes. The few she possessed were beginning to pull across her blossoming breasts. The market stalls were crowded with cheaply-priced remnants of material: flowered cottons and winceyettes. Charlotte told Miss Kitty that she could easily make Alice some new dresses and nightgowns.

'You really care for my great-niece, don't you?' Miss Kitty said. 'I wonder why. She is not a very attractive girl to look at. Do you pity her because she tried to drown herself?'

'I suppose pity must be a large part of what I feel for her,' Charlotte said slowly, 'but there's more to it than that. I think that Alice might really begin to blossom if she felt loved and wanted again, as she did when her father was alive. I *am* sorry for her, but I don't want to be. Pity, after all, somehow rubs off on the person to be pitied. It cannot be all that elevating to know that people pity you because you are thin and under-privileged.'

'So you think that Alice is under-privileged, do you?'

'No. I believe she *thinks* herself to be under-privileged, as her father was. That kind of stigma cannot be washed away in five minutes.'

Kitty smiled. 'If ever I am up in court on a serious charge, Charlotte, I shall want you as my advocate,' she said teasingly. 'You have a way of putting things into clear perspective. You are quite right, of course. You have my permission to buy as much pretty material as you think fit to make my great-niece "blossom", as you put it.'

Realizing Romilly's loneliness in a strange place, Rowan took his wife to London. Emily was in Scotland, and so they had to stay with his parents. He did not relish the idea, but he put his own wishes aside for Romilly's sake. She seemed physically ill, vaguely irritable, petulant and lack-lustre, wanting constant expressions of his love, demanding his reassurance that he found her attractive. But the strain of returning to his old home in Eaton Square was almost more than he could bear so soon after his enforced marriage. He could scarcely be civil to his mother, but he had to be for his wife's sake. And then began the puppet-show he detested, as Romilly's friends came to call on her, and she babbled on about having them to visit her in Scarborough when she and Rowan had found a house of their own.

What a bloody charade, he thought, as he went through the

motions of being an attentive young husband in love with his wife. It was when the guests departed; when he found himself alone with Romilly in their bedroom, that he hated himself most. He remembered a poem he had read and loved as a boy – 'Cynara: Non Sum Qualis Eram Bonae Sub Regno Cynarae'.

> 'I cried for madder music and for stronger wine,
> But when the feast is finished and the lamps expire,
> Then falls thy shadow, Cynara! the night is thine;
> And I am desolate and sick of an old passion,
> Yea, hungry for the lips of my desire:
> I have been faithful to thee, Cynara! in my fashion.'

When it was time to go back to Scarborough, Romilly sat on his lap and teased his hair with her fingers.

'I don't want to go back just yet,' she said. 'I want to go to Scotland to see my mother. Would you mind very much, Rowan?'

'No, of course not. Do whatever will make you happy.'

'I want you to come too,' she wheedled. 'I want to show you off to Grandmother Beresford.'

'I'm sorry, that's impossible. I must go back to work.'

'Oh yes,' she snapped. 'I know, to your precious cargoes of stones and fish-manure!'

'To my job,' he said patiently. 'But you go to Scotland if you wish. You could do with a holiday in the fresh air. You look so pale . . .'

She said, in an excited whisper, 'There could be a reason for that. I'm not quite sure, but I think I'm going to have a baby. I was close to my period when we got married, but it hasn't come yet. Of course it could be all the excitement – and everything, but I don't think so. I hope not. Oh Rowan, aren't you thrilled to know that I might be pregnant?'

> 'Dancing to put thy pale, lost lilies out of mind'.

A great tide of loneliness overwhelmed him.

Rowan looked down at Grey Wethers from the crest of a hill. The house seemed to have grown from the rich earth, an integral part of the ripe, fruitful soil of Wiltshire which he remembered from his childhood visits to Aunt Kitty. Those yearly visits had been his only respite from the hard demands of his upbringing, when he had been packed off by his parents at the old woman's insistence that she should see at least something of her great-nephew.

He had never dared betray his excitement as the carriage jogged him from Eaton Square to Paddington station, but his legs had come out in goose-pimples when he was put onto the great, grunting train, in charge of the guard; when his mother had given him a cool kiss on the cheek and walked back along the platform to the waiting landau.

The minute she was out of sight, he had pulled off his cap and chucked it, with careless abandon, on to the rack; had leaned out of the window to revel in the sight of porters wheeling their clanking handbarrows; long-skirted women, in high-heeled boots, mincing along beside the train, their arms filled with magazines and boxes of chocolates, followed by servants carrying their pet dogs and jewel-cases, or military-looking men marching uprightly along the platform, barking orders to the valets who carried their pie-filled hampers, guns and shooting-sticks.

He had whistled, blithely, the latest tune beloved of errand-boys on their rounds as he nipped off the train to buy a cup of tea and a sandwich from a passing barrow, had felt in his jacket pocket for a sixpenny piece; told the man, doling out the tea from a polished brass urn, to keep the twopence change; wished himself to be a guard with a green flag and a whistle, a station porter, or even the man in charge of the urn – anything else on earth but the son of Gervaise Tanquillan.

When the engine moved majestically away from the platform, his scalp had begun to tingle to the rhythm of the wheels. He had watched the great plumes of steam billowing up under the station roof with an overwhelming sense of gladness that a fortnight's freedom lay ahead of him.

Nothing had changed. He had looked down at the house, from this vantage point, a hundred times before. His flesh still tingled at the sight of long furrows heavy with ripening corn;

the flocks of grey-woolled sheep grazing on the tiered, wind-rippled grass of the Downs. He knew of no other grass the exact colour of Wiltshire grass – the green of willow trees misted over with the first touch of spring.

Time had wrought few changes in the landscape he loved. Cattle were still led, at evening, to the milking-sheds. The ground, after rain, was still churned to mud by the steady trampling of their hooves. The farm lads who followed the reapers at harvest time were exact replicas of their fathers and grandfathers before them. Change lay only in himself, a man who had exchanged freedom for bondage. He had not realized, in his youth and innocence, how precious freedom was. And yet it had always seemed to be his heritage, as England was his heritage, and the heritage of the men who had gone before him; simple men who had worked the earth through countless centuries, who now lay sleeping in the graveyard of the Norman church in the valley. Men who had lived their lives quietly with the sun on their faces, the wind in their hair, the women they loved beside them.

Looking down at the house, he knew as intimately as his own hands what each room contained. Not the stiff Constables of Eaton Square which he so detested, but tiny, glowing miracles of Renaissance art which Aunt Kitty had brought back with her from her visits to Italy when she was young. Glorious, haloed madonnas: sorrowing over the body of the crucified Christ.

Nor did Aunt Kitty's house contain plumcake-rich patterned chairs and sofas. Her furniture was earth-plain and functional: tables fashioned from seasoned oak by long-dead village craftsmen. Nothing there was too ordered or carefully arranged. The tack-room contained gaberdine coats slung on pegs; saddles, riding-whips; a plethora of rosettes and tarnished silver trophies; brushes and curry-combs, worn leggings and bowler hats; looped-up reins and stirrups; the clutter of an old woman who no longer rode to hounds, who lived in her memories of the past when she was young and beautiful.

Why she had never married remained her secret. She lived surrounded by her secrets, a deeply sensitive, humorous woman who now bred sheep as she had once bred horses, who still occasionally rode her old mare, Sally, at daybreak, stirring the willow-tinted grass of the downs with the thunder of her hooves.

Rowan had ridden after her on many a summer morning long ago, clinging to his saddle while she streaked ahead of him, laughing at him over her shoulder, her bright brown hair streaming in the wind, loving him as only a childless woman with memories to keep could love a town boy afraid of horses. And yet, in time, under her patient tutelage, he had learned not to be afraid, had learned how to handle the reins, to leap fences, to control his mount. It had seemed to him like flying then, when he and the horse were one, and its great horny pasterns lifted to the rhythm of his swiftly-beating heart, when the smell of the grass came up to meet him and the world seemed to be compounded of flying hooves, with clouds racing overhead, when the breath of his body was driven out of him in great gasps by the mass of thundering bone, muscle and sinew between his legs.

He had left his luggage at the village pub. His tongue felt as dry as sticks in his mouth as he plunged down the hill, past the clustered cottages at the lane end and the tiny post-office-cum-sweet shop where he had once purchased all those blissful gob-stoppers and strips of liquorice which would have shocked his mother had she known about them. Boys of his class were not expected to walk about with bulging cheeks and black-stained teeth, nor to whistle or make fists in their blazer pockets, nor lie on their backs in the hay watching the clouds sailing overhead; to revel in rain, to walk in it, face upturned, soaked to the skin, loving the smell of it on the roses in the cottage gardens.

He walked briskly up the drive and rang the bell.

'Why, if it isn't Mr Rowan.' Rivers's face crinkled with pleasure. 'Bless my soul, sir, the mistress will be surprised to see you.'

Rowan grasped the old man's hand. 'How are you, Rivers? How's the rheumatism?'

'Not too bad at the moment, sir. But where's your luggage?'

'I'm staying at the White Swan.'

'The mistress won't like that, sir.'

'I'm going back to Scarborough tomorrow. I didn't want to cause a disturbance. Where is my aunt now?'

'In the study, sir, doing the accounts. Shall I tell her you're here?'

'No. I want to surprise her.' He moved forward slowly, savouring his memories of the house, the dark panelled walls, broad window-sills with their familiar clutter of blue and white vases, the smell of beeswax polish; copper jugs filled with garden flowers; crimson peonies, larkspur and delphiniums. He rested his hand momentarily on the carved newel and glanced up at the landing in the hope that he might catch a glimpse of Charlotte.

His great-aunt was seated at her desk, her shoulders hunched over a ledger. 'Yes, Rivers, what is it?' she said absently, not looking up from her work. Rowan covered her face with his hands.

'What on earth!' She swung round in her chair. 'Oh, Rowan, my dear boy. This calls for a celebration! Rivers! I know you are there! Fetch the Madeira! Tell Cook that we shall be one extra for lunch.' Her face wrinkled with pleasure. 'Well, what are you doing here? And where is your wife?'

'Romilly has gone to Scotland to visit her grandmother. I happened to be in London. I decided to break my journey. How are you, Aunt Kitty?'

She glanced up at him sharply. 'I'm well enough. But you. I have known you all these years. You never could pull the wool over my eyes. I watched you, as a youngster, wrestling with your problems, keeping them to yourself. I fancy those problems have not changed much, or the pressures that were brought to bear on you.' She rose to her feet and placed her hands on his shoulders. 'You are not happy, Rowan. I can see it in your face.'

He knew better than to lie to her. 'No,' he said, 'I am not very happy.'

Rivers came in with the wine. 'Put the tray on the desk,' she said. 'No, don't bother to pour. I'll do so myself.' But her hand trembled slightly on the decanter. Rowan realized, with a sense of shock, that this woman who had seemed indestructible to him was nothing but skin and bone now. And yet her mind was a bright as ever. Her shrunken body seemed to him a frail chalice lit by the incandescent flame of the spirit. Time had not changed her capacity for understanding, her almost clairvoyant power to see beneath the masks people wore.

'This wife of yours,' she said sharply, 'you are obviously not in love with her.' She nodded, noticing the sudden closed expression in his eyes, the same look she had seen so often when he was a boy trying to come to terms with life, asking no pity for his lovelessness. How like Oliver he was. 'But you are in love with someone else.' This was not a question but a statement of fact. Two and two added up to four. It was quite clear to Kitty Tanquillan now – the reason why Rachel had written to her, why she had sent Charlotte Grayler out of harm's way – out of Rowan's way. 'And unless I am very much mistaken, the girl you are in love with is under this roof at this very moment.' Kitty wrinkled her brow. 'But is it wise, your coming here? What's to be gained by it?'

Rowan twisted the stem of his glass between his fingers. 'I didn't think in terms of gain. I simply wanted to see her again.'

'But why, if you felt so strongly about Charlotte, did you marry Romilly Beresford?' When Rowan did not answer, she said quietly, 'I'm sorry. That was a stupid question. Parental pressure again. What did they threaten you with this time – penury?'

'Do you think I'd have cared a damn about that?'

'No, of course not. It must have been something far worse. Whatever it was, you will never divulge the truth.'

A sudden knock came at the door. Alice Tanquillan waltzed into the room, her new white and pink sprigged dress twitching about her ankles and her hair caught back in a pink ribbon. 'Oh Aunt Kitty, may we have a picnic lunch? It's such a beautiful day.' She had not realized that anyone else was in the room.

'Hello, Alice,' Rowan said, stepping forward. She turned quickly at the sound of his voice, held back for a moment, then ran to him, her face alight with joy. 'Oh Rowan, Rowan,' she gasped, 'I knew that you would come to me sooner or later. I've missed you so much.'

There was no mistaking the look of adoration in the girl's face. Kitty Tanquillan realized at once that the little fool was in love with Rowan, that he did not guess the nature or extent of Alice's affection. His kiss was perfunctory, then he held her at arm's length saying how pretty she looked – the kind of thing a man says unthinkingly to a child. Kitty looked into the past with a strange sense of foreboding, seeing there another bright-eyed excitable girl – Martha Tanquillan – Alice's mother. It was all there, reborn in her daughter: Martha's febrile excitement, shrill laughter bordering on hysteria, the way she had of tossing her head and brushing her hand quickly across her forehead as if to dispel imaginary cobwebs.

'How long are you staying, Rowan?' Alice clung to his hand. 'He must stay for a long time, mustn't he, Aunt Kitty?'

'I'm afraid not, Scrap,' the old nickname sprang easily to his lips. 'This is just a flying visit. I simply came to . . .'

'To see me.' Alice finished the sentence for him. 'But you *must* stay. I have so much to show you – the farm and the horses. Besides, I want you to take me rowing on the lake.'

'That will do, Alice,' Kitty said firmly. 'You have my permission to go and ask Cook about the picnic.'

'But Rowan must come on the picnic too,' Alice said pertly.

'Certainly not. Rowan will have luncheon with me.' Kitty's tone of voice brooked no further argument. 'We have things to discuss. I have not seen your cousin for a long time, remember.'

Alice coloured up. 'Neither have I,' she said rudely.

'I shall not speak to you again, child. May I remind you that you are a guest under my roof. You will do as I ask!'

'You are just a jealous old woman, and I hate you,' Alice cried as she turned and fled from the room.

When she had gone, Kitty shivered and pulled her shawl more closely about her shoulders. 'I have tried not to believe it, but it is quite unmistakable,' she said.

'What do you mean, Aunt?'

'I have never spoken to you of Alice's mother before. I never saw the necessity until now.'

Seeing the old woman's distress, Rowan guided her to a chair by the fire. 'Sit down and get warm,' he said. 'You're shivering.'

He poured a little brandy into a glass from the decanter on the sideboard, and made her drink it. 'I'm sorry Alice has upset you so much. But you mustn't take too much notice of her, she is just young and excitable.'

'No, it's much more than that,' Kitty said. 'Alice is unbalanced, and it frightens me to think what might become of her if something is not done to help her. What I am about to say has a bearing on your own future, that is why I must talk to you. You have heard, I daresay, that Alice's mother died in an insane asylum.' The old woman's eyes were bright with tears. 'I loved Oliver Tanquillan, and I loved his wife, Martha. God forgive me, I left it too late to help her. That is why I must not leave it too late to help Alice.'

'Take another sip of brandy,' Rowan said gently. 'Don't you think we should leave all this until another time, when you are feeling better?' Kitty shook her head. 'No, I must speak of it now. Sit down, Rowan, and listen to me.' She caught hold of his hand.

'Oliver and Martha were a pair of babes in the wood, so much in love with each other, yet totally ill-equipped to face the world of reality. What a charming man Oliver was, to be sure. You are very like him, you know. The same dark, curly hair, the same characteristics. Poor Oliver failed because no-one can live entirely on dreams, especially a man with a sick wife and a delicate child to care for. I offered them a home here, but he would not accept that offer. He was too proud, you see; utterly convinced that he could make his own way in life.'

Kitty stared into the fire. 'He may have been a great writer for all I know, but he was born out of his time. No-one cared to publish what he wrote. It was too fanciful, too harsh for modern tastes. All people want nowadays is escapism: romance. But Oliver wrote of the future, of poverty, of man's purpose in the scheme of things. Meanwhile Martha became increasingly ill.' The old woman shivered, caught in a web of memories of Oliver and his tiny, bird-like wife with her high-pitched laughter and inexplicable changes of mood – laughing one minute, crying the next over a drop of spilt milk or something she had lost and could not find.

'The last time I saw her was in that dreadful institution. Her mind was quite gone. She recognized no-one, not even Oliver. She was under restraint for her own good and the safety of others. You see, she had attacked a wardress with a knife. It was – terrible!'

'Please don't, Aunt Kitty. It's all over now.'

The old woman shook her head. Her fingers dug into the back of his hands. 'No, it isn't! The symptoms of mental disturbance are all present in Martha's daughter. She loves and hates with equal intensity. I am so afraid that, if Alice ever really hated anyone enough, she would cause harm to that person. Even you, my dear.'

'*Me*? But why?' All this was beyond him. 'Alice doesn't hate me . . .'

'No,' Kitty Tanquillan said slowly, 'because she's in love with you. But she could hate, very intensely indeed, anyone you loved. Ah, I see you don't believe me. You think that I am just a foolish, fanciful old woman.'

'No, indeed I don't. I am simply trying to understand what you are saying.' Rowan ran his fingers perplexedly through his hair. 'But Alice is just a child . . .'

'That's where you are wrong,' Kitty said quietly. 'Alice is not a child. She is a young woman desperately in need of sexual fulfilment.'

Silence fell between them. Rowan said heavily, 'What do you intend to do?'

She touched his cheek gently with her fingers. 'I always meant to leave Grey Wethers to you,' she said. 'You have been as precious to me as my own son. I thought that I could trust Rachel and Gervaise to do what is best for Alice. I see now that I was mistaken. I made Charlotte tell me the truth about what happened to the girl in Scarborough, the rest I gleaned from Alice. Then it became increasingly clear to me that the child must receive medical treatment; must be given stability. That is why I have decided to leave Grey Wethers to her when I die.' Kitty knotted her hands together beseechingly. 'You do understand, my dear, that I must keep the girl safe for Oliver and Martha's sake?'

'Of course I understand.' Rowan gathered the old woman's hands and kissed them. 'I have never wanted anything from you save your love, and I've had that in good measure.'

'One more thing.' She gazed at him through her tears. 'I think that you should not stay here any longer. Not see Charlotte under this roof. Alice is very quick, very perceptive. I should not like her to guess the truth.'

'My God! You cannot believe that Alice would harm Charlotte?'

'I scarcely know what to believe any longer,' Kitty said wearily. 'I simply think that we dare not take unnecessary risks.'

'But I came here to see Charlotte. I must see her!'

Kitty smiled faintly. 'Yes, I suppose you must. Well, you'll have to leave it to me, that's all. Will you trust me?'

'Haven't I always trusted you?'

'Then go to the desk and write what I dictate.'

Alice turned on Kitty Tanquillan in a fury. 'You never meant me to see Rowan at all,' she cried. 'You said he was staying for lunch. Now he's gone, and it's all your fault!'

Equally devastated because Rowan had gone away so suddenly, Charlotte said firmly, 'You must not speak to Miss Kitty like that.'

'But I wanted to show him the farm. I wanted him to take me rowing. Now it's all ruined!'

'Jenny and I will take you rowing,' Charlotte promised.

'I don't want you and Jenny! I don't want anyone but Rowan!' Alice ran, sobbing, from the room. They heard the scurry of her feet on the stairs, the slam of her bedroom door.

Charlotte went after her. 'Alice, please let me in,' she called, but the bedroom door was locked. 'Go away and leave me alone,' the girl shouted.

'But you can't possibly stay locked in your room on a day like this.'

'I can, because I have something to do. Something very special and very private. You'll see!'

'Alice! Open the door at once!' But it was no use. Charlotte could hear her moving about the room, laughing hysterically.

Jenny was in the schoolroom. She looked up as Charlotte entered. 'Oh God,' she said, 'I thought things were going too smoothly. What do you suppose she is up to?'

'I don't know.' Charlotte stared out at the garden. 'I think she has started writing. I walked into her room unexpectedly the other day. She was scribbling away at something. She had the strangest look on her face.'

Jenny shivered slightly. 'Do you suppose she's taken to writing love letters to one of the farm lads? Or perhaps she's trying her hand at a penny novelette. Her father was a writer, wasn't he? Oh lord, I hate this kind of thing. And why do you suppose Rowan went off in such a hurry?'

'I don't know that either,' Charlotte said bleakly.

'Oh God, I'm sorry. I didn't mean to upset you.' Jenny vented her wrath on the blackboard. 'By the way, Miss Kitty wants to see you in her study.'

Charlotte knocked, and closed the door behind her. The old woman looked up from her desk. 'I have something for you,' she said, handing her a letter. 'Rowan asked me to give you this. Be sure not to let Alice see it.'

Mist of early morning lay over the fields as Rowan shaved, dressed, and went downstairs. Everything was quiet. He unlocked the door and walked quickly away from the White Swan where he had spent a restless night. Through the haze he heard the song of a lark, the quiet movement of cattle behind the hedgerows, the sudden, urgent bleating of a lamb wanting its mother.

He hurried to the spinney, unlatched the gate, and moved silently through the meadow encircling the lake until he reached the old summerhouse. He was too early, but far happier here than tossing sleeplessly in bed. The door of the summerhouse was open, hanging on its hinges, sadly in need of a lick of paint. Dust lay thick on the broken furniture. Nobody used the old, rickety building any more, but it had been the village cricket pavilion he remembered, where, after a hard-won match he had sunk his teeth blissfully into potted meat sandwiches and listened to the laughter of his friends – the village postman, the shop-keeper, the farm-hands, to whom he was just 'Maister Rowan' – a boy with a strong batting arm and a good eye for a wicket.

He could understand why Sweet Water Meadow was no longer used for matches. The lake had caught far more cricket balls than he ever had. Even so, his most vital memories of childhood were contained here.

He thought if he had a son, he would give him all the things he had never known: freedom above all else. He could not believe that Romilly was going to have a child. He preferred not to believe it. How could a child be conceived of such a passionless marriage? But wasn't he the living proof that a child could be born of nothing more than a sense of duty, for the sake of a name, a business?

Touching the dust-covered tables and deck-chairs, he remembered how, as a child, he had been made to accompany his father to his offices in the Strand, sitting stiffly beside him in the carriage, wearing a sailor suit and a wide-brimmed straw hat, dreading the moment of arrival at the board-room of his father's 'empire'. He had never been able to understand why so many old, bearded men chose to sit shuffling papers, talking interminably of profit and loss, when they might be outdoors in the sunshine, while he squirmed on a slippery leather chair, his feet not touching the ground, the leather sticking to his tender behind as cigar smoke circled lazily towards the ceiling and his eyelids began to close.

Never would a son of his undergo such torture. He thought, too, of the day he had plucked up enough courage to tell his father that he wanted to become a musician, a concert pianist. His music teacher had told him that if he worked hard enough he could achieve his ambition. 'You have the necessary touch of brilliance,' he said. He was sixteen at the time. His music lessons were discontinued from that day. Never, in his life, had he possessed the weapons to fight back. And yet, if the rest of his life was not to be wasted, he must begin to fight. He thought of Oliver Tanquillan, a man who had fought and lost, but he at least was worthy of respect.

He waited, counting the minutes, afraid that Charlotte might not come after all.

She walked swiftly across the meadow in a green and white dress pintucked to a nineteen-inch waist, wearing a straw hat with green ribbons. She had scarcely slept for wondering what she would say to Rowan when she met him again. She could not understand why he had not stayed for lunch yesterday. Alice was full of it at the time, happy because he had arrived, full of plans for the afternoon, primping and preening herself, wanting to change her dress because the pink and white one had a mark on the skirt: complaining because her aunt wanted to keep Rowan all to herself. Then, just as suddenly as he had arrived, he went away again, and Miss Kitty had handed her his letter asking her to meet him near the summerhouse before breakfast.

'I don't think I should go,' she confided in Jenny. But Jenny had laughed at her primness. 'You must do as you please. All I can say, if he had asked me to a secret assignation, I'd be there with bells on. Nothing could keep me away.'

'It's the secret part of it I don't understand,' Charlotte frowned. 'Why did Kitty say "don't tell Alice"?'

'That's as plain as the nose on your face,' Jenny said, 'the kid's head-over-heels in love with Rowan. She would probably attack you with a dinner-knife if she knew how he feels about you.' She glanced at Charlotte quizzically over her spectacles. 'You know very well you *will* go. Whether you should, is another matter entirely.'

Now, as Charlotte trod a path between the buttercups, she told herself, 'I must remain cool and calm; remember that he is a married man.' But when she saw him standing there near the summerhouse, her footsteps quickened with her heartbeats. She could never remain cool or detached where Rowan was concerned. The mind was one thing, the heart another.

He turned at the sound of her footsteps, and held out his arms to her. A lark rose up singing from the long grass. Suddenly the sun came slanting through the mist, dazzling on the water of the lake.

'I was so afraid you wouldn't come.'

'I very nearly didn't.' She took off her hat and swung it by the ribbons. 'Alice was very upset when you didn't stay for lunch.'

'Blow Alice,' he said, 'I came to see you.' He felt buoyant with relief: glad of the morning, the sun, of being alive and young with Charlotte in his arms. 'I like your dress,' he said.

'You know you shouldn't have come, not to see me . . .'

'Please, darling, try to understand. I *had* to come. I couldn't bear being away from you a minute longer. Don't turn away. Look at me. I love you! I didn't stop to question the right and wrong of the situation. For once in my life I acted on impulse.' He paused. 'But no, that is not quite true. The first time I yielded to an impulse was when I kissed you on the back stairs, and I shall never regret doing that.'

'You are not free to love me,' she said slowly, clinging to a shred of integrity and conscience.

'You think I don't know that?' A trace of bitterness crept into his voice. 'Do you think this is easier for me than it is for you? I wanted to tell you, that night in the garden, on my "wedding" night, about the girl in the stained-glass window. I don't know if she was real or imagined, but it was to her I made my vows . . .'

'No! *Don't*!' She pulled away from him. 'Oh, Rowan, don't you see? I know. I *know*! But it can't change anything now. Perhaps you don't love Romilly, but she is your wife!' Her voice caught on a sob.

'I'm sorry, darling. I should have known. I should not have come here after all.' He released her from his arms. 'Forgive me!'

'Oh, *Rowan*!' She could not bear to see him so unhappy, so defeated. 'Don't go! We mustn't part like this!' She held out her arms to him.

Turning, he smoothed back her hair, and drew her down into the grass, kissing her lips, whispering her name over and over again.

CHAPTER TWENTY

She had hoped to gain her room without being seen, but breakfast had already begun and the dining-room door was open. Alice rushed out to confront her.

'Where have you been?' she demanded. 'I've been looking for you everywhere.' She had apparently forgotten that yesterday she had not wanted to see Charlotte at all. 'What have you been doing?' She stared suspiciously at Charlotte's flushed cheeks. 'We've finished our porridge, and Aunt Kitty is in a foul mood this morning.'

'I've been for a walk in the meadow.'

Alice seized her hands and pulled her towards the dining-room. Miss Kitty was at the sideboard, helping herself to bacon and kidneys from the domed silver dishes.

'You are late, Charlotte,' she said coldly. 'I expect my guests to be punctual at mealtimes.'

'I'm sorry, ma'am.' Was Miss Kitty really angry or merely play-acting? It was difficult to tell.

Charlotte caught Jenny's eye and felt like laughing. Jenny was sitting there, staring owlishly over her spectacles, looking as if butter would not melt in her mouth, making a little O of her lips, fairly bursting with curiosity, knowing where Charlotte had been, dying to ask questions.

Rivers came in with the morning mail on a salver, his face as ruddy and crumpled as a Cox's orange pippin in wintertime. There was a letter for Jenny.

'Who's that from?' Alice enquired as Jenny slipped it into her cardigan pocket.

'I haven't the least idea,' Jenny said primly.

'Why don't you open it then?'

'Really, Alice, you are being very tiresome and ill-mannered this morning,' her great-aunt reprimanded her, as Charlotte scooped up a tiny portion of scrambled egg and returned to the table, to make some pretence of eating it. All she could think of was Rowan, and some lines from Alice Meynell's poem 'Renouncement'.

> "With the first dream that comes with the first sleep
> I run, I run, I am gathered to thy heart."

Jenny tore open her letter. 'It's from Harry,' she announced, settling on the school-room window-seat to read it.

'From Harry?' Charlotte puckered her forehead disbelievingly. 'How strange. I've never known Harry to set pen to paper before, except to write thank-you letters at Christmas.'

'I must have made an impression on him then!' Jenny laughed, her cheeks flushed with pleasure. She said slowly, 'What if I told you that I am half way to being in love with your brother?'

'I don't know. I'd be pleased if you really loved him, but what does "half way in love" mean? I'm fond of you, Jenny, but Harry's my brother. I wouldn't want him to get hurt.'

'I'm sorry, Lottie. I didn't mean to sound flippant. I have no intention of hurting him. My mind's in a muddle at the moment, that's all. One part of me wants to settle down to being a good wife and mother, while the other warns me not to, not until I have got rid of my anger and wanderlust. It's hard to explain, Carlotta, exactly how I feel at the moment. I think that I do love Harry very much, but I'd make him a poor wife, feeling as strongly as I do about women's suffrage.' She smiled. 'Don't worry, Lottie, you can trust me to do the right thing.'

She went on reading the letter. 'Oh,' she said, 'there's a message for you from Joe! I'm to tell you that he is officially engaged to Annie! The tea-party's on Sunday!

'Joe says: "Please tell Charlotte that Grandma's bowl with the silver rim has been taken out of mothballs again." Does that make sense to you?'

'Yes, it does.' Charlotte said, experiencing a sudden longing to be at home helping her mother with Joe and Annie's engagement tea. Then, bringing her mind back to practicalities, she asked Jenny, 'Have you seen Alice? I wonder where she has got to?'

'She's upstairs in her room, I think.' Jenny replied, as she set about preparing the morning's lessons.

'She didn't – suspect anything, did she?'

'About Rowan? No, I don't think so. Why should she?' Jenny looked up from what she was doing. 'How did it go, by the way?'

'I'll tell you later. I'd better go and find Alice.'

Rivers was in the hall. 'I was just coming to find you and Miss Jenny,' he said. 'Madam wants to see you in her study.'

'Now what?' Jenny smoothed her hair. 'I rather gathered that something was up at breakfast. The old girl seemed in a fearful ruck about something or other.'

It appeared that a book had been taken from Miss Kitty's room without her permission. Her face was hawk-like above the collar of her black dress. She stood erectly, one veined hand on the walking-stick she used when her rheumatism was troubling her. She was evidently angry.

'This room is my personal and private sanctum,' she said coldly. 'Have you seen the book?'

'It is scarcely possible to say without knowing the title,' Jenny said coolly.

'The title of the book is *Country Lore, Superstition and Witchcraft*.'

'Good lord!' Jenny pulled a face. 'No, I haven't seen it.' She added warmly, 'And I am not in the habit of taking books without the consent of the owner. Neither, I imagine, is Charlotte.'

'No, of course not,' Kitty said testily, waving aside the suggestion. 'I did not accuse you of taking it. Alice must be the culprit. I simply wished to know if you had seen it in her room. It is a dangerous book for a child like Alice to read.'

Charlotte suddenly remembered Alice's odd behaviour the other day, the strange, almost triumphant expression on her sharp little face, the way she had pushed whatever she had been writing into the top drawer of her desk.

'Ah, I see that you have thought of something. Have you seen the book, Charlotte?'

'No, Miss Kitty.'

'But you think you know where it is?' She sighed impatiently, 'Come, speak out. This is of vital importance.'

'I think it might be in the drawer of her desk.'

'Thank you. I shall look into the matter at once. That is all. You may go now.'

'Oh God,' Jenny said, closing the door, 'what the hell does Alice want with a book on witchcraft? You don't suppose she's trying to put a love spell on Rowan? Legs of toad, eye of newt, belladonna and ragwort – all that stuff? You know, Carlotta. I'm beginning to dislike this job intensely.'

In her room, Alice unlocked the drawer of her writing-desk and took out the book she had hidden there. Smiling to herself, she laid the roughly-shaped female figure she had fashioned from modelling clay on top of it, picked up a long sharp pin she had stolen from Charlotte's work-basket and jabbed it hard into the figure.

'There, Romilly Beresford,' she muttered, 'suffer as you have made me suffer. It's all your fault. Rowan would never have gone away and left me if it hadn't been for you. Suffer, suffer, suffer!'

It was late when Kitty Tanquillan called Charlotte into her room. She was sitting by fire and candlelight. Shadows were trapped eerily in dark corners, the draught from the door moved the candle flames in a curious, flickering dance. Shadowy bars moved and elongated on the ceiling, firelight caught the gleam of golden haloes of sad-faced madonnas. The scent of dried rose petals lingered in the air.

'Sit down, my dear.' Kitty indicated the chair opposite. Her voice was cracked and dry, the voice of a very old woman. 'I wanted to talk to you alone.' She moved her chair a little closer to the fire which was kept lit winter and summer because of the sudden chills she was prone to, which found their way into her bones in a way she had never thought possible when she was young. 'I have something to show you.' She placed the roughly-made doll she had found in Alice's room on Charlotte's lap. 'What do you make of that? Do you know what it is?'

'It's a kind of fetish.'

'And do you understand the purpose of the pin?'

'Yes, I think so.' Charlotte fingered the obscene thing with a feeling of disgust.

'Do you know who it is meant to represent? Can't you guess? Think, child.'

With a quick gesture of distaste, Charlotte brushed the unclean thing into the hearth. 'It could be anyone. Myself, you, Jenny – or . . .'

'Or Romilly Tanquillan?'

'But surely you don't believe in this kind of mumbo-jumbo?'

'Whether I believe in it or not is immaterial,' Kitty said. 'It is the intention behind it that worries me. Alice is in need of help. More help than you or I alone can give her. I am convinced that I should take the girl to see a specialist in mental disorders. The best man I know lives in London. It is my intention to take Alice there at once.'

Charlotte glanced compassionately at the old woman; noticed the trembling of her hands on the silver-knobbed walking-stick. 'But are you well enough to stand the strain?'

Kitty Tanquillan lifted her head proudly. 'I shall make myself well enough. I will do anything in my power to help my great-niece.' She smiled suddenly. 'But I am not so foolish and stubborn to think that I could manage alone. That is why I should like you and Jenny to go with me.'

Romilly Tanquillan stared out of her bedroom window at the spinney of Scotch firs bordering the garden, trees twisted and gnarled through a century of wind scouring down from the mountains. Benn Chaorach and Benn Mhanaich stood like grim sentinels to the east, wreathed in eternal mist – or so it seemed to Romilly, tapping her fingers restlessly on the window-sill.

In Scarborough she had wanted to be in London, in London she could not rest until she went to Scotland. Now she wished she was back in London. She could not think why she had wanted to come here in the first place. She hated those mountains, and disliked intensely her grandmother's house, built of solid grey stone, turreted, with uncarpeted staircases, long echoing passages, a shortage of bathrooms and hot water, and a baronial hall filled with ghastly sporting trophies mounted on mahogany plaques. In her present mood, she could not bear the sight of all the glassy-eyed stags her grandfather had slaughtered in the wild, heather-clad hills, nor the cases of stuffed pike and perch he had fished from the water of Garelochead.

She remembered her grandfather as a stubborn, irascible man in tweeds, usually with a gun or fishing-rod in his hand, sporting a nicotine-stained moustache above a mouthful of discoloured teeth. A rich man with a nose for blood sport, who had filled his home with reminders of his forays into the hills, and his long, costly expeditions to the Americas, Africa, India and Afghanistan, and left behind him a grim legacy of severed heads: buffalo, bison, wildebeest, elephant and giraffe, besides all the brightly-coloured Oriental rugs, mother-of-pearl inlaid cabinets, curved kukris, copper-topped tables, and carved ivory tusks.

He had died eventually in a bed he had shipped home from Louisiana, a monstrosity with scrolled ends, in which, he boasted to his wife, he had lain with half the Creole women of the Deep South: had given instructions before he died for the erection of his own tomb – of Aberdeen granite – within sight of his home. Romilly could see that tomb now, beyond the gaunt line of Scotch firs at the garden's end, surmounted with a glittering gold cross.

She had believed that having Rowan's child would bring untold joy and contentment; had pictured herself as the epitome of charming young motherhood, wheeling her son in the London parks with Rowan beside her.

Now, although quite certain of her pregnancy, that dream had little to do with reality; the wretchedness of early morning sickness, and constant depression made worse by her surroundings. She had half forgotten why she had wanted to come to Scotland – to impart the glad news of her pregnancy, to be fussed over and petted by her grandmother and her family of aunts, uncles and cousins who lived close by; to flaunt the thick gold wedding-ring on her finger.

She had been petted and made a fuss of. Now she felt sick, cold and very frightened. She glanced at the calendar. The thirteenth of July. Romilly had a superstitious dread of number thirteen.

She turned away from the window as Emily came into the room, smiling, holding out her hands to her. 'How do you feel this morning?' she asked brightly.

'I feel awful,' Romilly said. 'I never thought that having a baby would make me feel so bloated – so ugly!'

Emily noticed, with a feeling of misgiving, Romilly's lacklustre eyes and petulant expression. 'I'm so sorry,' she said. 'You see, I've arranged a picnic. I thought it would do you good. George and Arthur are coming, Cecily, Fiona and the children. David McClean is coming too, and Alastair is driving us. I thought you could wear your new purple dress and cloak. Oh, darling, what's wrong? I thought you'd be pleased.'

'I don't want to go,' Romilly said. 'I can't face people looking like this.'

'Darling, don't you realize that women are most beautiful when they are pregnant? When they know they are loved.'

Romilly said slowly, 'Rowan doesn't love me. He just feels sorry for me.' She stared at her mother's tell-tale face. 'You have known it all along, haven't you?' she asked accusingly.

'I don't know what you are talking about.' Too late now, Emily thought desperately, for the truth.

'Yes you do. You think me a fool, but I know now that Rowan doesn't love me. I thought our wedding night would be so wonderful, but it wasn't. It all started that day we travelled to Scarborough, when he wasn't there to meet me at the station. I've tried so hard to make him love me.'

'You are talking nonsense, my dear, because you are not feeling well.'

'No, I'm not. I *know*. If Rowan had really loved me, do you think that he would have let me come here alone? The truth is, he did not want to come with me – he preferred his stones and fish-manure to me.'

Suddenly she was in her mother's arms, crying her eyes out against her shoulder.

'Oh, my dear, you mustn't upset yourself so,' Emily murmured. 'Come now, get dressed. You'll be back with Rowan soon, and then you'll realize . . . you'll look on this as a bad dream.'

Romilly smiled wanly as David McClean, a near neighbour of Grandmother Beresford's, helped her into the carriage. They would be meeting the rest of the party – her cousins George and Arthur Beresford, their wives and children, at the picnic spot near Garelochead. The estate gillie, Alastair McNab, shook the reins and the carriage bowled forward smoothly between the pine trees bordering the drive.

Suddenly Romilly began to enjoy herself. David McClean was making a great fuss of her, tucking the plaid travelling-rug more closely about her skirts; keeping up a running commentary on the beauty of the scenery. He was a very earnest young man, tall, with receding fair hair, ruddy cheeks, a flourishing blonde moustache, and grey-blue eyes above a hooked beak of a nose. He wore the kilt of the McClean clan proudly and easily, and spoke in a soft Scottish accent. He was rich, attentive, and very handsome, apart from his thinning hair and his prominent nose. But there was a firmness and strength about him that appealed strongly to Romilly. She placed her hand trustingly in his as he sprang down to help her from the carriage, and laughed into his eyes when he complimented her on her hat with ostrich feathers curving about the brim.

The gillie unpacked the hamper beneath a clump of rowan trees; spread the checked tablecloth on the springy turf, got out the wine which he strung into the river to cool. And then, when he had set out the veal and ham pies, the cold chicken and salad, the cheese and fruit, and covered them with muslin to keep off the flies, he began to unpack tennis rackets and balls for the children to play with; Emily's easel, canvas and paintbrush, fishing-rods for the men, and sunshades for their wives.

There was a great flurry of welcome when the other carriages arrived. The children were charming, Romilly thought, calling her 'Auntie Rommy' and begging her to play bat and ball with them.

After lunch, Emily settled down to her painting, the children flopped down in the shade of the trees to sleep; the women gathered under their sunshades to watch their husbands fish, while Romilly and David McClean wandered away together to explore the river bank.

'Oh, this is so peaceful, so beautiful,' Romilly said dreamily, watching an eagle in flight above the great pointed fir trees on the distant hills. She was revelling now in the afternoon sun on her face, the sound of a waterfall in the distance. The path before her was dappled with shade and sunlight. She waved her hand at a cloud of midges.

'Are the flies bothering you?' David asked.

'Yes, a little. I wish I had brought my sunshade.'

'I'll go back for it,' David said gallantly.

'Oh, how kind of you.'

'You'll wait here for me?'

'Yes, of course.' But Romilly did not wait. When he had gone, she walked a little further along the river bank, wanting to see the waterfall. Suddenly, there it was, sandwiched between savage grey rocks in a treeless ravine; tumbling and foaming with a noise like thunder.

She had no presentiment of danger. Suddenly the grass beneath her feet gave way. She fell, with a long scream of anguish. A sharp stake, at water-level, pierced her leg. She lay there, screaming, impaled on the pointed shaft, the bubbling torrent stained red with her blood.

The water sucked about her, threatening to drag her under. But she remained pinioned to the shore.

The pain was indescribable. She screamed as the water surged about her. She was drowning in a red tide of pain and confusion. Her skirts were waterlogged, her hair floated out like seaweed. Her hat with the ostrich feathers swirled away on the tide.

Suddenly, somewhere above her, she heard a hoarse cry for help. Then someone scrambled down the slippery bank to lift her head clear of the water.

She lay for a long time in merciful oblivion. When she opened her eyes, she could not think where she was. The pain in her leg was excruciating. As memory flooded back to her, she uttered a hoarse cry of distress. Emily was beside her in a moment. 'Hush, darling. You are safe now. You must keep very still; try not to think about your accident. Rowan's coming. He will be here tomorrow.'

Romilly turned her head away. 'I don't want Rowan,' she said fretfully. 'David saved me. I want David. Where is he?'

'David was here before you gained consciousness,' Emily told her in a soothing voice. 'He brought you some flowers.'

'But he will come back?'

Concern lay in Emily's eyes that it was David McClean who came uppermost in her daughter's mind. 'I'm afraid not for a little while,' she said, feeling that she was treading on eggshells. 'He has gone to London on business.'

'London?' Romilly rolled her head on the pillow; tears flooded down her cheeks. 'Oh, God! I'm going to die! I'm going to die!'

'No, Romilly, you are going to get well!' Emily spoke more firmly. 'But you must try to rest now.' Oh, dear Lord, she thought, I wish Rowan were here.

A nurse entered the room to check the patient's pulse and administer a mild sleeping-draught. When Romilly fell asleep. Emily rose stiffly to her feet. She had not slept for twenty-four hours. Her eyelids felt as heavy as lead, her mind dull with worry. What had gone wrong between Romilly and Rowan?

The nurse brought her a cup of tea which she could not drink for the tight lump of misery in her throat. Everyone was being so kind, but if only Rowan would come . . .

She must have fallen asleep briefly in the chair beside

Romilly's bed. When she opened her eyes, Rowan was standing beside her in the shadows.

'Oh, my dear. I'm so glad you are here.' She half-rose to her feet, stumbled, and felt his strong arms about her.

'Poor Tante Emily,' he said. 'You must be tired out with all the worry.'

Next day, Rowan walked with Dr Manton down the hospital corridor. He was elderly, with receding grey hair, and deep-set blue eyes which missed nothing.

'Sit down, Mr Tanquillan.' Manton closed the office door behind them. 'Your wife's accident must have come as a great shock to you.'

'Yes, it has,' Rowan said heavily, 'and I blame myself. If only I had come to Scotland with her it might not have happened.'

'Oh, why not?' Manton wished to hear more. The circumstances puzzled him: a handsome young husband, a bride of a few weeks who had refused to speak to him. Manton prided himself on his understanding of human nature but he could not, for the life of him, see why Mrs Tanquillan had brushed aside her husband's flowers as if they meant less than nothing to her. Manton was scarcely surprised when he received no answer to his question. He said, easily. 'No use dwelling on imponderables. We must feel thankful that your wife has not lost the child she is carrying.'

'Her child?' Rowan raised his head to stare at the doctor.

'Good heavens, man,' Manton frowned, 'you must have known that your wife is pregnant! It's early days, of course, but didn't she tell you?'

It was true then, Rowan thought, Romilly was going to have their child and he had not believed her: had preferred not to believe her.

Manton said quietly, 'There is a great deal to feel thankful for, Mr Tanquillan. The injury to your wife's leg is superficial. It will heal in time, as long as the wound is kept free from infection. All things considered, Mrs Tanquillan has had a very lucky escape.' He plucked his underlip thoughtfully. 'To be frank with you, I am more concerned, at the moment, with her mental health. Your wife is a very highly-strung young woman.'

'Yes, I realize that,' Rowan said, rubbing his hand wearily across his forehead. 'What do you suggest?'

'No use beating about the bush,' Manton walked over to the window to stare out at the bright June sky filled with scurrying white clouds. 'I would like you to talk things over with Mrs Beresford. Your wife wishes to go back to London. *I* should much prefer that she stayed here under my care. Her leg-wound is clear of infection at the moment, but she is still in a state of shock after her accident. It is really a case of choosing between two evils. Move her, and her leg may become re-infected: leave her here, and she might suffer a complete mental breakdown.'

Manton said kindly, 'I cannot be the final arbiter. It is up to you and Mrs Beresford to decide on the best course of action.' He paused. 'But my own private and personal experience of doctoring is that mental ailments are far more difficult to cure than the purely physical.'

Romilly, who had once clung to Rowan as to a lifeline, said bitterly, 'It's all his fault. If he had really cared for me, none of this would have happened! He need not come fussing round me now, it's too late!'

'You mustn't say such things,' Emily said wearily, 'they are quite untrue. Rowan is beside himself with worry over you. You must not shut him out! Think of your child!'

'I don't want his child,' Romilly retorted 'I wish it was dead! I wish I were dead! Why didn't he tell me he didn't love me? I don't want a child born of pity! I just want to go home!' Tears flooded her cheeks. '*Please* take me home! I'll die if you don't!'

CHAPTER TWENTY-ONE

A series of stretchers, reserved train compartments, nurses and ambulances were organized to take Romilly back to London, a complicated business involving two days travel and an overnight stay at a York nursing-home where the fretful invalid's wound was treated before she was given a sleeping-draught.

Emily had wired ahead to the house in Eaton Square to have a room prepared for Romilly: had made arrangements for nurses to care for her day and night.

Over dinner at the George Hotel where they were staying Emily asked Rowan if he would mind sleeping in the dressing-room adjoining Romilly's bedroom.

'Of course not, Tante Emily. I leave everything to you.' He pushed his food away, untasted. 'I only wish to God that I had come to Scotland with you. All this is my fault.'

'No, my dear! You mustn't blame yourself!' Emily felt intensely weary. 'I rely on your strength, as I have always done. There is so much to look forward to now, the baby above all!'

'Ah, yes,' Rowan said dully, 'the – baby . . .'

On the last stage of the journey, when Romilly was carried on a stretcher to a waiting ambulance, Rowan heard the cry of a newsboy near the entrance to King's Cross station.

The ragged urchin was standing near a placard on which was scrawled:
ASSASSINATION AT SARAJEVO. ARCHDUKE FERDINAND AND WIFE MURDERED IN COLD BLOOD!

Rowan thrust a penny into the lad's hand, and stuffed the

paper into his pocket to read later. His thoughts were concentrated on Romilly, lying pale and wan in the ambulance; their arrival at Eaton Square; the fuss and bustle as her stretcher was carried upstairs to her bedroom; his feeling of helplessness as he was chivvied out of the way by the nurse in attendance.

It was past midnight when he remembered the paper, and sat up in bed to read it, a stranger in an alien atmosphere, listening to faint movements in the adjoining room where his wife lay in charge of a pseudo Florence Nightingale, a heavy-bosomed lady with grey hair, and starched cuffs to her uniform.

He read: "The Archduke Franz Ferdinand and his wife, the Countess Sophie, were to-day murdered during an army review in Bosnia. Their assassin, a student named as Princip Gavrilo, was arrested at the scene of the shooting."

It was a sad story. Countess Sophie had not measured up to the requirements necessary to an Imperial Hapsburg marriage, but Franz Ferdinand had married her anyway, because he loved her; had signed away the rights of his children born of that marriage. The saddest thing of all was that Franz Ferdinand and his beloved Sophie had gone to their deaths together on their wedding anniversary. But perhaps that was what they would have wished, given the choice.

Rowan was to remember, later, that he had once asked himself what it would take to trigger off the coming Armageddon.

This was the first time he had set foot in Eaton Square since his wedding day. Now the wheel had turned full circle. He was back in the city he loathed: back to the old regime. His parental puppeteers jerked his strings remorselessly as they had always done.

At dinner in Emily Beresford's dining-room, Gervaise Tanquillan held sway: treating the occasion as a board-meeting; laying down the law over roast beef and glazed carrots.

'Someone,' Gervaise said, slicing into a roast potato, 'must go to Scarborough at once to look after things there. And you, Rowan, had better take charge here!'

Never so much as an enquiry into his own feelings, Rowan thought bitterly, or Romilly's, or Emily's. All his father cared about was the smooth running of the Tanquillan Company. Christ! How he hated him!

He could not help but feel sorry for Romilly. Poor little Romilly who had hitherto tripped through life like a gadfly, who was now faced with untold pain and suffering as the child clamoured to be born.

His mother came daily to the house, bringing fruit and flowers, so that Romilly's bedroom resembled a hot-house; an over-heated, shrouded conservatory, since Romilly refused to have the curtains opened to let in a breath of fresh air and sunshine. And nothing he could do or say made any difference.

Ever since she came home from Scotland, Romilly's face had remained a pale blob on the pillows in that darkened room, and whatever he said to her fell on deaf ears, no matter how hard he tried to penetrate her deep, inmost thoughts: to persuade her to a happier frame of mind. And then that brightly irritating nurse would appear to shoo him away before she settled her patient down for the night, when he would wander back to his own room to make ready for bed, and lie there, staring into the darkness, until daylight came with the first jubilant bird song from the trees in the Eaton Square gardens.

Courtesy demanded that he should speak to his mother but he did so coldly, with a correctness and formality which irked Rachel past bearing. She had never really wanted a child: had never felt strong maternal love for her son, but she did care a great deal about family honour. She lay wide awake, one night, thinking about it.

She had married Gervaise Tanquillan to save her father from bankruptcy: had given birth to a child as an expedient to safeguard the future of the Tanquillan Import, Export and Lighterman Company. It then came as a bitter blow when her father died soon after Rowan was born, and his estate was sold to the highest bidder.

She had watched then, with a tight feeling of misery at her heart, her childhood home desecrated by the curious crowds who had flocked there on the day of the auction to bid for the treasures she had grown up with.

She would always feel grateful to Gervaise for saving at least a few of those treasures. His sexual demands upon her ice-cool unreceptive body had seemed a necessary price to pay at the time, but the years had taught them how to evaluate and appreciate each other's fastidiousness in sexual matters. Far beyond all that lay their respect for wealth and social intercourse, the special niche they had carved for themselves.

Certain family misfortunes had drawn them closer: the importunate Oliver Tanquillan and his crazy offspring on Gervaise's side; a bankrupt father on Rachel's. And yet, even now, Rachel often yearned after her childhood home, Carlton Abbas, a russet Elizabethan house with tall chimneys and wide oak staircase, which had suited, to perfection, her affinity with its ghosts and shades; the great staircase window with its view of the garden: the clipped yew hedges and widespread lawns. She had felt no desire to procreate so long as she remained the ice-cool chatelaine of her heritage.

Rowan knew nothing of this, but Rachel had always seen her son as the result of her own misfortune. And yet he had been a charming, handsome little boy, and she had felt some pride in showing him off to her friends, in shaping his destiny, frowning upon his weaknesses, so that he would never commit the folly of marrying beneath him, as she had been obliged to do. And now the stupid, insolent young pup was all angles and elbows with her since she had scotched his love affair with a grocer's daughter.

She told her son that she wished to speak to him in private. He walked with her up the steps into the drawing-room where she shrugged off the sealskin cape, and unpinned her hat.

'Well, Rowan,' she said, 'you have scarcely spoken a civil word to me since you came to London.'

He stared hostilely at her slim, upright figure. 'Does that surprise you?'

'Yes, frankly it does.' She regarded him coolly. 'I suppose you are still harbouring a grudge against me. What a fool you are, Rowan. Did you really think that I would send Alice away? You spoke of "emotional blackmail" at the time. That is a harsh accusation for a son to level against his mother. I realized, of course, that you were overwrought, not thinking clearly about the future. That is why I chose to ignore your hurtful attitude towards me. Now you appear to be carrying on some kind of vendetta against your father and myself. I really cannot tolerate your ungentlemanly conduct any longer.'

He faced her squarely. 'But you did send Alice away.'

She laughed. 'Oh yes, for good and sufficient reasons, but not to the place you supposed.'

'What place was that, Mother?'

'Oh, come now,' she said lightly, arranging her hair in front of a mirror, 'you know that as well as I do.'

'An institution, you mean, for mentally sick and unwanted children?'

Stung to anger, Rachel asked, 'Is this some kind of game? Truth or dare?'

'Whichever,' Rowan retorted. 'It is your game, Mother.'

She said coldly, 'I resent your attitude toward me. All I have ever asked of you is to honour your commitments: to behave as a Tanquillan should behave . . .'

'To which end you felt obliged to apply emotional black-mail,' Rowan cut in. 'You knew that I would not stand by to see that child put into an orphanage – or worse. You sicken me, Mother, with your talk of family honour and behaving as a Tanquillan should behave, as if we were chesspieces, not human beings.'

Goaded to even greater anger, Rachel said, 'But it wasn't just Alice. Your concern for her was merely a subterfuge. Did you really think that I would stand by and watch you make a fool of yourself over the Grayler girl? I have met her kind before, the servant class is rife with them: cheap little housemaids with dreams of grandeur, who believed that a few furtive kisses with the master's son meant that they would one day become mistress of the house. Rest assured, Rowan, that Charlotte Grayler will never become the mistress of mine!'

'So now we come to the real truth,' he said scornfully. 'Very well, I do love Charlotte, I shall always love her. Nothing on earth can change that. I would have married her, but she made it quite clear to me that we live in different worlds. She wanted nothing from the Tanquillans. Looking at you, Mother, I can see why, because we – because you – have nothing to give a girl like Charlotte – not decency or compassion or understanding. Nothing but bloody money and a name that stinks in my nostrils!' He turned away abruptly. 'I think that is all we have to say to each other.'

The weather was humid, as if a storm was brewing. The Beresfords' house was silent apart from the rustling, white-aproned figures gliding along landings and down the staircases and the white-faced Emily moving about like a ghost, and yet the air was electric, almost, with tension, sickly with the scent of flowers in Romilly's dark and overheated room.

Sometimes the bell rang, and a servant would show Romilly's friends into the hall, bringing more flowers, making discreet enquiries. But Romilly would not see them. When Emily suggested that she should, Romilly became hysterical.

'What are we to do, Rowan? We can't go on like this,' Emily said wearily. They were at dinner together, sitting at one end of the long table, toying with the food that neither of them wanted.

'I don't know.' Rowan glanced compassionately at Emily's drawn and suffering face. 'I can't get her to respond at all.'

'If only we could make her see that she will be able to walk again eventually. I wish she would begin to take an interest in life, that we could persuade her to have the curtains open. I can't bear to think of her lying there in the dark all the time.'

'I'll see what I can do.' Rowan waved aside the dessert, feeling that sick, restless churning inside him which had made eating a near impossibility ever since his wife's accident. 'If you'll excuse me, I'll go up to her now.' He gave Emily a warm, wry little smile as he left the table. 'Wish me luck.'

Sitting beside Romilly's bed, he told her about silks and spices from the Orient, painting a vivid verbal picture of the ships coming up the Thames to dock, the glowing colours of the fabrics, the strange exotic aroma of the warehouse where the spices were unpacked. 'When you are better,' he said casually, 'we'll drive down there together.'

The room had never felt so oppressive before, with the curtains tightly closed against a warm summer evening, and the cloying scent of roses.

'Go away and leave me alone,' Romilly said wearily.

'No, I'm damned if I will!' He got up, and with a quick movement swished back the curtains.

'How *dare* you!' She covered her face with her hands, screaming at him to close the curtains, to let her die in peace.

'Stop that!' He spoke sharply; held her wrists. 'Look at me! You are not going to die. Whether you like it or not, you are going to live – and you are going to walk again!'

The nurse skittered into the room, wringing her hands. 'What has happened?'

'The curtains,' Romilly moaned, 'close the curtains!'

'For shame, sir, upsetting the patient! There, there, my dear. Yes, of course I'll close the curtains for you.'

'You'll do no such thing,' Rowan said quietly, 'I forbid it. If you have my wife's welfare at heart, you will start letting sunshine and fresh air into this room. I'd have thought that anyone in your profession would have realized that.'

The woman was trembling now with righteous indignation. 'I will report this to Madam,' she rasped. 'I have never been spoken to in such a fashion before. I think you had better leave now and let me attend to my patient.'

'Do so by all means. Turn all your attention to getting my wife up and about again as quickly as possible: start encouraging her to think about living – not dying.'

Emily was on the landing, her hand trembling slightly on the banister. 'Rowan?' She took a step forward. 'I couldn't help overhearing.'

'I'm sorry, Tante Emily. I'm afraid I didn't handle that very well.'

'Ah, but you did. Thank you, my dear. You may leave things to me now.' She touched his cheek with her lips. 'By the way, a letter has just arrived for you. It's in your room.'

The letter had been redirected from Scarborough. He recognized Aunt Kitty's handwriting at once. Of course, his aunt would not have known that he was in London. She had written to tell him that she was taking Alice to London to consult a specialist; that they, with Charlotte and Jenny, would be staying for a few days at the Gateway Hotel in Northumberland Avenue.

He glanced at the dates. Suddenly a feeling of peace came over him, that curious sensation of warmth and contentment as he realized that Charlotte was here in the city with him. He stood near the window, looking out at the square. Daylight was beginning to fade. Soon the stars would come out over the rooftops of London. It comforted him to think that Charlotte might be standing near a window somewhere, looking up at the same sky, the same stars, thinking of him.

Alice was enjoying all the fuss and novelty connected with the unexpected visit to London – staying in a hotel with porters and chambermaids, and a lift.

She had, at first, been suspicious of Aunt Kitty's motives. 'If this is a trick to get me back to that house in Eaton Square,' she cried, 'you'll have to drag me there in chains.'

'Don't be so foolish, child! I wish to go shopping among other things, and to entertain an old friend of mine, Mr Latimer.'

It had been decided beforehand that a private meeting at the hotel with the specialist in the role of a family friend would be advisable, rather than attempt to take a recalcitrant child to his consulting-room in Harley Street. Alice was delighted when her great-aunt suggested a new dress for the occasion. It was by far the most beautiful dress she had ever owned – dark blue velveteen with a cream lace collar. Swirling round her bedroom in the new creation, Alice tossed her head and laughed. 'When I am rich,' she said, stopping to admire her reflection in a cheval glass, 'I shall sort out the wheat from the chaff and – and delegate the unworthy to the bonfire.'

Half amused, half irritated by the girl's vanity, Jenny said, 'You should pay more attention to your verbs before you start chucking people on bonfires.'

Alice regarded her coolly. 'When I am rich, I shall have all the new clothes I want. Will Oakleigh will teach me to ride. I shall ride to hounds, you know, and I will be very beautiful. I shall have my hair dressed in the latest fashion, and I will throw the most wonderful parties when Aunt Kitty is dead.'

'There's gratitude for you.' Jenny got up from where she was sitting, certain in her own mind that she had had enough of Alice for the time being. 'I shouldn't let your aunt hear you talk like that if I were you.'

'I don't care. Aunt Kitty told me that I shall be rich one day.' Alice giggled suddenly. 'Then I shall marry Rowan. We will be married at Grey Wethers, in the village church, you know.'

Jenny turned at the door. 'What's wrong with Westminster Abbey?' she said scathingly.

London excited Charlotte. She had thought at first she would hate it, the noise and bustle of the crowds, the churning of the traffic, the buildings which seemed so immense, so dwarfing. But there was more to it than that, she discovered: the emerald oases of the parks, the grey-green river like a throbbing artery with its ships and bridges; the balconied crescents and unexpected squares with their tucked-away churches.

She saw, with a sense of awakening from a long, dream-filled sleep, the tombs of the kings in Westminster Abbey, the vaulted aisles and cool grey stones, and suddenly all that she had read about and pictured in her mind became real to her at last, filling her with an ecstatic awareness of other dimensions to life, so that the young Charlotte who had grown up within the confines of Scarborough with all its limitations, seemed lost to her.

She told Jenny, haltingly, of her feelings as they walked together, arm in arm, past the shops and galleries, stopping now and then to browse at bookstalls or look in antique shop windows. Jenny, with her wider experience of life, knew what Charlotte meant. The same thing had happened to her at Somerville when her old life had suddenly seemed to her like a worn-out chrysalis, when her mind was emptied of old attitudes and shibboleths. Jenny had realized a long time ago, when she came up against new ideas and ideals in an atmosphere of concentrated learning, that only certain memories and values were worth retaining, that only two things in life, intellectual freedom, and love, mattered a damn.

She had seen Charlotte as too moulded, suppressed and influenced by her upbringing, a girl who had lived vicariously through books and poetry, too gentle, withdrawn and introverted to take life by the throat and live it as it should be lived, passionately and to the full. She herself had not yet succeeded in so doing, but it was all there inside her awaiting release in her writing or intense physical action. Whichever way Jenny turned she saw challenges, things to spark off fresh ideas, new avenues to be explored. Even now she was seeking wider fields to conquer. But she had not been idle. Night after night, in Scarborough and at Grey Wethers, she had been working away at her writing, burning the midnight oil, using up her abundant mental energy in the time left over from teaching.

This was the day that Kitty Tanquillan had chosen to invite Mr Latimer to lunch. The specialist knew the girl's background; the incident of the fetish. Kitty knew of course that there was little Latimer could do at the moment except observe Alice and form certain opinions. The mania which had overtaken the mother could not be dealt with unless it occurred in the child. Kitty prayed that, in tracing and treating the symptoms early on, Alice might be spared the fate which had overtaken Martha Tanquillan.

Jenny treated Charlotte to lunch in the Lyons Corner House near Trafalgar Square. They had walked and ridden all morning, scrambling aboard omnibuses, riding on the top deck with the sun in their faces. They had just been to the National Gallery where Charlotte's thoughts had turned to those pictures she had seen in books from the penny library. Suddenly, there they were in the reality of glowing colours, far more breathtaking than she had imagined, the great Titians and Gainsboroughs in their massive gilt frames, the Turners and Reynolds, Constables and Rembrandts. She had looked at them until she felt sated with so much beauty, noticing the intricate brushmarks, thinking that the eyes and hands of those great master painters had once lingered over those very canvases. It was like looking into their souls; sharing their vision. And then, when Jenny said she was hungry, they had walked out into Trafalgar Square, and there was Nelson on his column, dominating the square with its sauntering crowds, and strutting pigeons fluttering for thrown crumbs.

'Come on, let's sit upstairs,' Jenny said, leading the way into the cafe with its bustling nippies and hot food smells. 'Over there near the window.' She laid her handbag on the table and looked quizzically at Charlotte, the quiet girl from a northern seaside town who had just realized something of the world beyond her former limited existence. London was looking its loveliest today with its hazy greens and cloudless blue sky: the flower-sellers' baskets a riot of colour, and the constant kaleidoscopic movement of people and vehicles. It struck Jenny, when they had ordered tea and Welsh rarebit, what a marvellously outgoing and expansive era they were living in, with everything changing so quickly.

'What are you thinking?' Charlotte asked.

Jenny cupped her chin in her hands and looked down at the jigsaw street patterns below: brightly-coloured hats, horses and omnibuses. 'Do you realize that horses are on their way out?' she asked, frowning. 'Just take a look at all the motor vehicles down there. Doesn't it excite you to think that, in years to come, we will look back on this as the start of a new era?'

'I hadn't really thought about it.'

'Well, *do* think about it. Doesn't it strike you as incredible that men are taking to the skies? Actually *flying*! And not just men but women, too. What was the name of that woman who flew a biplane in the aerial Derby? Mrs Buller! That's it! And what about the wireless telephone? Everything's in embryo at the moment, but it's all really happening.'

'It scares me to think of it,' Charlotte said.

'Why should it?'

'I don't know. Perhaps because everything is happening too fast. It's like going downhill on a toboggan. Once you've started you can't stop.'

233

'I don't want to stop,' Jenny said decisively. 'I want things to happen fast.' She paused. 'You know, Carlotta, I've been thinking about this job of mine. It isn't right for me. I want to be a part of all – this.' She waved her hands expansively to encompass the scene from the window. 'Perhaps coming here to London has made me more aware of what I should be doing with my life. I thought I could settle for a job that wouldn't stretch me too much, but I can't.'

'You mean you are thinking of handing in your notice? But what would you do?'

Jenny sighed. 'I'm not sure yet. I have a little money put by. I just have this awful, glorious restlessness inside me.' She laughed. 'I'm sorry, perhaps I'm talking through my hat.' They ate in silence for a while, finishing their lunch. Suddenly Jenny peered intently across the square. 'Hell,' she said, 'something's going on over there – near the gallery. I wonder what's up. Let's go and see.'

They gathered up their things, Jenny paid the bill, and they hurried out into the sunshine. Jenny grabbed Charlotte's elbow as a horse-drawn police-van, driven at speed, rounded the corner, scattering the onlookers. A great cloud of pigeons rose up, flapping their wings, startled by the thundering of hooves and the movement of the crowd.

'What is it? What's wrong?' Charlotte held onto her hat as she hurried along, propelled by Jenny.

'Suffragettes! Chained to the railings!'

Charlotte saw, between the heads and shoulders of the people straining forward to get a better view, two ordinary-looking, neatly-dressed women shackled to the railings fronting the National Gallery. There was nothing bold or brazen about them, Charlotte thought. On the contrary, they looked rather pale and nervous confronted by the gaping, jeering, laughing crowd – like people put into stocks in the old days, or pilloried for some minor offence.

But these women had committed no offence apart from causing a disturbance. All they wanted was to draw attention to their right to vote. As mothers and housewives, caring for their husbands and children; bearing, as they did, the brunt of responsibility for their families in the face of poor wages, bad housing and slum conditions. And now, as the all-important child-bearers, deprived of any say in how their country's affairs should be run, they had taken matters into their own hands at last, led by the indomitable women's freedom fighter, Emily Pankhurst.

And so it wasn't just the poor or middle-class women who saw freedom to vote as every woman's birthright, for the elegant Mrs Pankhurst was very much upper-bracket, and so was her staunchest supporter, Lady Barclay, Jenny said. But they were jeered at just the same by men who still believed, as they had always done, that a woman had no right to a say in anything, not even how many children she should bring into the world.

Other women, supporters of the ones chained to the railings, were handing out leaflets to the crowd. Two more were holding up placards: 'What do Doctors think of Women Torture?'.

Grim-faced policemen waded into the melee. Some struggled to push back the crowd while others attempted to unchain the women. Others swarmed in a body to arrest the leaflet distributors and the women holding the placards.

Charlotte watched, heart in mouth, as one of the two placards was snatched from the hands of a little woman, wearing a decent black coat and skirt, by an over-zealous policeman. The placard was trampled underfoot in the ensuing skirmish. The woman in black made no attempt to resist arrest, she simply cried out, as she was hustled away, 'Doesn't anybody *care*?'

'Yes! I do! *I* care!' Jenny shouted.

Suddenly, she darted across the road, bent down to retrieve the fallen placard, raised it aloft, and stood there, facing the crowd, a defiant, laughing figure, her hat awry, shouting to other women to join her. 'What are you afraid of?' she yelled in a high, clear voice.

'*Jenny*!' Charlotte pushed with all her might against the sheer weight of the crowd forcing her back. '*Jenny*!' She fought frantically to push her way forward. '*Jenny*!'

Suddenly the mass of bodies gave way to her insistent pushing and hammering, and she was standing on the pavement edge, trembling, with Jenny just a few feet away from her, on the other side of the road, waving her placard, grinning like a monkey, shouting gaily, '"Oh, who will stand at my right hand and keep the bridge with me?"'

'*Jenny*!'

The other placard fell as the woman carrying it was lifted up bodily by a sweating policeman and carted away to the waiting police-van.

A rough-looking man jostled Charlotte. Dirty, unshaven, wearing a cloth cap and a knotted handkerchief round his throat, he spat out, 'Bloody suffragettes! They want crucifying, the lot of them!'

Charlotte stared in disgust at his cruel, leering face. Anger boiled up in her – an anger she had never known before. Her heart was pounding in her chest. She felt suddenly recklessly angry and alive, pulsating with a strange kind of energy and purpose. She saw Jenny, the bright, indomitable Jenny, standing there waving her placard; saw the pale yet determined faces of the women chained to the railings.

The fallen placard lay where it had been thrown, on the ground, in the dust. A far cry, all this, from the books and poetry she had read. Books merely reflected reality. She had never come up against this kind of reality before, something which demanded not thought, but action.

The surging crowd about her pulsated a white-heat passion, from the spitting man beside her to those who applauded the action of the suffragettes. Some laughed, others catcalled. None was indifferent to the situation. How, then, could she simply stand there, saying nothing, doing nothing? Her eyes were fixed on the fallen placard.

With a sudden spring, she raced across the road to pick it up and lifted it high into the air, feeling a surge of pride and comradeship as she caught Jenny's eye.

CHAPTER TWENTY-TWO

Rowan and the specialist arrived at the hotel at almost the same time. Latimer had just gone up in the lift when Rowan walked into the foyer. The receptionist told him that he believed Miss Tanquillan to be engaged. 'In that case, I'll leave a note,' Rowan said. 'Will you see that my aunt receives it as soon as possible?'

He had explained briefly, in the note, that Romilly had met with an accident. Handing it to the man behind the desk, he enquired if Miss Grayler was in the hotel.

'No, sir. Miss Grayler and Miss Carfax went out directly after breakfast.'

'I see. Thank you.' He would have given anything to see Charlotte at that moment, to take courage from the touch of her hand, to pour out to her his fears for the future, his dark thoughts and loneliness, knowing that she would understand.

Love had opened up so many new dimensions. That morning in the meadow at Grey Wethers . . . Love seemed to him a great warm tide bubbling into the deepest recesses of his being. He wanted Charlotte in every way that a man wants the woman he loves – passionately, physically and forever. Poor Romilly, why had he never wanted her like that?

His meeting with Charlotte had happened too late, but he had known from the beginning that he wanted her for his wife. He still railed against the inevitability of their situation. Life without her was intolerable. The thought of her being somewhere in this city, not knowing where, when they might be together, tormented him. In desperation, he wrote a second note, addressed it to her, and left it with the man behind the desk.

Charlotte and Jenny were not detained long at the police station. The heavily moustached desk-sergeant made careful enquiries: wrote everything down laboriously in a thick ledger. The two young women confronting him were not bona-fide members of the suffrage movement, simply onlookers carried away on the spur of the moment to involve themselves in the demonstration. None of the chained or picketing women, detained for further questioning, knew them. The sergeant, inured to this kind of partisanship, let them go with a warning to behave themselves in future.

'And what if we refuse?' Jenny asked him mischievously.

The man sighed deeply. 'Then I hope to God you'll misbehave yourselves somewhere else next time.'

Alice was cock-a-hoop over her meeting with Mr Latimer. So far as she was concerned, he was simply an old friend of her great-aunt's who had paid her a great deal of attention and asked her a lot of interesting questions which she had answered in her own startling, inimitable fashion, making him laugh and raise his bushy eyebrows in surprise. She had had a wonderful time, she later told Charlotte, and Mr Latimer had complimented her on her dress.

'By the way, Aunt Kitty wants to see you,' she said lazily, when she had run out of steam about her dress and the favourable impression she had made on the attentive Mr Latimer.

As Charlotte went along to Miss Kitty's room, she could not help thinking how much Alice had changed in the past weeks. That air of sweetness and vulnerability which had first captured her heart was gone now. Alice seemed very sure of herself all of a sudden; proud, sly and somewhat cruel. She wondered if the old woman had done a wise thing in telling the girl that she would be rich one day. She knew, with a feeling of loss, that Alice no longer needed her as she used to.

Kitty Tanquillan was seated in a high-backed chair near the window, looking down at the busy London street below, the threading carriages and motor-cars, the people thronging the pavements. The windows were slightly open, letting in the sound of the traffic.

'Ah, there you are,' the old woman said. 'Close the door. I want to talk to you.'

'Is anything wrong? Is it bad news about Alice?'

Kitty Tanquillan looked up at Charlotte, struck anew by her beauty, her air of breeding, the amazing sheen and colour of her hair.

'No,' she said, 'the news concerning Alice is far brighter than I thought. Mr Latimer was greatly impressed by what he termed her "engaging personality, honesty and originality". My fears for her sanity were, apparently, groundless. Alice, in Latimer's view, is just as sane as you or I. She is highly-strung, of course, but he has prescribed for that. All she needs is security, new interests to keep her mind off the past and, in time, a loving relationship with a member of the opposite sex.'

Kitty pulled a wry face. 'Indeed, all Alice needs is what every other woman has needed since the world began. But that is not why I sent for you. You had better sit down, my dear.' She paused. 'I have received a letter from Rowan, saying that his wife has met with an accident.'

Charlotte leaned forward to grip Miss Kitty's hand. 'An – accident? Is it serious?'

Kitty said bleakly, 'She was very nearly drowned. She might have been swept away except that . . .' the old woman's voice faltered, 'her leg was impaled on a spike in the river.'

A sudden memory of Alice sticking a pin into a witchcraft doll invaded Charlotte's mind. 'Oh God,' she whispered. 'But surely you don't think that . . .' Her voice died away, but she knew the same thought had occurred to Miss Tanquillan.

Kitty shrugged her shoulders helplessly. 'I don't know what to think. Commonsense tells me that it cannot be true, and yet . . .' She cast a worried glance at Charlotte. For all her quiet self-containment, the girl was a child in Miss Kitty's eyes, a child with little experience of the world, who could be easily hurt, but the whole truth must be told.

The old woman's voice was both level and compassionate as she said, 'One thing we must feel thankful for is that Romilly did not lose the child she is expecting.'

Charlotte brushed her forehead with her hand, as if the words had not sunk in, a puzzled gesture which touched Kitty to the heart.

'I am sorry, my dear,' she said kindly. 'Unfortunately, there is no way to make palatable an unpalatable truth.' She paused. 'Rowan handed in my letter to the receptionist when I was otherwise engaged. He left one for you also.' She handed Charlotte the envelope. 'He cares for you a great deal, you know.'

'Does he?' Charlotte turned the envelope listlessly, making no attempt to open it.

'You know he does!' Kitty sighed. 'Please close the window. The noise of the traffic has given me a headache.'

When Charlotte had done so, Kitty said, 'Aren't you going to open the letter?'

Charlotte attempted to smile. 'It might be as well if I tore it up without reading it.'

'You mustn't do that.' Kitty spread out her hands in a gesture of supplication. 'Oh, my dear, try not to feel bitter. You must not throw away your chance of happiness as I once did, when I was too young, too stupid, and too proud to realize that nothing else matters except taking everything that life has to offer while you are young and in love. There'll be all the time in the world afterwards for regrets, when you are an old woman like me.'

'But Romilly is going to have Rowan's child!' Charlotte turned desperately to face Miss Kitty. 'What kind of person would I be to come between them now?'

'But you love him, and he loves you,' Kitty reminded her.

'Yes, I do love him!' The floodgates opened at last as Charlotte spilled out her thoughts unchecked. 'I loved him from the moment I saw him at the house in Chalice Walk. He was so gentle, so kind, so thoughtful. I had never felt that way before. I wanted him to touch me, to hold me in his arms! Then I felt ashamed of myself when I knew he was engaged to marry Romilly.'

She turned her head away, fighting to hold back her tears. 'Then when he did marry her, I couldn't bear being under the same roof with them. I used to hear her voice on the stairs, calling to him. I would hear music behind closed doors as he played to her. I would stand in the garden in the early hours of the morning when I couldn't sleep, and look up at the windows of their room, and hate myself . . . I felt so cheap, so – so sick with jealousy!'

'Oh, my child. My dear child . . .'

'No, please listen to me, Miss Kitty. All I wanted then was to get away from him! When I came to Grey Wethers, I felt more at peace. I felt I could make a new life for myself. I thought I had succeeded, until he followed me there. I knew that I should not have seen him again, but I wanted to! I could not prevent myself!' Her breath caught on a sob. 'Then, when we came to London, I felt more sure of myself; less vulnerable. Jenny helped me. I saw in her the kind of person I wished to be, strong and independent. Can't you see, Miss Kitty, how hard I have tried not to give in? How hard I've struggled to put Rowan out of my mind? But if I saw him again, how strong would I be then?'

'Open the letter,' Kitty advised. 'Find out what he has to say.'

Charlotte tore open the envelope. 'He wants me to meet him tomorrow, near the National Gallery! Oh, how – funny!'

The National Gallery, scene of her recent involvement with the suffragettes. There seemed a bitter irony in that as she remembered how strong and independent had felt then, with Jenny beside her. Now she realized that she could never be strong and independent where Rowan was concerned.

'You will go,' Kitty asked, 'to please me?'

'Yes, if you really want me to,' Charlotte said dully, 'but only to tell him that it is all over between us.'

She settled her wide-brimmed hat more firmly on her head as she waited for Rowan, anchoring her hat-pins in place against a capricious breeze.

She had rehearsed, all the way to Trafalgar Square, what she would say to him: had felt proudly defiant as she stepped from the omnibus onto a pigeon-crowded pavement. But as the minutes ticked by, her confidence slowly dissolved. Her legs felt like jelly beneath her skirts, her hat kept bouncing up on her newly-washed hair, and the stand-up frill of her bodice felt both hot and uncomfortable beneath her chin.

She saw Rowan before he saw her, and stepped back, in alarm, to delay the moment of their meeting. But how worried he looked; how careworn.

She watched him coming towards her, knowing the dull pain at her heart was caused by jealousy. She was eaten up with jealousy of Romilly.

Were all men liars and cheats, she wondered, professing to love one woman while impregnating another?

Heat surged up beneath her undergarments. Cheeks scarlet with shame, she turned, intending to hurry away, but found she could not. As a cloud of pigeons rose up, flapping, she heard him call out her name. 'Charlotte! Thank God you're here!'

'I came because Miss Kitty asked me to,' she said defiantly.

'You are angry with me,' he said. 'I can't blame you for that. I know what you're thinking.'

She looked so vulnerable, standing there, her cheeks flushed, her eyes downcast.

'Look at me, Charlotte,' he said firmly, taking hold of her hands. 'Look at me!'

'I'd rather not.'

'Because if you did, you would realize that everything I have ever told you is true. You are the only woman I have ever loved.'

She looked up at him then, her hazel-green eyes flashing fire. 'Why don't you go away and leave me alone? What is it you want of me? Go back to your wife!' She hated herself for her bitterness and – envy. She had never known what it was to feel jealous of anyone before. Perhaps this was a lesson the Lord, in His wisdom, had decided to teach her to topple her from her perch. It was so easy to stand back from life as an onlooker, to feel sorry for the afflicted – the deaf and dumb, the lonely, the fat and grotesque people of the world – never having been deaf, dumb, lonely, fat or grotesque oneself. Now she understood something of Maggie's jealousy towards herself that day on

Oliver's Mount; Alice's possessive jealousy concerning Rowan. 'Oh, God! Please, *please* go away and leave me alone!'

He gave her his handkerchief to dry her eyes. 'You know that's impossible, because I love you so much. Give me this one day, at least. Come with me . . .'

'Where to?'

'I don't know. Anywhere! Does it really matter? I don't give a damn, just as long as we are together.'

He strode to the pavement's edge and hailed a taxi; told the driver to take them to the Embankment, where they stood, side by side, staring down at the oily green water running down to the sea.

'I never thought that I would come back to my old job,' he said, watching the dazzle of the sun on the water: the widespread ripples fanned out from a passing tug butting its way upstream. 'I have always hated London, or thought I did. It's different today: an enchanted city, because you are with me.'

'We are leaving London tomorrow,' Charlotte said dully, noticing Rowan's hand on the parapet, thinking how strong and warm it was; fighting desperately against the love she felt for him.

'Leaving? But you can't! I won't let you! I need you so much, Charlotte! I can't bear the thought of losing you!' His hands were suddenly on her face, tracing the curve of her cheekbones with gentle fingers.

'I must,' she said harshly, fighting a silent, inner battle against her feelings. 'Alice has seen the specialist. Miss Kitty wants to go home. There's nothing to stay here for now.'

Rowan frowned suddenly. 'The specialist! What did he say about Alice?'

'There's nothing to worry about . . .'

'Thank God for that!'

Charlotte unpinned her hat with the green ribbons, letting the breeze from the river ruffle her hair; easing the collar of her dress with nervous fingers, her mind in a turmoil as Rowan said gently, 'I need you, Charlotte! Please don't leave me! Stay with me!'

She frowned. 'Stay here, in London, you mean?' The very thought of so doing almost weakened her resolve – until she remembered Romilly. 'But that's impossible! I have my living to earn, my own life to live!' Then, gazing down at the river, she knew how much she wanted to stay with Rowan. Alice no longer needed her as she used to, but there were other people who did: her own family, Dadda, her mother, and Joey.

'I can't,' she said wearily. And then, because she was so much in love with Rowan, and so tired of fighting her emotions, she said, with a catch in her voice, 'Let us just live for today; not think about tomorrow.'

Rowan caught hold of her hand, and they walked along together for a while, two people in love in a teeming city full of people who, if they noticed them at all, did so because they were beautiful to behold, a tall, handsome young man and a girl with copper-coloured hair walking together in the bright sunshine of a July morning.

Presently, they crossed the road near Chelsea Bridge to look at the tall Georgian houses with their canopied balconies covered with clustering wisteria and purple clematis.

'I wonder who stood on those balconies long ago,' Charlotte said wistfully, imagining the flutter of fans, the wide-skirted dresses and periwigs of another age, another time. 'You know, Rowan, they might still be watching us.'

'Who, darling?'

She shivered suddenly. 'Nobody. Just – ghosts!' And yet a trick of light on a window-pane could have been the shimmer of a white dress near a drawn-back shutter, and perhaps all the people who had once trodden those shallow, worn steps to the front door were still inside the house, trapped in an eternal time bubble.

'What are you thinking?' Rowan asked.

'That nothing ever dies. I have always held the notion that, one day, somehow, somewhere, we shall be given the chance to relive our loveliest moments on earth; to rectify all our mistakes; to make amends for the wrong we have done to others. I can't quite explain, but I think that, when we die, we will see the world laid out like a great contour map, with all its rivers and valleys clearly marked; that we shall be able to pinpoint the exact moments we wish to live again and again. That would be heaven! But there would be hell, too, if we were obliged to relive all our mistakes.'

'It would be hell indeed, if I were obliged to relive mine,' Rowan said. 'I have not been the kindest of husbands. But at least Romilly would be given the chance to rectify her mistake in marrying me.'

'And if ever I came back,' Charlotte said desperately, 'I would want to go back to watching the tugs on the river, before I started this foolish conversation.'

They ate, when they were hungry, at a small restaurant near Westminster Abbey. When Rowan suggested they went into the church, they sat for a while in a side chapel listening to the soft swish of women's skirts, the tap, tapping of feet on the cool stone slabs.

Charlotte's cheeks were pale now, her face shadowed by her hat-brim, her hands clasped together as if she were praying. Perhaps she was, if thought concentrated on the person beside her could be called praying, or attempting, in that quiet place, to come to terms with her emotions concerning him.

The silence was broken suddenly by the opening notes of Bach's Toccata and Fugue in D Minor. Sensing Rowan's tenseness, she glanced up at him. He had lifted his head to listen with a raptness that puzzled her. It occurred to her that he looked the way she felt when she first read 'Adonais', and she knew instinctively that she must not intrude. No matter how deep the feeling between them, there were moments impossible to share with anyone else.

They did not speak until they were outside in the sunshine. 'I wanted to be a musician,' he said at last. 'A concert pianist. I've never told you before how much music means to me. I'm sorry, darling, if I seemed to withdraw from you a little while ago. It simply struck me what a desert my life has become. What things might have been possible if I had not been born a Tanquillan. I wished – prayed – back there, that things might, one day, be different, for us. I wonder if God, if there is a God, listens to prayers like that. Do you believe in God?'

'Sometimes I do, when I am happy. Other times, I'm not so sure. But I prayed too; prayed that He would forgive my petty spite and jealousy. I have fought so hard against loving you, knowing it was wrong. But I can't help it.'

'Have you thought, my darling, as I have, that this has been our wedding day?' he asked gently. 'Whether or not we deserve it.'

He stopped at a flower-seller's barrow to buy her a sheaf of roses. 'Your wedding bouquet,' he said hoarsely, bending to kiss her.

Then suddenly he was gone, snatched away from her by the crowds thronging the pavement, because there was nothing left to say.

In the distance came the bright, brassy music of a military band. As people pressed forward to watch the parade pass by, Charlotte remembered, with a terrible fear at her heart, her dream of marching men in a wilderness of skeletal trees where no birds sang.

Clutching her bouquet, she went up to Jenny's room on the first floor.

Jenny was packing her things. 'It's no use,' she said, 'I can't go back to Grey Wethers. I must stay here in London where I belong. I'll stay with a friend of mine in Bloomsbury: find a job to tide me over for the time being, until . . .'

'Until – what?'

'Until war comes, I suppose. It *is* coming, you know, and if it does, I want to be in the thick of it. I shall go to France as a nurse or an ambulance-driver.' She looked up from her packing. 'I wish you would stay on in London too, Carlotta.'

'No. I'm sorry, Jenny, I can't! If war comes, I must go home to my own people. My parents will need me if my brothers are called up.' Her lips trembled. 'But what about Harry? I thought you cared for him.'

'I do,' Jenny said unhappily. 'I care for him a great deal, but tell him I'm sorry. Tell him he'll be far better off without a crazy, muddled girl like me.'

'Perhaps he won't think so.'

'It isn't just the war,' Jenny shrugged her shoulders uneasily, 'it's – everything! Alice is beginning to get on my nerves, and I'm not very happy at Grey Wethers.' She folded a blouse and stowed it inside her suitcase. 'I guess Oxford spoilt me for the country life. But I'll miss you, Carlotta, more than I can say, and I suppose that I shall miss Kitty Tanquillan too in a strange kind of way, but life's for living, and I intend to live mine to the full for as long as it lasts.'

It was dusking over when Kitty, Charlotte and Alice returned to Grey Wethers. Alice was petulant because her holiday in London was over, because she had seen the city from a different angle: had found it a pleasant experience shopping for pretty clothes instead of half-rotten bananas and savoury ducks; living in a luxurious hotel with a lift to all floors, scarlet flock wallpaper, shining brass, and potted palms in the foyer, with a top-hatted commissionaire to open the doors for her. A taste of wealth had made her greedy for more wealth, lazy and bad-tempered; irritable with Charlotte and her aunt.

Kitty Tanquillan, on the other hand, could scarcely wait to get home, away from the roar and clatter of London beyond her bedroom windows. Did people never go to sleep there? The noise seemed to go on all night, and she was too old to appreciate being robbed of her sleep.

When Jenny told Miss Kitty of her decision to stay on in London, the old woman said sharply, 'Don't you think you are being very foolish and headstrong?' Then her face softened at Jenny's flushed cheeks and concerned expression. She sighed. 'But you are young and must do as you think best. What have you planned to do?'

'I know someone in Bloomsbury who might put me up for the time being. I'm sorry, Miss Tanquillan, I don't want to let you down over Alice. Indeed, if you wish me to go back with you to Grey Wethers until you find a replacement, I will do so.'

'That is generous of you, but it is summertime and I see no harm in allowing Alice to run free for a while. There will be plenty to occupy her time. I'll get Will to teach her to ride. The fresh air and exercise will build her up. In September, once she has gained her confidence, I shall send her to a day-school in Devizes.'

And so Jenny had stayed behind. She saw them off at Paddington, an indomitable figure in her shapeless oatmeal skirt and broad-brimmed black hat. Charlotte had clung to her briefly, knowing that she would miss Jenny's outgoing personality and sensitive intelligent mind.

'Take care. Keep in touch,' Charlotte said, as the carriage doors began to slam and the guard unfurled his green flag. But she had not realized just how much she would miss Jenny until the journey was over and the carriage swept up the drive of Grey Wethers.

When Alice and Miss Kitty had gone to bed, Charlotte sat near her bedroom window drinking in the sweetness of the night. The scent of stocks and roses was almost unbearably heady. She glanced at the flowers in a blue and white bowl on her dressing-table – her 'wedding bouquet'.

Filled with an intense longing for Rowan and Jenny, she began jotting down the words of a poem. The words had been clamouring all day for release. She wrote:

> 'When I am dead, you will find me
> In the wind that ruffles the young wheat,
> Where I have longed to be.
> I shall dwell in leaves that whirl on autumn days,
> And the still plenitude that holds the earth
> After the summer's heat.
> I shall be
> That shade that flecks the dappled ground
> Under the lilac tree.
> All wheeling, light and moving things,
> The sun that glances on a window-pane,
> Stars, ice-brilliant, aflame
> In winter skies;
> Fir-tips stung by frost;
> Complexity of light between boughs,
> The last glow before the ashes sink.

The intangible I shall live in fleeting things
Which mock my helplessness, in life,
To give them substance.
Dazzled ever by a seagull's flight,
Thick leaves, a bonfire's smoke
Blue against twilight,
Pain is closely bound with my delight.
But when Death comes to bring release,
Then I will move
Swiftly as clouds among the distant hills,
Nebulous as mist, at peace,
Inheritor of all I love.'

She looked critically at what she had written, and put it away.
She had no death-wish; life was too beautiful and precious for
that. Jenny had imbued her with something of her own
eagerness for change and new experiences.

She remembered her schooldays. Her teachers were genteel
elderly ladies who ran a small private school in Ramshill Road,
delicate maiden ladies who taught their pupils good manners,
cooking, sewing and the three 'R's'. Extra-curricular lessons –
French, German and music – were provided, at extra cost, by
peripatetic teachers, but her parents, with four other children
to feed and clothe, were unable to afford such luxuries. 'In any
case,' Filly had said, 'what's the use of Charlotte learning a
foreign language? Who would she be able to speak it to if she
did?' As for music, how could she practise that, since they did
not possess a piano?

And so she had been educated in a kind of mental nunnery,
conditioned in gentleness and correct deportment, her mind
fed on what the genteel ladies termed 'nice' poetry and
Arthurian legends. She had emerged from that dame-school
with a questing mind which her sketchy education had done
nothing to feed or stretch.

But the hours she had spent with Jenny had honed her mind
to a sharper awareness of all she had missed, and her
relationship with Rowan had made her realize the enduring
nature of love. At least she had one shining day to remember,

and if life contained only a few such days, it was better to have lived them, like a butterfly in the sun, than to face the rest of one's life without memories. Smiling sadly, she thought that the butterfly simile was an apt one. She felt, at this moment, like a bright-winged Red Admiral newly emerged from its chrysalis, a creature released from the inactive larva state, from the hard sheath of her old ignorance which, foolishly, she had once believed to be wisdom.

It had taken London, Jenny, Rowan and Kitty Tanquillan to teach her that life could be lived freely, expressively – even dangerously – without damaging the soul. As long as there was love.

Romilly thought, as long as I lie here, as long as I make no attempt to walk, I am not a beastly cripple but a whole woman.

Her former, sympathetic nurse had been replaced by a more efficient but impartial woman with a cheerful smile and a 'now, now, this won't do,' attitude towards her patient, whom Romilly loathed. This woman, Nurse Brown, had said, when Romilly begged her to draw the curtains, 'If you want them closed so badly, Mrs Tanquillan, why don't you try walking? Your leg's on the mend now, and I'm here to help you. I won't let you fall. Just think how pleased your husband would be if I told him that you had made the effort.'

'I can't. I can't!' She had dissolved into tears. Nobody knew what she was suffering, and no-one apparently cared, least of all Rowan. The hand-mirror she kept in the drawer beside her bed confirmed her worst fears. Her face was pale and drawn, with great dark circles beneath her eyes. Her hair was lank, the bump on her nose seemed bigger than ever.

She turned her face to her pillow and wept for herself and her misfortunes, remembering the night she had hacked off her hair by candlelight. She had felt herself to be ugly and unloved then – but now! She could not bear the thought of getting out of her safe, warm bed to appear before her friends holding onto a stick; misshapen, bloated and repulsive.

If she had known then what she knew now, she would not

have cared tuppence about her hair – or Rowan either. She had wasted her most precious years worrying about Rowan, wanting to appear beautiful in his eyes. How could she have been so blind, so stupid. Rowan had never loved her, she knew that now. He was cruel and insensitive. She stored up in her mind all the hurt he had done her. One night, when he came to her room, she unleashed those pent-up accusations in a torrent of words.

He had bent down to kiss her, saying how much better she looked, pleased because she seemed to be making progress at last.

'I'm not better,' she said in a low, harsh voice. 'How dare you come to my room to patronize me in such a fashion? I will never be "better" as you put it, thanks to you.'

'You will be, in time,' he said patiently.

'Oh, you'd like to believe that, wouldn't you?' she said scornfully. 'It would ease your conscience to see me crawling round this house like a maimed animal. It is all your fault. Everything that has happened to me is your fault. This child I'm carrying! What it must have cost you to make love to me after the way you treated me on our wedding night: standing there like a block of wood, letting a servant insult me; admonishing *me*, not her! I shall never forgive you for that. And afterwards, leaving me in that damned house all by myself for hours on end! Not caring that I was half out of my mind with boredom. You cared more for that bloody half-witted cousin of yours than you ever cared for me!'

'Romilly, please . . .'

'It's the truth,' she cried. 'I saw the way you carried her into the house that night she made such a fool of herself. She fitted very snugly into your arms. Are you in love with Alice? Is that it?'

'For God's sake, Romilly, you don't know what you are saying!'

'Oh don't I? You have never looked at me that way. *Never*! It has always been Alice, Alice, Alice! God, what kind of a man are you to want to make love to a child?'

Her face was bloated with tears, she could hardly speak for

sobbing, and yet she went on accusing him. 'And when I told you that I thought I was pregnant, what did you say? Nothing! Not even that you were glad or happy! You looked at me as if I were a stranger; as if you didn't really believe me. But I *am* pregnant! I am going to have your child! Or is the thought so repugnant to you? Was it so repugnant to you that you could not bear to go with me to Scotland? I asked you to go with me, but what did you say? You said no. You had to get back to Scarborough, to your bloody, boring job.'

'I'm sorry, my dear. So sorry . . .'

Her whiplashing words went on. 'Sorry? You weren't there when I needed you most! I might have been drowned if it hadn't been for David McClean! It was David who saved my life, not you. Not you, my – reluctant husband! David is more a man than you could ever be. That is why I want you to leave this house now. Go back to your beloved Scarborough – to Alice – or go to the devil if you like, but go away and leave me alone! I never want to see you again!'

Rowan turned away, tight-lipped, powerless to defend himself against her abuse, knowing her precariously-balanced mental state.

Turning at the door, he said slowly, 'Forgive me for having made you so unhappy.'

'Where are you going?' she asked shrilly.

'I don't know. There are so few avenues of escape left to me.'

He walked along the dark avenues of his mind, the Hound of Heaven at his heels.

> 'I fled Him, down the night and down the days;
> I fled Him, down the arches of the years;
> I fled Him, down the labyrinthine ways
> Of my own mind; and in the midst of tears . . .'

London seemed a desert once more now that Charlotte had gone away from him. He was powerless to help Romilly. He had no liking for the past, no hopes for the future. All he possessed was the memory of one shining day – the rest was failure; failure

252

as a man, a son, a husband and lover. He would be given no chance to fail as a father.

War was coming, that much was certain. He clung to that one certainty as a condemned man to a rosary. Perhaps that was the reason for his failure. He had never wholly believed in God, not as some people did. He had always hoped there might be a God, a loving Father watching over His children, but he doubted it.

He walked slowly along the Chelsea Embankment where he and Charlotte had walked together what seemed like a million light-years ago, remembering the colour of her hair, the sweetness of her smile, the touch of her hand on his; every word they had spoken to each other, how she had stopped to gaze at the Georgian houses opposite: her words, 'I have always held the notion that, one day, somehow, somewhere, we shall be given the chance to relive our loveliest moments on earth.'

Nothing had changed very much. The river still ran, green and oily between its banks; tugs still butted against the tide.

He saw himself as a misfit, as Oliver Tanquillan had been. He could never go back to his peaceful life in Scarborough. He had put his cottage up for sale. He could not go back to his old life at his parents' house in Eaton Square, nor did he wish to do so. His life as the son of Sir Gervaise Tanquillan was over, he knew that. He could never live under the same roof again with his father and mother. He had sacrificed all that he was prepared to sacrifice: his honour, his independence.

He remembered, in a dark dream of despair, his early life, his formative years, spent as a small, helpless puppet on a string, dancing to their tune; the misery of his realization that they did not love him; all those sad days when he had wanted nothing more than to run barefoot on warm golden sand as the poor children did; to study music, to become a musician. He wondered what his life would have been like had he possessed the courage to break free, as Oliver Tanquillan had broken free.

Now, not only the Hound of Heaven but the hounds of war were at his heels. Europe was a great melting-pot of discontent. The tapestry of war was already woven in vivid, unalterable colours. The assassination of Archduke Ferdinand at Sarajevo had put the match to the gunpowder.

He was sick and tired of fighting meaningless battles with his parents; tired of trying to justify his own existence in an alien atmosphere of soft, clinging wealth and emotional blackmail. Life must have more to offer than this. If not, why live at all?

He watched, for a while, the oily river flowing between its imprisoning embankments; the ships and tugs heading towards the freedom of the sea. Suddenly the weather changed. A thin, diaphanous mist curled inland, bringing with it a light, silvery rain which reminded him of Wiltshire and the piercingly sweet scent of roses in the cottage gardens; the joy he had once felt in a fortnight's freedom, as a child released from his parental prison, with a gob-stopper in his cheek and his teeth stained black with liquorice.

He walked, face uplifted to the falling rain, along the Embankment, thinking of Charlotte, loving her, knowing at last what he must do to make things right, to salve his conscience, to live up to his quintessential ideals of manhood.

He had so much to thank Charlotte for: his new awareness of beauty, of poetry. He smiled. 'To Lucasta, on going to the Wars', he thought. How did it go? Ah yes.

'I could not love thee, Dear, so much,
Loved I not Honour more.'

PART TWO

CHAPTER ONE

Filly Grayler sallied forth, in her best navy skirt and jacket, to watch the aerial display from the Esplanade. But even as she joined the crowd lining the railings, she knew that there was something in the air beside those new-fangled aeroplanes, a kind of restless expectancy which made her flesh creep beneath her stiff whalebone corsets, her scalp tingle beneath her daring new hat with the artificial roses.

If God had meant us to fly, He'd have given us wings, she thought, shading her eyes with a gloved hand. She had no patience with this Aviation Week which had set the skies over Scarborough buzzing with the sound of engines, and yet she had been unable to resist the temptation to see for herself the exploits of the daredevil pilot, B. C. Hucks, whom the newspapers had dubbed: 'the cleverest looping airman'.

She stood breathlessly looking out to sea as a plane rose higher and higher in a cloudless sky. Her heart almost stopped beating as the plane hovered momentarily, like a bird of prey, then zoomed down towards the shining expanse of blue water. Good God, she thought, he's going to crash, and turned her head away, not daring to look. Then, peeping between her fingers, she saw that seemingly frail structure of stretched canvas and struts lifting skyward again as the pilot effortlessly looped the loop.

Mercy on us, Filly thought, what is the world coming to? All this to ensnare bits of lads into joining the Royal Flying Corps.

War restlessness was eating into all their lives. She was sick and tired of listening to Albert reading aloud from the newspapers, asking questions she could not answer. How did she know why the British Fleet had visited Russia? Why the

Czar and Czaritza had been photographed with Admiral and Lady Beatty aboard the flagship of the British squadron?

All Frank and Harry talked about these days was war, when it would start, how long it would last. Frank said, his face beaded with sweat, his eyes brilliant with hope, that he wanted to get in it, to have a go at the Germans before it was all over. She knew why. Frank fancied himself in a smart uniform; saw himself as the saviour of his country, the swashbuckling young Frank Grayler beating the Germans single-handed; indomitable and undefeatable in his smiling, youthful conceit.

'Oh! And what do you suppose will happen to your dad and me if you go away?'

'Aw, come on, Ma. It can't last all that long . . .'

She had raised her head like an animal scenting danger. 'Promise me you won't do anything silly.'

'Like what?'

'Like taking it into your head to join up without telling me.'

Filly possessed an uncanny propensity for reading Frank's mind. Only last week, he had been tempted to nip into The Green Howards' drill hall in North Street and take the King's shilling. He would have done it too, had it not been for Joe's restraining hand on his sleeve.

'Don't do it like this, Frank,' he said quietly, 'not without telling them first. Ma would never get over it.'

Harry was with them at the time, peering in at the drill hall's flag-draped vestibule.

'What about you, Harry?' Frank asked in a taut voice. 'What do you think?'

'I think Joe's right. If you join now, so will I.' He and Frank had always done things together. 'But that would mean leaving Dad in the lurch. We can't just spring it on him. Who would see to the warehouse; the deliveries?'

Frank sighed impatiently. His feet were itching to get inside that drill hall. 'And what about you, Joe? When Harry and I go, will you come with us?' He was never too sure about Joe, the weaker brother.

'Of course I will,' Joe said loyally.

'Great!' Frank seized his brothers' arms. 'We'll leave it for

258

the time being then. but one of these days . . .'

They had marched together along North Street, arms linked, the three Grayler lads, all for one and one for all, secure in their brotherly trinity, laughing and unafraid.

Watching the plane looping the loop over the watered-silk sea, Filly thought how little children knew about their parents. She supposed that Frank in particular found his job restrictive, and that was why he railed at times against working for his father; always wanting to change things, to modernize the shop, growing impatient when Albert pointed out the drawbacks. *She* knew all the drawbacks, because they discussed them at night in the privacy of their bedroom: shortage of money, and the fact that the shop didn't belong to them. Now, with this new worry about war, Albert said that if it came there were bound to be food shortages, perhaps even rationing. Then it was left up to Filly to comfort him as she had done all through their life together; to make excuses for Frank's impatience.

'Frank's young and daft,' she would say. 'Besides, if rationing comes, we'll all be in the same boat. All the other grocers too. It won't be just us.'

'I know, love. But I've worked hard to build up the business; to serve my customers, to give you and the children the best of everything.'

'You have given us the best. We'll manage somehow. We always have. You worry far too much.'

One night, when they were getting undressed and Filly was standing in front of the mirror brushing her hair, Albert said, 'I thought, when I lost my first dog, that I would never have another. A grand little dog, she was, a border collie. I was twelve years old at the time. I nearly broke my heart when Bess died. Then my father bought me another dog for my thirteenth birthday.' He smiled. 'I think I resented it at first because it wasn't Bess. Then, after a while, I grew to love the other dog just as much.'

Filly stopped brushing her hair to stare at him. 'I know now that happiness in any shape or form can never be written off as a loss.'

'What do you mean?' Filly asked. 'Whatever made you say that?'

Albert shook his head. 'I don't know. I was just thinking that love is never wasted. No matter what happens now, we've had a lot of good years, a lot of happiness together, haven't we, Mother?'

'Yes. But I can't bear to hear you talk like that, as if it is all over and done with.'

Albert smiled sadly. 'I'm sorry, love. I just wanted you to know how I feel.'

The incident unnerved Filly. She had taken to watching him carefully afterwards, but Albert seemed much as usual except – that his feet seemed unsteady on the stairs, and his hand trembled slightly on the banister rail.

Towards the end of June, Frank had bunched up the pillows on his bed and lit a cheroot. His wedding to Madge was fixed for next Easter. By that time they hoped to have saved up enough money for a house of their own, but things weren't going too well in the savings department. Most of the money Madge earned as secretary to a wealthy old man, engaged in writing his memoirs, was soon frittered away on new clothes and fripperies: shoes, gloves, outrageous hats, and French perfume. Now, Frank thought, with war looming on the horizon, he and Madge should get married as soon as possible. He did not fancy going off to fight for his country and leaving Madge as a single woman – prey to the thousand natural shocks the flesh is heir to. It wasn't that he didn't trust her, but she was a damned attractive girl who made no secret of the fact that she had had any amount of admirers before he came along.

'What's worrying you?' Harry asked, acutely aware of his brother's moodiness; his preoccupation with the cracks on the ceiling.

'I want to get married,' Frank said, getting up and striding about the room like Jove irritated by his own thunder. 'Not next Easter, but now!' He turned fiercely to his brother. 'Have you ever had the feeling that you want to run, but can't because your legs are shackled? That's the way I feel. I want to fly like that bloody airman chap, Hucks. I want things to start happening fast. But nothing's happening to me at all. I'm bogged down, Harry! Bogged down to that bloody warehouse, to all those kegs of currants and sultanas! I'm sick and tired of it! War's coming! I want to be a part of it! I wish like hell it would start tomorrow or the next day. I can't stand all this hanging about!'

Harry knew exactly what Frank meant. He was tinged with the same kind of restlessness since his meeting with Jenny. He had never mentioned that night to Frank. At times he could scarcely believe that it had happened at all; Jenny's lips on his; their sudden, warm and thrilling contact in a dark, mysterious shelter, with the sound of the sea in the distance and stars burning overhead. But Harry was more level-headed than Frank, far more thoughtful and circumspect.

'Don't be soft,' he said, 'if you did get married right away, where would you live? You haven't saved enough money for your own place yet.' He added scornfully, 'At the rate you are going, you never will.'

Frank paced rapidly the strip of haircord carpet between their beds. 'Madge's parents would let us have a couple of rooms,' he said eagerly, 'and Madge wants to get married just as much as I do. Well, you know how it is – all that messing about in shelters and sitting in front parlours as if butter wouldn't melt in your mouth. I'm randy, our kid! I want Madge now!' He grinned shamefacedly.

'I know. But starting married life with your in-laws . . .' Harry shook his head and stuck out his bottom lip. 'You might feel shackled now, but how would you feel then?' He didn't think much of Madge's parents who lived in a stuccoed Victorian villa in Beulah Terrace overlooking the railway lines, a house with iron railings fronting a be-laurelled garden with the smell of cabbage – or it could have been cauliflower – permeating the entrance hall; getting tangled up in the heavy chenille curtains shrouding the windows. The smell vied for pride of place with Mrs Robinson's bad-back embrocation and the violet-scented cachous she sucked continually to keep her breath fresh. The whole house stank to him of genteel decay and vegetable water, and the back living-room, where Madge's delicate father stuck stamps into albums amid a plethora of Biblical texts and Victorian daguerreotypes, seemed to him as dank and dreary as a dungeon. How Madge's parents had ever managed to raise an outgoing, buck-toothed, bright-eyed, voluptuous daughter in such surroundings, he had no idea. But he could not, for the life of him, see Frank winceyetting his way up the Robinsons' staircase to a couple of rooms on the top floor to make violent physical love in an atmosphere of 'Thou, God, See'st Me' overhung with the effluvium of boiled cabbage.

'I don't care tuppence where we live,' Frank said desperately, stopping to knock the ash from his cheroot into his mother's best rose and forget-me-not-embellished dressing-table tray. 'Madge is driving me mad! She won't let me – well, you know what – until we're married. Oh, it's all very well for you to loll there like a bloody nodding mandarin, but you don't know what it's like, wanting a woman so much.'

Harry settled back on his pillows. 'You'd better not let Ma see that ash in her dressing-table tray,' he observed. 'She'll have your hide if she does.'

'God,' Frank groaned, 'this bloody family drives me crazy at times.' He opened the window and emptied the ash out of it. 'Has it ever struck you, Harry, what a queer lot we are?'

'What do you mean – queer?'

'Oh, I don't know.' Frank sat down on the edge of his bed to expound his views, an irritable young man wielding a cheroot instead of a rifle. 'I mean, there's you and me and Maggie. We're alike. Then there's Charlotte and Joe; they're not like us at all. I know Joe said he would come with us if – well – if things boil up, but he doesn't really want to. As for Charlotte, I'll never understand her if I live to be a hundred.'

He was, had he realized it, expounding the truth about families the world over, that every member of every family is individually contained within a precise framework. And yet he knew, as he spoke, that he would fight to the death to defend Joe and Charlotte. He was simply railing against his own frustrations, a handsome young fellow who wanted his own way in everything: freedom to run with the wind, freedom to make love whenever he felt like it, to smoke a cigar in peace without feeling compelled to empty the ashtray out of the window.

'If that's the way you feel about it, you'd better get things settled. The sooner the better,' Harry said, rolling over on one elbow. 'Go and live with Madge's parents if that's what you want.'

'It isn't what I want,' Frank groaned, slumping on his bed, cradling his head with his hands.

'What, then?'

'I'm not sure.' But he did know. He wanted to stand up and fight, to expel the great driving force of his manhood in physical action, to love, march, suffer – or even die gloriously – as long as he lived life to the full while it lasted. He raised his head. It was all clear to him now. He said simply, 'I want to – *live*!'

'What? Get married and go to live with *her* parents? I've never heard anything so ridiculous in all my born days.' Filly wiped her eyes with her handkerchief. 'A son of mine starting married life as a lodger! Wait till your father hears about this.'

'I've already talked to Dad,' Frank said moodily.

'And what did he have to say?'

Frank shrugged his shoulders. 'What could he say? Dad sees me as a man. You see me as a child. I'm sorry, Ma.' He slipped a placating arm round his mother's waist. 'Don't worry, it'll be all right, you'll see. It's just that you never seem to realize that things are changing. Why not accept it? I'm a grown man now. I want to get married. What's wrong with that?'

He knew, even as he spoke, that he would never be able to bridge the gulf of years between himself and his mother.

'Oh, do as you please then,' she said despairingly. 'I'll write to Charlotte. It's high time that girl came back home. Your father has never been right since she went away. Now, with all this war-talk, it's only right that she should think of us for a change.' Tears flooded down her cheeks. 'If ever you have children, you'll know what it's like, worrying about them all the time.'

And so Filly wrote to Charlotte, begging her to come home.

'Frank and Madge Robinson are getting married on the third of August,' she set down in her best handwriting, 'and your father is not at all well. I don't know quite what's the matter with him, but he's not himself, and all this war-talk is getting everyone down, me most of all. I really don't know if I'm on my head or my heels at the moment, worrying about this wedding and our Frank going to live in rented rooms at the Robinsons' house, and thinking that war might break out at any minute. It's like living on the edge of a crater. I wouldn't mind so much if Frank and that Madge Robinson had a home of their own to go to. What's upsetting me so much is the thought of them starting out together in a couple of furnished rooms. Whatever will the neighbours say?'

Charlotte read quickly through the letter. The words, 'and your father is not at all well' stood out from the page. Her heart contracted with fear. If Dadda was not well, if he needed her, she must go home at once. She had never known her father to be ill before.

She took her leave of Miss Kitty and Alice on the twenty-eighth of July; did so with regret. But Alice no longer needed her as she used to, although she cried bitterly when she knew Charlotte was leaving. It was Miss Kitty Charlotte most regretted saying goodbye to – a woman she had learned to love and trust, the only person on earth – apart from Jenny – who knew how things stood between herself and Rowan.

As the moment for departure drew near, Charlotte saw, with an ache in her heart, the summer sun touching to fire the windows of Grey Wethers; smelt, perhaps for the last time, the scent of the lavender bordering the terrace, knowing that this brief sojourn of hers in the West Country had given her memories she would always treasure.

Nothing would ever be the same for her again once she had left Grey Wethers. She would remember, to her life's end, the enfolding hills, the colour of the grass, the grey boulders which gave the house its name, the old summerhouse in Sweet Water Meadow, the song of a lark in dew-pearled grass; smoke rising from the cottage chimneys, the golden-haloed madonnas in

Kitty Tanquillan's study. There was a shine and shimmer about Grey Wethers, a kind of glamour touched on during those nights in a darkened picture house with Maggie beside her, when the pair of them had stared entranced at flickering images on a screen and lived, for an hour or two, in a different world, an enchanted, make-believe world.

Will Oakleigh was to drive her to Devizes station. She watched him pile her luggage into the trap, a slow-moving countryman making sure that everything was stowed away correctly, that the horse was easy and comfortable, its breeching properly adjusted. Kitty Tanquillan walked with Charlotte to the trap, saying all the last-minute things: 'Are you sure you've got enough money? Have you remembered your sandwiches? You will take a taxi from Paddington?'

'Yes, thank you. Thank you for everything . . .'

'Nonsense! And remember, you are welcome to come back here at any time. If ever you need me . . .' The old woman smiled and patted the girl's shoulder.

'It's time we were off,' Will reminded her.

'Goodbye, then, my dear.' Kitty kissed Charlotte warmly, as Will held out his hand to help her into the trap. Gravel crunched beneath the wheels as they moved away down the drive to the gates.

Will said nothing for a while. Charlotte surreptitiously dried her eyes and blew her nose. The passing breeze lifted her hat-brim; ruffled Will's hair. His hands were brown and firm, he held the reins loosely between his fingers; wrinkled his eyes against the glare of the sun, unable to make light conversation. He was a silent, lonely man who had learned to put a curb-rein on his emotions since the death of his wife and child; a man who felt infinitely more at ease with animals than human beings.

Charlotte wondered if Will was angry with her, he seemed so taciturn. Perhaps she had taken him away from his work. They were passing the field where the grey wethers were crowded together like grazing sheep beneath the sweeping outline of the Downs. Suddenly the wind softly parted the grass, making it ripple and sparkle in the bright, clear sunlight. 'I'll miss all this,' she said simply.

'You are not looking forward to going home then?' Will asked gruffly.

'Oh, yes, of course I am. But I've been happy here, too. Now my mother needs me at home. My father's not very well, and my brother's getting married . . .' She stopped speaking, thinking that she sounded like a child making excuses to an indifferent headmaster; squared her shoulders and settled her hat more firmly on her head.

When Will said, 'I'll miss you, Charlotte. That is, we'll all miss you,' she stared at him in surprise, noticing a warm flush of colour beneath his sunburnt skin. Although he did not even turn his head to look at her, or relax for an instant the grim set of his lips, his concentration on the road ahead, she knew he meant what he said; knew that she had not had time to come to terms with Wiltshire folk, so different from blunt, outspoken Yorkshiremen.

Paddington station was choc-a-bloc with men in uniform; territorials returning from summer camp to join their fighting units; men in khaki, putteed, carrying packs and rifles, with water-bottles strapped to their belts.

As she rode from Paddington to King's Cross in a taxi, she saw the anxious crowds thronging the streets of London; the placards and banners and Union Jacks. Watching the passing parade, she thought about Jenny's words, that one day they would look back on this as the end of an era, the beginning of a new way of life.

The taxi was caught up in a mob crowding towards Whitehall: to the seat of government. People were chanting and singing as if they wanted war to come; lifting high the Union Jack. And yet she sensed their fear, their desperation, as if they were singing in the face of Armageddon: the place where the kings of the earth were gathered together for the battle of that great day of God Almighty.

'All together like the folks of Shields' had always been Filly's favourite saying, conjuring up for her the warmth and togetherness of family life. As she baked cakes in the kitchen,

266

made jellies and blancmanges in various colours and shapes, she forgot for a little while Frank's wedding and the worsening European situation and turned her mind and her hands to preparing a homecoming welcome for Charlotte; the 'Prodigal Daughter'. She had been up since the crack of dawn, cleaning and scouring, singing about her work; spreading Charlotte's bed with clean linen, dusting and polishing her room – though why Charlotte had ever chosen to sleep in the attic she could not imagine. Still, the view from the window was rather nice, with a glimpse of the sea in the distance, above and beyond all the slate roofs and chimney-pots; a window framed in rose-sprigged cotton which she had washed and re-hung on stretched wire the day before.

Filly thought, as she viewed Charlotte's books on a white-painted shelf near the plain iron bedstead, that she had always preferred good high ceilings to sloping ones; brown paint and graining to white; that this attic room reflected all her younger daughter's oddities which came, she supposed, from Charlotte having red hair and green eyes. Even so, she could scarcely curb her impatience, her joy, until train time, until her mysterious, beautiful girl came back to her.

The scenes she had witnessed in London seemed like a dream to Charlotte as she was gathered back to the family circle. Excitement lent a new brilliance to her eyes, a high colour to her cheeks as she walked with her brothers across the Valley Bridge, and saw in the distance the welcoming curve of the South Bay, the blue line of the horizon, the sea a deep sapphire blue beneath an evening sky threaded with the deepening gold of sunset. Joey held her arm, Frank carried one of her cases, Harry the other as they bore her back, in triumph, to the waiting house, to Filly's pink blancmanges and scarlet jellies, hard-boiled eggs, salad, cakes and fruit salad set out in state amid a plethora of starched doilies and best china on the dining-room table; to Filly's arms and Albert's; to an evening of chatter, comment and critical glances from Filly.

Her mother thought that Charlotte looked well enough, but thinner, more withdrawn than ever, not understanding that

Charlotte felt herself overwhelmed by her homecoming, that the house seemed strange to her, squeezed and narrow after Grey Wethers, with all the people crowded together round the dining-room table; that, no matter how much she loved them, she could not immediately come to terms with them. She felt strangely disorientated, missing the scent of flowers through open latticed windows; Guernsey copper jugs filled with delphiniums; Kitty Tanquillan's drawing-room with its terrace-facing windows, sprawling armchairs and grand piano; the blessedness of the fragrance of newly-mown grass blown in on an evening breeze. Her head ached after the long journey. She could not eat the quivering mound of fruit, jelly and blancmange her mother had provided.

'But I made it especially for you,' Filly cried, affronted.

'Leave the girl alone,' Albert said quietly. 'She's tired out.'

Spooning up his own portion of jelly, reaching for the cream-jug, Frank wanted to know what it was like in London.

Suddenly all Filly's dread of the future settled on her like a cloud as Charlotte described the taxi-ride from Paddington to King's Cross.

Curiously enough, speaking of what she had seen in London released Charlotte somewhat from the strangeness of homecoming.

After supper, she tucked her hand into Albert's arm. 'Are you all right, Dadda?' she asked. 'Mother said in her letter that you had not been very well lately.' Her voice was laced with anxiety.

Albert smiled. 'Me, not well?' He seemed genuinely surprised. 'I wonder what made her say that? I'm – fine. A bit worried, maybe, about what will happen if war comes, if supplies are cut off, but then so is every other grocer in town.'

He cradled her chin with his hands; tilted her face to the light. 'But you, Copper, are *you* all right?'

'Yes, of course I am. Why do you ask?'

'I don't know.' He touched her cheeks with gentle fingers. 'There's something – different about you. You seem much older somehow. You were just my little girl when you went away. You're a woman now. What happened, I wonder, to

268

make you grow up so quickly?'

The old rapport was as strong as ever. She smiled. 'I'll tell you all about it one day, Dadda.' She knew that he would never probe or pry, that she would tell him about Rowan when the time was right. 'I'd better get back to Mum,' she said, 'she'll need me to help with the washing-up.'

Filly blurted, when she and Charlotte were alone in the kitchen, 'I'm worried sick, if you must know, about Frank getting married in such a rush. You know what people are! The way their minds work! They'll say that he and Madge Robinson *had* to get married in a hurry!' Her cheeks flushed scarlet. 'Well, you know what I mean. People talk so! What I can't get over is the idea of Frank going to that woman's house to live. Why couldn't he have waited a bit longer?' She answered her own question in the next breath. 'It's this damned war-talk that's made him muddle-headed!' she snorted, getting the bile out of her system as she dipped the dishes in hot water laced with soapflakes and a scattering of soda crystals to kill the grease. 'Frank's a fool! That Madge Robinson has him – bewitched! Maybe there won't be a war after all, then he'll be in a nice fix! He thinks he's badly done to here, but wait until he starts cigar-ashing Mrs Robinson's best dressing-table set, then see what happens!'

Charlotte bit her lip, trying not to laugh. Filly's way of speaking was unintentionally funny at times.

When the washing-up was dried and put away, she went to Joe's room. He was whistling lightly, brushing his hair in front of the swing-mirror on his dressing-table, preparatory to meeting Annie Crystal on that warm-scented summer evening. The window was open to catch a sea-breeze. The sky was dark now, filled with stars.

'I've brought you and Annie an engagement present,' Charlotte said. 'It isn't much, just a few hand-embroidered serviettes.'

'They're lovely. Really beautiful!' Joe spread the serviettes on his bed-cover, smiling his pleasure. 'Annie will be thrilled.' Then, understanding Charlotte's withdrawal, her strangeness at homecoming, he said simply, taking her hands in his, 'I know how you feel. Nothing's quite real any more, is it? We are not entirely at ease with each other, are we? Not as we used to be, I mean, before you went away.' He observed her carefully, smiling at her. 'Time has a way of changing things and people: making them strange with each other. It isn't a one-sided thing, you know. Even you seem different. . . .'

'Different? How?'

'I'm not quite sure. You seem much wiser somehow. You're not in love by any chance?'

Her colour deepened. 'Yes, Joey, I am.'

'I thought so. Do you want to tell me about it?'

'I can't,' she said quietly, 'not just now. It isn't straightforward, you see, not like you and Annie.' She laid her hand on his sleeve. 'I'm sorry, Joe. But thank you for understanding how I feel.' Looking into his eyes, she said softly, 'I just wish that we could all go back to being young again.'

'I wish that too, at times. But never to live, never to suffer, never to evolve as human beings; do you really believe that human beings are so afraid of life, so frightened of their God-given instincts that they would wish to remain eternal embryo?' He smiled. 'In any case, time, however much we might wish to lay hands on it, to hold it back, has a way of moving on, taking us with it. That is the way of the world, Charlotte, that is the rule of life.'

She said, 'If Frank and Harry join up, will you go with them?'

'Oh yes,' he said quietly, 'we've made a pact, you see. "One for all, all for one"; the Dumas interpretation of – brotherly love. Frank, Harry and myself are the Three Musketeers. I would not have it otherwise.'

Maggie and Bob arrived later that evening, Maggie burgeoning like a full-blown cabbage rose in a flowered smock gathered above her sagging breasts, wearing a summer skirt wide enough to accommodate her growing baby, while Bob, instrument of his wife's blossoming fecundity, dangled his cap in the doorway, as tongue-tied as ever in the face of his relations by marriage. Maggie, on the other hand, appeared to be taking her pregnancy quite philosophically, her fears, voiced on a windy April afternoon, quite forgotten. Charlotte thought, as she hugged her sister, how quickly Maggie had changed from a frightened bride-to-be into a smug, self-satisfied matron.

Harry, nervous and fidgety since Charlotte's arrival, hung about on the landing until he managed to catch her alone for a few minutes. 'I thought Jenny might have come back with you,' he said offhandedly, as if he didn't care one way or the other, although he had thought of nothing else since he knew Charlotte was coming home again, 'but I guess she decided to stay in Wiltshire after all.'

'Well, no, Harry. Jenny has gone to London,' Charlotte said. 'She left Wiltshire some time ago to stay with a friend of hers in Bloomsbury.'

'Bloomsbury!' Harry uttered the name as if Bloomsbury was on the other side of the world. 'But why?'

'She talked of going to France if war comes, as a nurse or an ambulance-driver. She couldn't stand being a governess. Jenny's a very unusual person, you know.'

'Yes, I know that.' Harry's blue-grey eyes were bright with hope beneath his mop of curling brown hair, his high intelligent forehead was beaded with perspiration, his cheeks flushed, as he looked earnestly at his sister. 'But didn't she leave me a message?' He blurted, overcome with shame, the sudden realization of his own ignorance, 'I love her, you see.' He had not thought to tell anyone, much less his sister whom he had always thought of as a child. But there was something different about her now. He couldn't begin to lay a finger on it, but Charlotte had grown up somehow since she went away. In any case, she was the only one who could answer his question.

Looking up at Harry's flushed, eager face, Charlotte knew that she could not bear to tell him the truth, that Jenny had said, 'Tell Harry he's much better off without a girl like me.' She hesitated momentarily, then lied like a trooper. 'Oh yes,' she said, smiling, 'Jenny sent you her love.'

'Really?' He went upstairs to his room like a man in a dream.

In her own room, Charlotte left the gas unlit. Shadows and heat

271

were trapped in corners. The open window, framed with rose-sprigged cotton, admitted a wash of starlit night; the scent of rocks and seaweed, the sound of the sea in the distance. This was one of the hottest summers for a long time. Albert had said the Bank Holiday looked like being a scorcher. The town was already packed with visitors, and more would flock to the sands when the day-trippers arrived, then the beach would be choked solid with people turning their faces to the sun.

Charlotte leaned her arms on the window-sill. Gas-lamps glowed softly in the sultry darkness, necklacing the square with amber lights. Her sense of disorientation was still strong, as if she existed in two places at the same time and the two parts of her had not yet merged into one body. She thought about Will Oakleigh unloading her belongings from the trap and standing with her on the station platform waiting for the train to arrive. She had felt more at ease with him by that time. Indeed, when the train came and she got into the compartment, Will had seemed to her a rock in a rough sea, her only link with the shore, as familiar to her as her own hand, and she had been glad of his firm handshake, the smile which softened his face as he wished her a safe journey.

Now she was home again among her own folk, and yet the transition had not been fully made from her more immediate past to the present. Her family appeared much the same as usual, and yet there were subtle differences in all of them. Time had shifted them about like grains of sand on the seashore, altering the pattern of their lives, faced as they were with events which threatened their very existence. Her father and Joey had noticed the changes in herself. Joe was right when he said that time had a way of moving on. Time had moved on relentlessly since her last meeting with Rowan.

Looking up at the stars, brightly eternal in the summer sky, she pondered the power and mystery of memory. Perhaps the Great Architect of Life had known, in His wisdom, that human beings could never live each day as it came without memories of the past; dreams, and hope for the future.

The power of the human mind never ceased to amaze her. Here she stood in a tiny room, bounded by four walls and sloping ceiling, and yet by a trick of memory she was back in London with Rowan, walking beside him near the river, sitting with him in Westminster Abbey, reliving their perfect day together as if time had ceased to exist.

Tomorrow, she would help her mother with the housework in preparation for Frank's wedding. Perhaps she would go into town to do some shopping, and the day after tomorrow she would remember that she had done all these things, then tomorrow would slip into the past along with all the other days of her life, but she would never forget any of them. Delving back into memory, she would recall at least the essence of a day, the sadness, joy or laughter it contained. So it was with very old men and women who conjured up youth from the past.

At that moment, Charlotte was with Rowan again, remembering him as she had last seen him, a tall figure hurrying away from her in a crowded London street.

CHAPTER TWO

The blend of international crisis and domestic upheaval imparted a curious sense of urgency to the days before Frank's wedding. The bridegroom said irritably that he saw no reason why the house should be turned upside-down since the Robinsons were seeing to things this time – not like Maggie's 'do'.

'Ah well,' Filly nodded mysteriously, 'you never know who will drop in.'

Frank, who had envisaged his marriage as a romantic elopement, found himself bogged down with arrangements. He and Madge had had a few words when she mentioned that she was having four bridesmaids. 'Four bloody bridesmaids,' he told Charlotte lugubriously as she pegged out the washing in the back yard. 'Why *four*, I ask you?' He was leaning against the warehouse door at the time, smoking a cigarette, his normally good-natured face puckered with indignation.

Charlotte laughed. 'Oh, come off it, Frank. Madge is sure to want a nice wedding. Most girls do. It's a kind of milestone in their lives.'

'I might have known you would side with her,' Frank said moodily. 'Nobody cares how I feel about it. *Women*! What with Madgie, Mother, and Mrs Robinson rushing round like scalded cats, I get the distinct impression that nobody would give a hoot if I didn't turn up at the church at all!'

He sighed impatiently and ground his cigarette-stub savagely under his heel. 'The way Ma's going on, anyone would think that Mrs Robinson was coming round here with a magnifying-glass to look under the beds!'

All he wanted was to marry his Madgie as quietly as possible.

He saw the ceremony in church as a barrier between himself and the marriage-bed. 'I wish we could have got married, at the crack of dawn, at the registry office,' he said, lighting another cigarette.

'Aren't you being rather selfish?' Charlotte asked, feeling in her apron pocket for a peg.

'Selfish? Me?' Frank stared at his sister in amazement.

'I'm sorry. But things will be tough for everyone when you and Harry and Joe join up. We'll need something pleasant to look back on then.'

'Pleasant! Like me making a fool of myself at the reception, you mean, when I stand up to read my speech?' Frank scoffed.

'Is that what is really worrying you?'

'Yeah, if you must know.' Frank grinned shamefacedly. 'Well, one of the things.'

'You needn't say much,' Charlotte advised. 'Just thank everyone. No-one will remember, afterwards, what you said.'

He said nervously, 'You know war's coming, don't you?'

'Yes, I know that.' Charlotte continued to peg out the washing.

'Mother won't admit it.' Frank threw down his cigarette half smoked. 'She gets my back up at times with her damned head in the sand attitude.'

'Aren't you being a bit hard on her?' Charlotte said. 'Have you ever really tried to understand her point of view? What it will mean to her when you and Harry and Joey have gone?'

'No, I suppose not.' Frank turned away. He had never felt very close to Charlotte before. He wondered why not. She was quite a sensible kid after all. A bit sharp-tongued, of course, but she was, after all, a red-head.

It seemed impossible to equate the worsening European situation with life in a seaside resort at Bank Holiday, with visitors almost wilting in the scorching hot sunshine.

Albert seemed bowed down with the news that the English food-market was already being hard-hit as a result of the crisis. The price of flour, butter, sugar, eggs, bacon and tinned goods had shot up overnight: bacon and butter supplies from Siberia would be inevitably cut off by Russia's mobilization.

'I wish you'd stop worrying,' Filly reprimanded him. 'I'll cancel the newspapers if you carry on like this much longer! What's the point of you sitting there, night after night, pulling a long face over something that might never happen?'

'But it *is* happening,' Albert said heavily. 'Holland has declared its neutrality in case of war. Crack Cossack regiments are being called to the colours. Germany has announced that even a partial Russian mobilization will be followed by immediate retaliatory action!'

He walked down to his shop, seeing an end to the world he had built up so lovingly over the years. Charlotte went after him. 'Don't worry, Dadda,' she said, filled with a longing to take the weight of disappointment from his shoulders and lift it onto her own. 'I'm here.'

'It's not just this,' he said, indicating the shop with a gesture of his hand, 'it's the boys. My sons.'

'I know, Dad. I know.'

Later that day, he read that a squad of fifty territorials of the 5th Yorkshire Regiment had returned to their headquarters in Scarborough and marched to the drill hall in North Street where they were issued with ball cartridges before their dispersal to guard the town's vantage points.

On Saturday the first of August, the news was graver still. All Russian forces were being mobilized. The Belgians had declared a state of siege. Their country was now under martial law.

France was making ready for war. The French premier had given orders for six army corps on the German front to mobilize. According to reports, German forces on the Alsace-Lorraine border were already concentrated for action.

Besides Russia, Austria, Serbia, Holland, and Belgium were mobilizing. Precautionary measures were being taken by Germany, Norway, France, Italy, Great Britain and Spain.

'Oh, my God,' Filly cried, starching valances as if her life depended on it, 'I feel half out of my head with worry.'

Charlotte, standing near her by the sink, ready to dash down to the yard with the washing, remembered the day she and Jenny had rushed to the help of those suffragettes chained to the railings in Trafalgar Square; memory jogged by an item in the morning paper. The Women's Social and Political Union had forbidden further militancy during the present crisis. She wondered, as she pegged out the clean linen to dry, what Jenny would make of that.

Dear Jenny. Charlotte wondered where she was now, what she was doing at the moment. The days they had spent together in London seemed like a dream to her now that her world was overshadowed by the grim war news. Above all, where was Rowan?

'I must not think of thee; and, tired yet strong,
I shun the thought that lurks in all delight –
The thought of thee – and in the blue Heaven's height,
And in the sweetest passage of a song.'

Charlotte's only consolation lay in the feel of wet linen beneath her fingers, the ordinary daily tasks which anchored her to reality. Her brief moment of optimism was forgotten when she read in the evening paper that the war clouds were gathering ever more deeply over Europe. Germany had sent its ultimatum to Russia and France. Franz Joseph of Austria had ordered general mobilization.

On Sunday the second of August, Germany declared war on Russia. Charlotte picked up a special edition of the local paper. 'Will England be drawn in?' she read. 'Agitation against war in this country is growing.'

German troops had invaded Luxembourg, were moving towards the French frontiers. The invasion of Luxembourg was seen as a provocative act which might lead to the intervention of other powers, including Britain.

She heard Frank coming downstairs, a bridegroom on the eve of his wedding. She would have known that confident whistle of his anywhere. She looked up as he came into the kitchen.

'Well, Sis, what's new?' he asked brightly, filling the kettle.

'All the excursion trains to Scarborough have been cancelled. Scarborough members of the Naval Reserve have been called up. They're off to Chatham first thing tomorrow morning.'

'Things are really hotting up then,' Frank said cheerfully. 'It won't be long now! Madge and I will be in for a bit of excitement when we get to London.' He felt pleased with himself that he had decided to take his bride to London for their honeymoon: about the only thing he had done right lately, he thought ruefully. But he knew his Madgie so well; knew that she would love poking round the shops, going to the theatre . . . He sighed blissfully, his stomach beginning to churn with excitement.

'It says here that British intervention is almost inevitable,' Charlotte continued. 'Sir Edward Grey said, in the House of Commons, that if a foreign fleet came down the Channel and bombarded the French coast, we could not stand aside.'

'I should think not.' Frank poured himself a mug of tea and flopped down on a chair to drink it, wondering if he should join the Navy instead of the Army. He shrugged that notion aside. He had never seen himself as a sailor. He thought instead of tomorrow night in London; walking with Madge into the foyer of the King's Arms Hotel in the Strand; signing the register 'Mr and Mrs Frank Grayler'.

He could picture it all. Madgie lying flat on her back in bed; arms extended, the teasing touch of her fingers in his hair, her magnificent teeth biting into his bottom lip: a female vampire intent on drawing blood. He swallowed hard, imagining his first night of bliss with his Madgie naked and unashamed. The ends of his moustache twitched upwards at the thought of being male, alive and virile, a bridegroom to boot. He would get through the bloody wedding ceremony somehow, then he and Madge would fly away to their first blissful mating.

Filly had insisted on a new outfit for Frank's wedding: a neat French navy marocain two-piece from Hopper and Mason's summer sale, with a white-frilled blouse, white gloves, and a white straw hat trimmed with navy blue ribbons. As mother of the bridegroom she felt it her duty to appear, like those ships at the Spithead review, with all flags flying.

'Now you can just forget all about the shop for one day, Albert Grayler,' she said severely to her husband, 'about that meeting as well. I'm not having you standing beside me at the reception looking like a leashed bloodhound, so there!'

'But I should go to the meeting' Albert said, standing impatiently while Filly arranged his tie to her satisfaction, 'it's important.'

'And your son's wedding isn't, I suppose! Oh, stand still, man. Stop fidgeting!'

'All the first-class grocers in town will be there,' he said stubbornly. 'I'm a first-class grocer, so I'm going, Mother, whether you like it or not!'

'Oh, please yourself then!' She sighed. 'You usually do.'

'Please don't be angry, Filly. We've got to discuss what's to be done about food-rationing.'

She smoothed his lapels. 'I'm not angry.' She remembered suddenly that framed First-Class Grocer certificate hanging in the shop above the tilted, tiered, glass-lidded biscuit-boxes; forgot for a moment the great dark bird of war hovering like a black cloud on the horizon as she thought of her family: the pride she felt in all of them. Her sons, Frank so tall and handsome, somewhat subdued this morning in his dark wedding-suit; his crinkly ginger hair plastered to his scalp with brilliantine, his moustache upturned above his full red lips.

Harry, his best man, equally subdued, constantly fiddling in his waistcoat pocket for the ring, his feet nervously tapping the kitchen oilcloth as he waited for the taxis to arrive. Joe, dear little Joe with his bright blue eyes, dark curly hair and warm skin touched, on his left cheekbone, with a tiny outcrop of moles like pencil dots, standing quietly beside Annie; holding her hand, smiling down at her, his eyes crinkling at the corners as he touched the spray of carnations pinned to the lapel of her neat silver-grey costume.

Maggie, as plump and self-satisfied as a duck in a blue flowered smock and a wide-brimmed hat decorated with artificial daisies, her cheeks flushed with excitement, with broken capillaries and the scraping of Bob's beard in the night; her lips as moist as pink rose petals, her baby a bulge beneath her smock.

Charlotte, her serene and lovely Charlotte wearing a pale green dress and jacket; a hat with floating green ribbons perched atop her glorious red hair. Filly knew, with a choking sensation, that no matter what Madge Robinson wore for her wedding, she could not possibly outshine her Charlotte.

The girl had always possessed amazing dignity, evident in the proud uplift of her head on the slim column of her throat. But today, today, that cool dignity of hers seemed touched with a new warmth. Her eyes, beneath uptilted brows, were as tender as springtime.

Filly held her breath momentarily as she always had done when she looked at this youngest child of hers, who was worth every moment of the pain she had suffered bringing her into the world.

She pushed aside the thought, as she marched downstairs to the side door with its jewelled prisms, that she had taken a mental photograph of her children standing all together, perhaps for the last time.

Albert slipped his arm round her waist as she sniffed, and fumbled in her handbag for a handkerchief. 'Come on, love,' he smiled, 'no tears. This is supposed to be a happy occasion.'

'It's all very well for you,' she said, dabbing her eyes. 'You're not a mother! Men don't feel things the same as women! Things will never be the same again after today. And don't you give me any of that "you're not losing a son but gaining a daughter" rubbish, because that's what it is, *rubbish*! Besides, I don't like St Saviour's church. Nasty, cold place! Why couldn't they have got married at St Martin's?'

'Because Madge isn't a spinster of this parish, I suppose.' Albert said mildly.

'No. Soon she won't be a spinster of *any* parish, that's what's worrying me. Why did she have to pick on our poor Frank?'

'You'd better pull yourself together,' Albert suggested slyly, 'the neighbours are watching.'

'Oh, are they?' With that, Filly put away her handkerchief,

straightened her hat, and marched out proudly to the waiting taxi.

Madge Grayler hung like grim death to her husband's arm. Tired and irritable after the excitement of her wedding day, the long journey to London, and the strange non-event of her wedding night, she felt like a vessel in tow against a rough sea as Frank tugged her remorselessly along The Mall towards Buckingham Palace. Her feet in her narrow patent-leather shoes were beginning to blister, her feelings towards Frank were evident in her mutinously narrowed lips. To think that, after all her teasing and cajoling, he had been unable to consummate the marriage, seemed to her a reflection on her womanhood. She had spent the night in a fever of anticipation. When, at four in the morning she had fallen into a sleep of utter exhaustion, she was still a virgin. She had not believed such a thing possible.

'I'm sorry, love. I guess I'm just too excited,' Frank had groaned from the depths of his humiliation. 'I've waited so long, and now . . .' The spectre of impotency had stared him in the face in the squeezed confines of their hotel bedroom. He had wept silent tears of frustration when Madge finally turned away from him.

Now, at close on eleven o'clock the following night, he gave vent to his frustration in dragging his wife through the streets of London. Glowing gaslight illuminated the crowds thronging the pavements outside Buckingham Palace. People were perched precariously on the edge of the stone parapet surrounding the statue of Queen Victoria, a moat of dark water behind them, the lights of the palace shining before them.

'For God's sake, Frank, slow down!' Madge berated him, but her voice was lost to him as he pushed his way to a vantage point near the palace gates. She fell silent as a palace official appeared from the inner courtyard to post on the high, spiked railings the Royal Proclamation announcing that Great Britain had declared war on Germany.

'Owing to the summary rejection by the German Government

that the neutrality of Belgium will be respected, His Majesty's Ambassador at Berlin has received his passport, and His Majesty's Government has declared to the German Government that a state of war exists between Great Britain and Germany as from 11 p.m. on August 4th.'

'Christ, Madgie, it's happened at last!' Frank's heart was beating like a drum as word spread and the crowd roared its approval. Some started singing 'Rule Britannia'. Another faction began the National Anthem. Cheers roared to a mighty crescendo; hats went spinning into the air, curving crazily against the dark summer sky, against the great gas-lamps bracketed to the palace railings; the shining palace windows.

'Oh, Frank!' Tears spilled down Madge's cheeks. She had never wanted him more than she did at that minute. She clung to him, knowing that soon he would be taken away from her, her tall handsome husband with his bright eyes and gleaming moustache. She regretted now all those nights in the darkness of shelters bordering the Spa paths when she had refused to succumb to his lovemaking. She hit hazily on the truth in thinking that their wedding night had lacked the magic of stolen kisses, of risk and chance. She had felt stultified in the overwarm hotel bedroom, an official houri in a white nightgown.

His lips sought hers eagerly. Lost in each other's arms, they did not notice the opening of the balcony windows until the shout went up: 'It's the King! The Royal Family!' and there appeared the head of a nation at war, with his queen, their sons and daughters; remote figures smiling and waving their hands in salute to the shouting, singing, cheering people below: of them, yet strangely removed from them, like puppet figures on a bright, shining stage.

At the hotel, Frank undressed slowly, his eager young flesh quivering with desire, nervousness making him hang back. What if the same thing happened? He tried to curb his desire; approached the bed with misgiving. Frank Grayler had never known defeat before in the whole of his young confident life;

now his mouth was dry with nerves, he experienced a gnawing ache in the pit of his stomach, aware for the first time of the weakness of human flesh – his own flesh. Realization of his vulnerability saved him from a second fiasco. Madge was tired, quiescent, forgiving. He sought love as a comfort, not simply an expression of his own virility. He put his arms around her; felt her warm tears on his face, and took her, not proudly but humbly.

Next day, excitement reigned supreme. People seemed stunned by the sudden transition of war-talk into positive action. Frank had risen from bed like a giant refreshed, wanting to be in the thick of things.

Street arabs with toy flags and paper helmets beat soap-boxes for drums as they marched the streets singing 'Rule Britannia', holding out tin boxes nailed on sticks to catch the thrown pennies of the laughing onlookers.

'Isn't it bloody marvellous?' Frank cried, gripping Madgie's elbow, trying to instil into his reluctant bride a little of his own enthusiasm. But Madge, tired and out of sorts, had begged him to stay in bed with her for another hour or two. 'After all, this is our honeymoon,' she said, snuggling down among the pillows, wanting him to make love to her again, hating the thought of traipsing the streets to watch people making fools of themselves simply because war had been declared.

'But just think, Madgie! History's in the making! We'll never see another day like this one,' Frank said eagerly, sensing the excitement which lay beyond the shrouded hotel windows.

He had never known such excitement before! Volunteers were storming the recruiting offices. Music was in the air: the skirl of pipes: brass bands playing the National Anthem. Tears filled Frank's eyes; he felt so proud to be British! He applauded a stalwart company of post office workers marching in a wavering undrilled line through Regent's Park: longed to go home, back to Scarborough, to join up with his brothers.

In Scarborough, the visitors streamed away, leaving the hotels empty, the beaches deserted. It was all over now, that hot, fraught August Bank Holiday. Sandbags were stacked across Eastborough. Steps leading to the sands were barricaded with barbed wire as the troops moved in.

Grocers had announced that there was no need for panic buying. Food supplies were safe; there was hope of grain from America. But housewives panicked just the same. Shelves were denuded in the stampede to buy up all the sugar, flour, tea, bacon and tinned goods they could lay their hands on. Albert was forced then to the realization that he must impose some kind of unofficial rationing.

Filly said it was the same at the shops in South Street. Women were rushing to buy eggs to put down in waterglass; meat to pickle in brine, fruit and vegetables to jam and preserve against the winter months. It was the rich folk who came off best. The poor ones seemed likely to go short in the grey months ahead.

'I don't care what I go short of,' Filly said doggedly, 'as long as Maggie gets her fair share of food. After all, she is carrying our grandchild.' Her hopes were centred on that child. She would need it to fulfil her maternal instincts when her sons were taken away from her.

In a surge of patriotic fervour, and because she couldn't very well refuse, she allowed the vicar's wife to put her name forward as a Red Cross helper at the local hospital, seven to nine o'clock two evenings a week.

CHAPTER THREE

Rowan Tanquillan quickened his steps. The river ran turgidly beside him, touched with brownish swirls of mud and silt. He passed Cleopatra's Needle and the flight of steps leading down to the Thames; the dolphined lamps spaced out along the Embankment. He walked until he came to the grey bulk of Scotland Yard, and hurried across the road to join a queue of men waiting to enlist.

Thin rain was falling as he shuffled forward in the queue listening to the talk going on around him, the earthy, often bawdy humour of men like himself with their own reasons for wanting to join up.

'My old woman'll make mincemeat out of me when she knows what I've done,' proclaimed a cheerful Cockney with a mouthful of broken, discoloured teeth, 'but I'd rather be shot at by the Germans than her when she's in one of her tempers.'

'Which regiment are you gonna join then, Bert?'

'The Cock-Ups,' came the unhesitating reply.

The recruiting office was painted green with benches ranged round the walls, filing-cabinets, and long trestle tables behind which sat army clerks leafing through sheaves of blue attestation forms. An army sergeant with cropped hair and a flourishing military moustache ran his eyes over the men waiting to be interviewed with the air of knowing at a glance what they had on beneath their outer clothing, what kind of soldiers they would make.

Rowan felt that he had been weighed up as 'soft, rich, in need of hammering into shape' and began whistling softly to himself until his turn came to be interviewed.

'Name?'

'Rowan Tanquillan.'

'Occupation?'

'Shipping clerk,' he said quickly.

'Sit over there. The Medical Officer will see you in a few minutes.'

His heart was pounding so fast, he prayed to God the M.O. would understand it was excitement, not heart disease that afflicted him. He need not have worried. The grey-faced man who confronted him, who made a cursory examination of his chest and eyesight, seemed far more breathless than himself. 'Any recent illnesses?' the M.O. enquired laconically.

'No. I'm pretty fit on the whole.'

'No epilepsy or venereal disease?'

'No, thank God!'

'In that case . . .' The Medical Officer scrawled 'Fit for Active Service', told him to dress, handed him his medical card, and sent him back to the outer office.

'Tanquillan. Over here!' He sat down at one of the trestle tables. The clerk looked at him woodenly. 'Which regiment?' he sasked.

'I'm sorry, I haven't the least idea,' Rowan admitted.

'You a Londoner?'

'Yes.'

'What about The London Regiment, County of London Battalion, The Rangers, Infantry Division?'

'Yes, that's fine with me.' Rowan flexed his fingers on the edge of the table. 'Now what?'

'Need any time to sort out your personal affairs?'

'Yes, perhaps I shall,' Rowan said thoughtfully.

'In that case, you'll come back here the day after tomorrow to swear your Oath of Allegiance before a qualified recruiting officer, you'll be given your first day's pay, after which you'll be posted. Is that clear?'

'Perfectly clear.' Rowan stood up. Now all that remained for him to do was face his wife and family, to tell them that he had enlisted in the Army.

On his way out, he remembered, with a smile, the Cockney's assertion that he would rather be shot at by the Germans than face his wife when she was in one of her tempers.

On the Embankment, he lifted his face to the rain and leaned over to look at the river flowing along so silently, so purposefully between its banks, feeling himself to be, as the river was, channelled to an inevitable destination, clogged at times by impediments; striving always to reach the open sea. He imagined, looking down into the oily water, that great burst of energy at the river's end when it flowed out unimpeded to become a part of a richer, freer existence.

He had never liked London, but he liked this old River Thames which seemed now, as never before, an integral part of his being. It was as if the river and he understood each other at last.

The house was very silent, very quiet. The rain had stopped an hour since but the atmosphere was still heavy and overcast.

The study door opened and Emily stood there. She looked at him uneasily, as if she sensed that something untoward had happened to him. 'You are home early,' she said with a question mark in her voice. 'What is it? What's wrong?'

'May I talk to you, Emily?'

'Of course. In here.'

He followed her into the study and stood by the desk as she closed the door behind them. 'Something has happened. You look – different,' she said. She spoke the truth. There was a peaceful expression in his eyes, a new air of resoluteness about him, evident in his squared shoulders and the smile hovering about his lips. The old look of harassment, of despair almost, had been expunged. The lines about his mouth and the shadows under his eyes, etched and deepened by Romilly's illness, were still there, but smoothed over and nullified by his new air of peace. He resembled a renegade priest brought back to the realization of his faith.

She moved forward slowly, and they stood facing each other for a while, not speaking. 'What have you done?' she said at last.

'I think you have already guessed. I'm sorry, Emily, I had to do it.' He laid his hand lightly on her arm. 'Please say you understand.' He spoke to her, not as Romilly's mother, but as a woman he cared for.

'Oh yes, I understand.' She looked up into his handsome, ravaged young face. 'But will Romilly?' She turned her head away suddenly, afraid that if she kept on looking at him she might betray her own feelings towards him. What a foolish old woman she was. Rowan was not in love with herself or Romilly, and yet, as she had watched him grow and mature, she had known that she loved him, not as a son-in-law, but as a woman in her own right. What she could never come to terms with, would never forgive herself for, was listening to Rachel Tanquillan, for having played her part in engineering a marriage between Romilly and Rowan which was bound to end in disaster. She did not blame him for loving Charlotte Grayler, but how she wished it might have been herself he loved. Had she been twenty years younger . . . She smiled sadly to herself.

Rowan said, 'I think that Romilly will not care very much one way or the other. She told me she never wanted to see me again.'

She stared out of the window. 'I'm so sorry, my dear. I feel that I am somehow to blame for all this.'

'Oh no!' He seized her shoulders, swung her round to face him. 'You mustn't think that; you who have been my best and dearest friend. Forgive me, but you have meant more to me than my own flesh and blood. If you knew how much I admire you, Emily!' He kissed her gently on the cheek.

'And now what?' She smoothed her burning cheek with her fingertips.

He smiled ruefully. 'Now I must face the music.'

'Have you thought how deeply shocked your parents will be?'

'No, I'm afraid I haven't. This was something I had to do for my own reasons. I have simply come home to make arrangements for Romilly's future. I shall go to the bank tomorrow. Everything I have in the world is hers. The day after tomorrow I shall swear my Oath of Allegiance.'

'But . . .'

He held her hands tightly in his. 'No, don't try to talk me out of it. When I take that oath, I shall go into the Army with nothing but the clothes I stand up in. I must discover what kind of man I really am. Do you understand, Emily?'

'Oh yes, my dear, I think so. But I can't help feeling that there is something – something you haven't told me – have not told Romilly even . . .' She paused. 'You know you can trust me.'

He smiled sadly. 'My mother knows. I'm surprised she hasn't told you. Or perhaps she has?'

'About – Charlotte Grayler, you mean?' Emily laid her hand on his shoulder, her eyes bright with tears.

'She did tell you then! I might have known!'

'I'm so sorry, Rowan. I wish she hadn't. I hated myself for listening.'

'It's all right, Emily. I can't blame you for that. But Charlotte has done nothing wrong. I have never been unfaithful to Romilly, though, God knows, I wished to be. I do love Charlotte. I married Romilly under false pretences. I have never loved Romilly the way I love Charlotte!'

He turned away. 'I'm sorry. Now you see me for what I really am, a cheat and a liar!'

'No, my dear,' she said gently. 'I am the cheat and the liar because of my own weakness and folly. I have known, all along, that you did not love my daughter as a man should love his wife, but I was too weak and stupid, too bound up with convention; too lonely and selfish, at the time, to face the truth. Forgive me, Rowan. Please forgive me.'

'There is nothing to forgive,' he said slowly, bending down to kiss her. 'Now I must go to Romilly.'

'You can't mean that you are going to leave me?' Romilly stared at Rowan from her pillows. 'Of all the mean, despicable tricks! But I know why. You can't bear the sight of a helpless, pregnant cripple!'

'Please, Romilly,' Rowan said wearily, 'you cannot believe that.'

'I don't know what to believe any longer.'

'Then believe this. I am sorry for everything that has happened; sorry I have made you so unhappy. I have made provision for you and – and our child. I know you'll be safe with your mother. And you will get well again soon, whether or not you believe it.'

'You *have* made me unhappy,' she sobbed. 'Why did you marry me if you didn't love me? Why were you never there when I needed you? You have made a fool of me, and I will never forgive you for that! Now you are going away. *Why* are you going?'

'Because I cannot live with myself as I am any longer,' he said hoarsely. 'Because . . .'

'Because I threw myself at you, didn't I?' Romilly whimpered. 'It's the truth! I see it all now! God, how you must have pitied me, a stupid girl so much in love with you that she couldn't even begin to imagine how much you loathed her!'

'I have never – loathed you,' he said quietly. 'I have always looked upon you as the sister I never had.' He clenched his hands on the coverlet, knowing that he could never explain his feelings to her in a thousand years, faced as he was by the brick wall of her hostility. 'I wanted you to be happy. I thought, in marrying you, I could make you happy.'

'But you never wanted to marry me at all, did you? That's true, isn't it?' Her voice rose hysterically. 'God, what kind of a man are you? How did you feel in church, that day, making vows which you intended to break even as you made them? But I know why now. It was always Alice, Alice, Alice! It was always Alice you wanted, never me, never *me* . . .'

He rose to his feet, knowing there was nothing left to say.

'You are going to find her now, I suppose?' she cried accusingly as he reached the door.

He turned, his face a mask of suffering. 'No, Romilly,' he said. 'God willing, I am going to find myself.'

'What bloody tomfoolery is this?' Gervaise Tanquillan stared at Rowan in amazement. 'My son joining the Army as a private! Christ! I refuse to believe that even you are capable of such lunacy! What about the business? What about your mother and me?'

He poured himself a stiff glass of brandy, unnerved by the realization that his hand was shaking. The veins in his cheeks stood out like scarlet embroidery cotton, his eyes narrowed to slits behind his gold-framed spectacles. 'We'll see about this,' he snapped. 'You haven't actually taken the oath, so you are not yet fully committed.' He tilted the glass to his lips, his mind busy with ways and means of extricating his son from what he saw as an act of folly perpetrated in a moment of youthful fervour.

Standing there in his father's study, scene of so many lectures connected with the duties and responsibilities of a Tanquillan towards that insatiable god, the Family Business, Rowan said implacably, 'But I *am* committed, Father, because I want to be, and nothing you can do or say will prevent me.'

Gervaise slumped into a chair. 'For Christ's sake, Rowan, does it mean nothing to you that you are about to ruin all that I have built up for you over the years?'

'You have built nothing for me, Father, that I value,' Rowan said levelly. 'What you have done has been for the Company. When have you ever looked on me as anything but an extension of your own vanity; the continuance of a name?'

Gervaise rose unsteadily to his feet. 'How dare you say such a thing? I have given you – everything!'

'In the physical sense, perhaps, I admit that. The one thing you never gave me, which I needed above all else, was – love. No, listen, Father! Do you remember the day I tried to explain to you my love of music? I reached out to you then in the hope that you would understand how deeply I felt about it. You did not even pay me the compliment of taking me seriously. All you did was cancel my lessons.'

Rowan fingered the silver inkwell on his father's desk. 'If you had spoken to me kindly then, if you had only taken the time and the trouble to explain your reasons for not wanting me to become a musician: if you had said: "I understand your feelings, but I need you, my son," I would have gone to the end of the earth and back to please you. But never once, in the whole of my life, have you told me you love me, and neither has my mother. That is why I intend to break away from this curious prison you think of as a family, which has to do with money, not love.'

He strode from the room, closing the door firmly behind him.

Later, Rachel said charmingly, 'Rowan, my dear, your father has told me what you intend doing. But you won't join that stupid Army, will you, for my sake?'

She was dressed for dinner in an emerald silk gown, smelling excitingly of Houbigant's 'Quelques Fleurs'; her hair drawn back into a chignon, her arms and neck lightly powdered, with diamond and emerald bracelets clasped about her wrists. But her eyes, he saw, were as chilly as marble chippings beneath her pencilled eyebrows. The eyes of an emotional blackmailer.

He touched her extended hand coolly with his lips, and smiled up at her. 'I wouldn't dream of doing this for your sake, Maman,' he said levelly. 'This is something I intend doing for my own sake.'

It was over at last, the sham and the fake, the lies and tears, the emotional blackmail, the accusations and recriminations.

He had ridden out the storm; the anger, the business dealings, the settling of his affairs, with one thought in mind – freedom.

And yet, as he stood up to swear his Oath of Allegiance, Rowan knew that he would never be free of loving Charlotte Grayler.

CHAPTER FOUR

Albert dreaded Frank's return from his honeymoon. Looking out at the square, at a newsboy dropping papers through letterboxes, he thought that when Frank – the leader – got back, it would be a question of hours before the lads enlisted. He wished he was young and fit enough to go with them. Age had crept up on him suddenly, filling him with a sense of bewilderment, of hurt pride that his limbs no longer moved as quickly as they used to.

It was almost closing time. He called to Harry to send the apprentices home. Harry came through the shop, lugging the shutters, those long heavy green boards to latch into place – against what? Since that panic-buying invasion of local house-wives there was precious little left to protect against thieves. But old habits died hard. He heard the slam of the back door as the apprentices went away, whistling. His once firm muscles ached abominably as he helped Harry to lift and secure the shutters. His breath caught in his throat as he hoisted them into position. He could scarcely bear it when Harry said, 'Don't worry, Dad, I can manage on my own.' He wondered, as he went upstairs for his supper, who would do all the humping and lifting when Frank and Harry joined the army.

When he had eaten, he sat down to read the evening paper. Spies were being rounded up. He glanced at a picture of two unhappy-looking foreigners being escorted to the police station for questioning. The King's chef had been arrested too, but wasn't it a bit thick to categorize all the honest, decent men working as chefs and waiters as spies? It seemed to Albert the height of stupidity to send men who had chosen to live in England back to their own countries to face a no man's land of despair. He flicked through the pages. Horses were being commandeered by the Army for immediate shipment to France.

Horses! Christ, Albert thought, what if they take Nobby?

They did take Nobby. Albert had never felt so sick and helpless in his life as when, next day, an army sergeant appeared on his doorstep.

'I understand you have a horse, sir?'

'It's not my horse. It belongs to my son!' The colour drained from Albert's cheeks, his legs began to tremble.

'Quite so, sir.' The sergeant hated this job – taking away people's horses. The ones he had so far commandeered were strung together in the lane, the poor brutes, ready for branding and shipment overseas. Nobody could tell him they didn't know what was happening. They knew all right by the look in their eyes, their frantic neighing when they were led away. 'I'm sorry, but it's my duty. If your son's horse is fit for service, I've got to take it.'

Harry came through from the warehouse. 'What's happening? What's going on?' He wiped his hands nervously on his corduroys.

'It's Nobby, son. They're commandeering Nobby.'

'They're bloody well not,' Harry burst forth, 'nobody's taking my horse! I'll kill the bastards if they lay a finger on him!'

'No use taking that attitude, sir. We've got to take it.'

'Oh yes?' Harry rounded on the man, hands clenched. 'And who are you to come here laying the law down? What about my father? How do you suppose he'll manage the deliveries when my brothers and I join up, if you take the horse as well?'

'I'm sorry. It isn't my fault. You don't suppose I like doing it. Now if I could just see the animal.'

'Oh, Christ!'

Albert had not seen Harry cry since he was a little boy. 'Don't, son,' he said unsteadily, 'I can't bear it.'

Harry lifted his red-rimmed, grief-stricken eyes to his father. 'But the bloody bastards are taking Nobby!'

Filly and Charlotte came downstairs, white-faced. Filly

began to cry. Charlotte slipped her arm round Harry's waist. She turned to the sergeant standing there at a loss to know how to proceed. 'Please, can't you give us just a little while longer?' she begged. 'This isn't just a horse, it's part of us; our family.'

He was a youngish man with an eye for a pretty face. 'Well, I don't know, miss. I have my orders.'

'My brother will be all right when he's had time to get used to the idea, I promise.'

'Half an hour then, no more.'

'Come on, Harry,' Charlotte said gently. She thought, as she watched him walk down the yard to the stable, that this was a facet of war none of them had envisaged.

'I'm going too,' Filly said, but Charlotte laid a restraining hand on her arm. 'Best not,' she said, 'this is Harry's time.' Firmly she took command of the situation. 'We'll wait in the kitchen. I'll make some tea.'

It was the worst half-hour of her life, sitting at the table with her parents, unable even to swallow the tea she had made. She sprang to her feet as she heard the clatter of hooves in the yard below. She could see, from the window, a long string of horses in the lane behind the house. Then Harry led his horse from the stable, his head against its neck, his strong young fingers caressing its muzzle. There was a quiet dignity about Harry now as he hitched Nobby to the leather strap held by a young corporal. When the string of horses moved away, Harry hunched himself against the wall, his arm across his eyes.

'I'm going down to him,' Filly cried, jumping up, knocking over her teacup.

'No, Mother. He'll be better on his own for a while.' Knowing Harry, he would need time to get over the shock. There was nothing anyone could say or do to mitigate his suffering.

'I don't know what's come over you, our Charlotte,' Filly cried accusingly. 'How you can stand there so calm and cool and collected, I don't know.'

'Don't, Mother,' Albert said wearily. 'Copper's right. Leave the lad alone.'

Filly turned on him. 'Oh yes, it's always the same with you.

Charlotte can do no wrong in your eyes. But I know Harry better than she does. After all, I am his mother!'

'Sit down, Filly!'

'*What?*'

'I said, sit down! Can't you see that Copper is just as upset as we are?' He remembered something Filly had said to him what seemed a lifetime ago: 'Don't you realize that Charlotte has outgrown us?'

Frank could not bear to stay on in London a minute longer. War had been declared, and there he was incarcerated in a stuffy hotel bedroom. Even the pattern on the curtains was beginning to get on his nerves since he had viewed it from all angles during the past twenty-four hours.

Sated and sore with love-making, with his bottom lip swollen and a hunger pain in his stomach, he pulled away from Madge. 'Look, love,' he said irritably, 'I've just got to get back to Scarborough. I can't hang about here any longer doing nothing.'

'*Doing nothing!* Well, I like that!' Madge sat up in bed. 'Why, you rotten, selfish bastard! What about me?'

Having overcome the spectre of impotency, having proved his manhood time and time again amid a bewildering mass of kicked-aside sheets and blankets, Frank felt hurt and misunderstood by Madge's condemnation of him as a 'selfish bastard'. He was bloody hungry now, and sick to death of sex. The glorious energy bottled up in his lean young frame demanded other, more purposeful outlets. He had had enough of plunging and panting for the time being, enough of that damned pattern on the curtains.

Madge, with the sheet tucked under her chin, had no clear understanding of male psychology. Having discovered the pleasures of the marriage-bed, she wished to remain in it indefinitely, although she too was hungry for a good steak dinner in the hotel restaurant. Too angry to speak, she began to cry.

'Aw, Madgie,' Frank said awkwardly, pulling on his trousers, 'don't turn on the waterworks.'

As he bent down to kiss her, he received a stinging blow on the cheek, and watched in amazement as she rose up, stark naked, and began throwing the contents of the dressing-table pell-mell into a suitcase, muttering under her breath as she did so, hurt and humiliated that her fine buxom body aroused no further passion in him.

'What the hell are you doing?' he asked.

'What do you think I'm doing?' She threw her wedding negligée across her shoulders. 'There doesn't seem much point in staying on here since you are tired of me already.'

'Tired of you?' He would never understand women if he lived to be a hundred. 'How can you say that when I've had you seven times in the past twelve hours!'

They caught the train back to Scarborough in a wordless fury of misunderstanding.

Charlotte knew at once that something was wrong. She had never cared much for Madge, but this distraught girl was now her sister-in-law, Frank's wife. It did not take much guessing to know what had happened. Frank strode into the house like a giant refreshed, Madge was on the verge of tears. Their appearance surprised Filly in particular. When Frank asked where Harry was, she said she didn't know. He had gone off somewhere since they had taken his horse away that morning.

'Taken Nobby? Christ Almighty!' Frank said in a shocked voice. 'But why?'

'If you'll come with me, Frank, I'll tell you.' Charlotte hustled him into the dining-room and closed the door firmly behind her.

'What the hell's going on here?' He had never seen Charlotte so angry before. 'What's come over you all of a sudden?'

'More to the point, what's come over you, dragging Madge back to Scarborough like this,' she said hotly. 'No, don't try to explain. I know why you've come. But I'm telling you straight, Frank, we've had all the heartache we can stand for one day. If you breathe one word about joining up now, I'll never speak to you again as long as I live!'

'But Charlotte. . . .'

'Don't you "but Charlotte" me! Since you are here, since you have taken it into your head to spoil Madge's honeymoon, just give a thought to Mother and Dad. How dare you breeze in to add to their troubles? The army's taken Nobby, just as it will take you and Harry and Joey in time.' She felt in her pocket for a handkerchief. 'I'm ashamed of you, Frank Grayler! So just have your supper, and keep quiet for once in your life!'

'My God,' he said, bemused. 'What's happened to you?'

'Never mind what's happened to me. I don't give a damn for myself. It's Mum and Dad I'm concerned about. We're having no more unhappiness in this house today!'

He had the grace to admit that he was sorry. 'I'm sorry, too,' she said. 'I didn't mean to fly off the handle like that. It's just that everything is happening too fast. It's this war. This damned, bloody war!'

'But Harry, Joe and me, we're all going to enlist,' he said moodily.

'I know that. So do Mum and Dad. But surely you can spare them just a little more time after all the years they have given to us.'

'Yeah, I suppose so, but. . . .'

'But nothing! If this war means an end to kindness, the sooner we are all dead the better. And you haven't been very kind to Madge, have you? Can't you see how upset she is?'

He had never seen Charlotte so determined before, or realized how beautiful she was. Frank had always thought of his sister as a skinny, meek and mild kid. Now, as she stood before him with her eyes flashing fire, her cheeks reddened with anger, her bright flame-coloured hair standing like an aureole about her oval face, her shoulders drawn back proudly above her slightly swelling breasts, he caught his breath in surprise.

'All right,' he said, 'I'll do as you ask.' He smiled suddenly, the old indomitable Frank Grayler smile. 'But just for tonight. Tomorrow or the next day, Harry, Joe and I are off to that recruiting office.'

'I know that, Frankie. Just give us tonight.'

Harry came in later, subdued and red-eyed. Nobody asked him

where he had been and he did not tell them that he had spent the entire day walking, until the sheer physical exercise had numbed the pain of his despair. The sight of Frank surprised and cheered him. 'I thought you weren't coming back until Saturday,' he said, and wondered why Madge looked so miserable, sitting there in the front room with her honeymoon hat perched on her head, her lips quivering.

'Sorry about Nobby,' Frank said, gripping his brother's shoulder.

'Ay, well, what's done is done,' Harry replied shortly, unable even to talk about it.

When Joe came in, he too evinced surprise that Frank had come back from his honeymoon so soon, then wished that he had kept his mouth shut when he caught sight of Madge. Joe, the most perceptive of the brothers, quick to sense atmosphere, weighed things up at a glance. Even Frank seemed curiously restrained. Glancing at Charlotte, Joe knew why, that she had 'had it out' with Frank. He breathed a sigh of relief.

He had heard, when he came up from the harbour for his dinner, that Nobby had been commandeered, that Harry was missing. It was so like Charlotte to have fettled Frank to save their parents further distress on this curiously eventful day.

He had brought home with him a bass-bag full of fish for supper, gleaming herring, mackerel, and plaice landed from the cobles that afternoon. The muscles of his throat tightened as he looked into the void of the future when there would be no more gifts of fish to his mother. This fraught family amnesty could not last forever. He called Filly into the kitchen; saw her smile as she emptied the fish into the sink and began to clean it.

He knew that a main contingent of Green Howards had left Scarborough by the afternoon train, that men were flocking to the recruiting centres to enlist. There would be little or no delay in kitting out recruits once they had sworn their Oath of Allegiance to the Crown. Joe had no stomach for war, for fighting, for killing. He loved his home and his girl, his quiet little Annie Crystal. But he was no coward. He was not afraid of dying. What he most regretted giving up was the quietude of home, his peaceful existence in the town he loved. He gave his mother a brief hug; thought, with a pang of guilt, that he had lied to her all along about the fish he brought home being a perk of his job. He had paid for every fillet from his wages.

Madge ate practically nothing despite Frank's coaxing. Charlotte's 'telling-off' had hit home and he was doing his best to jolly his wife into a better frame of mind – without much success. 'I'm sorry, love,' he murmured as they went into the dining-room, but Madge's pride had been stung.

'That's all very fine,' she snapped. 'A nice fool you've made of me, Frank Grayler. What will my parents say when they know how you've treated me? I'll never be able to hold my head up again.'

Frank got his mother alone in the kitchen afterwards. Filly had never liked Madge Robinson but she did possess a sharp sense of fair play, and she berated Frank soundly for his thoughtlessness in dragging his wife home so soon. Knowing in her heart of hearts why he had done so did not improve matters. She dared not think about that at present.

'Could we stay here tonight, Ma?' he wheedled.

'Certainly not! She's your wife. You've got rooms of your own to go to, so you'd best go to them, hadn't you?' She could not help getting that dig in. She relented later, not for Frank's sake but for Madge's, and because she did not really want her son shown up in a bad light to the Robinsons.

'All right, you can have the spare room,' she said at last. 'That lass looks all in. Fancy, after all that money she spent on her wedding duds.' She sighed, her face flushed after the cooking and washing-up. 'I shan't be sorry to get to bed myself after all the goings-on we've had today.'

'Look, Madgie,' Frank said when they were alone together, 'I'm sorry about everything. It's just that Harry and Joe and I made a pact. We'll be joining up tomorrow.'

'Join up then! See if I care!'

'You don't mean that!' His desire was aroused anew at the sight of her in her wedding nightgown with her hair unbraided.

He slipped his arm round her waist.

'Oh, stop pawing me!' She was coolly matter-of-fact now. 'I'm here because I have to be, not because I want to. The honeymoon's over!'

Because nothing, no situation, emotion – anger, grief or happiness – ever remains static, by morning Madge had relented somewhat, tickled because she had proved her power over Frank in denying him his conjugal rights until she saw fit to restore them. But attempting to coax him out of his intention to join up, she came up against the brick wall of his resistance, so Madge's triumph was shortlived and Frank, staring up at the ceiling, thought the sooner he was in the army the better.

Filly pressed her hands to her eyes to shut out the sight of her uniformed sons. She had not thought that the Army would snap them up so quickly. She sank to her knees near a highbacked chair which had belonged to her mother and lifted her hands in an attitude of prayer and bewilderment. 'Oh God, I can't bear it,' she sobbed.

'Aw, come on, Ma,' Frank said uneasily, 'we don't look all that bad, do we?' He felt strangely out of place standing there in the front room in his ill-fitting khaki uniform, ranged up with his brothers near the fireplace, thinking that this reminded him of when they were kids about to go on a Sunday school outing, lined up to have their ears and knees inspected. And yet how proud, how purposeful he had felt when he marched out of that drill hall with the King's shilling in his pocket. This was the moment he had dreaded all along: his mother's tears.

Harry said, 'We haven't got long, Ma. Our train leaves in half an hour.'

It was Charlotte who rallied. 'I'd better pack you something for your journey. Come and help me, Madge.'

She opened a tin of corned beef; gave Madge a loaf to cut and butter. The starch had gone out of Madge now, her hands were shaking, tears rolled down her cheeks. 'Oh God,' she whimpered.

'Here, let me!' Charlotte took charge of the bread-knife. 'I'll see to the bread while you put the meat in the sandwiches. We'll have to hurry to get to the station on time.'

'The station?' Madge's face puckered. 'I'm not going to the station!'

'You must go! Please, Madge. We must give them a proper send-off. Mum can't go, so it's up to us.' She cut into a currant cake which she wrapped in greaseproof paper. 'There, that's about it,' she mused. 'Heaven knows when they'll get their next proper meal. Come on, Madge, put your hat and coat on.'

Madge made no further demur. Shocked by the suddenness of events, she did as Charlotte told her. But she could not bear to go back into the living-room where Filly was saying goodbye to her sons. Albert walked unsteadily onto the landing, grey-faced, his eyes filled with tears. 'Are you all right, Mr Grayler?' Madge asked, thinking how ill he looked. Strangely, he and Madge drew comfort from each other in the few minutes before the boys appeared. Albert said, 'I'm sorry, Madge. This can't be easy for you.' She laid her hand on his sleeve. 'It isn't easy for any of us, is it?' she said. 'Are you — are you going to the station?' Albert shook his head. 'I'd like to, but I can't leave their mother alone in the house. It will seem very empty without them.'

Annie was at the station when they arrived, a lonely figure in grey, standing beneath the clock-tower. Her face lit up when she saw Joe. She hurried towards him, hands outstretched. 'Oh, Joe, I was so afraid I wouldn't get here on time . . .' She glanced up at him shyly. 'You look so — so grand in your uniform.' They walked hand in hand to the train.

'Everything happened so fast,' Joe explained, keeping tight hold of his girl's hand. 'I think even Harry and Frank were surprised. The doctor scarcely bothered to examine us properly, there were so many of us waiting for medicals. When we had signed the attestation forms and sworn the Oath of Allegiance, we were kitted out and given travel warrants straight away.'

'Oh, Joey. What a shock for your poor mother. I'll go up and see her tonight. . . .'

'Bless you, Annie.' He gripped her hand more tightly as they pushed their way through the crowds on the platform. 'Thank God I was able to get a message to you in time. I just shoved a tanner in a kid's hand and told him to run round to the cafe.'

Annie worked as a waitress at Rowntrees Old Time Cafe in Westborough. When a breathless little lad had run in asking for her, she had simply pinned on her hat, put her coat over her uniform, and hurried to the station.

Madge, subdued and tearful, clung to Frank's arm as they threaded their way to the train. Harry and Charlotte walked together. The music of a brass band vied with the noise of steam-letting from the engine. People were laughing, weeping, waving Union Jacks. The band played the old Boer War song, 'Soldiers of the Queen'. Great clouds of steam rose up to the station roof. Charlotte held Harry's arm; walked beside him proudly upright. He said, 'Take care of Mum and Dad for us.' the pain of leave-taking had hit Harry amidships. He could scarcely speak for the lump in his throat. Strangely, his father's brief handshake, his words, 'Goodbye, my son. Take care,' uttered in a low, hoarse voice, had touched him far more than his mother's tears.

'I'll do my best, Harry,' Charlotte said, thinking how unreal everything seemed. 'You've got your sandwiches, and you will write as soon as possible?'

'You bet.' He had never felt so strange in his life before. His uniform seemed big enough for two men. He could scarcely believe that he was now a soldier. He felt like a small boy dressed for a charade.

'It's almost time,' Frank said nervously. 'Give us a kiss, Madgie.'

Madge wished, as she dug her teeth into Frank's bottom lip, that she had been more compliant during the night. She loved him now as she had loved him outside Buckingham Palace the night war was declared. God, but he was handsome. But, even as she kissed him again and again, she knew that the essential Frank Grayler had already left her. She noticed the elation in his eyes as the whistle blew, the eager way he swung himself into the carriage.

As the train moved slowly away from the platform, the

windows were filled with faces; a forest of waving arms appeared. When the train was out of sight, there was nothing left but loneliness, memories and fast-falling tears beneath a pall of smoke as the band packed their instruments and departed. The platform was strewn with torn paper Union flags.

Outside the station, Charlotte, Annie and Madge stood together for a few minutes, bound momentarily by a strange feeling of anti-climax, with tomorrow, and so many tomorrows to face as best they could without the men they loved.

CHAPTER FIVE

Station morning! Charlotte stood in the yard gripping the shafts of the hardcart she had borrowed from Mr Roe, the fishmonger, while the apprentices, young Billy Sowerby and Tommy Chambers, hurried from the warehouse lugging the empty kegs and crates to stack on the barrow.

'Yer niver gonna wheel that thing down to't station by yourself, miss, are yer?' gasped the breathless Billy. 'Why, it'll run away wi' thee on't hills!'

'In that case, Billy Sowerby,' Charlotte said briskly, 'you and Tommy had better come with me to see that it doesn't.'

'Eee, me an' Tommy can't leave t'warehouse,' Billy said nervously. 'T'Maister 'ull hev our hides if we does.'

'No, he won't,' Charlotte assured the lad. 'Things have changed now. There's a war on. But this lot of empties had better be at the station on time, or *I'll* have your hides! Understood?'

'Yes miss.'

'Right then. Is that the lot?'

'Yes miss.'

'Very well. Come on.'

The curious procession wended its way round the square to Ramshill Road, Charlotte and Billy holding the cart handles; Tommy straining against the front of it on the downhill slope to the station, his short-trousered legs splaying out like pipe-stems, the heels of his boots seeking purchase on the flinty road surface.

Sweating and panting, her hat bouncing on her head, Charlotte realized what this war would mean to the women left behind to carry on the work of men and horses in their absence, but she clung to the cart handles like grim death, determined that, even though Harry and Nobby were gone, she would somehow continue where they had left off.

She had been up since the crack of dawn, struggling to take down the shutters, buckling at the knees as she swung back the heavy iron latches which secured them, thinking that she might easily be crushed if the great solid slabs of wood fell on top of her. And yet she had managed somehow to hold them, to 'walk' them, one by one, to the warehouse. But her arms were scraped and bruised by their contact with the thick, unyielding planks, and she had been obliged to sit down on the back step afterwards to get her breath back.

'My God, girl,' Filly cried when she came down with her Brasso and cleaning rags, 'whatever have you been up to? Look at those bruises on your arms!'

'Don't fuss, Mum. I'll wear long sleeves next time.'

'But taking down those shutters on your own! Your dad will have a fit when he hears about this!'

'Don't tell him then.'

'But you can't go on like this, a skinny bit of a lass like you trying to do a man's work.'

'It will get easier as I go along,' Charlotte said stubbornly. 'By the way, I've arranged with Annie to borrow her bicycle so that I can get round to take the orders.'

'Orders!' Filly snapped, 'what's the use of that? We've hardly anything left to sell!'

'That's not the point, Mum. We must keep in touch with the customers; explain how things stand. If nobody bothers, they'll think we don't care.'

'That's all very well, but when you've taken the orders – just supposing there are any – what about the deliveries now that Harry and Nobby have gone?' Filly's eyes filled with tears as she spoke. She wiped them away with a clean corner of her Brasso rag.

'I've borrowed Mr Roe's old handcart for the time being,' Charlotte explained, 'until we can get one of our own.'

Filly was horrified. 'What? My daughter shoving a handcart round town! Whatever next! I won't let you do it!'

'Women will end up doing worse things than pushing handcarts before this war is over,' Charlotte reminded her. 'This is no time for false pride. It's a matter of survival.'

Filly, who had scarcely slept all night for worrying about her sons, felt out of sorts with herself and the world at large as a result. 'Survival!' she sniffed. 'What worries me is the thought of those lads of mine not getting enough to eat. You know how faddy Frank is about his food. I've heard tell they give them nothing but porridge for breakfast, and Frank hates porridge. He won't survive long on that!'

'Cheer up, Mum,' Charlotte said, squeezing Filly's hand, 'it won't do Frank any harm to eat something he doesn't like for a change.'

But Filly was in no mood to be cheered up, 'I don't know what's come over you lately,' she said. 'You've been different ever since you came back from Wiltshire. I don't like it. You're much harder than you used to be. I haven't forgotten the way you spoke to me they day they took the horse.'

'I'm sorry, I didn't mean to upset you. I just thought Harry would be better on his own. He wouldn't have wanted us to see him crying.' She glanced at her mother, longing to confide in her that she was different because she had learned more about life since she went away. It was on the tip of her tongue to tell Filly that she had fallen in love, but the words died on her lips. She loved her mother, but she knew her so well. Filly would throw up her hands in horror if the truth came out.

The warehouse smelt mustily of tea, and despite Filly's grouse of there being nothing left to sell, the shelves were still far from denuded, due to Albert's careful husbandry. Filly had perched herself on an upturned keg beneath stalactites of muslin-covered bacon rolls. 'That yard wants swilling,' she said, staring out through the open door.

'I'll see to it when I get back from the station,' Charlotte replied, standing up. She had pushed Mr Roe's handcart out of sight in the stable for the time being; now she went to fetch it and wheeled it out into the yard, ready to load up when the apprentices arrived.

'Oh my God,' cried Filly, 'it reeks of fish!'

'Well, it's bound to, isn't it?'

'*Charlotte*! I won't let you!' But Charlotte was already giving instructions to the apprentices as they came in by the back gate.

They waited avidly for news. When it came, it told of blisters and backaches, cramped accommodation, ditch-digging and route marches. The boys were billeted for the time being in a Darlington drill hall while a camp in Hummersknott Park was under preparation. Meanwhile the Grayler lads were sleeping in a barrack-type room with hardly any space between the beds. 'It's the snoring that gets me,' Frank wrote. 'I thought the bloody roof would lift off the first night.' He had scratched out the more pithy adjective and substituted the word 'blooming'. 'The food isn't much cop neither, so if you could see your way clear to sending us a good cut-and-come-again cake, I'd be much obliged.'

Rowan sat on an upturned barrel to write to Charlotte; the first opportunity he had had to set pen to paper since joining The Rangers. It was a bright, clear Sunday morning, the first rest day his Company had enjoyed since leaving London at the outbreak of war.

On the evening of 4 August, the rank and file were marched away to spend the night at the central Y.M.C.A. in Tottenham Court Road. During the days that followed, rumours had run rife as to where they would be sent next. Bert Hoskins, the cheerful Cockney Rowan first met in the enlistment queue outside Scotland Yard, had tapped his nose with his forefinger and said it was bound to be overseas, whereupon a mate of his scoffed, 'G'arn, Bert, we ain't even been taught to fire a gun yet. What bloody good would we be overseas? Stands to reason, we've gotta be trained first.'

It had come as a shock to the chirpy Cockney when they ended up in Regent's Park for rifle training; when their first route march landed them at Hampstead Heath. From there they were marched to Staines. Now, sitting close to Rowan, nursing his blistered feet and swearing softly under his breath, Bert muttered that his old woman would have the laugh on him right enough if she found out he was still pussyfooting about in the South of England, hardly a cock-stride from where he'd set off, after all he'd said about wanting to get over to France to have a go at the Germans.

Rowan stopped writing to grin at him. 'Cheer up, Bert. We'll get there soon enough.'

'What I can't understand,' Bert said, 'is what a toff like you is doing in an outfit like this. A well-educated bloke like you, chucking in with this mucky lot, don't seem right to me.' He scratched his head as he spoke. 'The bleeder in the bed next to mine is lousy. Gawd's truth, guv, I don't know which to scratch first, me feet or me napper.'

Bert was sharp-faced, keenly intelligent, with an engaging smile despite his broken teeth, a whippet of a man with slightly bandy legs and tattooed forearms embellished with lovers' knots, doves, and the name 'Ada' which, he confessed, was one of the reasons why he and his old woman didn't see eye-to-eye at times since her name was Bertha.

He cocked an eyebrow at the writing-pad on Rowan's knee. 'Writing to the missis, are yer?' he enquired. 'Suppose I oughta write to mine, but I ain't gonna. Not till I gets well out of harm's way, that is. If she knew where I was, she'd be after me, an' she's a big woman is my Bertha.'

Rowan laughed and returned to his letter.

'Dearest Charlotte,

I knew, when I said goodbye to you in London, that life as I had lived it was over for me. The love I feel for you could no longer be denied whatever the consequences, nor could my desire to change what I could no longer endure. That is why I have enlisted with The First County of London Battalion, The Rangers, as an infantryman. I discovered that the original Regimental title was The Gentlemen Members of Grays Inn, nick-named 'The Devil's Own' which seems apt in my case.

Today, Sunday 16 August, is fine and fair, our first rest day since war was declared. Sitting here with the sun on my face, memories of our last meeting come flooding back to me. Loving you imbued me with enough courage to break free at last. I had breathed freedom on our day of days together. Selfishly, perhaps, I could no longer deny myself that freedom to live and love as my heart dictates.

Whatever my faults and failings, and they are many, I offer you one unalterable truth – I love you. I shall go on loving you.'

Not knowing that Charlotte had left Grey Wethers, he posted the letter there, care of his Aunt Kitty, who re-addressed and sent it on to Scarborough where it arrived on the morning of 20 August, along with a letter from Jenny.

Charlotte, down early to open the shop, saw the two envelopes side by side on the doormat. When Filly came down to wash the step, Charlotte was standing near the side door, her apron splashed with bright coloured lights from the stained glass, eyes shining, cheeks flushed with excitement. 'What are you standing there for?' Filly asked suspiciously. 'What's that you're reading?'

'It – it's a letter.'

'A letter? Who from?'

'It's from Jenny.' Charlotte's heart missed a beat. Suppose her mother asked to read the letter? But Filly's mind was elsewhere. 'Oh, by the way, the vicar's wife will be glad of our help at the hospital tonight. Seems they've brought in some Belgian soldiers.' She sighed deeply. 'I don't know what the world's coming to – our lads going over there to be shot at and theirs coming over here to be nursed. It seems all wrong to me.'

Scarborough Hospital, a red-brick gabled building with a creaking lift, iron bedsteads, pulleys, and an occasional aspidistra in the wards, seemed overlaid with the smell of disinfectant which permeated everywhere from the lobby to the lavatories, along with the odour of boiled fish, stewed mutton and rice pudding.

Friends of the Hospital, mainly large-bosomed ladies in sweeping hats, had settled themselves in a basement room where they handed out, to their smaller-bosomed helpers, quantities of wool, knitting needles, newly washed and dis-infected bandages to be re-rolled, and zinc buckets, mops and

Jeyes fluid to those unfortunate enough to be called on to swab the floors. They were estimable women with a high sense of public duty, mainly the wives of aldermen and vicars, whose wide experience of getting things done had certainly borne fruit if the boxes of socks, comforters, Balaclava helmets and blanket squares they had collected were anything to go by. They spoke of 'Our Brave Lads' in capital letters and took it in turn to read from the Bible or the works of Jane Austen as their minions swabbed, rolled or knitted: always ready with a word of advice if a heel went wrong or a sloppily-rolled bandage went bouncing across the linoed floor from the shaking fingers of a new recruit.

Charlotte elected to swab floors. Anything was better than being incarcerated in a stuffy basement listening to Job, Chapter Three, Verse One. Despite her hard day wheeling Mr Roe's handcart round town delivering orders, her abundant energy was not exhausted, and so she lugged her zinc bucket upstairs to the lobby, swabbed, squeezed out the mop, swabbed and squeezed again until her arms ached, smiling inwardly as she thought of Jenny doing much the same kind of thing in one of the big London hospitals, since she had embarked on her nursing career, 'doing,' as she put it, 'the most menial, boring jobs imaginable, my dear Carlotta. But I face quite cheerfully the fact that I shall probably end up doing far worse things than cleaning sluices and polishing floors when I get to France. And get there I must and *shall!*' Darling Jenny. Even a hastily scrawled letter breathed something of her warm, vital personality.

She had tucked Rowan's letter in her apron pocket. If only she could feel certain that he would never regret leaving his wife and unborn child. She could not quite believe that he would not, and yet her heart was filled with a wild, singing gladness that he still loved her and, whatever the outcome, she would always love him.

She thought, as she swabbed the long corridors between the wards, that all she wanted at this moment was to deaden her emotions with hard work; to fall into bed too physically exhausted to do anything but sleep soundly. But even when her limbs felt as heavy as lead, her brain played traitor as she tossed from side to side worrying about her brothers; Rowan; and her father. She could not fathom what was wrong with Dadda, but she had noticed, since the boys went away, how confused he seemed, like a child in need of constant direction; a clock with the mainspring damaged.

That night, despite her weariness, sleep would not come. She paced her room until the small hours, wanting to run to Rowan, to feel his arms about her. Moonlight was streaming in when she sat near the window to write to him, but the words would not flow. She tore up page after page despairingly, afraid that what she wrote was too fulsome or too stiff. What she wanted to say was: 'Please, my darling, do not think that I would blame you if, in the end, you felt that you must go back to Romilly. All this – your sudden decision to enlist, your longing for freedom, might turn to dust in your mouth one day. A living child, flesh of your flesh, might prove to be more important than your love for me. I would never wish that love which exists between us to blind you to reality or to prevent you from changing your mind one day.'

In the end, after a long and exhausting battle with her emotions, Charlotte wrote just that, and slipped out of the house to post the letter in the pillar-box at the end of the square as the light of a new day was breaking over the sea.

She walked to the Esplanade to watch the play of light on the water, the first flush of pink and gold touching the horizon. How quiet the town looked, how peaceful with the fishermen's cottages clustered about the harbour and the tide washing up on the sand. Impossible to believe that somewhere beyond that sun-tinged horizon, men were engaged in battle, that great guns breathed fire and smoke; and monstrous shells ploughed up the unresisting earth of France and Belgium, that men were dying, even now, in fields and orchards far from home.

She turned away, unable to equate those nightmare visions with the untouched beauty of her town; the symmetrical lines of the Victorian hotels on the Esplanade; the gracious Crown Hotel with its balconies and French windows; the Prince of Wales; the chateau-like Villa Esplanade, and all the solid, balconied houses in between.

It seemd to Charlotte that war could never touch this town she loved so dearly, that guns and shells could never penetrate the great bulk of the Grand Hotel which lay beneath her, shining and shimmering in the first rays of the sun. And yet, as she turned away, she felt suddenly cold with fear.

CHAPTER SIX

Albert read, with relief, that huge food imports were arriving from Denmark. The situation had stabilized somewhat after those early days of the war when most of the town's grocers had closed their doors against panic-buying. But other tradesmen had been hit too: the clothiers, outfitters, drapers and dressmakers had felt the pinch as housewives held onto their money, fearful of overspending as the news worsened.

The worst recession had come when the Germans entered Brussels. Albert's pity flowed out to the hordes of weary refugees pushing handcarts away from the beleaguered city.

Japan had entered the war against Germany. Now the Hun was closing in on Paris, and Lord Kitchener had put out an appeal for more men for the Army. Albert read, with tears in his eyes, of the maimed and wounded British soldiers arriving daily at Southampton.

Filly, on the other hand, refused to even look at the papers. Life was bad enough as it was, without making it worse by reading about it.

'You'll make yourself poorly,' she said one evening after supper, when Albert seemed particularly quiet and withdrawn, 'worriting on so much about the war. In any case, I don't believe all I hear.' She clattered the dishes into the sink as she spoke. 'All I'm bothered about is those poor lads of ours up to their knees in mud after all that rain at the end of August, and queuing up at Mrs Franks's in case there's a bit of extra meat going. It's a pity those damned politicians don't know what it's like for mothers these days. They'd soon make peace if they did!'

Albert made no reply. It wasn't just the war he was worried

about, not that he would ever mention to his wife the real reason for his sudden lapses into silence at mealtimes: the lump he had discovered in the region of his groin, a hard, unyielding lump which made him sweat occasionally as he realized the reason for his increasing physical weakness. But nothing on earth would make him see a doctor about it. With God's help, he would keep going until the war was over, until his sons came back to him. This was Albert Grayler's own silently-fought battle against a foe far more deadly and implacable than the Germans. He thought back to the night when he had discovered the lump, when he had rambled on to Filly about that old dog of his. He had a strange notion that his Copper half guessed the truth about himself, as he had half guessed the truth about her.

One night, when Filly had gone to bed and he and Charlotte were alone together in the front room, he said quietly, 'I haven't thanked you for all you have done for me since you came home. We couldn't have managed without you. But you are working far too hard.'

Charlotte, tidying the room for the night, turned to him, knowing that the moment for truth had come at last. 'I don't mind hard work,' she said. 'I'm glad of it. It takes my mind off things.'

'What – things?' He laid his hands on her shoulders. 'You can trust me, Copper.'

'I'm in love, Dadda.'

'So that's it. I thought as much. Is it someone you met in Wiltshire?'

'No, Dadda. I met him here, the day I took Alice Tanquillan back to her family. He is Alice's cousin, Rowan Tanquillan.'

'Sit down, Copper, and tell me about him.'

'You're not – angry?' she asked, when the story was told.

'Why should I be angry?' he said slowly. 'This is your life. Nobody but you has the right to live it.'

She turned her head away. 'I wanted to tell Mother. I tried to tell her, but she wouldn't understand.'

'No, perhaps not, and I don't think you should tell her, not yet. The right time will come.' He smiled. 'Or perhaps not even the right time, but the necessary time.'

Charlotte met her father's eyes unflinchingly. 'Will your – necessary time come too, Dadda?'

'Oh yes,' he said softly, smoothing her hair, 'but until it does, we shall keep faith with each other. Life is so short, my Copper. One day you are young and the years stretch in front of you like a great shining river. In no time at all, the river becomes a stream dried up at its source. I have no regrets about my particular river. I've had a good life. I've lived my life as I wanted to live it. I want you to do the same.'

She knelt at his feet. 'Are you very ill, Dadda? Can nothing be done to help you?' Tears ran down her cheeks unchecked.

'I want nothing done,' he said. 'All I want is to carry on as best I can for as long as possible. Why worry your mother with all this when she has so much to worry about already? This is our secret. Promise?'

She rested her head wearily against his shoulder, feeling the warmth of his arms around her. Nothing had ever come between their perfect love and understanding of each other, nothing ever would, but to let him go without a fight . . .

'Promise, Copper,' he said urgently.

She could scarcely speak. Her throat felt dry, constricted, her body drained of energy as she saw, through her tears, his well-loved face, gentle and compassionate, looking down at her. She took hold of his hands, those hands which had guided her, with understanding, every step of her life, and kissed his fingers one by one, remembering – 'This little piggy went to market, this little piggy stayed at home . . .'

She tried to smile. 'It is still your river,' she said.

'We've been in this bloody army for over two months now,' Bert Hoskins grumbled, 'and I ain't set foot no further than Haywards Heath. Now we're back in flaming London.'

The battalion had received orders to guard the railway from Waterloo along the South Western main line, to Bert's disgust, a boring job if ever there was one, with nothing to look at except a high railway cutting, a couple of sets of lines, and trains chuntering past. Night duty was the worst. Then he couldn't see anything at all except fog or stars and the patch of ground he was standing on. 'I asks you,' he said plaintively to Rowan, 'if a ruddy German spy came up on me all of a sudden like, what the hell could I do about it? Even if I could see to shoot him, which I couldn't, me ruddy fingers 'ud be too cold to press the trigger.'

Rowan had long since come to the conclusion that war was nothing more than an endurance test of will and stamina, unglorious and deadly dull at times, a matter of obeying orders, of learning how to apportion the mind and body equally between watchfulness and memories, so that a part of the brain remained alert to a sudden footfall in the dark, while the other part of it wandered at will down the avenues of time.

In the dark watches of the night, he paced up and down, up and down, thinking of Charlotte, of Romilly; his parents, his unborn child, wondering how he should reply to Charlotte's letter. He wanted to tell her that the child Romilly was carrying was conceived of pity, not love, that he had long since set aside any notion of becoming a real father to it. He wanted his child to know the happiness of unity, not strife. He had delayed answering Charlotte's letter because he wanted to be certain that, when he did answer it, he would be able to find the right words to explain to her exactly how he felt, but that would not be easy because a part of every man on earth was committed to caring for his children: seed of his seed, an essential part of himself.

Frank Grayler, Harry and Joe, had been posted on 16 October to billets in Newcastle-on-Tyne, after what seemed an eternity of slopping about in the mud of Hummersknott Park. Harry and Joe were glad of the posting, not so Frank. Army life was not living up to his expectations. He had not bargained for the dullness of training, the unexpected sense of being nothing but a small cog in the wheel of military discipline. He had joined the 5th Battalion, The Green Howards, to fight the Germans. In Newcastle, he could fight nothing more than an overwhelming feeling of boredom. But there was more to it than that. He was sick with worry because Madge had stopped writing to him. He had not received a letter from her for almost three weeks.

'I'll tell you this much, Harry,' he said, ruffling his hair with his hands, 'if I don't hear from her soon, I'm getting out of here. I'm going home to find out for myself what she's doing.'

'For God's sake, Frank, don't be such a fool,' Harry warned him. 'Why don't you write to Charlotte; ask her to go and see Madge. She'll find out for you.'

Charlotte did not relish the commission, but she could not refuse it.

Filly was up in arms when she knew that Madge had stopped writing to Frank. '*I'll* go and see her,' she said indignantly.

'You had better leave it to Copper,' Albert said, knowing his wife's penchant for losing her temper. 'Perhaps the girl's ill . . .'

'And perhaps she isn't,' Filly snapped. 'Perhaps she has found herself another feller!'

In the end, Charlotte went by herself.

The door was opened by Madge's mother. 'Oh, it's you,' she said off-handedly.

'Is Madge at home?'

'No, she isn't.' The woman folded her arms belligerently across her sagging breasts and felt in the pocket of her apron for a cachou to pop into her mouth since she could smell her own breath at times. She wore bulging carpet slippers. The smell of cabbage-water emanated from the back room where her husband was having his tea.

Madge's voice floated down from the landing. 'If that's Jack, tell him to wait in the parlour. I'll be ready in a few minutes.'

'It isn't Jack,' Mrs Robinson called back, 'it's Charlotte Grayler poking her nose in where it isn't wanted.' Her nostrils quivered. She was a common woman at heart, as Charlotte had always suspected her to be, despite her genteel bad-breath cachous.

'You might as well let me in,' Charlotte said, 'I'm not leaving until I've spoken to Madge.'

'Oh, please yourself then.' Mrs Robinson stepped back, in awe of Charlotte, though she couldn't think why. 'But don't you go upsetting her,' she blustered. 'She's had a bad time with that brother of yours. I told her straight, I did, right from the start, that he wasn't good enough for her. And I was right about that.' She sniffed, encouraged by the sound of her own voice. 'Dragging her home from London the way he did, then joining up the next day. That poor girl came home crying her eyes out. I told her straight, I did, that she should see a solicitor about it . . .'

Madge appeared on the stairs in a flurry of petticoats with a shawl about her shoulders. Her cheeks were flushed, her hair in disarray. 'I don't know why you've come here,' she said hostilely, 'I've got nothing to say to you.' She had always disliked Frank's younger sister with all her airs and graces.

'You know why I've come. Frank's worried sick about you.'

'Oh, is he?' Madge interrupted sarcastically. 'It's the first time then. He didn't worry about spoiling our honeymoon.'

'I agree with you, and I told him what I felt about that, but to have stopped writing to him . . .' Charlotte paused, uncomfortably aware of being an interloper; a female Daniel in the lions' den. She could not bear the smell of the house or the Biblical texts on the walls, the dusty, rose-embellished wallpaper or the narrow passage with its strip of worn, cabbage-impregnated carpet, but she must, for Frank's sake. 'I think it such a pity to let what happened in London come between you.'

Madge, saucer-eyed, buck-toothed, laughed unpleasantly. 'It would take the starch out of you if you knew what really happened in London,' she said. 'You have a great opinion of that brother of yours, haven't you? But he wasn't up to much on our wedding night.' She twitched the ends of her shawl, displaying her naked shoulders. 'Oh, have I shocked you? Sorry. I daresay you don't know much about that kind of thing.'

'Perhaps not,' Charlotte said, feeling her anger rise but keeping tight hold of it, 'what I do know is that this should be discussed in private, not shouted aloud in a passage with the front door wide open and half the street listening.'

'Well, really!' Mrs Robinson bridled, itching to have her say. 'I told Madge straight, I did, that any chap who can't perform his marital duties on his wedding night, ain't worth bothering about. I said straight out that she had good grounds for an – an

319

annulment of the marriage, and I for one wouldn't be sorry to see her shot of that selfish young brute. As for discussing things in private, who asked you to come here to discuss anything at all?'

Charlotte was out of her depth now. She said, 'I came to ask Madge to write to Frank, that's all.'

'Leave this to me, Ma,' Madge snapped, tugging Charlotte towards the front parlour, a dismal room overlooking the railway lines, with a drooping aspidistra on a bamboo table, a sagging settee in front of the paper fan-embellished fire-grate, and a what-not crowded with Goss china ornaments. Closing the door firmly behind them, she said, 'Now let me put you straight about a few things. Frank doesn't care about me. All he cares about is this bloody war. I'll show you his letters if you don't believe me. Why the hell did he marry me in the first place, that's what I'd like to know, when all he really wants is to kill Germans?' She added bitterly, 'I wish to God I had never set eyes on him, and that's the truth. Everything went wrong from the start.'

Her face crumpled suddenly, and Charlotte knew that she was speaking the truth as she saw it. 'I did love Frank, I do still love him in a funny kind of way, but we'll never be happy together. I'm young and attractive, I want to be happy. I can't face a lifetime of misunderstanding with Frank or anyone else. Life's for living, isn't it? I want to have fun. The way things are going, who knows what tomorrow may bring?' She began to cry.

'I'm sorry, Madge,' Charlotte said quietly. 'I understand how you feel, but marriage isn't just for a day or a year . . .'

'Oh yes, I know,' Madge was suddenly hostile again, 'it's a bloody life sentence, isn't it? Well I'm not wasting my life on your brother.' She dried her eyes with the edge of her shawl. 'I've found myself a man who really cares for me. Oh, you needn't look so shocked. Jack's nice, a real gentleman who knows how to treat a woman, and we're going to get married one day . . .'

'Another "life sentence"?' Charlotte said. 'You're not very consistent, are you?' She felt sick at heart.

'You'd better go now,' Madge said. 'I don't expect you to understand about Jack and me, but I can't help the way I feel.'

'It doesn't make any difference whether I understand or not,' Charlotte turned with her hand on the doorknob, 'it's what Frank thinks that matters. At least promise me that you will write to him.'

'Oh, all right.' Madge sighed. 'But I'll only tell him what I've told you. It's all over between us.'

Charlotte scarcely knew, as she carried on with the work of the shop and the hospital, whom to worry about most – her father, Frank or Rowan. Work seemed the only antidote to pain: pushing the handcart around town delivering orders, swabbing floors, rolling bandages, helping her mother with the cooking and cleaning. She had no time for books or poetry. She felt at times like a very old woman easing herself into bed after the long, difficult days, not bothering to say her prayers because she no longer believed in a God of love, not bothering to brush her hair because she was too tired, just feeling with her toes the warmth and benison of her eiderdown, hoping against hope that she would sleep until morning, until it was time to get up and begin the meaningless charade all over again.

Maggie came to see her parents less frequently these days since the weight of her baby, her bulk and girth made walking difficult. She would arrive, puffing and panting, to spread herself in an armchair in the sitting-room where she would regale Filly with details of her heartburn, flatulence and dyspepsia, while Charlotte, making tea for her sister, forbore to mention that, so far as she knew, they were one and the same thing, brought about by Maggie's fondness for rich, greasy food. Maggie's complacency irritated Charlotte these days: the impression she gave that she considered herself to be, by way of her condition, on a higher plane of existence than the rest of womankind. She could scarcely bite back her anger when Maggie dismissed Frank's marital problems with the comment that it served him right for marrying such a daft lass in the first place. Although Charlotte could not condone Madge's unfairness in not writing to Frank, she understood enough about the strange workings of the human heart to realize that nothing pertaining to love could ever be cut and dried, docketed and dismissed so lightly. She wondered, as Maggie tucked into quantities of chocolate biscuits, if her sister ever looked back to that April afternoon when her own problems came uppermost, when she was faced with fears and doubts about her own marriage.

One day, when Maggie had waddled upstairs to the sitting-room, she said, out of the blue, 'Oh, by the way, I picked up this letter as I came in. It's from London. Who do you know in London, Charlotte?' She held the letter in her hand and tapped it teasingly against her palm, reminding Charlotte of the days when Maggie would wrest away her books of poetry to make game of them. 'I think I'd better open it and see for myself,' she taunted.

Colour drained suddenly from Charlotte's face as she recognized Rowan's handwriting. Her legs began to tremble. She said, as coolly as she could, 'It's from Jenny, I expect. Please give it to me, Maggie.'

Filly, pouring out the tea, said, 'Oh, that nice governess girl. I wonder how she's getting on. Go on, open it, Charlotte.' But Maggie did not relinquish the letter. '*I'll* open it,' she said, 'and read it out to you.'

'Give me that letter!' With a sudden spring, Charlotte tore it away from Maggie. Colour returned to her cheeks as suddenly as it had departed. Incensed with anger, she cried, 'How dare you pry into my affairs?'

'*Charlotte!*' Filly was shocked. 'Maggie meant no harm. You shouldn't upset her so, in her condition.' She turned appealingly to her elder daughter. 'You mustn't take any notice of her, Maggie, Charlotte's just tired these days, and no wonder.'

But Maggie, still tinged with envy of her beautiful sister, said slyly, 'I don't believe the letter is from Jenny at all. It's from some chap or other she's taken up with.'

Throwing caution to the winds, knowing that her 'necessary' time was here, was now, Charlotte said, 'You are quite right, Maggie. But it isn't from a chap I have just taken up with, it is

322

from a man I happen to love very deeply.' She turned and ran from the room, leaving Maggie and Filly open-mouthed.

Lying on her bed, Charlotte knew that she had not meant to break the news of her love affair with Rowan like this. She felt demeaned by her reaction to Maggie's teasing, but she was not sorry that it was out in the open at last. Later would come Filly's questions, her mother's righteous indignation and condemnation over her love affair, but this was something she must weather and overcome; ride out as fishermen rode out a storm at sea, bravely; without fear.

When she was calmer, she opened Rowan's letter; drew comfort from it:

'My dear Charlotte,

I had to be sure, when I replied to your letter, that I could do so in all honesty. Night after night, on guard duty, I have gone over and over again the question of my feelings towards my wife and child.

It would be untrue to say that I shall not often think about that child. I should feel myself to be less than a man if at least a part of me did not yearn towards it. This is something that you have already understood and accepted. What else can I say except that I harbour no such yearnings towards the mother. Romilly and I have known each other all our lives, we grew up together. I respect her, I feel compassion towards her, I have never loved her nor ever shall. I cannot say more, nor, I think, would you wish me to do so.

Love cannot be bidden, or told not to exist, at will. It is a frail flower, but a hardy one, like snowdrops that push their way to the sun no matter how deep the snow of winter . . .'

Now it was time to face the music. Charlotte tidied herself and went down to the kitchen. Maggie had gone home, but Filly was there, preparing supper, cheeks flushed, lips drawn into a narrow line of disapproval.

She wasted no time in getting things into the open. 'Well, this is a nice state of affairs.' She clattered the saucepans angrily to underline her displeasure. 'No wonder you've been acting so queer lately. Who is this man you've taken up with?'

'His name is Rowan Tanquillan . . .'

'*Tanquillan!* There, I might have known it! I knew no good would come of you going off to Wiltshire! Tanquillan! Huh! I expect you were carrying on with him all the time you were away! Why have you kept him such a secret? He can't be worth much if you are so ashamed of him.'

'He is Lady Tanquillan's son. I'm sorry, Mother. I meant to tell you about him. I thought you wouldn't understand.'

'No more I do,' Filly cried, beside herself with worry transmuted to anger by her ignorance of the situation. But there was more to it than that, something she herself hardly understood, a feeling of being shut out; resentment that Charlotte had not confided in her, her old dread of the abnormal. Then memory pierced a clear beam through her confusion. 'Rowan Tanquillan. But he's a married man!' A saucepan lid clattered to the floor unheeded. 'You've been carrying on with a married man!' There was no worse crime in Filly's book than this.

'I haven't been "carrying on" with him, not in the way you suggest,' Charlotte said desperately, facing her mother, hating herself as she spoke for what she saw as a betrayal of her inmost feelings, knowing that her love for Rowan was on trial. She said, 'Please don't ask me any more questions because I shall not answer them. You have no right to condemn what you don't understand.'

'No right! I am your mother!' Filly still believed that giving birth to a child meant that the child should forever remain fastened to her by an umbilical cord of unquestioning love and devotion. And that was the crux of her resentment, that Charlotte had grown away from her over the years, that she had never been able to understand her even as a child. The disgust she felt was not totally directed towards Charlotte. Filly knew that she had somehow failed as a mother, that her beautiful girl had slipped through her fingers.

She said, more gently, 'I'm sorry I spoke so harshly. All I want is your happiness. Just promise me that you will put an end to this affair, and I'll say no more about it.'

Charlotte said quietly, 'But I want to talk about Rowan. I want you to understand how I feel about him. Please, Mother.'

'No.' Filly was adamant; missing her chance with Charlotte, seeing things in black and white with no subtle shades between the two. 'I've brought you up to understand the difference between right and wrong. You know as well as I do that what you've done is wrong . . .'

There was no point in pursuing the conversation. Charlotte went back to her room knowing that failure to stand on her own two feet now would mean a return to her role in life as a cipher, that nothing had been solved or settled between herself and her mother.

She clung to Rowan's letter as a talisman; replied to it at once, making no mention of the scene with her mother or her father's illness; writing amusingly of her work at the hospital, smiling through tears as she wrote:

'The older ladies are adept at directing tea-making operations, telling the younger ones how the kettle should be filled and where the cups and saucers are kept, nagging us to remember, since tea and sugar are in short supply, not to add "one for the pot".

'They adore arranging flowers and sailing up to the wards with them – for "Our Brave Lads". Mrs Monckton, our Chief Do-Gooder, even left a vase of Michaelmas daisies in the Maternity Ward, where most of the "Brave Lads" had just given birth to squalling infants.

'But it was the "Poor Brave Belgians" on the top floor who came in for the most attention. I was mopping the ward when Mrs Monckton bowled in with a vase of chrysanthemums and said, in schoolgirl French, "Ah, mes pauvres braves soldats" – which must have seemed very odd to them since they were the crew of a fishing vessel found drifting in the North Sea, suffering from dehydration.

'I'm sorry, darling, if all this sounds rather puerile. I know it is, but where would we be without laughter?' She ended the letter, 'I love you. I pray for you day and night. Yours ever, lovingly, Charlotte.'

In mid-December, Rowan's battalion received orders to proceed to France. He was given 36 hours leave commencing at midday 16 December. A letter would never reach her in time. He sent a telegram. The message was poignantly brief: 'Short leave commencing 16 December. Must see you. Please come. I'll meet every train. Rowan.'

Filly threw down the telegram in disgust. 'You're not going,' she cried. 'I had rather you had been born dead than this.'

Albert said, 'Don't be too harsh, Filly. We have no right to prevent her. The girl's in love.'

'*In love!*' Filly's anger was beyond anything Charlotte had ever known before. Her words were incensed, vitriolic, born of fear and ignorance, the scathing words of a woman brought up to believe in the sanctity of marriage vows, who saw her daughter's affair with a married man as a wicked betrayal of her upbringing. 'If Charlotte goes to London,' she said hoarsely, 'I'm done with her! No daughter of mine would go traipsing off to London to meet a married man. No, you can't wheedle your way round me, Albert Grayler! I'm ashamed of you, too! What kind of a father are you to condone such wickedness! And what kind of a man is this – this Rowan Tanquillan – to entice a young girl away from her family?' Tears spilled down her cheeks. 'Well, I hope to God he'll pay for it one day!'

'Filly,' Albert protested.

'Don't you "Filly" me! I've wasted my life if this is all the thanks I get for trying to bring up my children properly, in the fear of God! Perhaps I've never understood Charlotte. Now I know why, because she's a whore at heart, a wicked wanton young hussy who does not give a damn for her family. I never saw it before, but I see it now!'

'No, Mother! It isn't true!' Charlotte ran from the room, pressing her ears against her mother's condemnation, knowing that nothing Filly could say or do would prevent her from catching the early morning train to London.

The German High Seas Fleet was spoiling for a fight. Britain's recent victory at the Battle of the Falkland Islands had proved a stinging blow to German Commander-in-Chief Admiral Von Ingenohl's pride. This new raid he had planned was a daring one, a fitting reprisal for the humiliation of defeat. His ships lay, in worsening weather conditions, north-west of the Dogger Bank, fifty miles from where the British Fleet, under Vice Admiral Sir George Warrender, awaited events.

British Intelligence knew the Germans were planning an attack. Commander-in-Chief Admiral Jellicoe, reluctant to risk an engagement close to the British coast, mined by the Germans, had fixed his Fleet's rendezvous 25 miles south-east of Dogger. Von Ingenohl's plan was comparatively simple: an advance force would lure out a British squadron, lead it to the waiting guns of the German warships, and the advance force would then strike against the British coast.

At first light on 16 December, six battleships, the mighty *Seydlitz*, *Moltke* and *Blucher*, *Derrflinger*, *Von der Tann* and *Kolberg*, purled off from the main German force to bombard the north-east coast of England. In grey December mist, the force sub-divided. *Seydlitz*, *Moltke* and *Blucher* steamed silently towards Hartlepool; *Derrflinger*, *Von der Tann* and *Kolberg* towards Scarborough. *Kolberg* veered south to lay mines, *Derrflinger* and *Von der Tann* opened fire on the sleeping town.

Charlotte was halfway across the Valley Bridge when the first shell struck. She heard a noise like thunder from the sea; a flash of light lit up the grey December sky. But wasn't that the wrong way round? Did not lightning come first, thunder afterwards? She stopped, knowing instinctively that what she had seen and heard was more than an approaching storm. She could see, from where she stood above the valley's leafless trees, the mist-shrouded South Bay, the faint outline of Castle Hill. Suddenly, there was a crimson ball of fire; black plumes of smoke rose from the summit of the hill. She could dimly discern, through the mist, two great grey shapes, like whales, ploughing across the bay. She heard the unmistakable whine of shells, other explosions as *Derrflinger*'s mighty guns pounded the sea-front.

She began to run, seeing tongues of fire shooting upwards,

327

staining the sky a dull blood-red. The ground seemed to heave and lift beneath her feet. She stared wildly about her. People were appearing from their houses: half-dressed women wearing shawls and petticoats, looking helplessly up at the sky, not understanding what was happening, surprised in the act of getting up to start the day, cooking breakfast and dressing their children ready for school. One woman, hair spread about her shoulders, held a comb in her hand. Men wore hastily donned trousers with dangling braces.

At that hour of the morning the life of the town was scarcely under way except for the street-cleaners, and milkmen making their rounds. Postmen were delivering letters; housemaids, of necessity early risers, were sweeping doorsteps, lighting fires, setting trays, making tea when the first shells struck. Then china began dancing and rattling on tables, pictures crashed to the ground, kettles juddered from stoves, and panic came uppermost as chimneys toppled, windows were blown in, slates were ripped off, and ceilings collapsed, bringing down with them clouds of plaster and choking dust.

Doors were blown off their hinges as shell-splinters ripped through solid masonry; walls were stripped to the lathes; upper storeys sagged; mattresses were torn to ribbons; brass bed-steads tilted crazily through gaping holes in floorless rooms. In one house, a young father snatched up his baby from its cradle as a shell-cap pierced the roof. He watched, in silent horror, as it nosed, creaking and grinding through the ceiling, mesmerized by the grey snout, unable to speak or move until the crying of the baby broke the spell and he stumbled downstairs seconds before it crushed the child's cradle to dust.

The German ships were no more than 500 yards offshore, sailing southwards, firing broadside. At the end of the run, they turned almost lazily, to begin firing portside; pumping shells into the defenceless town.

People were running blindly into the streets, taking with them whatever they could carry; piling pots and pans on perambulators or handcarts, with one thought in mind, to get away from the shelling, not stopping to think that they might well run even greater risks away from their houses, snatching

328

up whatever they considered worth saving: food, photographs; family pets; canaries in cages.

A poor woman in Eastborough who had saved up to buy enough butter and fruit for a Christmas cake to send to her husband in France, ran into the street with it under one arm, pulling along a crying child and a dog on a lead with her free hand, running, panic-stricken, to get to the station as a shell whined overhead; struck; and the ground behind her was littered with red-hot, jagged shell-splinters, while a shopkeeper who lived nearby emerged from his side door wearing a top-hat, carrying a cash-box, with seven pair of boots strung round his neck by the laces.

The priest in charge of Holy Communion at St Martin's church continued the service even when the building was holed by a shell. Better to die in fear of the Lord than to live in fear of the Germans. 'Our Father, Who art in Heaven . . .' He spread his hands upon the altar-rail, as clouds of dust billowed like fog about himself and his congregation.

In a Methodist chapel in the town centre, the caretaker took his wife and children to the cellars where they sang the Doxology. Meanwhile, the girls of Queen Margaret's School left their breakfast uneaten and filed out of the refectory to hurry down the long road skirting Oliver's Mount, towards Seamer, while telegraphers at the Sandybed wireless station a mile or so from the town centre transmitted urgent messages to the Admiralty that Scarborough was under attack from the sea.

At Scarborough Hospital, wards were thick with soot and brickdust from wrecked chimneys. As clouds of choking fumes enveloped their beds, wounded Belgian soldiers on the top floor took command of the situation. These were men accustomed to gunfire, to warfare against innocent civilians. Those able to walk spoke soothingly in broken English to the bewildered nurses; organized the removal, by creaking lift, of mobile patients to the ground floor.

Charlotte could not turn back now. Half out of her mind with worry about her parents, she was forced along by a seething mass of humanity hurrying towards the station; as helpless as a cork in a rough sea.

Mazed with the horror of the shelling, she found herself pressed up against the platform barrier by half-crazed people fighting to escape the holocaust. She had given up hope of finding room on the train when an old woman wearing a red flannel dressing-gown seized her arm.

'Please, miss. *Please* help me,' the old woman cried, her teeth chattering with cold and shock.

'Where are you going?' Charlotte asked gently, holding the old woman's elbow, feeling the shaking of her body; reading desperation in her eyes.

'I must get to Seamer! I have a son there. I'll be all right if I can get to him. He'll take care of me. For God's sake, miss, please help me!'

Soldiers, trying to cope impartially with the mass of hysterical people attempting to force their way through the barrier, let Charlotte and the old woman through.

Carriages were packed like sardine-tins. Those who could not find room in the compartments clung to the door-handles. Few of the travellers had tickets. The soldiers were fighting a losing battle in attempting to restore order from chaos.

The sky above the station roof was as black as night, suffused with an unearthly red glow. The smell of cordite lingered suffocatingly in the cold, foggy, December air.

Wild rumours had begun to circulate that the Germans had landed, that the bombardment of Scarborough was the forerunner of an invasion by enemy forces.

Charlotte had managed to find the old woman in red flannel a seat in the crowded carriage. At the back of her mind lay the thought that she should not be here at all but with her parents. Then she remembered that Rowan would be waiting for her in London, and her torment began. Where did she really belong? With whom?

Suddenly she noticed an old man, holding a parrot in a cage, wandering aimlessly along beside the train; a man wearing a striped nightshirt tucked into his trousers with a tasselled nightcap on his head.

'In here,' she cried, flinging open the door as the train began to move away from the platform, extending her hand to help the old man and his parrot into the carriage.

As the train slid away from the station, Charlotte stood near the carriage window, seeing, through the misted glass, a long procession of refugees pushing perambulators and handcarts stacked high with their worldly goods, just as the Belgian refugees she had read about had streamed away from Brussels as the Germans entered their capital city.

She felt suddenly sick and empty and lonely, as the train sped on through a gaunt winter landscape of shorn fields, brown earth and leafless trees.

CHAPTER SEVEN

Special editions of the London papers blazoned news of the bombardment. 'East coast towns under attack by German warships. Scarborough, Hartlepool and Whitby hit,' called the newsboys.

Rowan had booked a room at a hotel in Lancaster Gate, where he changed into civilian clothing before catching the tube to King's Cross, pausing, en route, to buy a bunch of gold and white chrysanthemums at a flower-seller's barrow.

A placard bearing news of the bombardment caught his eye as he strode from the Underground. He bought and read a paper. Fear clutched his heart. What if Charlotte . . . ?

King's Cross was busier than he had ever known it before with people coming and going, baggage being stowed away in the guards' vans, with companies of soldiers standing at ease while the officers strode along the platform making enquiries about travel arrangements.

Some of the soldiers had their wives with them, concentrating on the last precious words to each other before the men were marched away to board the trains. Some of the women were weeping. One could sense the emotion beneath the vaulted station roof; not just sorrow, but joy, too, as other trains came in and happy reunions took place at the barriers. But Rowan's feelings of pleasure at his meeting with Charlotte were overlaid now with anxiety. He could scarcely bear to wait for the York train to be signalled. His mind flicked over endless, alarming possibilities. How could he be sure that she would come at all? If she did not, he would go at once to Scarborough; find out what had happened to her.

Everything which had seemed so simple, so right, so

inevitable that afternoon when he had booked the room at the hotel, now seemed laced with imponderables; the nagging worry that he had done wrong in booking just one room. What if Charlotte was shocked by his assumption that she would want to spend the night with him?

His leave had started at one o'clock; would end at midnight on the 18th. He cursed himself inwardly. Of course he should have left it up to her to decide. He had acted on an impulse, believing that Charlotte would want what he wanted, if she came at all. God, she *must* come!

The train drew in slowly. People craned forward anxiously, knowing that it had come from the stricken north. News of the bombardment had stunned and shocked. Wild rumour had it that the Germans had landed at Whitby, Scarborough and Hartlepool. People felt threatened now; uneasy, speaking in hushed tones of German atrocities in Belgium, the massacre of innocent people at Badonviller. They had believed Britain to be impregnable; now they weren't so sure.

Exhausted by the long journey, sick at heart with the scenes she had witnessed, Charlotte stumbled along the platform to the barrier. Suddenly Rowan's arms were about her. Too tired and bewildered to speak, she leaned her head against his shoulder as he guided her to a taxi, shocked by her pallor, the dark shadows beneath her eyes.

At the hotel, he carried her case to the lift; held her tightly as it bore them swiftly to the top floor. Waving aside the lift-boy's offer of assistance, he tipped the lad half a crown, supported Charlotte along the landing, opened the door of their room and carried her inside.

'You need rest,' he said gently, unpinning her hat and helping her off with her coat. 'Try to sleep.' He laid her on the bed and covered her with the eiderdown.

'Have you had anything to eat?' he asked quietly, smoothing her hair. When she shook her head, he said, 'I'll fetch you some tea and sandwiches. You are here. You are safe, thank God. That is all that matters.'

When he returned with the tea, she was fast asleep, tucked up like a weary child beneath the sprigged eiderdown, the bedside lamp shining on her hair. Quietly he drew the curtains against the deepening gloom of a winter afternoon, then sat down to watch her as she slept, marvelling at her beauty, thinking of her as his true wife.

Her nearness filled him with longing. He wanted her as he had never wanted a woman before. But he would never ask more of her than she was prepared to give of her own free will.

He remembered his wedding night with Romilly, his lack of emotion towards her, the strain of pretence as she covered his face and lips with kisses. She had taken off her nightclothes and stood naked in front of him, repelling him by her immodesty, revealing a new facet of her personality, a curious wantonness, a kind of excitement in displaying her nakedness, her insistence on intimacy before the time was right.

No wonder he had been so clumsy with her. He had not been prepared for her passionate approach to love-making; her strange elation as she attempted to arouse him with urgent, whispered words of love, thrusting forward the frugal cones of her breasts for him to kiss; pressing his hands to her quivering belly.

When that had failed, she had resorted to tears, crying out how much she missed her father. Then the feel of her shaking shoulders, his pity for her, had made him more gentle, more compassionate towards her. When at last she lay sobbing against his shoulder, he had made love to her, albeit unskilfully, thrusting into her without tenderness.

How strange, he thought, when the act was over, he had always imagined compassion and tenderness to be one and the same thing, but they were not. Compassion meant 'to spare or succour'. Tenderness meant 'loving, affectionate, fond'. He had wished to spare and succour his wife: to spare her the humiliation of knowing that he did not love her, that her naked body did not excite him: to succour her because he felt sorry for her. He could not imagine, for one moment, that he had satisfied her lust as he lay beside her in the dark, listening to her uneven breathing.

It was dark outside when Charlotte stirred, and opened her

eyes. She lay for a moment looking up at the ceiling, uncertain where she was. She had slept deeply, an exhausted plunge into oblivion. Now she experienced the slow gathering-together of memory, and sat up with a low cry of terror.

Rowan rose quickly to take her in his arms: rocked her gently as a father might soothe a child afraid of the dark. Clinging to him, she felt the steady beat of his heart, the warmth of his hands on her back. He could feel her tears through the thin stuff of his shirt. He shrugged off his jacket, took off his collar and tie, and lay down beside her, catching the fragrance of her hair, holding her tightly in his arms, speaking to her gently, telling her not to be afraid, drawing her close to him for comfort.

They lay like that for a long time, until she stopped trembling, Rowan understanding her needs, her fears, her uncertainty, her courage in being there at all. It could not have been easy for her to fly in the face of her upbringing to come to him. Perhaps he had asked too much of her, had taken too much for granted in booking this one room.

He waited patiently until she raised her lips to be kissed. 'Feeling better?' he asked.

'Yes.' Her voice was little more than a whisper.

'This room. Our room. You don't mind?' He had to be sure, sensing her shyness.

'No. I wanted to be with you.'

'I'm glad.' He kissed her again, very gently. The moment was delicately poised. He wanted her with every fibre of his being, but the time was not now, not yet.

Realizing how hungry she must be, he got up, taking command of the situation, knowing that she would need some time to herself to bath, and change her clothes. Catching sight of the flowers, he handed them to her, smiling. 'I bought you these,' he said.

'They're beautiful.' She smiled back at him. 'Would you put them in water for me? There's a vase on the mantelpiece.'

He went into the adjoining bathroom where he filled the vase; arranged the flowers as best he could, then washed his face, brushed his hair, and put on his collar and tie, whistling softly under his breath as he did so, an old habit of his which had irritated Romilly past bearing. 'Why must you always whistle in the bathroom?' she had asked.

Why indeed? But even as a small, lonely boy, he had whistled in the dark.

When he was ready, he carried the flowers back to the bedroom, placed the vase on the mantelpiece, and put on his jacket.

'I pressed the last flowers you gave me,' Charlotte said, watching him. 'My – wedding bouquet – do you remember?'

'Remember?' he said quietly. 'My dear girl, I shall never forget anything that we have ever said or done together.' Bending down, he kissed her lightly on the lips. 'I'll meet you downstairs, when you are ready.'

Charlotte lay for a while in blissfully hot water, seeing with a kind of detached wonder the outlines of her slender young body as a pale, mysterious creature in a rock-pool, knowing that, before the night was through, this body of hers would belong to Rowan. She was not afraid. The fears and stresses of the day seemed laved away by the caressing touch of the water on her skin.

Her mind was at peace now, soothed and healed by Rowan's quiet understanding, his arms about her, the long silence between them as they had lain together on the bed. She had known then all the tenderness and quietude of love, and yet she had felt a strong desire to lie naked beside him, a desire made even stronger by the thought of their parting. How could she let him go away without the fullest expression of her love for him?

She thought, as the water laved her body, that perhaps her mother was right in calling her wicked and wanton. Nothing had changed. Rowan was still married to Romilly. But, despite that, how could it be wrong or wicked to take life and love on such an overwhelming tide of certainty? She remembered, as she stepped out of the bath to dry herself, Kitty Tanquillan's words: 'There'll be all the time left in the world for regrets, when you are an old woman like me.'

Now, love seemed to Charlotte an act of faith, a tiny candle lit against the darkness of the world.

She put on a long, leaf-brown velvet skirt, a cream lace blouse with an upstanding collar; brushed her hair until it shone, and gathered it into a loose chignon at the nape of her neck. The skirt was the exact colour of her hair, the lace blouse complemented the creaminess of her skin. When she was ready, she walked downstairs, her legs trembling slightly with excitement, her hand resting lightly on the banister.

The foyer was crowded with people, men in uniform, girls, elderly dowagers. Rowan watched her as she moved down the staircase, thinking she held herself like a queen. Others thought so too. He noticed the way heads turned her way; admiration on the faces of the men, envy on the women's, because of her shining quality of poise. She might have worn something quite ordinary, the result would have been the same. No matter what she wore, nothing could diminish Charlotte's beauty which had to do with the way she carried herself, the way her head, crowned with the deep, glowing copper hair, was set upon her shoulders.

Rowan's heart beat strongly with pride as he walked forward to meet her, took her hand and led her to the dining-room, to a table in a corner near the bandstand, sensing her shyness as the maître d'hôtel fussily pulled back her chair for her, and snapped his fingers for the wine waiter.

She sat very still, smiling but not speaking, hoping she would not make a fool of herself when it came to choosing food from the bewildering variety of dishes listed on the menu the waiter handed her, with everything in French. She knew that coq meant chicken, she understood the meaning of boeuf and porc, but how could she possible confess that she wasn't very hungry, that all she really wanted was a little soup and a plain omelette? That she was, by choice, a vegetarian?

Rowan laid aside his menu. 'We will have the soup,' he said, 'and omelettes fines herbes.' The waiter looked pained, but bowed slightly and hurried away.

'How did you guess?' Charlotte asked, thinking that she had never loved Rowan more than she did at that moment for his refusal to embarrass her by ordering in French.

337

'I didn't guess, I knew. Call it a sixth sense if you like, where you are concerned.' He took her hand across the table. 'Happy?'

'Oh yes, very happy.'

'Before I go away,' he said, 'I want to know everything about you from the minute you were born to the moment you walked into this dining-room.'

'Please don't talk about – going away. I want to pretend that this will never end, that we shall still be here a hundred years from now, alive, together, and eternally young . . .'

'We will be, perhaps not for a hundred years, but as long as we live, for as long as we – remember. And, when we die, we shall come back to live it all over again. Remember what you said that day on the Embankment? I think you were right. Nothing ever dies. I read once that every word we speak remains forever a part of the universe. I didn't believe it at the time, but I do now.' He held her hand tightly in his. The orchestra played a waltz. 'Will you dance with me? I want to hold you in my arms.'

A silver witchball cast a myriad whirling diamonds on the heads of the dancers. As she stepped with him onto the floor, she felt herself to be floating in a silver snowstorm in a magical, make-believe world; sensed the slow, pulsating rhythm of life in Rowan's heartbeats. No matter what had been, or what was to come, all that mattered was the here and now, this sublime moment with his arms about her, and the certainty of their love for each other.

They walked slowly upstairs together, her head resting against his shoulder. He opened the door of their room and carried her across the threshold.

Setting her down, he loosened her hair; caught his breath as it spilled about her shoulders. Very gently, he began to unbutton her blouse, saw the naked curve of her shoulders, the swelling breasts above the cotton modesty vest; touched to the heart by her trust in him.

He carried her then to the bed, and laid her down, smoothing the pillows for her head, and looked down at her with infinite understanding of her childlike innocence. He could have wept when she held out her arms to him, and raised her lips to be kissed. Their loving, when it came, would be a mutual thing born of their deep need of each other.

He buried his face in the soft, fragrant mass of her hair; touched, with gentle fingers, her pink-starred breasts, then gave himself up to the slow, sweet rhythm of life, soothing her pain with whispered words of love until all the pain was gone, dissipated in the confluent act of love in which each gave to the other gladly and freely, without restraint; with a passionate awareness of each other's needs.

When the loving was over, she covered him as a mother might cover a sleeping child, and held his head close to her breast. He lay with his arm about her as though, even in sleep, he could not bear to relinquish her.

He awoke to a sublime feeling of peace. His limbs felt heavy and relaxed, his mind crystal clear with happiness. Raising himself on his elbow, he looked at his sleeping Charlotte lying beside him, her hair spread upon the pillows; one arm extended, the quiet pulse of life beating steadily in her throat. Leaning over, he touched that pulse with his lips.

She stirred then, opened her eyes and smiled up at him. As he lay in peace beside her, he remembered that this was the last day of his leave. Daylight was straggling through the drawn curtains. They had eight hours left together. Eight short hours.

She knew what he was thinking. It had seemed during the long dark hours of the night that time would never end. Now there was so little of it left.

'I can't bear the thought of losing you,' he said.

'You are not going to lose me. Nothing can ever separate us now.'

'I never knew it would be like this, that so much love could exist in the world.'

It was a bitterly cold day, grey with low-hanging clouds, threaded with blistering hail showers. After breakfast, they boarded a bus to the Embankment and walked beside the river, oblivious of the cold, leaning their arms on the parapet to watch hailstones scurrying across the water.

Rowan said, 'If I died, you would always know I was there beside you. I should prove a very persistent ghost, turning up at the most unexpected and possibly embarrassing times. I would not blame you if, one day, you told me to go away, to leave you in peace to live your own life.' He spoke lightly, but she knew what he was trying to say. Glowing youth and strength were no longer a guarantee of man's allotted span of threescore years and ten. She knew he had faced the possibility that he might not return from France. That shared knowledge had imbued their loving with passionate urgency; these few fleeting hours were overlaid with the need for truth and understanding, to say all the things they had never said before.

She told him about her family; her love for her father and Joey, as they walked hand in hand towards Chelsea Bridge, about Joey's girl, Annie Crystal, Maggie's wedding, about Frank and Harry. She could not bring herself to speak of the misunderstanding between herself and her mother. What they said to each other today would be tomorrow's memories. She did not want to burden him with her troubles.

Over coffee, she listened intently to the story of Rowan's early life, sketching a picture in her mind of the way his hair sprang from his forehead, the colour and texture of it, the way his mouth curved in sudden laughter, the cleft in his chin, the widely-spaced dark eyes; straight nose, his hands, shoulders, everything about him. And yet features in themselves meant little, it was what they added up to that mattered. No picture, however carefully painted on canvas or in the imagination, could ever capture the living tissue, the little quirks and slight imperfections that made the picture come to life.

He had a way, she thought, of slightly raising one eyebrow when he smiled, a tiny mole on his right cheek, a few grey hairs at his temples; an overwhelming presence which came from his upbringing and education, a warmth and charm which sprang from the heart of him; a shining integrity about him, a deep voice; an innate modesty and shyness, an understanding of human nature; a kind of spiritual grace.

And now the sands of time were running out for both of them. Her train was due to leave King's Cross at five minutes past three.

Strange how, at the last moment, there seemed nothing left to say; that one somehow anticipated the loneliness, almost willing the unbearable parting over and done with.

He bought her violets for her coat. The train was packed to overflowing. He found her a seat; put her case on the rack. She left her gloves on the seat; stood beside him on the crowded platform watching the hands of the clock moving inexorably towards three.

At the last minute, he bent down to kiss her, crushing the violets. She got into the carriage; lowered the window; clung to his hands until the train began to move, her eyes misted over with tears.

CHAPTER EIGHT

She slept to the rhythm of the wheels, awoke bemused to the high, keening whistle of the engine as the train moved through a limbo of hailstones borne on moaning wind-gusts. For one terrible moment the wind sounded like the whine of shells, and she remembered that she was moving relentlessly towards Scarborough to face what must be faced there: ravages perpetrated by the guns; buildings she loved torn and holed; her mother's anger, things she had pushed to the back of her mind for Rowan's sake. Now the realization of what lay ahead made her shiver with nervous tension. She had left the house like a thief in the night, stealing silently downstairs, leaving a note to say she was catching the early train to London. Facing Filly's condemnation would not be easy.

After the bombardment, soldiers, detailed to help with the casualties, had brought out the injured and laid them on the pavements until the arrival of the ambulances. A special edition of the local paper had appealed to householders to take in families whose homes had been destroyed. Day long the soldiers had worked to clear away debris from the streets so that life and movement might continue unimpeded by the rubble of toppled chimneys, broken glass and shell-splinters. Troops had been sent in to restore confidence in face of an invasion panic. In the afternoon, two destroyers of coastal patrol had ploughed the waters of the South Bay to cheers from the disorientated populace who viewed their arrival with a feeling of comfort and fresh optimism.

A lifetime of experience separated Charlotte, the woman, from the girl who had crossed the Valley Bridge a few crowded hours ago. She could still smell cordite in the air. The wind had dropped now. It was terrifyingly dark and quiet, as if the grieving people of a town had withdrawn behind closed blinds to pray for their dead. A feeling of unease, a presentiment of danger quickened her footsteps as she turned into St Martin's Square.

The house stood as eyeless as a skeleton, its windows blown out. The iron latches which once held the shutters were bent like arthritic fingers beneath the pitted fascia board. She saw, by the feeble light of a gas-lamp, a gaping black hole near the dining-room window.

Trembling, she hurried forward to ring the bell, praying that a light would appear behind the jewelled glass of the side door as someone came downstairs to answer her insistent summons. But there was no light, no shine, no comforting sound of footsteps on the stairs. She felt suddenly like a little girl waking up in the terrifying strangeness of a darkened room, crying because her nightlight floating in a saucer of water had been extinguished.

She fled to the next house and rang the bell until the clamour roused one of its occupants. The woman, their neighbour Mrs Winters, held up a candle in a metal stick. 'Who's there?' she cried. 'What do you want at this time of night?'

'It's me, Charlotte Grayler . . .'

'Charlotte? Oh yes. I couldn't see.'

'Please. What has happened to my parents?'

The woman, in a red dressing-gown, held up a hand to her mouth. Her hair was plaited in grizzled pigtails. Embarrassed because she had forgotten to put in her false teeth, she mumbled, 'But surely you must know . . .'

'No. I – I've been away.'

Tears began to course down the woman's wrinkled cheeks, her eyes were blank holes of despair. 'Your father – poor Mr Grayler. They laid him on the pavement until the ambulance came. Always his first customer, I was, on a Monday morning, living so near, I mean.' She made a vague gesture with her hand. 'Our house was hit, too. You should see the attics, the

343

state they're in.'

'I'm sorry, Mrs Winters, but what about my father?'

'I'm not sure. He wasn't hit. He fell down the stairs. Some kind of a seizure. I don't know. Shock, I suppose. Two men were killed outright, you know, on the corner of South Street. Just talking, they were, near the Montpelier Boarding-House. Funny, the shell went in the front and out the side, and suddenly there they were as dead as mutton. Terrible, isn't it, that you can be alive and kicking one minute, dead the next?'

'I – I'm so sorry. But where is my father now?'

'They took him to hospital.'

'And – my mother?'

'Oh, she went down to your sister's house. Well, I mean, she couldn't have stayed on here, could she, not with Mr Grayler in hospital and the house the mess it's in?'

Charlotte ran back over the bridge into town. One of the duty nurses at the hospital recognized her as a Red Cross helper. 'I'm sorry,' she said, 'you can't possibly see your father now.' She viewed with a dispassionate, professional eye, Charlotte's trembling lips and paper-white face. 'You'd best get a good night's sleep. Come back tomorrow.'

'But how is he? Please, you must tell me!'

'Very ill, I'm afraid. He had a seizure. He wasn't wounded, if that's any comfort. Please, you must go now. I can't spare any more time. Come back tomorrow.'

Go now? Where to, Charlotte wondered. To Maggie's house? She could not bring herself to do that. She thought, with relief, of Annie Crystal, Joe's girl, who lived with her elderly widowed mother not far from the hospital. Desperately tired, Charlotte dragged herself to Annie's house where, in minutes, she found herself encompassed with quiet understanding in Annie's back parlour beside the dying embers of the fire which Annie quickly replenished with coal and wood-chippings.

'I'll make up the bed in the spare room,' Annie said, putting a pan of soup on the cooker to heat; getting out a loaf of bread, some butter and cheese. 'Poor Charlotte, you look all in.'

'Don't waste your sympathy on me,' Charlotte said bleakly,

'I don't deserve it. You don't know what I've done.' Her voice caught on a sob. 'All I know is, if anything happens to my father, I'll regret it for the rest of my life.'

'Yes, I do know,' Annie said. 'Your mother told me. But if the shoe had been on the other foot, if it had been Joe and me, do you imagine I wouldn't have done exactly the same thing? I'm just so lucky that Joe isn't married to someone else, that's all.' She placed a comforting hand on Charlotte's shoulder. 'As for your father . . . forgive me, but the doctor said his seizure could have happened at any minute, bombardment or no bombardment. Albert has been seriously ill for some time now. Perhaps you knew that. It was only a question of time.'

'But I might have given him more time!'

'Time for what? To watch you waste your life? He wouldn't have wanted that. He glories in you, Charlotte, in your spirit of independence. If Albert dies and you give up fighting for what you believe in, you *will* have something to regret for the rest of your life.' She poured the soup into a dish. 'They say the onlooker sees most of the game. I have always seen you and my Joe as the strong ones of the Grayler family. Whatever happens now, Charlotte, please keep strong for all our sakes.'

'But I'm not strong, Annie.'

'Oh yes you are. Stronger than you realize. I know. Just think how you helped Harry when his horse was commandeered, how you've pushed your way round town with Mr Roe's old handcart, how busy you've been at the hospital. Don't you see how much we all depend on you?'

'My mother doesn't. She'll never forgive me for not being here when I was needed.'

'Not now, perhaps,' Annie said, 'but she will in time.'

Albert died two days later. Charlotte, Filly and Maggie were at his bedside. The boys had been sent for.

The ward was freezing cold, lit by a smoking stove at the far end of the room. The nurses had tacked up Christmas decorations. Vases of stiff chrysanthemums were arrayed on the central table. It was two o'clock on a bleak December afternoon.

Albert opened his eyes. 'I'm thirsty,' he said.

When the nurse had given him a sip of water from a feeding-cup, he asked where his sons were.

'They're coming soon, Albert,' Filly said faintly, wiping her eyes.

'I'm not sure I can wait much longer.' He turned his head painfully. 'Maggie? Are you getting enough to eat?'

'Yes, Dad.' Maggie collapsed weeping against her mother's shoulder.

'Copper?'

'I'm here, Dadda.' She held his hand tightly in hers.

'Remember – the river?' He smiled.

'Yes, Dadda. Of course I remember.'

'Funny,' he murmured, closing his eyes, 'it's all wide and shining again.'

The funeral was held from Maggie's house. The boys had been granted compassionate leave. The blinds were tightly closed, filtering green light into the room where the coffin rested on trestles, surrounded with wreaths.

Maggie and Filly had slept together in the back bedroom, Bob on the parlour sofa until the day of the funeral. Harry, Joe and Charlotte put up at Annie's house while Frank, to Mrs Robinson's disgust, had turned up at the house in Beulah Terrace to claim his conjugal rights which Madge, in view of the circumstances, seemed reluctant to deny him.

'Well, it's your funeral,' sniffed Mrs Robinson, whereupon Madge burst into tears and snapped, 'No, it isn't. It's Mr Grayler's funeral, and he was always decent to me. Besides, Frank *is* my husband!'

And so Frank and Madge were reunited in a creaking brass bedstead beneath a sloping roof to the occasional grunting and puffing of trains from the station below which vibrated the ewer in the washbasin on the marble-topped wash-hand stand and shook the lid of the soap-dish to a frenzied, rattling dance. It seemed to Frank, moving and grunting to the rhythm of the train-wheels, somehow wrong of him to reach a pulsating, physical climax when his father lay dead. He cried, then, in

Madge's arms, remembering all that his father had meant to him: the pennies he had given him for ice-cream cornets and donkey-rides on the sands as a boy. Madge stroked his hair and whispered, 'I know, love, I know,' forgetting all about Jack for the moment and Frank's cavalier treatment of her on their honeymoon; living only for the moment, for the feel of a sexually awakened man in her arms. There was no real badness in Madge. Like Frank, she simply wanted to live life to the full as long as it lasted. She thought of her body as a finely-honed tool; her pouting lips, strong teeth, and long, dark hair as a ticket to a world of continuous physical excitement and pleasure. She knew, from old photographs of her mother, how quickly life could dissolve from the questing certainty of youth and physical attraction to the mediocrity of middle-age, how soon death could come to put an end to everything.

After the funeral, Filly said bitterly to Charlotte, 'None of this would have happened if you hadn't gone away. I don't want you near me any more. You are no daughter of mine. I'm staying here with Maggie and Bob. I'm to have their back room.' She began to cry. 'My old life's over now. All those happy days I spent with your father. I don't understand any of this. All I wanted was to be happy, to do my best for my children. I loved to see everything bright and shining. But nothing shines now. That house. I remember the day Albert and I went to look at it. I hated it, but he wanted it. He was so set on it, that I couldn't very well refuse him. Now it's all gone, my home, my sons. There's only Maggie left. Maggie's been good to me. I'm staying with Maggie. She'll need me when the baby comes.'

'Please, Mother,' Charlotte said brokenly, 'I'm here, too. Won't you try to forgive me?'

'No,' Filly cried, 'I'll never forgive you for going off with that chap the way you did. You've made your bed, now lie in it! All your life, ever since you were born, there were secrets between you and your father. His last words on earth were spoken to you, not me. What did he mean about that river? There were always secrets I couldn't share, as if I was an outsider. It was always him you turned to, never me. Well, he's gone now, so take your secrets somewhere else in future. Take them to that fancy man of yours!'

Charlotte turned away, lacerated by her mother's jealousy and misunderstanding. Her old life was over too, just as Filly's was.

She stayed with Annie over Christmas, trying to gather her thoughts, crying out her grief over her father in Annie's spare room, talking to Annie over the fire in the back parlour when her invalid mother had been settled down for the night. The boys had gone back to Newcastle. Annie's tiny back sitting-room seemed a haven against the searching December winds.

'I've got to get away from Scarborough,' Charlotte said, shivering despite the warm fire.

Annie said sensibly, 'You are not going anywhere for the time being. Certainly not until you have had time to think things over. Please stay here with me until after the new year. I'll be so glad of your help.'

And so Charlotte had helped Annie with her Christmas shopping, had gone to market with her to buy a goose, a piece of belly-pork, a stone of potatoes; sprouts, carrots and onions; holly to decorate the house; had helped her to gum together paper-chains to loop lopsidedly round mirrors and pictures; to carry in coal from the yard; to arrange the Christmas cards on the mantelpiece in the front room.

In a bazaar in town, she had bought a special Christmas card for Kitty Tanquillan; had written a letter asking her permission to return to Wiltshire sometime in January.

She had heard nothing from Rowan, not that she had expected to since she knew that, on Christmas Eve, he would be sailing for France.

The spirit of Christmas was lacking. The war, the bombardment, had left their mark. She went to midnight service with Annie because Annie asked her to; found that she could not sing the carols for the lump in her throat. Then, glancing sideways at Annie, Charlotte knew that she could not sing either. They simply stood together, drawing comfort from each other.

It was a still night with a full moon and clouds as feathery as dandelion clocks. After the service, they stood together looking out to sea, listening to the wash of the tide on the shore. Suddenly a curious thing happened. Charlotte sensed Rowan's presence, as if he had held out his hand to her in the great silver arc of the night. Gripping the cold iron railings, the dull misery in her heart was replaced by a warm feeling of peace. 'What is it?' Annie asked, but Charlotte could not reply. Wherever Rowan was at that moment, she knew he was thinking about her.

Rowan turned away from the ship's rail. For one shining moment he had believed himself to be with Charlotte. At daybreak, the battalion marched towards a rest camp on the outskirts of Le Havre.

Bert Hoskins's stomach was rumbling with hunger. He remembered suddenly that this was Christmas Day, and thought of his 'old woman', his 'Big Bertha', shopping for a nice little duck in Walthamstow market on Christmas Eve, stuffing it full of sage and boiled onions and shoving it in the oven to cook along with a panful of taters. His mouth watered thinking about that duck; his heart ached thinking about that warm little kitchen at home, with a lop-sided, bauble-hung Christmas tree in the corner, and Bertha clouting the kids' ears whenever they got under her feet. His own Christmas dinner was nothing but an omelette in a local estaminet, washed down with rough red wine instead of beer, along with the rest of his Company. The smell of garlic worried him a good deal too.

Boxing Day was filmed over with brittle white frost like icing on a Christmas cake. On the night of 28 December, a storm broke over the camp; rain came down like stair-rods, turning the ground to a quagmire. Orders for entrainment came next morning. Horses had broken loose during the night, dragging their pickets from the soft mud. Limbers and waggons had sunk wheel-deep in the morass. Men not engaged in fatigue work stood frozen to the marrow by stinging hailstones until the waggons were dug out. Rowan whistled a snatch of the Marseillaise as the column set off, in cattle trucks, to St Omer.

Charlotte could not bear to leave the situation with her mother unresolved over Christmas. On Boxing Day, she and Annie went down to Maggie's. 'Beware Greeks bearing gifts,' she said wryly as they waited on the doorstep. Annie laughed. 'Don't worry,' she said, 'after all, this is the season of goodwill.'

But Maggie's squeezed parlour contained little evidence of goodwill apart from a coal fire. Maggie had not forgiven Charlotte for her outburst over Rowan's letter. She made it plain that she was not very pleased to see Annie either, since she had given her sister houseroom.

'If you've come here to upset Ma,' she snapped, 'you'd better not stay. She's upset enough as it is.'

'That's the last thing I came for. I'd just like to talk to her, that's all,' Charlotte said, 'and to give her a present.'

The broken veins on Maggie's cheeks blobbed a deep scarlet. 'Ma doesn't want anything from you, not after what you've done.'

'Isn't that for her to say?' Charlotte met her sister's hostility unflinchingly.

'You'd best go into the front room then. You come with me, Annie,' Maggie said grudgingly. 'I expect she'll want to see *you*.'

Maggie's furniture was brand new, formally arranged. The house still smelt of fresh paint and wallpaper. There had been no attempt at Christmas decorations, out of respect for Albert. The hearth contained a 'tidy' with neatly-hung firetongs, shovel, brush and poker – a wedding present from Aunt Clara. The curtains were half drawn across the bay window, imparting a Stygian gloom to the painfully clean and polished room; russet chrysanthemums stood to attention in a vase on the sideboard. Warming her hands at the fire, Charlotte felt like a patient in a doctor's waiting-room.

The door opened and Filly came in. Charlotte was shocked by her pallor, the violet smudges under her eyes. She wanted to run to her, to beg her forgiveness, to tell her she loved her, but Filly's expression did not soften. Her attitudes had hardened since Albert's funeral, fed by Maggie's bitterness that Charlotte had been vouchsafed the kind of experience she could only read about in penny novelettes. Nor had Maggie forgotten how Bob had looked at Charlotte that day tobogganing on Oliver's Mount. Filly's dependence on her had imbued Maggie with a smug self-righteousness. Fat and sloppily pregnant, she could scarcely bear the sight of her beautiful sister.

'Mother,' Charlotte said, 'we must talk. I know I've made you angry, and I'm sorry.'

'There's nothing to talk about. I said all I had to say to you after your father's funeral.'

'But we can't leave things as they are. Won't you at least try to understand my feelings?'

Filly turned her head away. 'You were always good with words,' she said bitterly.

'What do words matter? I'm trying to tell you how I feel . . .'

'Oh yes,' Filly said scornfully, 'it's always how *you* feel, isn't it? Never mind how *I* feel! I want nothing more to do with you, Charlotte. You've chosen your path, now stick to it.' Her face puckered suddenly. 'It makes me ill to think of it, you and that – that chap – in bed together. That's why you went to London, isn't it? So that you could sleep with him?' Her lips tightened. 'Well, pack your things and go back to him. See how much he cares for you then. Men like him use girls like you for their own selfish pleasure, the way they use the servants in those posh houses they live in . . .'

'It isn't true!' But Charlotte knew that nothing she could say or do would break down her mother's barrier of resentment. She said wearily, 'Very well, Mother, if that's what you choose to believe, I shall go away.'

She paused, hoping that even now her mother would relent, but Filly remained bound up in all her old shibboleths of right and wrong, her deep fear of the abnormal: of moral laxity.

Annie offered to accompany her to the house to collect her things, but Charlotte preferred to go there alone.

She slipped the key in the lock; saw, with an ache in her heart, the jewel colours on the carpet. The stairs were covered with fine white dust. She trod carefully, her shoes making imprints.

The dining-room door had been blown off its hinges. That room, scene of Maggie's wedding reception, of so many Grayler family discussions, was sagging now, the sideboard upended, spilling forth a tattered waterfall of lace-edged cloths. Her grandmother's cut-glass salad bowl lay smashed beyond repair, but the silver rim rocked, intact, a bright silver circlet, on the shredded carpet.

The sitting-room windows admitted the bright watery sunshine of a cold December morning. The curtains and the rods which held them had been torn down. Pictures hung awry, but, curiously, her father's pipes were untouched on the mantelpiece, even though the hearth was piled deep with soot and cinders. She dared not enter the room; even her light footsteps on the threshold caused a tremor. She saw, with tear-filled eyes, that Albert's chair had been riddled with shell-splinters.

In the kitchen, Filly's cooker had been wrenched away from the buckled wall. The flue had blown in sideways, scattering the floor inches thick with soot and brick-dust.

She felt as audiences feel when the curtains part to reveal the setting for a stage play. But there would be no more players on this stage. The final act was over, the lights dimmed forever. And yet, as one hears, in an empty theatre, ghost voices from the past, as the very brickwork tingles with memories, so Charlotte listened to the words and laughter trapped beneath the roof of this house where she was born.

She remembered her brothers, Frank, Harry and Joey, as children; remembered all the inconsequential words they had spoken to each other over the years. She remembered her mother as a bright-eyed young woman forever cooking and cleaning, polishing stair-rods, washing and mending, starching and ironing, scolding and forgiving; her father in his clean white Monday-morning coat going down to open the shop, a proud figure of a man with his bright golden-red hair and upturned moustache; remembered herself and Maggie hurrying home from school in their starched linen petticoats and brown stiff dresses, as hungry as hunters, waiting in the kitchen for their mother to spread freshly-baked oven-bottom cakes thick with butter and strawberry jam.

Now the rooms were silent and empty, with all the laughter and love gone out of them, as if they had somehow been bewitched; frozen to a dreadful immobility.

Nothing but the thunder of guns, the whine of shells, would have persuaded Filly to leave her bed unmade, the sheet pushed back untidily over the blankets. Charlotte saw, with the ache of tears in her throat, the imprint of her parents' heads upon the pillows, a scattering of her mother's hairpins on the Victorian dressing-table, her father's dressing-gown thrown across a chair.

The boys' rooms had long since been tidied of their personal possessions. Blankets lay neatly folded on the beds in the room Frank and Harry had shared. A film of dust, like grey cigar-ash, lay over the carpet and furniture. In Joe's room, the swing-mirror on the tallboy had shattered; splintered glass had gouged into the oilcloth.

In the room she had once shared with Maggie, Charlotte saw the old brass bedstead, the blind with its dangling ivory acorn, the honeysuckle wallpaper, the narrow fireplace with its torn paper fan to hide the grate. The wardrobe mirror was zig-zagged with cracks. The room seemed colder than ever now, covered in grey, insidious dust blown down from the chimneys when the shell struck.

She picked her way slowly up the creaking attic stairs to her own room; cried out when she saw the havoc the shell had wreaked there. The ceiling near the blown-out window had collapsed amid a welter of slates and plaster. The bed was piled high with the wreckage of a fallen chimney. She realized that had she been in that bed when the shell struck, she would have been killed outright. The floor was holed. The shell must have come through the roof, deflected, then torn through the wall of the dining-room. Or perhaps there were two shells. Who could tell?

The floorboards groaned beneath her feet as she began to empty her wardrobe of clothes. She tiptoed, heart in mouth, to the chest of drawers where she had kept her underclothes. The gathered-together petticoats fell from her hands as she picked

353

up a calf-bound volume of poetry she had bought in London the day she and Jenny went to the aid of those suffragettes in Trafalgar Square. Percy Bysshe Shelley! Flicking its pages, she read,

> I arise from dreams of Thee
> In the first sweet sleep of night,
> When the winds are breathing low,
> And the stars are shining bright:
> I arise from dreams of thee,
> And a spirit in my feet
> Hath led me – who knows how?
> To thy chamber window, Sweet! . . .
>
> O lift me from the grass!
> I die, I faint, I fail!
> Let thy love in kisses rain
> On my lips and eyelids pale.
> My cheek is cold and white, alas!
> My heart beats loud and fast:
> O press it to thine own again
> Where it will break at last!

There was nothing more she needed now of this place except to say goodbye to it, as she must say goodbye to the town she loved which had always seemed part and parcel of her own self and being.

She closed the side door quietly behind her.

Perhaps she would come back again one day.

CHAPTER NINE

Will Oakleigh was at the station to meet her.

'I thought we had seen the last of you,' he said gruffly as he helped Charlotte into the trap.

'You sound almost sorry that you had not,' she said lightly. 'I'm sorry to have put you to so much trouble.'

He smiled as she climbed up beside him. 'Who says I'm sorry?' He shook the reins over the horse's back. 'I've missed you, Charlotte. We've all missed you.'

She glanced round her at well-remembered scenery; experienced a strange sense of homecoming although the willow-tinted grass was frost-rimed now, the trees all bare.

'You look peaky,' Will observed. 'Have you been ill?'

'Not exactly.' She paused. 'My father died just before Christmas.'

'I'm sorry.' He drove in silence for a while. 'I read about the bombardment in the newspapers. It must have been terrible.'

'Yes, it was. Very terrible.'

'I prayed for you,' he said. 'Prayed you'd keep safe.'

'That was kind of you, Will.'

'I know what it's like losing someone you love. I don't suppose you want to talk about it now, but if ever you do . . .'

'Thanks, Will. Perhaps I shall one day.' What a nice man, she thought, not effusive but kind and somehow – strong.

He said nothing more as he turned the horse's head between the gateposts, but she sensed his companionship and was glad of it.

The flowers edging the terrace were all dead now, filmed over with a light sprinkling of snow. The house was in darkness because of the blackout regulations, but a light shone forth briefly as the front door opened and Kitty Tanquillan stepped forward to greet her.

'Oh, my dear! I'm so pleased to see you! Come inside quickly. You must feel half-frozen. Will, hand down her luggage!'

Charlotte was suddenly overwhelmed by the flying figure of Alice Tanquillan as the girl raced downstairs to cover her cheeks with kisses. Scarcely five months had passed since their last meeting, but Alice had grown much taller. She wore a red velvet dress and her hair was neatly braided, giving her face a more mature, less gipsy appearance.

'Charlotte,' she said breathlessly, 'I haven't had a bite to eat all day for excitement! Aunt Kitty was so cross with me when I turned my nose up at Cook's fish pie. Do you like my hair, my dress?' She twirled round for inspection, her eyes brilliant with delight beneath dark, up-tilted brows. 'I can ride now! Will has been teaching me. I go to school in Devizes. It's frightfully dull and boring, of course, but it's a cross I must bear, I suppose.' She frowned. 'But why have you come back so soon? I thought you had gone away for good.'

'*Alice!*' Kitty halted the flow of words with a gesture. 'All that can come later. Charlotte will want to go to her room before dinner. You'll stay, of course, Will. Rivers! Miss Charlotte is here! Tell Cook we'll dine in half an hour.'

'Rivers!' Charlotte shook the old man's hand. 'How are you?'

'He's as right as a trivet,' Kitty said drily. 'Will, carry Charlotte's things upstairs. You, Alice, stay here with me!'

The girl pouted and shrugged her shoulders. And yes, Charlotte thought as she went up to her room, it is still there, the old, febrile excitement. She looks older, more mature, but she is still the same unbalanced child I remember so well.

A fire had been lit in her room. Pausing on the threshold, Charlotte thought that this house seemed indestructible. Time had imparted an ageless quality to its solidity, its stones, beams and fireplaces. And yet the air was still tinged with the transient scent of lavender and rose-petals, a fragrance as fleeting as bygone summers.

As Will set down her cases, she experienced a feeling of relief that he was staying to dinner, as if his presence would prove a barrier against a thousand questions she felt too tired to answer.

Reading her thoughts, Will said levelly, 'Don't worry, I won't let Alice bother you too much.'

He felt stiff and awkward in Charlotte's presence because he was in love with her. He had loved her from the moment he saw her at his farmhouse door with the summer sun on her face. Not a day had passed since then that he had not thought about her. Now, piling her luggage inside her room, suppressing a desire to kiss her, he thought that there was no fool like an old fool.

She had Will to thank time and time again during dinner for drawing the conversation away from herself. Whenever Alice blurted a question in that disconcertingly blunt way of hers, Will led her back to the topic of horses.

Riding had become a passion with the girl. 'She has taken to the saddle as a duck takes to water,' Will said, touching on her vanity.

He spoke the truth. Riding had imbued the reckless Alice Tanquillan with a feeling of self-importance. The once poverty-stricken child who had run away from Queen Margaret's School with suicide in mind, who had stood poised above splintering waves running in on the rocks of Scarborough's South Beach, was now the equal of her schoolmates at Devizes. She was a rich, well-dressed young woman who cared not a jot for anyone else's opinion of her, since she thought so highly of herself now that she had money, fine clothes, and horses to ride.

Kitty Tanquillan, at the head of the table, said little but observed a great deal. Charlotte ate little. It was obvious that Will was in love with her. Her shoulders stiffened when Alice said, apropos of nothing, 'My cousin Rowan's in the Army now, you know. We had a Christmas card from him just before he sailed for France. Poor darling Rowan! I don't see why he had to join up so quickly, but I expect it was all that beastly Romilly's fault!'

'*Alice!*'

The girl stared at her aunt, wide-eyed. 'But you said yourself, Aunt Kitty, that he had no need to volunteer. You were very upset about it at the time.'

Glancing across the table at Charlotte, Will noticed that her hand trembled suddenly on the stem of her wine glass. Her face was very lovely, very serious by candleshine, framed by that lustrous hair of hers. Kitty said abruptly, 'I had hoped not to discuss the war this evening. It is not a pleasant topic of conversation.'

But Alice was in an argumentative mood. She retorted, 'I don't see why we should ignore it, how can we ignore it since it is at the back of everyone's minds? You are thinking about it all the time, aren't you Charlotte? So are you, Aunt Kitty, and you, Will! It isn't fair on Rowan to shut him out when he's out there somewhere fighting for us!' Her voice rose hysterically.

Kitty ignored the outburst. Rising to her feet, she told Rivers to serve coffee in the drawing-room. 'You will go to your room now, child,' she said to Alice. 'You are very tired, and certainly not in need of further stimulant.'

Alice's eyes flashed fire. 'I am not in the least bit tired!'

'Perhaps not, but you will say goodnight now to our guests.' Kitty's tone of voice brooked no further argument from the wayward girl. Alice flounced from the room without a word, slamming the door behind her. Glancing at Kitty Tanquillan's drawn, set features, Charlotte knew how much the battle of wills had cost the old lady in terms of mental and physical effort. The day would surely come when Alice would ride roughshod over her benefactress. She was reminded of a circus act: a lion-tamer holding in check, by sheer personal magnetism, a tawny young lioness.

Maggie was sitting having breakfast with Filly in the back room of the house in Garibaldi Street when her pains started. Bob had just gone to work. The fire which Bob had laid and put a match to when he got up at six o'clock, was now burning brightly in the hearth, lighting up the pictures on the walls, the ornaments on the mantelpiece, flickering on the table set with Maggie's second-best china. Filly had made the toast by the fire, holding out the slabs of bread on a pronged toasting-fork. The butter was set on the hearth to soften.

Breakfast with her mother had become a ritual, something they enjoyed together when Bob had been got out of the way. Lately, since Maggie's time drew near and she felt disinclined to get up at the crack of dawn, Filly had taken to cooking Bob's breakfast in the scullery adjoining the back room, fussing over him as she used to fuss over Albert and the boys, making sure that his eggs were bloomed as he liked them, that the bacon, if they were lucky enough to have any, was crisply done. Then, when Bob had eaten, he would hunch his shoulders into his greatcoat and call up the stairs to his wife that he was off to work. When the back door had closed behind him, Maggie would come downstairs, huddled in a padded dressing-gown, to the warm little room redolent with toasting bread. She would hold her slippered feet to the fire to get warm, and lather her slices of toast with melted butter and marmalade.

Now, between mouthfuls of toast, she felt a queer trickle of fluid between her legs, a tug of pain in her belly. 'Oh, Ma!' she cried out, 'it's starting! My baby! It's starting!' She bent forward, pressing her hands to her abdomen.

Half fainting with fear and ignorance, she leaned heavily on Filly's arm as her mother led her back upstairs to the front bedroom, and sat on the edge of the unmade bed as Filly began rummaging in the top drawer of the tallboy for a clean nightgown.

'Just stand up a minute while I make the bed,' Filly said authoritatively, 'then slip into this clean nightdress while I run next door and tell Mrs Smith to send for the midwife.'

'Christ, Ma! Don't leave me!' But Filly, who had given birth to five babies, said placatingly, 'Don't worry, nothing will happen for a long time yet. Just lie down, I'll be back in a few minutes.'

When Filly returned, she wound a clean sheet between the rods of the brass bedstead, twisted it expertly between her hands, and shoved the ends of it between Maggie's fingers. 'There,' she said, 'hold onto that when your pains come fierce.' She crossed to the window to part the curtains, but Maggie could not bear that. 'Leave them closed,' she muttered between clenched teeth. It was an animal instinct to want to give birth in the dark.

Agony bucked Maggie's body as her birth canal began slowly to open. She screamed aloud with the impossible-to-bear pain of it, tearing with her fingernails at the sheet her mother had given her to hold. When her screams of pain and terror rose to a crescendo, Filly moistened a face-flannel in the ewer on the wash-stand and thrust it between her daughter's lips. 'Bite on that,' she said firmly.

Maggie stared up at her mother in bewilderment as the gag was applied; felt, with a sense of horror, the wet flannel between her teeth, and yet as pain overwhelmed her, she bit deeply into it and twisted the sheet more desperately between her sweating hands.

When Bob came home for his dinner at twelve o'clock, he stared in dismay at the ashes of a dead fire in the grate; heard the cries of his wife in labour, a queer banshee wail that filled the house. 'Oh, my God,' he cried, dashing to the foot of the stairs, certain that Maggie was dying. Halfway up, he met his mother-in-law coming down. 'I must go to her,' he stammered, but Filly advised him not to. 'Everything's all right,' she said, 'just go and sit down and I'll get you something to eat.'

'Eat! I don't want anything to eat,' Bob mumbled. 'How do you expect me to eat at a time like this?' He lifted his head to stare wildly up the staircase as his wife's cries floated down to him. 'How long has she been like this?'

'It's nothing unusual,' Filly said calmly, 'first babies take a long time coming.' She forced him towards the little back room. 'Either go back to work or sit down and keep quiet. This is woman's business. I'm expecting the midwife at any minute.' She sighed. 'Why don't you go back to work? You'll be far better off doing something useful.'

'Yes,' Bob said unsteadily, 'yes, I think I'd better.' He remembered briefly the pleasure he had found in exploring his wife's body, all the grunting and puffing and that supreme, godlike feeling when his climax came, how proud he had felt when he knew that he had implanted his child in Maggie's womb. Now he felt nothing but a deep sense of despair that the simple act of procreation had been desecrated by so much pain and suffering. He walked blindly towards the back door.

The midwife appeared at last, a fat, blowsy little woman with a penchant for endless cups of tea, wearing a pinafore beneath a green coat, and a wide-brimmed hat which remained firmly on her head throughout Maggie's travail. Sitting in a chair beside the bed, drinking her third cup of tea, she nodded sagely: said, 'Your womb's fully opened now, my dear. The baby's head is in the birth canal. You'd better start bearing down now, love. Just push, and keep on pushing. What a lucky girl you are, Mrs Masters. Most first babies take a whole day and night. You've almost managed yours in ten hours!'

Maggie had never realized that such pain was possible. She lay, twisting and writhing, moaning and belching, on a bed of pain, holding on like grim death to the sheet between her hands, biting on the wet flannel between her lips, until the midwife threw back the bedclothes and shoved an ice-cold macintosh sheet between her legs.

'There,' the midwife crooned encouragingly between mouthfuls of tea, 'you've brought its head. The worst is over now.'

I'm dying, Maggie thought. I'm dying and no-one cares. Her hair clung wetly to her forehead, her eyes were filled with dripping perspiration. She felt like an animal brought to slaughter. Then, with a final heave, she expelled the burden from her womb and lay panting, groaning and uncaring as the midwife cut the umbilical cord and smacked her child into lusty life.

'You have a beautiful little girl,' the woman said, but Maggie, torn and lacerated in mind and body, turned her head away, experiencing no joy in motherhood, simply a deep-rooted feeling of injury that her tender flesh had been so desecrated with pain; that nobody had warned her what to expect. Whatever happened, she would never have another baby, she decided, as the child was put beside her to suckle. Nor could she bear her husband's obvious delight in his child. It was all very well for him to come up to her room, to pick it up and make such

361

a fuss of it, but she was the one who had to feed it. She could scarcely bear the sight of it, a red-faced scrap of humanity with a fuzz of dark hair, latching onto her breast like a leech.

Annie wrote to Charlotte that Maggie had given birth to a beautiful little girl with dark hair and blue eyes. 'Bob is over the moon with her,' she penned. 'He calls her "Peg-o-my-heart", and I fancy the name will stick. I've never seen Bob so happy before, but Maggie isn't very well. She seems depressed, but some women are when they have just had a baby. I expect we'll all buck up a bit when the days begin to lengthen; when springtime pokes its nose round the corner.'

Charlotte read the news in her room at Grey Wethers. Annie's letter was posted on the last day of January. It was now February, a bitterly cold day with a searching, hailstone-laced wind. Soon it would be time to set off with Will on the feed-wagon. Kitty Tanquillan had said, 'I warn you, Charlotte, it will be hard, rough work for a woman out there on the Downs, taking food to the sheep. You'll need to learn how to handle a pitchfork.'

'I don't mind that, as long as I earn my salt.'

'But I've already told you, I can find lighter work for you about the house.'

'I don't want that . . .'

'No,' Kitty sighed, 'you want to drive yourself to forget what happened in Scarborough. That's the truth, isn't it?'

'Yes, I suppose it is.'

'Very well then, since you are so stubborn and pig-headed, I'll say no more.'

And so Charlotte had set about helping Will with the sheep, driving with him to where the animals nosed among the boulders in the snow and wind-scoured earth, her cheeks stung crimson with hailstones, her hair bound with a tugging scarf; forking bales from the cart as the shearing wind almost tore the breath from her body, struggling to hold back the strange feelings of nausea which attacked her as soon as she got out of bed these mornings.

Kitty read the letter from London with a frown: mistrustful as ever of Rachel's motives in writing to her. Now what is Madam up to? she wondered.

'Gervaise is not at all well at the moment,' Rachel had written in her decisive hand, 'and wishes to see you. There are things to discuss better not touched on in a letter. You will be most welcome to stay with us for as long as it pleases you to do so. This is an anxious time for us since our daughter-in-law is expecting her baby at any moment, whilst I am naturally involved in fund-raising for Belgian Relief, as most women are these days . . .'

Kitty spread out the letter on her desk. Gervaise must have suffered a brainstorm if he had really asked for her. Shrewd commonsense warned her that Gervaise's illness must be a ploy, an excuse to discuss something of vital importance to him – and only one thing mattered to her nephew. Money!

Curiosity got the better of her. She wanted to know what Gervaise and Rachel were up to, not that she relished the notion of travelling to London alone. But if, as she suspected, this summons had to do with Alice, Grey Wethers, and Rowan, she would have no hesitation in dealing firmly with the pair of them.

Kitty arrived at the house in Eaton Square, cold, tired, and not in the best of tempers, to find Gervaise, as pink and portly as ever, standing in the hall to greet her.

The same old mausoleum, she thought with distaste, glancing at the frowning portraits on the walls, the branching staircase, and the black and white marble squares at her feet.

'Well, Aunt, how are you?' Gervaise planted a peck on her cheek – like a robin redbreast pecking at a worm, she thought, beginning to take off her gloves, finger-by-finger, thumb-by-thumb, knowing that this would irritate him past bearing.

'More to the point, how are *you*?' She considered him coolly.

'I'm well enough,' he replied, signalling a servant to take her things upstairs.

'Oh? I'm pleased to hear it. I thought, by Rachel's letter, that

I should find you at death's door. Where is Rachel, by the way?'

'God knows! She's seldom at home these days!'

Kitty was halfway upstairs when Rachel appeared at the front door as breathless as if she had run all the way from wherever she had been, to greet her guest on time. This subtlety amused Miss Tanquillan, since Rachel looked the picture of elegance in a green costume, fashionably braided in darker green, with a matching feather-trimmed hat, and fox furs about her shoulders.

Rachel's war effort certainly did not include standing about on cold station platforms handing cups of tea to soldiers, the old woman thought as Rachel rustled up to her, kissed her cheek, and walked with her to the guest-room.

'I do hope you'll be comfortable here,' Rachel said, after enquiries about the journey and Kitty's state of health. 'Tea will be served in the drawing-room when you are ready.' She smiled, but seemed in no hurry to leave. 'You will remember to keep the curtains tightly drawn? We have to be so careful here, though I imagine the blackout regulations are far stricter here than they are at Grey Wethers.'

Ah, Kitty thought, the tip of the iceberg. 'What is wrong with Gervaise?' she asked, holding her hands to the fire. 'He looks well enough to me.'

Rachel toyed with the pearls at her throat. 'He's worried. We both are. Things are rather – difficult – at the moment.'

'Not for Gervaise, surely?' Kitty unpinned her hat. 'I imagined that he would be riding a tidal wave of success with all his government contracts.'

'I was not referring to financial matters.' Rachel frowned slightly. 'It is Romilly we feel concerned about, and Rowan. Gervaise was deeply wounded when he joined up without a word. Oh, you know what young people are these days, and the early days of marriage are often emotional ones.' She paused to let her words sink in. 'Poor Romilly has had a particularly hard time of it: first the accident, now with the baby due at any minute. I daresay that she had not stopped to consider her position in society as a divorced woman with a child to bring up.'

364

'Divorced?' Kitty raised her eyebrows in surprise. 'I had no idea that matters had gone that far.'

'They haven't – yet.' Rachel smiled. 'Romilly has been very ill, you know. Her mental state gave cause for concern. Inevitably, when Rowan went away, the idea of divorcing him became implanted in her mind and took root there.'

'On what grounds?' Kitty asked. 'Not desertion surely, since Rowan simply felt the urge to serve his country, and hardly non-consummation of the marriage?'

Rachel shrugged her shoulders disarmingly. 'You are right, of course, these would prove unacceptable grounds for divorce. I imagine that only Rowan's adultery – had he committed it – would have sufficed.' A smile hovered about her lips. 'But impetuous young men do sometimes fall from grace, don't they?'

A warning bell clamoured in Kitty's brain. She felt strangely ill at ease; cold, despite the warmth of the fire.

'Of course,' Rachel continued, 'it has taken a great deal of persuasion to make Romilly see that divorce would be out of the question. Neither Gervaise nor I would tolerate such a slur on the family name, or the notoriety connected with such a scandalous procedure. As a Tanquillan yourself, you will understand what I mean. Gervaise hopes to gain a seat in Parliament in the next election. It is unthinkable that a man in his position, who has already earned a knighthood for his services to his country, should find himself involved in a sordid domestic squabble.'

Oh God, Kitty thought. Now I begin to understand why I was sent for.

Rachel straightened a picture above the mantelpiece. 'Gervaise and I have reached the only possible conclusion, that whatever occurred between my son and his wife to bring about this unhappy state of affairs should be healed as quickly as possible, not only for the sake of my daughter-in-law and her child, but for Rowan's sake too.' Again that disarming smile of hers. 'Naturally, Gervaise has not yet altered his will, made in our son's favour. My husband is far too generous and forbearing for that, since he lives in hope of Rowan returning to the family business when the war is over.'

'And if Rowan chooses not to do so?' Kitty asked. 'Then, I suppose that Gervaise would disinherit him just as my brother disinherited Oliver Tanquillan?'

'Exactly.' Rachel picked up her furs.

'I hardly think that that would worry my great-nephew unduly,' Kitty said, drawing back her shoulders, knowing that nothing had changed between herself and Rachel, that she heartily detested her, as she had always done, despite her charming veneer.

'Possibly not,' Rachel said, 'but it might worry Romilly and her child a great deal in time to come. One makes allowances, of course. I scarcely think that my daughter-in-law has realized the implications of bringing up a child on her own, but I think that you, Aunt, will understand. Society is unforgiving to those who flout its conventions . . .'

'Which you, no doubt, have pointed out to Romilly?' Kitty said scornfully.

'Why, yes,' Rachel admitted. 'Of course I have, for the child's own sake, which is why she now feels inclined to seek a reconciliation with that headstrong son of mine.' She paused, her hand on the door. 'That is why Gervaise and I decided to seek your help . . .'

'*My* help?'

'Why yes. Knowing how close you are to Rowan, how much he relies on your judgement and commonsense: as virtual head of the Tanquillans, he would listen to you.'

Kitty felt suddenly very old, tired and confused. She had forgotten, to some extent, had preferred to forget Rachel's powerful, almost hypnotic influence; the cold, calculating personality beneath the flummery of beads and furs.

'But you must be terribly tired and hungry after your long journey. Shall we go down and have tea now?' Rachel said serenely.

They were at dinner when a servant came in with an urgent message for her ladyship. Rachel, elegant in black lace, rose to her feet. 'I must go at once,' she said. 'Romilly is in labour. She wishes to see me. Please go on with dessert.'

Gervaise asked moodily over coffee in the drawing-room, 'Is it true that you intend leaving Grey Wethers to Alice Tanquillan?'

'Quite true,' Kitty replied levelly. 'I have made no secret of the fact, which is why you came by the information, I suppose. What did you do, Gervaise, bribe one of my solicitor's clerks?'

Ignoring the thrust, Gervaise continued: 'And so, when you die, a valuable estate will belong to a mentally retarded child?' His eyes were as cold as marble chippings behind his gold-rimmed glasses. 'You have no right, in my opinion, to squander a property which belongs, lawfully, to the Tanquillans.'

'Aren't you forgetting that Alice is a Tanquillan too?' Kitty said coolly. 'What I choose to do with my property is my business. Willing Grey Wethers to Alice is my way of making up to Oliver Tanquillan the wrong he suffered at my brother's hands – and yours!'

'But the girl is quite mad!'

'According to Claude Latimer, the eminent psychiatrist, Alice is just as sane as you or I,' Kitty retorted.

Charlotte thought at first her sickness had to do with exhaustion, the shock of her father's death, the bitter quarrel with Filly: saying goodbye to her home, and coming to Wiltshire, linked with worry about Rowan.

She waited, every day, for a letter, but there had been nothing apart from one postcard addressed to Miss Kitty to say that he had arrived safely in France. She had written to him saying she had left Scarborough, but perhaps he had not received that letter. Uncertainty had brought her to a low physical ebb, which was why Miss Tanquillan had suggested light work about the house if she really insisted on 'earning her salt'. But Charlotte knew that she would prefer to be outdoors, helping Will to care for the animals, to work so hard that she would tire herself out both mentally and physically. Her mind had seemed like a mouse on a treadmill since the death of her father; laced with guilt and remorse. And now another worry chewed away remorselessly at the back of her mind . . .

367

She stood nervously at the gate leading to the doctor's house. Will had driven her into Devizes in a snowstorm to meet Alice from school; to visit first a seed merchants in the Brittox.

'I'll meet you in an hour from now,' he said, 'when you have finished your shopping.'

When he was out of sight, she turned her footsteps towards a doctor's surgery tucked away down a side street near the Corn Exchange.

She sat for a long time in the waiting-room before the doctor was ready to see her. When the nurse, seated at a desk in the corner, called her name, Charlotte walked along a passage to the surgery, knocked and entered.

The man facing her was elderly, with cold grey eyes. His bony fingers tapped lightly the edge of his desk. 'Yes, Miss Grayler, what can I do for you?' He glanced at his watch impatiently, as if she was taking up his precious time.

She told him reluctantly, feeling that he was undressing her with his eyes.

'Sickness?' He frowned, his lips drawn into a disapproving line. 'Any other symptoms? Your periods?'

Charlotte flushed crimson, remembering that day, just after her twelfth birthday, when she had hung about the house in agony of mind, not daring to tell her mother that she was bleeding to death. How, when she plucked up enough courage, Filly had told her it was nothing to worry about, but she must not mention it to anyone else. She had called it 'a woman's carry-on'. But her tone of voice, and her insistence that Charlotte should never divulge it to a living soul, nor ever discuss it with her sister, or her schoolfriends, had made her feel that this was something dirty, to be ashamed of, something to be brushed under the carpet along with childbirth.

Now, admitting to a strange man that she had not bled for the past two months deeply shocked her, especially when the doctor glanced distastefully at her bare left hand and said coldly, 'When did you last have sexual intercourse?'

Tears sprang to her eyes. 'Oh come now, Miss Grayler,' the man said acidly, 'don't look so shocked. Quite frankly, it always amazes me when young unmarried women like yourself turn up at my surgery pretending they don't know what ails them, and sit there as if butter wouldn't melt in their mouths. You are pregnant, Miss Grayler, and my advice is to get the man responsible to make an honest woman of you. Here! Just a minute! Where are you going?'

In the street, Charlotte leaned against a wall to regain her composure, in an agony of distress, her heart hammering against her ribs; sick at heart; lacerated by the doctor's brutality, because he had made her feel unclean, had somehow diminished the love she had shared with Rowan.

Sobbing, she remembered that her mother had called her 'wanton: a whore at heart'. Was that how Rowan saw her? Her mind in a turmoil, she stumbled back to the market square; snow flurries laced with stinging hailstones mingling with her tears.

Will Oakleigh was standing near the trap, glancing around the square with anxious eyes. 'Where on earth have you been?' he asked. 'I've been standing here for the past twenty minutes.'

'I'm sorry, Will. I – I don't feel very well.'

'You'd best get in the trap then,' he said gruffly. 'We'll pick up Alice and get home before the road becomes impassable.'

Before the road becomes impassable, she thought dully, taking his hand outstretched to help her into the vehicle.

Kitty Tanquillan arrived home a week later, and took to her bed for a few days, suffering from what Rivers described as 'tired-outness'.

'My lady should never have gone to visit those relations of hers,' the old man said dolefully, shaking his head. 'I've seen it happen before. They seem to forget she's not as young as she used to be. Well, I told her, but she wouldn't listen to me. Now she's just lying there, not eating, worried to death about something or other.' He turned his rheumy old eyes trustingly to Charlotte. 'You go up to her, miss. Perhaps if you took up a nice drop of broth, she'd take it from you. And try to make her say what's on her mind. There's something bothering her, I'm sure of that.'

'I'll try,' Charlotte said, carrying the tray upstairs.

Kitty was lying in bed with the curtains drawn. 'So that dear old fool Rivers has sent you to see to me, has he?' she greeted Charlotte, resignedly. 'I wish he would stop fussing over me. I'm not ill, you know. I'd just like to be alone for a little while to get my mind in order.'

'How is Sir Gervaise?' Charlotte enquired, filled with pity for the old woman's frailness.

'Ha,' Kitty snorted, 'there's nothing wrong with my nephew that abstinence from eating and drinking would not cure, and I told him so.' She appeared to derive some pleasure from the memory. 'But sit down, my dear. No, I don't want anything to eat!' She hesitated. 'I have things to tell you which you may not wish to hear, but I have never been one to beat about the bush, as you well know.'

She stretched out a withered hand appealingly. 'You know that I love and respect you, Charlotte,' she said. 'How much I had hoped that you and Rowan . . .' Her voice broke suddenly. 'How much I had hoped that you and Rowan might find happiness together one day . . .'

'Please don't try to talk if it tires you. I'll come back later. Try to sleep now.'

'Sleep! I can't sleep!' The old woman turned restlessly on her pillows. 'I blame myself for throwing you and Rowan together. I did so for my own private and personal reasons. But now . . . Please forgive me . . .'

'I don't understand,' Charlotte said. 'What is there to forgive?'

'I told you, my mind's not quite clear at the moment. I have been through a harrowing experience. It's an exhausting business for me staying under the same roof with my nephew and his wife. What a precious pair they are to be sure! The undertones and subtleties, the plotting and scheming.' Kitty sighed. 'I would have returned home after two days except that another crisis occurred when Romilly gave birth to her baby, a son. What a commotion that caused!'

A wave of faintness swept over Charlotte. Her face drained suddenly of colour. She bent forward to steady herself, fighting against the sick feeling which threatened to overwhelm her.

'Oh, my dear! What a fool of a woman I am. I shouldn't have blurted out that news so carelessly!' Kitty scrambled out of bed to hold on to Charlotte. 'You should see a doctor,' she said. 'I'll send for mine; get him to prescribe a tonic for you.'

'No. I'll be all right.' Charlotte straightened up, and rose to her feet. 'I'll go to my room for a little while.'

'Take what you want, saith the Lord. Take it and pay for it.'

Charlotte sank down on her bed. What use now were tears or regrets? She had known that Romilly was going to have a baby: had learned to live with that knowledge. Now she felt lacerated in spirit, torn with guilt and remorse. She had never felt so alone before, with Rowan far away, and her father gone forever. If only she could see him once more; ask him what to do, feel the warmth of his arms around her. The pain of loneliness closed in on her. What should she do?

She loved Rowan; would always love him. But how could she face the thought of becoming a burden to him? She did not want his money or his pity. Sick at heart, she knew that she must bring up her child by herself. In her present low state, she could see no alternative. Then she remembered the doctor's cruel words: 'my advice to you is to get the man responsible to make an honest woman of you.' But what honour would there be in writing to Rowan to burden him with her troubles? Her pride would never allow her to do that. And pride was all she had left now.

She went, later, to Miss Kitty's room. The old woman was seated in front of the fire, in her dressing-gown.

'Are you feeling better?' Charlotte asked.

'Never mind about me. How are *you* feeling?' Kitty wrinkled her forehead. 'I have been worried about you. I wish you would stop working so hard; driving yourself as if the devil were after you! It is extremely foolish of you in view of all you have suffered recently: the death of your father . . .' She paused. 'I'm sorry, I didn't mean to remind you of that. Oh dear. I seem unable to think straight at the moment. I keep blundering on, saying all the wrong things. I'm so very worried, you see. I scarcely know which way to turn.'

She continued, bitterly, 'I should never have gone to London. Poor Rowan! No wonder he wished to break free of parental pressure. I had half forgotten how implacable that could be, or how – deadly.'

'Don't you think that you had better go back to bed?' Charlotte asked quietly, forgetting her own troubles in her concern for Miss Tanquillan. 'Try to sleep. You are very tired.'

'I wish to God I could sleep,' Kitty said restlessly, 'but I can't. I have allowed myself to be drawn, against my will, into a situation that, quite frankly, horrifies me.' She shivered suddenly despite the warmth of the fire. 'What frightens me most is that I, of all people, should find myself coerced into doing something alien to my nature: attempting to bring about a reconciliation between Rowan and his wife.'

'A – reconciliation?'

'I said, at first, that I would not consider it,' Kitty declared proudly, 'until Romilly asked for me, and begged me to use my influence on her behalf.' Kitty's eyes were pain-shadowed, her mouth trembled. 'How could I refuse her, a young woman who had very nearly died giving birth to Rowan's child, knowing that, if I did not at least make some attempt to do so, that precious, money-grubbing nephew of mine would have no compunction in making a new will disinheriting both his son and his grandchild.'

Tears filled the old woman's eyes. 'I have never cared very deeply for money, but I do care a great deal about right and wrong. I have seen one member of the Tanquillan family disinherited, and lived all my life with the pain of what happened to poor Oliver as a result. I cannot bear to think of Rowan being so mistreated.'

'Yes, I see. I understand,' Charlotte said slowly.

'But you *don't*,' the old woman insisted, 'not the whole story; how much I had wanted you and Rowan to be happy together one day!' She smiled sadly. 'Poor Judas Iscariot! I never understood the man before. Now I begin to see why he hanged himself!'

Charlotte raised her head in alarm. All her own fears were forgotten as she said quietly, to cut through Miss Kitty's distress, 'But that is nonsense! You must do what you believe to be right for Rowan's sake! You knew, as I did, that we never had any kind of future together! I told you once, in London, that I could never stand between a man and his wife.'

'Yes, I remember,' Kitty said hoarsely. 'I remember, too, that I begged you to meet Rowan again. That is why I find it so hard to forgive myself. If I had not interfered, that day, I should have less to reproach myself with now.'

Charlotte said gently, 'But just think, Miss Kitty, had I been stronger, I would not have listened to you. The blame does not rest on your shoulders. I wanted to see Rowan again. I did see him, and I shall never, regret that.' She smiled. 'We had a wonderful day together, thanks to you. Now, please Miss Kitty, go to bed and try to sleep.'

The barn was warm, hay-scented, lit by a kerosene lamp. Charlotte knelt beside Will as he gently pulled a lamb from a heaving, prostrate ewe.

Uttering low words of encouragement, Will persuaded the ewe to stagger to its feet, to begin laving the lamb with its tongue. The lamb began to bleat, and then to suckle. Tears streamed down Charlotte's cheeks.

'What is it? What's wrong?' Will asked.

Charlotte said simply, 'I am going to have a baby.'

She heard the sudden grunt of his indrawn breath. '*You*, Charlotte? I don't believe it!'

'It's true, Will! I'm sorry, I shouldn't have told you.'

'No, lass, you did right to tell me.' Jealousy clutched at his heart as he asked, 'Who is the father?'

'I'm sorry, I can't tell you that.'

'Won't he marry you? Is that it? Is that why you are crying?'

'No,' she said, 'I cried because of the lamb. Because I had never seen anything so beautiful or so touching in my life before.'

'The birth of a lamb?' Will frowned, bemused, he who had seen the birth of so many lambs. He said awkwardly, 'I had no

373

right to question you, except that – I love you. I loved you from the moment I set eyes on you.'

The truth was out at last, but he felt no relief at the admission. 'Don't you want the baby?' he asked gruffly.

'Yes, I do. I want it very much.'

'But have you thought what it will mean, a lass like you giving birth to an illegitimate child?'

'I haven't had much time to think at all yet,' she confessed.

'But you *must* think, girl! I know this village: the people who live in it! They can be very cruel, very unjust! About the man: the father . . .'

'He is already married,' Charlotte said quietly, laying her hand on Will's arm, 'and before you jump to the wrong conclusion, he is someone I love very much. That is why I want this child. I am not afraid!'

The lamb was suckling hard now, butting its head against the ewe's milky udder. Will's throat worked awkwardly as he looked at Charlotte; her pain-shadowed eyes and trembling lips, her bright red hair spilling about her shoulders. Loving her as much as he did, he could not bear to think of her as the butt of cruel, mindless jokes and harsh criticism. The village women, he knew, would turn their spite on her when her baby began to show.

He said slowly, 'I know I'm old, and not very clever, but I would make you a good husband. I would never trouble you – physically. I would respect and honour you always; give your child a good home, my own name. I have always wanted a child, you see.' He bowed his head, half ashamed of his declaration of love: his proposal of marriage.

Charlotte knew he meant what he said. A man who cared so much for dumb animals could never be less than compassionate towards a tiny, helpless human being. She knew she did not love Will in the way she loved Rowan Tanquillan, but nothing about him was repellent to her. He was a man she had learned to trust and respect, whom she looked on as a friend, a father figure with his strong, capable hands, and his pride in his work. But she had to be honest with him. 'I don't love you, Will,' she said. 'I like and admire you, but that isn't the same thing.'

'You think I don't know that?' He rose to unhook the lantern. 'I've made a fool of myself, haven't I.' His face was seamed with the pain of rejection.

Charlotte stood beside him, her hand on his sleeve. 'No, you haven't. I am honoured that you should want me for your wife – especially now . . .' Her lips trembled. 'Will you give me time to think about it?'

'Take all the time you want,' he said. 'Just remember that I love you. I would never give you cause for regret.'

Kitty Tanquillan stared into her dressing-table mirror, remembering the days when her hair was dark and thick, held in a snood beneath her riding hat. Remembering how she once strode, booted and spurred, about Grey Wethers, how at dawn she would ride out to meet Gilbert Stapleford, exercising the horses. She saw again that ruined cottage on the Downs where they clung together in desperation, knowing that they were not free to love at all.

She knew how quickly the youth of the heart could be swallowed up in tears and regrets, that first love, when it happened, came as both a joy and torment, a never to be forgotten experience, something she had urged upon Charlotte, to her cost.

Her own story had ended bitterly. Gilbert had gone back to his wife and children in the end, pressurised, as Rowan had been, by those who claimed to have his welfare at heart, and she had let him go, knowing the day would come when he would miss his children.

She had not even told him that she was going to have his child. Pride had forbidden that. When the affair ended, she went abroad for the summer, to Italy, where their son was born, and died. Perhaps the ageing process had started then, for when she returned to Grey Wethers, she had noticed that her hair was threaded with silver.

Now history seemed to be repeating itself, and her visit to London had resurrected a host of painful memories, not simply of her own abortive love affair and the secret she had never divulged to a living soul, but memories of Oliver Tanquillan and his wife Martha; the cruelty of her brother in disinheriting his younger son, the kind of cruelty he had bequeathed in full measure to Gervaise.

She had not told Charlotte the whole truth, that the Beresfords were in dire financial straits. Sir Edmund's business had been on the verge of collapse, due to the war, when Emily approached Gervaise for help and advice. She could see it all: how smoothly he would have told her not to worry, that he would take care of her problems, how willingly Emily had trusted him when she had signed certain papers giving him control over her affairs.

Yes, I can see it all quite clearly now, Kitty thought; how my nephew must have revelled in the knowledge that he now possessed another weapon to hold over Rowan's head if he refused to conform.

Staring at her face in the glass, Kitty shivered suddenly as she remembered Rachel's slight shrug of the shoulders when she said: 'I imagine that only Rowan's adultery – had he committed it – would have sufficed. But impetuous young men do sometimes fall from grace, don't they?'

Kitty had seen in those words, and the way they were uttered, a veiled threat to Charlotte.

Now she was faced with a deadly kind of emotional blackmail. But, as old as she was, as tired and dispirited as she had felt since her return from London, she still had some pride and spirit left. No, I'll be damned if I will act as a mediator between Rowan and his wife, she thought. If Romilly wants Rowan back, she must be the one to tell him so. That benighted nephew of mine and his wife shall not get the better of me.

Her mind was clear again, and functioning as it had always done before. Smiling grimly, she went back to bed, and rang the bell for Rivers to bring her some food before she starved to death.

Next morning, she was up and about again as usual, seeing to the accounts, sitting at her desk in the study, pen in hand, making out the week's menus.

She looked up, frowning slightly with concentration, as a knock came at the door, and Charlotte entered. 'Yes, my dear, what is it?'

'I – I have something to tell you.' Charlotte stood nervously in the doorway.

'Well, don't just stand there. Come in. Sit down by the fire.' The old woman spoke brusquely, noticing how strained Charlotte looked, how pale her cheeks were. 'I was just about to take my mid-morning glass of Madeira. You'll join me?'

'No, thank you. I'd rather not, if you don't mind.' Charlotte held back the sudden feeling of nausea that threatened to overwhelm her at the thought of drinking a glass of wine.

A sudden memory of herself, a lifetime ago, assailed the old woman: a tiny flicker of knowledge in the way Charlotte held herself as she moved towards the fire.

'Well, what have you come to tell me?' Kitty took the chair opposite, forgetting all about her glass of Madeira.

Charlotte said quietly, 'Will Oakleigh has asked me to marry him, and I have said yes.'

'But you don't love Will,' Kitty said, deeply shaken.

'Nevertheless, I am going to marry him, and I intend to make him a good wife.'

'But – *why*? For God's sake, girl!'

'Because I am going to have a child.'

'Will's child, you mean?'

Charlotte shook her head. 'No, not Will's child. Rowan's!'

'Does Will know?'

'That I am going to have a child, yes. But not the name of the father,' Charlotte said dully.

'Oh, my God, what fools we mortals be! But you cannot possibly marry a man you are not in love with for the sake of your child! Does Rowan know?'

'No, and I couldn't bear it if he did!' Charlotte raised her head proudly. 'And you are wrong in thinking that I don't love Will. I *do* love him for his kindness and compassion.' Her voice faltered as she continued, 'Don't you see, Miss Kitty, it's the only way left open to me if my child is to be given a decent home and a secure future? And I want that above everything else! I

377

don't matter any more, but my child means everything to me! Oh, I thought, at first, that I could bring it up by myself, but I wasn't thinking very clearly at the time. I could not bear it if my baby – Rowan's baby – had to face the stigma of not having a father – a name!' She covered her face with her hands. 'Rowan has a legitimate son now. Don't ask me to become a burden to him. I would rather try to make him believe that I never loved him at all, than that!'

'Oh, my dear. I know. I understand,' Kitty said compassionately, remembering Gilbert Stapleford. 'I have often thought that we are two of a kind, you and I. Now I know I was right. She paused. 'When do you and Will intend to get married?'

'As quickly as possibly,' Charlotte replied, 'at the register office in Devizes.'

'Oh no, that won't do at all,' Kitty said quickly. 'This must be no hole-and-corner affair. I know these villagers. Please, won't you let me give you a church wedding, and a reception here at Grey Wethers, as my – my gift of love to you.'

She wore a silver-grey outfit and carried a posy of snowdrops Will had gathered for her under the hedgerows near the farm. The church was cold, the altar lit with candles and decorated with Christmas roses. Charlotte's hand shook as Will slipped the wedding-ring on her finger.

Half turning her head, Charlotte caught a glimpse of Alice Tanquillan's red velvet dress, the tilt of her hat above swallow-wing eyebrows. The pews were packed with tenants, farmhands and their wives, who knew and respected Will Oakleigh, and yet only one person mattered to Charlotte.

'Forgive me, Rowan,' she prayed, 'for wanting to give our child a secure home, a certain future.' When he and Romilly came back together, he need never again feel torn between them: never have to answer questions about the past, or admit to his wife that he had fathered an illegitimate child. If she were convincing enough, he might, in time, forget about her, or remember her only as a girl he once knew whom he had imagined himself to be in love with, a wayward creature with a shallow, butterfly mind, whose love was as fickle as swallows gathering for flight when the long hot summer days ended.

But this was wintertime, and the swallows had long since flown away, leaving her desolate. And her mind was not a butterfly mind, nor could she forget Rowan as long as she lived, as, she suspected, he would never forget her. But she was a married woman now, with a ring on her finger and her husband beside her, holding her hand, smiling down at her, and they were walking together down the aisle to their waiting carriage, about to drive to their wedding reception at Grey Wethers, amid whirling snowflakes thickening the drifts in the hedge-rows. And this was a man who loved her, this strangely unfamiliar husband of hers who held her hands and kissed her fingers one by one and whispered how happy she had made him.

Kitty meant what she said, and although Charlotte had not wished for a church wedding, the old woman was insistent, and gave her reasons in her usual authoritative manner, bringing Will into the discussion. A simple church wedding was by far the best thing, she said. People would be far more likely to gossip if they went about getting married in a hole and corner fashion. There would be gossip later, of course, that was inevitable. She spoke drily, with humour. No need to make a mountain out of a molehill, the situation was a familiar one in village life, girls got pregnant all the time; married, settled down and had their babies and, sooner or later, tongues stopped wagging.

She glanced at Will sitting quietly on the edge of a chair. 'If you intend to bring up the child as your own,' she said, 'there is no reason why people should not suppose it to be yours. Is that what you want?'

Will nodded. 'Good, that's settled then,' Miss Kitty declared. But Charlotte proved herself the old lady's match when it came to the question of what she would wear. Nothing would persuade her to marry in white, nor did she wish to go away with Will after the wedding, and Kitty Tanquillan did not press the matter.

'I'm still in mourning for my father,' Charlotte said, 'and

379

there's work to do on the farm.' But that was not the whole truth. Deep down lay the feeling that white was a virgin colour – and honeymoons were for lovers. But she could not deny Kitty the pleasure of giving her a proper wedding reception.

Grey Wethers was decorated with scarlet poinsettias. Fires and lamps threw warm pools of light on walls and ceilings, expelling the gloom of a winter day. Miss Tanquillan had engaged a trio to play soft background music, mainly popular music-hall tunes of the day and songs from the shows, *The Quaker Girl*, *The Chocolate Soldier*, *The Count of Luxembourg*. The buffet table was white-covered, looped with smilax; spread with succulent cold food – roast ham, beef, chicken in aspic, salmon mousse; cheeses from Devizes market; pâtés, trifles; petits fours.

Rivers had brought up claret, hock, and Madeira from Miss Kitty's cellar. The wedding-cake stood in pristine glory on a separate table, with the champagne she had bought from Devizes Vintners.

Alice Tanquillan, a bright butterfly figure in her red dress, felt herself to be the centre of attention since the bride had chosen to wear such a dull outfit, of which she had been sharply critical when Charlotte was busy making it.

'Why aren't you having a proper wedding-dress?' she'd asked, cupping her chin with her hands, as Charlotte treadled away at the sewing-machine. 'Brides should wear white satin, a veil, and carry roses.' She sighed. 'When I marry Rowan, I shan't choose dull old grey. I shall wear a dress like a crinoline, a diamond tiara, and carry a bouquet of crimson roses; the colour of blood.'

Charlotte had sworn softly as the thread snapped.

'You never used to swear,' Alice observed coolly. 'Why haven't you invited anyone from Scarborough to the wedding? Are you ashamed of Will? Is that it? But of course he is only a farm manager, and quite old. Don't you mind marrying an older man?' Alice was in her most tiresome, questioning mood. She continued, 'And why aren't you having a honeymoon? When I marry Rowan, I'll make him take me to the South of

France, or Venice.' She giggled suddenly. 'I'm very atractive to men, you know. Aunt Kitty has invited Mr Latimer to the wedding, and I can twist *him* round my little finger. But it's Rowan I love. I think about him from the minute I wake up to the minute I fall asleep.'

Charlotte's irritation mounted. Life was difficult enough, sewing a dress for her wedding to a man she was not in love with, without listening to Alice's foolish chatter. She said coldly, rethreading the needle, aware of a dull ache of misery at her heart, 'Then you should stop thinking about Rowan.'

The girl's mood changed suddenly. Her face darkened. 'Who are you to tell me what I should do?'

'It's foolish to dream impossible dreams,' Charlotte said, remembering that she had dreamed too many of her own. 'I don't want to see you hurt.'

'I don't see anything impossible about it,' Alice retorted. 'Why shouldn't I marry Rowan one day? He's not in love with that stupid, whey-faced Romilly. He went away because he couldn't stand the sight of her, because he has always been in love with me! I know that no-one believes me, but I *know!* My aunt can't bear me to speak of Rowan because she knows as well as I do that when he comes back, when I am grown-up, we will get married.'

Charlotte's hand trembled on the wheel of the sewing-machine. 'When Rowan comes home,' she said in a low voice, 'he will return to his wife and child.'

'His – *child!*' Alice's reaction to Charlotte's words was electrifying. Her cheeks went deathly pale. Tears began to rain down her face. She sprang up, arms outflung, fingers clawing the air. Then, sobbing wildly, she sank to the floor and lay, face down on the carpet, her body convulsed with sobs.

'I'm sorry, I thought you knew that Romilly had had a baby,' Charlotte said helplessly, attempting to gather Alice in her arms; shocked when she saw the expression of hatred in the girl's eyes. Then commonsense took over. 'Get up,' Charlotte said, realizing that Alice was play-acting but frightened by the child's need to dramatize; her slyness and cunning.

Alice sat up and smiled, a mysterious little smile which

masked her intense inner excitement. Her body-racking sobs all forgotten, her little masquerade over, she said coolly, matter-of-factly, 'You are no fun any more, Charlotte. I like people who give in to me, like Aunt Kitty. I love the way she handles me with kid gloves and makes allowances for me. It's the most exciting game I know. Of course I knew that Romilly had had a baby.' She giggled. 'Perhaps it is time I made another doll and stuck pins into it.'

'*Alice!*'

'Oh, don't worry,' Alice laughed gaily as she picked herself up off the floor, 'I shan't do it. But if you could see your face, Charlotte.' She turned at the door. 'Well, never mind. If I can't have Rowan, I'll take Mr Latimer instead. He's terribly handsome, you know, and it will be such fun making him fall in love with me.'

The room was crowded with people. The trio on the dais in the hall played the waltz from *The Chocolate Soldier* as mouths closed greedily over the rims of champagne glasses. Alice, in her red dress, searched with her eyes until she noticed Kitty Tanquillan talking to a tall, elderly man with startlingly blue eyes beneath finely-shaped eyebrows.

So that is Claude Latimer, Charlotte thought, watching intently as Alice forced her way into the conversation; clinging to the man's arm and laughing up at him so blatantly that he was obliged to take notice of her. His late arrival had prevented Charlotte meeting him officially when she and Will stood together at the door to welcome the guests; to receive their good wishes for a long and happy married life.

But Kitty Tanquillan, conscious of her duties, made up the omission. 'Charlotte, Will, this is my good friend, Claude Latimer,' she said, after the cake had been cut.

'How do you do, Mr Latimer,' Charlotte said coolly, looking up into his aesthetically handsome face; knowing, as she shook hands with him, that she had not seen the last of him.

When the reception was over, she and Will walked quietly down the lane to the farmhouse.

On the doorstep, Will swung Charlotte into his arms and

carried his bride over the threshold.

'Well, Charlotte, here we are.'

'Yes, Will, here we are.'

The restraint between them was only natural. They smiled uncertainly at each other, a bewildered eighteen-year-old girl and a man in his forties, two people who had married for the wrong reasons. It was a fraught moment. Now they were alone together, neither knew what the other expected. Charlotte saw Will as a kindly, understanding father figure. Will saw Charlotte as his wife, a beautiful, desirable woman, with whom he was deeply in love.

He said brusquely, 'Your room's at the head of the stairs. I laid a fire earlier on. It only wants a match to it.'

'I'd best go up then and change into my working things,' she said awkwardly.

'Working things! On your wedding day! We should have had a proper honeymoon. I should have taken you to a hotel in Bristol or Bath . . .'

'Oh no, Will! I'm glad to be home. I'm much happier in familiar surroundings.' She smiled up at him. 'Besides, there's the ewes to see to.'

'I had better change into my working clothes too, then,' he said, following her upstairs, the dogs lolloping behind them, breaking the tension between them.

She came down, minutes later, wearing an apron; busied herself in the kitchen, drawing the curtains, stirring the fire, cooking Will's supper, glad, when he came in from the fold across the yard, that he was wearing his old familiar clothes. And yet they were still ill at ease with each other.

After supper, when he had helped her to wash and dry the dishes, they sat together in front of the fire, the cats and dogs at their feet.

What now, and what for the rest of my life, Charlotte wondered, listening to the slow heartbeats of the clock in the corner, the fall of cinders in the hearth. Gazing into the leaping flames, she suddenly remembered the witchball in a London hotel, how it had slowly revolved, scattering light on the heads of the dancers. Rowan, she thought. Oh, Rowan.

Watching the play of firelight on her face, Will said gruffly, 'Are you sorry you married me?'

'It hasn't really dawned on me yet that we are married.'

'That doesn't answer my question.' A full feeling of jealousy invaded his heart. 'It wouldn't be like this if I were younger, sitting here like Darby and Joan, an old man and a young girl.' He covered his face with his hands.

'Don't Will.' She scarcely knew what to say or do to comfort him. Slipping to her knees beside him, she said softly, 'There are so many ways of loving – the way you loved your wife . . .'

He looked at her then, and held her hands tightly in his. 'Yes, the way I loved Abby; the way you love the father of your child. I want you to tell me about him.'

'No!' She attempted to loosen his grasp, frightened suddenly by the intensity of his expression. 'I can't talk about it. I want to forget him.'

'But you never will, that's true, isn't it?'

'Please, Will, I'm very tired.'

He groaned suddenly. It was as if a kind of madness had come over him. But he had known, as she looked into the fire, that she was thinking of that other man, still loving him, still wanting him. 'I – I'm sorry, Charlotte. Forgive me. I had no right to question you.' He smiled then. 'Poor little lass. It has been a long hard day for you, hasn't it? The wedding, the reception. I watched you all the time.' He laughed bitterly. 'A woman's wedding day is supposed to be the happiest day of her life, and here you are landed with a man old enough to be your father.'

He bent forward to kiss her cheek, found his lips suddenly on hers. He could not help it. Desire for her was a burning pain forcing up through his loins. He felt her stiffen suddenly as if repelled by his kiss, although she did nothing to prevent it. When he released her, she said in a low voice, 'I would not want you to think that I had married you not loving you at all.' She paused, lips trembling. 'The past is over and done with. I did love someone once, but you are my husband. If you want me to sleep with you, I will.'

'No,' he said hoarsely, 'we made a bargain, let's stick to it.

The time is not now, not yet.' He cradled her face gently with his hands, his momentary madness over and done with. 'I want you, Charlotte, make no mistake about that, but not as a duty.' He stroked her hair, angry with himself because he had made her unhappy. 'One day, perhaps, you will come to love me as much as I love you.'

Withdrawing his hands, he said, 'Get off to bed now. We've a long hard day ahead of us.'

Master of himself once more, he got up, lighted a candle, and gave it to her.

She turned on the stairs, candle in hand. 'Goodnight, Will,' she said.

'Goodnight, Charlotte, and – forgive me for loving you so much.'

CHAPTER TEN

The Grayler boys sailed for France on 17 April, crossing from Folkestone to Boulogne in the troop-carrier *Onward*.

At last the adventure's beginning, Frank thought, leaning against the rail, looking down at the water churning against the ship's side. The long training behind him, he felt more alive now than he had ever done before, knowing how to shoot straight and use a bayonet. He had spent his 36 hours embarkation leave with Madgie. All was right with his world. He began to whistle between his teeth.

Harry and Joe were beside him. Harry looked grey about the gills as his stomach heaved to the motion of the ship. Joe's face was serious. He stared out at the horizon, seeing nothing. Frank guessed what ailed him. The family split-up had affected Joe more deeply than himself and Harry. Joe, the thoughtful, sensitive one, had not come to terms with the death of their father, that their mother and Charlotte were at loggerheads, but then Joe had always been a funny kind of kid. 'Cheer up, young 'un,' he urged, nudging Joe's elbow.

Joe smiled with his lips but the smile did not reach as far as his eyes. He could not believe that his old life had passed away so swiftly, as if someone had taken a sponge to a blackboard to wipe away in a moment the happy years of his youth and childhood.

Charlotte's letter telling him of her marriage to Will Oakleigh was in the breast-pocket of his uniform. 'Will is a good man, a kind man,' she had written. But what did Charlotte want with a man old enough to be her father? He had worried over it like a dog with a bone until Annie told him the truth, that Charlotte had had an affair with Rowan Tanquillan. He had put two and two together then; guessed why Charlotte had married so quickly, why his mother withdrew into her shell whenever Charlotte's name was mentioned, plumping up her shoulders, refusing to say what had gone wrong between them.

Sensitive Joe Grayler blamed himself for what had happened. 'It all started that day Charlotte brought Alice Tanquillan home,' he told Annie. 'If only I had taken the girl back to the house in Chalice Walk.'

'It's no use blaming yourself, Joey,' Annie pointed out to him. 'What has happened is all in the past. Nothing can change it now.'

'But I should have known! I should have seen! I knew that Charlotte was in love with someone! She did not want to talk about it, but I should have made her!' He said anxiously, 'Promise me that you will never lose touch with Charlotte.'

'I promise.'

'I never thought my mother could be so – cruel . . .'

'Don't, Joey. It isn't her fault! She's been hurt, that's all. Your mother belongs to a different generation, but she still loves Charlotte.'

'How do you know? How can you be so sure?' Joe cradled his head in his hands.

'Because, without love, there can be no hurt, no pain or disappointment.'

Joe had smoothed back her hair then with a gentle hand. 'How wise you are, Annie, and how beautiful.'

'Beautiful!' Annie laughed, 'I'm as plain as a pikestaff, and you know it.'

'Not to me.' Her little, pale heart-shaped face lit with eyes as grey-blue as the sea in winter, framed with straight ash-blonde hair drawn back from a high forehead, seemed as beautiful to Joe as a springtime wood with slender birch saplings coming into leaf. She was well named Annie Crystal since her lovely simplicity echoed the beauty of dewdrops on flower-stalks, trembling and radiant at early morning.

Now, Annie, Charlotte, his mother, his old home, all the things Joe Grayler most cared for were far behind him. The only reality was war, the reverberating chunk-chunk of the engine, the deck of the troop-ship beneath his feet, the tightly-packed khaki-uniformed figures around him, the coast of France before him.

The battalion spent a cold, uncomfortable night at Boulogne. Now they were there, no-one seemed sure what to do with them except feed them great hunks of dripping bread and watery soup. At midnight they marched to the railway station, en route to Cassel. Next day, tired and hungry, they marched to Steenvoorde, hearing in the distance the heavy cannonade of the German guns, seeing, in the sky, bright flashes like summer lightning. On 23 April, they were hustled aboard khaki-painted London buses; trundled, by way of Abeele, Poperinghe and Vlamertinghe to a camp at Bielen, north-west of Ypres, where the road was blocked with hundreds of Belgian refugees fleeing the beleaguered town, their worldly goods piled on carts and wagons.

'My Christ, the poor devils,' Frank muttered, brought at last to the realization that this war, which he had looked on as an adventure, was nothing of the sort. It was the faces of the children, hungry and crying, clinging desperately to their mothers' skirts, trudging through the churned-up morass that was once a decent country road; the stricken faces of the old people forced to flee their homes with nothing but a few poor bundles on their backs; the handful of stragglers from the Allied armies, suffering the after effects of a gas attack; men without respirators who lay choking, half-dead or blinded behind the slow-moving column of refugees, that stripped the veil from his eyes. He sat stunned, holding his rifle between his knees, as men without sight, clinging trustfully to the shoulders of the man in front, came into view, shuffling and stumbling over the rough surface of the road.

A long procession of doomed men flooded towards beleaguered Ypres. On 19 February, a week after Maggie Masters was delivered of her child, Rowan Tanquillan, Bert Hoskins and the men of their Company, were busily engaged in digging trenches near Ypres in the pouring rain. Rain beat down on their macintoshed backs. There seemed to be nothing else in the world save rain and wet earth as they dug deeper and deeper, with entrenching tools, into the soft, wet sticky clay sucking about their ankles.

On 16 March they spent the night in huts near Vlamertinghe with rain dripping through the roofs. Not that they noticed. They were too exhausted to care. All they wanted was the panacea of sleep.

On 28 March, A and B Companies were sent up to the front line to join the 2nd Northumberland Fusiliers and the Second Cheshire Regiment.

How odd, Rowan thought, it's almost Easter; Easter, the great Christian festival in the Church calendar, and here we are, rifles in hand, bent upon killing our fellow men.

The day after Good Friday, the battalion marched through frost-rimed countryside to hear the Bishop of London preach a sermon for which his Lordship was an hour late. His tardiness upset the men who had marched eight long miles to hear him speak. His opening remark, 'As you could not come to the Church, I have brought the Church to you,' caused an uproar in the ranks.

'Pity you didn't bring it a bit nearer,' Bert Hoskins called out, shaking off Rowan's restraining hand on his arm. 'No, I don't care,' he muttered, 'they can court-martial and shoot me if they want to! It's all very well for him to preach about God! There ain't no God in this bloody war if you ask me, an' his Lordship can stuff 'is bleedin' Church where the monkey stuffs its nuts!'

On 23 April, as The Green Howards were pressing on to the north-west of Ypres, Rowan's Company relieved the Welch Regiment on their left. The Rangers bivouacked in open fields, near Verloerenhoek, in flimsy straw-covered shelters, hearing in the distance the continuous muted roar of the German guns, watching helplessly as a stream of Canadian soldiers, wounded, gassed and exhausted, crawled back slowly from St Julien.

'I know that my Redeemer Liveth!' The boys they buried that morning were no more than nineteen years old. The stretcher-bearers brought them in; reverently searched their pockets for family photographs and other personal mementos to send back to their relatives. Buglers blew Reveille over their graves.

Spring came slowly to Wiltshire, bending the orchards with pink and white blossoms under azure or rain-swept skies. The Downs came brilliantly alive with willow-tinted grass. The baby in Charlotte's womb began to stir.

On 25 April, the 5th Battalion The Green Howards were ordered to retire from St Julien to make room for The Seaforth Highlanders and The Royal Irish Fusiliers coming up to relieve them for a much-needed rest.

Frank, Harry and Joe Grayler halted, with the rest of their battalion, in a field south of the Zaaerebeke stream near the road to Wieltje. Sweating, lice-covered, exhausted, they lay on the ground awhile to recover.

'Christ, I'm tired!' Frank wiped the sweat from his eyes and grinned at his brothers. 'I could sleep forever!'

'Don't say that!'

'What's up, Harry? Come over superstitious all of a sudden?' Frank laughed up at his brother; teeth glinting in the sun, his moustache upturned above his smiling lips. The Laughing Cavalier. He rolled over on his back and lay looking up at the sky. His limbs felt heavy and relaxed. Frank had never thought much about God before, now he wondered if He existed. Perhaps He did, after all.

He picked a flower idly and looked at it curiously, as if he had never seen a flower before. It was only a common-or-garden daisy, but how exquisitely fashioned it was, how intricately designed. Perhaps there was someone in heaven who made daisies in his spare time between all the killing and maiming. He tucked the flower in his breast-pocket and thought about Madgie; the joy of being a man with a beautiful woman between his legs. His eyelids closed with the benison of sunshine and tiredness, to the sweet sound of the wind sighing about his exhausted body.

He awoke to the digging of Harry's arm in his ribs. 'What's up now?' he asked, yawning.

'Come on, Frank, get up. We're off again!' Harry heaved up his pack and rifle.

'Where's Joe?'

'Over here!' Joe grinned at his brother.

Frank rose to his feet like a young Greek god, stretching his arms above his head as he had always stretched them after sleep. He was wide awake now; ready for action.

They recrossed the Zaaerebeke stream towards St Julien. 'I thought we'd seen the last of this bloody place,' Frank laughed. 'It's starting to look like home to me now.'

They advanced slowly in face of withering fire from the German guns . . . Suddenly Frank fell, shot through the heart.

'Frank! *Frankie*! Oh Christ, *Frankie*!' Joe sank to his knees beside his brother.

Frank smiled as he slept. A wilting daisy hung from the breast-pocket of his blood-stained uniform.

The worst thing of all was leaving Frank where he had fallen. Others had fallen too, men Joe knew well. The stretcher-bearers would come later to bring in the casualties. Even so, he could not bear to leave Frank, but the battalion was advancing despite his grief, firing and advancing, resting, firing and advancing in a kind of slow cotillion amid the blossoming smoke from the German guns: scrambling across the torn earth, fissures ploughed up by shrapnel. The enemy was advancing too. It was still early morning. The sky above the billowing gunsmoke was patched with April sunshine, the ground beneath his feet exuded a curiously rich smell of good earth blended with human sweat and blood. At ten o'clock, the Germans halted and began to consolidate the trenches they had captured.

Joe rested, at his superior officer's command, half lying, half squatting on a bank of seamed earth where a scattering of windflowers still blew, rifle at the ready; eyes blurred with tears, heart frozen with grief. Sweat trickled down into his eyes, almost blinding him. He could see nothing, feel nothing. He knew then that the human sweat he had scented was his own sweat. His body was bathed in it. And then, from the churning depths of his bowels to his thickly thudding heart, feeling began slowly to return. What he felt was hatred. Hatred of the Germans who had killed his brother. He stood up, swaying on his feet, shambled forward, rifle cocked.

'Get down, man!' Joe sprawled forward, his face in contact with the sweet-smelling earth. He lay there for a moment, winded. Then he noticed, with surprise, that his right hand was spattered with blood. He began to shake. Tears coursed down his cheeks. A roughly sympathetic voice spoke in his ear. 'Come on, Grayler, there's work to be done.'

He struggled to his feet. Harry, entrenching tool in hand, was one of a working party hastily digging for cover. 'Where's Frank?' he demanded.

'Frank's – dead.' Joe scarcely recognized his own voice.

Harry sounded angry. 'he can't be. Not – Frank. I saw him not twenty minutes ago.'

Joe had cried for his brother. He could not bear the frozen expression on Harry's face. He said, 'It's true. It's just you and me now, Harry.'

Harry said bleakly, 'But he can't be dead.' All through their lives he and Frank had been together, as one. How was it possible that a man could be alive one minute, dead the next?

Watery sunlight struck suddenly through the clouds, lighting up for a second the scarred earth beneath their feet, touching to a sudden beauty the tiny flowers struggling for survival amid the wilderness of war.

CHAPTER ELEVEN

She had composed the letter a hundred times over in her mind before she sat down to write it.

If Rowan was to know happiness with his wife and child, she must convince him that the affair was over, as indeed it was and must be now that she was married to Will. 'Being cruel to be kind', Filly would call it. Perhaps she should simply say that she no longer loved him, but when the moment came, she found she could not write such a palpable untruth, nor would Rowan believe her if she did.

She chose her words carefully, beginning with the aftermath of the bombardment, the death of her father.

'I blame myself for what happened,' she wrote. 'Had I not gone to London to meet you, I might have been able to prevent my father's death. I would at least have been there when he needed me.' This much was true: she had lived with her guilt over Albert ever since, and paused to wonder if, knowing the consequences of her journey to London, she would have gone anyway. Oh yes, she thought, yes, I would have, because Dadda knew and understood . . .

'I suppose I knew, all along, that I was never cut out as . . .' a – a mistress, she thought. Strange, but I never thought of myself as that, not with Rowan . . . 'a mistress. Deep down I hated all the lies and subterfuge.' Oh, God forgive me, my darling. . . .

'When Will Oakleigh asked me to marry him, I realized how much I needed a settled home; a husband to care for me. We were married in the village church at Cloud Merridon a week ago.

'I'm sorry, Rowan, if you are disappointed in me.' Here the

pen-nib sputtered, flecking the page with a myriad drops of ink so fine that Charlotte decided to leave them as they were. She could scarcely see the page through her tears. 'Our love, as sweet as it was, would have worn me down in the end. Please forgive me.'

She signed the letter, 'Charlotte Oakleigh', and wept over it.

When Will asked her why she had been so preoccupied the past few days, she said truthfully that she had had an important letter to write.

Will did not pursue the matter. He discovered, by chance who it was she had written to when he met Jack Kent, the village postman, gathering mail into his sack at the village letter-box. The man said, with a broad, conspiratorial grin, 'Young Maister Rowan Tanquillan's in luck today. Three letters for him. One from his aunt, one from that barmy young Alice, and . . .' he screwed up his eyes, 'I don't recognize the writing on the other envelope, but it's fair bulky.'

Will recognized the handwriting at once. He said nothing, merely shook the reins over the horse's back and went on his way.

Near the village pub, he stopped, eaten up with a sick feeling of jealousy. He climbed down from the trap, pretending to adjust the bit in the animal's mouth, fighting to overcome the shock of knowing who was the father of Charlotte's child. Never, in his wildest imaginings, had he thought of Rowan Tanquillan. But then all the pieces slotted together like a jigsaw puzzle. Why else had Kitty Tanquillan gone to so much trouble over the wedding? Everything fitted together neatly at last. She had done so because she knew that Charlotte's child was flesh of her flesh, her great-nephew Rowan's child.

Will leaned his head to the horse's neck momentarily, feeling that the world was swimming away from him: looked up to see the landlord of the White Swan, thumbs tucked into braces, staring at him from the doorway of his public house.

'Now then, Will,' the man said, 'anything I can do for you?'

Will said, between clenched lips, 'You can give me a drink. I'm parched.' He tethered the horse in the pub yard and entered the bar-parlour, Will Oakleigh who, so far as the publican remembered, had never set foot in the place before during the day, Will not being a drinking man – not like some of the farm-hands who came down from the fields and drank until their money ran out or the pub closed.

Billy Smith, landlord of the White Swan, wiped down his counter and rested his hands on it, curious to know why Will Oakleigh had developed such a thirst all of a sudden. There was something distinctly odd about him. His lips were set in a grim line, his usual slow-paced charm of manner was gone; he seemed hard put to it to be civil, which was decidedly odd in Will's case since his civility and good looks, tanned face and greying hair, had given many of the village widows ideas when Abby Oakleigh died a few years back.

Billy Smith remembered that the widows who had set their caps at Will: worthy women who believed that every present-able man in his forties needed a capable woman to look after him, had not been best suited when Will Oakleigh had turned them down, one by one.

The scorned ones, the women who knew how to wash clothes, bake bread, put up preserves, scour doorsteps, pluck chickens, and lend a hand with the sheep-dipping if necessary, said that losing his wife must have turned Will Oakleigh queer. Then Will had confounded the entire village in marrying a bit of a lass with red hair, and so quickly that eyebrows had been raised into hat-brims with the suddenness of it all.

Gossip had run rife. They respected Will, of course. That did not prevent them having their say. 'Ah well, just wait and see,' was the consensus of opinion, 'she won't make him much of a wife.'

Even the ones who had been at the wedding: guests of Miss Tanquillan, who had eaten her food and drunk her champagne, had said as much. Billy felt bad about that. It seemed all wrong to him that people spoke behind their hands about Will's wife even as they drank her health. But women, in his opinion, were nothing but a bunch of nasty-minded bitches, sharp of eye and slow of intellect: women who watched, like hawks, for signs of a thickening waistline.

Then Betsy Overfield, the farm-hand's wife who used to 'do' for Will Oakleigh before his marriage, added fuel to the bonfire in saying that she had been to the farmhouse one day to collect an apron she'd left there; had got the shock of her life when she happened to go upstairs to find Mrs Oakleigh's things in one bedroom, Will's in another.

Now the village was agog with rumours. Its inhabitants spoke slowly, with lengthened A's.

'You mean they ain't sleeping together? Well, faancy thaat. Poor Will.'

'But she is thaat way, you caan depend on it,' Betsy nodded.

'They must have been intimate, then, before they got wed. But she's only been here since Januaary. She an' Will haaven't been married long enough yet for her to begin showing.'

'Aaaaah!'

'He ain't the faather, then?'

'Thaat's what it looks like to me!'

Now here was Will slaking his thirst at midday. The conscientious Billy Smith wiped down his counter and thought what a bloody fool Will Oakleigh had been to take on a pretty young redhead as wife. Red-headed women were well known for their uncontrollable fits of temper. He drew the only possible conclusion, that Will and his missus had quarrelled.

Rowan read Charlotte's letter disbelievingly. Something about it did not ring true. But there it was in black and white. She was married, he had lost her.

He rose to his feet and stumbled unseeingly from the tent into the fresh air.

Bert Hoskins went after him. 'What's up, guv?' He grasped Rowan's arm concernedly. 'Is it bad news?'

'Leave me alone, Bert.'

'Strewth, mate, you look terrible!' Bert had never seen Rowan like this before, his face drained of colour. He had been young a few minutes ago, now he looked like an old man weary of life, every line on his face etched and deepened with suffering.

'Leave me alone, I said! For Christ's sake, just go away, will you?'

'Right, guv, if you say so. But I'm here if you need me.' Bert turned away.

'I'm sorry! No offence!' Rowan reached out blindly.

'Course not, guv. I understand.'

Bert Hoskins thought, as he went back to the tent to polish his boots, that he had never met a real gent like Rowan Tanquillan before.

Roughly brought up in the East End of London, obliged to lie and pilfer, to hate and despise all the gentry stood for, he had revised his opinions ever since he and Rowan were thrown together in the war. He had grown to love Tanquillan as a brother. Not that Tanquillan was rich – not so far as Bert knew anyway, since Rowan was always as hard up as he was. But what Tanquillan possessed by way of breeding was evident in the way he wore his uniform, the way he spoke, the way he had of making light of danger and fatigues; his cheerfulness, his quality of leadership.

Bert knew officer-material when he saw it, and Rowan Tanquillan should, by right, be leading men into battle, not wasting his time crowded into a tent with the rank and file, the loud-mouthed, brutish and insensitive.

Bert Hoskins was prouder of his friendship with Rowan Tanquillan than he had ever been of anything in his life before. He remembered, hazily, something his mother, who believed in the Bible, had once said to him: 'Greater love hath no man than this, that a man lay down his life for his friend.' Perhaps he'd got it all wrong. Perhaps his mother had misquoted or he had not remembered exactly, but he knew what she meant. Funny thing was, he had no great belief in God or the Bible, only in loyalty and love, which again seemed queer since he had been loyal to no-one in his whole life, especially not the woman he had vowed 'to love and to cherish till death us do part'. But Bertha was a silly sort of a woman when all was said and done. He wondered, briefly, if he was 'queer', then bucked up because he knew he wasn't. No man with a whatsit the size of his and a hankering after the mademoiselles in the bistros he and his mates frequented could ever be dubbed as queer. And yet, above and beyond all that, lay his deep love of Rowan Tanquillan.

He thought, as he buffed away at his boots, that something had happened to upset the guv right enough. Woman trouble, no doubt. Bound to be. Well, Rowan had leave due to him, as he himself had. No doubt he'd go back to England and sort things out when he got there.

But Rowan did not go on leave. Two days later, skirmishing across open ground between the Allied and German trenches, relieving the Suffolk Regiment bogged down in shell-holes raked with withering machine-gun fire, Bert, following closely in Rowan's wake, saw him buckle and fall.

Heedless of his own safety, Bert rolled, between a hail of machine-gun bullets, to his friend's side.

'Christ, guv,' he muttered, then saw, with a gut feeling of relief, that Rowan's eyes were open: heard him grunt with pain. He had a bullet wound in his shoulder.

'Come on, guv, lean on me,' Bert said between clenched teeth, 'we'll make for that shell-hole over yonder.'

Heaving and pulling, he dragged Rowan across the few yards separating them from the bullet-raked battlefield to the comparative safety of the hole in the ground. 'Those bastards,' he muttered, as machine-gun bullets zipped past his head too close for comfort.

In the hole, he laid Rowan on the ground; ripped open his uniform, attempted to staunch the blood-let with his handkerchief. When that failed, as the blood continued to flow from the wound in Rowan's shoulder, Bert ripped off his shirt and fashioned a rough tourniquet of wood and shirt-strips.

Rowan lay where Bert had left him until dusk, until the stretcher parties came out to bring in the dead and wounded, when someone stuck a lighted fag between his lips.

'I think I can walk,' Rowan said, but when he tried to stand his legs felt like nursery-tea blancmange. He staggered and would have fallen had it not been for a supporting arm in the darkness.

'Take it easy, guv,' Bert Hoskins advised. 'Better get on the stretcher, you've lost a lot of blood.'

'Bert! What the hell are you doing here?' Rowan grinned weakly, 'you're not a stretcher-bearer.'

Bert said gruffly, 'I came with the blokes to show them where I'd put you, that's all.'

Men were moved as pawns in a chess game. Places they had never heard of before, St Julien, Vlamertinghe, Zonnebeke, were wefted into their very existence with the stench of blood and sweat, the muck and mire of the trenches after heavy downpour, the sight of ruined villages and hungry children. Day and night long they heard the roar of the guns, the stutter of machine-gun fire. Down once peaceful country roads they came, exhausted columns of men and horses, the stretchers and ambulances. Forests of simple wooden crosses marked the graves of the fallen.

Joe understood Harry's anger, the misery too deep for words or tears which kept him white-faced and taciturn throughout the following day and night. The brothers moved together and were together as they had always been, but the mainspring of their existence was gone and neither could believe that such a tremendous force in their lives had been removed in seconds; that all Frank's vitality and joy in living had been snuffed out as a breeze flickers and snuffs out a candleflame.

The Lahore Division and the 149th Brigade had succeeded in entering and occupying the southern outskirts of St Julien. The German gunfire was appalling, enemy planes were constantly overhead, flying low, bombing, with deadly accuracy, the Allied positions.

On the night of 27 April – relieving a battalion of the London Regiment – Harry was hit in the leg with shrapnel. Buckling onto his side, he rolled down a shallow incline to lie, mazed with pain, in the mud of a shell-hole.

'Harry!' Joe was beside him. Kneeling in the soft, stinking mire, he eased his brother into a sitting position.

'I wish to Christ the buggers had killed me outright,' Harry groaned, sweat gathering on his forehead. He smiled up for an instant into Joe's face. 'It's up to you now, young 'un,' he said, then fainted from loss of blood.

He became conscious of movement, the bumping of the ambulance over uneven ground. There were other men beside him. It crossed Harry's mind that there must be a sight more wounded than ambulances. No-one spoke much. A man with a bandaged head unearthed a packet of cigarettes from his breast-pocket, a match flared. 'Fag, mate?' he asked. Harry nodded. 'Thanks.' The tobacco tasted good. 'Where are they taking us?'

The man inhaled deeply. 'Base hospital.' He grinned wearily. 'They'll patch us up, give us a bit of leave, then send us back to that bloody lot.'

Harry lay back. The pain in his leg shut out all other feeling. He was being carried. The murmur of voices sounded like the buzzing of flies in his ears. Pain and weariness rendered him incurious to his surroundings. There seemed to be a great emptiness inside him. Then someone spoke his name in a gentle, persuasive voice. 'Harry. Harry, my dear.'

He thought he was dreaming. He had dreamed so often of hearing Jenny's voice again. He opened his eyes to see her standing beside him in her VAD uniform, her hair haloed against the light, that soft brown hair he remembered so well.

'Jenny!'

The smile that lit up his face touched her to the heart. She held his hand. 'Hush,' she said, 'you must lie quite still and not try to talk.' He looked so much older, she thought, than the shy boy who had walked beside her on the sands that night in Scarborough.

'You won't go away again, will you Jenny?' His clasp on her hand tightened.

'No, I won't go away. Promise!'

How curious, she thought, that within the past few hours she had come into contact with two people Charlotte Grayler loved – her brother Harry, and Rowan Tanquillan.

Romilly Tanquillan looked at her sleeping child in its cot. Beresford Tanquillan – Berry – was a beautiful child, perfect in every detail, not red and puckered and squalling like some babies she had seen. A child to be proud of, evoking cries of delight from her friends who called to see her when she was well enough to receive them, in her flower-filled room with the curtains drawn back to admit the hazy winter sunlight of Eaton Square.

Everyone said admiringly how brave she was to have come through her illness and childbirth so pluckily, and how well and attractive she was looking. Tactfully, no-one mentioned Rowan – no-one except her mother and Tante Rachel, and Romilly was left in no doubt about Rachel's feelings in particular: it was Lady Tanquillan who first spoke of a reconciliation between herself and Rowan for their child's sake, if for no other reason, except of course there were so many reasons why they should heal their differences.

She had spoken quietly and persuasively, never saying too much, lightly touching on memories, sketching pictures of the past with brushstroke words: 'Do you remember your first party? You wore a blue dress with forget-me-nots, and Rowan saved up his pocket money to buy you a doll . . .'

Romilly still had that doll, scuffed and slightly battered. She had never been able to bear to part with it.

Then the memories had become more immediate. 'Do you remember your coming-of-age party? Your wedding day?' Rachel had been clever enough to stop there, had changed the subject adroitly, knowing that she had successfully planted the seeds she wished to plant in her daughter-in-law's mind, leaving it up to Emily to touch on more dangerous topics. Not that there was collusion between Emily and Rachel nowadays, since Emily had learned to mistrust Rachel's motives, and those of her husband.

What Emily said to her daughter was spoken from the heart for the sake of her grandchild, and in defence of Rowan.

'Romilly, my dear,' she said softly, 'you must not go on blaming Rowan for what happened. It all began with the death of your father. Had he not died when he did, you would have had your white wedding, your honeymoon. Don't you see, darling, it was all circumstantial?'

When Romilly's lips narrowed mutinously, Emily said, 'You blamed Rowan for your accident, but have you forgotten that it was he who put you on the road to recovery? It was Rowan who cared enough about you to send that nurse packing. It was Rowan who made you see that you could walk again if you really wanted to. Now you *can* walk, and you have Rowan's child to consider.'

When Romilly failed to reply, she continued, 'Do you imagine for one moment that I don't know what is on your mind? You imagine yourself to be in love with David McClean. That's true, isn't it?'

'David saved my life,' Romilly said dully, flushing to the roots of her hair. 'Can you blame me for loving him?'

'I'm not blaming you for anything, my dear. Of course you are a little in love with David, but Rowan is your husband, the father of your child. It is Berry, and your future with Rowan you should consider now.'

And so Romilly sat down to write to Rowan on delicately scented notepaper, certain of her own power to get what she wanted. She was slim and able to wear her prettiest frocks again, since her leg had healed and she could walk without a trace of a limp. She had given birth to a beautiful child and the world seemed a lovely place once more, despite the war which could have been a million miles away from her. London was still an exciting place to live, with handsome young officers in smart uniforms crowding the restaurants where she lunched occasionally with her friends.

The letter was re-addressed to Rowan in hospital. He had designated his Aunt Kitty as next-of-kin, not Romilly or his parents. He read:

'My dear Rowan,
I have been terribly ill and miserable since you went away. I had hoped your Aunt Kitty would have written to explain things to you. Sir Gervaise and Tante Rachel asked her to do so. So did I.

Apparently she refused, for what reason I cannot imagine.

However, since it is left up to me, I must tell you that I have given birth to a son. It was a difficult birth. I had a terrible, *terrible* time bringing him into the world. His name is Beresford Tanquillan, Berry for short.

While I cannot quite forgive you for all the pain and anxiety you have caused me, I think that our child should be brought up against a secure family background. He is, after all, a Tanquillan.

I am, therefore, prepared to forgive and forget the past for the sake of our son . . .'

Jenny Carfax had fought her way from London's Charing Cross Hospital to overseas service, letting nothing prevent her from getting where she wanted to be, in the thick of things, ministering to the badly wounded soldiers brought in daily from the bloody battlefields of Belgium. She was determined to prove to the surgeons, who performed almost impossible operations under extreme difficulties, that women had their part to play, too, in nursing back to health the seriously injured soldiers in their care, or, as too often happened, easing the passing of those with no chance of survival.

And yet, at times, even the stout-hearted Jenny wondered if women were strong enough to stomach all the suffering and deprivation; the long hard days and even longer spells of night duty. She watched, with a kind of savage helplessness, the sweet flowering of young manhood condemned to die before it had even begun to live.

The work was back-breaking as the ambulances poured in a steady stream of critically wounded men to the operating theatres. Her mind felt numb, at times, with exhaustion. She moved and spoke as an automaton as she cleaned up the theatre, swabbed the wards, changed dressings, boiled blood-soaked bandages, and wrote letters to parents who had lost their sons in bloody, wasteful battle. She scarcely remembered the pleasure of a good night's sleep. She looked back on her days at Somerville as a kind of lazy, sunlit dream, the flat in Bloomsbury she had shared with her friend as a much-desired haven of peace and quiet; London as a cultural oasis in a war-torn desert.

Her friend, Esme Pierce, had left the Bloomsbury flat now, but Jenny had kept it on. The key to it lay in her handbag. It was such a lovely flat: high ceilings sloping suddenly to interesting dormer windows overlooking roofs and treetops; London skies full of trembling stars; washed with London light and London sounds; pale grey dawns that rose, with hint of rain or sun, from the eastern reaches of the City; the chirping of sparrows in the plane trees in the squares below; the chiming of bells in the air. The monotone of chimney-pots etched against fog; the curious blueness of wet slates in a London downpour.

All Jenny's books were there, packed tightly into white-painted shelves. Her bed, covered with brightly-coloured Mexican blankets, was set beneath a great glass skylight through which she could view the moon and stars. She wanted to go back there one day, to her books and dreams and gramophone records. But even if she did, she would never be quite the same person again, as Harry Grayler would never be the same person again – or Rowan Tanquillan. They had all seen too much suffering to regain that first, fine careless rapture in living.

She walked down the ward to Rowan's bedside. Pulse and temperature were normal. His wound was healing well, and yet he looked strangely ill and unhappy. She said cheerfully, 'You'll be able to go home soon, on leave.'

'Home?' He laughed bitterly. 'I'm not sure where that is any longer.'

'What is it? What's wrong? You can trust me.'

'Charlotte's married. Did you know?'

'Yes, she wrote to me.'

'And I thought . . .' He closed his eyes. 'I'm sorry, Jenny. For-give me. I seem to be in a trap, an old, old trap. I thought I had escaped it but I haven't. Perhaps there is no escape in this life.'

'For what it's worth,' she said slowly, 'I came to the same conclusion a long time ago. The trouble is, I don't believe in a hereafter, do you?'

'Oh, yes.' He opened his eyes; smiled faintly without bitterness. 'I never used to until I met Charlotte, but then I thought that such love, such happiness, could never be without point or purpose.' He quoted softly, '"What were the use of my creation if I were entirely contained here"?'

'I didn't realize you were a Brontëophile,' Jenny said.

'I'm not really. I scarcely know what I am any longer.' He stirred uneasily, 'A misfit, I suppose. I've always had this feeling of – rebellion – if you like; rebellion against my so-called class, my upbringing. Dreams came to nothing, until I met Charlotte. Suddenly everything changed. I felt strong and certain then. She gave me courage. Now . . .' He turned his face away, and Jenny noticed the dark shadows under his eyes.

'Has it occurred to you that Charlotte might have had her reasons for marrying?' She asked quietly.

'I know her reasons,' Rowan replied, 'she made them perfectly clear in her letter to me.' The bitterness was back in his voice. 'Every line of that letter is branded in my mind.'

Jenny poured a sleeping-draught with a practised hand. 'Then obviously you have made no attempt to read between the lines,' she said. 'Now, sit up and drink this.'

She walked on down the ward, smoothing a pillow here, straightening a coverlet there; taking pulses, temperatures, administering sleeping-draughts. A veritable Florence Nightingale, she thought wryly. Everything was quiet save for the muted barrage of German guns in the distance.

She stood for a while near the door, breathing in the scent of a May night. Winter had slipped away unnoticed. There, in the semi-darkness, stood a single cherry tree, its branches weighted with pink blossom, while high in the sky a slip of a moon played hide and seek in the clouds.

Turning, she walked slowly to Harry Grayler's bedside, thinking to find him asleep. But Harry was not asleep. He had been waiting for her to come to him, fighting back the drowsiness of a sleeping-draught, aware of the throbbing of his leg beneath the closely tucked-in blanket. He had something to say which could not wait, something he had churned over and over in his mind since the first time he met Jenny.

Nothing in the world, except love, made much sense to him now. Since Frank's death, since the senseless slaughter he had witnessed in the trenches, only love: the love of a man for his brother, his home and family, the love of a man for a woman, the love of men for their country; their beliefs – even their horses – now came paramount.

When he saw Jenny coming towards him, smiling, he held out his hands to her and simply said what was in his heart.

'Will you marry me?'

'Oh yes,' she said through tears. 'Yes, Harry, I will.'

News that Frank had been killed, Rowan wounded, reached Charlotte on the same day. Annie wrote from Scarborough to say that Filly was heartbroken when the telegram arrived: 'Nothing we can say or do to comfort her makes the slightest impression,' Annie put in her letter. 'All she wants is the baby, little Peggy. All she does is sit in the rocking-chair near the kitchen fire, nursing the little thing in her lap.' She added, 'Poor dear Frank. None of us can quite believe that we shall never see him again, that he will not come striding back to us one day as large as life. Now Maggie is upset because Bob is talking of joining up. I often think back to before the war when Frank was so anxious to join the Green Howards. No-one thought then what the war would mean to all of us; how it would change all our lives.'

Charlotte plumped a load of washing into hot soapy water in the sink. The only way she could bear her grief lay in doing something useful with her hands, in possing the clothes, twisting, wringing and starching. Tears rolled down her cheeks to plop into the water. She pushed back her hair with the palm of her hand as she rinsed and starched and remembered her brother Frank: delving into memories; recalling things about him that she had half forgotten, the way he had always taken the lead, how, as a little boy, he had taken charge of the pennies for donkey rides and ice-cream cornets. How, when she had cried for a ride on a donkey, Frank had hoisted her up into the saddle in front of him and held onto her tightly to keep her from falling off. How, once, he had disappeared for a whole day while their mother wept and worried and, as darkness fell, threatened to run for a policeman, while Albert said soothingly there was no need for that.

'What makes you so sure?' the distraught Filly had snapped. 'For all you know, Albert Grayler, your son may be lying dead somewhere . . .'

Albert smiled. 'If I know my son, he'll be off somewhere enjoying himself.'

And so it had proved. Frank turned up, dirty, tired, hungry – and radiantly happy – having spent the entire day at camp with the Boys' Brigade.

'But you're not a member of the Boys' Brigade,' Filly said faintly, uncertain whether to kiss or kill him.

'I am now,' Frank grinned.

When Kitty Tanquillan walked into the farmyard, she found Charlotte pegging out her washing on the line, a sturdy figure harnessed with a white pinafore. As she approached, she could see that the girl had been crying. Kitty had chosen her moment carefully, knowing that Will was out shooting on the Downs.

News from the War Office that Rowan was wounded had affected the old woman deeply, since there was no way of knowing how badly or what were his chances of survival.

Charlotte knew at once that Miss Kitty, who found walking painful, had not come from Grey Wethers to the farm for nothing. Rowan, she thought. Something has happened to Rowan. She hurried forward, leaving a trail of scattered clothes-pegs on the ground behind her, this new anxiety superimposed on her grief about Frank; mouth trembling; cheeks wet with tears, a dull feeling of misery at her heart. She said, despairingly, 'Rowan! You've had news of Rowan! He's not . . .?'

'Take me inside. Let me sit down,' Kitty said.

They entered the kitchen together.

CHAPTER TWELVE

News spread like wildfire through the village that Kitty Tanquillan's nephew had been wounded; Charlotte Oakleigh's brother killed.

Mrs Battye, the churchwarden's wife, felt more charitable then towards Charlotte, and very curious about her. When it was decided, at a meeting of the Mothers' Union, that Mrs Oakleigh should be invited to bake scones and buns for the Belgian Relief Fund and help to arrange the church flowers, the redoubtable Mrs Battye led a delegation of ladies to the farmhouse, hoping against hope that they would find the place in chaos so that she could nod her head afterwards and say, 'I told you so'.

But the house was in apple-pie order, a line of crisp white linen was blowing in the yard, and Mrs Oakleigh met them at the door with her bright red hair neatly braided, and wearing a clean white apron about her thickening waistline. 'Won't you come in?' she asked. 'I'll make you some tea. Please sit down.'

The hearth was spotlessly clean, Mrs Battye noticed, and the air was filled with the scent of stew from a bubbling pot suspended from a hook above the fire. Disappointed, the churchwarden's wife said, 'We are sorry to disturb you, but we just felt it our duty to bring you and your husband back to the church. Will has such a fine voice.' She smiled ingratiatingly. 'Unless, of course, you are an atheist, Mrs Oakleigh.'

'No, I'm not, Mrs Battye,' Charlotte said pleasantly, 'I'll be happy to help in any way I can.' Disliking the woman intensely, she continued (disliking herself even more as she spouted something taught to her by her dame school teacher), 'After all, as Proverbs, Chapter 26, Verse 4, has it – "Answer not a fool according to his folly, lest thou also be like unto him".'

'Oh dear. Oh well, I see that you know your Bible,' Mrs Battye said, bridling at the implication that she was the fool referred to. The rotten little bitch, she thought, making me look small. How dare she? No wonder Will had been acting so strange lately, drinking at the White Swan of a dinnertime, which he had never thought of doing when he was married to Abby. Mrs Battye thought that Will was so miserable because he knew he was not the father of his wife's child. But if Will was not, who was?

Jenny Carfax and Harry Grayler were married by an English padre in a wooden church surmounted with a simple wooden cross.

The bridegroom, in hospital blue, walked with a stick. The bride wore the only clothes she had with her apart from her V.A.D. uniform – an oatmeal-coloured skirt and cardigan, and a floppy black hat with an ostrich feather curled round its brim.

But the other nurses decided that Jenny's outfit needed 'lifting'. One of them came in with a handful of roses, gathered from the hospital grounds, which she tucked between the fronds of the ostrich feather. Another gathered a handful of May blossom and bound it with a silvery ribbon from a birthday card, for Jenny's bouquet.

Rowan Tanquillan gave the bride away. A young, off-duty doctor was Harry's best man.

The hospital cooks had put their heads together to bake the bride and groom a wedding-cake consisting of more flour than fruit. The nurses had decorated the church with sprays of wilting apple blossom and roses.

A wounded captain of the Lahore Division gladly gave up a bottle of champagne to toast the health of the bride and groom after the ceremony.

The padre, white-surpliced, smiled upon the young couple as they entered his church; accepted that the soldier could not kneel down to make his vows; that the bride also preferred to remain standing during the most solemn part of the ceremony, as if defending, with her own upright young body, her maimed young husband-to-be.

'Wilt thou have this man to thy wedded husband . . .?'

'I will,' Jenny said tenderly.

'Those whom God hath joined together let no man put asunder.'

And then came the kissing and congratulations, the wedding feast consisting of one bottle of champagne, several bottles of French wine from the local estaminet, the floury wedding-cake, and piles of roughly-cut sandwiches. but no-one drinking a toast to the bride and groom could doubt that this was a love match, that something fine and good had emerged from the waste of war, for Jenny's face, beneath her rose-bedecked hat-brim, was the face of a woman in love, while Harry Grayler's eyes betrayed all the love he felt for her – his Jenny, his love – his wife.

At the beginning of June, Rowan was sent home on sick leave. Events had made it impossible for him to reply to Romilly's letter, but he knew he would have to go to London and see her.

The old shackles fell about him as he arrived at Eaton Square in a taxi and saw the familiar buildings: the imposing pillared façades, the lamp brackets beneath the handsome porticos. A man was delivering groceries in the basement area. He caught a glimpse of a maid's white-streamered cap and heard a great deal of giggling before the delivery man whistled his way up the curved basement steps.

The plane trees in the gardens were in new leaf. He could see, at the end of the square, the sun-washed façade of St Peter's church. He rang the bell and waited, looking up at his father's house next door, seeing behind the glass of the balconied French windows the heavily-lined red velvet curtains.

He wished very much to see his son and Emily Beresford. He tried to convince himself that he wished to see Romilly also, but knew that he did not. Nor did he wish to see his parents. Freedom had taught him that life was too short for lies and pretences. Experience had stiffened his backbone. He had changed a great deal from the old Rowan Tanquillan whose life had been spent in living up to other people's expectations. Guilt was the hardest enemy of all to conquer. Once that was overcome – and fear – human beings emerged much stronger. Why then, if he had overcome the two greatest enemies to a man's peace of mind, did he dread entering the house in Eaton Square?

The butler recognized him at once, but Rowan's uniform made a poor impression on the man who felt it beneath the dignity of Eaton Square that a soldier should appear in anything less than the uniform of a captain or lieutenant. He said stiffly that Madam, Miss Romilly and her son had gone yesterday to Scotland to visit old Mrs Beresford. 'We were not expecting you, sir,' he added reproachfully, 'but I will give orders at once for your room to be made ready for you.'

'It doesn't matter. I shall not be staying.' Rowan could scarcely disguise his relief that the moment of meeting Romilly had been postponed. The tone of her letter had convinced him that nothing had really changed between them. He could not have borne to go through the scenes of recrimination all over again.

He strode to the end of the square and hailed a taxi to Paddington.

Charlotte had gone into marriage with some misgiving. From her own point of view, would she make Will a good wife? But above and beyond the inevitable doubts and fears lay the knowledge that this marriage was for the sake of Rowan and her child. Therein lay her strength. Her deep gratitude to Will made acceptable the unimagined difficulties. Despite her willingness to become part of village life, to polish the church brasses and turn her hand to the work of the farm, she knew that the village women in particular did not regard her as one of themselves. Will said that anyone who had not lived there for ten years at least was looked on as a stranger. 'I did warn you,' he added, 'and so did Kitty Tanquillan.'

'You warned me of the stigma attached to unmarried mothers,' she said. They were sitting together at supper. Will wore a shirt open at the neck with the stud showing. He had not bothered to wash or change into a clean shirt as he usually did when he came in from the yard. He ate quickly and carelessly, shovelling up his food scarcely bothering to talk to her. She could stand the indifference of the villagers, not that of Will. Since the death of Frank, and news that Harry had been wounded following on so quickly, her only release lay in talking about them to her husband. Will had been sympathetic, of course, but she had been aware of a watchful expression in his eyes, as if he were waiting for her to say something he wanted to hear.

Just after the news of Frank and Harry, 'They say things always come in threes,' he said.

'What do you mean?' She had been busy about the kitchen at the time, not paying much attention to what he was saying.

'Bad luck, misfortunate, that kind of thing. It's true in your case, isn't it?'

Suddenly she knew what he was driving at, that he had guessed the truth. While she had wanted to talk about her brothers, she had not felt able to speak to him about Rowan. Now there seemed no point in attempting to keep her very personal and private feelings about him to herself any longer, and yet she had not wanted it to be like this. She would have told Will the truth in her own good time, when the truth might not hurt so much as it did at present.

That Will knew, explained a great many things which had happened between them recently, his unaccustomed moodiness and waiting, watchful expression, his frequent visits to the village pub.

'I would have told you in time,' she said, putting down the crock of eggs she had been washing.

'But you did not trust me enough to tell me when I asked you,' Will replied bitterly. 'That day in the barn. Perhaps you thought I would not offer to marry you if you had told me the truth then.'

'That's unfair!' She turned to face him, bewildered by the injustice of his accusation.

'Is it? Perhaps it was all a put-up job between you and Kitty Tanquillan. You knew, as she did, that I was in love with you.'

'*Will!*' She crossed the room quickly towards him and laid a conciliatory hand on his arm. 'Please try to be fair. In any case, what does it matter now? I wrote to Rowan just after we were married. I told him it was all over between us.'

Will said thickly, 'But it isn't all over, is it? You are still in love with him!' He shook off her hand. 'Or are you going to lie about that, too?'

'I have never lied to you,' she said quietly, 'nor shall I ever do so. I respect you, Will. I thought that you respected me, too. I married you because I thought we could build up a decent life together. What has happened to change all that?'

Breathing heavily, he clamped his hands about her skull as if, by continued pressure, he might blot out her memories of the past.

She threw off his hands and stepped away from him. 'You're drunk,' she said in a low voice, half afraid, yet understanding his jealousy; bewildered by the change in him; wanting to make things right between them because Will was all she had now: Will, the farmhouse, and her baby, in an alien world. 'Won't you try to sleep for a little while?'

He said brokenly, 'I'm sorry, Charlotte. I'm so – so sorry, my lass.' He was quiet now, deeply ashamed of himself. 'A fine husband I've turned out to be.' He touched her hair with fumbling fingers. 'It's just that I love you so much . . .'

'I know, my dear, I know.' She helped him upstairs to his room where he sprawled, face down, on his bed.

Charlotte was up early to gather mushrooms for Will's breakfast, wanting to please him, to bridge the widening gulf between them. She walked to Sweet Water Meadow, a basket over her arm, drinking in the warm, sweet summer air, feeling her child stirring beneath the loose, flowered smock she wore, remembering, as she bent down near the hedgerow to gather a handful of clover and buttercups, another morning, very much like this one, when she had run across this same meadow wearing a green dress pintucked to a tapering nineteen-inch waist, and a straw hat with green ribbons, to meet Rowan Tanquillan.

Now, everything was changed. She was changed. The war had taken away her old feeling of security, that blissful certainty of youth and hope and love which had seemed so indestructible only one short year ago. Now Frank and her father were gone away from her forever. Search as she might, she could not find them. Where, in all this waste of land and sea and air, are you absorbed: you, so simple, good and ordinary, she wondered, remembering the lines of a poem she had written about them. About her father in particular:

> 'A thousand old pretenders smile through other eyes
> And go about your business for you,
> But still I cannot find you . . .'

The sky above her head was pearled over with the mist of early morning, the grass beneath her feet was heavy with dew. A lark rose up singing near the old cricket pavilion. With a sense of déjà vu, she conjured up that morning last summer. In that instant she even imagined the figure of a man coming towards her through the mist.

Rowan had walked down from the house. He had come to Grey Wethers in the hope of seeing Charlotte, drawn to the meadow by the restless certainty that, if he waited long enough, she would come to him, sensing his presence perhaps. He had wakened to a feeling of telepathy, the self-same feeling he had experienced the night he sailed for France. Night long, he had wrestled with his emotions concerning Romilly and his child. The choice was open to him. He could have caught a train to Scotland; he had chosen to come to Wiltshire. There was no going back. Life demanded total honesty, total commitment to his chosen path. And then, as in a dream, he saw the woman, an unreal shape at first, standing quietly, holding a basket in her hand, perhaps a country woman, softly plump with child.

He walked forward, slowly, then more quickly, filled with a growing wonder and delight. He knew, as he held out his hands to her, that the woman was Charlotte, that the child she carried was his. She wore a hat of soft straw, tied, sunbonnet fashion, with a blue scarf. The sharp, clear contours of her young body were blurred now with the coming child. Her face was paler than he remembered, more sharply planed, touched with suffering. She neither spoke nor moved at first. He read disbelief in her eyes. Then, with a sigh, she stepped into his arms, like a small, weary bird glad of its nest.

'Why didn't you tell me?' he murmured. 'Oh, Charlotte, why didn't you? Why did you marry Will Oakleigh? Why, Charlotte, why?'

'Because of our child,' she said simply. 'Because I wanted you to be happy.'

He untied the scarf; gently took off her hat and let if fall to the ground; smoothed her hair with his fingers. 'Didn't you know that you are my happiness? Did you think that I could be happy without you? I've been in hell since you wrote me that letter. Such a long silence. You never replied to any of the letters I sent you.'

'Letters? But I never received any...' And then she understood why. He had posted them to Scarborough. Perhaps even now they were lying on the mat near that jewel-coloured side door. Or perhaps her mother had found them and torn them up. She felt cold and empty, sick at heart, utterly weary. Too late now. Even Rowan's arms could provide nothing more than a temporary refuge. 'I must go,' she said uneasily.

'But there's so much to say to each other.'

'You don't understand. If Will knew... if he saw us together. Please Rowan, you must go away. We mustn't see each other any more. I gave him my word that it is all over between us.'

Her body trembled against his. She had been through so much – the death of her father and brother, the knowledge that she was going to have a child; facing things alone, making decisions which affected both their lives. He could not leave things as they were. He realized the bitter irony of the situation.

'Are you in love with Will?'

'How can I answer that? Please, Rowan, I *must* go now.'

'Are you – afraid of him?'

'It isn't as cut and dried as that . . .' How could she begin to explain the bewildering complexity of her emotions in a few words?

'Very well, darling.' He spoke quietly, not wanting to add to her distress. 'I'll be leaving in a few days anyway. Romilly has taken my son to Scotland. What I have to say to her will not be cut and dried either, I imagine. But we can't leave things as they are.' He cupped her face with his hands. 'I must see you again. I'll wait for you tonight in the summerhouse.'

'I can't promise,' she said.

Very gently, he bent his lips to hers and knew, as her mouth met his, that nothing had changed since that first time he had kissed her on the stairs at the house in Chalice Walk. 'Remember always that I love you,' he said huskily.

As she returned to the farm, she remembered that she had once given Alice Tanquillan a sixpence for courage. How strange that human beings clung to remembered words, dead flowers pressed within the pages of a book, shells, coins and kisses, as talismans. She felt calmer now, remembering the touch of Rowan's lips on hers.

Will was in the kitchen. 'Where have you been?' he asked. 'I thought you had overslept. When I went to your room, the bed was made, and you'd gone out. I thought for a minute that . . .'

'I've gathered some mushrooms for breakfast.' She set the basket on the table, certain that he would notice something different about her, the way her hands shook slightly as she slipped into a pinafore and busied herself with the cooking. Soon enough, the village would be agog with the news that Rowan was home on leave. Would Will put two and two together then? Would he remember how ill at ease she had seemed when she walked into the house? Would he question her until she admitted the truth? Would he believe that her meeting with Rowan had been accidental?

Alice paid particular attention to her toilette that morning; hugged herself with joy that Rowan had come back to her. She had known all along that he would. The knowledge that he had chosen to come to Grey Wethers instead of going to Scotland to see Romilly, meant only one thing to her. Rowan was not happy, anyone could tell that, and she had kept her ears open to the murmur of voices from her great-aunt's private room when she was supposed to be in bed and asleep. It had been a simple matter to slip downstairs when the servants were in their own quarters and the staircase and hall were deep in shadows. It had seemed so mysterious and exciting to blend with those shadows, to stand as still and silent as a ghost to catch words and phrases through the slightly open door.

'. . . Scotland. You'll go, of course?'

'. . . suppose I must. It will make no difference in the long run.'

'All this. I'm so sorry, my dear.'

Then something about 'the child', which Alice could not catch. The voices became inaudible at that point. Alice stirred restlessly. Why didn't they speak up? Then she heard Rowan say, 'It was all over then, when I went away. Romilly knew that. Oh, I realize . . .' his voice dropped again.

Why did Aunt Kitty mutter so? Alice sighed impatiently. Then Kitty's voice rose a little as she said, 'I don't think I should be the one to speak of that. It is a very personal and private matter between yourselves . . .'

'Yes . . . but I still love her . . .'

At that moment, the door to the servants' quarters opened and Rivers appeared. 'The old fool,' Alice muttered under her breath. But the old man's eyes were dim, and it was an easy matter to slip away up the staircase to her room. Once there, Alice flung herself ecstatically on her bed. What did it matter that she had not heard all the conversation. She had heard enough. Rowan loved her! She rolled over on her back, arms outstretched, a child who harboured, within her fast developing body, the sensations of a sexually-awakened woman. She knew all about love. Not just the emotions connected with loving: its pain and heartbreak; the untold misery of waiting and longing; but how babies were conceived, because her father had told her a long time ago, before she was old enough to equate what he was saying with her own physical development and feelings.

She remembered clearly his words to her when, shortly before he died, she had gone to him and told him that she was bleeding. He had said, in that warm, wise way of his, 'It's nothing to be afraid of, Alice. It simply means that you are a woman now, capable of having children.' Nor had he stuffed her head full of nonsense about birds and bees and gooseberry bushes. Because Oliver Tanquillan was a man who believed in the truth, he had explained everything to her, clearly and simply. Because he had done so, she had accepted the facts of life, and gone on playing with her dolls, thinking no more about it – until she met Rowan.

Now, early on a pristine June morning, she stared at her reflection in the mirror and hugged herself with delight because Rowan loved her.

She felt wise and good now; somehow holy, because this was Sunday morning with the church bell tolling Matins across the warm, early summer meadows, because Rowan was under the same roof as herself, and somehow – somehow, she would have him all to herself at last; tell him how much she loved him, and feel his arms about her.

She had chosen her prettiest dress – one that Charlotte had made for her – a soft green muslin affair with a spreading skirt and a broderie anglaise collar. When she had brushed and braided her hair, she ran down to breakfast; cheeks flushed, eyes sparkling.

'Alice! How pretty you look,' Rowan said, thinking how much the girl had improved since his great-aunt had taken her in hand.

'Do you really think so, Rowan?'

'Yes, of course I do.' He answered mechanically, his thoughts far away as he remembered, with infinite longing, the blurred outline of a pregnant woman seen through the early morning mist of Sweet Water Meadow: urged the day towards dusk when, God willing, he might see her again. But there was a long, fruitless day to live through until then, punctuated with the ten-thirty church service, luncheon, the long afternoon, dinner, and Evensong. God, how he hated Sundays! This Sunday in particular. What if Charlotte was in church? How could he prevent himself from looking at her? If Will Oakleigh was beside her, how could he bear to sing the words of Te

Deum Laudamus: 'Also the Holy Ghost: the Comforter'? Or those of the Benedictus: 'To give light to them that sit in darkness and in the shadow of death'.

Death! He had lived in the shadow of death and pain and hopelessness and despair for the past six months. What he most needed now was hope for the future, but what right had he to expect absolution for his sins of omission; his inward rejection of Romilly; not being there when Charlotte needed him.

The war, which had once seemed to him a means of escape, his one chance of proving himself a man, now seemed to him a no man's land of waste: waste of land and living creatures; of trees and loveliness; crops and planting; a waste of the slow, necessary rhythm of life against the monstrous thunder of enemy gunfire which stilled the birdsong and the sound of laughter from human throats, and left, at sunrise, the dreadful tally of the newly dead, surprised by death, lying in the mud and muck of hastily-dug graves which the powers-that-be called trenches.

When, after lunch, Alice begged him to take her rowing on Sweet Water Lake, he could not help but smile at her and say yes to what he saw as her innocent pleading for fun and relaxation. Why, after all, should the very young suffer for the mistakes of an older generation? He looked upon Alice as a child, a girl who had weathered and surmounted her own particular hell quite bravely, far more bravely than he had weathered his own.

Smiling, he pushed off the boat from the shore; thought how quickly she was growing up, his funny little scrap of a cousin with her adult hair-style and unfurled parasol, dabbling her fingertips in the water.

The sun was high now, in a cloudless June sky. The sound of the oars dipping into quiet water was balm to Rowan's restless spirit. In the middle of the lake he stopped rowing and lay back on the cushions, glad of the sun on his face, the peaceful lapping of the water about the sides of the boat.

Almost asleep, he became aware of Alice Tanquillan's body close to his, her warm kisses on his cheeks and hair; her voice;

whispered words in his ear, 'Oh, darling Rowan, please, *please*, make love to me! I know you want to! Why don't you, then? There's no-one to see! No-one in the whole world.'

He opened his eyes to the sight of her, skirts tucked up about her thighs, lying beside him in the boat, her child's body quivering with desire.

'For Christ's sake, Alice!' He laughed, then saw the naked longing in her eyes.

He said, 'Dear Scrap, I love you, but not in the way you imagine.' Straightening her skirts, he hated himself for even wanting to laugh at her, understanding the emotional hell she was in: akin to his own. After all, who was he to weigh or evaluate one kind of loving against another?

Alice said dully, 'I'll make you pay for this, you know. Take me home now! I loved you once, now I shall hate you till the day I die!'

CHAPTER THIRTEEN

The weather changed abruptly as storm clouds gathered over the Downs, turning the sky inky black. Thunder growled incessantly about the hills, a sound which reminded Rowan of gunfire over the fields and valleys of Belgium, as the intermittent lightning reminded him of gun-flashes, those curious bursts of light followed by plumes of dense black smoke. Then the rain came in a deluge, with a pattering noise like rapid machine-gun fire. Rowan watched it from the drawing-room windows, hitting the terrace, bouncing up again, bending the flowers, blotting out the world in a thin grey veil of concentrated fury.

The incident with Alice had unsettled him. I should have been more understanding, he thought, should have talked to her quietly and reasonably. He sat down at the piano; began playing Chopin's Revolutionary Study. Kitty Tanquillan came into the room. Sensing her presence, he stopped playing. 'What is it?' she asked. 'What's wrong with Alice? The child has locked herself in her room and refuses to come down to dinner.'

'It's my fault,' Rowan said. 'I did the unforgivable thing. I laughed at her. Oh, *God*!'

'You need not say any more, I think I understand.' Kitty sighed and turned to stare out at the rain. 'You know, Rowan, I thought that growing old would mean happiness and peace of mind, an end to emotional upheaval. I once pictured myself as a very old lady living out my life here in peace and tranquillity. How stupid I was to imagine that old age brings a kind of amnesty to one's problems.' She pulled a wry face. 'It might be different if I were senile, if my mind had aged along with my body. I should be thankful that it has not, but I often wish it had.'

She said, 'What are you going to do, my dear? What are you going to do about Romilly? When you go to Scotland, what are you going to say to her? Remember, there's your child to consider.'

'There's Charlotte and our child to consider too,' he said quietly.

'Yes, but Charlotte is married now. You must not interfere with that. The girl did what she thought best to ensure that her child would be given a name; a secure future . . .'

'If I thought that Charlotte was happy with Will Oakleigh, I would not interfere,' Rowan said, closing the piano, 'but she is far from happy. She's – afraid . . .'

'You know how much I love you,' Kitty said, 'but I cannot help wishing that you had not come here just now.'

Rowan bowed his head. 'I'm sorry, Aunt Kitty. I'll go away tomorrow then . . .'

'Rowan!'

He smiled at her. 'No, don't worry, I understand. You are quite right, as usual. I must see Romilly; settle matters between us. But I must warn you, right or wrong, no matter what the consequences, I intend to see Charlotte again before I leave. I must hear it from her own lips that she *is* happy.'

He walked, in the rain, to the summerhouse.

The wet summer grass squelched beneath his feet. He thought wryly as he went through the spinney, that the Irish described rain as liquid sunshine; call it what you will, there was a great deal of the stuff falling on his bare head from the branches of the trees. But, ah, the clean smell of it; the memories it revived of rained-off cricket matches. If anyone asked him to describe the one scent above all others to conjure the essence of an English summer, it would be rain at evening which unlocked the deep warm fragrance of the earth, and dogroses.

It was dusking over. The spinney and meadow were threaded with shadows, lengthening and deepening. The rain was soft now and gentle, murmuring and pattering; the lake moved and rippled to the rhythm of the drops, and washed along the margin of stones near the landing-stage. Some work had been done to the summerhouse. Kitty had told him that she had intended to have it taken down last autumn, since it was scarcely worth the cost of repair. It was Alice who had begged her not to because she liked to go there on wet afternoons, to shut herself in and listen to the rain on the roof. This Rowan understood: the sense of peace and loneliness, the thrill of make-believe, of secret kingdoms of the imagination was something he had known too and loved as a child.

The door was open. The interior smelt of new wood. Some of the floorboards had been replaced with sturdy oak, and there was the paraphernalia of bygone years, wicker chairs and rickety tables, mouldering tennis rackets with broken strings, oars propped up in a corner along with discarded shoes and galoshes; old boat-cushions, frayed and torn, sagging benches where the cricket teams had once sat to eat their sandwiches. Rain pattered on the roof as Rowan struck a match to light a small oil lamp on one of the tables. Now that he was here, waiting, he realized how unlikely it was that Charlotte would come, a married woman sitting at home with her husband. What excuse could she make to get away, even if she wanted to? He toyed with the idea of going to the farm as bold as brass, remembering Will Oakleigh as a decent man, gentle and caring of his stock, the archetypal slow-moving, slow-thinking countryman, well liked, thorough, conscientious, as stubborn as a mule, but certainly no villain. And yet Rowan could not get out of his mind that Charlotte was afraid of him.

If only things had been different. If Charlotte had received his letters from France telling her how much he loved her. If he had known about the child in time to prevent her marrying Will. Her sacrifice was too great: he would have made provision for her. But Charlotte had married Will in the mistaken notion that she would make life easier for himself. He had his parents to thank for their meddling. His aunt had told him about her visit to London, how Rachel had talked Romilly into the idea of a reconciliation for the sake of their child. Again the bitter irony

423

of the situation occurred to him: the woman he loved who had put herself and her child beyond his reach; and the woman he did not love, with Romilly's child the innocent pawn in the Tanquillan power game.

Charlotte hurried across Sweet Water Meadow. The rain had stopped now, the sky was faintly luminous with stars. Will had spoken little all evening. When the clock struck nine he got up, put on his jacket and said he was going to the village for an hour. She knew what that meant. Will would come back when the pub closed, unsteady of step, smelling of beer and tobacco smoke. 'Please don't go,' she said, knowing how he would be when he returned: slightly aggressive, critical, or worse – maudlin.

'A man must have some pleasure in life,' he said briefly. 'There's precious little here.' She knew what he meant – with a wife in name only.

While Charlotte hated his visits to the White Swan, she understood and pitied Will's unhappiness, the bitter jealousy which had invaded his mind since he discovered who had fathered her child. If the father had been some unknown boy with whom she had shared a moment's passion, some nameless, faceless youth who had died in the trenches, this Will would have come to terms with. It was Tanquillan he could never accept: Tanquillan who had destroyed his peace of mind. Tanquillan – not some unknown, dead youth but Rowan, alive, rich, handsome and vital. What she most feared was a confrontation between the two of them; bitter words spoken in anger that could never be recalled.

She sat by the fire for a while after Will had left the house, listening to the slow, inevitable ticking of the clock, willing herself to stay where she was. But it was no use. Rowan would be waiting for her. She could not live like this, in fear. Suddenly she remembered the old Charlotte Grayler who had seized the shafts of Mr Roe's handcart and wheeled it down to the station, the girl who had stood beside Jenny Carfax waving a fallen suffragette banner. Fear was a killer – the enemy of human dignity and strength. Love remained the one great shining star in a war-darkened world, but if the world ended tomorrow, the stars would still remain.

'Thank God you've come!' Rowan held out his arms to her.

'No, please don't kiss me.' She stood quietly, trembling, wrapped in a dark cloak with the hood thrown back. 'I can't stay long. Will might come back unexpectedly.'

'You are afraid of him, then?'

'Not for myself. Only for you . . .'

'I never saw Will as a violent man,' Rowan said.

'He isn't. It's just that . . .'

'Come, sit down.' He took her hands in his. 'I promise not to make things difficult for you, but asking me not to kiss you is like asking a starving man not to eat.' He drew her to a bench. 'I want to know the truth, darling. What about Will?'

'I feel so disloyal, talking about him behind his back.'

Rowan said, 'I'm going away tomorrow. Aunt Kitty was right when she said she wished I hadn't come here just now, but I can't go away not knowing how things stand between you and Will; how you feel about our child. Oh, Charlotte!'

'Going away?'

He saw, by the feeble light of the lamp, the sudden anguish in her eyes. 'Where?' she asked. 'Not back to France?'

'I'm going to Scotland to see Romilly and – and my son. I want to see him. God knows how I shall feel when I do. Oh God, Charlotte, what has happened to our lives? I married Romilly for the same kind of reasons you married Will, because I was afraid for others . . .'

'What – others?'

'You and Alice. Never mind why, that isn't important now. Christ, what a fool I was. I was weak and cowardly. I succumbed to emotional blackmail.' He buried his face in his hands.

'You mustn't blame yourself.' She touched his hair with her fingertips, wanting to comfort him. The barrier between them was broken as she felt his arms about her, his lips on hers.

Rowan said passionately, 'Come away with me, Charlotte! Let us go away together now!'

'No,' she said wearily, 'we can't. We must not! Running away will solve nothing. I'm married to Will, you are married to Romilly. Selfish love is no use at all, I see that now. How could we be happy together if we simply took the easy way out? Don't you see, darling?'

'Yes.' He smiled down at her, aware suddenly of a new dimension to loving, a freshness and revitalization of his spirit which seemed to him like a song – a psalm – Exaltabo te, Domine. 'Thou didst turn thy face from me; and I was troubled. Then cried I unto thee O Lord; and gat me to my Lord right humbly. What profit is there in my blood when I go down to the pit? Shall the dust give thanks to thee: or shall it declare thy truth?' How could he consider himself to be anything more than a coward if he dared not face Romilly or his emotions when he saw his son for the first time?

He said, 'No matter what the future brings, I shall always love you. Nothing can ever change that. If we never meet again in this life, you will always remain the greater part of myself. You, and our child.' He rested his hand gently on the curve of her belly.

'I shall christen her Shelley Katherine. Katherine after your Aunt Kitty.' Tears starred Charlotte's lashes. 'You asked me how I felt about – our child. Oh, Rowan, I want it so much, so very much . . .'

'And – Will?' he asked urgently.

'Will is a good man. I would not have married him otherwise. He is – jealous, that's all. You see, we occupy separate rooms . . .'

'Don't say any more, my darling.' Rowan pressed his fingertips to her lips. 'I understand.' He smiled. '"I have been faithful to thee, Cynara, in my fashion."'

They sat quietly together for a while, then Rowan said, 'I have news for you. Jenny and Harry were married a few days ago.'

Charlotte's face radiated happiness. 'Jenny and Harry? Oh, Rowan! How is Harry? How did Jenny look? What did she say?'

'So far as I remember,' Rowan laughed, 'she said, "I take thee, Harry Grayler, to my wedded husband." I don't think she cared two hoots how she looked. She wore that same loose oatmeal-coloured skirt and cardigan she wore in Scarborough, and the same hat. But somehow it looked exactly right for the occasion; most fitting and proper. She carried a bunch of wild flowers, and someone had found a few roses for her hat-brim. After the wedding, we drank champagne. God only knows where it came from. We had cake, too, and sandwiches, and I made a speech. Quite a good speech, looking back.'

'What did you say?'

'Simply that I felt myself privileged to have known the bride before the war; that I could imagine no finer example of womanhood, dedicated to the ideals of freedom, loyalty and love. I said that I had known the bridegroom more recently, since our incarceration in the same hospital ward, but that I knew his – family – well; that this was a man who had grown up to the best that family life had to offer, who would make a fitting husband for so lovely a bride.'

'Oh, Rowan!'

'Just before they left for their honeymoon, Jenny said, "Tell Charlotte I love her, and thank her for her discretion. Giving Harry my love was much kinder than telling him that he would be far better off without a girl like me."'

'If only Frank and Joe had been there,' Charlotte said. Then, urgently, 'What time is it? I must be going now!'

And this was the moment they dreaded. Saying goodbye to each other.

'We'll meet again, my darling,' Rowan said. 'Will you kiss me goodbye?'

'Oh, Rowan, of course I will.' She held up her face to his.

'Don't say goodbye. Never goodbye, just – au revoir, my love; my dearest love.'

She knew, as she hurried back across the meadow, that she would remember that kiss to her life's end.

CHAPTER FOURTEEN

Alice Tanquillan made no move to leave her room until the taxi appeared to take Rowan to Devizes station, when she waltzed downstairs, smiling, to bid him goodbye.

'Alice,' he said, thankfully, thinking that yesterday was forgotten, 'I'm so glad you came. I hoped you would . . .'

'Did you, Rowan?' she said artlessly. 'But yes, of course. Perhaps you wanted to tell me how pretty I look. I *do* look pretty this morning, don't I? Charlotte made this dress for me. Mrs Oakleigh, you know. Dear Mrs Will Oakleigh!' She giggled delightedly. 'It's the one I wore yesterday in the boat. You haven't forgotten, have you?'

They were alone for the moment. The taxi had just arrived. Rivers was busy handing his luggage to the driver, and Kitty had gone to her sitting-room to find an unopened bottle of Madeira for Rowan to take with him.

'No, I haven't forgotten,' Rowan said levelly. 'I rather hoped that you had.'

'Ah, but I haven't,' she replied brightly; smiling up at him. 'And I meant what I said. I do hate you now!'

'Alice!' My God, he thought, Aunt Kitty was right, she *is* mad.

'I'm sorry if I hurt you. I never meant to,' he said.

She laughed excitedly. 'Hurt me? Because you laughed at me? How could you possibly think that? Nobody in the world can hurt *me*! I'm immune to hurt, as my father was. Nobody ever really hurt him either because he was stronger than anyone else on earth. Stronger than Uncle Gervaise or Aunt Rachel, because he knew much more than they did, and so do I.'

'What do you mean?' But there was no more time. Kitty Tanquillan came out of the house at that moment, his luggage was safely stowed away, the driver climbed into his seat, and the taxi moved off down the pebbled drive.

'Will,' Alice asked that afternoon, after her riding lesson, as they led their horses back to the stable, 'what does "cuckold" mean? Is it just another word for a cuckoo?'

'No,' Will said unthinkingly, used to the girl's suddenly blurted questions, 'so far as I know, it means the husband of a faithless wife. Why do you ask?'

'No special reason. I just wondered, that's all,' Alice smiled, unsaddling her pony. But Will wasn't satisfied. He said, clutching the girl's arm, 'That isn't good enough! I asked you a question.'

'And I gave you an answer,' Alice laughed. 'Why, what's the matter, Will? Are you a cuckold?' She continued unsaddling her pony, patting its head, offering a handful of sugar-lumps from the pocket of her riding-habit.

Will swung her round to face him. 'What exactly do you mean? What are you trying to tell me?'

'Nothing,' Alice said airily, 'except that I happened to take a walk in Sweet Water Meadow last night . . .'

'And?'

'Well, I expect it was after you had gone down to the pub. You do go down to the White Swan quite often these days, don't you?' Alice giggled at Will's discomfiture.

'What if I do?' he snapped. 'What business have you to pry into my affairs?'

'Let go of my arm, Will,' Alice said coldly, 'you're hurting me.' She laughed then. 'Don't you think I handled Tosca quite nicely over that last jump? We must raise the jumps tomorrow! You must teach me to jump as high as the moon!' She paused. 'All the Tanquillans are good riders: my Aunt Kitty; my cousin Rowan. Aunt Kitty never tires of telling me how she taught Rowan to ride . . .'

'For Christ's sake,' Will said hoarsely, 'what are you driving at?'

Alice smiled serenely. 'I saw my cousin Rowan and your wife together last night in the old summerhouse in Sweet Water

Meadow. He laid a pile of cushions on the floor – you know, those old boat-cushions? When he had done that, they lay together on top of them and made love. At least, I suppose they were making love because they moved together in a funny kind of way.'

Alice laughed to herself as Will turned away from her, a shambling, distraught figure who believed that she was telling the truth.

Now, Alice Tanquillan thought triumphantly, you, Rowan, and you, Charlotte, suffer as I have suffered. But, in the crazy wilderness of her mind, it was Charlotte she most wished to destroy. Charlotte, whom she had once loved with all her heart. Charlotte who had betrayed her. Charlotte who was carrying Rowan's child.

Rowan had not suspected for one minute that she had followed him from the house the night before, that she had listened to every word he and Charlotte had said to each other in the summerhouse. Nor did she regret lying to Will Oakleigh. All she wanted was revenge. Now she had it! Now she reigned supreme, the arbiter of justice, the sower of seeds, the great destroyer. And yet, in her finest, most triumphant hour, she could scarcely bear the pain in her head, the feeling that the world was swimming away from her, the hot tears which coursed down her cheeks: the taste of salt on her tongue, the sensation that she had suddenly been cast adrift in a small boat on a flood of tears. She knew then that she would always love Rowan and Charlotte. How strange: she had never realized before that love and hatred could be so bound together, so one, that there was no telling where one ended, the other began.

Will ate his supper, saying nothing, glancing at his wife across the table. At nine o'clock, he went down to the village pub where he drank several pints of beer. At ten-thirty, he returned to the house. Charlotte was in bed. The dogs rose up to meet him, wagging their tails, the cats miaowed about his feet.

He walked upstairs to the landing; threw open the door of Charlotte's bedroom, and stood, swaying, on the threshold, holding a lamp in his right hand; cheeks waxen, hair awry – a colourless Othello to a bewildered Desdemona.

'Will,' Charlotte said, 'what is it? What do you want?'

'I want you,' he said, 'and I intend to have you, you bitch!' He moved slowly towards the bed, unbuttoning his clothing.

'No, Will! For God's sake! What's the matter?' Charlotte slipped out of bed, not fully awake. And this was like some horrible nightmare, the fury in Will's voice, the naked lust in his eyes, his stumbling footsteps as he came towards her, the foul smell of drink on his breath. Fear rose up in her as she pressed her body against the wall, hands outstretched to fend him off. 'Don't, Will! For God's sake, don't!'

'That's not what you said to him, is it? Last night in the summerhouse, when you lay with Tanquillan! Alice saw you!' He came closer. 'If he could have you, so shall I!'

Lurching forward, he pinned her to the wall with his hands, speaking in a low, rough voice. 'You think I'm not good enough for you. You think I'm not capable of doing what he did to you.'

She thought she would choke with fear. For a moment, she seemed hypnotized, incapable of action. But Will was unsteady on his feet. Bringing up her hands, she pushed him away from her with all her might. He stumbled backward against the bed. She heard the grunt of his indrawn breath as his legs buckled beneath him and he sprawled to the floor. In that second, Charlotte ran for the door; hurried downstairs to the kitchen.

Will had locked and bolted the outer door for the night. The dogs rose up and frolicked about her as she tore at the bolts, but the key was not in the lock. Suddenly she remembered that Will always hung the key on a hook near the fireplace at night. Turning, impeded by the dogs, she heard him coming downstairs after her as she wrenched the key from its hook and tried to insert it in the lock. The key fell from her shaking fingers. The dogs loped towards Will, jumping up at him, barking excitedly. Charlotte found the key, jammed it in the lock, turned it, tugged open the door, and raced for the barn.

The barn door was heavy. It creaked on its hinges as she swung it open. Will was coming across the yard as she crashed the door shut behind her and shot the bolts. Her breath came in shuddering gasps as she sank down on the floor among the sweet-smelling hay. Will was outside, hammering the door with his fists, shouting to her to let him in. The lower edge of the door trembled to his kicks. Charlotte scrambled on her knees to the piled-up hay near the mangers. Two gentle-eyed calves stared at her as she lay sobbing and gasping close to their stalls. At least the hay provided some warmth. Her feet were bare, she had nothing on but a thin cotton nightgown. Stunned with shock, she glanced up at the pale outline of a window. What if Will gained entry that way? He was quiet now. She imagined him prowling round outside. One of the dogs barked suddenly. The barn was filled with the scuttering sounds of mice in the hayloft, the calves made licking noises, softly comforting sounds which brought her back to reality.

If Will gained entry, she must be prepared to run for the door or get up the ladder into the loft. She had reason now to be thankful for muscles strengthened by heaving down those heavy shutters of her father's shop. Will was drunk. Sooner or later the effects would wear off. In the morning perhaps, he would be sorry for his actions; even so she could not live with him any longer. She could not help but weep for the waste of it all, their lives together; the future which she had envisaged as a calm, sweet business of growing warmth and understanding between them. Now she knew that Will would never accept her child as his own. Jealousy had eaten into him too deeply for that. The naked lust in his eyes had frightened her. And then she remembered his words: 'Alice saw you.'

Alice! So Alice had been there outside the summerhouse last night, listening to their conversation, peeping; playing the eavesdropper; had told Will she had seen them lying together. It was Alice who had filled her husband's ears with lies. But why? Then she knew why. The pieces clicked into place one by one. Alice knew that Rowan was the father of her child. Alice believed herself to be in love with Rowan; thought that Rowan was in love with her. Will's jealousy was nothing compared with that of an unbalanced girl intent on destruction. Hell hath no fury like a woman scorned.

Where could she turn now, for help? She lay, trembling, in the hay, cold and curiously empty, starting at every sound. If only Rowan were here. She remembered the day Will delivered the ewe of its lamb. How companionable they had been that day, how she had looked up to him then. Even now, she could not hate Will. All this is my fault, she thought. I should have told him the truth from the start. Too late now for regrets. She and Will had reached the point of no return. And yet she had offered to sleep with him. She could not equate her gentle husband with the gaunt, lustful man who had entered her bedroom intent on rape.

She slept briefly then; wakened to a stronger light through the window. All was quiet. Getting up, she crossed to the door, and pressed her ear against it, listening. A cock crowed in the farmyard. Shivering in her thin night-attire, she unbolted the door. If Will was there, waiting, if he forced her to the ground and took her against her will, she knew she would not have enough strength left to resist. But the yard was empty.

She scurried quickly to the house, quietly opened the door. The dogs lolloped towards her, whimpering. Will was asleep in a chair near the fireplace, snoring slightly. She tiptoed past him. The dogs stared at her curiously, wagging their tails. They followed her upstairs to her room, watched her, heads cocked, as she dressed; made a bundle of a few things she would need to take with her. Goldie, the oldest retriever, barked suddenly. 'Oh, hush,' she cried, bending to stroke the dog's head. 'Quiet, Goldie! Quiet!'

The dog thumped its tail on the floor. When she was ready, Charlotte picked up her purse containing her housekeeping money, a matter of a few pounds in loose change, and stole onto the landing. She wore her cloak. She had not even stopped to tidy her hair. Clutching her bundle, she walked slowly downstairs. A board creaked. Will opened his eyes momentarily, then sank back to sleep. The cats were awake now, stalking about the kitchen, looking for food.

She knelt briefly at the door to caress the dogs; looked round the kitchen, then closed the door carefully behind her and hurried away down the long, empty road to Devizes station. If she walked steadily, fairly quickly, she might be in time to catch the milk-train to London.

CHAPTER FIFTEEN

Charlotte travelled to London with no idea what to do when she got there. She had simply remembered London as a place where she was happy once with Rowan and Jenny, a place in which a pregnant woman carrying a bundle containing a few clothes and books, might lose herself. She had had enough of village life: the small-mindedness of men and women who saw the hills as a stockade against the world, people who paid lip-service to God, who cleaned His brasses and arranged His flowers, yet had no real conception of Christianity. Not one woman had stretched out the hand of friendship to her. Not one of them had said, 'I am your friend. I will help you.' No-one except Kitty Tanquillan. But Kitty Tanquillan was the last person on earth she could have turned to in her present crisis, because of Alice.

She had spent a precious five shillings on her fare. She spent another shilling on a cup of tea and a sandwich in the station buffet. She sat, wrapped in her cloak, her hair spilling about her shoulders, wondering what to do next, aware of veiled glances in her direction, with no way of knowing that people looked at her because, sitting there in a crowded station buffet, swaddled in a cloak, with her red hair loose, she resembled a Michel-angelo madonna: motherhood incarnate.

She wondered, as she ate her sandwich, if that were nourishment sufficient for her growing child. She spoke to that child in her own language; inwardly, with love. 'Don't worry, my little one. I'll think of something.' Her child meant everything to her. Somewhere, in this great sprawling city, she would find a home for herself and her child. Then she remembered Jenny: Jenny's flat in Bloomsbury. She knew the address. Strengthened with the tea, and the sandwich, she made her way to a bus queue.

But London was a tricky, private city, she discovered, as she walked its pavements and alleyways looking for Jenny's apartment. A city full of confusingly similar squares, churches and spires, throbbing with life, filled with uncaring strangers, with trees and Methodist meeting-places, with shops and stalls, and houses curving away in side streets, tall houses, balconied, fronted with iron railings. And now the sun was high and hot, and Charlotte's feet were weary with traipsing London for a resting place. She sat down on a park bench for a while. Bloomsbury seemed to her a maze of endless streets and hard pavements. She was lonely, lonelier than she had ever been in her life. Solitude was something she had always sought, something inborn: she had never been a gregarious person. Loneliness was something different, loneliness was linked with fear, and yet she had wanted anonymity, to lose herself in a crowd after the numbing terror of last night.

Even on the train, she had not felt safe lest Will had followed her. The nightmare was still upon her, the memory of Will's eyes, cruel and lustful, was something she would never forget. In that moment, something horrible and vile beyond belief had entered her life. She had encountered naked, human jealousy which prompted a decent man to attempt an indecent act. Part of the nightmare was Alice Tanquillan's role in that. She shivered suddenly despite the warmth of the day, brought back to reality by the chiming of bells from a nearby steeple. Faint and hungry, she got up from the seat and walked on to continue her search for Jenny's flat.

When at last she came to a tall house in a terrace, with steps to the front door, she could scarcely find strength enough to ring the bell. When the door opened, her eyes blurred suddenly.

'Yes, what is it? What do you want?' The voice was that of a woman, a warm, lively voice laced with an unmistakable Scottish accent.

'I – I'm so sorry.' Charlotte stretched out her hand to the voice. 'So – sorry.' The voice and the world swam away from her suddenly as she sank to the ground in a dead faint.

When she opened her eyes, she was lying on a couch in a room with sunlight coming in through the window, filtering through starched lace curtains. The couch was horsehair, covered with a crocheted blanket made from colourful scraps of wool. Two canaries, in a cage near the window, filled the room with song. Someone had placed a cool bandage on her forehead. A woman sat beside her, gently massaging her hand.

'So you've decided to come round, have you?' the woman said. 'Praise God for small mercies! I thought, for one awful minute, I had a corpse on my hands, and you wouldn't believe the trouble I had to get you inside. My name's Bridie McKenna, by the way. What's yours?'

Charlotte focused her eyes on a thin, smiling face with intensely blue eyes beneath a mop of grey-gold hair, the colour of dusky wheat, drawn up in a kind of knob stuck through with carelessly placed hairpins.

'Does Jenny Carfax live here?'

'Jenny? Aye, she does, when she's at home. Do you know Jenny?'

'Jenny's my sister-in-law.'

Bridie McKenna narrowed her eyes. 'Jenny isn't married,' she said.

'She married my brother Harry, in France, a little while ago.' Charlotte smiled faintly. 'She's Jenny Grayler now. My name is Charlotte . . .'

'Charlotte!' Bridie's expression lightened. 'Of course! Jenny spoke of you quite often. So you are Charlotte Grayler. But what a state you're in!' She stood up, a slight figure dressed in a black skirt and a spotless white blouse. 'I'm not going to ask you any more questions just now,' she said firmly, 'I'm going to get you something to eat. You look half starved, if you don't mind my saying so. That won't do, you know, since you are obviously eating for two at the moment.'

She came back presently carrying a tray with Scotch broth, scrambled eggs and potato pancakes. Charlotte ate hungrily. When she had finished, she smiled gratefully at Bridie.

'You're in some kind of trouble, aren't you?' Bridie said. 'But you needn't tell me unless you want to. God knows, I've been in trouble myself often enough. Now I'm forty-five years old, and at peace with myself and the world. I've neither chick nor child, and my husband is dead.' She smiled ruefully. 'We weren't very happy together, but at least he left me this house and enough money to live on. Truth to tell, I wasn't sorry when he died. He was an awkward kind of man was Bruce McKenna, with a penchant for whisky and an eye for the women.'

She glanced at Charlotte's left hand. 'You're married I see, but you are not much more than a child yourself. Hark at me, blethering away while you are half asleep. Come now, I'm going to put you to bed in Jenny's room. Things will look a lot better tomorrow.'

She explained, as she led the way to the top floor, that she let rooms for the company as much as the extra income. 'What would a woman like me do all by myself in a house this size? But I'm fond of it.' She ran her hand caressingly along the polished banister rail. The gesture reminded Charlotte of her mother. 'Well, here we are.'

She opened the door to a new world for Charlotte. Peace enveloped her as she saw Jenny's books and pictures. Pillows had never seemed so soft before. She awoke, hours later, to look up at the stars through the great glass windows over Jenny's bed. Covered with Jenny's Mexican blankets, she felt her baby kicking ferociously against the wall of her womb. Even unfamiliar sounds were not alarming. The soft closing of a door on a lower landing seemed strangely comforting; the sighing of the wind round the chimney-pots, the rattling of a catch, were happy sounds. She lay for a while absorbing the miraculous feeling that tomorrow – tomorrow she would get up strong and refreshed to face life anew.

Rowan spent the night in Edinburgh, breaking the long journey to the Trossachs, sending a wire announcing his arrival the next day. Money was tight, but he booked in at the Cockburn Hotel where he had stayed before in more affluent circumstances, a hotel noted for its good cuisine and comfortable beds, which seemed to him Dickensian in flavour. Edinburgh's topography, its blend of old and new buildings, gracious crescents and monuments, had always appealed to him.

He walked to the Castle before dinner, but there were sentries on duty behind wefts of barbed wire; great searchlights mounted on the terraces. He stood for a while looking down at the crawling, panting trains beneath, making for the station on glittering lines. Trees sprayed soft green fountains of leaves in the public gardens edging Prince's Street. Day long he had wrestled with an overriding sense of unrest, the feeling that Charlotte was in danger.

Scotch beef was the finest in the world, but he had little appetite for dinner after all. The dining-room was filled with smart women escorted by uniformed men. He remembered the hotel in London. How curious that good hotels everywhere radiated the same aura of unreality, of transience, the same bee-like hum of conversation and discreet laughter, with under-stated lighting and soft carpets to muffle the sound of passing footsteps.

The war seemed far away from him now, a rapacious monster awaiting his return to the trenches. He was not afraid of dying. Death seemed, at times, an easy escape from the painful business of living. He strove to remember, as he drank his coffee, Hamlet's soliloquy. Charlotte would know the exact words:

> 'To die, to sleep –
> No more; and by a sleep to say we end
> The heart-ache and the thousand natural shocks
> That flesh is heir to. 'Tis a consummation
> Devoutly to be wish'd . . .'

Charlotte. He could not live without her, but he must. Shakespeare knew all about madness too, but Rowan could never hate or despise poor Alice Tanquillan. He pitied her with all his heart: a child born for tragedy. He remembered the sweetness and charm of her the night she stood on the terrace of the house in Chalice Walk, hands newly washed, her hair tied with a blue ribbon, saying in a light, clear voice: 'I feel I could take off and fly like an eagle. Oh, look at the sky. Isn't it beautiful? All those little, delicious pink clouds.'

Romilly stood in a fever of nervous apprehension, awaiting Rowan's arrival. She had combed and rearranged her hair ten times over during the past hour, had changed her dress three times; snapped at the servants; clung to Emily, driving her mother to the point of anger by her idiotic vanity.

'For heaven's sake, Romilly,' Emily said, 'try to behave naturally. I daresay Rowan is feeling apprehensive too.'

When the carriage arrived at the front door, Romilly ran onto the landing. 'He's here,' she cried, nervously twisting the beads at her throat, staring down the long staircase at the scene below: the driver carrying indoors a somewhat battered suitcase; Rowan standing on the threshold looking about him at the mounted heads on the walls, evidence of her grandfather's preoccupation with blood sport.

She remained half hidden by the turn of the stairs, thinking that he was much thinner than she remembered him, that his right arm looked stiff and awkward in the sleeve of his uniform. Her husband seemed like a stranger to her now. She clung despairingly to Emily's arm. 'I can't go down,' she said in a low voice, 'I just – can't!'

'Then I will,' Emily replied calmly, walking slowly to the head of the stairs; holding out her hands in a gesture of welcome, then hurrying as she saw his face uplifted to hers, the smile about his lips, his genuine pleasure at seeing her again.

'Emily,' he said, kissing first her hands then her cheeks, 'oh, Tante Emily, how well you look!'

'I wish I could say the same about you, Rowan,' she murmured. 'How – thin you are! Oh, my dear, forgive me. How tactless of me, but I have been so worried about you. How is your arm?'

'Much better.' He smiled down at her. 'If you knew how much I've looked forward to seeing you again.'

'This – all this – can't be very easy for you,' she said.

'It isn't.' He frowned slightly, remembering the reason why he had come; something he had half forgotten for the moment in his pleasure at meeting Emily. 'Where's Romilly?'

'I'm here, Rowan.'

He turned at the sound of her voice, and saw her, dressed in pink, hands worrying at the beads about her throat, standing on the staircase above him; hair drawn back in a loose chignon, the inevitable fringe curling softly above her eyes to cover the bump of her forehead.

'Romilly,' he said, moving towards her, knowing, as he did so, that he did not love her, that nothing had changed between them, that all he felt for her was the old compassion – the kind of compassion he felt for poor Alice Tanquillan. Suddenly, Alice and Romilly melted together in his mind as one person: the child and the child-woman, sharing similar ideas about love; seeing love as a kind of game linked to ensnaring; dressing up; a flaunting of sexual attractiveness. But love was nothing like that. Love was a meeting of minds; a blurred outline; an ideal. It was contentment; peace, rightness. It was a pregnant woman seen against the mist of early morning; a girl wearing a green dress pintucked to a tapering nineteen-inch waist; a woman with a bunch of violets pinned to her coat. Love was the quiet running of a great river making its way to the sea. Love, as he knew it, gave no quarter; asked none. Love was a constant torment. Love, when it happened, was bread, wine and meat; all that man could desire to fill to overflowing mind, heart, and eternity.

'Did you have a good journey?' Romilly asked stiffly.

'Very pleasant indeed, thank you.'

'We had better go to the drawing-room. My grandmother is anxious to meet you.' Romilly added, 'She knows nothing about – us. She's a very old lady. Oh lord, Rowan, did you have to wear that awful uniform?'

'Awful uniform?' He raised his eyebrows quizzically. 'I happen to feel rather proud of it.'

Romilly shrugged her shoulders. Somewhere, he thought, as they walked together to the drawing-room, in this great mausoleum of a house, is my son: flesh of my flesh. He said, looking with distaste at the carved elephant-tusks and kukris, the glassy-eyed antelope, stag and wildebeest staring down at him from the walls, 'I should like to see Berry. I thought we might have seen him first.'

'He's asleep,' Romilly replied. 'You can see him later, before he's settled down for the night.'

Emily said quietly, 'I see no reason why Rowan should not see his son now, asleep or awake. Grandma Beresford is probably sleeping too.' She smiled at Rowan, understanding his impatience. 'We could slip away for a few minutes. Grandmother scarcely knows one day from another now, bless her. When she meets you, she will not quite understand who you are or what you are doing here. That is the tragedy and blessing of old age, that memories, even unpleasant memories, are often more vital than the present. She still thinks Grandfather Beresford is alive and kicking, although she had a hell of a life with him when he was.'

'*Mother!*' Romilly pursed her lips. But Emily laughed. 'Come with me, Rowan,' she said conspiratorially. 'You go ahead, darling. Warn Grannie. We'll be down in a few minutes.' Truth to tell, Emily wanted Rowan to herself for a little while. She spoke lightly, but her heart was heavy, knowing that the situation between Rowan and Romilly would never be resolved. But she wanted Rowan to see his son; wanted to be alone with him when he did so, to see the expression in his eyes; just to be there in the room with him, to say whatever needed to be said by way of comfort or understanding.

She watched him as he crossed the room to the cot where his son lay sleeping; dismissed the nursemaid with a pleasant gesture; a smile. 'Wait in the other room,' she said in a low voice. The girl bobbed a curtsey, and withdrew.

The curtains were drawn; the room was in semi-darkness. The child's cheeks were as plump and pink as a Botticelli cherub's: starred with downturned lashes. He had fallen asleep sucking his thumb. His mouth was puckered.

Moved almost to tears, Rowan remembered a poem of Coventry Patmore's:

'Then, fatherly not less
Than I whom Thou hast moulded from the clay,

Thou'lt leave Thy wrath, and say,
"I will be sorry for their childishness."'

'Oh, Emily, I never knew it could be like this,' he said huskily. 'My son! My son!'

'I know, my dear.' She held out her hand to him. He clasped it momentarily, then covered his face with his hands. 'What the hell am I going to do?'

'How can I possibly tell you that?' she said quietly. 'How can anyone tell you? But, whatever you decide, remember that I want you to be happy. There has been too much grief already.'

'Romilly wrote me wanting a reconciliation. I saw my parents' influence behind it. They want me back, and they want my son. A good, obedient line of Tanquillans to ensure the continued flow of money into the coffers.' He looked down at his child. 'It will not happen, not if I can help it. I must talk to you, Emily.'

'Later. After dinner. Grandmother goes to bed early. By the way, I thought it expedient to give you a room along the landing from Romilly's.'

Grandmother Beresford resembled a very old toad spread panting on a rock. Her skin was dull and mottled, rubbery in texture, seamed with countless lines forming a network about lips and eyes. Her hands were flaccid, surprisingly big for a woman. Rowan thought that she resembled a Belgian peasant, one of those very old, quiet women who looked upon their vanished world with a kind of quiescent apathy, seeing the past as the only reality.

'She's deteriorated a lot since Christmas,' Emily said when the elderly nurse-companion had helped Mrs Beresford to the room on the ground floor which she used as a bedroom. 'The deterioration started when Edmund died. The suddenness of my husband's death was too much for her. She began living in the past. I daresay she will have forgotten who you are by morning.'

Romilly stared at Rowan across the table, a carved mahogany affair of banqueting-hall dimensions, laid for dinner at one end and lighted with a candelabra. She had spoken little since Rowan's arrival, as tongue-tied now as she used to be in the old days before their engagement, her finishing-school charm extinguished by recent events and the solid stone mansion which she so disliked. Old grievances welled up in her mind as she toyed with her food; solid slabs of mutton served with vegetables, Irish stew fashion, followed by a hearty suet pudding with custard, the usual kind of fare served by a dour servant; cooked by a woman who understood the value of starch and fat to keep out the cold of the Scottish winters, who made no concession to lighter menus even in summertime, for the house itself was always cold, winter and summer alike.

Romilly could think of nothing to say to Rowan; no questions to ask. She left the talking to Emily. War talk bored her to distraction. She compared Rowan to David McClean. Rowan was handsomer than David, but David looked splendid in his uniform whenever she met him in London, on leave from his regiment. Now she had no wish to listen to a re-hash of the sinking of the *Lusitania*; zeppelin raids, one as recently as last month on the outskirts of London, when Emily had insisted on taking the baby and herself, along with the servants, to the cellars of the house in Eaton Square until the sirens sounded the All Clear: a wretchedly chilling, frightening and uncomfortable experience.

Romilly wished to be alone with Rowan, to speak of things that really mattered, or so she had believed until, finding herself alone with him in the drawing-room after dinner, she remained tongue-tied. What she really wanted was to hear him say that he was sorry for all the heartbreak he had caused her, to tell her how grateful he was for her letter suggesting a reconciliation, not to stand there by the great stone fireplace looking down at the smouldering logs in the hearth, stirring them occasionally with the toe of his shoe. It seemed to her a breach of social etiquette that he had not changed for dinner. When, at last, she broke the silence to say so, Rowan smiled. 'I had nothing to change into,' he said. 'I gave up changing for dinner when I joined The Rangers. I'm no longer the Tanquillan son and heir. I gave up that kind of nonsense when I enlisted. I'm a poor man now, my dear, but surely you haven't forgotten? I thought the settlement between us was entirely fair. All my worldly goods in exchange for – freedom.'

'But surely, now that you are here, presumably in response to my letter – though you did not take the trouble to reply to it – things are different?'

'I could not reply to it,' he said quietly, 'since my right shoulder was shot to pieces at the time, and I am not ambidextrous.'

'Ambi– ?' She frowned. 'I don't understand the meaning of the word. Are you laughing at me?'

'God forbid that I should do that. I am simply trying to explain why I did not reply to your letter. I could not write with my left hand.'

'You haven't said a word about how I look; how well I am able to walk,' she said accusingly.

Rowan turned from his contemplation of the fireplace. 'You look charming,' he replied. 'Pink suits you. That dress must have cost a small fortune, and I always knew you would walk again one day if you put your mind to it.'

'And what about my son?' She stared at him hostilely beneath her carefully arranged fringe, angry because he was not saying what she had expected to hear. 'Why is it,' she blurted, 'that you always mock me? Why are you always so bloody heartless and superior?'

'Heartless? Superior? Is that how I strike you?' He smiled ruefully. '"Wad some power the giftie gie us, tae see ourselves as others see us." I never saw myself as being either, especially when I looked at my son – our son.'

'I had a terrible time bringing him into the world,' she said flatly, aware as she spoke, that she had somehow missed her chance with him, seeing the sudden bleakness in his eyes, knowing that if she had been content to say nothing at that moment, he might have turned to her with pride and pleasure in the small miracle their physical union had created. She made things worse. 'I'm sorry, Rowan,' she floundered, 'but it's the truth. I did have a horrible time. I very nearly died.' She flushed to the roots of her hair. 'Ask Mummy if you don't believe me.'

'I believe you, Romilly,' he said quietly, turning back to the fireplace, remembering Charlotte as he did so.

She clutched his arm, beside herself with anger because she had mismanaged the conversation. 'Is that all you have to say? I am still your wife. Berry is our child. I have a right to know what you intend to do about us. I made my intentions clear enough in my letter. You are a Tanquillan. My son is a Tanquillan! You made your point when you left me to enlist in the Army! But what exactly did you hope to achieve by that stupid gesture? Just look at yourself, Rowan, think how you have demeaned yourself and your family, your child, and me, by your damned – conceit. What are you now except a face, a number, a – a commonplace soldier!'

'You may be right. I am a soldier. Perhaps I was conceited in believing that in giving up wealth and position, I might learn some essential truth about myself. I imagined that somewhere existed a man I scarcely knew, whom I had never come to terms with, free and incorruptible. The idea was born a long time ago in my uncle, Oliver Tanquillan. You wondered once why I had never talked about him – because his name, his mode of living, was an embarrassment to my father. Yet Oliver Tanquillan was true to his own beliefs. Oliver wished to be a writer, I wanted to be a musician. The difference between us lay in that Oliver did what he wanted to do – unsuccessfully, I admit. I never even had the courage to try.'

Rowan's voice deepened. 'Oliver Tanquillan believed that he had something of importance to tell the world in his writing. And yet I saw that man smashed to the dust by the Tanquillans, by the mean spirit of my grandfather who disowned him because he dared to go his own way; by the even meaner spirit of my father; the snobbery of my mother. I saw him buried as a renegade who failed to live up to the Tanquillan concept of right and wrong. They buried him without compassion, with not one spark of regret. They buried him on a wild, winter day, and buried him right gladly, with a minimum of ritual, a maximum of hypocrisy in the shape of a decent oak coffin and a splendid wreath. Not from any sense of loyalty or love, but because, in their pride, they could not have borne to follow a pauper's coffin to its last resting place. I know. I heard them talking together before the funeral.'

Rowan's voice was hoarse now, with emotion. 'All Oliver Tanquillan had, by way of love, was a handful of snowdrops thrown on his coffin-lid by his child; in my own awareness of him as a man I had always admired . . .'

'Why are you telling me all this?' Romilly interrupted. 'I don't want to hear any more. It's macabre; horrible.'

'Because I hoped to make you understand why I enlisted. Why I became a – commonplace soldier.'

'But what has all this to do with us?'

'A great deal,' Rowan said in a softer voice, taking her hands in his. 'You asked me a question: what I intend to do about you and our son.' He paused. 'If I come through this war, I intend to find myself a job; any kind of job, I don't care what. It is too late now to become a musician, I know that, but I know shipping. I know about imports and exports. I speak French, German and Italian passably well . . .'

'What are you saying?' Romilly's face was a study of incredulity; disbelief laced with horror. 'You mean that you actually intend to carry on this stupid vendetta against your own parents?' She shook off his hands and swirled a pace or two in her pleated chiffon dress, then turned again angrily to face him, her cheeks suffused a deeper shade of pink than her frock. 'Are you seriously suggesting that I become the wife of a – a dock labourer, a shipping-clerk, or worse? You must be out of your mind if you imagine that I intend having my son brought up in a back street . . .'

'You haven't much faith in me,' he said ruefully.

'You have not given me much reason,' she replied coldly.

'I had rather you said nothing more for the time being. All I ask is that you think it over.'

'There's nothing to think over!'

'I thought you wanted a reconciliation,' he said slowly, noticing the old petulant expression about her lips and eyes, the spoilt child in her which never seemed far from the surface.

'What I want is a continuation of my standard of living for myself and my child,' she snapped, 'a husband of some

446

standing, doing the work he was brought up to do . . .'

'The old Tanquillan cipher, you mean?' He knew then that nothing he had tried to tell her had penetrated her mind.

'I'm going to bed now,' she said. 'You asked me to think things over. I suggest that you do the same.' She felt all-powerful, very sure of herself now, believing that she held the strongest weapon of all, her child, for she still generally thought of Berry as being solely her child. She turned at the door. 'The idea of our reconciliation came from your mother, a person I respect and admire. She at least has the name Tanquillan at heart if you have not. She and Sir Gervaise care what happens to me and my son, if you do not. And I imagine that you believe me to be as unattractive to other men as I am to yourself.' She gave a high-pitched laugh of triumph. 'What a fool you are, Rowan, if you believe that. I could marry again tomorrow if I were free of you. I could marry a man who would give me all that you never have; love and affection, a settled home for my son. Think about it!'

He smoked for a little while in contemplative silence. Half an hour later, he went upstairs to his room. A little before eleven o'clock, a knock came at his door. Emily Beresford entered. 'Forgive me, Rowan,' she said, 'I heard you come upstairs ages ago. You wanted to talk to me. Shall we go down to the drawing-room? I could do with a nightcap.'

He threw a handful of kindling, a fresh log on the fire, then crossed to the tray on the side-table, poured two glasses of whisky, handed one to Emily, and sat down in a chair opposite.

'I shall leave here tomorrow,' he said, cradling the glass in his hands, watching the kindling take hold from the fire-embers: tongues of flame licking a pine branch. 'I was a fool to have come in the first place.' He stirred, and smiled across at his mother-in-law, his beloved Tante Emily, a woman he loved and trusted.

'It's no use,' he said. 'The price is too high. Emotional blackmail . . .'

'Oh, my dear.'

'Perhaps it's my fault,' he said slowly, 'perhaps I am being stupid and bloody-minded in wanting to change the world a little, as Oliver Tanquillan wanted to change it. Romilly does not want her world changed, at any rate. I can't blame her for that.'

'You said you wanted to talk to me,' she reminded him, watching the firelight on his face, speaking in a low voice. The house was wrapped in darkness and silence apart from the staircase light and the pools of lamp and fireglow within the room. 'It is something private and personal. Something you haven't told Romilly?'

He glanced up at her, amazed by her perspicacity. 'I wanted you to know that I had not lied to you that day I told you I had been faithful to my wife. It was true at the time.'

'But not now?' Emily's voice held no reproach.

'Charlotte is expecting our child. Romilly will have reason enough to divorce me if she wants to.'

'You are going to tell her then?'

'Oh yes, eventually. Perhaps not here, not now. But she has a right to know.'

'Then you will be free to marry your Charlotte.' Emily's eyes were sad but understanding.

Rowan said heavily, 'No, that will not be possible. Charlotte is married to someone else now. She married to give our child a name, to give Romilly and myself a chance of happiness.'

'Then why spoil her gesture?' Emily asked, leaning forward, touching his hand. 'Why tell Romilly at all?'

'Because I hardly think that Romilly wants a reconciliation on my terms.' He smiled ruefully, tilting the whisky against the sides of the glass, noticing the way the firelight turned the liquid a deep, shining amber, how the intricately cut pattern on the glass sparkled and scintillated in a spurt of orange flame. 'What we said to each other in this room convinced me of that. I said I didn't blame her, and I don't. It was unfair of me to expect her to leap at the prospect of – love in a cottage.' He raised his head. 'I can never go back, you see, to my old life.'

'Not even for the sake of your son?'

'My son.' Rowan's eyes darkened as he remembered the sleeping child in its cot, the indescribable feeling of love and tenderness he had experienced on seeing Berry for the first time. 'That is why I asked you what the hell am I going to do. Whichever way I turn, I face a blank wall. If I stick to my guns, I shall lose Romilly and my son. If I do not, I shall lose myself and Charlotte.' He laid his hand urgently on Emily's. 'What *shall* I do?'

He's so young, so vulnerable, she thought. She had never loved him more than she did at that moment. She said quietly. 'Why ask me? You answered your own question when you said that you could never go back to your old life.' Her face was very tender by firelight, the lines of maturity washed over and softened with the glow from the burning logs, so that Rowan saw her as she must have looked as a young woman. 'But for what it's worth, why leave here tomorrow? Give yourself more time. Be gentle with yourself and Romilly. Get to know your son.' She smiled to ease his tension. 'Besides, you need fattening, and fresh air. Above all, you need peace and quiet. There's an abundance of everything you need here. The hills around this ghastly old house are full of fresh air. I suggest you walk in them until you are so ravenous that even Cook's boiled beef, carrots, dumplings, Irish stew and steamed puddings will seem akin to Tournedos Parisien, Noisettes of Lamb Garni, and Crème Brulée served by an attentive French waiter in the dining-room at the Ritz Hotel. Grandfather Beresford laid down a good cellar, and I know you have a palate for wine, though how Gevrey Chambertin Clos St Jacques and Grand Montrachet will go down with boiled beef and dumplings, I'm not too sure. Besides, there's a splendid, overstrung German grand piano in the music room, and a library full of books. So won't you stay on for a while, if only for my sake?'

'If you really want me to,' he said softly, wondering why Romilly possessed so little of her mother's warmth, charm – and kindness.

CHAPTER SIXTEEN

Charlotte's new day was here, was now. Awakening, deeply refreshed, her first sensation was that of holiday in a great city bathed with warm sunshine, laced with unexpected sounds from the street outside: the churning of a barrel-organ, the clattering wheels of trams sparking their way along wide, lively thoroughfares, the clip-clop of horses' hooves as the milkman made his deliveries, the clanging of churn-lids, the man's cheerful whistling and called-out greetings as maids and housewives hurried outdoors clutching milk jugs draped with bead-hung muslin to keep out the flies.

Charlotte watched from the hall passage as Bridie McKenna joined a group of women on the pavement, milk-jug in hand. The milkman was a thickset elderly man wearing leggings polished to the sheen of horse-chestnuts in autumn. For one moment he reminded her of Will, and the clanking of the churns, the dipping of the ladle brought back to her a memory of home: the milkman's horse and float turning into St Martin's Square; of Filly rushing out with her bead-covered milk jug on summer mornings long ago; how the milkman had always dipped his ladle once, and once again, for good measure.

She turned away then, her sense of holiday suddenly expelled as the truth dawned on her that she was virtually homeless and penniless, reliant on a stranger's goodwill for her very existence. Perhaps she had been too optimistic, too trusting in seeing Bridie McKenna as her salvation. How could she rely on a nature as warm and outgoing even as Bridie's to see her through this present crisis? Bridie had done her best for her, but she could not impose upon her good nature any longer.

'What on earth's the matter with you this morning?' Bridie asked as they sat together over breakfast in the back room with the horsehair sofa and the singing canaries. 'You look as if you had lost a penny and found a farthing.'

Charlotte said, 'I must find myself a job; somewhere to live.'

Bridie raised her eyebrows in surprise. 'Why? Don't you like it here? Weren't you comfortable last night?'

'Please don't think that. I love it here, but I can't afford to stay. I counted up last night and I have exactly two pounds, ten shillings and fivepence in the world.'

'You're not thinking very straight are you, my dear?' Bridie said, pouring herself a second cup of tea. 'If you can't afford to stay here, where could you afford to stay? Do you imagine I would turn you out in the street in your condition? As for finding a job . . .' She raised her eyebrows and smiled. Her skin, Charlotte noticed, was paperfine, seamed with tiny lines about her eyes and lips, as if the years had begun a drying-out process of the fine living tissue, and yet there was something youthful about her in the clearness of her eyes, the quick way she moved and spoke. In common with most Scotswomen, Bridie possessed a forthright compassion neither fulsome nor maudlin.

She said, 'I don't wish to pry, but don't you think you had better tell me something about yourself so that I can help you? Nothing you say to me will go any further.' She touched Charlotte's hand lightly across the table. 'You can talk to me while I feed the birds.'

And so Charlotte told her story haltingly, in a low voice, knotting her hands together when she came to the night she had spent in the barn. She described how, in the early hours of next morning, she had gone back to the house to gather up a few belongings and walked the three miles to Devizes, glancing back over her shoulder all the way to make sure she wasn't being followed.

Bridie listened in silence as she filled the seed-dishes in the cages and replenished the water-pots. When Charlotte had finished speaking, Bridie said, 'Thank you for confiding in me. What we have to consider next is how to proceed. First and foremost, you may put aside any notion of leaving this house. You are welcome to stay for as long as you like.'

'But I must pay my way,' Charlotte said.

451

'But what could you possibly do?'

'I was trained as a dressmaker. That is something I could do sitting down if I could find someone willing to employ me.'

'A dressmaker!' Bridie laughed delightedly. 'My dear. That's it!' She opened the windows leading to a long, overgrown garden, letting in the sunlight. 'I have a sewing-machine. We could place an advertisement in the corner-shop window. I'll be your first customer.' She sat down at the table, face aglow. 'There are lots of women in the neighbourhood who would be glad of a dressmaker. I could rent you a room on the first landing at five shillings a week, and provide free board until you've had time to build up a clientele. When you've started earning, you can pay me back at so much a week.' She laughed. 'Knowing your fiercely independent nature – which sticks out like a sore thumb, if you don't mind my saying so – this would seem an ideal solution. What do you think? Is it a deal?'

'It's a deal. And – thank you. Thank you.' Charlotte's eyes blurred. Laying her head on her arms, she wept slow tears of relief, not realizing until that minute how tired she was both physically and mentally. Bridie let her cry, understanding that this was something necessary, a release from the traumatic events of the past few days.

Kitty Tanquillan tethered the trap in the yard and entered the farmhouse, walking stiffly, her face betraying the anxiety she felt at Charlotte's disappearance. 'Will,' she called, 'where are you?' It was a warm morning but the room felt chill and inhospitable. The hearth was filled with the ashes of a dead fire, the table was littered with soiled cups and plates. The curtains had not been drawn back. Clicking her tongue, she remedied that at once as the dogs came bounding downstairs and Will appeared on the landing.

'Well,' she snapped, ensconcing herself in the wing chair near the empty hearth and shooing away the dogs, 'what have you got to say for yourself? Just look at you. And have you any idea of the time? You should have been at work hours ago! What do you think I am running, a farm or a home for inebriates? What in God's name is happening? What have you done to

Charlotte? She was seen at Devizes station early this morning. If any harm comes to her, I warn you, Will Oakleigh, that you will find no friend in me.'

Will came slowly downstairs, sat in the chair opposite and buried his head in his hands. 'It's like a nightmare,' he muttered. 'I don't know what came over me. As God is my witness, I never meant to touch her. I would never hurt Charlotte. I love her too much.'

He raised his head, seeing Miss Kitty's face through a mist, eyes red-rimmed from sleeplessness. He had wakened from his drunken stupor in the early hours of the morning, had roamed the house and the fields, the barn and outhouses, looking for Charlotte; and gone to the summerhouse in Sweet Water Meadow thinking to find her there. Had he done so he would have thrown himself at her feet and begged her forgiveness. He said, brokenly, 'You say she went to Devizes station? Oh, God. She must have walked all the way there. But are you sure?'

'Quite sure,' Kitty said coldly. 'News has a way of travelling fast in this village. Cook's son is a porter there. She bought a ticket to London. According to him, she was in a dreadful state, as well she might be. Did you beat her, Will, in your drunken rage, after you left the White Swan?' Contempt curled the old woman's lips.

'No, I did not beat her,' he said thickly. 'I wanted to. I wanted to hurt her when Alice told me that she had been with Tanquillan.' He stared into the bewildering vortex of his own jealousy. 'I couldn't bear it,' he muttered between clenched teeth, 'I tried to, but I couldn't. I kept on seeing them together, making love. Oh, Christ!'

'Alice told you that?' Kitty wrinkled her forehead, beginning to understand, 'And you believed her? How could you?' She recalled what Rowan had said to her in the drawing-room, 'I did the unforgivable thing, I laughed at her.' So that was it. Jealousy, the bitterest, cruellest of all human emotions, lay at the bottom of all this. She would have been glad at that moment of a blurred brain in a stronger body, a kind of mumbling forgetfulness common to most women of her age. 'If you really loved Charlotte,' she said, 'you would have trusted her, and if you were not man enough to accept the truth, the fact of her pregnancy, you should not have asked her to marry you.' She leaned forward in her chair, speaking in a clear cold voice. 'Presumably you would have treated her more kindly had she indulged in a sexual fling with some man she did not care tuppence about. This destructive jealousy of yours came about when you knew who the father was. That's true, isn't it?'

'I knew she still loved him,' Will said, rubbing his hand wearily over his eyes. 'She married me not loving me.'

'You knew that at the time. But she trusted and respected you. She believed, as I did, that in time you would build a good life together. But you gave her no time at all. Worse still, you were prepared to listen to lies about her, to drive her away. I find that hard to forgive. But where is she? We must find her. How much money did she take with her? Think, man!'

Will shrugged helplessly. 'I don't know. Not much. She had about three pounds in her purse, I reckon.' His mouth worked awkwardly.

'Does she know anyone in London? Did she ever receive any letters?'

'Yes. Someone called Annie wrote to her regularly, and the governess who was here last summer.'

'Jenny! Of course, Jenny Carfax. But she's nursing somewhere in France,' Kitty said sharply. 'Are the letters in Charlotte's room?'

'I don't know.' Will shook his head.

'Then go and look!'

He got up, went upstairs, and came back with a small bundle of letters tied with blue ribbon.

'Give them to me.' Kitty rose stiffly to her feet, leaning heavily on her silver-knobbed walking-cane. 'And now do something about your appearance, then get about your work. Keep your own counsel, above all keep away from the White Swan.' As she turned to leave, she remembered an old French saying: 'tout comprendre c'est tout pardonner' – to know everything is to understand everything. Her face softened slightly. Poor Will was paying a high price for his jealousy, an all too human emotion. Now she must deal with Alice

454

Tanquillan whose lying tongue had brought about this state of affairs, and decide what to do about her. If necessary, the girl must go to Latimer for treatment.

At Grey Wethers, she sent for Alice to come to her study. The school in Devizes had not yet broken up for the summer, but the building was under repair and the girls had been given a few days' holiday until the builders had finished re-slating the roof.

Alice appeared jauntily, dressed in her riding-habit. Her eyes were exceptionally bright, her cheeks flushed with excitement at the prospect of riding her horse, Tosca. Today was the day Will Oakleigh had promised to raise the jumps for her.

Kitty turned away from the window as the girl entered the room. 'I think you know why I have sent for you,' she said in a clear voice.

'No, Aunt.' Alice surveyed the old woman serenely, all wide-eyed innocence.

Perhaps she really does not know what she has done, Kitty thought, any more than her poor mother knew what she was doing when she attacked that prison wardress. 'Why did you lie to Will Oakleigh?' she asked. 'Why did you tell him that you had seen Charlotte and Rowan together in the summerhouse?'

Alice raised her eyebrows in surprise. 'Because I did see them together.'

'Doing what?'

'I don't know what you mean.' Alice lowered her eyes suddenly as she saw Kitty Tanquillan's cold expression.

'I think that you do. You lied, didn't you, when you told Will that you had seen them – making love?'

Alice laughed defiantly as she looked up. 'What if I did? I just wanted to get even with them, that's all, for loving each other more than they loved me! I heard every silly, simpering word they said to each other! It made me sick to hear them! Rowan laughed at me when I told him how much I loved him, but he didn't laugh at Charlotte.' Her face twisted suddenly into an expression of hatred. 'If it wasn't for Charlotte, Rowan might have loved me . . .'

'Alice,' Kitty said quietly, 'you are only a child.'

'No, I'm not! I'm a woman! That is the mistake you've all made! I think as a woman! I feel as a woman! I hate all of you because no-one has ever understood that: the way I feel!' She ran out of the room, tears streaming down her cheeks, her mind in a turmoil.

'Come back, Alice! Where are you going?' But the girl was running blindly along the terrace, snapping off flower-heads with her riding crop as she went, her long skirt brushing the paving-stones as she stumbled towards the stables where the stable-lad, young Alan Feetenby, was busy saddling Tosca.

'Where's Will Oakleigh?' she demanded.

'Will? I dunno. I ain't seen hide nor hair of him this morning, miss.'

'Then I'll ride without him! You can raise the hurdles for me!'

'Not without Will's permission,' the lad said decisively. 'I'd get the rough end of his tongue if I did anything without his say so.' Alan was sixteen, a brawny youth slow of speech but quick of intellect. 'It would be more than my job's worth. Just calm down, miss. He'll be here in a few minutes, I reckon.' He grinned amiably, thinking that Miss Tanquillan's niece was a proper little spitfire and no mistake, a bit young and skinny, but quite beddable. Then, 'Here, what are you doing?' he gasped as Alice snatched the reins from his hands and led Tosca to the stone mounting-block in the stable yard. A fearful thought struck him. 'You ain't gonna take that horse over the jumps by yourself, are you? You know Miss Tanquillan's instructions! You know you ain't supposed to do that!'

Alice laughed as she looped her knee over the side-saddle, dug her heel hard into the mare's flank and cantered smartly towards the paddock.

The sun was extraordinarily bright, glinting on each branch and twig of the trees surrounding the paddock. The whole world seemed ablaze with sunlight as the mare lifted its hooves in rhythm to her fast-beating heart. She loved the glare, the thump, thump of the saddle beneath her, the brilliance of the sunshine which matched the feeling she had of fireworks exploding inside her head. Her mind was ablaze with colour and light; shredded with sounds and memories, like the brightly-coloured pieces of a kaleidoscope shifting and changing so quickly that she could scarcely catch at one memory before another edged in to take its place. She saw the jumps in front of her, as tiny and inconsequential as a pile of matchsticks. The far end of the paddock with its perimeter of trees and fences seemed nothing more to her than another pile of matchsticks. The drumming of the mare's hooves was like a heady drug. She whipped the horse to a mad gallop, dug her heel more firmly into its quivering flesh as she approached the high, split-rail fence beneath the trees. The mare uttered a high-pitched whinny as it rose into the air . . .

Will Oakleigh walked, head uplifted to the sky, breathing in the scent of summer grass and earth beneath his feet. He had been driven to the Downs by his dire need to be alone for a while among the silent hills, to ask God's forgiveness for what he had done to Charlotte.

'What kind of a man am I?' He asked the question aloud, remembering Charlotte's sweetness and beauty, the way she had worked about the farm, how bravely she had faced up to the death of her brother, asking nothing more of him than his quiet understanding of her heartbreak, how much he had hurt her by his narrow-minded jealousy. He thought, despairingly, that he would give anything to have her back again. Kitty Tanquillan's words had bitten into him deeply, making him realize what a poor fool he had been to doubt Charlotte's integrity.

I must find her, he thought, turning on the crest of the hill to look down at the farm and village spread below him like a child's toy; the intricacy of grey buildings and fields hedged about with the burgeoning trees of summer, like a patchwork quilt of green and grey and gold washed over with the quiet blue of the sky, with tiny white cloud-patterns chequering the fields, clouds which might blow up later into massed galleons sailing before a rising wind.

He had shaved off his overnight growth of stubble, swilled his head under the kitchen tap and changed into a clean shirt. Now, walking quickly downhill, he glanced at his pocket-watch; remembered that he had promised Alice Tanquillan a riding-lesson at eleven o'clock. Alice Tanquillan. He stood for a moment looking down at the farm-buildings; the paddock. The last person he wanted to see today of all days was the girl responsible for his troubles. He screwed up his eyes against the sun, wrestling with his conscience, realizing that Alice was not entirely to blame for his misery. And then he saw her taking the mare over the jumps, faster and faster.

Gripped with a sudden fear, he started to run downhill; felt the soft grass and earth cascading, with showers of dislodged pebbles, beneath his feet as the mare, with a terrified whinny, cleared the paddock fence and galloped, out of control, towards the plantation where, on spring evenings, he went shooting to bring the crow population under control. Alice was clinging to the mare's saddle. He heard her shrill scream of terror as the low-hanging boughs closed in on her.

Scrambling, sliding and cursing, Will plunged through the trees to reach the runaway mare before the girl was unseated, and stood, for a minute, winded, arms outstretched, as the horse galloped into view. Tosca reared up, pawing the air with her hooves as Will caught at the bridle. He felt the burning pain of running leather between his outstretched hands before the mare's front hooves came down on him, smashing him to the ground. He lay sprawled on the grass, a trickle of blood staining his lips as the mare stood quietly, twitching its ears, now that its headlong flight was over.

Alice got down from Tosca's back as best she could. She was kneeling beside Will when the stable-lad came running through the paddock gate. Will had fallen on a sharp stone. The back of his head was covered with blood. Alice remembered the day she had found her father lying in a pool of blood in the room above the pawnbroker's shop. The kaleidoscope images were crowding in faster now. She saw, not Will Oakleigh, but her father lying there. She remembered with a terrible clarity, the sharp, sour smell of whisky; drawn blinds with yellowing calico strips, a typewriter on a green chenille tablecloth. She was a child again, crying for her dead father, uncaring of her fine clothes.

She stared up unseeingly at the stable-lad as he knelt beside

Will, chafing his hands, pressing his ear to Will's breast to catch a heartbeat. 'It's no use,' the lad said bleakly, 'he's gone. Will's dead.'

'No, he isn't. He can't be!' Alice began to whimper like a little girl lost in the dark. 'Will, listen to me. I lied about Rowan and Charlotte. You must forgive me, Will! Please say that you forgive me!'

'It's no use, miss. I'd best fetch someone from the house. Leave him be, Miss Alice, there ain't nothing you can say to him now that will do any good.' The lad snatched off his cap as he rose unsteadily to his feet. 'He were a good man, Will Oakleigh. One of the best.' He said vehemently, 'He died saving your bloody neck!' His anger broke suddenly. 'Well, I hope you're satisfied! It's all your fault! I told you not to go riding alone, but would you take any notice of me? Not you, you spoilt little bitch! You bloody, spoilt little bitch!'

Later, kneeling at Kitty Tanquillan's feet in the study, Alice said, 'I don't know what's wrong with me, but it must be something terrible.' She brushed her hand across her forehead as if dispelling imaginary spiders' webs. 'I don't mean to be wicked, but I can't help it. It's as if I'm two different people in one body. One minute I'm calm and quiet and the world seems such a beautiful place to be alive in. The next minute, I want to hurt people. My brain runs hot with mischief. I feel like a goddess when that happens, as if I were all-powerful, as if the people around me were puppets dancing to my tune. That's the way I felt today, in the paddock. I knew I could jump as high as the moon if I wanted to.' She laid her head in Kitty's lap. 'My brain feels like a great dead weight inside my skull at times, then nothing I do or say or feel is real any more. Why am I like this? Please help me, Aunt Kitty! Please, *please*, help me!'

'I will help you, my dear,' Kitty said, laying compassionate hands on the girl's trembling shoulders. 'I'll speak to Mr Latimer . . .'

'Latimer?' Alice crinkled her brow. 'What has he to do with this?'

'Claude Latimer is a – psychiatrist – the best man in his field.

He will be able to help you if anyone can . . .'

'A – psychiatrist?' Alice stared up into Kitty's eyes. 'Am I mad, then? Was my mother mad? Is that why she left us so suddenly? Is that why my father would never speak of her? Why he would never tell me what had become of her? I'm damned then, aren't I?' She rose to her feet. The shock of Will's death had had a sobering effect on her. She still could not believe that he was dead. She had not believed it even when the doctor came, and men from the farm, to carry Will's body back to the farmhouse on a hurdle. She had stood, unnoticed, holding Tosca's reins, as people came and went, speaking in low voices, asking questions. 'How did the accident happen?' 'Where had Will been all morning?' Then the stable-lad said something, and all eyes were suddenly turned on Alice, standing quietly under the trees, staring at Will's body like someone in a trance. The the doctor said to one of the farm-hands, 'She shouldn't be here. Take her back to the house! Has anyone told Miss Tanquillan?'

The man, dangling his cap, said that young Alan Feetenby had been up to the house to tell the mistress what had happened; that the old lady had taken the news badly. 'I'd better get along to attend to her,' the doctor said, 'since there's nothing to be done for Will Oakleigh.'

Alice remembered that someone had taken Tosca's reins from her at that moment, and led her away from the clearing where Will lay on his back, a light breeze ruffling his hair, looking for all the world as if he had lain down to sleep for a little while beneath the outspread trees, amid a myriad gentle, fluttering, early summer leaves, with dappled sun-spots, like golden pennies, touching his cheeks.

Now, standing quietly in Kitty Tanquillan's study, Alice said, 'I tried to tell Will how sorry I was that I had lied to him, but he wouldn't listen. Now I'm going to see Charlotte, to ask her forgiveness.'

Kitty said dully, 'Charlotte isn't here. She – she's gone away.' The old woman's eyes were filled with tears. 'Just go to your room, child, and try to rest.' Will's death had shocked her beyond belief. She felt old and very tired, incapable of coping with the tragedy which had overtaken all of them. If only Rowan were here. She wondered if she had tempted fate in wishing that she had a blurred mind in an ageing body, for she could not think clearly any longer; scarcely knew what to do first to bring order from chaos. But at least she had discovered Jenny Carfax's address in London from the little bundle of letters tied in blue ribbon.

As Alice walked slowly upstairs to her room, Kitty Tanquillan knew that she must begin to think clearly again; that everything depended on her. Her eyes fell suddenly on the face of a golden-haloed madonna. She stood quietly for a moment looking at it, until her brain began to function again.

Sitting at her desk, she wrote two letters in a shaky hand. One to Rowan, the other to Claude Latimer. That done, she gave them to Rivers to post. Then, waving aside the old man's help, she draped a shawl about her shoulders, grasped the handle of her walking-stick, and walked uprightly down the lane to the farmhouse to pay her last respects to Will Oakleigh.

The house was filled with quiet folk in need of guidance: farm-labourers and their wives solemnly gathered together, not knowing what to do in the absence of Will's wife. And so Kitty Tanquillan gave her orders succinctly: 'You, Fred Taylor, take the dogs for the time being. You, Joseph, put the cats out in the barn. Mary Taylor, you had best put the kettle on to boil; make tea for everyone.'

And, 'Yes, ma'am,' they said respectfully, recognizing the voice of authority. Then Mrs Battye, the churchwarden's wife who had got wind of the trouble and stuck her nose in where it wasn't wanted, said slyly, 'We didn't know quite what to do for the best with Will's wife away so suddenly, and no-one knowing where to find her. Seems odd, doesn't it, Mrs Oakleigh going off to London in such a hurry, at the crack of dawn; in such a state by all accounts.'

Kitty Tanquillan drew back her shoulders proudly and stared Mrs Battye straight in the eye. 'By whose account?' she asked. 'Don't tell me that you, of all people, listen to gossip! And you a good Christian woman! Mrs Oakleigh went to London urgently to say goodbye to her brother before he sails for France!' She had dealt with the Mrs Battyes of this world a hundred times before.

'Oh, I'm sorry. Then Mrs Oakleigh will be back in time for her husband's funeral?' Mrs Battye asked, subdued by the towering presence of Kitty Tanquillan.

'Most certainly,' Kitty said, turning away. 'And now, I'm going upstairs to Will.'

In her room, Alice Tanquillan slowly divested herself of her riding-habit and put on the green dress that Charlotte had made for her. The only person in the world who mattered to her now was Charlotte. Charlotte, who had stolen her way into her heart on that bleak morning long ago, when she had stood poised on the jetty staring down at the hidden rocks beneath, listening to the mesmerizing whisper of the tide ebbing and flowing, ebbing and flowing with an eternal heartbeat. She remembered suddenly the words of 'Dover Beach', her father's favourite poem; put up her hand to smooth her hair; whispered,

> 'Listen! you hear the grating roar
> Of pebbles which the waves suck back, and fling,
> At their return, up the high strand,
> Begin, and cease, and then again begin,
> With tremulous cadence slow, and bring
> The eternal note of sadness in . . .
>
> Ah, love, let us be true
> To one another! . . .'

Smiling, Alice tucked a few pound notes inside a little Dorothy-bag Aunt Kitty had given her last birthday. She crept quietly down the carved oak staircase, and walked, in her fluttering green dress with the lace collar, down the long, empty road to Devizes station, where she bought a ticket to London.

The man in the ticket-office, who knew her, said, 'Where are you off to, young miss?'

Alice smiled at him charmingly; said primly, 'I'm going to see my father. He sent for me, you know, to stay with him for a little while.'

The man, a simple Wiltshire peasant, believed her.

CHAPTER SEVENTEEN

Emily's words, 'be gentle with yourself and Romilly', sprang to mind as Rowan walked the Scottish hills, the scent of pine, fir and spruce in his nostrils. The war seemed far away here among the singing burns and craggy heights. He had not realized how tired he was until he lay on springy turf beside bubbling water.

He thought, watching the sky between branches, that he had been too harsh with Romilly when, stung by her attitude, he had voiced his feelings about Oliver Tanquillan; his hopes for the future. Could he really expect his wife to leap insecurity? That was what Emily had meant by being gentle. Nothing could be solved in a moment; old wounds must be healed with tact and understanding. He smiled to himself, remembering the pleasure he had found in his son, already betraying signs of a decisive personality in his dislike of bathtime, his penchant for one particular teddy bear. Even Romilly seemed happier, more relaxed when she held her son in her arms.

He thought, on his way back to the house, which lay in the valley below, a grey stone mansion with dunce-capped turrets, that Emily in her quiet way had paved the road to a better understanding between himself and Romilly, realizing that he needed a period of rest and reflection. He had found considerable pleasure in the library and music room; delving into the works of Sir Walter Scott and Robert Louis Stevenson, playing the piano after dinner, although he knew that he would never play again as he used to, since his right arm felt stiff and awkward at times. Emily had even used her personal wizardry to persuade the cook to serve lighter meals; had spread her warmth and influence as a comforting cloak about the house, charming the servants and the nurse who cared for old Mrs Beresford.

Rowan could see, as he strode across the lawn, that tea had been set on the terrace. Romilly, in a light summer blouse and skirt, had the baby beside her in his perambulator. Old Mrs Beresford was seated in a high-backed cane chair next to Emily who was pouring the tea, her wide-brimmed straw hat tilted against the glare of the sun, smiling as he took the chair next to hers. 'Just in time,' she said. 'Did you enjoy your walk?'

'Very much.' He looked across at his son, thinking how much babies enjoyed the world they inhabited. Even the little children he had seen on those long, muddy roads in Belgium stared with solemn, lustrous eyes at birds in flight and pointed with delight at the farm animals tied to the backs of lumbering carts and wagons. He and Bert Hoskins had watched, with the rest of their battalion during enforced rests on their way to the Front, the children's slow smiles at proffered biscuits, bars of chocolate, or even slices of unbuttered bread. He remembered that men, very often short of rations themselves, never quite certain of their next meal, gained pleasure in giving away the precious contents of their food parcels to the tiny victims of a world gone mad.

Strange, he had thought the war far away from him out there on the hills among the curling bracken and lark-song. But how could he forget for more than a few hours the sights and sounds and impressions which had coloured his thinking for the past months?

Emily was being patient and kind with her mother-in-law, tucking a serviette beneath the old woman's chin, holding the teacup for her, feeding a cucumber sandwich between her slackened lips. He stirred uneasily in his chair, fighting back a feeling that this was a scene from a play; nothing whatever to do with reality. It occurred to him, as he watched Romilly nibbling a scone; raising her hand occasionally to smooth her hair, or to twitch away, with scarcely concealed irritation, an intrusive insect, that if he went back to his old life, all his days would be like this one – a moment's freedom, then back to the puppet-theatre with Romilly playing the part of a young wife and mother in love with her husband, his son being engineered to fit his role as a Tanquillan. He excluded Emily from the puppet-theatre image, Emily who had gained in stature since the death of her husband, who had taken life by the horns and come smiling through her own personal trials and tribulations. A woman who understood the deep, underlying passions of the human heart while preserving a calm, unruffled exterior. He felt, in that moment, that he wanted to lay his head in her lap, to feel her warm, compassionate fingers on his hair, to hear her say: 'I understand, my dear. I understand what you are going through.'

Almost against his will, he thought of Charlotte; longed for Charlotte: remembered the words of Alice Meynell's 'Renouncement':

> 'With the first dream that comes with the first sleep
> I run, I run, I am gathered to thy heart.'

Romilly had said something to him which he had not heard. He frowned perplexedly as he looked across at her. 'I'm sorry, my dear. What did you say?'

'It doesn't matter!' She was sulking now; cheeks reddened, staring at him beneath the absurd fringe of curls on her forehead. 'I asked you to pick up Berry's teddy bear, that's all. But you were obviously miles away.'

'Oh, I'm sorry.' He rose to his feet to retrieve his son's toy as a servant came towards them with a letter on a salver.

'This came by the late post, madam,' he said stiffly. 'It's for Mr Tanquillan.'

Rowan stooped to recover the teddy bear; straightened up, and glanced at the writing on the envelope. 'It's from Aunt Kitty,' he said, turning the letter in his fingers, smiling across the table at Emily. 'I'll read it later.'

'Perhaps you had better read it now,' Emily said, 'it might be important.'

'Very well, if you'll excuse me.' He tore open the letter, read it, and turned quickly to face Romilly. 'I – I'm so sorry,' he said dully, 'I must leave at once!'

Emily rose to her feet. 'Is it bad news?'

'Yes, I'm afraid it is. My aunt is in trouble. I must go back to

Wiltshire as quickly as possible. There has been an accident . . . Will Oakleigh, Aunt Kitty's farm manager, is dead. I'm so sorry, Tante Emily, but I must catch the first available train.' He excused himself and strode quickly to the house to begin packing.

Romilly came to his room as he was strapping his suitcase. 'I don't understand any of this,' she said petulantly. 'Why should you rush off to Wiltshire simply because your aunt's farm manager met with some kind of an accident? Surely to heaven there are plenty of servants about the place to help her? I don't want you to go! Why on earth should you? Your aunt must be a very possessive woman, ruining your leave this way.'

'There's more to it than that,' Rowan said quietly. 'You had better read the letter.'

He waited for her reaction; heard her sharp intake of breath, watched her cheeks flood with colour. 'So that's it!' She flung the letter on the floor as if she had touched something unclean. 'You intend rushing off to Wiltshire because of – *her*! Charlotte Grayler! No, don't touch me! I might have guessed. No wonder you went to Wiltshire in the first place instead of coming straight here! This letter makes it abundantly clear that something is going on between the pair of you. And I thought all along it was Alice.'

'You don't begin to understand,' he said wearily. 'Charlotte married my aunt's farm-manager, Will Oakleigh, the man who was killed. I don't understand any more than you do why she has disappeared.' Rowan's moment of truth had come. He said, 'But I must find her. She is expecting a child, you see. My child.'

He thought for a moment that Romilly was going to faint. The hot tide of colour in her cheeks drained away as suddenly as it had appeared. She clutched at the edge of a table for support. Her voice when it came was low and harsh. '*Your* child!'

'You had better sit down. I'll get you some brandy.' He attempted to hold onto her but she turned on him in a fury. 'I don't want any brandy! I don't want anything from you ever again. You have hurt me, lied to me, patronized me for the last time.' She stood with her back to the table, staring at him, mouthing her contempt. 'All that rubbish about what we would do when the war is over. All that cant and hypocrisy about wanting to start a new life with Berry and me.' She gave a low, scornful, hysterical laugh. 'Well, you can say goodbye to both of us now! Go to your bloody mistress. I'll divorce you, do you hear me? I'll divorce you!' Her eyes were brilliant with tears. She ran one hand carelessly through her hair, disarranging the curls on her forehead, revealing the high, bumpy brow which she had kept so carefully hidden throughout the years. He felt suddenly touched by the sight of it, as bare and scrubbed-looking as a child's knee.

'Yes, I expected you would when you knew the truth,' he said gently. 'I'm sorry you found out this way. I meant to tell you under less dramatic circumstances.' He smiled briefly. 'I had hoped you would understand.' His heart yearned after his son, but he knew where his heart belonged. He experienced, despite his anguish, a great shining moment of relief that there would be no more lies between them. He went on in a low voice, understanding the pain his wife was suffering, wanting to comfort her, 'You told me that you could marry again if you were free. I assume you meant David McClean . . .'

'Yes, David McClean,' she said proudly; defiantly. 'David is deeply in love with me, as I am with him.'

'Then I think that you should marry him if he can make you happy. Perhaps this is the right time to let go of your childhood dreams of me – the boy next door. I was never the right man for you, my dear Romilly.' He uttered the endearment in all sincerity, remembering her as the little girl who had always been a part of his life, whom he had never loved more than he did at that moment, as a man might love a small, unhappy sister.

He turned to the window to stare out at the rolling hills in the distance, at pine trees adumbrated against the blue summer sky, etched like pen-and-ink drawings on a vast azure canvas stretched tautly behind a vista of shimmering grass and fern threaded with glistening water, with tiny burns burbling down from the craggy heights where eagles built their nests and brought up their young to fly high, wide and free, with the wind

467

beneath their wings. He saw, in his mind's eye, a solemn little boy staring at a thrown-away teddy bear; felt the tug of tears in his throat as he thought of his son. 'The pity of it is, that I love Berry so much,' he said.

Romilly said dully, 'the pity of it is that I thought I loved you.'

Grey Wethers was in darkness when Rowan arrived there early next morning. He had walked from Devizes station watching the spread of dawn in the east; seeing all the old familiar landmarks – the humped Downs beneath an iridescent, mother-of-pearl sky; hedgerows and trees, blossom-bent; ditches alive with straggling campion and cow parsley, with birdsong, and the tiny scutterings of early morning creatures.

He knocked briefly at the front door; heard the drawing back of chains and bolts, the scrape of the key in the lock, and smiled apologetically at old Rivers standing there in his night-shirt, his feet encased in carpet slippers.

'Oh, it's you, Mr Rowan,' the old man said, throwing open the door. 'Thank goodness you've come, sir. The poor mistress . . .'

'I know. Rivers. I'm so sorry . . .'

'But you don't know the worst of it, sir.' The old man's lips trembled. 'Miss Alice has gone as well. God only knows where to. Just walked out of the house, she did, and caught a train to London, the same as poor Will Oakleigh's wife.'

'Is my aunt awake?'

'I don't rightly know, Mr Rowan . . .'

Rowan gripped the old man's arm. 'Never mind,' he said, smiling encouragement, 'I'll go up to her room. You go back to bed. I'm sorry I disturbed you.'

'No, I ain't going back to bed, sir,' Rivers said proudly, 'it's high time I was up and doing. I'll get dressed and make you and my lady some tea. You must be tired out, sir, after such a long journey.' He shuffled off towards the green baize door at the end of the passage.

Kitty Tanquillan was on the landing, huddled in a quilted dressing-gown. 'My dear boy. Thank God you've come!'

He tried to persuade her to get back into bed, but she would not hear of it. They went downstairs to the study where the ashes of yesterday's fire lay thick on the hearth.

'Just talk to me,' Rowan said briefly, 'while I get this going.' His aunt was shaking, he had noticed, with cold and nervous tension. Raking away the ashes, he found kindling in a copper scuttle, built a pyramid of sticks, set a match to it, and when it had taken hold, he eased a handful of coal and a log onto the blaze. 'Now come and get warm,' he said, taking Kitty's arm and helping her to a chair. 'Ah, here's Rivers with the tea.'

'I'll get you some breakfast now,' the old man said. 'Cook's not up yet.'

'Don't bother cooking breakfast for me,' Rowan told him. 'I'll be leaving again in a little while.'

Rivers looked shocked. 'But you must eat something, Mr Rowan.'

'Of course he must,' Kitty said firmly. 'There's a train to London from Devizes at ten o'clock. You have time for a good breakfast and a hot bath before you leave. I insist on it. Bacon and eggs, please Rivers, for my nephew; toast and coffee for myself. And – thank you.'

'Have you any idea where Charlotte might have gone to?' Rowan tucked a plaid rug round his aunt's knees; poured her a cup of tea.

'Will gave me those letters on the desk,' she replied with a slight shiver. 'Charlotte may well have gone to Jenny's address in Bloomsbury. As for poor Alice, God only knows where she has got to.' Kitty's mouth trembled. 'I shall never forgive myself if anything happens to either of them. It's all my fault. Everything is my fault. I was too harsh with Will, too blind with Charlotte, too soft with Alice. I should have realized that Will and Charlotte would never be happy together. I should have fought tooth and nail against their marrying. I should have seen what would happen, that Will, despite his kindness, was a lonely, passionate man, very much in love with Charlotte. I should have seen at once, when he was sitting where you are sitting now, when we were talking over the wedding arrangements, that he was eaten up with jealousy because he was not

469

the father of Charlotte's child. Oh, it wasn't what he said, it was the way he looked at her; such a queer, hungry, yearning look. I saw it, but I ignored it. I thought, in my blind stupidity, that I was acting for the best in giving them a decent wedding, a fine reception.' The old woman laid her head in her hands and wept. 'God forgive me for my blindness of heart; my cowardice. It was the same with you and Alice. I could see how much that girl loved you, how much she revelled in money and fine clothes, how uncaring, unthinking and unmanageable she had become since I made the mistake of telling her that she would one day inherit – all this . . .'

'Don't, Aunt Kitty,' Rowan said quietly, holding her hands tightly in his. 'What's done is done. In any case, I am far more to blame than you are. I should have been kinder to Alice. I knew how she felt about me, and I laughed at her. As for Charlotte . . .' He closed his eyes suddenly against the pain of having loved her not wisely but too well, seeing in his mind's eye a great shining star revolving slowly but inevitably in time and space, a bright burning mass spinning in the darkness of a lonely child's imagination as a kind of dream of belonging, as warm and comforting as the sand which ran between the toes of poor barefoot children far less fortunate than himself.

Suddenly, Charlotte Grayler had become that star of his, embodied in human flesh. Charlotte with her nimbus of bright, red-gold hair and quiet, shining eyes. Then he had known all the glory of loving, as if he had suddenly walked, unafraid, upon the sands of time, feeling the warmth of the world on his bare feet: the wash of a warm tide about his heart; the blinding sun on his eyelids, and all the quiet winds of heaven about his pillow as he had fallen asleep in Charlotte's arms.

CHAPTER EIGHTEEN

He took a taxi from Paddington to Bloomsbury. London was uncomfortably hot after Wiltshire. The city's old joie de vivre had been dispelled by ten months of war. There were fewer young men in evidence except those in uniform. Buildings seemed shabbier despite the warm summer sunshine.

Some of the women were in uniform too: members of the Women's Reserve Ambulance Corps, dressed in belted khaki jackets and unbecoming broad-brimmed hats, with their skirts hoisted inches above their black-stockinged ankles; W.A.A.Cs, in unfeminine sack-like garments, drilling in Hyde Park. He wondered briefly if they regretted their lost plumes and parasols. He did, if they did not. The world was ugly enough as it was without dressing women in such drab clothes. He had never realized so acutely before that the old world, with all its faults and failings, had gone forever; that the eager youth of his generation had grown old before its time. He wondered, as the taxi nosed through the traffic, if he would find Charlotte; how, if he did, he would break the news to her that Will Oakleigh was dead. His depression was all part and parcel of a London he had never cared very much for, which now seemed to him like a desert of drab khaki uniforms bereft of smiling women turning their heads bewitchingly beneath lace-frilled umbrellas.

'Here we are, guv.' The taxi-driver was a man in his fifties, too old for war service. Twelve months ago, he had driven a hansom cab; he still regretted the passing of horse-drawn vehicles, but he had been astute enough to move with the times.

Rowan stood for a moment looking up at the house; number 12 Walbrook Terrace, before he mounted the front steps and rang the bell.

In the front room over the porch, Charlotte was busily arranging the treadle sewing-machine Bridie had lent her, which a couple of strapping youths had carried upstairs for her less than an hour ago. When it came to finding willing helpers, Bridie certainly knew where to look for them, she thought, smiling with pleasure. The two lads, builders' apprentices engaged in pointing a house further down the street, had been bribed with a shilling apiece to haul the machine from the cellar, and given mugs of tea and slabs of cake when they had finished.

'When the infant arrives,' Bridie said decisively, 'we'll hide the bed and the cot with a screen when your clients come for a fitting.' She was busy with a duster, polishing the mahogany chest of drawers.

'Clients! Suppose I don't get any?' The riskiness of the venture suddenly overwhelmed Charlotte. She sat down on a chair. 'And if I do, what if the baby starts to cry just as I'm pinning up a hem?'

'Don't worry,' Bridie laughed, giving the chest of drawers a final rub, and moving on to the dressing-table, 'I'll take care of her.'

'Her? You think I'll have a girl then?'

'That's what you've set your heart on, isn't it?' Bridie raised an enquiring eyebrow. 'I'll just finish the polishing, then I'll make up your bed. I hope you'll be happy in this room, Charlotte.'

'Of course I shall. It's a lovely room.' Charlotte glanced round appreciatively at the solid, glowing furniture, liking above all else the bright sunshine which streamed in through the bay window, the little bookcase that Bridie had thoughtfully placed near the gleaming brass bedstead.

'Och, there's the bell! It will be the laundryman for his money, I expect.' Bridie deposited an armful of clean linen on the bed and bustled away. But it wasn't the laundryman.

She was back a minute later. 'There's someone to see you, my dear. He said it was urgent.' Her face was slightly puckered with anxiety.

'Will!' Charlotte clasped her hands tightly together, the

knuckles showing white. 'Oh, Bridie, I can't face him. What can I possibly say to him?'

'Charlotte, my dear, it isn't Will. It's Rowan Tanquillan.'

'Rowan?' Charlotte hurried onto the landing and leaned over the banister; heart pounding, breathless with excitement. She would have known him anywhere, even though his face was turned away from her in contemplation of the coloured etchings on the glass-panelled inner door – swags of deep purple grapes, leaf-entwined; heaped baskets of damsons; swallows and butterflies – a door which reminded her of Filly's side door at home except that the colours were different. Not emerald, ruby and aquamarine, but sapphire and amethyst; rich colours splashed by the sunshine of a June morning onto the plain khaki stuff of a soldier's uniform.

'Rowan!'

He turned as she called his name; held out his hands to her as she walked heavily downstairs. 'But I don't understand. How did you find me?' She stood a little apart from him, knowing that something was wrong. 'What is it?'

'It's about Will,' he said slowly. 'Is there anywhere private where we can talk?'

Bridie came quietly downstairs. 'Go into the parlour,' she said. 'You won't be disturbed there.'

Charlotte sat staring into the deep clouded well of her immediate past, too stricken by the news of Will's death to cry for him. What she most regretted was that she had never come close to understanding the proud, shy man she had married. She thought, in those terrible moments of tearless grief, how many other things she regretted, too: the gulf which had widened between herself and the people she loved – her mother and Maggie and Alice Tanquillan; Alice who was lost somewhere in London.

There was nothing she could do to bring Will back, but Alice . . . She said bleakly, 'We must find her, Rowan. All this is my fault. We found her once before – remember?'

'Yes, I remember,' Rowan said heavily, 'but this is not a matter of finding a lost girl in a garden. She could be anywhere,

anywhere at all. Besides, you need rest. . . .'

'Rest!' Charlotte cried, getting up from the sofa. 'I should never rest again if you did not let me help you look for her. She might have gone back to the old house in Highgate: to the pawnbroker's shop. Please, Rowan, let us not waste any more time . . .'

Alice, it appeared, *had* gone to the pawnbroker's shop. The pawnbroker, ill at ease, wiped his forehead with a handkerchief and said that Oliver Tanquillan's girl had been hanging about on the pavement for an hour or more before his wife had gone out and told her to move off. 'After all,' he whined, 'we didn't want no more upset here. I run a respectable business, I do, and we don't want no more truck with the police coming round asking questions like they did when Mr Tanquillan was found dead. A terrible experience that was, sir. Anyone would have thought I had murdered him: the questions they asked, and making out that I'd quarrelled with him about the rent owing and suchlike. No, we didn't want any more fuss over the likes of him or that barmy kid of his!'

'And you have no idea where the girl went to after you had sent her away?' Rowan asked grimly.

'No, sir, I haven't. That's the gospel truth! Like I told you, we want no more dealings with the Tanquillans or the kid. In fact, sir, you can take something he left behind, for what good it may do you or anyone else come to that.' He scurried away and came back minutes later with a brown paper parcel tied with knotted string. 'Here,' he said, thrusting the parcel at Rowan, 'you take it.'

'What is it?' Rowan asked, frowning.

'How the hell should I know? Some kind of a book, I reckon. A load of high-flown rubbish, not worth the paper he typed it on.'

'Where to now?' Rowan asked, as the shop door pinged shut behind himself and Charlotte. 'Where, in God's name, is she?'

Charlotte said slowly, 'I believe I know where she is. Poor Alice. She is with her father.'

* * *

The Highgate cemetery, even on a warm June day, exuded a certain chill: the eeriness of crowded-together gravestones and crumbling mausoleums overgrown with ivy.

Rowan remembered, as he and Charlotte walked together the weed-infested paths among the eyeless cherubs and towering marble angels, that bleak January day when Oliver Tanquillan, his shy knight errant, was buried; how he had pitied his strange, mentally-unbalanced cousin; how she had clung to him. The place seemed less terrible to him now than it had done then; with sunshine dappling the paths; a levelling-ground of all men's pride and passion, a place for truth and understanding.

Charlotte stopped suddenly and laid her hand on Rowan's sleeve. 'Over there,' she said quietly.

Alice Tanquillan had hung a daisy chain about her father's gravestone. She was sitting quietly in the sunshine in her pale green dress with its pointed lace collar, singing the words of an old French nursery rhyme: 'Sur le pont d'Avignon'.

Charlotte walked towards her with infinite care, so as not to startle her. 'Alice,' she whispered, 'Alice.'

The girl looked up at her, smiling. 'Hush,' she murmured, 'he's asleep now; at peace.'

'We have come to take you home, darling,' Charlotte said, holding out her hands.

Alice said, 'I don't deserve to go home. I've been a very bad girl. I'm wicked, you know. Very wicked.' She got slowly to her feet. 'But I am tired, and very hungry.' She spoke in the sing-song manner of a child learning its alphabet. 'I hurt poor Will. I didn't mean to. I wanted to tell everyone how sorry I was, but no-one was there, so I came to tell my father instead.' She smiled as she leaned her head against Charlotte's shoulder. 'It's all right now. My father said I mustn't worry any more.'

Charlotte braced herself for the ordeal of Will's funeral. Nothing eased or mitigated the pain until she remembered the beauty of the world in a raindrop.

She could not have explained to anyone what that meant to her. It was a trick of the mind: something she had experienced many times before, when Maggie had pried into her private world of books and poetry; a kind of withdrawal from the world in the contemplation of one perfect and lovely object, so that that object became a little world in itself, calming her troubled spirit.

Her heart held nothing save love and forgiveness for Will Oakleigh. She felt no bitterness towards him, merely regret that he had gone away from her so suddenly, that time had run out for both of them before its healing process had begun. Hours, days, weeks, months, perhaps years would eventually have bridged the gulf between them, bringing them to a closer understanding of each other. But there was no time left to them now.

Her mind was strung between the awful finality of death and the glad awareness of new life as her child kicked lustily inside her. It was then she clung to the memory of quiet rain, remembering how she had walked beneath the trees of home noticing the marvellous perfection of raindrops radiant on branches; pellucid drops as clear and clean as diamonds; each drop a secret wellspring of light and hope.

Her father had touched on his wellspring of light in his vision of a wide, shining river. That was the secret of their close understanding of each other: the secret of the whole meaning of love, the great strength and mystery of love, that all the people who loved the world and each other had touched upon its essential, unflawed simplicity.

CHAPTER NINETEEN

Harry Grayler received word that he was being sent back to England to an army convalescent home near Bognor Regis.

'Oh, God no,' he muttered, throwing aside the official letter. 'Can't you do anything about it, Jenny?' He could not bear the thought of leaving his wife in Belgium whilst he languished in some cockeyed rest home for wounded soldiers. 'My leg's fine now! Tell them I won't go!'

Jenny laughed as she teased him to a better humour. 'You should think yourself lucky, my lad. And who do you think I am to tell "them" anything at all? Besides, if you don't need a rest, I do.'

'Away from me, you mean?' Harry was in no mood for joking. His love for Jenny was a constant torment eating away at his guts. He could never come to terms with the feeling that he wasn't good enough for her, that she had married him out of pity. 'You don't understand,' he said dully. 'This war has a lot to answer for. I can't explain, but I feel so bloody helpless . . .'

'Harry, my darling.' Jenny stopped laughing. 'Do you think I don't understand how you feel? I love you . . .'

He looked into her face, afraid of reading nothing more than compassion in her eyes; pity for his helplessness.

She meant what she said. Harry was like a pool of clear water with no hidden depths. Perhaps that was why she loved him so much. She had had enough in her student days at Oxford of clever men whose brilliance had engendered the oddest behavioural patterns: the foppish, the over-earnest, the dilettante. 'The Owls and the Pussycats' she had secretly called them. But Harry was none of those things. Harry Grayler, with his fine physique and untutored mind, made a noble, clean thing of loving: imbued the act of physical union with decency and honour.

Harry said, 'When this war is over, I'd like to work close to the earth, with animals, with horses in particular.'

'You're still thinking of Nobby, aren't you?'

'Yes.' Harry turned his head away to hide his emotion. 'I've never forgotten that old horse of mine. I've looked for him everywhere, every day since I joined up. I think I love horses far more than my fellow men at times.' He remembered the blowing of a bugle across the war-torn fields of Belgium, sounding retreat to a cavalry division, how so many riderless horses had returned to stables across a wilderness of churned-up mud in answer to that forlorn bugle-note; great-hearted beasts, ears pricked for the sound of voices that would never come again. 'I'd like to go into farming. Would you mind if I became a farmer?'

'No, my darling. I'd like being a farmer's wife.'

'Oh, Jenny, my Jenny . . .'

The irony of the situation struck Jenny forcibly. The three Grayler brothers had joined up together at Frank's instigation. Now Frank, the devil-may-care leader of the trio, was dead; Harry wounded. Only Joey, the brother who had never wanted to fight at all, was left to carry on the battle.

How odd it was that she had never met Joe or Frank or Maggie Grayler, and yet she felt that she knew them all intimately. Frank, the oldest brother, who had gone into battle with such heroic intentions. She could not help thinking that death had surprised Frank the day he recrossed the Zaaerebeke stream, that he had never seen himself as being mortal. Frank Grayler was the archetypal British soldier who had answered the call to arms for the sheer excitement of getting into a scrap, who believed that he would survive the war and live to talk about it, in his old age, as a supreme test of valour. Few of the men she had nursed had seen the war as anything else but a proving-ground of their manhood, a skirmish that would be over and done with in six months at the most.

One day, Jenny thought, I will write a book about this war and all the people who were caught up in it: about the Frank

Graylers who died for nothing more than a glimpse of glory: about the women left to mourn their passing.

'What are you thinking, Jenny?' Harry asked, drawing her into his arms.

Jenny smiled. 'Only that I love you.'

They had received permission to spend their last night together in a small hotel a few miles away from the hospital. She said, beginning slowly to undress, 'But why waste time talking . . . ?'

Filly wakened from a deep sleep to hear the baby crying in the room across the landing. Getting up, she put on her dressing-gown and laid her ear to the door, listening intently, wanting to pick up the child and nurse it. Her maternal instincts warned her that Maggie was not feeding her child properly. There was something forlorn and hungry about Peggy's wailing. It had been the same in the early weeks of Charlotte's life when Filly was breast-feeding her youngest daughter. Then the doctor had told her that her milk was insufficient, that the child would be far better off fed from a bottle.

She had tried to tell Maggie that the baby cried so much because she wasn't getting enough milk, but Maggie had been queer and irritable since the birth of her child. She merely drew her forehead into a frown and said shortly that she supposed she knew what was best for the baby since she was its mother. She did not tell Filly to mind her own business in so many words, but Filly knew that was what she meant.

Suddenly the two-up, two-down house seemed too small to contain three adults and a baby, plus piles of washing and ironing; the perambulator blocking the narrow hallway, with the sitting-room fire permanently shrouded by a firescreen of wet nappies, and the kitchen chaotic with cooking.

Inevitably, mother and daughter exchanged heated words at times, when Maggie was dragging about the house like a half-drowned cat and Filly offered to see to the baby while her daughter got on with the housework. 'What, and have you spoil her to death?' Maggie snapped, unwilling to admit that she was bone tired with being up half the night, and frightened to death that Bob might make her pregnant again. She couldn't very well say so, but Maggie felt it indecent that Bob wanted to make love to her with her mother in the back room and almost certain to hear the creaking of the bed-springs whenever he demanded his conjugal rights.

'I wish to hell that your mother had never come to live with us,' Bob muttered one night when Maggie, tired out with all the feeding and washing and housework, told him to leave her alone. 'If she's going to lie there all night with her ear pressed to the wall, she had better pack her things and go somewhere else to live.' Then Maggie called him mean and unfeeling, after all her poor ma had been through.

'She's taken over the whole bloody house,' Bob grumbled, half ashamed of himself. 'If she hadn't fallen out with Charlotte, they could have lived together and left us alone.'

He could not have said anything more likely to cause another outburst. 'What do you mean — if she hadn't fallen out with Charlotte? It was all Charlotte's fault, carrying on the way she did. You always take her side, and I know why. You'd have liked to carry on with her yourself!'

'That's not true. Though one thing's for sure, Charlotte's got a lot more gumption than you have when it comes to . . .' He bit his tongue before it ran away with him.

'When it comes to what?' They were arguing fiercely under the bedclothes. 'Go on, Bob Masters. Finish what you were going to say.'

'When it comes to getting things organized, the way she did when your brothers joined up. Wheeling that hand-cart down to the station . . .'

'Making a spectacle of herself,' Maggie snorted bitterly.

'You've always been jealous of her, haven't you?' Bob demanded in a hoarse whisper. 'Nothing she ever did was right for you. But I always liked Charlotte. My God, you'd think she had broken the ten commandments the way you and Ma carry on about her. There now, you've wakened Peggy with your hollering.'

He flung his legs out of bed, lit the candle and walked softly to the cot where Peggy lay. 'What's the matter, Peg-o-my-heart?' he murmured, picking her up and kissing the soft tuft of dark hair above the wide-open blue eyes.

'What do you think's the matter with her?' Maggie sat up in bed and ripped open her nightgown. 'Here, give her to me.' Bob looked with distaste at the pendulous breasts ballooning like a cow's udders from his wife's unbuttoned nightdress, repulsed by her lack of modesty, the careless way she started to feed his child. Everything was beginning to get on his nerves. He felt crushed by the weight of two women in the house, constantly at loggerheads these days, always arguing about who should do what for himself or the baby.

Maggie had had a tough time bringing Peggy into the world, but no man wanted reminding of that twenty-four hours a day. He had tried to play fair with his wife, but he would never forget the first time he'd attempted to make love to her after what he considered to be a decent interval; the sheer humiliation of the act, with Maggie hissing frantically in his ear that her mother would hear the jingling of the bed-springs.

He thought, as he put Peggy back in her cot, that the best thing he could do was join up, and wondered as he got back into bed and blew out the candle, what had happened to the man who had gone into marriage with such high hopes. All he had ever wanted was to make a nice little home for Maggie. He could not help remembering, as he buried his head in the pillow, the early days of their courtship when Maggie was all smiles, with her hair drawn back in tight little curls from her eager, laughing face, holding up her mouth to be kissed.

Did marriage change every woman from a sweetheart into a worry-seamed matron who went to bed in curl-rags? He thought inevitably of Charlotte; could not imagine her going to bed in curl-rags. Time, he felt, would deal kindly with Charlotte, because Charlotte would always deal kindly with time.

He knew that Maggie was not asleep, that the quarrel between them had not been settled or solved. He felt his wife's silent disapproval as an invisible knife between his shoulder-blades, knowing that she had hit on the truth when she had accused him of wanting to 'carry on' with Charlotte. He remembered, with a warm feeling at his heart, that day on Oliver's Mount when he had turned to help Charlotte up the slope. In that moment he had sensed another dimension to living, in the touch of her hand. But he had been so callow, so unsure of himself. It occurred to him that that was the beginning of Maggie's jealousy. That was the day Charlotte had moved her belongings to the attic: the first time he had felt at odds with Maggie. Nothing had been the same since that day.

Bob had never thought so deeply or profoundly before, but then he had never felt so fed-up before. He heard, with a feeling of relief, Maggie's gentle snoring, and turned away from her, coming to certain conclusions about the future.

'I heard you and Bob going for each other last night,' Filly said sharply next morning when Bob had gone to work and Maggie was feeding Peggy. 'I couldn't quite hear what you were saying, but I can imagine. I'm a nuisance to you, aren't I? You want me out of the house. Well, I'll go. I'm not stopping where I'm not wanted.'

'Oh for heaven's sake, Ma, shut up,' Maggie snapped back at her. 'We were talking about Charlotte, if you must know.' She felt too tired and irritable to go into long-winded explanations: too scared of Filly's wrath to tell her the whole truth.

'Oh,' Filly said, 'what about Charlotte? What did Bob say about her?'

'Something that nettled me, that's all.' Maggie switched the baby laboriously from one breast to the other.

'What did he say exactly?'

Maggie's anger broke. 'You know as well as I do that Bob always had his eye on Charlotte! And she knew it. I daresay she thought she could take him away from me if she wanted to! She never stopped trying!'

'That's not true and you know it,' Filly retorted, rushing to Charlotte's defence as she had done so often in the past; scarcely realizing that she had done so. 'Charlotte never looked twice at Bob. And I've told you over and over again, that baby is not getting enough milk!' She added, sotto voce, 'And the way you are carrying on, it's a wonder the milk you have got hasn't turned sour!'

'Oh, that's right! Keep sticking your oar in,' Maggie cried, beside herself with anger at her mother's interference. 'Bob was right! It is time you went somewhere else to live! I'm sick and tired of your constant carping and criticism. Here!' She thrust the whimpering baby at Filly. 'You bloody well feed her!'

Filly stood up, wounded to the heart. 'Where are you going?' Maggie asked, knowing that she had gone too far.

'To pack my things,' Filly said.

'Don't be so silly, Ma,' Maggie cried, 'I didn't mean it.' But Filly was halfway up the stairs, almost blinded with tears, remembering, as she stood on the threshold of the little back room, the old days when she had reigned supreme in the house in St Martin's Square.

Memories rushed in on her as she dragged a suitcase from the top of the wardrobe and began opening drawers and cupboards. The scene with Maggie made her remember very clearly all the harsh words she had spoken against Charlotte, the bitterness she had felt towards her youngest child, and Albert, when she had realized the strength of the bond between them; the feeling she'd experienced of being shut out of their love for each other.

But where had her great upsurge of blinkered moral judgement led her? Albert was dead, and Charlotte no longer a part of her life. She felt the emptiness of life without them – and Frankie – as a great void which even Maggie and Bob and little Peggy could not fill.

Then Maggie came up the stairs after her, and put her arms round her shoulders. 'I'm sorry, Ma,' she said. 'Please don't go. I'm sorry if I upset you. I'm just worn out, that's all. Please, Ma!'

At dinnertime, Bob walked into the house, dressed in a khaki uniform.

'I've enlisted with The Green Howards,' he said. 'Well, Maggie, aren't you proud of me?'

'You silly, bloody fool,' Maggie sobbed, turning away from him. 'Why didn't you tell me what you were going to do? What do you think will happen to Peggy and me when you're gone?'

'I didn't think you'd mind all that much,' Bob said confusedly. 'After all, you've got your mother to take care of you. I just thought that things would be easier for you without me.'

CHAPTER TWENTY

Will Oakleigh had died a hero, and heroism was crowned with a certain glory. It was not simply a question of not speaking ill of the dead at his funeral, but lauding his bravery in saving a human life.

Charlotte, as his widow, found herself accorded the respect the villagers felt for her late husband. Rumour, fanned by the churchwarden's wife, that all had not been well between the dead man and his wife, was stilled by Charlotte's reappearance. Then Mrs Battye said that she might possibly have been wrong in supposing that Charlotte's sudden departure to London, early on the morning of Will's death, held any sinister connotation; though it did seem odd to her that Will had not driven his wife to Devizes station that day, and a pregnant woman walking all that way alone and arriving on the platform in such a state, did seem very strange to her.

A mother of five chipped in at that point to remind the churchwarden's wife that pregnant women did irrational things at times. But of course Mrs Battye could not be expected to understand that, since she had never had any children.

Everyone agreed afterwards that it had been a fine service, a fitting tribute to poor Will. Men and women turned up in church in their Sunday best clothes, and stood in respectful silence as Charlotte came in with Kitty Tanquillan, Rowan and Alice. The wilful girl, Mrs Battye noticed with satisfaction, seemed suitably chastened, as well she might be under the circumstances. The churchwarden's wife, with one finger in her hymn book, wondered what had really happened the day Will Oakleigh died, though she was unlikely to find out since the main protagonists in the drama had obviously closed ranks.

All the same, young Alan Feetenby had been sure that there had been some kind of a row between young Alice and the mistress of Grey Wethers the morning of Will's death.

Kitty Tanquillan had arranged for the funeral reception to be held in the church hall. Some folk, including Mrs Battye and her cronies, thought it might better have been held at Grey Wethers, while the more reasonable and compassionate said it was hardly likely poor Mrs Oakleigh would want reminding of her wedding reception held there a few short months ago. In any case, the food was marvellous despite the shortages imposed by war and the enemy blockade of Great Britain, with plenty of cold ham and chicken to go at.

How strange, Kitty thought, the solemnities over and done with, how quickly folk returned to normal. The last page in Will Oakleigh's life was written now, the book closed. He lay at peace in a place he had known and loved well, but life went on. Now the people who had seen him buried in the graveyard of Cloud Merridon were laughing and tucking into the food she had provided for them, as if he had never existed.

She shivered suddenly, then turned her gaze on the urns of flowers she had ordered to be brought down from the house to soften the severity of the church hall: glowing masses arranged by her own hands as a tribute to Will Oakleigh. She thought, as she sipped a glass of wine, that when she and Will were dust, different generations of people would come to Cloud Merridon, tucked away in the winding valley between green hills. The newcomers would know and care nothing about the people who had gone before them, who had lived out their lives, their little tragedies, sorrows and joys, in a different time, another world from theirs. God willing, it would be a happier, more peaceful world than she and Will had known.

Charlotte looked very tired and pale, she thought, while Alice, a law unto herself, stood apart from the rest, not eating or speaking until Rowan crossed the room to stand beside her. Kitty smiled then. How like Rowan, she thought, to act protectively towards his young cousin, to stand beside her as a shield against those who blamed her for Will's death.

Kitty sighed, knowing that the next few days would not be easily lived through. The farmhouse must be emptied of Will's belongings to make way for a new farm manager and his family, which meant that Charlotte would be faced with the painful business of deciding what to do with Will's personal effects: his clothes, and furniture.

She had told Charlotte that she would be welcome to stay on at Grey Wethers, but she had known, even as she made the offer, that Charlotte would refuse. Rowan's leave was drawing to a close. Another week, and he must return to France, to his battalion. As for Alice, the girl badly needed the help of Claude Latimer. Kitty Tanquillan mistrusted the child's present apathy far more than she mistrusted her usual febrile excitement. When all this was over and done with, she must take her to Latimer for treatment.

The farmhouse door stood wide open to sun and air. The kitchen, which Charlotte had always seen as the heart of the house, was almost stripped of Will's belongings. She had felt, as she was forced to pry into Will's private papers, old photograph albums and letters, like an intruder – a voyeuse – uncovering the secrets of the man she had married. A man she had scarcely known and never really understood. But as the farmhouse was cleared, there were certain things she could not bear to part with, for his sake. Abby Oakleigh's piano, for one thing; Will's chair; his grandfather clock.

At Rowan's suggestion, she asked the vicar of Cloud Merridon if he would like Abby's piano for the church hall, since the old one was so out of the tune. She decided to take Will's chair and the clock back to Bloomsbury with her.

Will's clothes presented less of a problem. They could be packed up and sent to the Belgian Relief Fund – a society continually in need of warm clothing for the constant stream of refugees crossing to England in small boats; people who had lost everything but the clothes they stood up in as the German Army overran their towns and villages.

Before one tea-chest full of Will's clothing was nailed down, Charlotte wrote, on a slip of paper, 'May God go with you', and slipped it into the pocket of a tweed jacket with patched elbows.

Rowan said compassionately, 'Don't you think you should rest now, darling?'

'I can't rest until all this is seen to,' she replied, glancing up at him with tears in her eyes. 'But I am so glad that you are here to help me.'

'I won't be here for very much longer,' Rowan said gently, taking her hands in his. I rejoin my Regiment tomorrow.'

'So soon?' Charlotte asked bleakly. 'Oh, my darling, so soon?' She had not been aware of the passage of time. It had seemed to her that the days at the farmhouse would go on forever.

Rowan said quietly, drawing her closer to his heart. 'Before I leave you, I must tell you that it is all over between Romilly and me. It was not a happy parting, how could it have been? But when this war is over, I'll come back to you, my darling. Somehow, I *will* come back to you.'

CHAPTER TWENTY-ONE

Charlotte returned to Bloomsbury a week later. The farmhouse had been cleared and arrangements made with a firm of carters to take the chair and the clock, along with a few pictures and ornaments she had decided to keep.

Bridie welcomed her calmly and sensibly, understanding that Charlotte would be better off if her mind and fingers were kept busy. Over supper, she handed Charlotte a list of potential clients. 'We've struck oil,' she said cheerfully. 'Mrs Mounsey at the corner shop wants a blouse and skirt. Her husband said he wouldn't mind a new suit of clothes, but I drew the line at that.' She laughed. 'And a Miss Atkinson would like you to make her a wedding-dress for when her young man comes home on leave.'

'Oh, Bridie. I'll never be able to repay you . . .'

'Of course you will. You'll be rich in no time at all.' Bridie gave Charlotte a searching glance: the girl looked tired and pale.

'I didn't mean money, I meant kindness,' Charlotte said. 'I can pay my way for a little while now because Will left me thirty-five pounds.' She felt in her pocket for a handkerchief. 'I came across a bank-book when I was looking through his things. There was a will of sorts too. It wasn't a proper will, it wasn't witnessed or anything. He must have written it just after we were married. It said, "I bequeath to my beloved wife, Charlotte, all my worldly possessions." That was the worst moment of all, realizing how much he loved me when it was too late.'

'Best not to dwell on that, my dear,' Bridie said quietly. 'From now on, start looking to the future. You have your child to live for – and this business venture of yours. I have the feeling that this is just the beginning, that one day you will be a rich, successful woman. Don't ask me how I know. I suppose I'm a bit fey, like most good Scotswomen.

Charlotte looked down at her hands, hoping that her fingers had lost none of their dexterity when it came to cutting out and adapting patterns. Suddenly, with a little lifting of the heart, she knew that handling material again would bring its own special magic; the joy she had always felt in creation.

Next day, the carters arrived with the furniture. Charlotte was upstairs in her room at the time, polishing the sewing-machine with linseed oil. 'All right, I'll answer the door,' Bridie sang out, 'before they start using the clock as a battering-ram.'

When everything was in place, with two pictures of Grey Wethers hung up, and a pair of Staffordshire dogs on the mantelpiece, Bridie stood, arms akimbo, admiring the effect, listening to the ticking of the clock in the corner.

Suddenly, long pent-up tears flooded down Charlotte's cheeks, and she was in Bridie's arms, sobbing against her shoulder. 'I'm sorry,' she faltered, drying her eyes when the storm was over.

'You needn't be,' Bridie said, 'I know how you feel. It was the same for me when my husband died. I couldn't rid myself of the notion that I had failed him. Then, as time went by, I started remembering the happy times when we were young and very much in love, and I realized that life must go on; that we must go along with it. Don't poison your young life with regrets, my dear. Make a little place in your heart for Will Oakleigh; keep him safe there always, then put him out of your mind once and for all. That is the best advice I have to give you.'

Filly Grayler glanced down the Births, Marriages and Deaths column of the *Scarborough Evening News*, and uttered a sharp little cry.

'What's the matter?' Maggie asked, on her way to the kitchen to make up Peggy's feed; much happier now that the baby had stopped its eternal, hungry wailing; easier in her mind since

Bob had joined the Army and since she and her mother had buried the hatchet for the time being.

'It's that Madge Robinson,' Filly said indignantly. 'She's gone and got married again! It says here, "On 14 July at St Saviour's Church, Margaret Phyllis Grayler, daughter of Frances and Arthur Robinson of 4 Beulah Terrace, to John (Jack) Kemp, younger son of Gladys and Edward Kemp of 24 Lyall Street." Well, of all things! And our poor Frank scarcely cold in his grave!'

'Aw, don't take on so, Ma.' Maggie sniffed. 'Madgie Robinson wasn't good enough for our Frank anyway. It's good riddance to bad rubbish, in my opinion.' Maggie had a way of never quite understanding or making allowances for other people.

'That's all very well,' Filly cried. 'What hurts me is that she couldn't have waited a bit longer. What will the neighbours think?'

Maggie could not have cared less what anyone thought since the constant dread of becoming pregnant again had receded to a safe, manageable distance.

Annie Crystal folded the latest letter from Joe back into its envelope. Poor Joey was having a hard time of it in Belgium. She had followed his every move with a growing feeling of anxiety. May had been a month of hard fighting for The Green Howards as they moved, like chess-pieces on a board, from Vlamertinghe to Brielen; from Brielen to trenches in Santuary Wood, in face of German gas attacks.

Annie could scarcely come to terms with the thought that, on Whit-Sunday, when she had been in church singing hymns of praise to the risen Christ, men were dying; choking to death for want of respirators. She could not help wondering how the war would affect a sensitive mind like Joe's. And yet he always wrote cheerfully, comfortingly, telling her how much he loved her, looking forward to their wedding day on his next leave.

But this last letter was different; more poignant. 'You are my guiding star,' he had written. 'Whenever the suffering seems too great to bear, I remember your sweet, smiling face, and the memory of you somehow eases the pain of this sad, unnecessary waste of human life. Whenever I see the moon riding high and serene in a cloudless sky over the great earth-weals of the trenches, I remember that same moon is shining down on the roof of the house where you, my darling, lie fast asleep.

'Then I recall all our quiet, happy days together, and find comfort in the memory of laughter borne on other winds, when the world seemed much younger than it does today. Sleep well, my Annie. Keep strong and calm and busy, for what you are thinking and feeling, and all the lovely, quiet things you believe in, somehow come across the miles that separate us . . .'

Material thudded quietly and sweetly beneath the foot of Charlotte's sewing-machine. She loved the feel of it between her fingers; the whisper of white satin, the harsher notes of twill and bombazine. She felt more alive now, knowing that none of the old magic of dressmaking had escaped her; that she was a born dressmaker, cutting out patterns with an instinctive flair for taking in or letting out seams; easing bustlines; nipping in waistlines; always ready with suggestions to enhance the finished garments – a bow here, a filet of lace there – to make her clients smile with delight; to turn a plain dress into a confection.

She remembered, with joy, the wedding-dress she had created for Miss Judith Atkinson; how she had lowered the high, plain neckline; inserted a froth of foaming lace to the décolletage, built up, layer on layer, so that the bride's shoulders emerged as two swan's wings floating on a tide of white satin.

As July moved into August, and people remembered that this was the first anniversary of the outbreak of war, Charlotte began to feel the strain of kneeling to pin up hemlines and sitting for hours at her machine, but the work kept her mind occupied, and letters from Annie and Jenny, au fait with family news. Bob Masters had not undergone a very long training period; had been posted abroad almost at once. Annie had, of necessity, left her job as a waitress since trade was so bad, and had gone into a clothing factory. Charlotte could read between the lines Annie's anxiety over Joe, who had had only one brief spell of leave since he went to France.

It was an anxious time all round for Annie Crystal, whose mother was now seriously ill in hospital after a fall.

'I know that she will not recover,' Annie wrote, 'and it is foolish of me to grieve so, but the house seems empty without her, and I cannot help remembering the happy old days when I was a child and my father was still alive. Mother was the pivot on which the house revolved in those days.'

Charlotte knew exactly what Annie meant, it had been the same with Filly when she was a young woman: a larger-than-life personality who ruled the roost with a rod of iron. Now Charlotte thought, as she bent over her sewing-machine, that while she had always been her father's girl when it came to secrets, it was her mother she missed most at the moment, as the days slipped by towards the birth of her child. If only Filly had taken the trouble to reply to the wedding invitation she had sent her, but she had not, nor to any of the letters, asking her for-giveness, that Charlotte had written to her since her wedding.

Then, inevitably, pride had forbidden Charlotte's writing any more letters, and she had begged Annie not to tell Filly that she was pregnant. She had no way of knowing that Maggie had burned her letters to her mother as they arrived.

On the fifteenth of August, Kitty came to the house in Walbrook Terrace to see Charlotte.

Her visit to London was planned initially to discuss, with Claude Latimer, Alice's progress at the clinic where the girl had been since the traumatic days following Will Oakleigh's funeral, when Alice had subsided into a state of apathy, refusing to eat or speak; forever singing snatches of an old French nursery rhyme; and knotting her fingers together as if fashion-ing an invisible daisy chain.

Bridie answered the bell; recognized at once, from Charlotte's description of her, Rowan Tanquillan's aunt. 'You must be Miss Tanquillan,' she said. 'Won't you come in?'

'And you are Mrs McKenna.' Kitty smiled briefly. 'I've heard about you too.'

'It's not more bad news, is it?' Bridie asked, reading the expression in Kitty Tanquillan's eyes. 'Oh, God, I hope not! That poor girl!'

'I'm afraid it is,' Kitty said quietly, 'but she has a right to hear it. I'm sorry, but you know as well as I do that Charlotte is not the kind of person to flinch from the truth.'

When Charlotte came downstairs, Kitty Tanquillan took from her handbag the telegram she had received from the War Office: 'Regret to inform you that your nephew, Rowan Tanquillan, is missing, believed dead.'

'Rowan can't be dead. I'd have known it if he were! Charlotte lifted her eyes to Kitty Tanquillan's face, bewildered by the brevity of the telegram: the cold black type on a yellow telegraph form.

'There's this letter from a friend of his,' Kitty said dully. 'I think you should read it.' The old woman sank down in a chair as Charlotte unfolded the letter.

'Dear Madam, she read.
I promised my mate Rowan that I would write to you if he copped it as he said he would write to my old woman if I did. Not that I am giving up hope that he is still alive, because I can't believe that he is dead. Not him, not the guv.

It happened like this. It was a bad night as black as pitch with the rain coming down like stair-rods. We was out trenching close to the enemy lines and they was giving us hell, picking us off the minnit we showed our heads, and there was a machine-gun high up on a ridge raking away at us apart from the snipers.

Well, Rowan laid beside me in the mud for a bit, then he said it was time somebody put paid to that bloody machine-gun (begging your pardon, but that's what he did say.) I told him not to be so soft, that there was nothing we could do about it except lay low, which we did for an hour or more, until he couldn't stand it no longer. Somebody's got to get them bastards, he said, before the whole bloody lot of us is wiped out.

The last I seen of the guv was when he started to crawl

forward on his belly towards the ridge. I started to go after him like I always went where the guvnor led, until I was hit in the leg and couldn't follow him no more. After that I seen nothing more of him. But that bloody machine-gune stopped firing.

I would just like to say that I was proud to be his friend. No finer gent ever lived than Rowan Tanquillan. But like I said before I still don't believe he's gone. Yours truely, Bert Hoskins.'

Charlotte walked slowly beside the shining river Thames, stopping now and then to lean her arms on the parapet. The evening sky was stained deep purple, blue and gold. The colours of the sunset were trapped in the oily water, shimmering far down to its secret depths where quick, silent currents tugged the great river inevitably down to the open sea.

It seemed to Charlotte, as she stared down at the expanse of flowing water, that Rowan stood beside her, his hand on hers: that the small candle she had once lit to love was still shining in the near darkness. Tugs hooted on the river: great ships lay at anchor; a solitary sea-bird uttered a keening cry as it turned on silent wings towards the marshes at the river-mouth.

Through the rumble of passing traffic, Charlotte listened for a well-known, well-loved voice: Just eight hours. That's all the time we have left together. It's not enough. I can't bear the thought of losing you.

But you are not going to lose me. Nothing can ever separate us now.

She remembered the river as it was then, scurried with stinging hailstones borne on a bleak December wind.

I will never leave you now, Charlotte. If I died, and you went on living, you would always know that I was there beside you. I should prove a very persistent ghost . . . This love of ours can never die. Whatever happens to me, you will never be alone . . .

She could almost smell, on a warm August evening, the scent of violets pinned to her coat: the overpowering sweetness of those crushed and bruised flowers as Rowan held her to his heart on a cold station platform.

She could not believe that he was dead. As long as she was

alive in the world, carrying his child in her womb, she would never give up hope of seeing him again. And yet it was such an empty, frightening world without him, and the pain of not knowing where he was, what had happened to him, was the greatest torment she had ever known.

She could scarcely remember now how she came to be on the Thames embankment. Bridie had begged her not to leave the house on her own, but she had felt compelled by an overwhelming need to be alone with her memories of Rowan, She vaguely remembered buying a ticket on a tramcar: another on an omnibus: walking from the bus-stop near the Chelsea bridge, and crossing the road near those Georgian houses where ghosts were trapped in eternal time-bubbles.

She began to walk along the Embankment, conscious of the heaviness of her body, the effort of putting one foot in front of the other. Her brain seemed numb with shock and grief; the world of hope and imagination had shrunk to the dimensions of a womb. The people around her appeared to her as blurred shapes lacking identity or substance. Then the pain began, a gripping pain which surged upwards through her body, making her sweat and tremble. Biting her lips to prevent herself from crying out, she leaned against the parapet, tearing at the stonework with her fingernails.

A few passers-by stared at her with fleeting curiosity and went on their way, laughing and talking, wrapped up in their own affairs. When the first wave of pain had subsided, she walked a few steps further, feeling her child as a dead weight inside her. And then the pain returned with such intensity that there seemed to be nothing else in the world. Shuddering and gasping, half fainting, she sank down on the pavement.

The woman who came up to her was poorly dressed, elderly, with the smell of gin on her breath. 'Don't worry, dearie,' she said, 'I'll help you. I've had six myself.' She stared about her. 'Ain't it the bleedin' truth, want a bobby and can you find one?'

A few people had stopped now to see what was happening. 'Well, don't just stand there gawping,' the woman cried, 'go and find a copper; get an ambulance. Can't you see she's going to have a baby?'

496

Pain came crashing in like waves on a seashore. Somewhere close by a woman was screaming. Charlotte could see above her a light like a pale sun; figures in white moving like shadows against a background of dark green walls, a screen, the sharp outline of white-painted trolley. One of the white figures leaned over her. 'You must fight, Mrs Oakleigh. You mustn't give in.'

They had discovered Charlotte's name and address in her handbag when she was admitted to hospital. A constable had then gone to the house in Walbrook Terrace. Now Bridie sat in the green-painted corridor near the maternity ward, waiting for news, glancing anxiously towards the ward whenever the swing doors parted. Charlotte had been in labour for four hours. The sister had asked her if there was anything to account for Mrs Oakleigh's apathy and physical weakness. 'Why?' Bridie's heart lurched. 'She's going to be all right, isn't she?'

'That's hard to say at the moment. She appears to have lost the will to fight.' As Bridie covered her eyes momentarily, the sister continued, 'Anything you can tell me might help. I don't know how to get through to her.'

'But Charlotte *is* a fighter. She has always been a fighter,' Bridie said urgently.

'She is not fighting now,' the woman replied quietly. 'If you know why not, you must tell me.'

Bridie nodded. She had given way briefly to panic, but that would not help Charlotte. She said, more calmly. 'Mrs Oakleigh received bad news today. Someone she cares for is missing, believed dead. She has been through a very hard time just lately. I suppose it's an old story these days, isn't it, people losing those who meant most to them? If Charlotte has stopped fighting, it is because the heart has gone out of her. First her father, then her brother. She had scarcely recovered from that when her husband was killed.' Bridie was speaking almost to herself now. 'I think that she has seen the world she knew and loved dwindling away so that her courage failed her. She could no longer withstand the loneliness; the mother who never writes to her. Friends are all very well, Sister, and I count myself her friend, but they cannot fill the emptiness. I suppose the news she received today was the last straw.'

Bridie McKenna's eyes were filled with tears as she glanced up at the sister's compassionate face. 'But she needs this child. More than anything else on earth, Charlotte wants and needs her baby.' She paused. 'Perhaps if I could see her; speak to her . . .'

'I'm sorry, that's not possible, Mrs McKenna. I appreciate your concern, but we cannot allow visitors to the labour ward. I really am sorry. We must just hope for a miracle.'

Bridie had half risen from the bench in that long, impersonal hospital corridor. Now she sank back on it, hands clenched, willing Charlotte to start fighting.

People came and went, but Bridie saw none of them. She had always believed in the power of prayer, and she prayed now as she had never prayed in her life before. She wondered, as she prayed, if God would forgive this unorthodox pew, a hard bench in a hospital corridor, with the smell of ether, and the constant opening and shutting of doors; the scurrying sound of footsteps coming and going.

She was so tired, so very tired and confused. It was five hours now since Charlotte had gone into labour . . .

Then, 'Bridie.' a voice said softly, insistently 'Oh, darling, we came as soon as we could.'

Bridie stared up at a well-known figure wearing a wide brimmed black hat with a curling ostrich feather. 'Jenny!'

'We went to the house first.' Jenny explained in a breathless whisper. 'Thank God the woman next door knew where you were. There's something to be said for gossipy neighbours after all.' Jenny smiled. 'Oh, this is my husband, Harry Grayler.'

Bridie rose to her feet. 'Just wait here a minute,' she said, mazed with relief: half frantic with relief; wanting to cry out with joy; to offer thanks to God that miracles still happened. She was not quite sure how to set about it, but she wanted Charlotte to know that she was not alone after all: that her brother Harry was here.

CHAPTER TWENTY-TWO

They waited at the hospital until a nurse padded along the corridor, smiling, to tell them that Mrs Oakleigh had been safely delivered of her child – a girl.

'Can we see her now?' Bridie asked.

'What, at this hour of the morning?' The young nurse laughed. 'No, you can come in this afternoon between two and four o'clock, with the rest of the visitors.'

Glancing at the clock above the swing doors, Bridie saw that it was five minutes past three.

At home in Walbrook Terrace, she made tea and sandwiches for the three of them. If she was tired, poor Jenny must be dropping with fatigue, since she had travelled from France the day before to meet Harry in London.

'We are rather like those little figures in a weather-clock at the moment,' Jenny said, unpinning her hat and running her fingers through her hair. 'Harry's going back to France in a few days to rejoin his battalion, whilst I languish here in England.' She glanced across at her husband with a questioning lift of her eyebrows. 'I suppose we might as well let Bridie into our secret. The truth is, the Army gave me my walking-papers when I started with morning sickness. I'm going to have a baby!'

Charlotte lay in bed with her baby beside her.

Her world, which had seemed so bleak and terrifying a few hours ago, had become warm and meaningful again. Holding Shelley Katherine to her heart, she scarcely now remembered the hours of her travail; the weariness of mind and body when she had believed that she was powerless to prevent herself being washed away on a tide of agony towards a vast ocean of forgetfulness. She remembered only that she had thought how good it would be to drown in the undertow; not to have to fight or suffer ever again.

As pain washed over her, she had believed herself back in Scarborough, watching the incoming tide racing up on the beach, seeing all the sand-castles she had built with so much care and concentration washed away by the bubbling, oncoming sea. She had built so many sand-castles in her brief lifetime; had built them with energy and hope, but none of them had withstood the pounding of time and tide. What she could not fight was loneliness: the feeling she had that all the people she loved had gone away from her: her father and Frank; her mother and Maggie; Will and Rowan. Above all – Rowan.

And then, amid all the pain and confusion, someone had bent over her and whispered, 'Your brother Harry is here,' and she had suddenly known that the sea would not claim her after all. She had started to fight then to bring her child into the world: had known the delight; the agony; the necessity of giving birth to Rowan's child.

Then had come the brief anxiety of wanting to know if her baby was whole and well and – perfect.

'You needn't worry, Mrs Oakleigh,' someone had said to her. 'You have a beautiful little girl with blue eyes and a strong pair of lungs.'

She had smiled then, on the edge of sleep, and whispered, 'Welcome to the World, my little one. My Shelley Katherine.'

Now, sitting up in bed, anxiously awaiting her visitors, she felt like 'lamb and salad'; remembered that Filly had always referred to anyone dressed-up as 'lamb and salad'; remembered too that, at Christmas, when snowflakes began to fall, Filly had always said, with a kind of breathless wonder, 'Look! The old woman is plucking her geese.'

Charlotte knew, as she glanced down at her baby, how much she needed her mother's forgiveness and approval. Then Jenny came down the ward towards her, arms outstretched, and there was Harry, following closely behind her yet hanging back a little, as Harry had always hung back in Frank's shadow.

Looking at him, holding out her arms to him, Charlotte seemed to see the tall figure of Frank walking beside him.

She knew then that people lived on for as long as one remembered them with love and gratitude; that death held no dominion over the continuance of life and hope and rebirth. How could anyone who had ever gloried in springtime possibly disbelieve the evidence of their own eyes?

Inevitably, profound thoughts about life and death were diminished by day to day living. Harry's return to France was a time of acute anxiety for both Charlotte and Jenny, and Charlotte's euphoria in hospital after the birth of her daughter was quickly succeeded by the realization that human emotions were too finely balanced to remain static for very long.

Harry's leave-taking was proof of this. The house seemed empty without him, and Charlotte knew what it had cost Jenny to say goodbye to him.

But Jenny was not the type to grieve openly. Very soon she began talking about getting herself a teaching job to fill in time and to earn some money before her baby began to show. Then Bridie suggested that she might well advertise for home tutorial work. And so another notice was placed in the corner-shop window, and Jenny laughingly dubbed number 12 Walbrook Terrace, 'The Bloomsbury Employment Agency'.

Meanwhile, Charlotte continued to stitch away at clothes for the neighbours; getting up in the early hours of the morning to feed little Kathy; washing her clothes and nappies at Bridie's sink whenever she had a spare minute; pegging out the washing in the long back garden; remembering Filly as she did so. Bridie reminded her so much of her mother, and yet there was a world of difference between the two women because of their upbringing and their experiences of life. What Filly condemned, Bridie condoned. It was as simple as that. And their lives were overshadowed by world events; by social and political upheaval. Great Britain had been blockaded by Germany as long ago as last February. Food was in short supply. The Allies had landed at Gallipoli; Italy had declared war against Austria; Warsaw had fallen into enemy hands, and German zeppelin raids were becoming more frequent over London.

One night in September, Charlotte was roused from sleep by the moaning of sirens. Jumping out of bed, she scooped up Kathy from her cot and ran downstairs with her child in her arms.

'Quickly, Charlotte, Jenny, downstairs to the cellar,' Bridie directed in a hoarse voice, 'the bloody thing's overhead!'

They huddled together, listening to the dull crump of falling bombs.

'What a strange experience,' Jenny said afterwards, 'the three of us sitting in the cellar with our hair down, like the Witches of Endor, wearing carpet-slippers, with poor Bridie rushing upstairs to grab hold of her canaries. What odd things people say and do under attack. What was it you said, Bridie, about the Prince of Wales?'

'I said I saw him coming out of Buckingham Palace the other day, and he looked as if a good meal would kill him.' Bridie reiterated, 'and that brought on a fit of grumbling about having to queue up for food.' She had been laughing seconds before. Now the laughter died out of her eyes. 'I wonder how much longer this war will last. I don't give a damn for myself, but I do care about the children.'

And still no word of Rowan Tanquillan. But his child, Charlotte thought, was so beautiful, an enchanting little creature with a mass of soft, curling chestnut hair and eyes as blue as speedwell.

As September sank, with early frosts and falling leaves, to a hazy October, Charlotte gave thanks for Bridie and Jenny, and her child. Bridie's commonsense approach to life cheered and sustained her, while Jenny's bright, quirky, intelligent conversation inspired her as it had always done before.

Sometimes she and Jenny would walk together in the park beyond the prim Victorian houses of Walbrook Terrace, with Jenny pushing Kathy's perambulator, practising, she said, for the day when she would be wheeling one of her own.

Annie wrote, the third week in September, to say that her mother had died peacefully in hospital. In the early days of October came another letter from Annie saying that Joe was coming home at last. Happiness and relief lay in every line of that letter. Wedding plans had been made a long time ago. Annie's wedding-dress was made, and so was the wedding-cake.

'I can scarcely believe it,' Annie wrote. It seems too good to be true! Joe is leaving for England on the seventh. He'll be in London the next day! Charlotte, my dear, I want you and Kathy and Jenny to come to Scarborough with him. I should not feel properly married if you were not there at our wedding, and Joe feels the same. Please, *please* come! Joey will wait for you at King's Cross to catch the midday train. Yours, lovingly, Annie.'

Walking in the park with Charlotte that afternoon, Jenny was deeply conscious of her sister-in-law's silence. 'What is it?' What's wrong?' she asked at last. 'I thought you would be so delighted about all the good news. But you're not, are you? You look like someone who has lost a shilling and found a sixpence!'

Aggravated past bearing by Charlotte's downcast expression, Jenny drew her to a bench under a tree. 'I could shake you,' she said with mock severity 'Isn't this what you have been waiting for all along? We *are* going to Scarborough with Joe, aren't we?'

Charlotte clasped her hands and looked across the leaf-scattered grass towards the backs of the houses in Walbrook Terrace, seeing the brilliant daubs of scarlet-berried rowan trees above a line of sagging garden fences.

'You can go to Joe and Annie's wedding if you want to,' she said slowly, 'but I can't! Don't you see, it wouldn't be fair to Annie or Joe to spoil their wedding. I'll meet Joe at King's Cross and explain things to him. He'll understand.'

'Oh, Carlotta!' Jenny covered Charlotte's hands with hers. 'Don't you want to go back to Scarborough?'

'Not want to go back?' Charlotte said, her face alight with longing. 'I dream of going back there! Shall I tell you something, Jenny? At night in bed, I set myself a kind of mental test. I imagine myself setting off from Falsgrave to walk to St Martin's Square, or from Victoria Road to Sandside, so that I shall not forget one street or alleyway. I close my eyes and remember all the shops and houses; all the little things that gave me so much pleasure long ago. The coffee-machine in a grocer's window; sparks flying all bright and shining against the dusk of a winter afternoon; the way the street lamps looked like drowned primroses on wet pavements; the way the rooftops of my town stood up all high and peaked against a winter sunset. There is not one thing about Scarborough that I do not remember with joy: with a sense of belonging. But I can never go back there. Not now: not ever . . .'

'Do you remember that day in Trafalgar Square?' Jenny asked softly 'when those suffragettes were chained to the railings, and we stood there together waving placards?'

'Yes. Why do you ask?'

'Because you took life by the horns that day. Perhaps that is what you should do again.' Jenny said. 'Perhaps someone should give *you* sixpennyworth of courage. Alice Tanquillan used to show me the one you gave her. Did you know she kept it in a bit of an old purse under her pillow for the bad days?'

'Did she?' Charlotte smiled sadly. 'Poor little Alice. I think we have a lot in common.' She leaned forward to look at Kathy. 'Perhaps I was wrong in not telling Mother about my baby. But it's too late now. I'm not a natural born fighter like you. In any case, I have no fight left in me.'

Filly Grayler bumped into Madge Robinson in the market where she had gone to see if she could get hold of a bit of best butter. She and Maggie were reduced to eating what Filly termed 'scrape' with their bread – a kind of hard, yellow margarine. But the farmers' wives occasionally brought butter to market on a Thursday.

'Hello, Mrs Grayler,' Madge said uneasily, aware of Filly's scornful recognition, unsure what to do or say in the circumstances. 'How are you?'

'I'm well enough,' Filly said grudgingly, 'and so are you by the look of it.' She took in at a glance Madgie's smart clothes. 'I suppose congratulations are in order. I saw the announcement in the *Evening News*.'

'I thought you might have.' Madge frowned. 'I'm sorry, Mrs Grayler. I expect you're upset because of Frankie. But life must go on, mustn't it?'

'Apparently it must,' Filly replied bitterly, turning away.

'Mrs Grayler,' Madge said unexpectedly, 'I'm sorry that we have never seen eye to eye. Perhaps you never thought I was good enough for your son. That's the impression you gave. Well, we did have our ups and downs, but that was partly your fault. No, let me finish. I don't suppose I'll ever pluck up the courage again, but I did care for Frank. I liked Mr Grayler, too. He was a good, kind man, and I was sorry when he died. But you have no right to treat me as if I had done something wrong in getting married again. That's all I wanted to say. You have a way of turning people against you. It doesn't matter to me or to Frankie now, but we'd have had a hard time of it if he'd lived.'

Filly walked instinctively to the old house in St Martin's Square. It was nothing but a shell now, the shattered repository of so many hopes and unfulfilled dreams.

Her furniture had long since been removed and put into store because Maggie had not wanted her place cluttered with her mother's belongings, though Bob had said it was only right that Filly should hang up a couple of pictures in her room if she wanted to, and keep her ornaments in a cardboard box under her bed, as reminders of home.

Because it was a bright, fine day, Filly sat on a seat under a lilac tree to rest her feet and stare across at the old house.

The brasswork she had once kept polished to pristine glory was dull now and neglected. The sandstone edging to her steps had long since disappeared, but the jewel-coloured glass was still intact. Her face softened as she remembered how the sun used to shine through that glass, dappling the stairs and walls and polished stair-rods with glowing, jewel-lights.

She had deliberately kept away from the house before in case she made herself soft with weeping over the past, and yet it had always been there at the back of her mind. She had scarcely shed a tear since the day of Albert's funeral. As an oyster builds up layer upon layer against an irritant in its shell, so she had built up a protective barrier against grief.

Now, looking at the house where she had spent the best years of her life, she imagined the tall figure of Frank lifting down the shutters; whistling; smiling at her as she knelt to wash the steps; Albert behind the shop counter, note-pad in hand, counting the tins of salmon on the high mahogany shelves. She imagined another figure too, the slight figure of a girl in a green dress, wheeling a handcart to town: hat bouncing on an abundance of red hair. 'Charlotte,' she whispered, 'oh, Charlotte.'

All this because she had met Madgie Robinson in town; because of something Madge said which had struck home to her: 'You have a way of turning people against you.'

Was that really true? She, who had wanted nothing more than her children's happiness? What had she ever done but try to instil into her family a sense of honour and decency? What if everyone rode roughshod over the code of ethics which she had had dinned into her as a child?

She remembered her own mother as a stern woman who, after the death of her husband, had ruled the roost with a rod of iron until the last days of her life when she was reduced to someone with the mentality of a baby. Then Filly wondered what she would have done had her mother, in the strong, implacable days of her youth, refused to let her marry Albert.

If Albert had been a different type of man: already married; a rake; would that have made any difference to her feelings for him? Supposing he had been married; had asked her to go away with him, would she have turned him away?

It seemed to her now that her life had been ruled by her mother's narrow-minded prejudices and fears. But as Madgie said, Albert was a good man, and Filly's mother knew that. But children did inherit a great deal from their parents, and there was no telling how the genes would separate to form other human beings. Filly thought that none of her children, except Maggie, had inherited her own faults and failings; that Frank, Harry, Joe, and Charlotte, had been fortunate enough to inherit all of Albert's great-hearted qualities.

She glanced, with worried eyes, across the square towards St Martin's church where, every Sunday in the old days, she had sung hymns and listened to the man in the pulpit preaching the forgiveness of sins; condemning in the same breath the sins that one was supposed to forgive.

But Felicity Grayler had never been one for deep, theological argument. She simply felt troubled, uneasy, lost and bewildered in a rapidly changing world where none of the old values which she had once believed in held sway any more.

Getting up from the seat, she knew that she needed someone to talk to. Not a parson – she had always stood in awe of parsons with their soft hands and Sunday surplices, but someone she knew and trusted.

'Come in, Mrs Grayler,' Annie Crystal said, smiling. 'I was just about to make myself a cup of tea. Sit down. I won't be more than a minute.'

Filly glanced round the room, drawing comfort from its order and neatness: the warm fire burning in the hearth; curtains closed against the encroaching darkness of an October evening.

When Annie came in with the tea, Filly blurted, 'I know that you are on your own now. I just wondered if you would consider renting me a room.'

Annie said carefully, puzzled by her visitor's obvious distress, 'I'm afraid not, Mrs Grayler, You are welcome to stay here if you want to; payment doesn't enter into it,' She poured out the tea. 'But I thought you were settled with Maggie.'

'So did I,' Filly said dully, 'but I'm not. Maggie doesn't want me.' She attempted a smile. 'I just need somewhere to go until I make up my mind about the future, I'm not an old woman. I could find myself a job; make a home of my own. I still have my own things, you know: my furniture. It's time I started living my own life again.

'But won't Maggie feel offended?' Annie asked quietly.

'Oh, yes,' Filly replied with an edge of bitterness to her voice, 'because Maggie is offended every time I open my mouth these days. 'It's "don't do this, don't do that" from morning to night! It's a terrible thing, Annie, the way my family is all split up and done for . . .'

Annie drew a deep breath and plunged straight in. 'That's what you think but it isn't necessarily true, is it?'

'What do you mean?' Even now, Filly was faintly hostile: bristling, ready to take umbrage, even with quiet little Annie.

Annie said calmly, 'You are hiding your head in the sand if you think the Grayler family is done for. I know that Frank and Albert are gone, but there's a whole new generation springing up to fill the empty places, and the only one who came make the family whole again, is *you*!'

She threw caution to the wind, remembering Albert Grayler as she did so: a man who had known and believed in the 'necessary time' for the truth.

'Apart from little Peggy, you have another grandchild, too. Charlotte's child, Kathy. So you see, the Grayler family is not finished at all. It is just beginning all over again!'

Filly raised her head, The tears she had kept back for such a long time rained down her cheeks. She caught the sudden gleam of firelight through her tear-blurred eyes, so that the whole room was filled with a kind of dancing radiance, melting the frost which had lain like a dead weight at her heart ever since Albert died.

Charlotte woke up early on the morning of the eighth of October to bath, feed and dress little Kathy, as nervous as a kitten at the thought of seeing Joe again, wondering if the war had changed him. She would know in a few hours from now.

She had tried to persuade Jenny to go to the wedding without her, but Jenny had remained obdurate. 'I'm not going without you, Carlotta,' she said.

'I can't go! I'm sorry, Jenny. I just can't, that's all.'

Bridie had gone down to the taxi-rank at the corner of Walbrook Terrace to order a car to take Charlotte to King's Cross at half-past ten, so that she would have at least an hour with Joey before his train left at midday.

The taxi arrived, drawing up at the door, as Charlotte, with

Kathy in her arms, walked out of the house.

At the same moment, a telegraph boy propped his bicycle against the railings and came whistling up the step towards her. 'Name of Oakleigh?' he asked laconically, unfastening the pouch at his waist, and handing her a telegram.

Bridie, standing near the front door, covered her mouth briefly with her hands. Then, 'Give me the baby,' she said, as Charlotte accepted the telegram and stared down at it, while the telegraph boy continued his tuneless whistling, awaiting a reply.

'You had better come indoors to read it,' Jenny said quietly as Charlotte's fingers trembled on the buff-coloured envelope.

'I can't, Jenny! I can't!'

'Do it!' Jenny ordered. 'No matter what it says, you've got to read it!'

'Yes,' Charlotte said, remembering the sixpennyworth of courage she had once given Alice Tanquillan; suffragettes chained to the railings in Trafalgar Square; the courage of Rowan crawling on his belly through mud and slime to silence an enemy machine-gun.

Without courage there could be no hope for the future. Frank's battle was over, perhaps Rowan's was too. If she failed now, her battle would be over before she had even begun to fight.

She wanted to go to Joe's wedding, to make her peace with Filly, to give the child conceived of her love for Rowan a decent future in the place she loved best on earth. None of these things would be possible without courage.

Squaring her shoulders, she opened the envelope.

'What does it say?' Jenny asked.

'You read it!'

'"News received. Rowan alive and well. In enemy hands. Kitty Tanquillan."'

Jenny drew in a shuddering breath. Slowly she went to the front door where the telegraph boy awaited a reply. 'Put this,' she said. 'Telegraph gratefully received. Thanks be to God. Charlotte.'

'Now go and pack, or we'll miss Joe at King's Cross,' said the indomitable Jenny. 'Bridie, tell the taxi to wait. We'll be out in a minute.'

Charlotte noticed an old man handing out tracts on a street corner, Greet ye one another with a kiss of charity. Smiling, she held her baby in her arms. A barrel-organ near King's Cross played Keep the Home Fires Burning.

Life seemed suddenly as wide and sparkling as a great shining river flowing towards a limitless sea of hope.
Dadda's river.

THE END

A SCATTERING OF DAISIES
by Susan Sallis

Will Rising had dragged himself from humble beginnings to his own small tailoring business in Gloucester – and on the way he'd fallen violently in love with Florence, refined, delicate, and wanting something better for her children.

March was the eldest girl, the least loved, the plain, unattractive one who, as the family grew, became more and more the household drudge. But March, a strange, intelligent, unhappy child, had inherited some of her mother's dreams. March Rising was determined to break out of the round of poverty and hard work, to find wealth, and love, and happiness.

0 552 12375 7 – £2.50

A SELECTED LIST OF FINE NOVELS
AVAILABLE FROM CORGI BOOKS

THE PRICES SHOWN BELOW WERE CORRECT AT THE TIME OF
GOING TO PRESS. HOWEVER TRANSWORLD PUBLISHERS RESERVE
THE RIGHT TO SHOW NEW RETAIL PRICES ON COVERS WHICH
MAY DIFFER FROM THOSE PREVIOUSLY ADVERTISED IN THE
TEXT OR ELSEWHERE.

12281 5		Jade	*Pat Barr*	£2.95
12142 8		A Woman of Two Continents	*Pixie Burger*	£2.50
12637 3		Proud Mary	*Iris Gower*	£2.50
12387 0		Copper Kingdom	*Iris Gower*	£1.95
12503 2		Three Girls	*Frances Paige*	£1.95
12641 1		The Summer of The Barshinskeys	*Diane Pearson*	£2.95
10375 6		Csardas	*Diane Pearson*	£2.95
09140 5		Sarah Whitman	*Diane Pearson*	£2.50
10271 7		The Marigold Field	*Diane Pearson*	£2.50
10249 0		Bride of Tancred	*Diane Pearson*	£1.75
12689 6		In the Shadow of the Castle	*Erin Pizzey*	£2.50
12462 1		The Watershed	*Erin Pizzey*	£2.95
11596 7		Feet in Chains	*Kate Roberts*	£1.95
11685 8		The Living Sleep	*Kate Roberts*	£2.50
12607 1		Doctor Rose	*Elvi Rhodes*	£1.95
12579 2		The Daffodils of Newent	*Susan Sallis*	£1.75
12375 7		A Scattering of Daisies	*Susan Sallis*	£2.50
12636 5		The Movie Set	*June Flaum Singer*	£2.95
12609 8		Star Dreams	*June Flaum Singer*	£2.50
12118 5		The Debutantes	*June Flaum Singer*	£2.50
12700 0		Light and Dark	*Margaret Thomson Davis*	£2.95
11575 4		A Necessary Woman	*Helen Van Slyke*	£2.50
12240 8		Public Smiles, Private Tears	*Helen Van Slyke*	£2.50
11321		Sisters and Strangers	*Helen Van Slyke*	£2.50
11779 X		No Love Lost	*Helen Van Slyke*	£2.50
12676 4		Grace Pensilva	*Michael Weston*	£2.95

All these books are available at your bookshop or newsagent, or can be ordered direct from the publisher. Just tick the titles you want and fill in the form below.

TRANSWORLD READERS' SERVICE 61–63 Uxbridge Road, Ealing, London, W5 5SA

Please send a cheque or postal order, not cash. All cheques and postal orders must be in £ sterling and made payable to Transworld Publishers Ltd.
Please allow cost of book(s) plus the following for postage and packing:

U.K./Republic of Ireland Customers:
Orders in excess of £5; no charge
Orders under £5; add 50p

Overseas Customers:
All orders; add £1.50

NAME (Block Letters) ....

ADDRESS ....

....